MAD

About The

SEVENTIES

TO Jim (Barley),
I hope it doesn't
make you MAD that
it bought you MAD,
because if I bought
MAD and your MAD
you wouldn't be very
GLAD and if you
weren't GLAD then
I would be SAD, So
don't get MAD, read MAD!
Tolga Crys...

MAD
About The
SEVENTIES
THE BEST OF THE DECADE

by "The Usual Gang of Idiots"

LITTLE, BROWN AND COMPANY
Boston New York Toronto London

Though Alfred E. Neuman wasn't the first to say "A fool and his money are soon parted," here's your chance to prove the old adage right—subscribe to *MAD!* Simply call 1-800-4-MADMAG and mention code 5BKB5. Operators are standing by (the water cooler).

FIRST EDITION

ISBN 0-316-32802-2

10 9 8 7 6 5 4 3 2 1

Q-HAW

Published simultaneously in Canada by Little, Brown & Company (Canada) Limited

Printed in the United States of America

In memory of John Putnam,
Arthur the Plant's illegitimate father,
and *MAD*'s beloved art director from
1955 through 1980.

— "The Usual Gang of Idiots"

Compiled and interior design by Grant Geissman

Special thanks to:
Charles Kochman and Cameron Crouch (DC Comics),
Nick Meglin, John Ficarra, and Annie Gaines (*MAD* magazine),
Geoffrey Kloske, Mark Chimsky, Clif Gaskill, Teresa LoConte (Little, Brown),
and especially "The Usual Gang of Idiots,"
those talented writers, artists, editors, and conspirators
who have rotted the minds of *MAD* readers for five decades.

FOREWORD

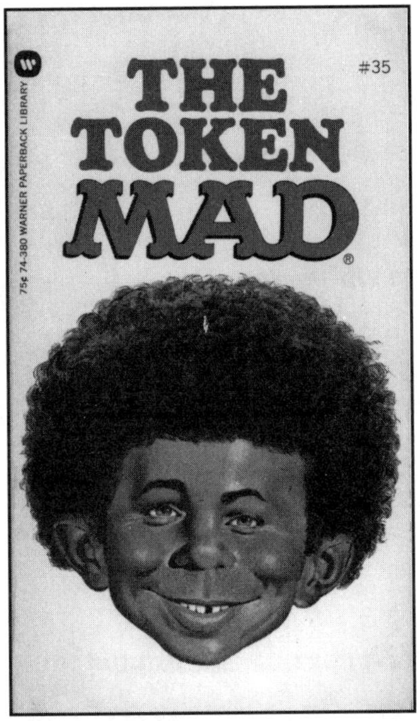

THE TOKEN MAD
#35
75¢ 74-380 WARNER PAPERBACK LIBRARY

By 1970 *MAD*, the publication that *Time* magazine once dubbed "a short-lived satirical pulp," had been rotting the minds of its readers for eighteen years—three years as a comic book and fifteen in its incarnation as a black-and-white magazine. Like it or not, *MAD* magazine had become a bona fide American institution, a pop cultural icon. Given this long a run, *MAD* could no longer count on the "shock of the new," the surprise of being fresh and different. Thankfully, though, what *MAD* *could* count on was a pool of exceptional and utterly unique talent with an uncommon allegiance to the magazine—artists, writers, and editors with an uncanny awareness of who and what they were: "The Usual Gang of Idiots." Under the somewhat eccentric but firm guidance of publisher William M. Gaines (and his full-time staffers Al Feldstein, Nick Meglin, Jerry De Fuccio, John Putnam, and Leonard Brenner), the artists and writers of *MAD* had made the magazine a phenomenal success, and in a cultural if not professional sense, *MAD* had helped "make" them: their names were known to millions of people, many of whom could recite their favorite feature, movie parody, or TV takeoff verbatim.

Nick Meglin: The seventies to us were—

You again? I thought we lost you in *MAD About the Sixties!*

N.M.: I should be so lucky! But here it is, another decade, and you're off and running at the mouth MAD infinitum!

Should I take that as a compliment?

N.M.: What do you think? But please continue, my good man . . .

With your kind permission. And feel free to jump in anytime you—

N.M.: Count on it!

Anyway, the decade of the seventies was kind to *MAD*, even if the magazine's parodies didn't exactly return the favor. While carrying on with *MAD*-ness as usual, in 1972 the magazine reached its all-time circulation peak of over two million copies per issue. The Usual Gang of Idiots were at the top of their game, and if by then the game wasn't exactly brand-new and experimental it hardly mattered, for the Idiot Gang had become a well-oiled satirical juggernaut. There is also a curious phenomenon at work with regard to *MAD:* the Golden Age of the magazine in any one person's mind is likely to be the time period in which he or she first discovered it. A survey of readers from various eras will produce similar responses: "Well, *MAD* is good now, but back in _____, now that's when it was *really* great!"

N.M.: I believe just the opposite happens when you're involved in the creative process, and I think that's one of the major reasons for our continued success. The artists feel their work improves with each job, and the writers, faced with the challenge of diminishing returns—how many really strong variations are there on a valid, sharp-edged premise?—are competing with themselves rather than against others. My co-editor John Ficarra and I still marvel when a brilliant script or piece of art crosses our desk from a "veteran" and wonder, "How do they continuously come up with the stuff?" In truth, though we certainly feel a reverence for the classic MAD articles in this collection, we're just as enthusiastic about some of the current efforts.

Like the sixties, the seventies (or, as the era came to be called, the "Me Decade") took labyrinthine turns. Just as a crew-cut college student in 1960 would have had difficulty predicting the hippie movement of the late sixties, no self-respecting flower child of 1970 could have predicted the polyester leisure suits and disco music of the late seventies.

Unlike the sixties, which was a decade that seemed to be driven and defined by the music we listened to, the seventies was a decade that seemed to be defined by the TV shows we watched and the films we went to see. Reacting to this, by the early seventies *MAD* had begun running a movie parody and a TV show takeoff in every issue. This began causing problems, for all of a sudden the magazine started to have trouble getting reference photos from production companies, who knew what they were in for and refused to cooperate. The artists desperately needed the photos; they had to have something to base their caricatures on. Coming to the magazine's rescue in this endeavor was a longtime staffer, associate editor Jerry De Fuccio.

N.M: Jerry had an uncanny ability to sweet-talk and cajole the all-important still photos from the producers, publicity people, secretaries, or whomever. With his great vocabulary and sonorous voice, he'd tell them he was a professor at Fordham (from which he himself had graduated) and that he needed this stuff as visual aids and research for some "Modern Cinema 1.01" or "Contemporary Media in a Complex Society" course he was teaching. And they always obliged. Jerry was MAD's class act—he dressed well, was very dignified, and often represented Bill or MAD at times when a certain sophistication (that the rest of us lacked) was called for. As an English Lit major, he was particularly strong with Alfredisms and the play-on-words stuff we did, like the "Department" headings in every issue. A very likable guy as well.

The Usual Gang of Idiots remained remarkably intact between the sixties and the seventies, a fact that added cohesiveness and a strong reader identification to the magazine. But there were some additions and changes to the magazine's regulars, a few born of dire necessity. In 1971 *MAD*'s star caricaturist and A-list movie parody artist Mort Drucker came down with hepatitis and was literally too weak to lift a pencil for the better part of a year. Says Drucker of the period, "My emotions ranged from sadness to anger because I couldn't work. Sometimes when I felt a little stronger I would try, but the strength soon ebbed and I knew the work was less than I was capable of. It was a very frustrating time for me."

Enter Angelo Torres, a friend of Nick Meglin's from their days as students at the School of Visual Arts. Torres's association with Bill Gaines went back to the mid-fifties, when he had done work on Gaines's EC science fiction and adventure comics, mostly as an assistant to artist Al Williamson. Since the 1956 demise of Gaines's much-acclaimed EC comics line, Torres had been toiling away at unheralded work in various mediocre and low-paying *MAD*

imitations, and doing highly regarded (but still low paying) work for Jim Warren's *Creepy* and *Eerie*. Looking for a temporary replacement for Drucker, Meglin put a call out to a somewhat reluctant Torres.

N.M.: Ange had no great love for what he was doing, but it paid the bills and his clients were more than satisfied with whatever this major talent turned in. He had moved to a cabin in the Pennsylvania woods and was happy having left comic-book pressures and tight deadlines behind him. His new publishers never asked for changes or corrections, often changing scripts around to fit his drawings should he have interpreted the scene wrong or illustrated the wrong person saying the wrong thing in the wrong panel. They paid little and demanded less, and this approach suited Ange just fine at the time. MAD represented a level of excellence that he would have to turn up his efforts a few notches to meet. That meant compromising his casual lifestyle and interfering with his tennis and trout fishing. Fortunately for MAD, he and his wife, Joan, were planning to start a family, and the magazine's page rates became very attractive indeed to this prospective father. I convinced him to abandon the world of MAD wannabes and join The Usual Gang, even if only for the time it took Mort Drucker to return to a full work schedule. Well, Mort returned not too long after, but like so many of us who became involved with Gaines and his paternal approach to publishing, Ange's "temporary" term of MAD employment can be measured in decades, continuing to this day.

In many people's minds, the relaxed attitudes of the late sixties led in the early seventies to what might be termed the "validation of the slob." Hairstyles of the period tended to be long and relatively unkempt, untrimmed facial hair was common, and clothing styles were loose and casual, to say the least. Just as *MAD* magazine's long-held "question authority"

Bill Gaines before

stance was contributing to cultural changes in the sixties, the sixties likewise were working their own changes on the *MAD* staff. By 1970 the dress code at *MAD*, never stringent to begin with, became downright nonexistent, and various staffers began sprouting beards, goatees, or mustaches of their own. Publisher Bill Gaines, not what one might call a fashion plate, seized upon this newly afforded opportunity and abandoned shaving, which he hated, and grew a beard, which he loved: it was something that required absolutely no effort. He likewise stopped making his regular trips to the barber to get his hair crew cut and started allowing his graying tresses to do just as they pleased. Like rocker David Crosby sings in "Almost Cut My Hair," Gaines was "letting his freak flag fly."

N.M.: To give credit where credit is due, assistant art director Len Brenner was the first resident "beard." The nickname "Beard" was an affectionate nom de un-groom that art director John Putnam bestowed upon him, one that still prevails today. However, it was Norm Mingo, that natty gentleman in English tweeds, starched collar, and shined shoes, who sported the first hair growth of any significance. With his white mus-

Photo by John Putnam

Bill Gaines after

tache and goatee and looking very much like a taller version of Monopoly's "little capitalist," no one would have guessed by his attire that MAD's foremost cover artist—a Saturday Evening Post *illustrator in the thirties—had delineated or, better, defined Alfred E. Neuman as MAD's omnipresent logo character.*

Another member of the staff intoxicated by seventies pop culture was writer Dick DeBartolo, who became addicted to disco music and its lifestyle. On any given night, DeBartolo could be found grooving to the beat at one of Manhattan's ultra-trendy discotheques.

N.M.: Dick was a real disco nut. He went so far as to gut his houseboat "office" moored at a New York City marina and outfit it with an expensive sound system, all kinds of floor and ceiling lights, fog machines, the works! "Disco Dick's" served as the site of many spirited disco parties. To his dismay, the IRS wouldn't allow as a deduction this $30,000 expense listed for "research" of a three-page MAD article on the subject of disco.

But not all was fun and games. There was great debate and concern in the seventies over such issues as prejudice, bigotry, race relations, and women's rights, all of which were addressed in various _MAD_ articles of the era, and some of these are featured in this anthology. As one looks over this material, however, one is reminded of the old adage "the more things change, the more they stay the same." In these overly cautious and "politically correct" times, some of the material _MAD_ published in the seventies to illuminate (and poke some fun at) society's ills would not be tolerated today. Regrettable as it seems, the "thought police" have been able to tone down even some of _MAD's_ ability to shock and enlighten through its satire, by oversensitizing people to

what is "appropriate." No stranger to controversy in its long history, the magazine got a little more than it bargained for with the 1974 publication of what has come to be known as "the finger cover" (issue #166). This is yet another example of something that probably wouldn't get published today, though in this instance, perhaps with good reason.

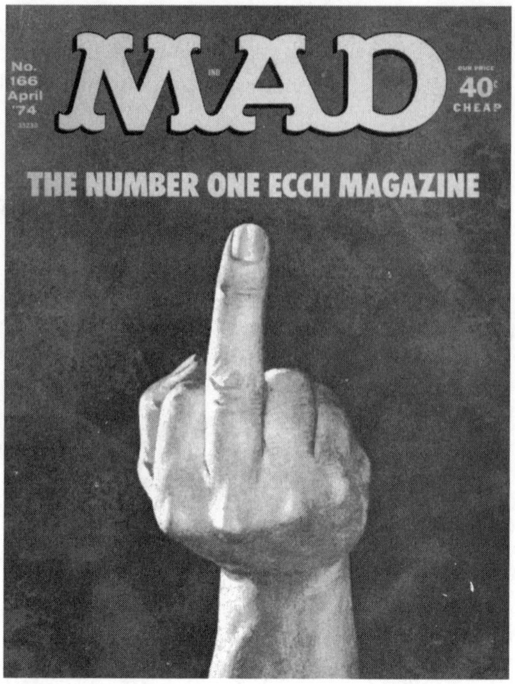

No. 166 April '74
MAD
OUR PRICE 40¢ CHEAP
THE NUMBER ONE ECCH MAGAZINE

N.M.: You would *bring that one up!*

You seem a trifle unsettled, editor Meglin!

N.M.: I am! More than a trifle! I know you'll maintain that the controversy makes it noteworthy to include, considering the integrity of your journalistic approach! Well, I got your "journalistic approach" right here! Admit it! You want to embarrass me!

No way! Please elaborate on that brilliant cover—I believe it was your idea, wasn't it?

N.M.: @#%^&! I just cursed you in comic code! Okay, let me explain. As in all conferences, there's a little horsing around and a lot is tossed about for our own mutual enjoyment. It's never a waste of time, since it helps set the mood you need for that type of discussion, and sometimes a dopey throwaway idea evolves into something usable. Like the King Kong cover (#94, April 1965), which I thought up as* *a private gag for Gaines since he was a King Kong collector and devotee (Bill insisted we use the idea—it was rare that he ever offered editorial input—so we did and to my surprise it was well received by fans). So this time I gave the middle finger salute and said, "How about this: 'MAD—Always Number One in Good Taste!'" Everyone laughed, but both Putnam and the Beard started to mount serious support for it as a viable MAD cover. I strongly objected to it at first, but lost out. The next thing I know, our editor, Al Feldstein, agreed to go with the cover, only he had changed the "explanation" line to the way it finally appeared in print. I was very upset. Not only did I think the image was a cheap laugh masquerading as audaciousness, now even the gag had been lost! Without the contradiction of the finger image with the "good taste" line, there was no joke here! I felt no satisfaction when the sales for that issue proved disastrous—wholesalers, except in the big cities, never sent copies out to distributors and retail markets. But I truly believe that would have happened with whatever line was used. As innocent as it seems today, that image isn't what people had grown to expect on a MAD cover, and readers didn't respond favorably. There! Are you happy now?*

Delighted!

N.M.: Your round, but I'll get you next time, ol' buddy! There's bound to be another book sometime. . . .

I'm looking forward to it!

    There are no doubt many readers who aren't quite up to speed on some of the history of _MAD_ that has been discussed here. With this in mind, we refer those readers to a companion title in this series, _MAD About the Sixties,_ by the same publisher, Little, Brown and Company. (The book con-

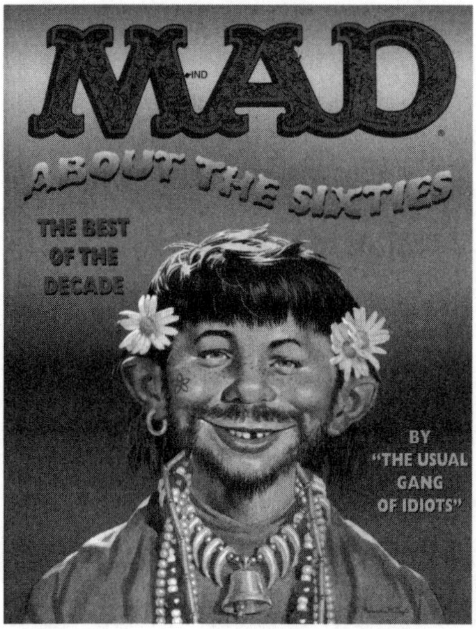
MAD
ABOUT THE SIXTIES
THE BEST OF THE DECADE
BY "THE USUAL GANG OF IDIOTS"

tains the very best material published by *MAD* during that decade, and its foreword has a lengthy and informative discussion of the unique origins of *MAD*. Besides, *MAD About the Sixties* is a title all *MAD* fans should have on their bookshelves.)

But with regard to the seventies, anyone curious about the politics, pop culture, attitudes, and fashion of the "Disco Decade" could do a lot worse than to examine this capsule history of the era—a history that has been ever so slightly skewed, of course, by The Usual Gang of Idiots.

So what are you waiting for? Sit back, grab a Billy Beer, and get down, get funky, and get it on with *MAD About the Seventies!*

—Grant Geissman, who was more than happy to be interrupted once again by Nick Meglin

GRANT GEISSMAN is the author of *Collectibly MAD* (Kitchen Sink Press), the history of *MAD* as shown by its own collectibles, and the compiler/annotator of *MAD About the Sixties* (Little, Brown and Company) and *MAD Grooves* (Rhino), a collection of the best from the *MAD* record albums. He is also an internationally known jazz/pop guitarist with ten albums released under his own name.

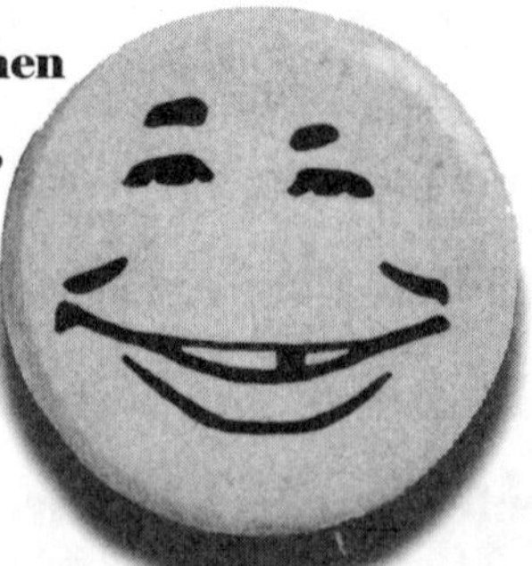

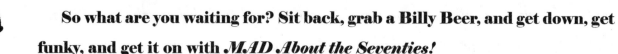

Spring 1970: The Beatles, the musical group that more than anything else defined the 1960s, have just announced that they are disbanding. The spacecraft *Apollo 13* is launched for man's third trip to the moon, but an oxygen leak forces the astronauts to abandon ship and return precariously in their lunar module. The number one song in the country is "ABC" by the Jackson Five, which features a prepubescent singer named Michael Jackson. And the *MAD* ship of fools sails on.

By the late 1960s, *MAD*'s covers began to be driven not only by clever gags that featured Alfred E. Neuman but also by illustrations that tied the "What—Me Worry?" kid in with an interior feature such as a movie parody or TV takeoff. The cover of issue #135 (June 1970) groups Alfred in with *MAD*'s parody of the hit counterculture film *Easy Rider*. Issue #138 (October 1970) parodies the popular "Peanuts" comic strip, while #140 (January 1971) morphs Alfred into George C. Scott in *Patton*. Other major cover tie-ins: *The Godfather* (#155, December 1972), *Planet of the Apes* (#157, March 1973), and *The Poseidon Adventure* (#161, September 1973). For absolutely no discernible reason, the *Poseidon Adventure* cover, which shows only Alfred's feet, has the distinction of having the highest sale of any issue of *MAD*, before or since.

The "*MAD* Paint" cover (#148, January 1972), rendered by longtime cover artist Norman Mingo, is a classic example of *MAD* humor: impossibly absurd, silly, and funny. Another wonderful absurdity, the apparently mis-cut cover of issue #151 (June 1972), actually backfired: a lot of prospective *MAD* purchasers didn't pay attention to the cover gag and kept digging deeper down into the stack to find a copy of the issue that was printed "correctly," an obviously pointless exercise.

The "smiley face" cover of issue #150 (April 1972) references the "smiley face" button fad of 1971 and the fad's attendant phrase, "Have a Nice Day." According to the book *Fads, Follies, and Manias*, more than 20 million "smiley face" buttons were sold in a six-month period, making the image one of the more instantly recognizable icons of the seventies.

The "TV Scene We'd Like to See" one-pager in this section is a takeoff on the popular *Mission: Impossible* TV show. Written by a young comic named Chevy Chase, this piece was the only one of his many submissions accepted for the pages of *MAD*. Chase, of course, would go on to great heights just a few years later as a charter member of the "Not Ready for Prime Time Players" on *Saturday Night Live*, proving his forte to be performance humor rather than printed-page satire.

The "*MAD* Fold-In," as created, written, and drawn by Al Jaffee, was begun in 1964 and quickly became a *MAD* institution. The first "Fold-In" in this section is a tour de force pasticcio of comic-strip characters that "folds in" seamlessly to make its political statement. The second "Fold-In" in this section considers the debate over the legalization of marijuana, a debate that still rages twenty-five years later. As usual, Jaffee's attention to detail makes the piece: note the beautifully rendered Tiffany lamp, which was de rigueur decor for potheads in the days when a Tiffany lamp could be found cheap at most any thrift shop. Another regular feature by the indefatigable Jaffee was "Hawkes and Doves," an amusing little military variation-on-a-theme that ran until President Richard Nixon finally brought the boys home from Vietnam in March 1973. The "Hawkes and Doves" piece appearing here is the very first one (from #137, September 1970) and the only one to appear in color.

"*MAD*'s Modern Believe It or Nuts," by writer Arnie Kogen and artist Bob Clarke, is a take on the well-known "Ripley's Believe It or Not" series. Noteworthy is the John Lennon and Yoko Ono appearance. It refers to the cover of the album *Two Virgins*, which bore a full-frontal-nude shot of the couple; the record had to be packaged in a special "plain brown wrapper" to get distributed into record stores (a practice customarily used more on "girlie" magazines than on record albums).

"*MAD*'s Updated Mother Goose" puts a seventies spin on Mother Goose's venerable children's verse, taking off on such luminaries as Hugh Hefner, Andy Warhol, Warren Beatty, Jack Benny, and Dr. (not Mr.) Spock. The stanza "Jane Be Naughty, Jane Be Bad" refers to Jane Fonda, who had recently appeared seminude in such films as *Klute* and *Barbarella*. The "When Onassis Goes Broke" stanza is a dig at Jacqueline Kennedy Onassis. After the tragic assassination of John F. Kennedy in 1963, both John and Jackie were off-limits as targets of *MAD*'s satire, but once Jackie married Aristotle Onassis and reinvented herself as the jet-setting Jackie O., she found herself on *MAD*'s satirical hit list once again.

"A *MAD* Look at Protest Demonstrations" is yet another example of why artist/writer Sergio Aragonés is the unchallenged master of pantomime cartooning. The protest demonstration scenarios illustrated in the piece are the quintessence of early seventies Flower Power concerns.

"Sleazy Riders" is *MAD*'s look at the ultimate biker/counterculture film, *Easy Rider*. This was the first feature to be directed by Dennis Hopper (who also starred along with Peter Fonda) and was the breakout film for newcomer Jack Nicholson. Interestingly, *Easy Rider* was financed largely by money that the film's producers, Bert Schneider and Bob Rafelson, had made as the creators of TV's original Prefab Four, The Monkees. Schneider and Rafelson's association with Jack Nicholson dated back to The Monkees' flawed but interesting film *Head*, for which Nicholson contributed to the screenplay. Artist Mort Drucker and writer Larry Siegel do *Easy Rider* one better in the last two pages of "Sleazy Riders," taking an unexpected left turn.

"Silent Majority — The Magazine for Middle America," by artist George Woodbridge and writer Larry Siegel, is the flip side of the "Hippie — The Magazine That Turns You On" piece collected in *MAD About the Sixties*. Best cover blurb: "Don't Be Afraid to Beat the Ten Commandments Into Your Kids!"

"Sports Cars We'd Like to See" was written and drawn by Basil Wolverton, a self-described proponent of the "spaghetti-and-meatball school" of illustration. Wolverton's grotesqueries date all the way back to the comic book *MAD* of the fifties. Another artist with a history dating back to the comic book *MAD* (this time all the way back to the first issue) is Wallace Wood, who is represented here with "Altar Ego," a dig at the opulence of the Catholic Church. When the piece was reprinted in a Brazilian edition of *MAD*, authorities in that heavily Catholic country arrested the hapless Brazilian publisher, temporarily putting a stop to *MAD*'s appearances in Brazil.

"Lover's Story," by Drucker and Siegel, sends up the ultimate date movie/weeper of the early 1970s, *Love Story*, starring Ryan O'Neal and Ali McGraw. Based on the number one bestseller by Erich Segal, the film version was the top-grossing film of 1970, bringing $50 million into the studio's coffers.

There were numerous attempts at relevance and social statements on the boob tube in the early seventies, many of which were ultimately skewered by the *MAD*-men. The most influential of these was producer Norman Lear's *All in the Family*, which is widely regarded as a breakthrough in television. Archie Bunker's loudly outspoken views on minorities and the attendant tensions this caused in his neighborhood were far from the bland fare typically served up on TV sitcoms. *MAD*'s take on the show, illustrated by Angelo Torres and written by Larry Siegel, is "Gall in the Family Fare" and centers on a visit from a certain World War II buddy. While not as abrasive as *All in the Family*, *The Mary Tyler Moore Show* (spoofed here as "The Mary Tailor-Made Show" by Angelo Torres and writer Tom Koch) could also be considered "relevant": the single, ambitious career woman Mary played was the symbol of the liberated woman. Even children's programming underwent a transformation: PBS's new and experimental educational show *Sesame Street* took place in an unspecified urban environment, and the main characters were neither black nor white but literally rainbow-colored: red, green, yellow, and blue. *MAD*'s "Reality Street," written by Dick DeBartolo and grittily pencil-rendered by Jack Davis, juxtaposes the mean streets of real urban living with the *Sesame Street* characters and trots the combination right out to its satirical edge.

Widely regarded as one of the best American films ever made, *The Godfather* was the top-grossing film of 1972, bringing in more than $86 million. It was, as *MAD* humorously points out, a "family" film. We meet the family, done *MAD*-style, in "The Oddfather," a magnum opus by writer Larry Siegel and artist Mort Drucker. All the ingredients of a *MAD* classic are here: Drucker's dead-on caricature and Siegel's brilliantly funny script, which touches upon and expertly skewers all the characters and plot points of this epoch film in a mere nine pages.

In these politically correct times, a piece like "You Can Never Win with a Bigot" (by writer Frank Jacobs and artist Paul Coker, Jr.) would probably be reconsidered, even at *MAD*, and more's the pity, for it is hard to imagine a better way to illuminate the pointlessness of prejudice and bigotry.

Ending this section is "One Day on a Transcontinental Jet," by "*MAD*'s Maddest Artist," Don Martin. In the early 1970s (before the introduction of X-ray security checks at airports), armed passengers hijacking commercial airliners and demanding to be flown to Cuba for political asylum was an all-too-common occurrence. As might be expected, Martin takes this to its logically MAD conclusion.

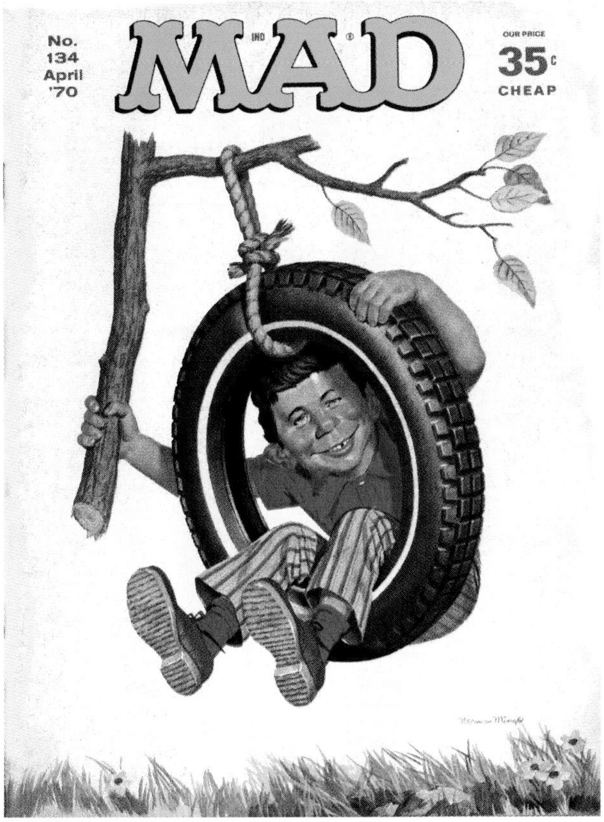
No.
134
April
'70
MAD
OUR PRICE
35¢
CHEAP

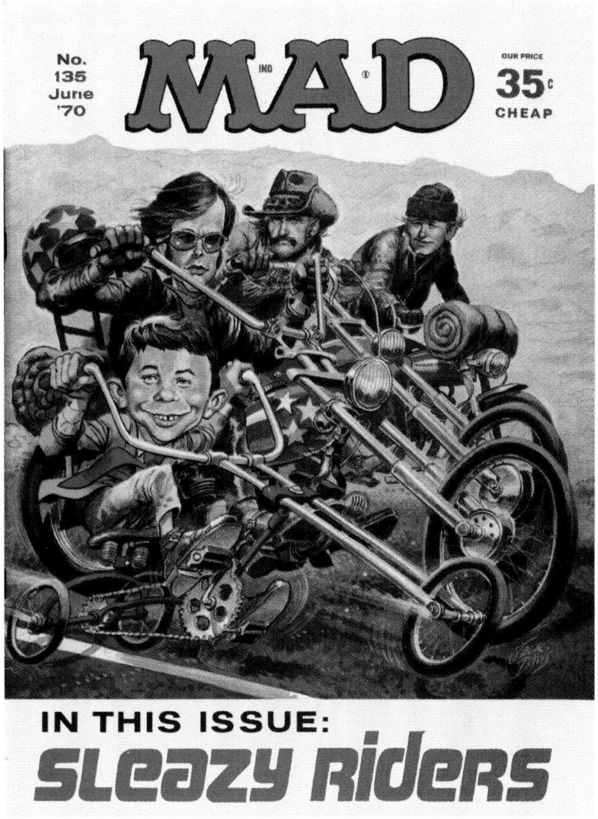
No.
135
June
'70
MAD
OUR PRICE
35¢
CHEAP
IN THIS ISSUE:
SLEAZY RIDERS

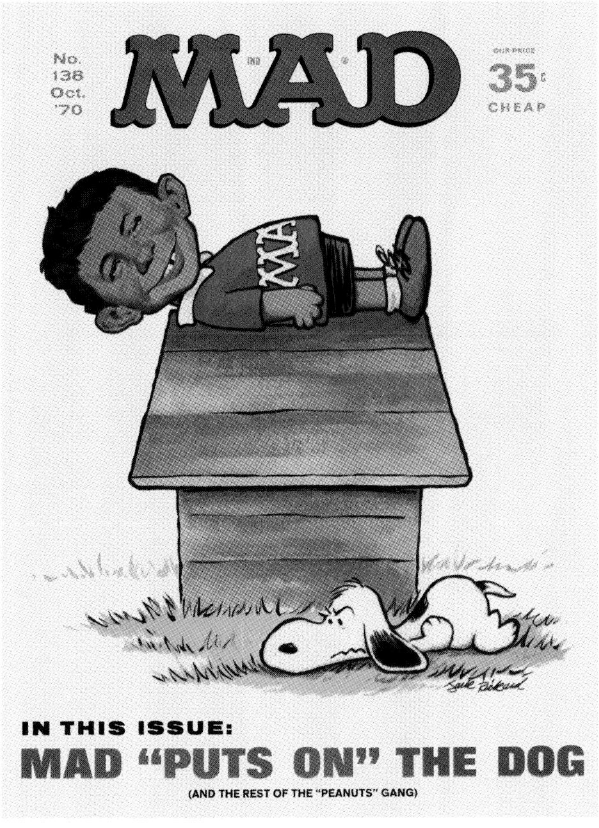
No.
138
Oct.
'70
MAD
OUR PRICE
35¢
CHEAP
IN THIS ISSUE:
MAD "PUTS ON" THE DOG
(AND THE REST OF THE "PEANUTS" GANG)

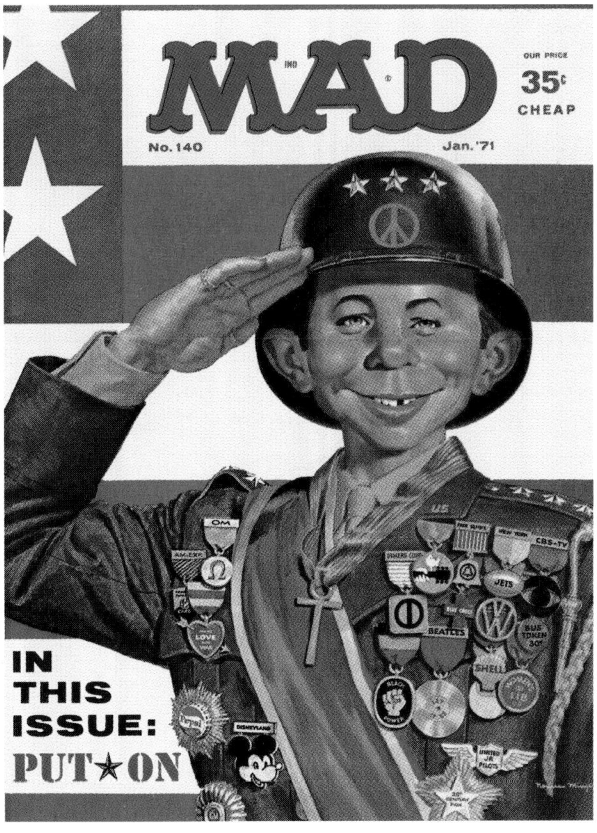
MAD
OUR PRICE
35¢
CHEAP
No.140
Jan.'71
IN
THIS
ISSUE:
PUT★ON

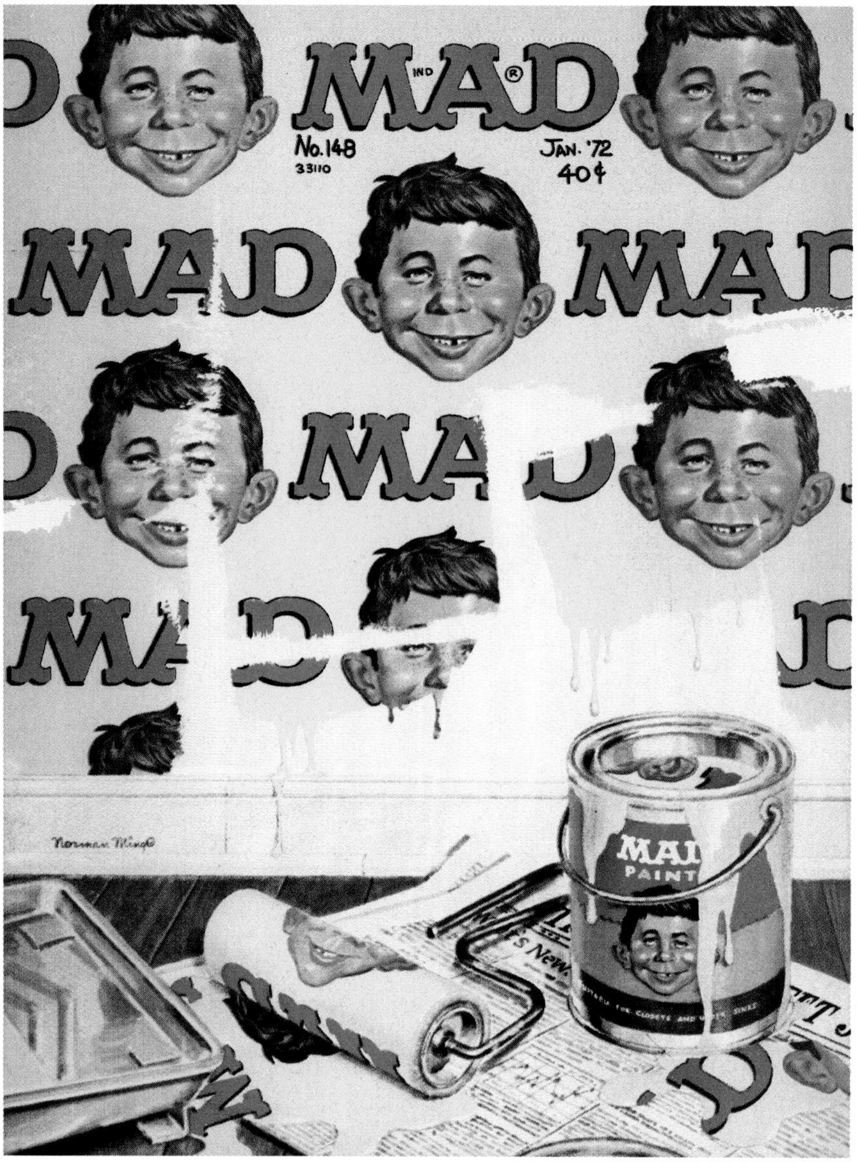
MAD
No.148
33110
JAN. '72
40¢
MAD
PAINT

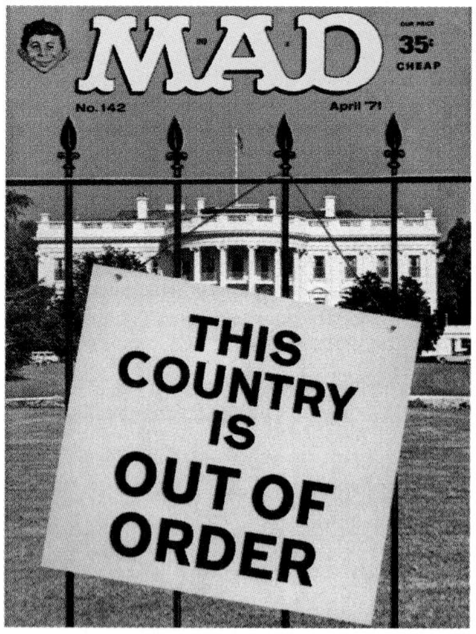
MAD
35¢
CHEAP
No. 142
April '71
THIS
COUNTRY
IS
OUT OF
ORDER

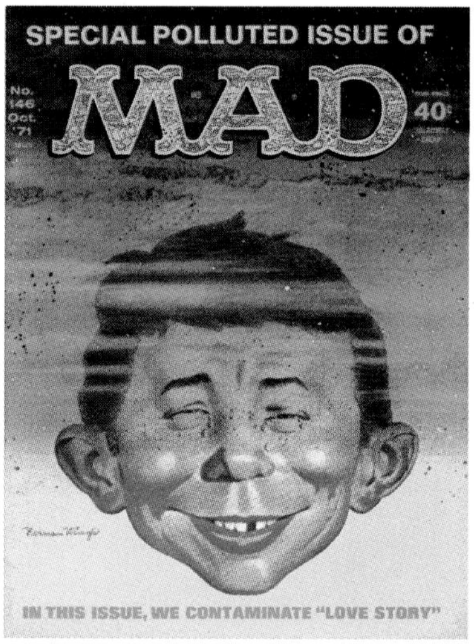
SPECIAL POLLUTED ISSUE OF
No.
146
Oct.
'71
MAD
40¢
IN THIS ISSUE, WE CONTAMINATE "LOVE STORY"

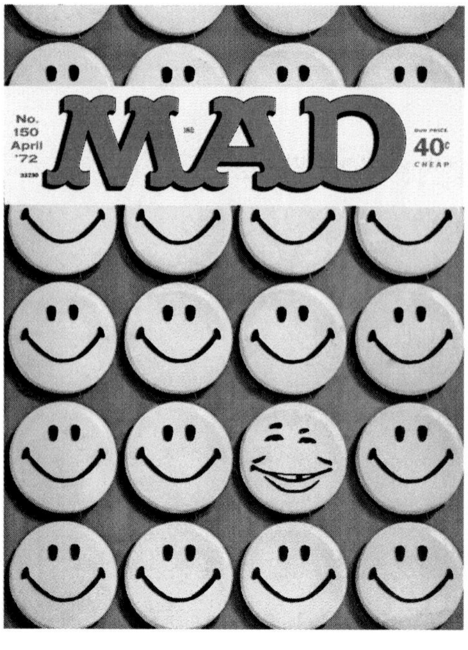
No.
150
April
'72
MAD
40¢
CHEAP

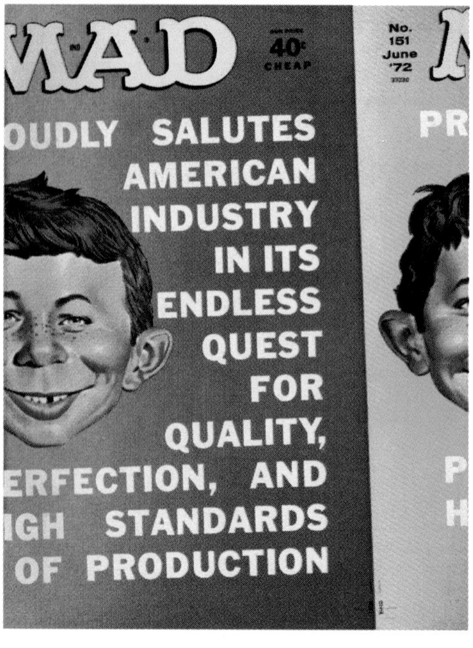
MAD
40¢
CHEAP
No.
151
June
'72
OUDLY SALUTES
AMERICAN
INDUSTRY
IN ITS
ENDLESS
QUEST
FOR
QUALITY,
ERFECTION, AND
IGH STANDARDS
OF PRODUCTION

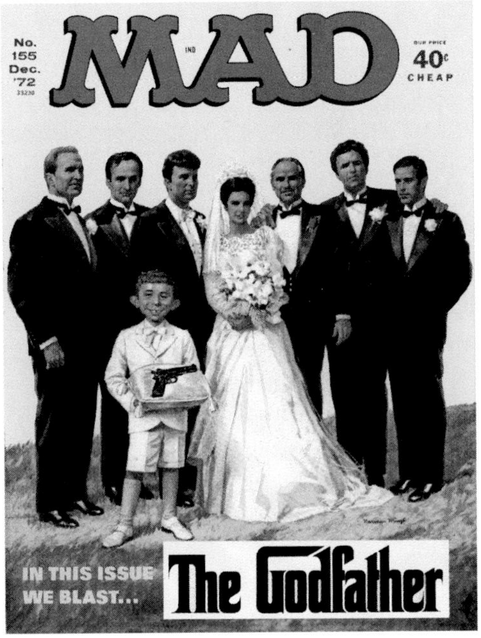
No. 155 Dec. '72
MAD
OUR PRICE 40¢ CHEAP
IN THIS ISSUE WE BLAST...
The Godfather

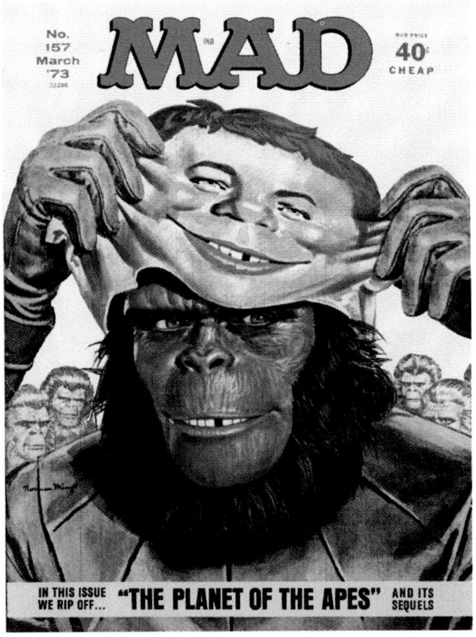
No. 157 March '73
MAD
OUR PRICE 40¢ CHEAP
IN THIS ISSUE WE RIP OFF...
"THE PLANET OF THE APES"
AND ITS SEQUELS

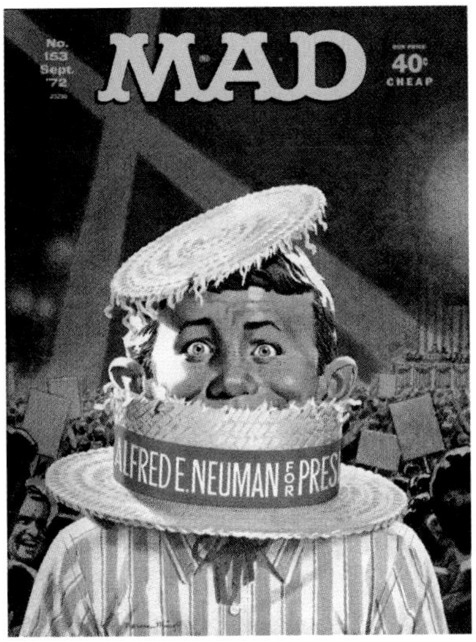
MAD
40¢ CHEAP
ALFRED E. NEUMAN FOR PRES

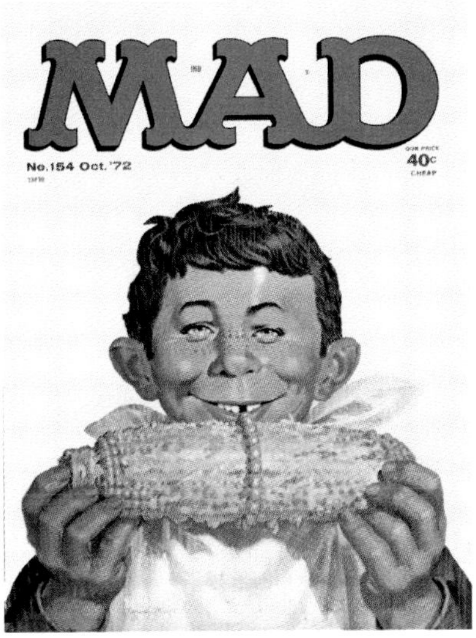
MAD
No.154 Oct.'72
OUR PRICE 40¢ CHEAP

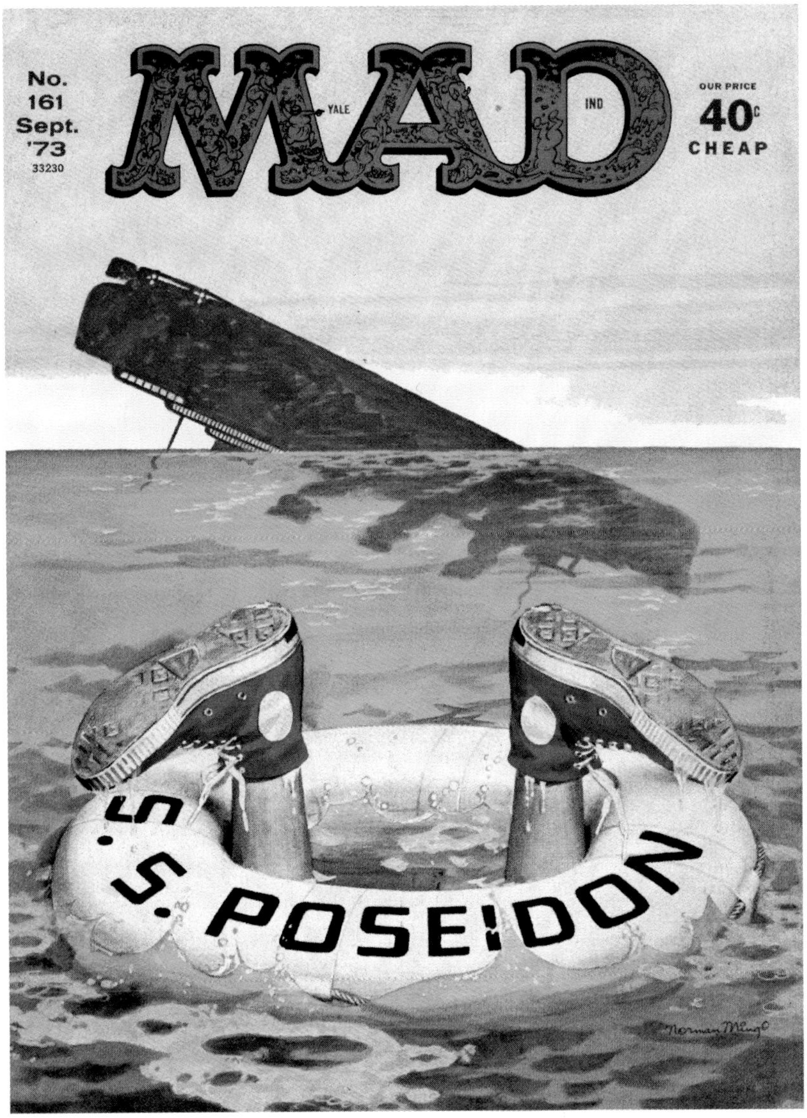
No. 161 Sept. '73 33230
MAD
YALE
IND
OUR PRICE 40¢ CHEAP
S.S. POSEIDON

A TV SCENE WE'D LIKE TO SEE

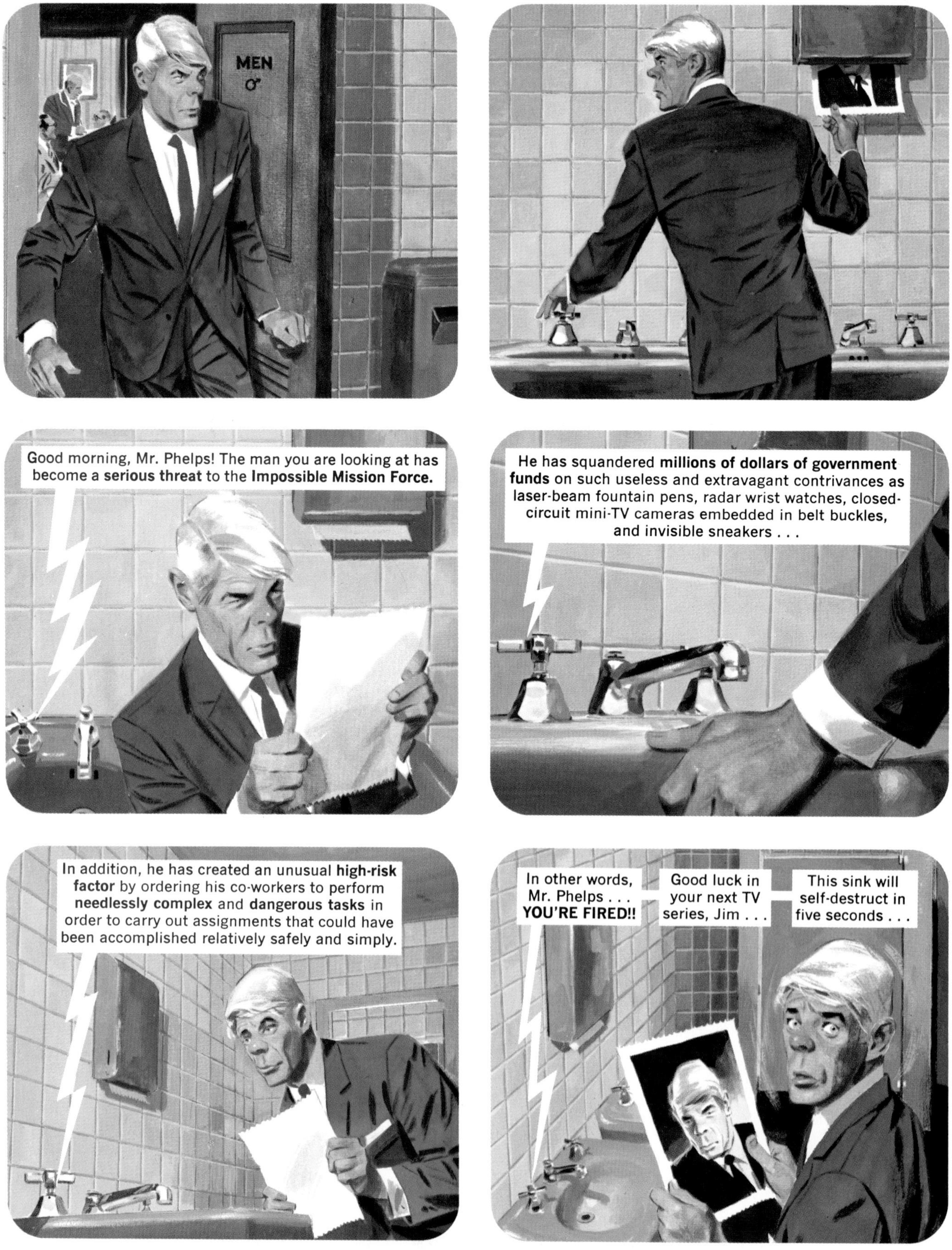
MEN
Good morning, Mr. Phelps! The man you are looking at has become a serious threat to the Impossible Mission Force.
He has squandered millions of dollars of government funds on such useless and extravagant contrivances as laser-beam fountain pens, radar wrist watches, closed-circuit mini-TV cameras embedded in belt buckles, and invisible sneakers . . .
In addition, he has created an unusual high-risk factor by ordering his co-workers to perform needlessly complex and dangerous tasks in order to carry out assignments that could have been accomplished relatively safely and simply.
In other words, Mr. Phelps . . . YOU'RE FIRED!!
Good luck in your next TV series, Jim . . .
This sink will self-destruct in five seconds . . .

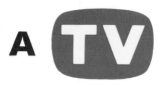

ARTIST: JOHN CULLEN MURPHY WRITER: CHEVY CHASE

WHO IS FAST BECOMING OUR ALL-TIME TOP COMIC CHARACTER?

HERE WE GO WITH ANOTHER RIDICULOUS

MAD FOLD-IN

Throughout the years, the United States has produced a fascinating parade of "Comic Characters". Recently, however, a brand new one has burst upon the scene who threatens to eclipse all the rest. To find out which one we're talking about, fold in the page as shown . . .

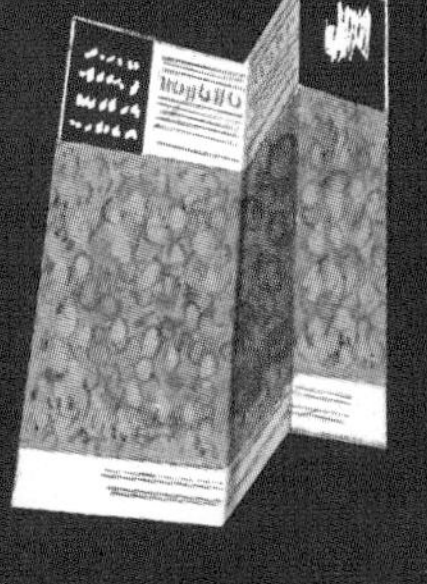

FOLD PAGE OVER LIKE THIS!

A▶ FOLD THIS SECTION OVER LEFT ◀B FOLD BACK SO "A" MEETS "B"

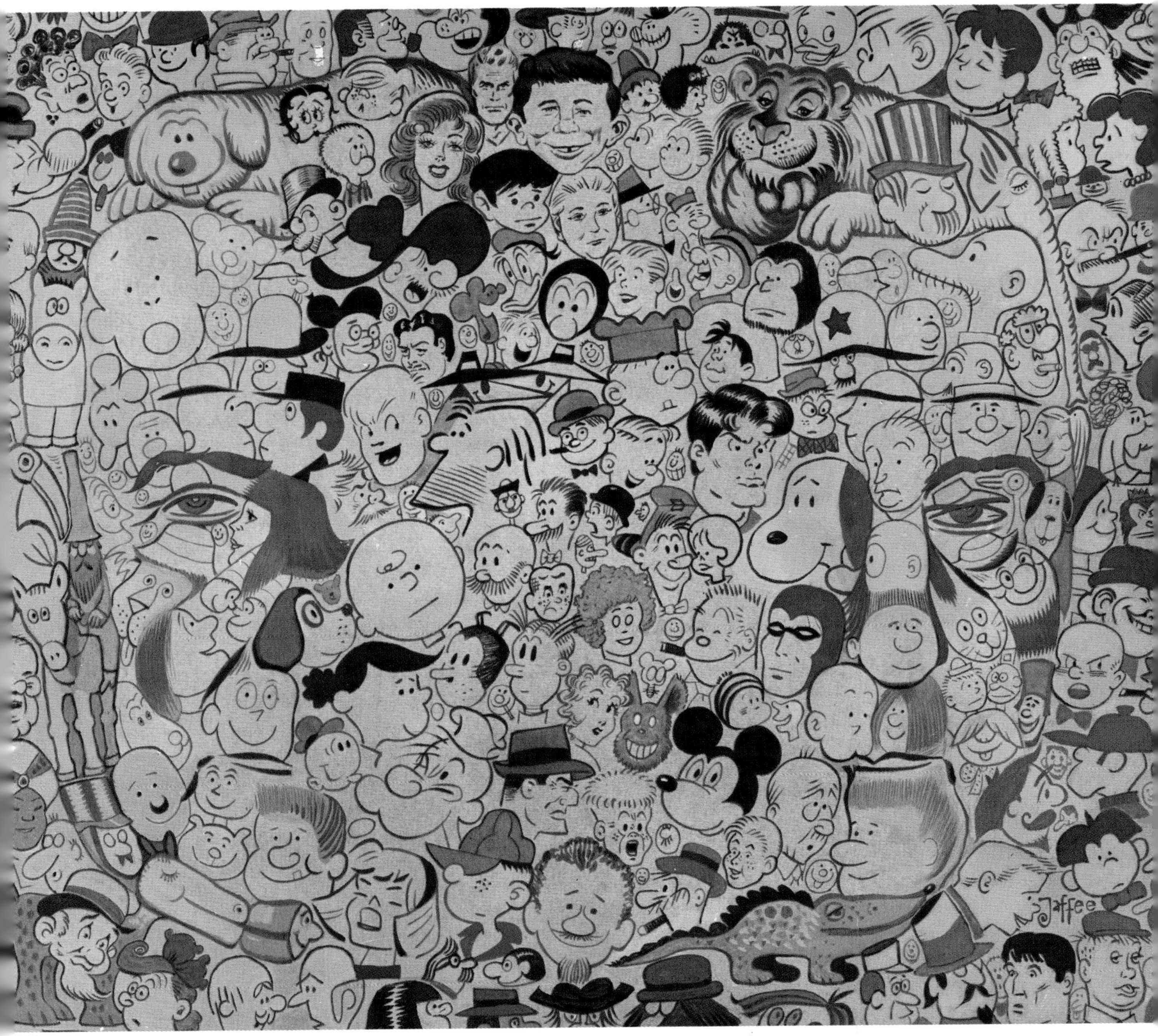
Jaffee

ARTIST & WRITER:
AL JAFFEE

SPINNING HIS WEB OF HUMOR, THE COMIC HERO AGAIN AND AGAIN CHARMS OLD FANS AND NEW

◀B

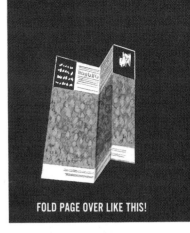

Introducing A New MAD Feature Which Takes A Humorous Look At The War Between

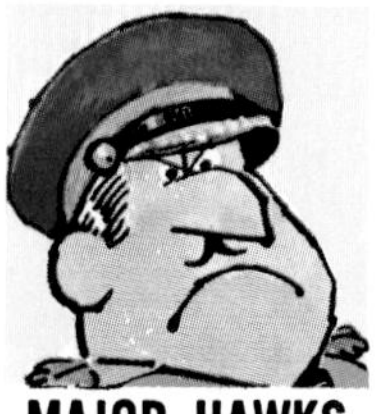

MAJOR HAWKS

HAWKS & DOVES

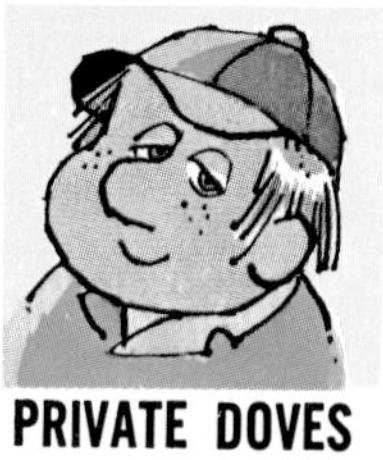

PRIVATE DOVES

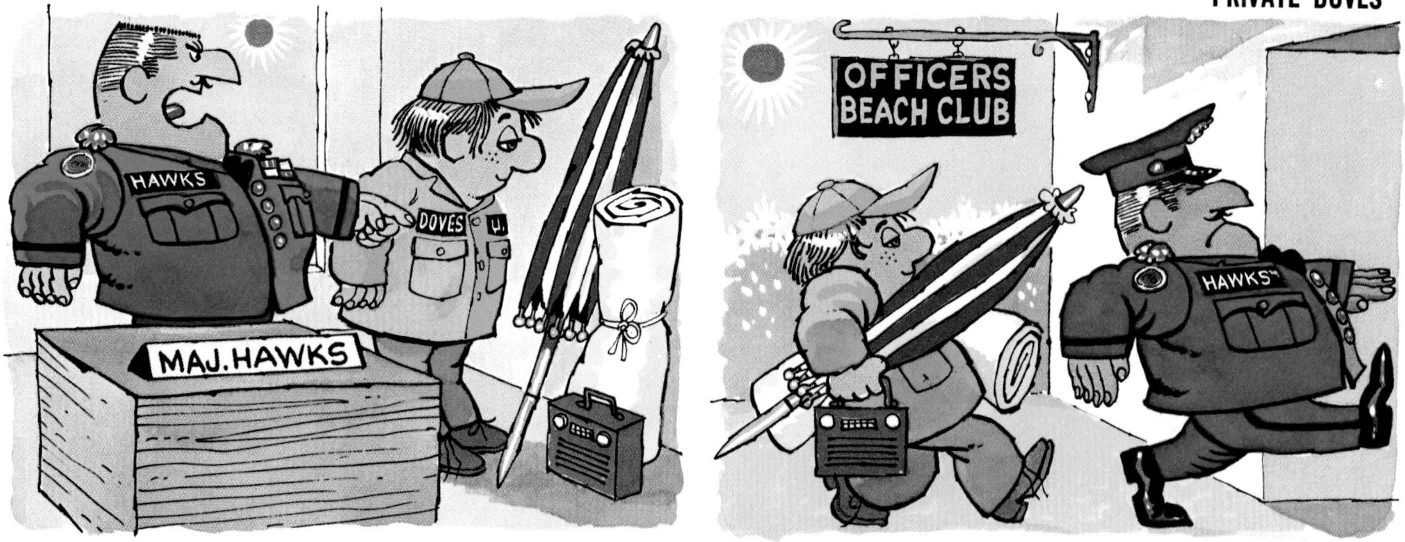
HAWKS
DOVES
MAJ. HAWKS
OFFICERS
BEACH CLUB
HAWKS

ARTIST & WRITER: AL JAFFEE

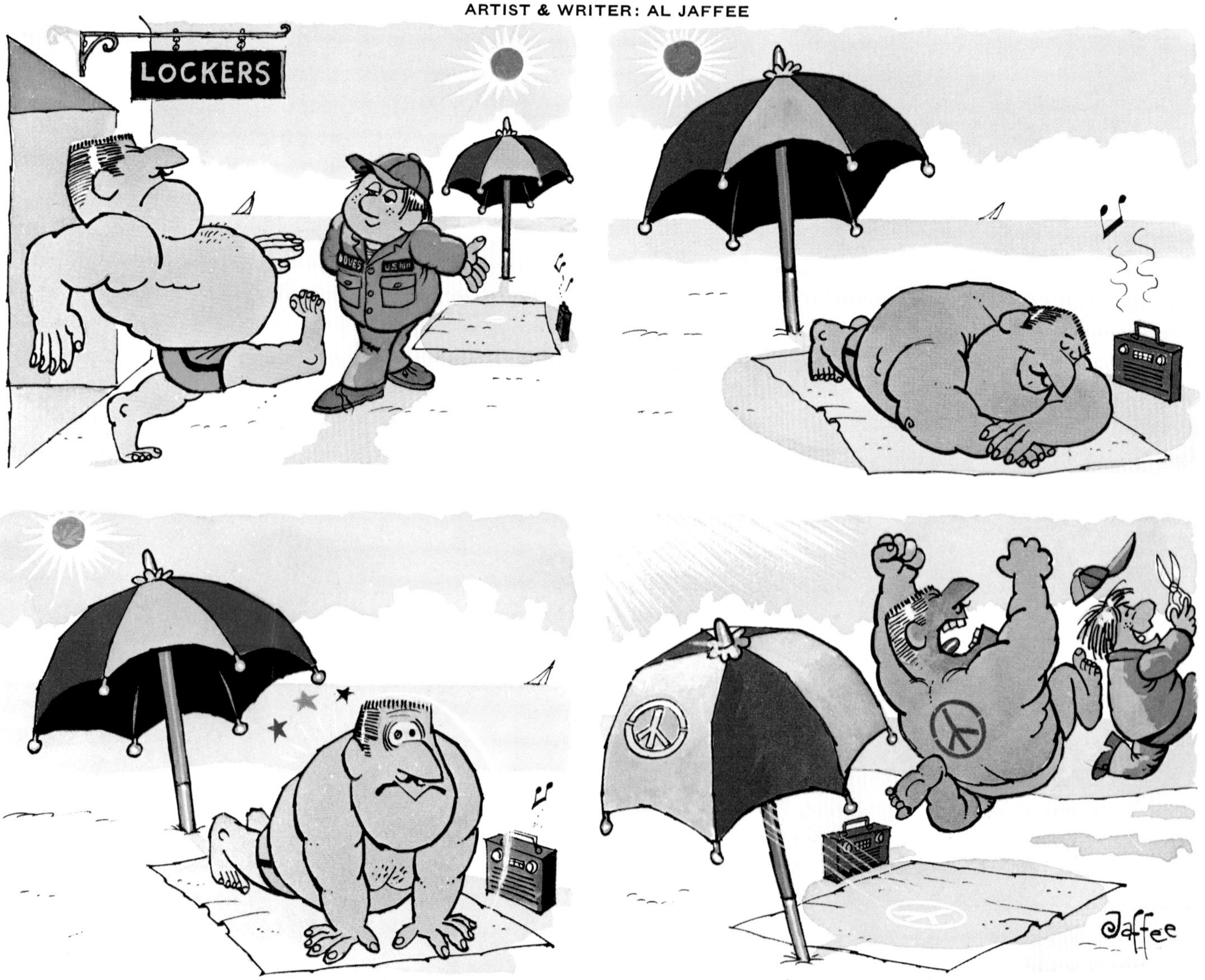
LOCKERS
DOVES
Jaffee

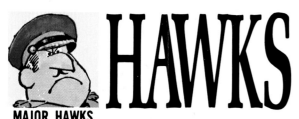

The Vampire

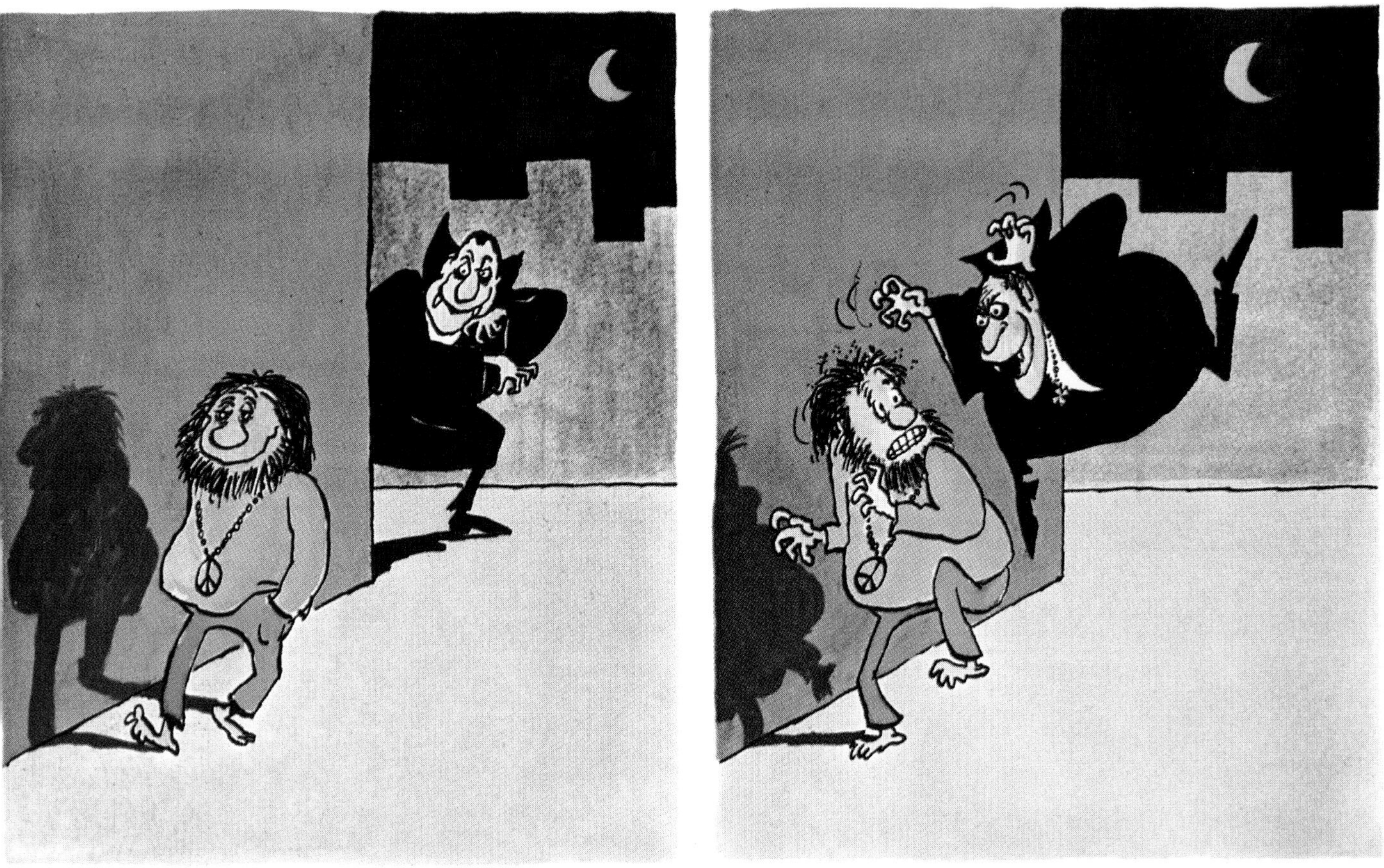

ARTIST & WRITER: SERGIO ARAGONES

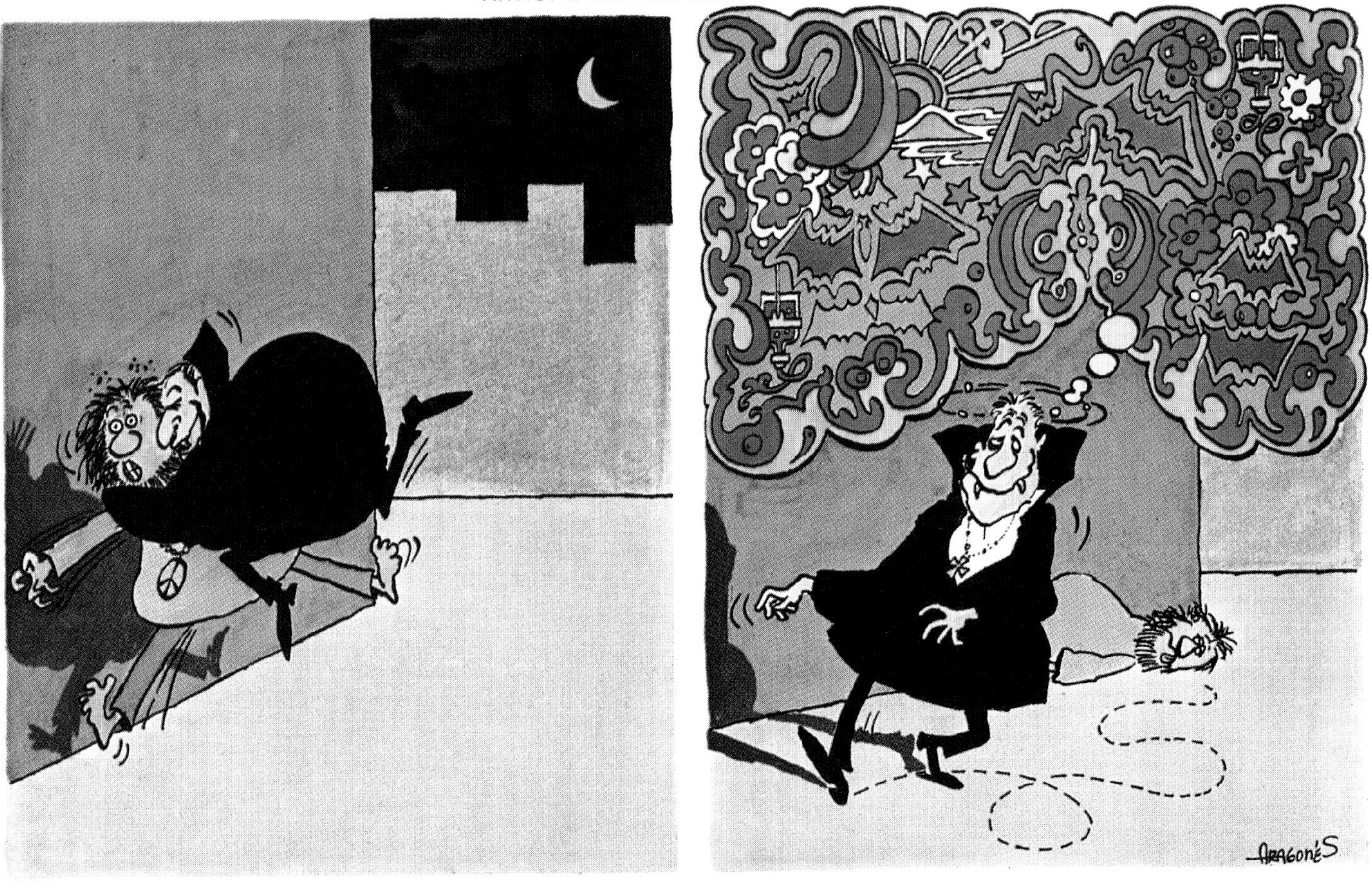
ARAGONÉS

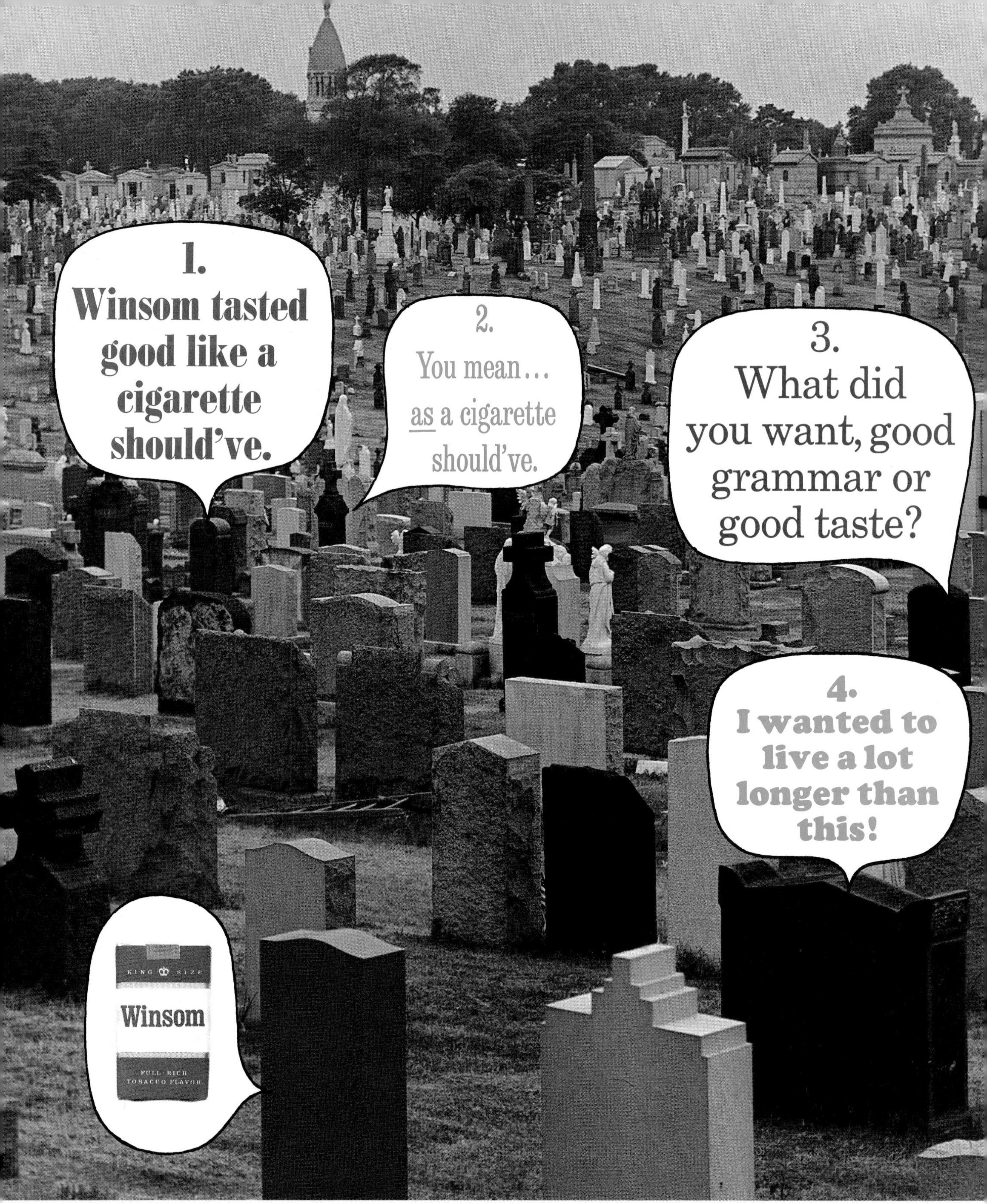
1. Winsom tasted good like a cigarette should've.
2. You mean… as a cigarette should've.
3. What did you want, good grammar or good taste?
4. I wanted to live a lot longer than this!
KING SIZE
Winsom
FULL-RICH TOBACCO FLAVOR

Winsom may not say it right, but they sure know how to put you right—
six feet under with CANCER BLEND tobaccos

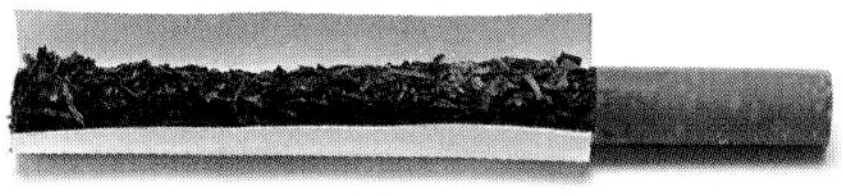

MAD's Modern Believe It or Nuts!

ARTIST: BOB CLARKE   WRITER: ARNIE KOGEN

DURING THE WORST HEAT WAVE OF THE SUMMER, **MYRON STANLEY FOOTSELMAN** DANCED THE **BOOGALOO** FOR **57 HOURS** WITHOUT STOPPING ...WHILE WEARING **ICE SKATES!**

DESPITE THIS UNIQUE EFFORT, THE ARMY **STILL** INDUCTED HIM!

CONTRARY TO POPULAR BELIEF...

KING KONG

WAS **NOT** KNOCKED OFF THE EMPIRE STATE BUILDING BY WORLD WAR I AIRPLANES--NOR DID HE **FALL** OFF!

HE WAS ACTUALLY **LURED** OFF ...BY A **BANANA** PLACED ON TOP OF THE **CHRYSLER BUILDING!**

2+2 = $27,000,000
submitted by
THE PRODUCERS OF
BOB & CAROL & TED & ALICE

JOHN **LENNON** & YOKO **ONO** **NEVER** POSED NUDE FOR THAT ALBUM COVER!!

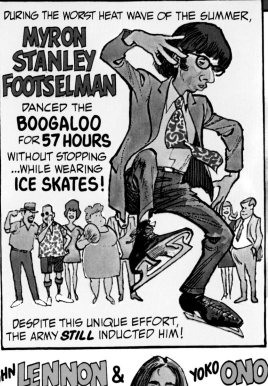

WAS MERELY TWO MORE INCREDIBLE IMPERSONATIONS BY [TH]OSE FANTASTIC MIMICS, RICH LITTLE AND DAVID FRYE!

ON THE NIGHT OF SEPT. 29, 1969 **PETER MURKEY** AN AMATEUR HYPNOTIST, AMAZED HIS FRIENDS BY ACTUALLY PUTTING **34 MILLION PEOPLE** TO SLEEP WITH ONE QUICK MOVEMENT OF HIS HAND!

IT WAS WHILE HE WAS PERFORMING HIS NIGHTTIME JOB AS AN ABC-TV ENGINEER WHEN HE FLICKED THE SWITCH WHICH SHOWED THE PREMIERE EPISODE OF "THE SURVIVORS"!

SIGN LANGUAGE

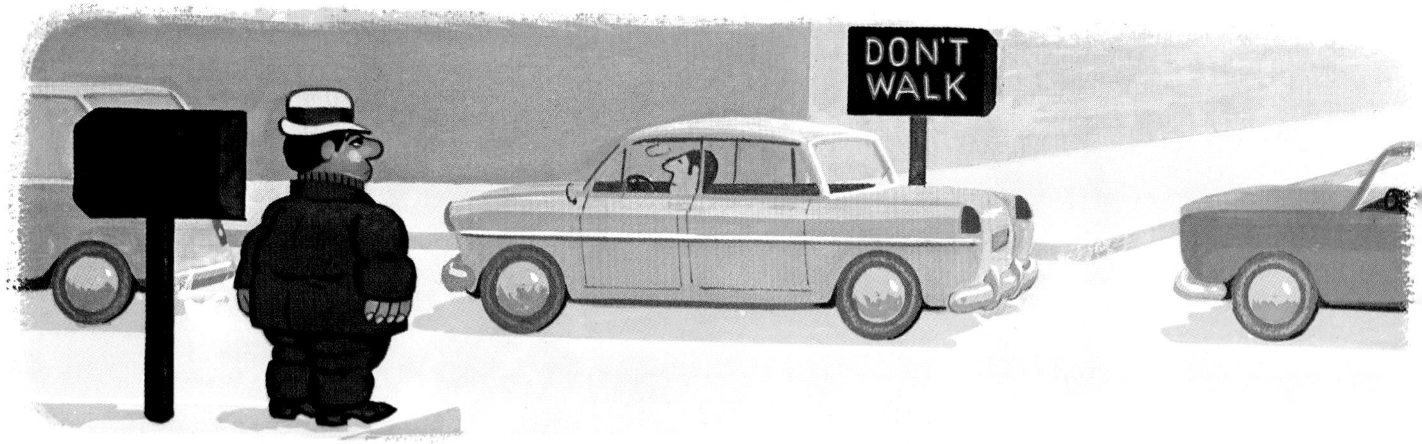

DON'T WALK

ARTIST & WRITER: AL JAFFEE

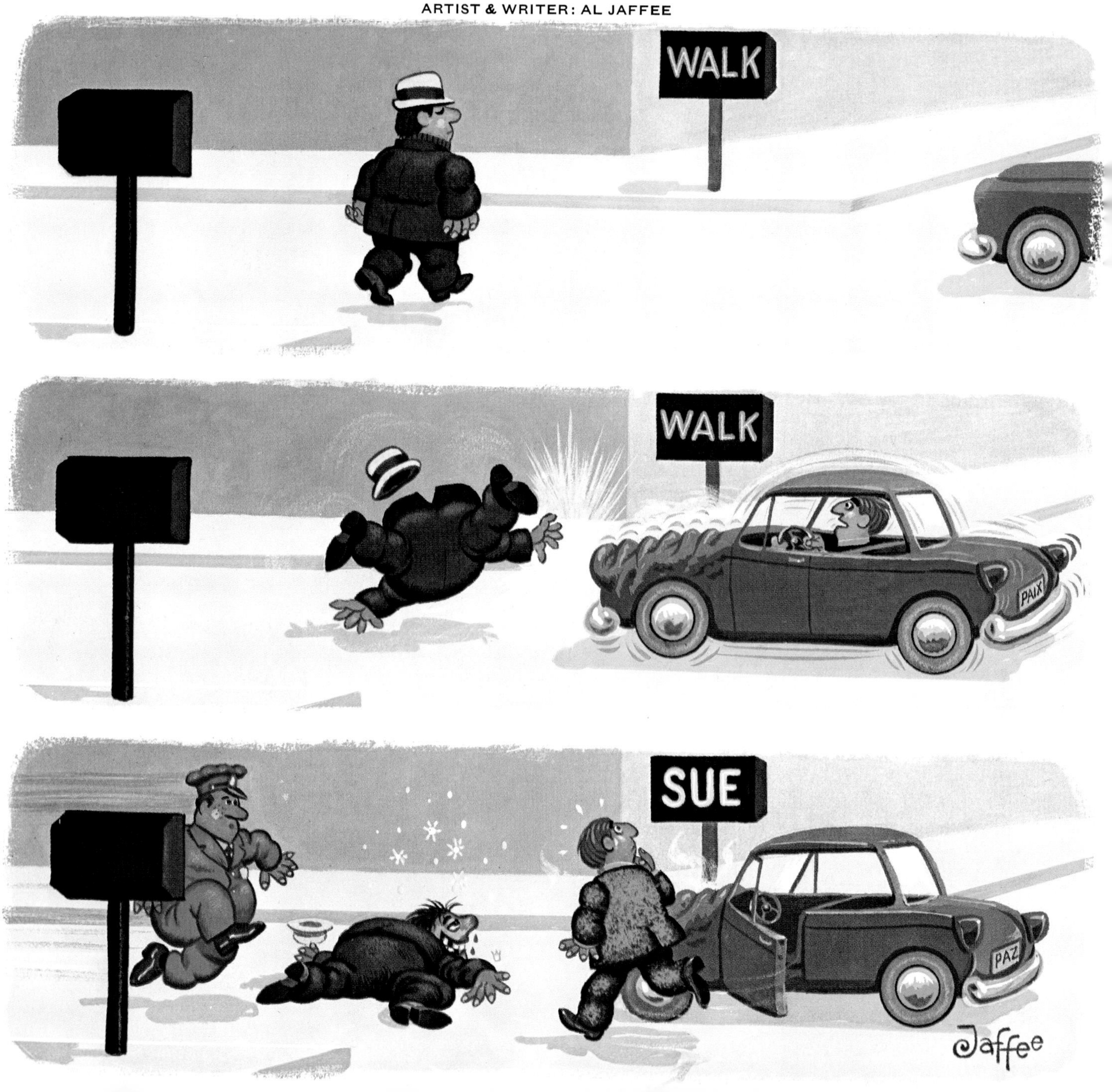

WALK
WALK
PAIX
SUE
PAZ
Jaffee

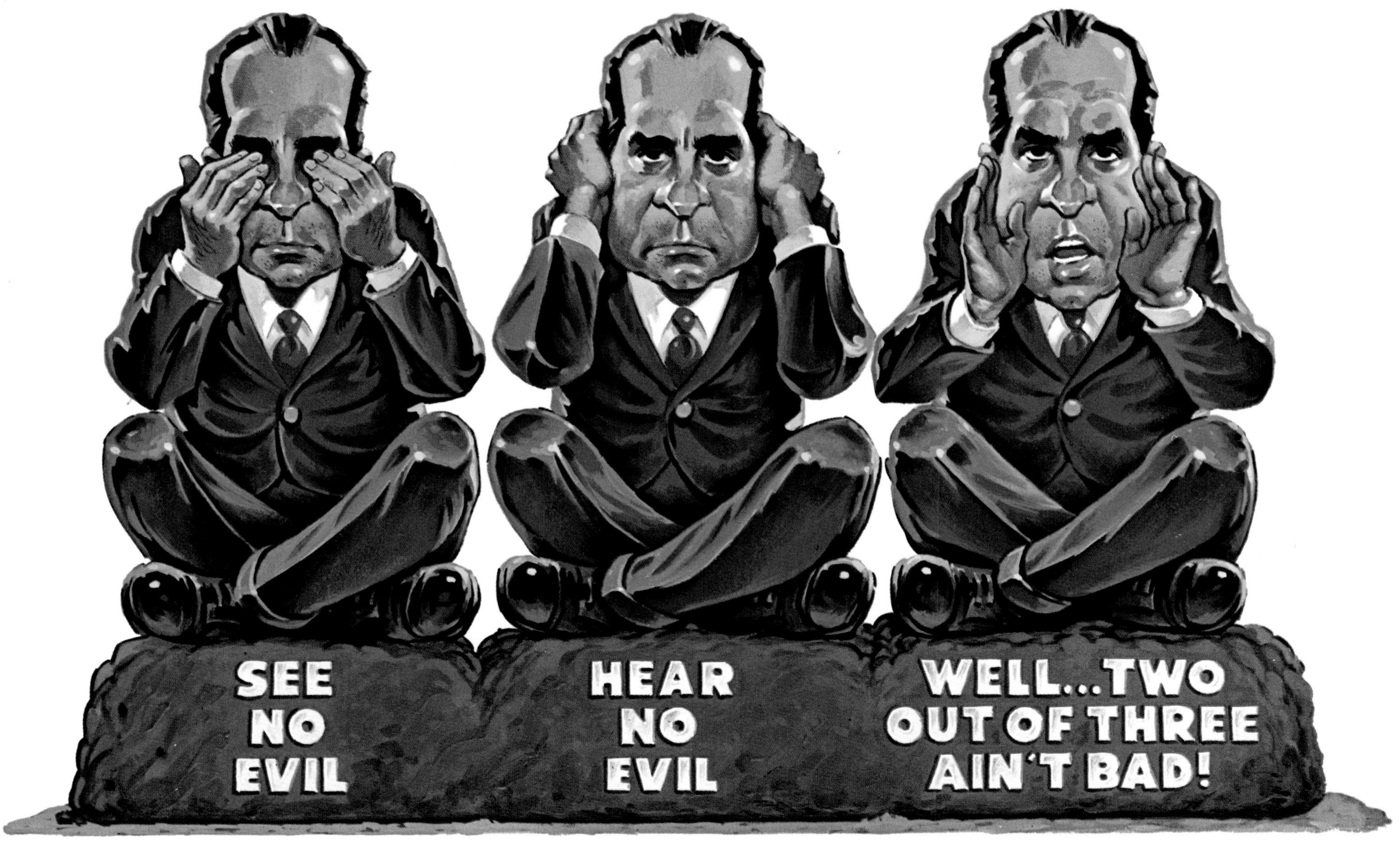
SEE NO EVIL
HEAR NO EVIL
WELL...TWO OUT OF THREE AIN'T BAD!

ARTIST: JACK RICKARD

WRITER: LARRY GORE

A GRIM FAIRY TALE

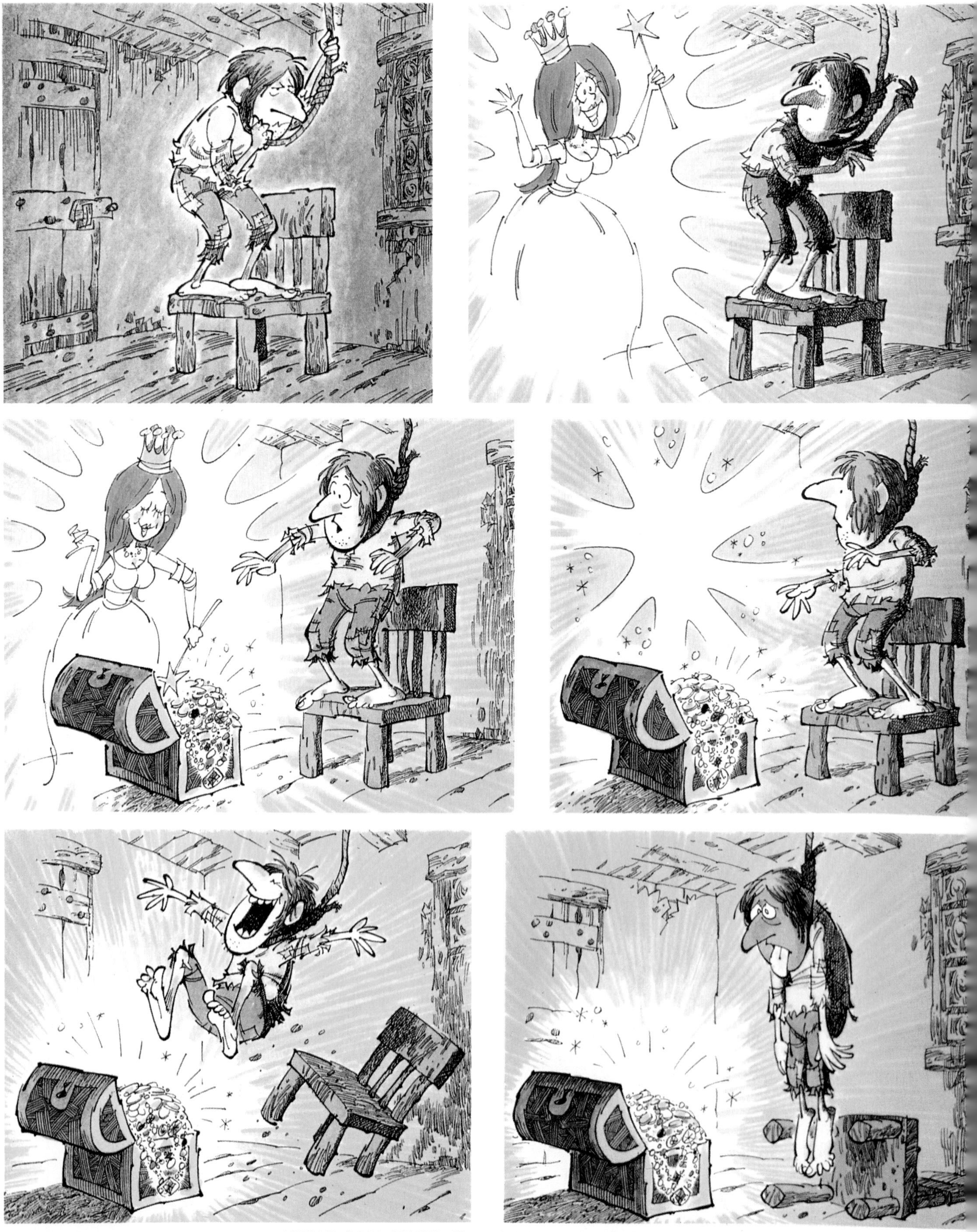

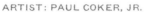

ARTIST: PAUL COKER, JR. WRITER: AL JAFFEE

WHOSE LIFE WOULD BE SERIOUSLY ENDANGERED IF POT WERE LEGALIZED?

HERE WE GO WITH ANOTHER RIDICULOUS

MAD FOLD-IN

Some people think that Pot is harmless, and some people think that Pot is harmful. But one thing is sure. Everyone agrees that, for some people, legalized Pot would have a murderous effect. To find out who they are, fold in the page as shown.

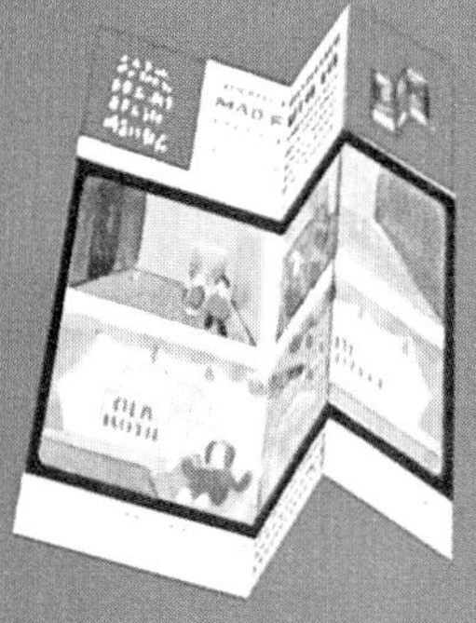

FOLD PAGE OVER LIKE THIS!

A▸ FOLD THIS SECTION OVER LEFT ◂B FOLD BACK SO "A" MEETS "B"

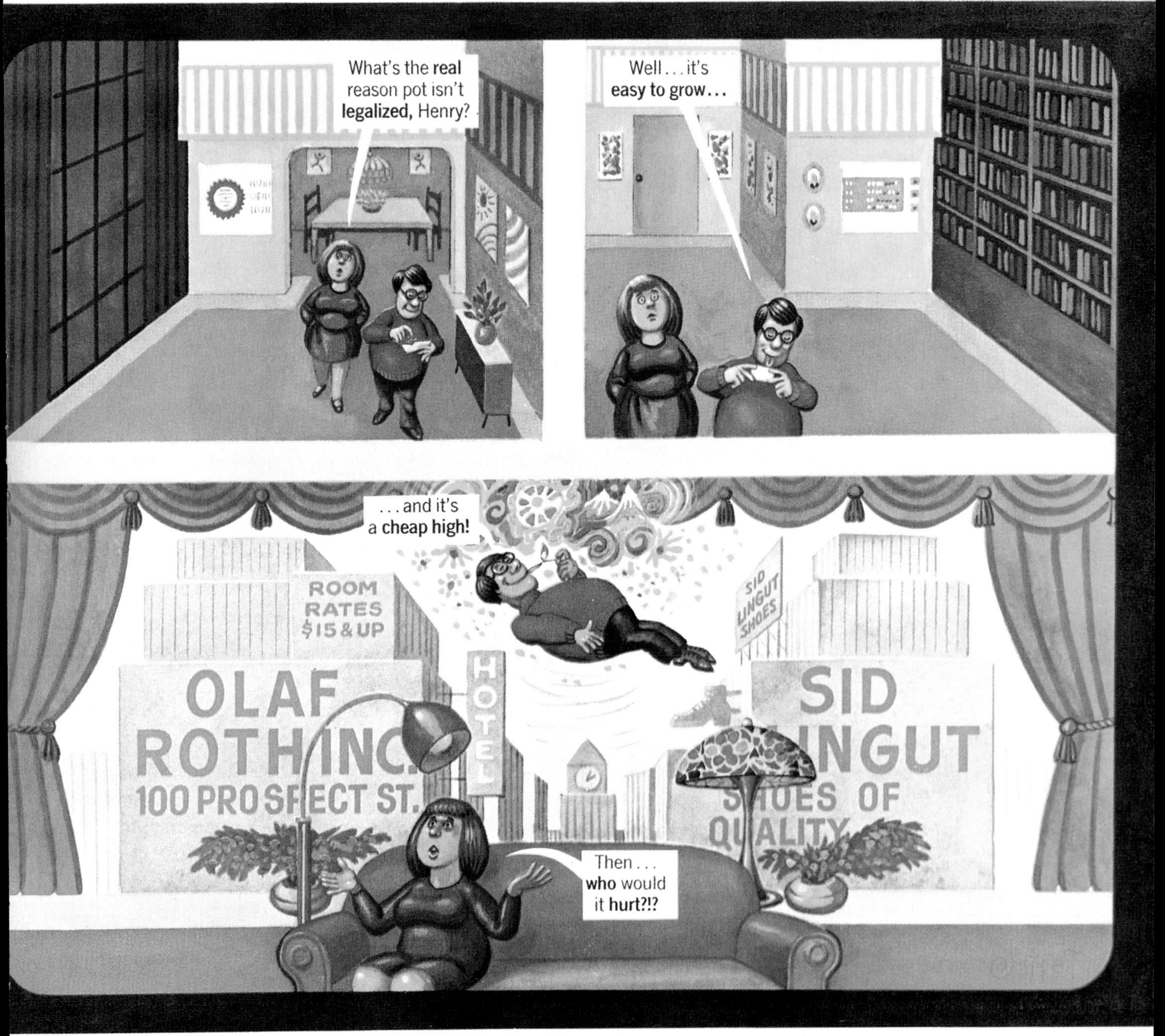

What's the **real** reason pot isn't **legalized,** Henry?
Well . . . it's **easy to grow . . .**
. . . and it's a **cheap high!**
ROOM RATES $15 & UP
SID LINGUT SHOES
HOTEL
OLAF ROTH INC. 100 PROSPECT ST.
SID LINGUT SHOES OF QUALITY
Then . . . **who would it hurt?!?**

THE MISGUIDED POT SMOKER IS MERELY A NAUGHTY BOOB TO MANY. BUT OTHERS WOULD PENALIZE BUSTED POTHEADS SEVERELY FOR THEIR SILLINESS

ARTIST & WRITER: AL JAFFEE

A▸ ◂B

A MOVING JUNGLE TALE

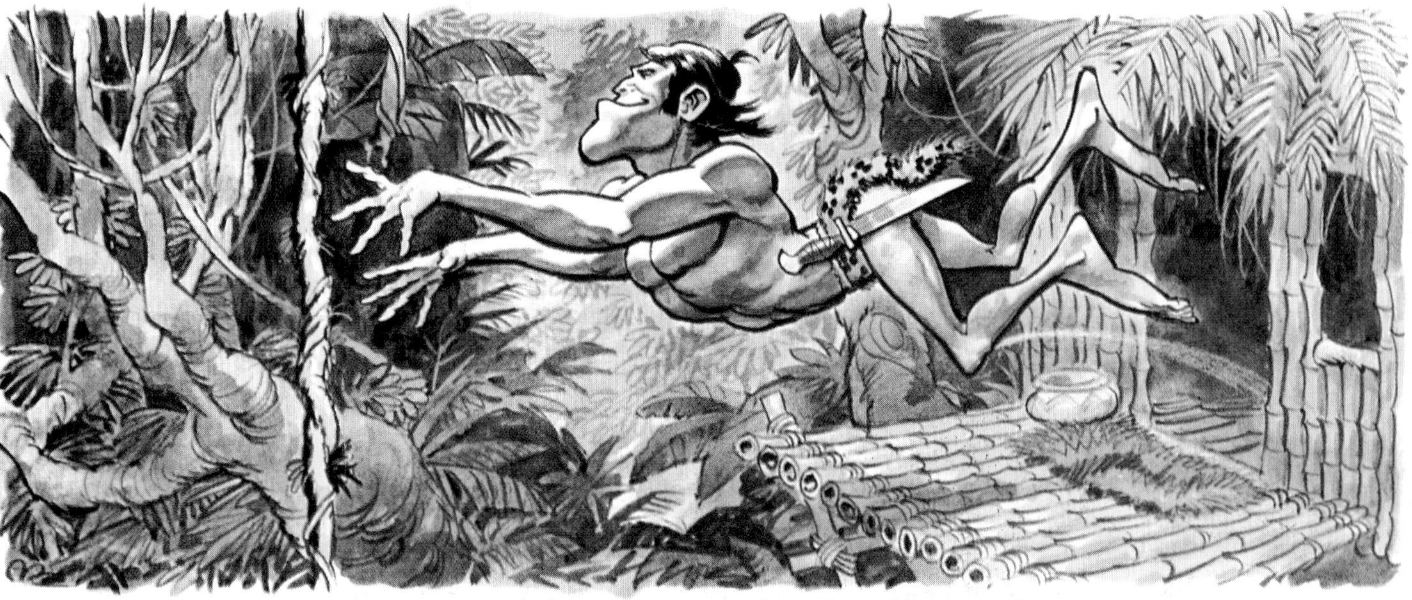

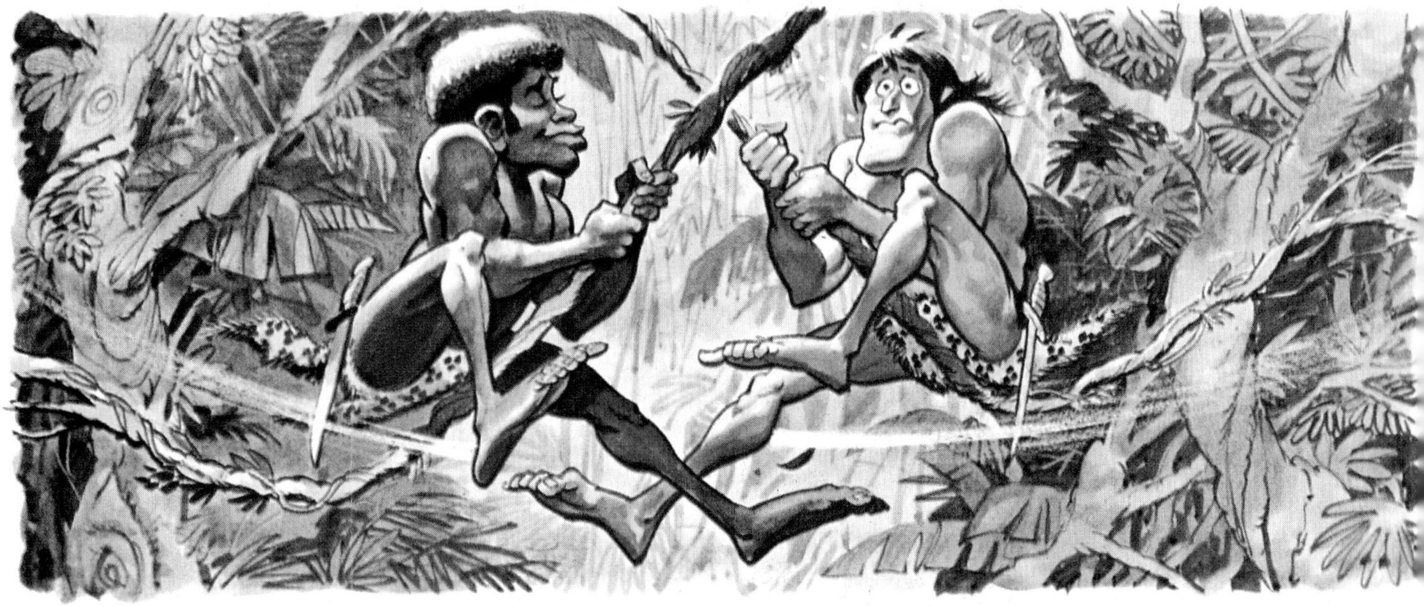

WRITER: DON EDWING ARTIST: JACK DAVIS

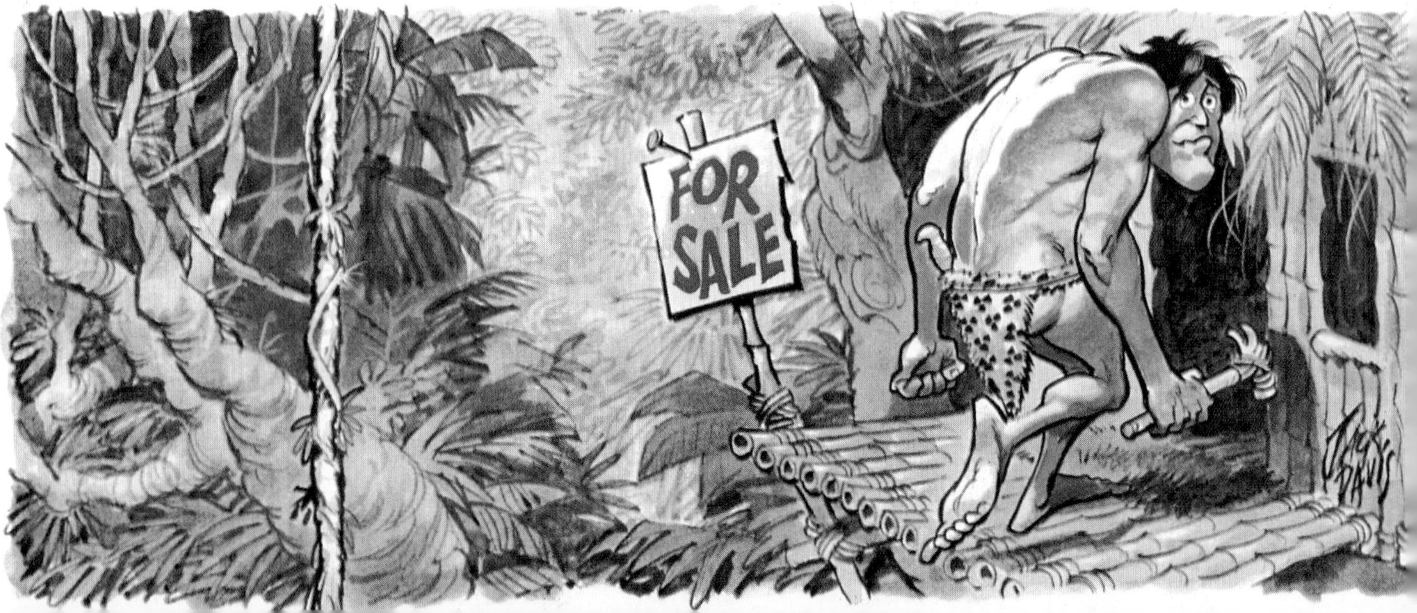
FOR SALE

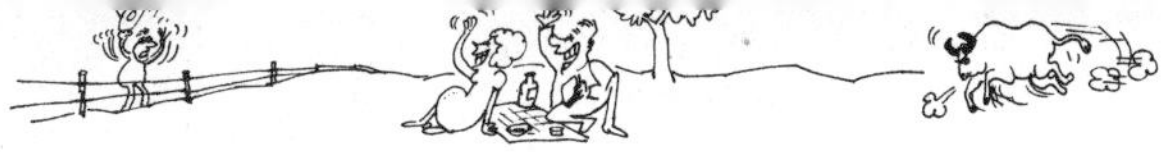

Let's face it. Mother Goose is out of date. Like what five-year-old really cares about Mary and her little lamb, or if Jack Horner really sat in a corner? Kids today are sharp, hip, forward-looking. They want to know about the Big Names of the Present. Let us, then, dedicate ourselves to the education of the Romper Set as we present

MAD'S UP-DATED MODERN DAY MOTHER GOOSE

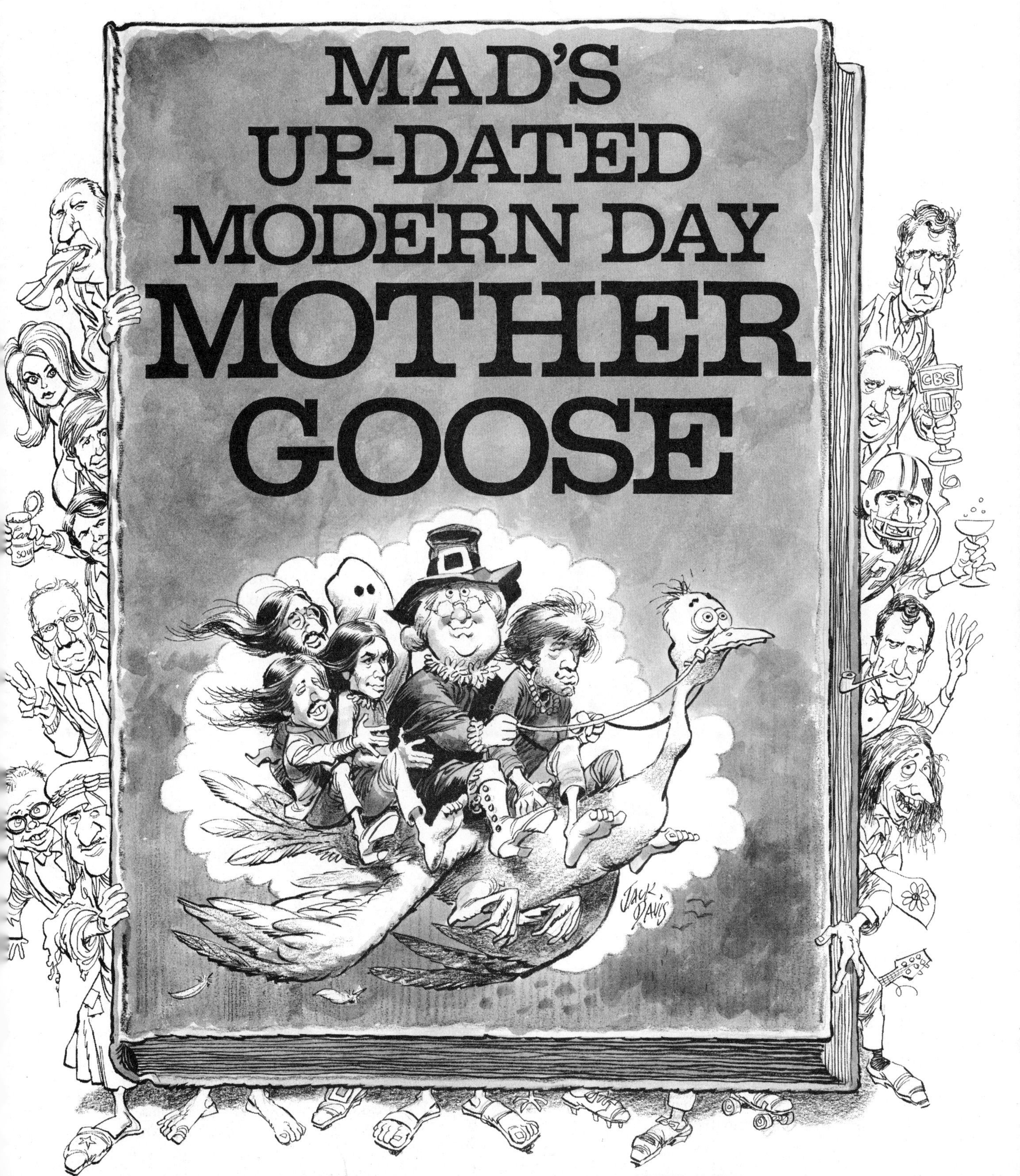
CBS
JACK DAVIS

ARTIST: JACK DAVIS WRITER: FRANK JACOBS

Spiro Agnew

Spiro Agnew spoke off the cuff;
Spiro Agnew spoke very tough;
All of his friends in the North and the South
Couldn't remove Spiro's foot from his mouth!

Hefner Had A Magazine

Hefner had a magazine,
Which first shocked many folks
With color spreads of half-nude girls
And sort-of-dirty jokes;

But now we're bombed with raunchy filth
And pornographic swill,
Which makes poor Hefner's magazine
Seem more like "Jack and Jill"!

Broadway Joe And Pete Rozelle

Broadway Joe and Pete Rozelle
Resolved to have a scrimmage,
For Pete Rozelle said Broadway Joe
Was spoiling football's image;

Although they had an awful fight
And very nearly parted,
You'll notice that they patched things up
Before the season started!

Pat-A-Cake, Pat-A-Cake, Tiny Tim

Pat-a-cake, pat-a-cake, Tiny Tim—
Are you a her, or are you a him?
Pat-a-cake, pat-a-cake, we won't guess,
Because, Tiny Tim, we couldn't care less!

Five Little Hippies

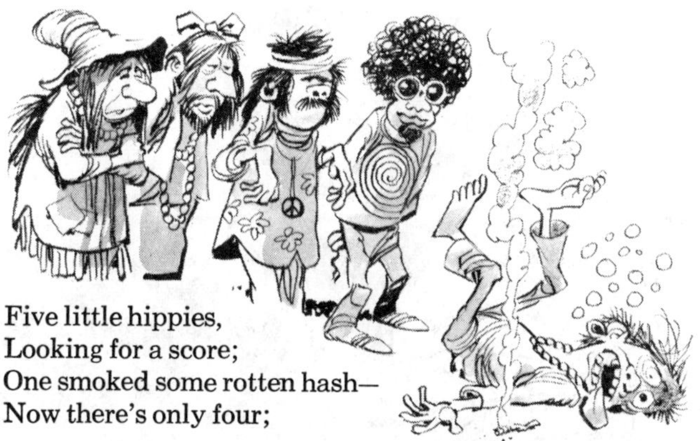

Five little hippies,
Looking for a score;
One smoked some rotten hash—
Now there's only four;

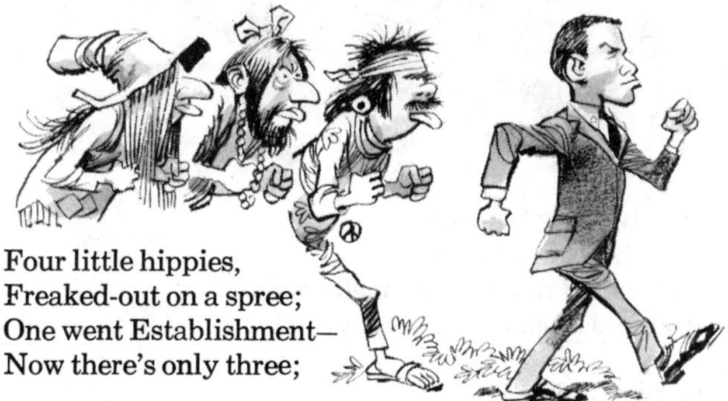

Four little hippies,
Freaked-out on a spree;
One went Establishment—
Now there's only three;

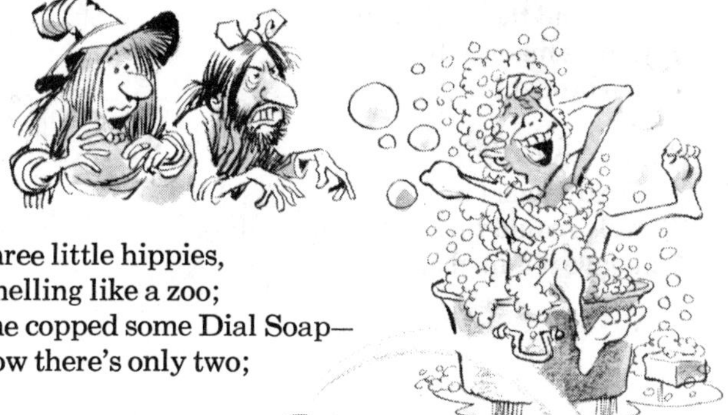

Three little hippies,
Smelling like a zoo;
One copped some Dial Soap—
Now there's only two;

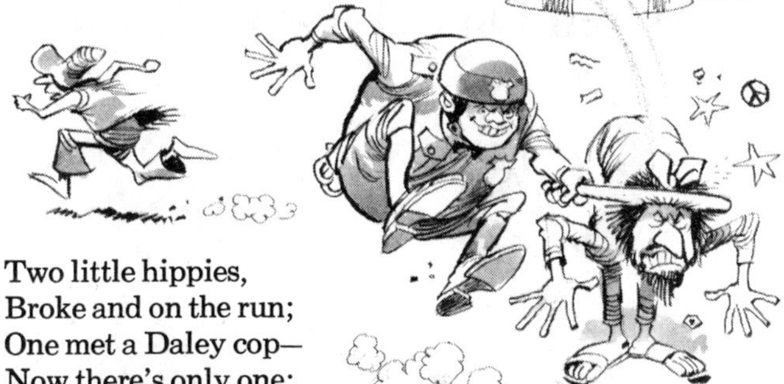

Two little hippies,
Broke and on the run;
One met a Daley cop—
Now there's only one;

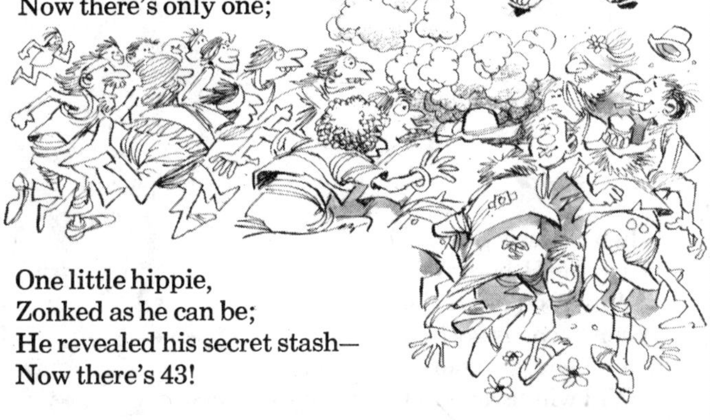

One little hippie,
Zonked as he can be;
He revealed his secret stash—
Now there's 43!

Gamel, Gamel, Bright As A Camel

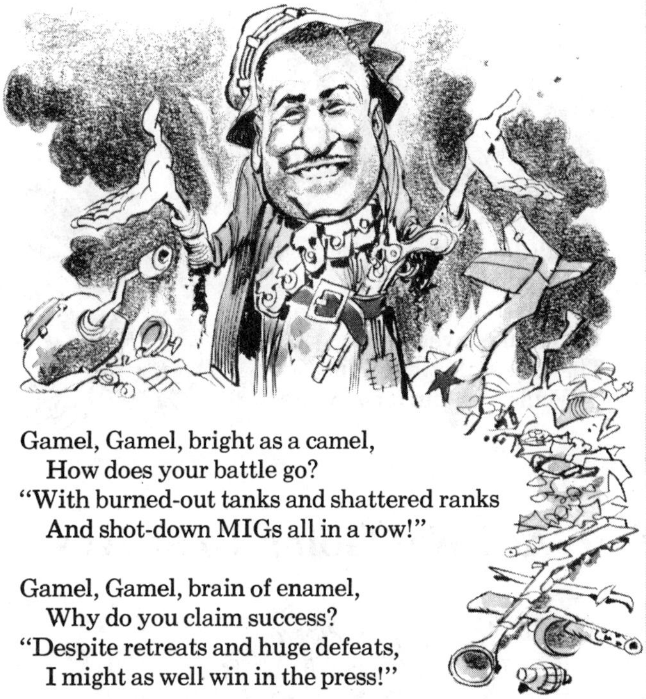

Gamel, Gamel, bright as a camel,
How does your battle go?
"With burned-out tanks and shattered ranks
And shot-down MIGs all in a row!"

Gamel, Gamel, brain of enamel,
Why do you claim success?
"Despite retreats and huge defeats,
I might as well win in the press!"

Ringo, Paul, George & John

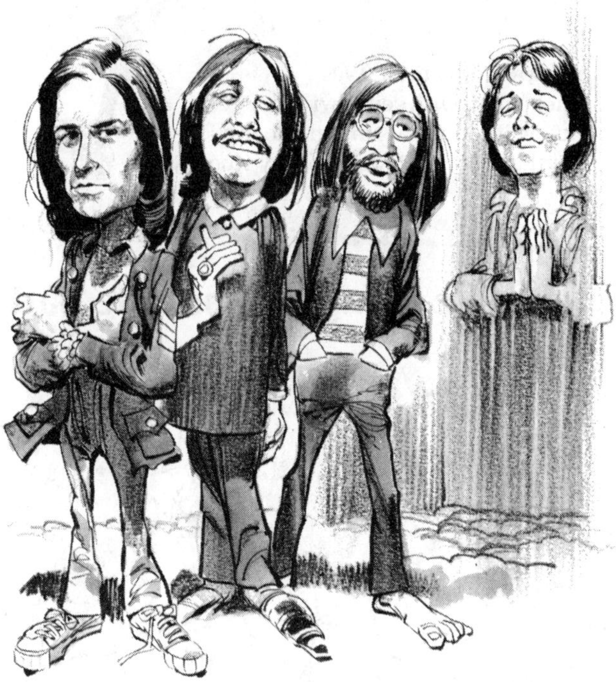

Ringo, Paul, George and John
Played a trick and put us on;
Dropped hints Paul was dead as nails—
And rocketed their record sales!

Stingy Jack Benny

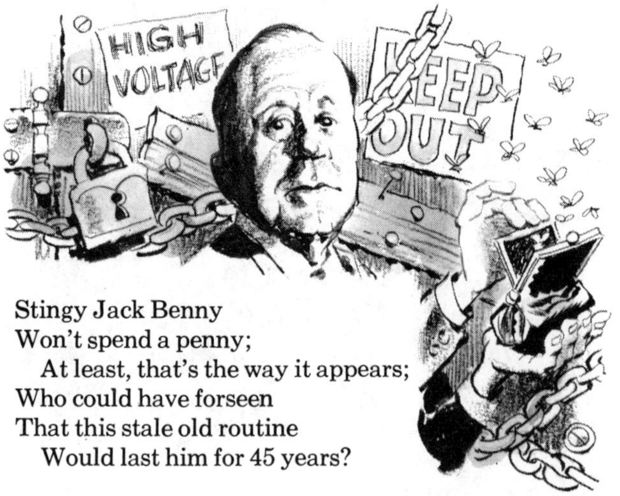
HIGH VOLTAGE
KEEP OUT

Stingy Jack Benny
Won't spend a penny;
At least, that's the way it appears;
Who could have forseen
That this stale old routine
Would last him for 45 years?

As I Was Going To St. Ives

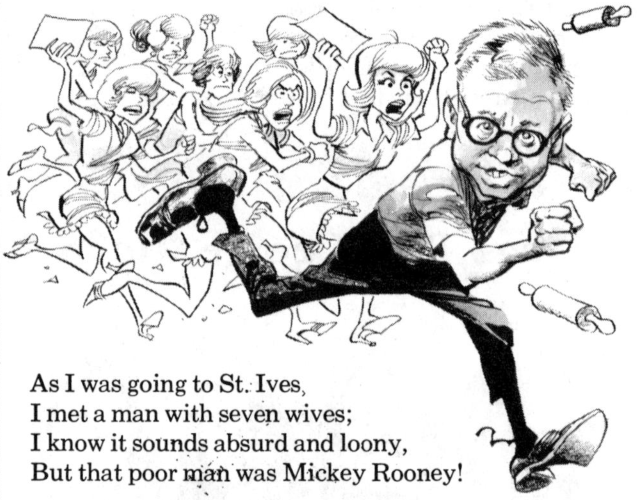

As I was going to St. Ives,
I met a man with seven wives;
I know it sounds absurd and loony,
But that poor man was Mickey Rooney!

Jane Be Naughty, Jane Be Bad

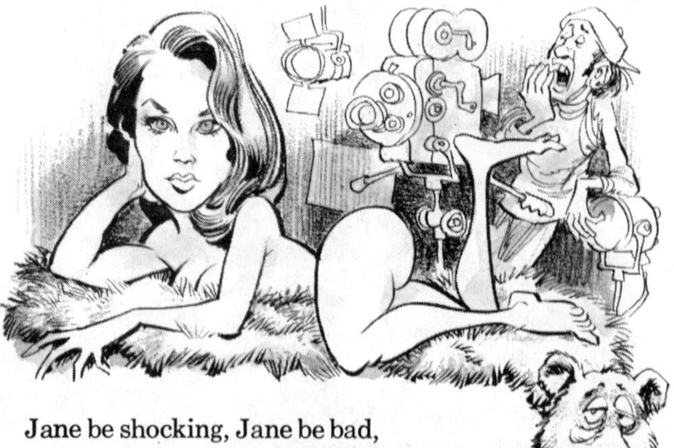

Jane be shocking, Jane be bad,
Jane pose in movies all unclad;
Jane big nothing, Jane big bore,
Jane please put on your clothes once more!

Handy Andy Warhol

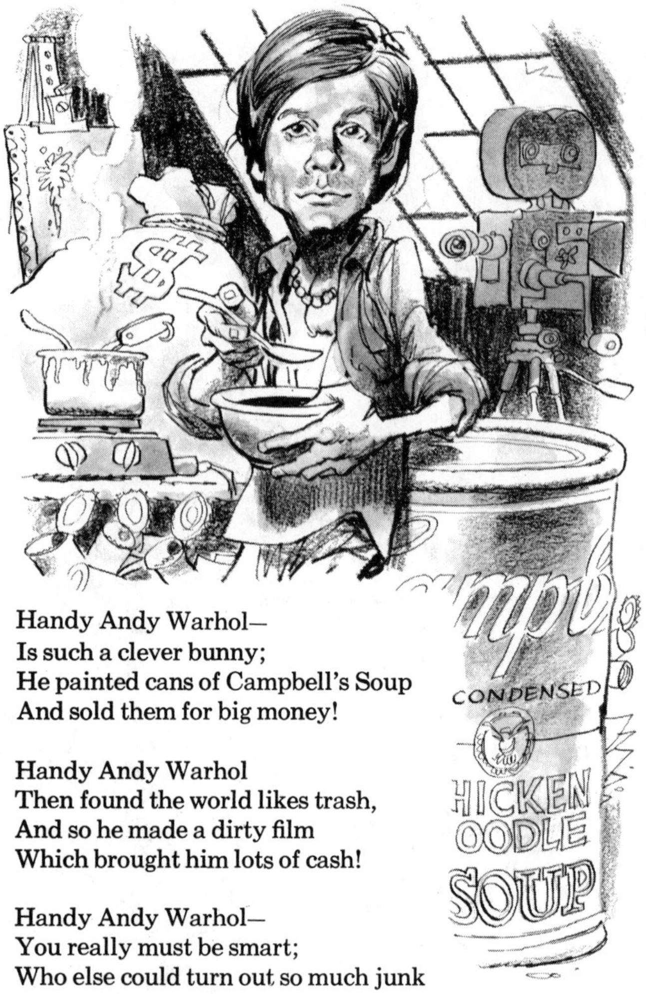
CONDENSED
HICKEN
OODLE
SOUP

Handy Andy Warhol—
Is such a clever bunny;
He painted cans of Campbell's Soup
And sold them for big money!

Handy Andy Warhol
Then found the world likes trash,
And so he made a dirty film
Which brought him lots of cash!

Handy Andy Warhol—
You really must be smart;
Who else could turn out so much junk
And have it hailed as "art"!

When Onassis Goes Broke

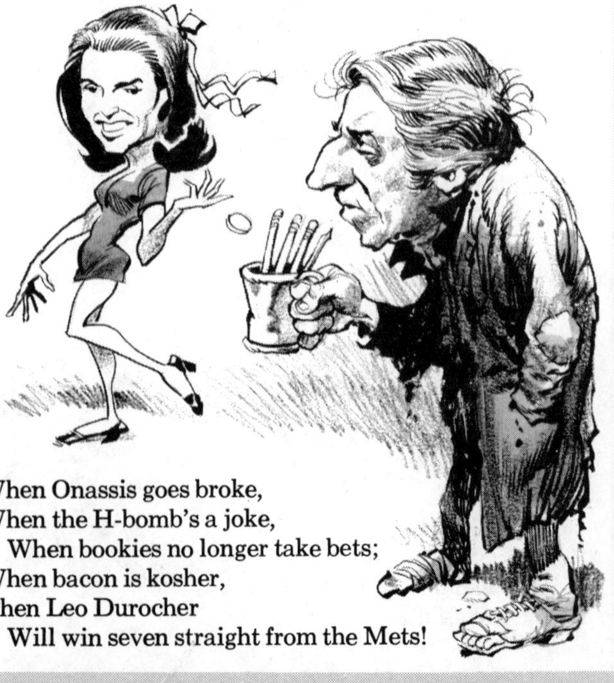

When Onassis goes broke,
When the H-bomb's a joke,
When bookies no longer take bets;
When bacon is kosher,
Then Leo Durocher
Will win seven straight from the Mets!

Wee Timmy Leary

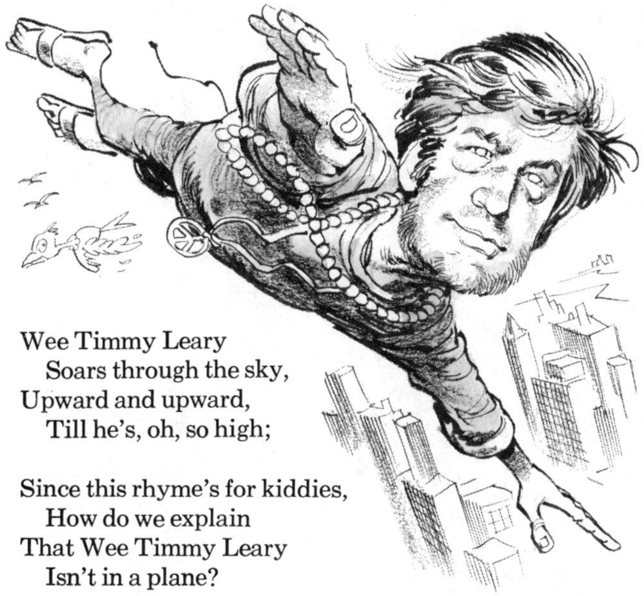

Wee Timmy Leary
  Soars through the sky,
Upward and upward,
  Till he's, oh, so high;

Since this rhyme's for kiddies,
  How do we explain
That Wee Timmy Leary
  Isn't in a plane?

Sing A Song Of Pitchmen

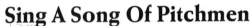

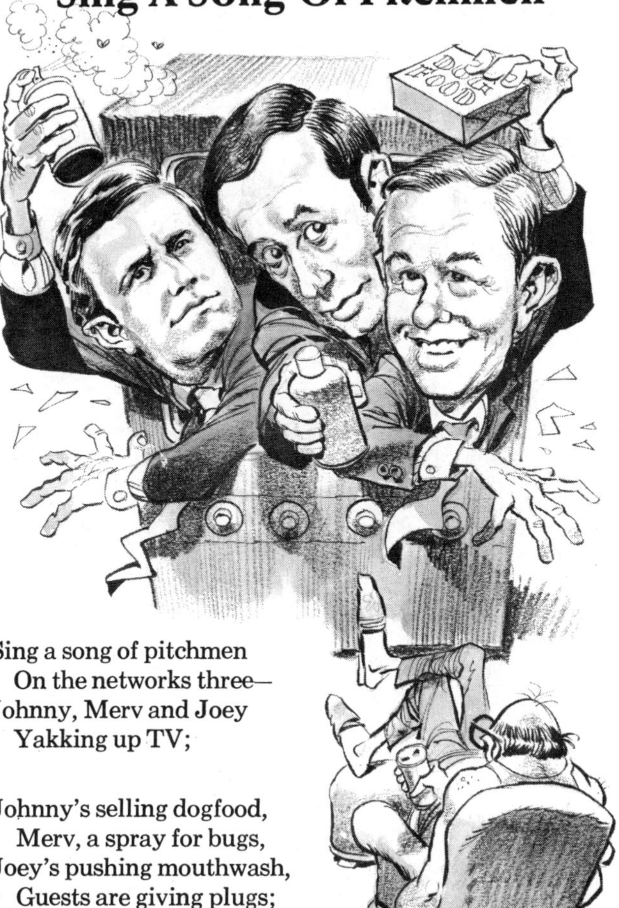
DOG FOOD

Sing a song of pitchmen
  On the networks three—
Johnny, Merv and Joey
  Yakking up TV;

Johnny's selling dogfood,
  Merv, a spray for bugs,
Joey's pushing mouthwash,
  Guests are giving plugs;

When their shows are over,
  And we've choked our grief,
Even David Susskind
  Seems a big relief!

Warren Beatty Had A Sweetie

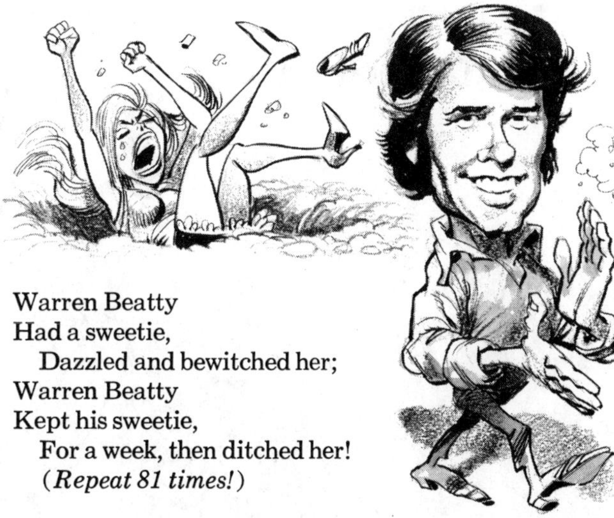

Warren Beatty
Had a sweetie,
  Dazzled and bewitched her;
Warren Beatty
Kept his sweetie,
  For a week, then ditched her!
  (*Repeat 81 times!*)

If Wishes Were Horses

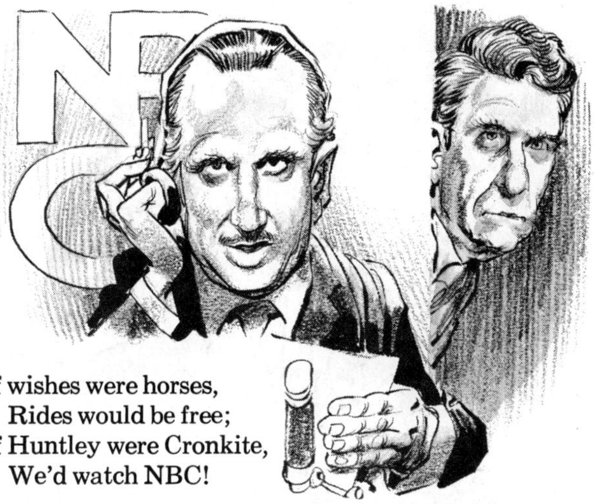

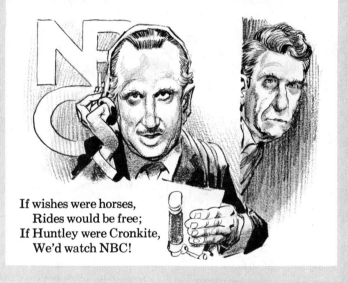

If wishes were horses,
  Rides would be free;
If Huntley were Cronkite,
  We'd watch NBC!

Spock, Spock, The Baby Doc

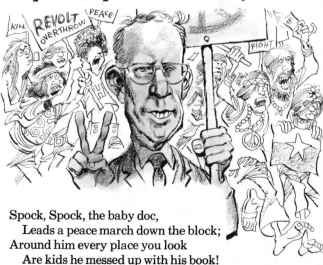

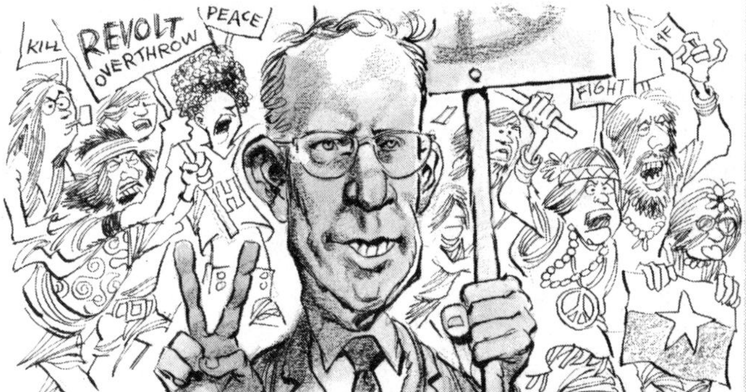
KILL
REVOLT
OVERTHROW
PEACE
FIGHT

Spock, Spock, the baby doc,
  Leads a peace march down the block;
Around him every place you look
  Are kids he messed up with his book!

BOMBING THE BAN-ERS DEPT.

SERGIO ARAGONES TAKES A MAD LOOK AT...

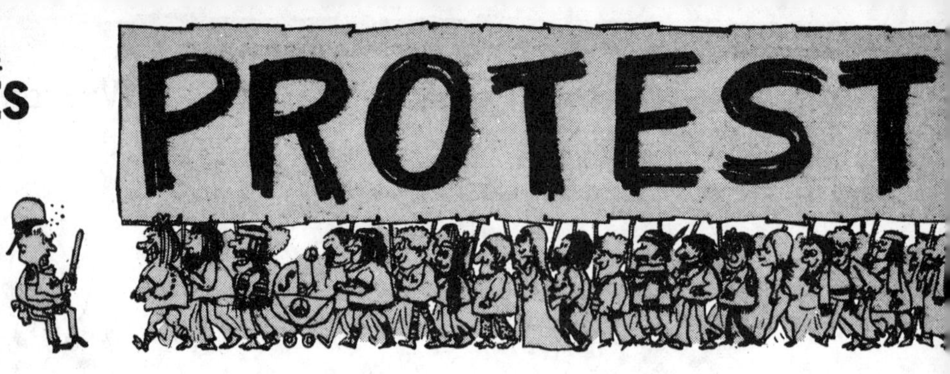
PROTEST

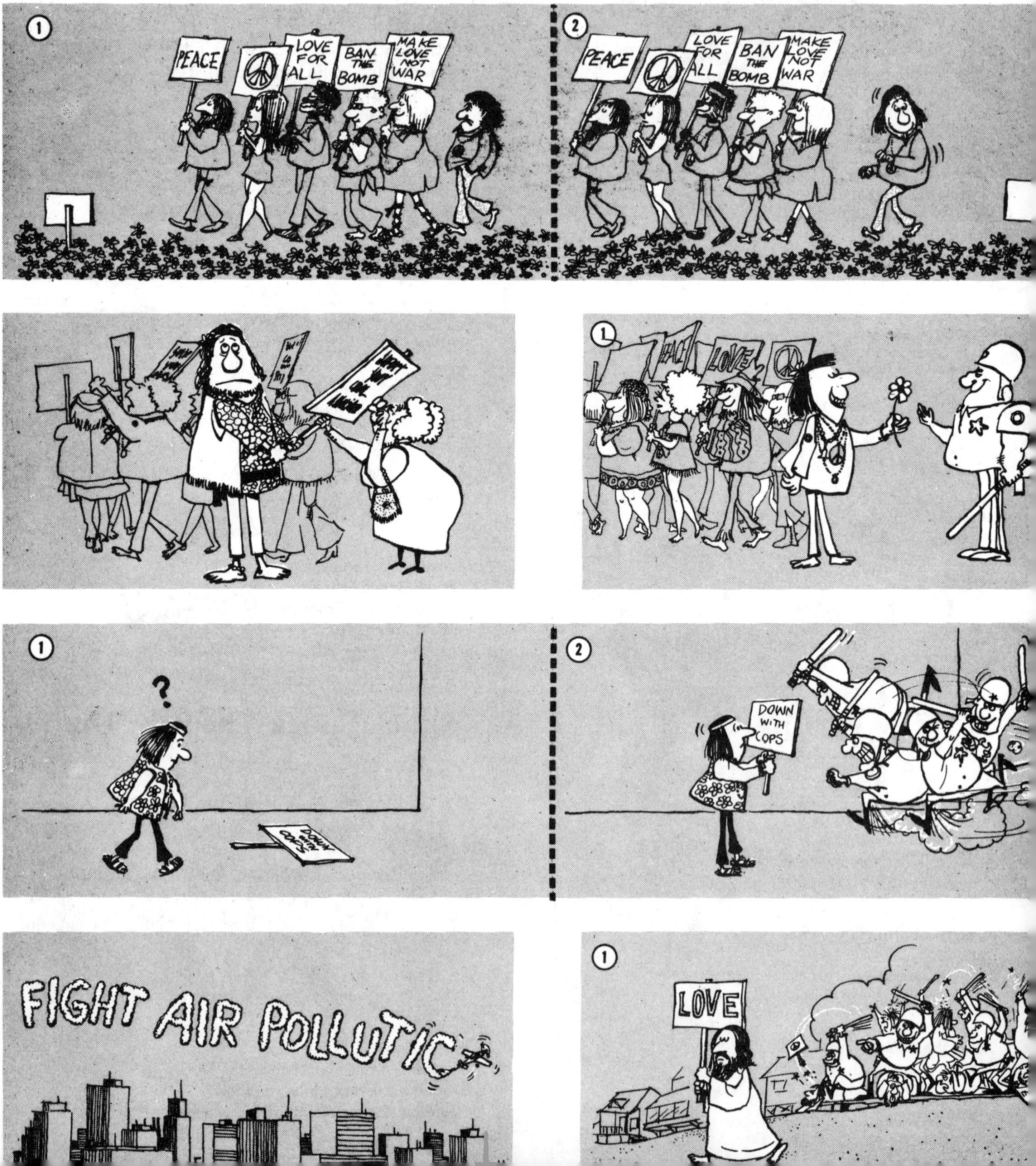
1
PEACE
LOVE FOR ALL
BAN THE BOMB
MAKE LOVE NOT WAR
2
PEACE
LOVE FOR ALL
BAN THE BOMB
MAKE LOVE NOT WAR
1
PEACE
LOVE
1
?
DOWN WITH COPS
2
DOWN WITH COPS
FIGHT AIR POLLUTIC
1
LOVE

DEMONSTRATIONS

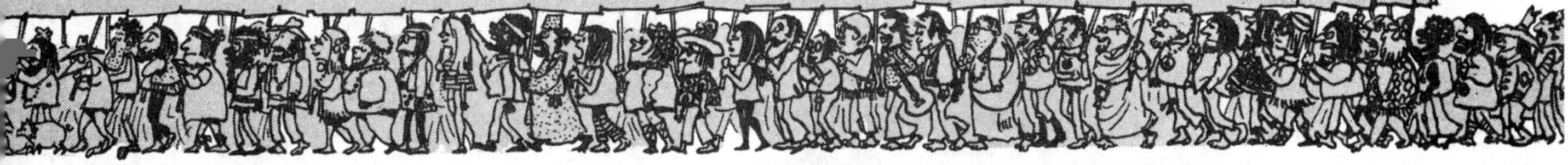

ARTIST & WRITER: SERGIO ARAGONES

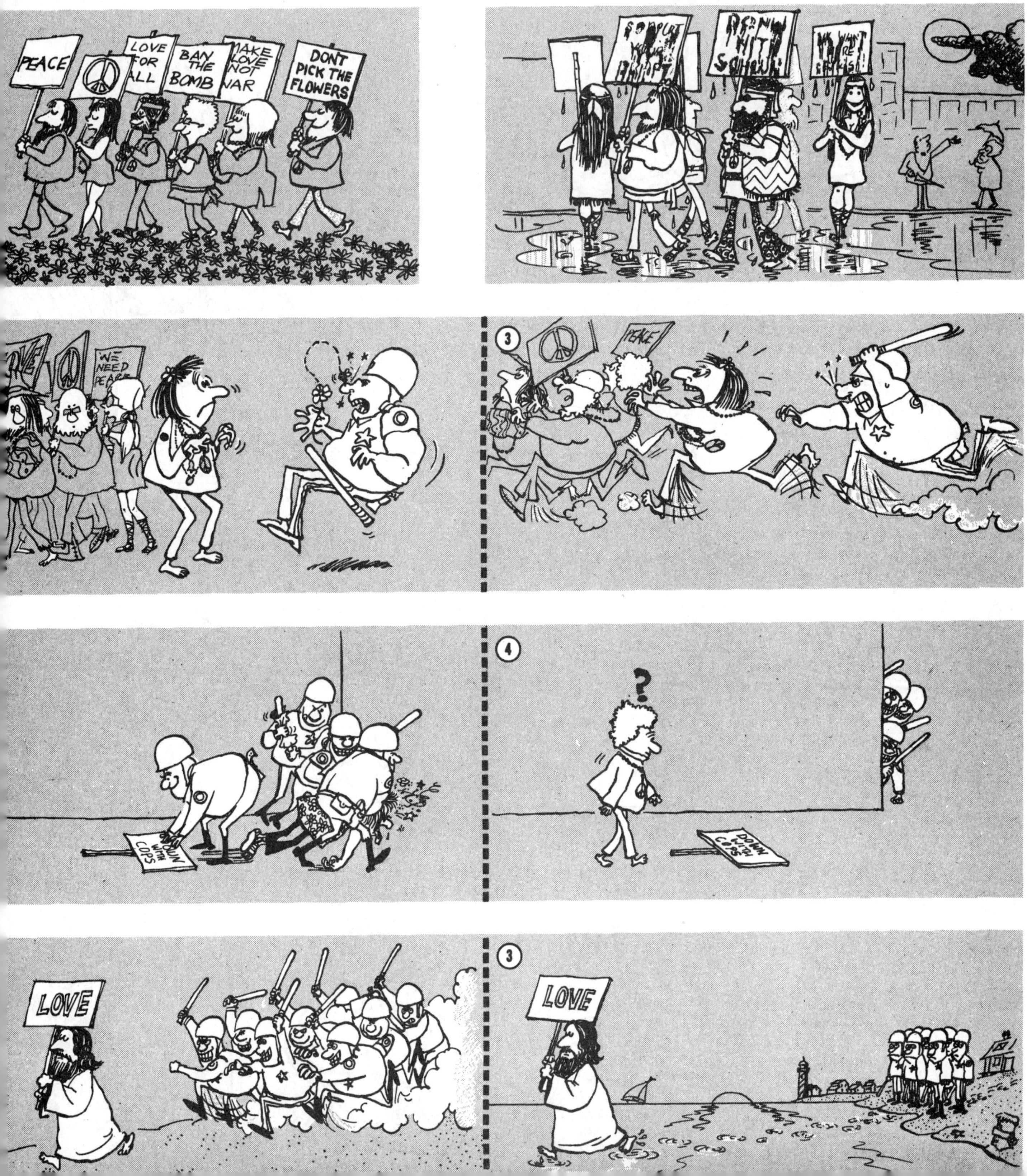
PEACE
LOVE FOR ALL
BAN THE BOMB
MAKE LOVE NOT WAR
DON'T PICK THE FLOWERS
WE NEED PEACE
3
PEACE
DOWN WITH COPS
4
DOWN WITH COPS
LOVE
3
LOVE

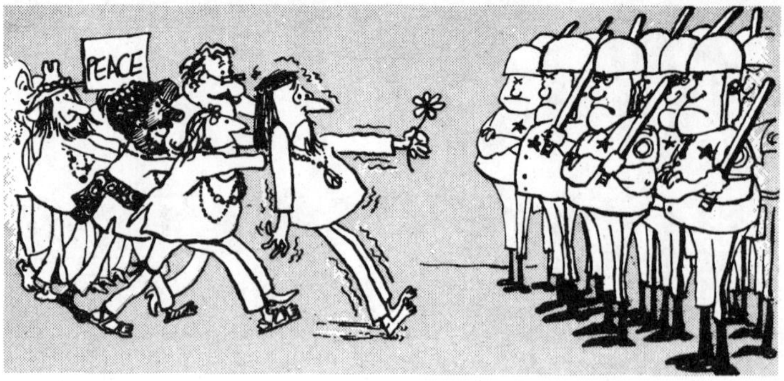
PEACE

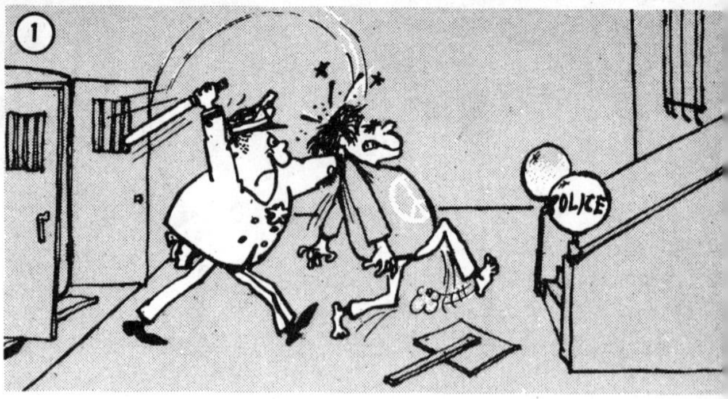
1
POLICE

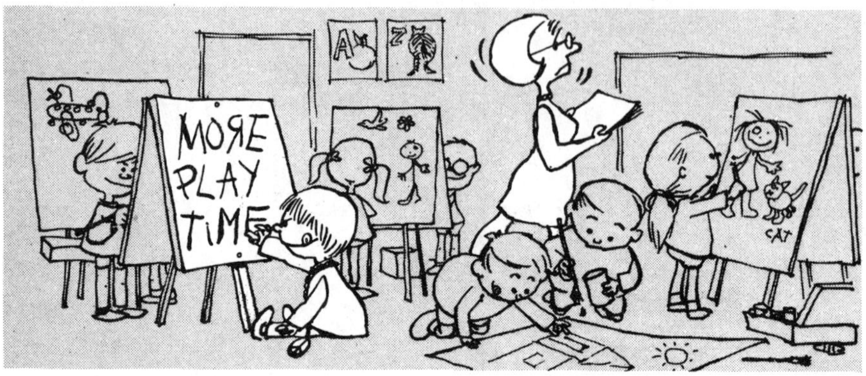
MORE PLAY TIME
CAT

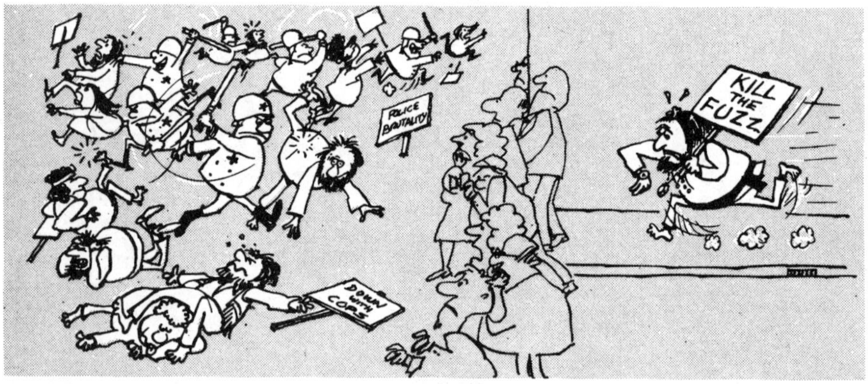
POLICE BRUTALITY
KILL THE FUZZ
DOWN WITH COPS

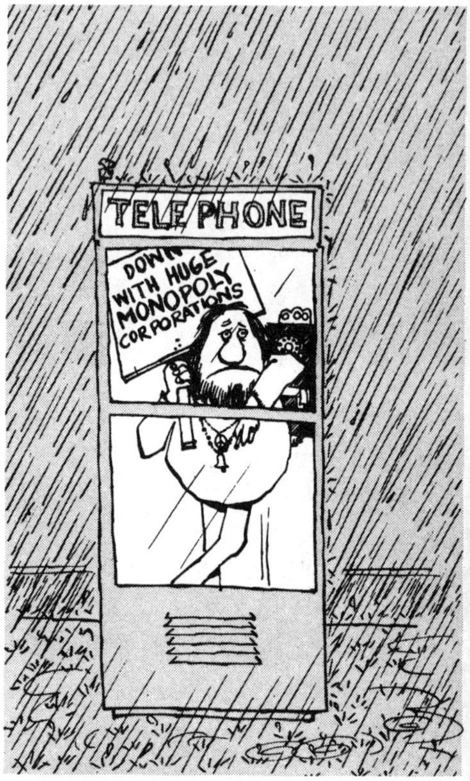
TELEPHONE
DOWN WITH HUGE MONOPOLY CORPORATIONS

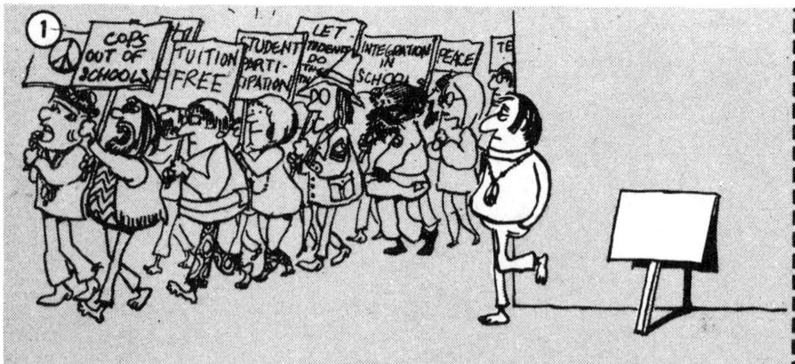
1
COPS OUT OF SCHOOLS
TUITION FREE
STUDENT PARTI-CIPATION
INTEGRATION IN SCHOOLS
PEACE

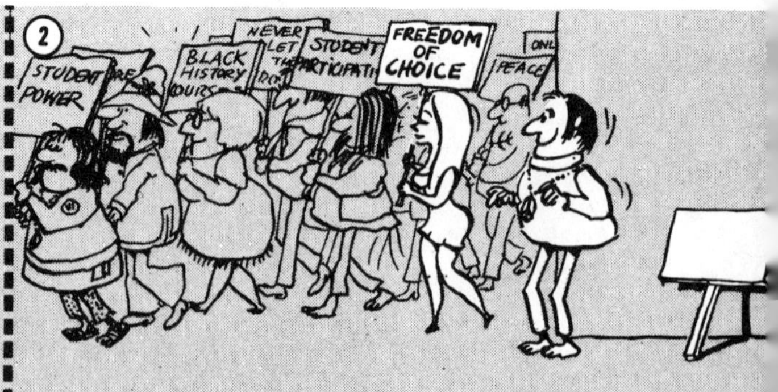
2
STUDENT POWER
FREEDOM OF CHOICE
PEACE

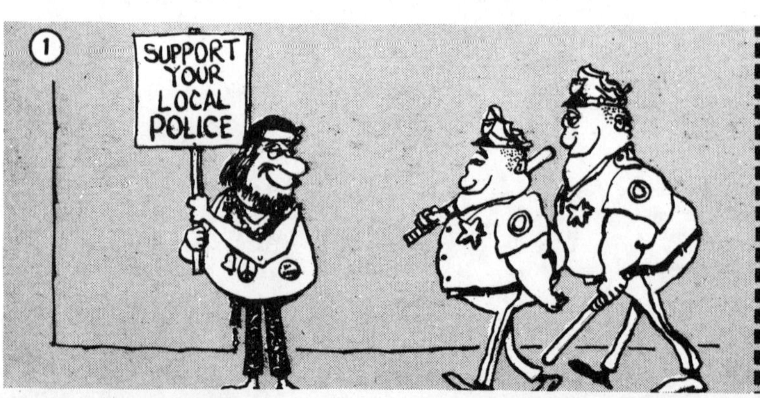
1
SUPPORT YOUR LOCAL POLICE

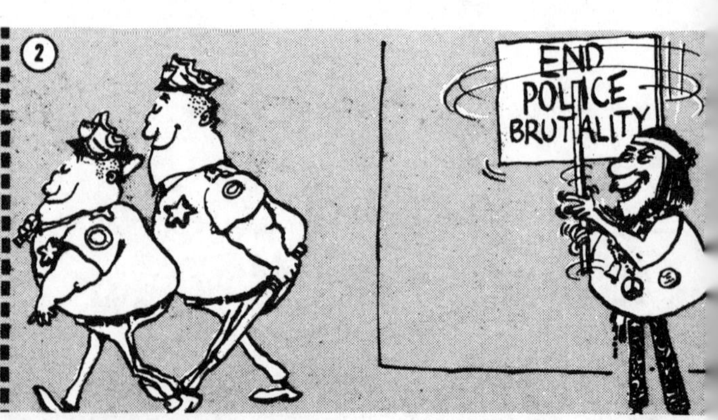
2
END POLICE BRUTALITY

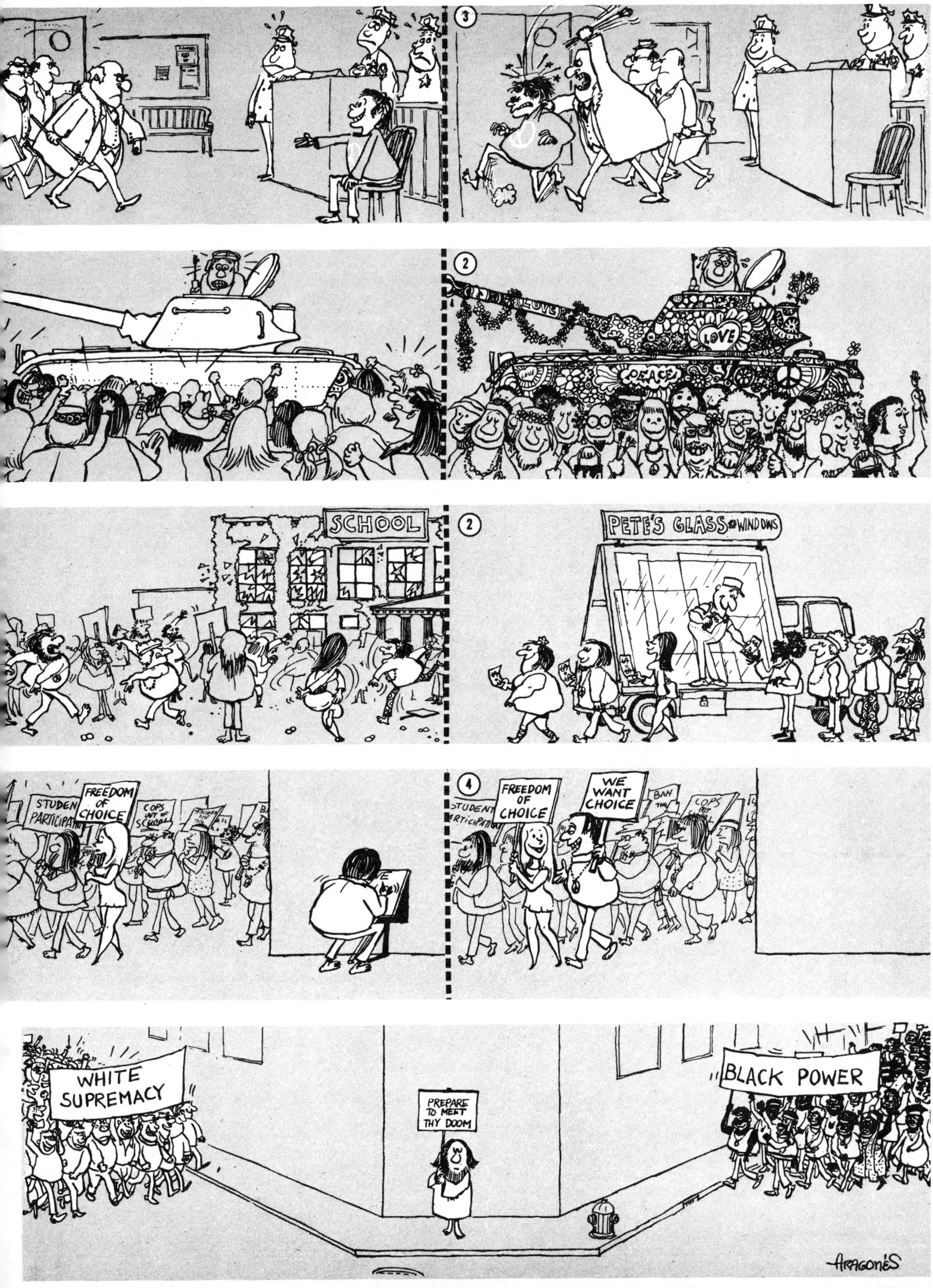

3
2
LOVE
LOVE
LOVE
PEACE
SCHOOL
2
PETE'S GLASS & WINDOWS
FREEDOM OF CHOICE
4
FREEDOM OF CHOICE
WE WANT CHOICE
WHITE SUPREMACY
PREPARE TO MEET THY DOOM
BLACK POWER
ARAGONÉS

There's a "now" movie around—about two "now" guys who ride on "now" wheels . . .

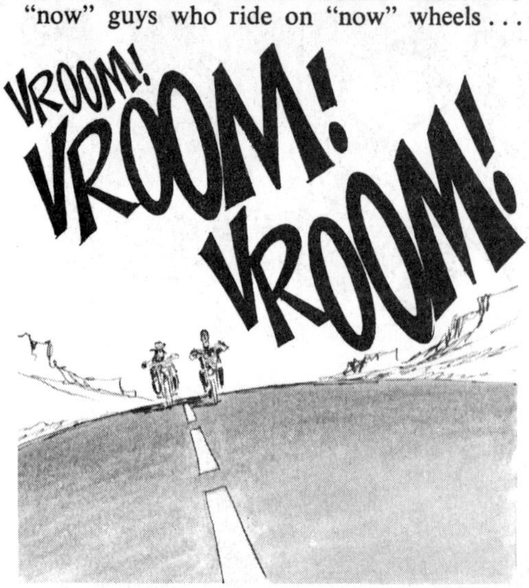
VROOM!
VROOM!
VROOM!

. . . and smoke "now" grass, and pop "now" pills and talk "now" talk . . .

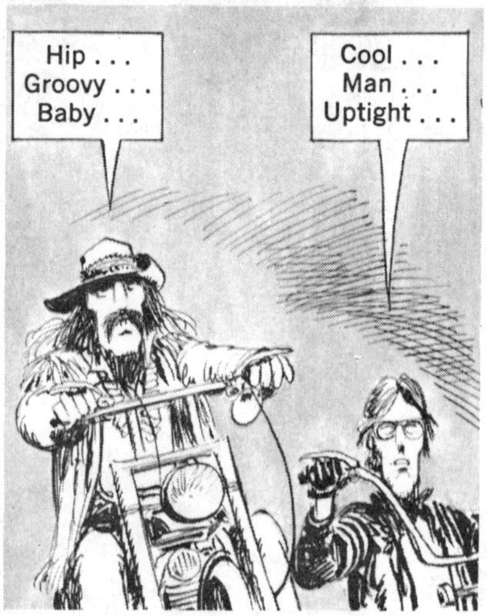
Hip . . . Groovy . . . Baby . . .
Cool . . . Man . . . Uptight . . .

. . . while some "now" performers pla and sing "now" music in the background

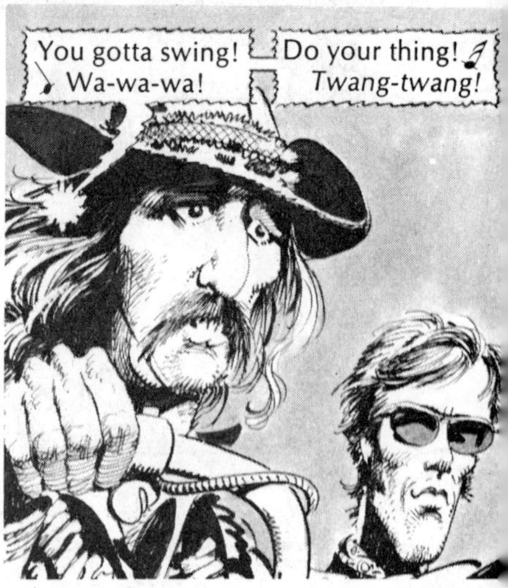
You gotta swing! Wa-wa-wa!
Do your thing! Twang-twang!

What are these two "now" guys looking for in this movie? Well, according to the newspaper ads, they're looking for "America", but they can't find it anywhere! And what are we "MAD" guys looking for in this movie? We're looking for a "plot", but we can't find *that* anywhere! You'll see what we mean as we bring you our "MAD" version of

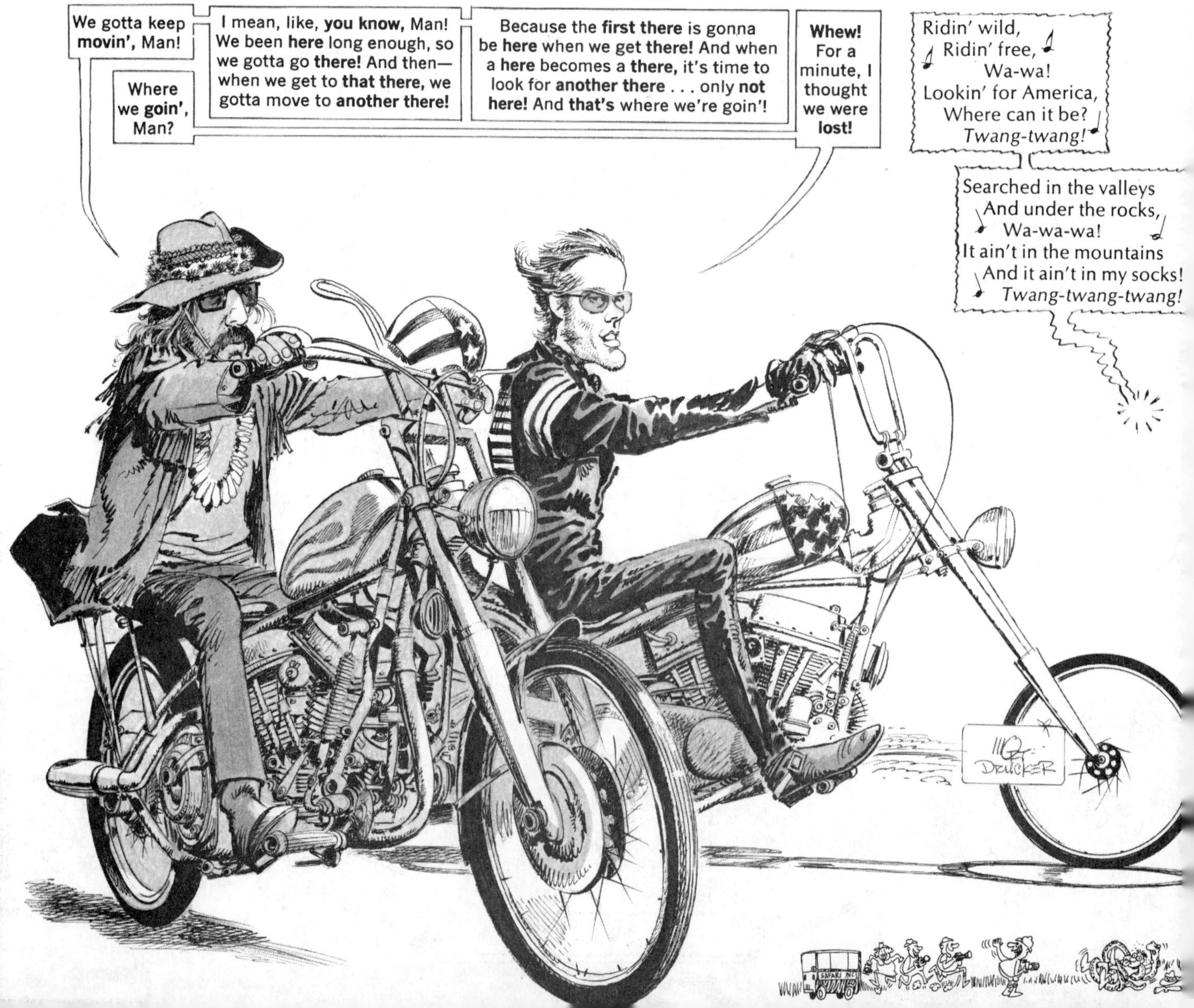
We gotta keep **movin'**, Man!
Where we **goin'**, Man?
I mean, like, **you know,** Man! We been **here** long enough, so we gotta go **there!** And then—when we get to **that there,** we gotta move to **another there!**
Because the **first there** is gonna be **here** when we get **there!** And when a **here** becomes a **there,** it's time to look for **another there** . . . only **not here!** And **that's** where we're goin'!
Whew! For a minute, I thought we were **lost!**
Ridin' wild, Ridin' free, Wa-wa! Lookin' for America, Where can it be? *Twang-twang!*
Searched in the valleys And under the rocks, Wa-wa-wa! It ain't in the mountains And it ain't in my socks! *Twang-twang-twang!*
DRUCKER

SLEAZY RIDERS

ARTIST: MORT DRUCKER WRITER: LARRY SIEGEL

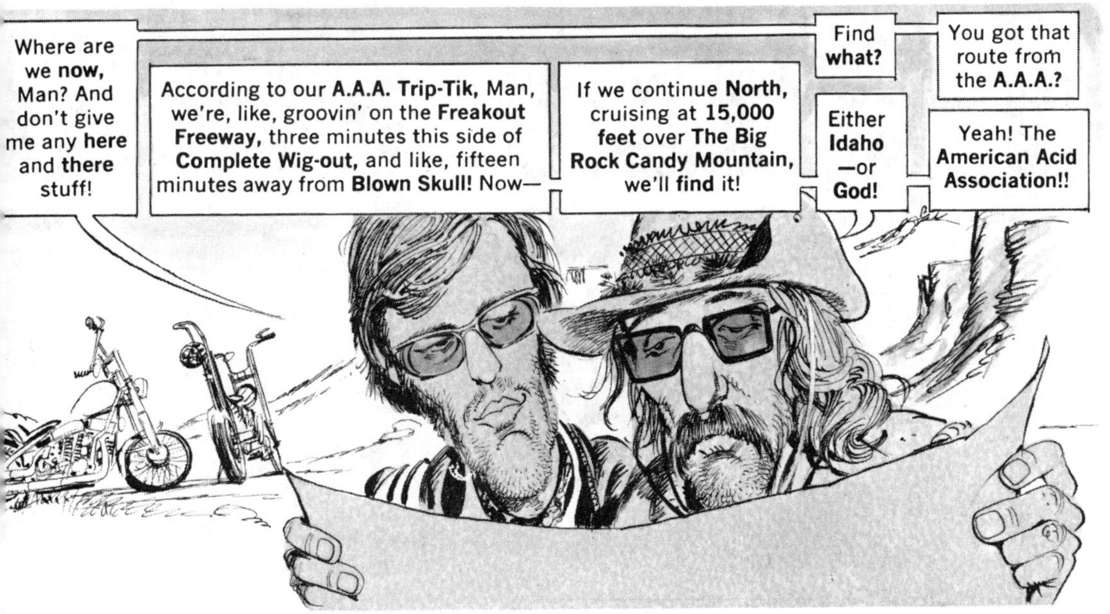
Where are we now, Man? And don't give me any here and there stuff!
According to our A.A.A. Trip-Tik, Man, we're, like, groovin' on the Freakout Freeway, three minutes this side of Complete Wig-out, and like, fifteen minutes away from Blown Skull! Now—
If we continue North, cruising at 15,000 feet over The Big Rock Candy Mountain, we'll find it!
Find what?
Either Idaho —or God!
You got that route from the A.A.A.?
Yeah! The American Acid Association!!

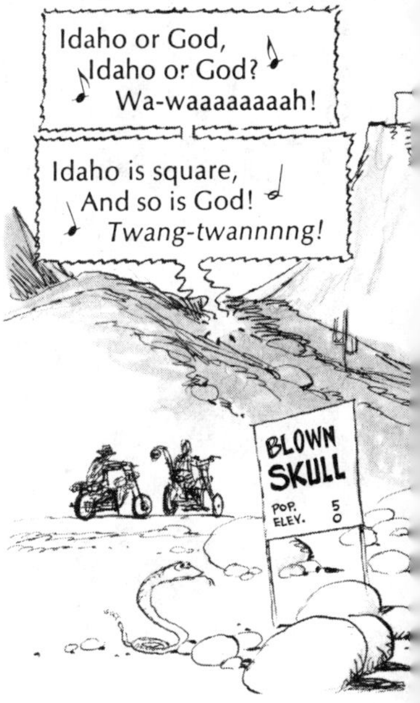
Idaho or God, Idaho or God? Wa-waaaaaaaah!
Idaho is square, And so is God! Twang-twannnng!
BLOWN SKULL
POP. 5
ELEV. 0

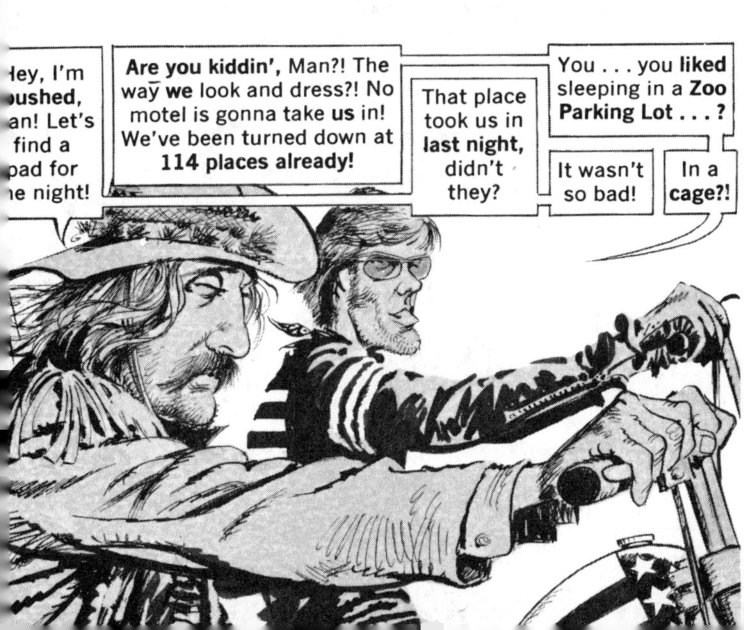
ley, I'm ushed, an! Let's find a pad for e night!
Are you kiddin', Man?! The way we look and dress?! No motel is gonna take us in! We've been turned down at 114 places already!
That place took us in last night, didn't they?
You . . . you liked sleeping in a Zoo Parking Lot . . . ?
It wasn't so bad!
In a cage?!

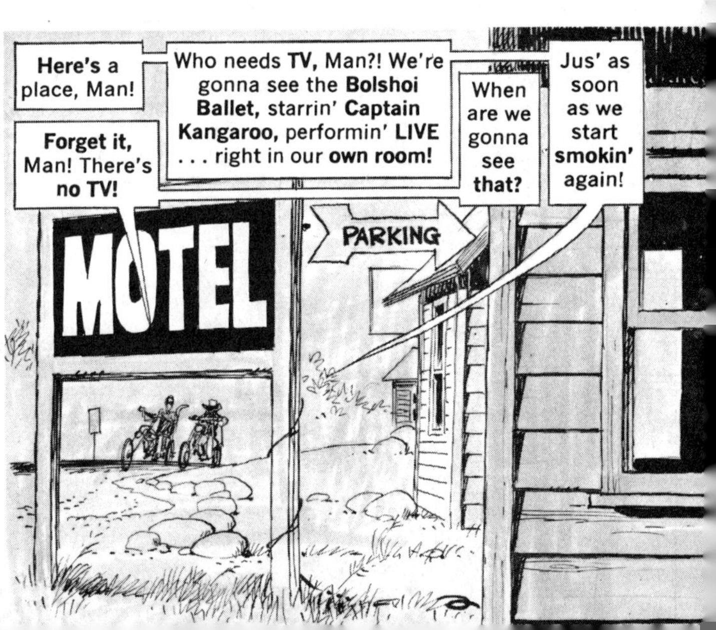
Here's a place, Man!
Forget it, Man! There's no TV!
Who needs TV, Man?! We're gonna see the Bolshoi Ballet, starrin' Captain Kangaroo, performin' LIVE . . . right in our own room!
When are we gonna see that?
Jus' as soon as we start smokin' again!
MOTEL
PARKING

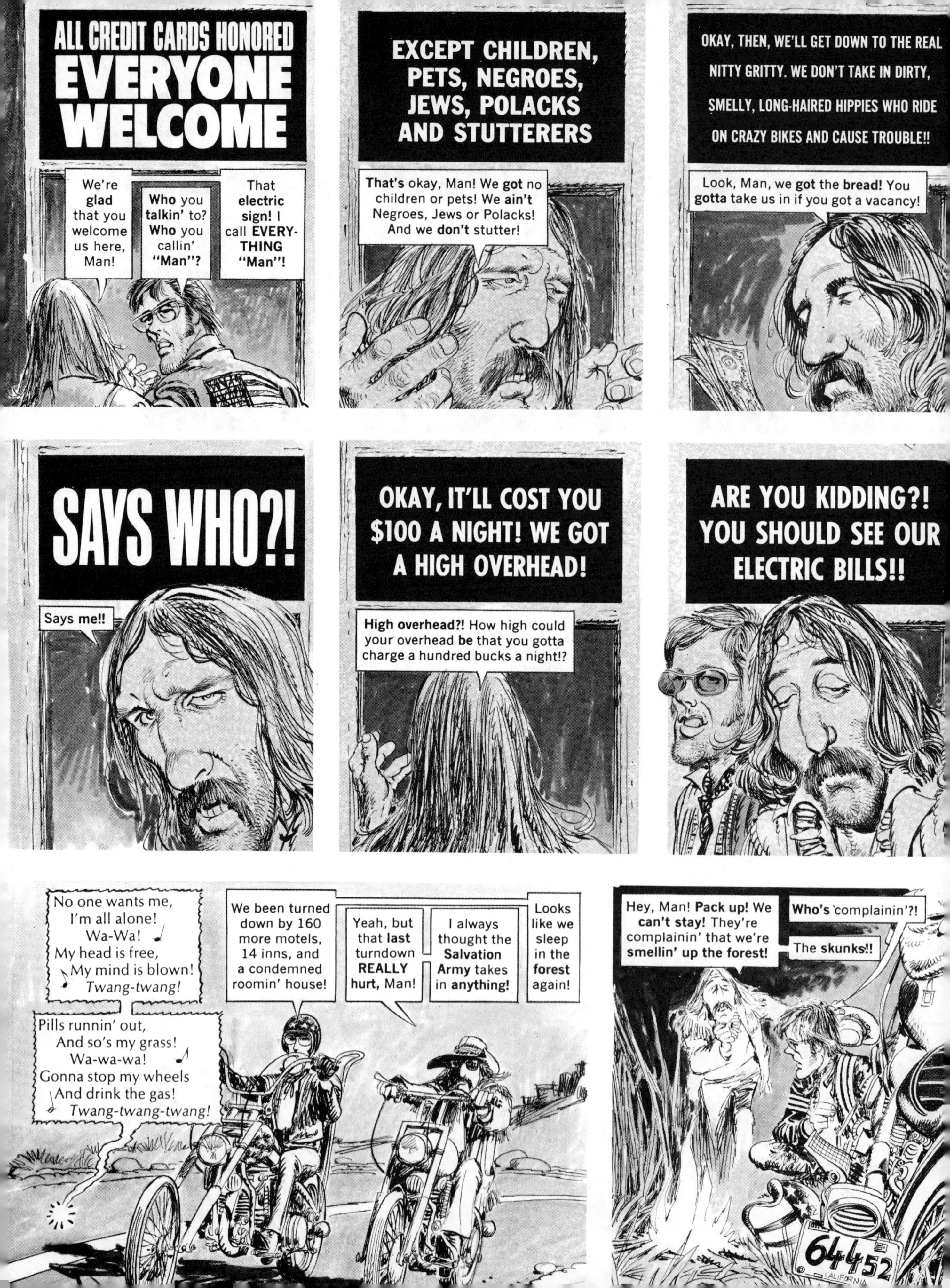
ALL CREDIT CARDS HONORED
EVERYONE WELCOME
We're glad that you welcome us here, Man!
Who you talkin' to? Who you callin' "Man"?
That electric sign! I call EVERYTHING "Man"!
EXCEPT CHILDREN, PETS, NEGROES, JEWS, POLACKS AND STUTTERERS
That's okay, Man! We got no children or pets! We ain't Negroes, Jews or Polacks! And we don't stutter!
OKAY, THEN, WE'LL GET DOWN TO THE REAL NITTY GRITTY. WE DON'T TAKE IN DIRTY, SMELLY, LONG-HAIRED HIPPIES WHO RIDE ON CRAZY BIKES AND CAUSE TROUBLE!!
Look, Man, we got the bread! You gotta take us in if you got a vacancy!
SAYS WHO?!
Says me!!
OKAY, IT'LL COST YOU $100 A NIGHT! WE GOT A HIGH OVERHEAD!
High overhead?! How high could your overhead be that you gotta charge a hundred bucks a night!?
ARE YOU KIDDING?! YOU SHOULD SEE OUR ELECTRIC BILLS!!
No one wants me, I'm all alone! Wa-Wa! My head is free, My mind is blown! Twang-twang!
Pills runnin' out, And so's my grass! Wa-wa-wa! Gonna stop my wheels And drink the gas! Twang-twang-twang!
We been turned down by 160 more motels, 14 inns, and a condemned roomin' house!
Yeah, but that last turndown REALLY hurt, Man!
I always thought the Salvation Army takes in anything!
Looks like we sleep in the forest again!
Hey, Man! Pack up! We can't stay! They're complainin' that we're smellin' up the forest!
Who's complainin'?!
The skunks!!
64452

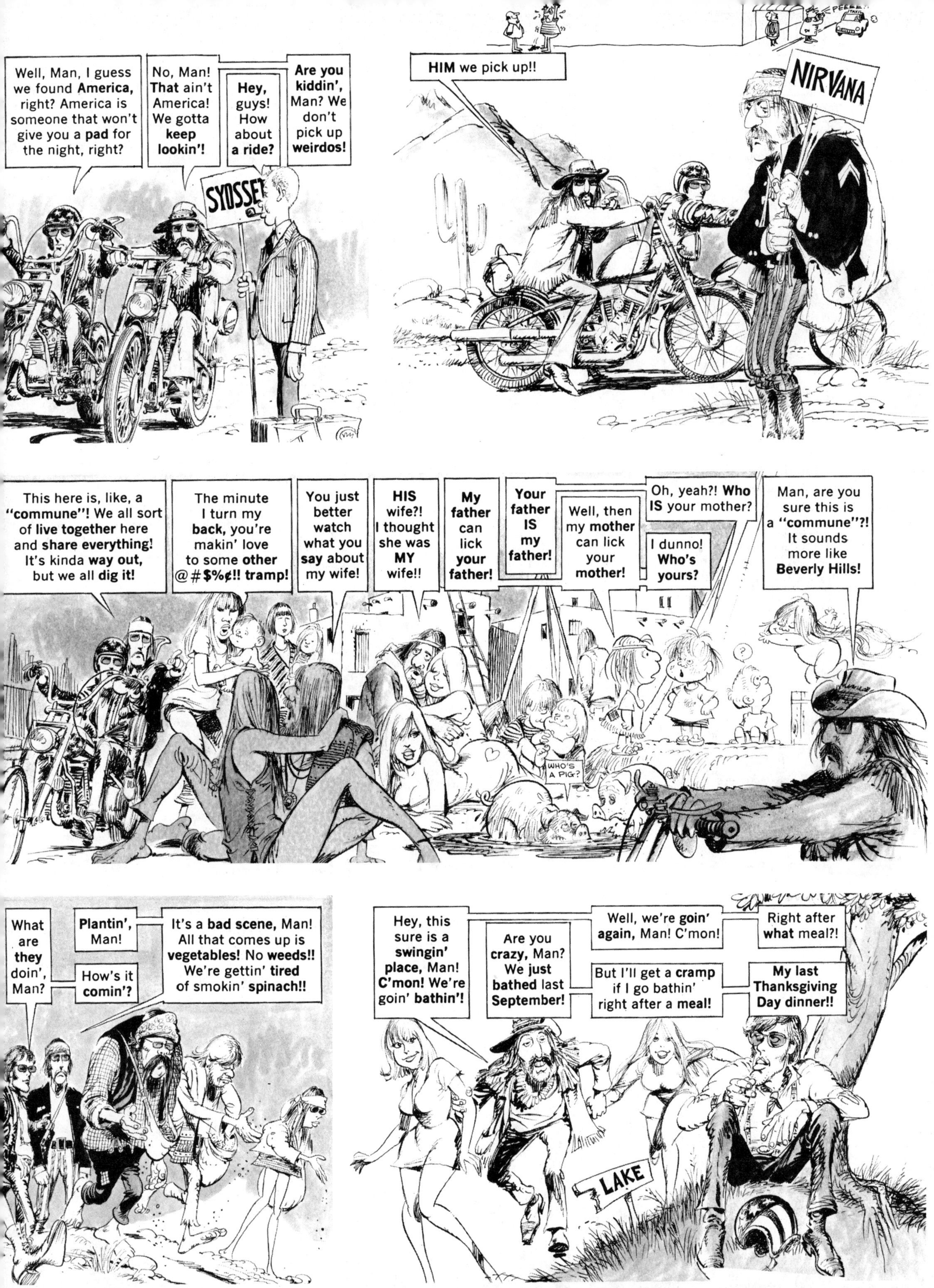

Well, Man, I guess we found America, right? America is someone that won't give you a pad for the night, right?
No, Man! That ain't America! We gotta keep lookin'!
Hey, guys! How about a ride?
Are you kiddin', Man? We don't pick up weirdos!
SYOSSET
HIM we pick up!!
NIRVANA
This here is, like, a "commune"! We all sort of live together here and share everything! It's kinda way out, but we all dig it!
The minute I turn my back, you're makin' love to some other @#$%¢!! tramp!
You just better watch what you say about my wife!
HIS wife?! I thought she was MY wife!!
My father can lick your father!
Your father IS my father!
Well, then my mother can lick your mother!
Oh, yeah?! Who IS your mother?
I dunno! Who's yours?
Man, are you sure this is a "commune"?! It sounds more like Beverly Hills!
WHO'S A PIG?
What are they doin', Man?
Plantin', Man!
How's it comin'?
It's a bad scene, Man! All that comes up is vegetables! No weeds!! We're gettin' tired of smokin' spinach!!
Hey, this sure is a swingin' place, Man! C'mon! We're goin' bathin'!
Are you crazy, Man? We just bathed last September!
Well, we're goin' again, Man! C'mon!
But I'll get a cramp if I go bathin' right after a meal!
Right after what meal?!
My last Thanksgiving Day dinner!!
LAKE

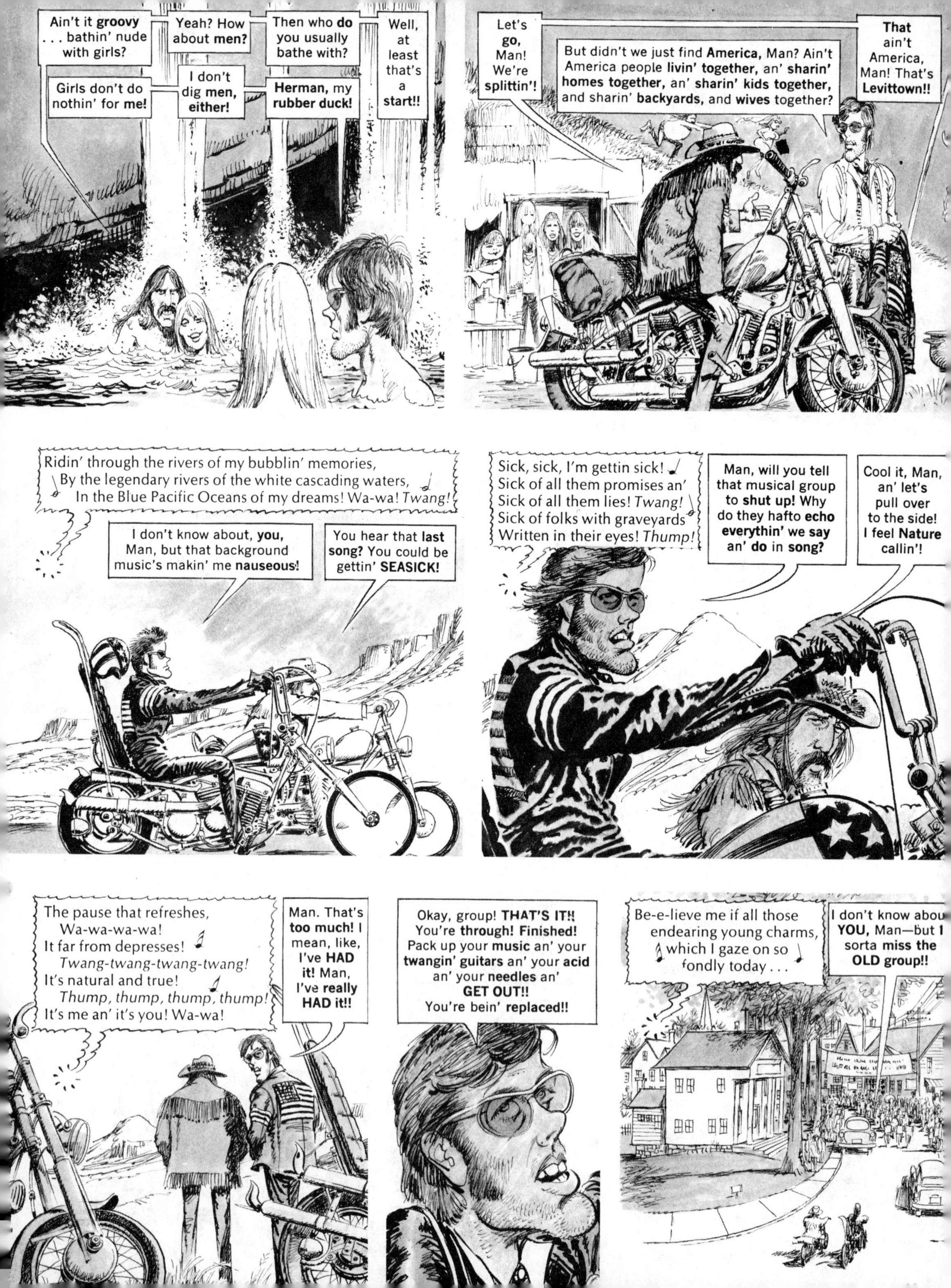

Ain't it groovy . . . bathin' nude with girls?
Girls don't do nothin' for me!
Yeah? How about men?
I don't dig men, either!
Then who do you usually bathe with?
Herman, my rubber duck!
Well, at least that's a start!!
Let's go, Man! We're splittin'!
But didn't we just find America, Man? Ain't America people livin' together, an' sharin' homes together, an' sharin' kids together, and sharin' backyards, and wives together?
That ain't America, Man! That's Levittown!!
Ridin' through the rivers of my bubblin' memories, By the legendary rivers of the white cascading waters, In the Blue Pacific Oceans of my dreams! Wa-wa! Twang!
I don't know about, you, Man, but that background music's makin' me nauseous!
You hear that last song? You could be gettin' SEASICK!
Sick, sick, I'm gettin sick! Sick of all them promises an' Sick of all them lies! Twang! Sick of folks with graveyards Written in their eyes! Thump!
Man, will you tell that musical group to shut up! Why do they hafto echo everythin' we say an' do in song?
Cool it, Man, an' let's pull over to the side! I feel Nature callin'!
The pause that refreshes, Wa-wa-wa-wa! It far from depresses! Twang-twang-twang-twang! It's natural and true! Thump, thump, thump, thump! It's me an' it's you! Wa-wa!
Man. That's too much! I mean, like, I've HAD it! Man, I've really HAD it!!
Okay, group! THAT'S IT!! You're through! Finished! Pack up your music an' your twangin' guitars an' your acid an' your needles an' GET OUT!! You're bein' replaced!!
Be-e-lieve me if all those endearing young charms, which I gaze on so fondly today . . .
I don't know abou YOU, Man—but I sorta miss the OLD group!!

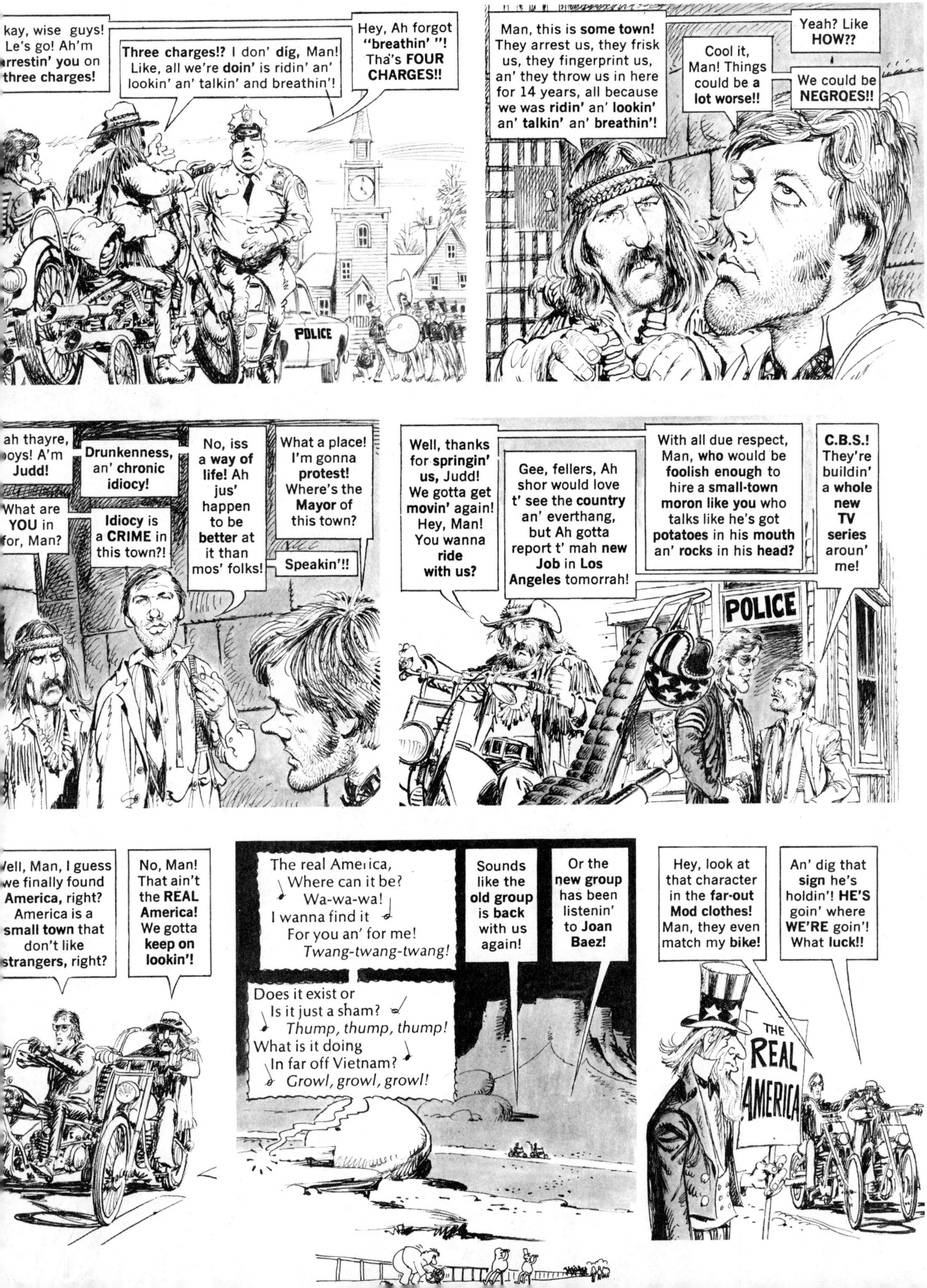
kay, wise guys! Le's go! Ah'm rrestin' you on three charges!
Three charges!? I don' dig, Man! Like, all we're doin' is ridin' an' lookin' an' talkin' and breathin'!
Hey, Ah forgot "breathin' "! Tha's FOUR CHARGES!!
POLICE
Man, this is some town! They arrest us, they frisk us, they fingerprint us, an' they throw us in here for 14 years, all because we was ridin' an' lookin' an' talkin' an' breathin'!
Cool it, Man! Things could be a lot worse!!
Yeah? Like HOW??
We could be NEGROES!!
ah thayre, oys! A'm Judd!
What are YOU in for, Man?
Drunkenness, an' chronic idiocy!
Idiocy is a CRIME in this town?!
No, iss a way of life! Ah jus' happen to be better at it than mos' folks!
What a place! I'm gonna protest! Where's the Mayor of this town?
Speakin'!!
Well, thanks for springin' us, Judd! We gotta get movin' again! Hey, Man! You wanna ride with us?
Gee, fellers, Ah shor would love t' see the country an' everthang, but Ah gotta report t' mah new Job in Los Angeles tomorrah!
With all due respect, Man, who would be foolish enough to hire a small-town moron like you who talks like he's got potatoes in his mouth an' rocks in his head?
C.B.S.! They're buildin' a whole new TV series aroun' me!
POLICE
ell, Man, I guess we finally found America, right? America is a small town that don't like strangers, right?
No, Man! That ain't the REAL America! We gotta keep on lookin'!
The real America,
Where can it be?
Wa-wa-wa!
I wanna find it
For you an' for me!
Twang-twang-twang!
Does it exist or
Is it just a sham?
Thump, thump, thump!
What is it doing
In far off Vietnam?
Growl, growl, growl!
Sounds like the old group is back with us again!
Or the new group has been listenin' to Joan Baez!
Hey, look at that character in the far-out Mod clothes! Man, they even match my bike!
An' dig that sign he's holdin'! HE'S goin' where WE'RE goin'! What luck!!
THE REAL AMERICA

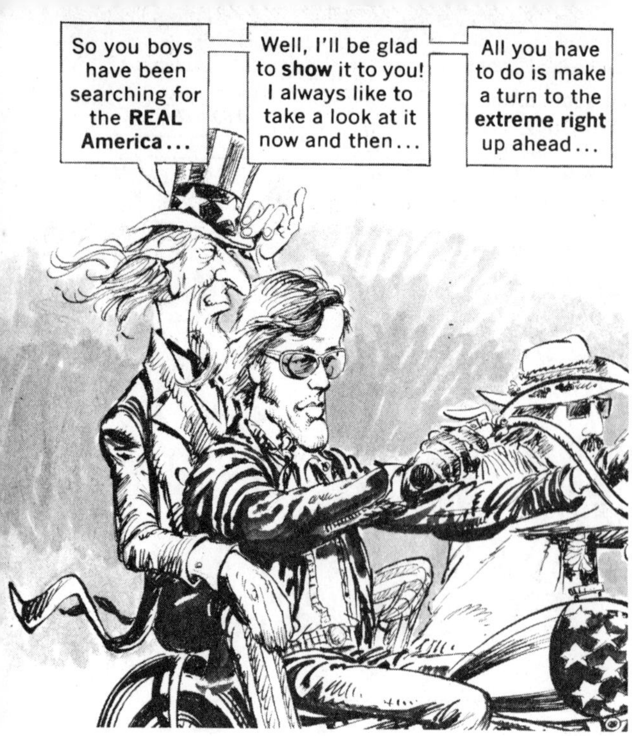
So you boys have been searching for the **REAL America** . . .
Well, I'll be glad to **show** it to you! I always like to take a look at it now and then . . .
All you have to do is make a turn to the **extreme right** up ahead . . .

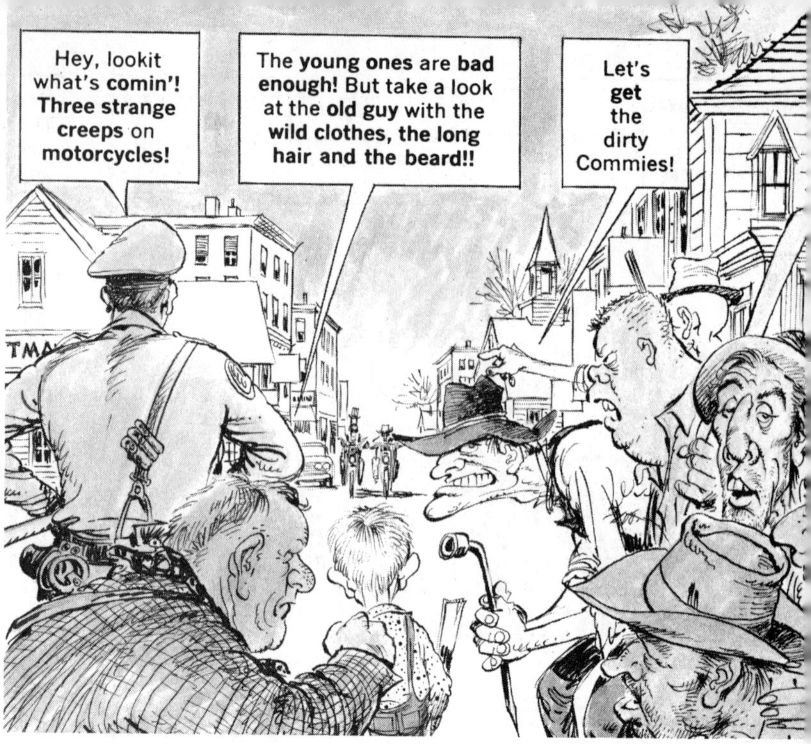
Hey, lookit what's **comin'! Three strange creeps** on **motorcycles!**
The **young ones** are **bad enough!** But take a look at the **old guy** with the **wild clothes, the long hair and the beard!!**
Let's **get** the dirty Commies!

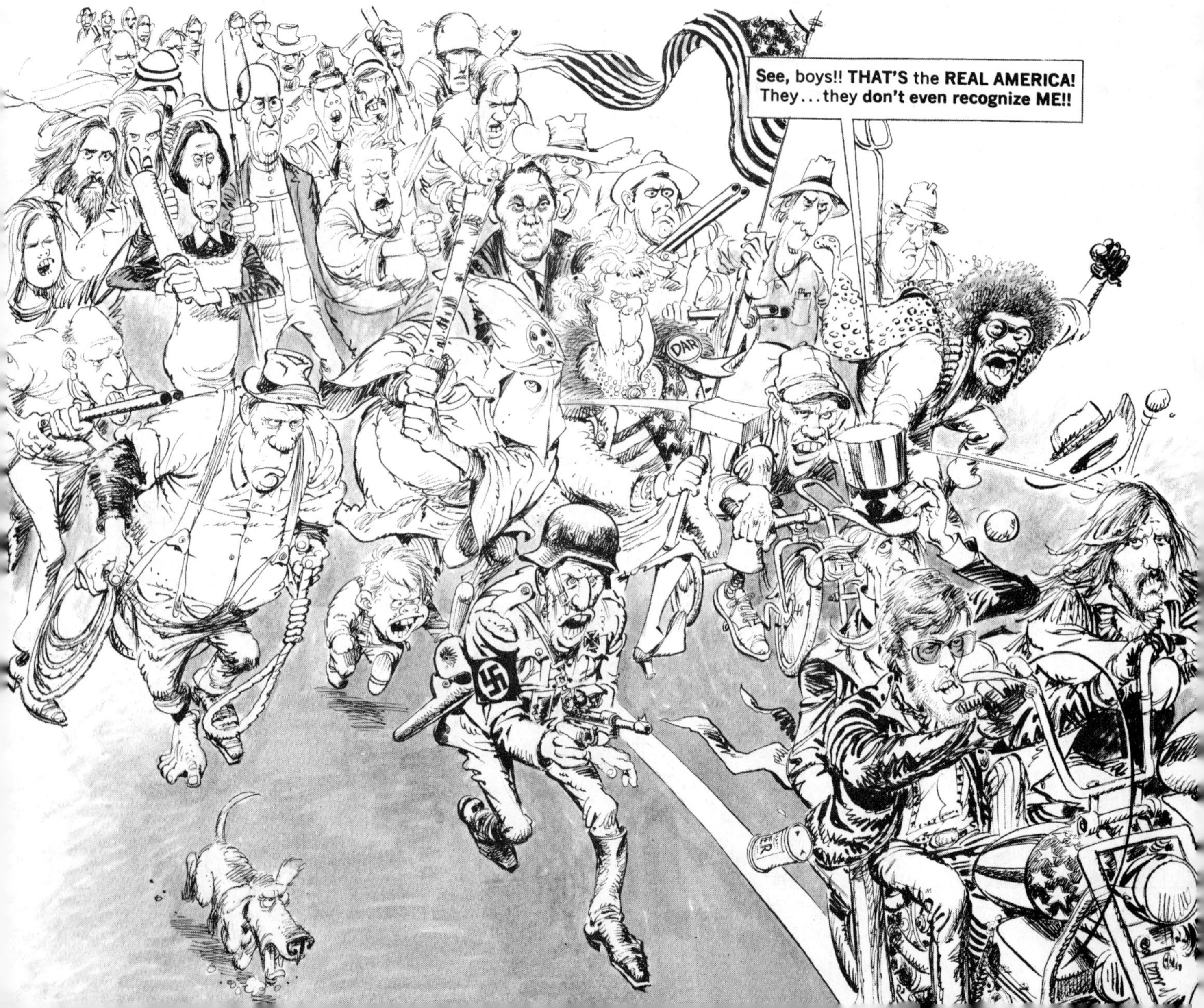
See, boys!! **THAT'S** the **REAL AMERICA!** They . . . they **don't even recognize ME!!**

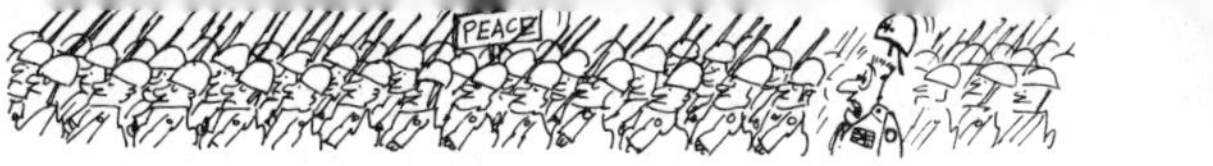
PEACE

PUTTING THE RIGHT ON DEPT.

As we all know, the Hippies, the Yippies, the SDS, the Black Panthers, and just about every activist group in the country has its own newspaper. Yes, the Underground Press is flourishing with such publications as "The East Village Other," "The Berkeley Barb," as well as other titles too numerous to mention, as well as still other titles we wouldn't **dare** mention! Well, whether you know it or not, the enemy is starting to fight back. Ever since Spiro Agnew came along, and Time Magazine named "The Middle American" as "Man of the Year," the pendulum has begun to swing in the other direction. So, Underground Press—Beware! Watch out for things to come—like THE OVERGROUND PRESS, and sickening publications like

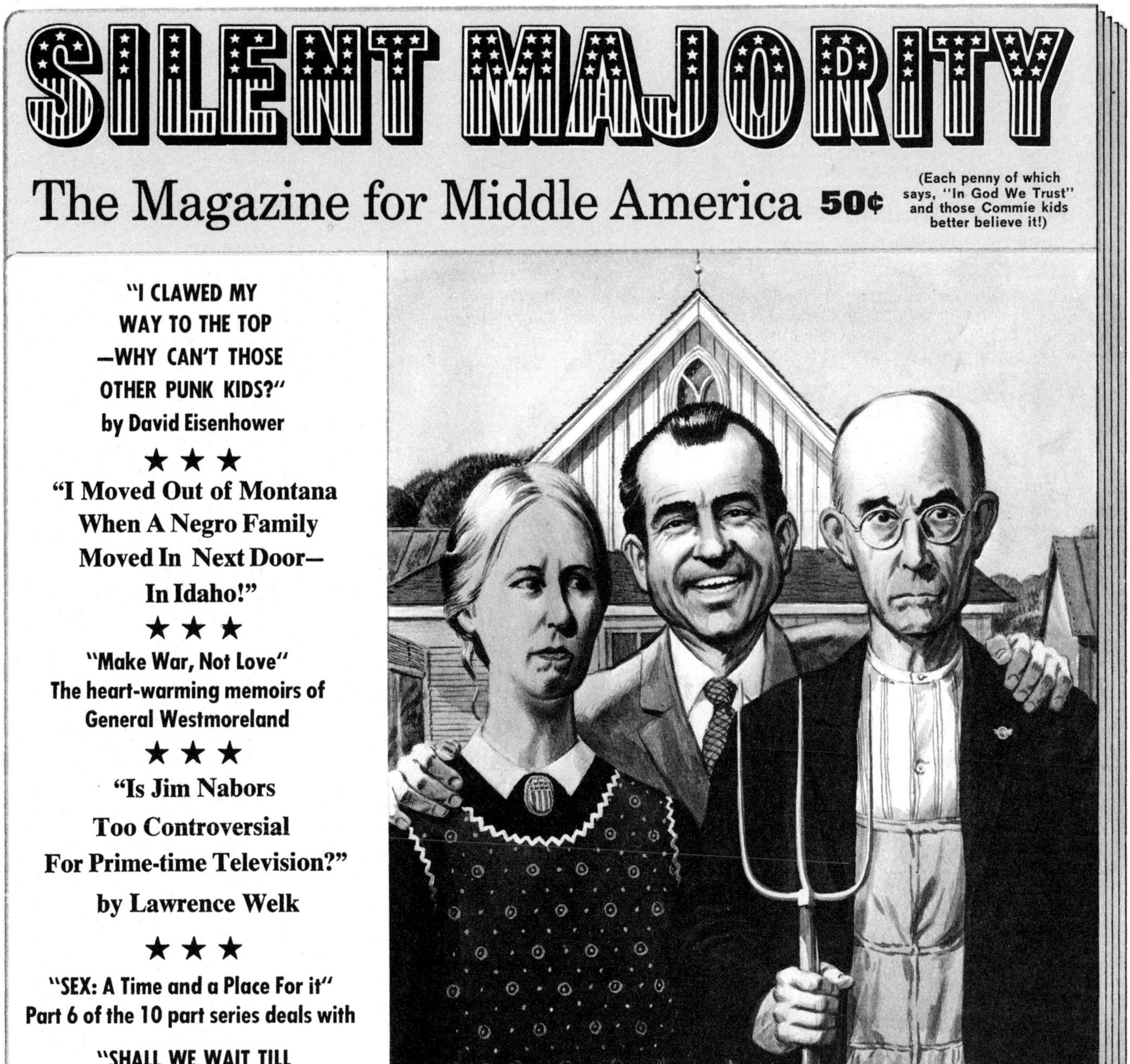
SILENT MAJORITY
The Magazine for Middle America 50¢
(Each penny of which says, "In God We Trust" and those Commie kids better believe it!)
"I CLAWED MY WAY TO THE TOP —WHY CAN'T THOSE OTHER PUNK KIDS?" by David Eisenhower
★ ★ ★
"I Moved Out of Montana When A Negro Family Moved In Next Door— In Idaho!"
★ ★ ★
"Make War, Not Love" The heart-warming memoirs of General Westmoreland
★ ★ ★
"Is Jim Nabors Too Controversial For Prime-time Television?" by Lawrence Welk
★ ★ ★
"SEX: A Time and a Place For it" Part 6 of the 10 part series deals with "SHALL WE WAIT TILL WE'RE MARRIED TO KISS?"
★ ★ ★
"Don't be afraid to beat the Ten Commandments into your kids!"
SPECIAL BONUS OFFER:
A Genuine 33 RPM record entitled, "PAT BOONE SINGS HAPPY ENDINGS TO JOAN BAEZ'S PROTEST SONGS"

ARTIST: GEORGE WOODBRIDGE WRITER: LARRY SIEGEL

Are you a bumbling idiot at parties? Do you always say the wrong things? Contact the MORRIS WILLIAMS AGENCY! We'll supply you with a top writer who'll transform you from a BUFFOON into a STATESMAN overnight!

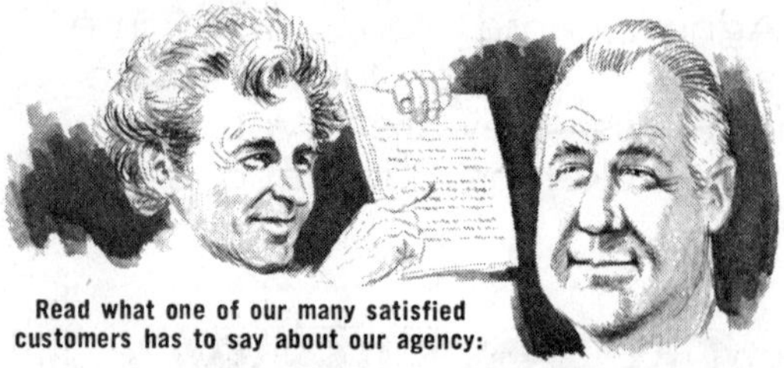

Read what one of our many satisfied customers has to say about our agency:

"I was always shooting my mouth off and saying ridiculous things like 'fat Jap' and 'when you've seen one slum, you've seen them all.' Then one day I fired my old writer and got a new one from Morris Williams. Well let me tell you that in practically no time at all I was a fountain of wisdom. I was saying things like 'effete snobs' just like I knew what it meant. And in no time at all I was the second most popular man in the nation, an outstanding statesman, and a living legend in my time."

THE MORRIS WILLIAMS AGENCY

New York, Beverly Hills, Chicago, London

Is your teenager endangering his health by smoking dreaded *grass*? Do you, as a parent, ever say, "If only I could get him to stop smoking marijuana?" N O W Y O U C A N ! !

With POT-O-BAN

Slip Pot-O-Ban into his joint when he's not looking. It's not magic, not a gimmick! Just a simple, all powerful *filter* that captures the *grass fumes* in its tenacious center and doesn't let them through to *blow his mind!*

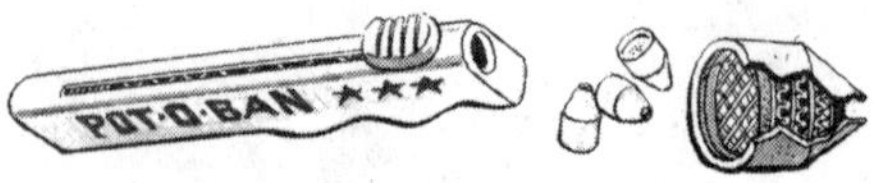
POT-O-BAN

Before you know it, your teenager will not be inhaling dreaded grass anymore – just pure, *clean* tobacco into his lungs, just like you and me! You *owe it* to your kids!

Try POT-O-BAN!

Giving a party for some *liberal friends?* No minority groups in your neighborhood (lucky you) to invite? Call . . .

HEARST RENT-A-NEGRO

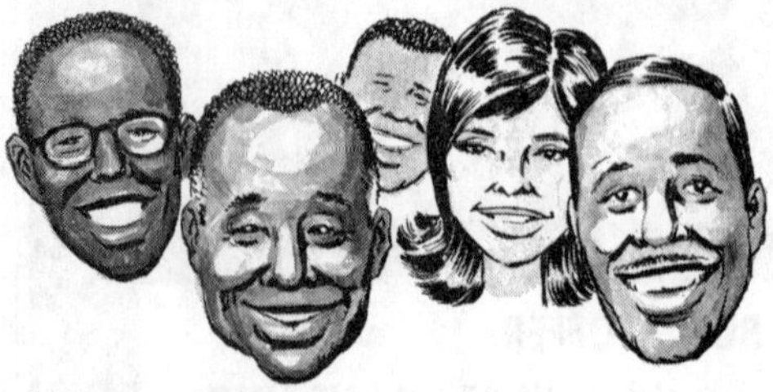

Take your choice of our collection of clean, light-colored token models, or try one of our darker models. All guaranteed to be well-mannered, no trouble, and non-violent. (Extra charge for tap-dancing or banjo playing). Remember, when you rent from **HEARST,** you're not just renting a **token Negro,** you're renting the entire membership of the **NAACP** and **CORE!**

"SILENT SAYS"

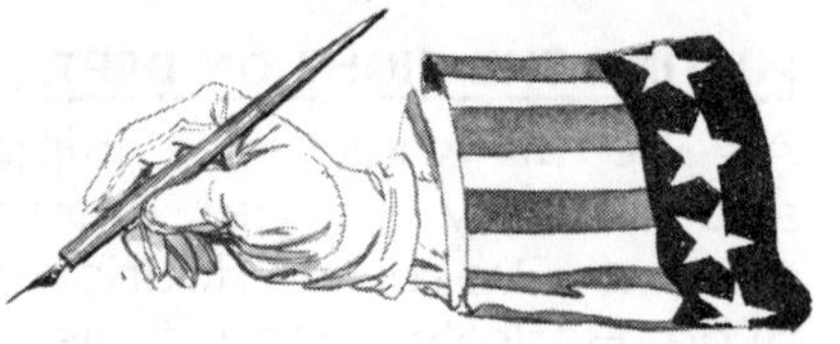

Each month, editor Sam Silent answers questions and tries to solve problems submitted by our readers.

Dear Silent:
I find it hard to tell one Cabinet member from another. In fact I heard a rumor the other day that you'll never see Sect. of State Rogers and Attorney General Mitchell photographed together because they're the same man. Is this true?

Brandon Edwing
Spokane, Washington

Dear Mr. Edwing:
I checked the rumor out with Sect. of Defense Laird (or as he is laughingly referred to by his friends—"Sect. of the Treasury Kennedy") and he said "That's ridiculous. They're talking about Sect. of Health, Education and Welfare FINCH!"

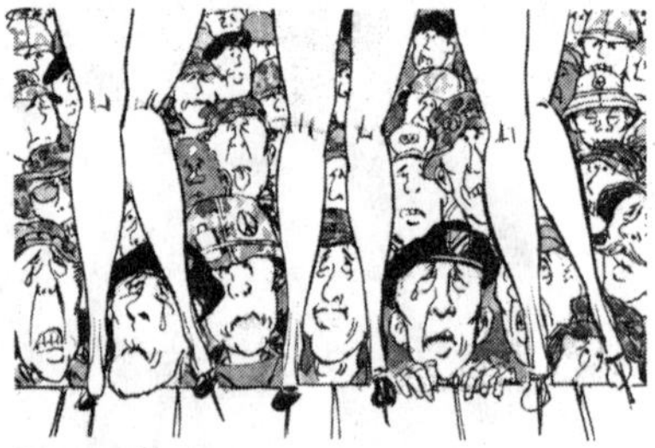

Dear Silent:
I think those anti-war demonstrators should be tarred and feathered. I think we should do all we can to help our boys in Vietnam. We send them letters and food packages and every Christmas Bob Hope goes to see them with Ann-Margret, Pamela Tiffin, and Raquel Welch. And yet when I see the boys on TV, they look disturbed. Why are they disturbed?

Grace Warbler
Mamaroneck, N.Y.

Dear Miss Warbler:
They're disturbed because every Christmas Bob Hope goes to see them with Ann-Margret, Pamela Tiffin, and Raquel Welch.

Dear Silent:
As a decent Middle American, I, like you and the editors of this magazine, do not believe in prejudice (only last month I swam in the same Pacific Ocean the Mexicans were swimming in). Which is why I find those Polish jokes that are going around so offensive. Some of our finest citizens are Polish-Americans. Who started those Polish jokes anyway?

Oliver Brack
Los Angeles, Cal.

Dear Mr. Brack:
It could have been a recalcitrant college youth, or perhaps an effusive monologist with a sense of perverse levity. And then again it might have been some Wop.

Dear Silent:
I have just returned from the South Pole, where I spent the last 10 years, and I feel a little out of touch with things. I'm looking for a new career to go into and I'm considering that of a College Policeman. I think it would be splendid to patrol a nice, friendly campus, smile a cheery hello at the students, and call them by name while they address me warmly by mine. What do you think of my idea?

James Pigg
Sioux City, Iowa

Dear Mr. Pigg:
Have you ever considered going into the plumbing business?

Dear Silent:
As a conscientious Middle American citizen living in Wyoming, I thought it might be a good idea to bring the world a little closer to my children. So next Christmas, instead of taking them to Disneyland again, I thought I would take them to look at a Negro. Can you help me? What do Negroes look like? Where do I find one? Are they friendly? Is it a good idea to feed them? Do they bite?

Ned Womber
Laramie, Wyoming

Dear Mr. Womber:
I admire your wonderful plan and think you have an excellent idea. However, I don't think you are ready for it just yet. I suggest you do something as traumatic as that GRADUALLY! Instead of jumping right in, and possibly "over your head," why not BUILD UP to a Negro by taking your children to see a Jew first?

ilent Majority's"
rize Fiction

TORY
)F
'HE
ИONTH

very month this magazine awards 10,000 Red, White,
ıd Blue Stamps to the fiction piece which best
irrors the clean, decent, patriotic thoughts of
day's Middle American. We are pleased to
esent this month's winning story.

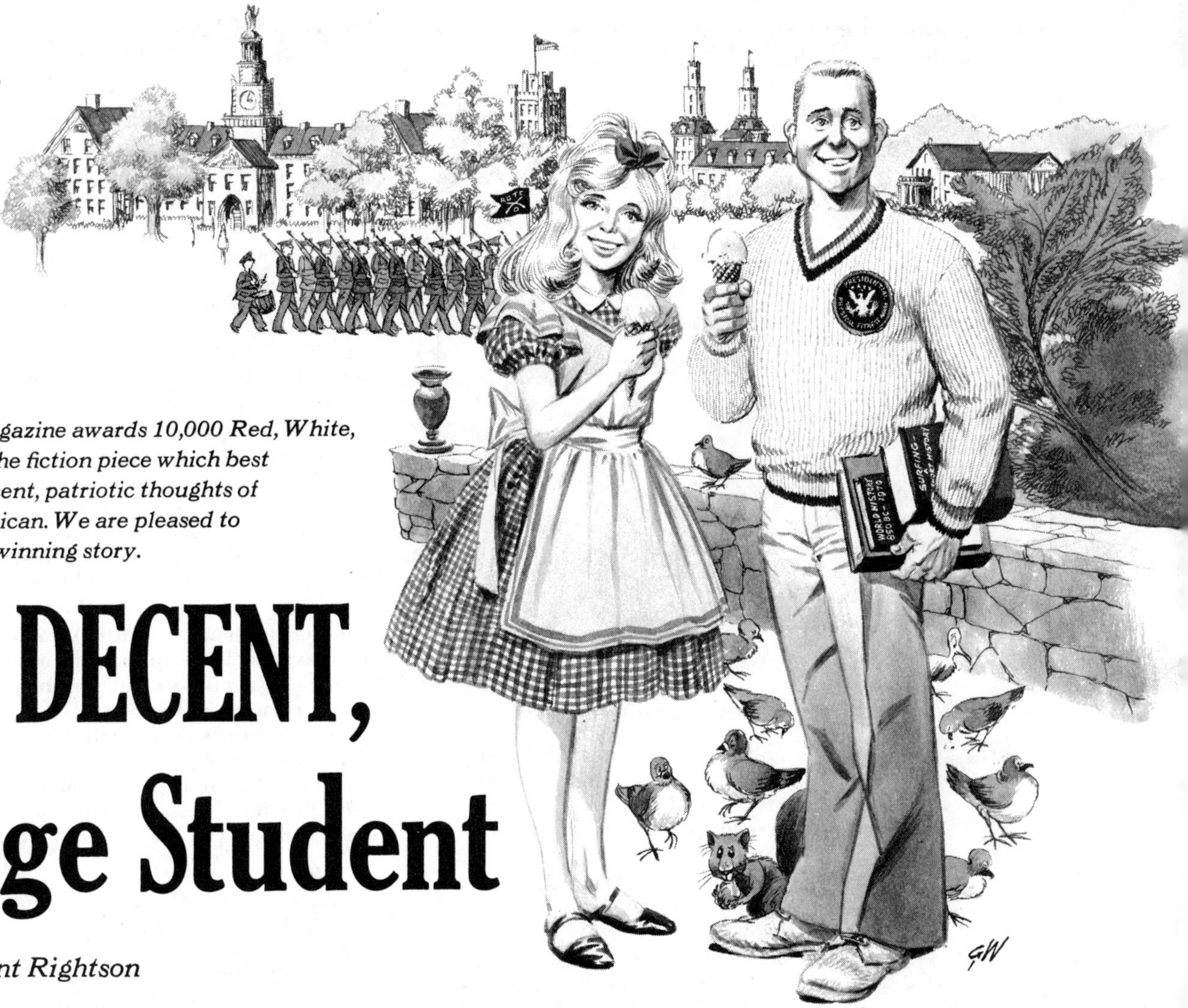

ROTC
SURFING
WORLD HISTORY

DICK DECENT,
;ollege Student

· Norman Vincent Rightson

"Like to go for a walk, Jane?" said Dick Decent to ; coed girl friend Jane Wasp, as they met on the mpus of State Agricultural College. She nodded eerily and they began to stroll.

Dick was a clean-cut, handsome lad of 19. He had neat crew-cut and wore a red and white tennis 'eater and white buckskin shoes. Jane, a lovely, ·sh-looking girl of 18, had long, neat hair and wore simple, fresh-laundered pinafore with a tiny Ameri-n flag sewn in the upper left hand corner near r heart. Together they looked like any two, plain, erage, ordinary, American college students.

"What a great day it is," said Dick. "And what a and school this is, and how lucky we both are to be re. Golly!"

"Dick, must you use *profanity?*" said Jane.

"Sorry," said Dick.

"Oh, look," said Jane, "there go some ROTC cadets."

"How tall and strong they look," said Dick. "What great bunch of fellows."

"They send a tingle of pride up and down my ine," said Jane.

"I doubt if anyone on campus is more beloved by e student body than they are," said Dick simply, as tear of joy crept out of his eye. He quickly brushed away.

"Oh, say, Jane," said Dick, "would you like to go to the Prom with me?"

"I'd like to, Dick," said Jane, "but..."

"I'm sorry about last night, Jane," said Dick. "I didn't mean to do what I did."

"It's not that I don't *want* you to kiss me," said Jane. "And I realize that there must be at least four or maybe five 'fast' girls on this campus who *do* kiss. It's just that I'm saving my kisses for Mr. Right."

At that moment along came Chancellor Valleyforge accompanied by another man.

"Hello, Dick and Jane," said the Chancellor.

"Hi, Chancellor," said Dick. "Classes are better than ever these days and we have *you* to thank for it."

"Pshaw, Dick," said the Chancellor. "I'm only doing my job. It's a pleasure working for you wholesome kids. By the way, Dick and Jane, I'd like you both to meet Mr. Eric Novotney, of the Dow Chemical Company."

"Mr. Novotney," said Jane, wringing the man's hand, "I can't tell you how proud we students here are of the wonderful job you're doing for our nation."

"Love your napalm," added Dick sincerely.

"We hope you'll join our company after you graduate, Dick," said Mr. Novotney.

"Nothing would give me more pleasure," said Dick, "but first I must go to Vietnam."

"If the Army will only have me," he added hopefully.

"What a nice man he seems *(Continued on Page 53)*

STATUS QUO-TES

Our roving cameraman gets opinions on the burning issues of the day from random Middle Americans. This month's question:

"How do you feel about today's attitudes towards sex?"

Fred Sashay, Fire Island, N.Y.

I don't pay much attention to today's attitudes towards sex. *My* attitude towards sex has been the same since I was four. My mummsy took care of that. But I can't complain—I've got a good interior decorating business going and my sweetheart and I recently rented a beautiful new apartment which we will move into as soon as his divorce comes through.

Harry Trefflick, Salem, Oregon

Maybe I'm a little different from most people in my generation, but I'm all for this new freedom of sexual expression for kids. I've always encouraged my son Ted to bring girls home to the house, ever since he was 15. Now that Ted is older and off to college, I miss him. I also miss the girls he used to bring home. Now if I can only think of a way to get my *wife* off to college!

Caleb Flint, Saginaw, Michigan

I think today's attitudes are disgusting. These kids are sick. We're raising a generation of perverts. I'd like to string up a few by there thumbs and whip 'em. But not just an ordinary whip. No, a nice, freshly oiled whip that's laid across their shoulders in clean, even strokes, until their skin welts and a little blood wells up in the gashes. That'll teach those sickies a little decency.

Paul (Pop) Armbruster, St. Petersburgh, Fla.

I'm glad you stopped me, young feller. Yes sir, always like to talk to folks. I'm just 84 years young and still the picture of health. Would you believe it, my mind's still as quick as a steel trap. Yes sir, I can remember clear back to the Blizzard of '88. Course I don't remember recent things too well. Now then, concerning your question . . . what's *sex*?

Along Middle America Avenue

What's Cooking With the Guys and Gals of the Establishment
by GRAY LIFESTYLE, JR.

Let's hear it for the congregation of Furd Township Church, Maryland. For the past eight Sundays they've given up services to picket the Supreme Court Building over the school prayer ruling. Atta-way, Furd Township! Let's get prayers out of the church and back into the public schools where they belong . . . Bad news and good news and bad news from Hominygrits, Georgia. Mel Duff, County Chicken Plucker, was just fired. Now for the good news. Mel has decided to throw all his experience behind his candidacy for Governor. Now for the bad news again. The new state constitution for Georgia dictates that a former chicken plucker cannot succeed a former chicken restaurant owner as Governor of the state. So now it looks like Mel may have to settle for the Supreme Court. You can't win 'em all . . .

* * * * * *

Tragedy Department: Friends of Hattie McLish were shocked to learn of her untimely death due to an overdose of sleeping pills. They say she'd been very despondent lately because she found out her children were taking drugs . . . Attention critics of Pres. Nixon who have been complaining about spending $26 billion to put a man on the moon instead of using that money to wipe out poverty. We've got news for you pinkos: There *is* no poverty on the moon . . . Trouble comes in double doses: Silent Majorityite Sandra Debbs was not only heartbroken to discover that her maid just left her, she also found out that her teenage children ran away from home last Christmas.

How about a word of praise for those patriots at Disneyland who refuse admittance to punk kids with long hair and silly mod clothes. Said Asst. Disneyland Manager Walt Lancer (in the "Goofy" costume on the left), "If they can't look like civilized human beings we don't want 'em in here!"

Three cheers for Dan and Philomene Humbolt of Biloxi, Mississippi, who have been educating their children at home since the Supreme Court school desegregation ruling in 1954. The Humbolt's oldest boy, 24 year old Donald, is already up to long division, and 23 year old daughter Billie Mae hardly moves her lips anymore when she reads . . . Soon-to-wed, hardworking D.A. Ed Shtarp has been so busy lately confiscating "I Am Curious—Yellow," "Medium Cool," and other filthy films being exhibited in his county that he was almost late for those fabulous showgirls performing at his stag party last Friday night!

* * * * * *

It looks like Spiro's pressure campaign against the TV networks is paying off. Following Pres. Nixon's next address to the nation, instead of a critical analysis, CBS has agreed to present a 15 minute program containing "The Best of Hee Haw" . . . It's a brand new six pound baby for the Felix Ungers. He's head of the National Clean Morals Committee and she's a noted anti-nudity crusader in Wesselville, Arizona. Obeying its parents wishes, the baby was born fully clothed. Keep an eye on this column in late 1983 for word of the baby's s-x!

THE ESTABLISHMENT IN ACTION

A Pictorial Run-Down of What's What in Middle Americas-ville

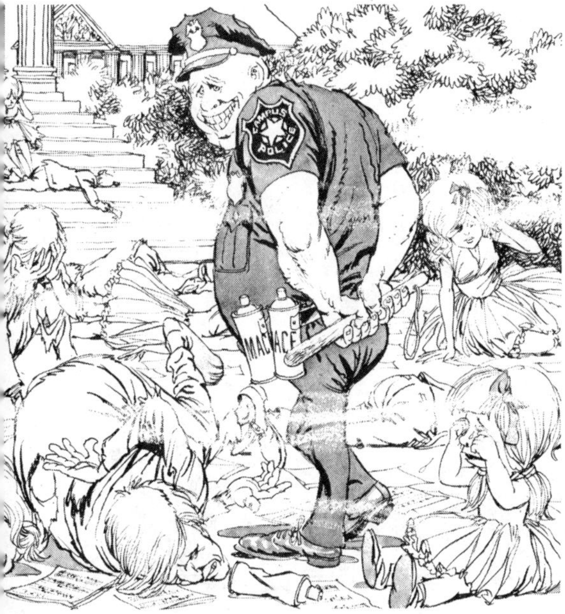
CAMPUS POLICE
MACE
MACE

CIDENTS WILL HAPPEN: Was ULCA campus cop Bull rnie's face red the other day! That large group thought was radical campus demonstrators and ich he hosed, clubbed, and sprayed with Mace, ned out to be the Establishment's own lovable ng Family who were showing up on campus to do Arbor Day concert. Try not to worry about it, ll. You'll have real fun next Friday afternoon en the Black Students Union have their meeting!

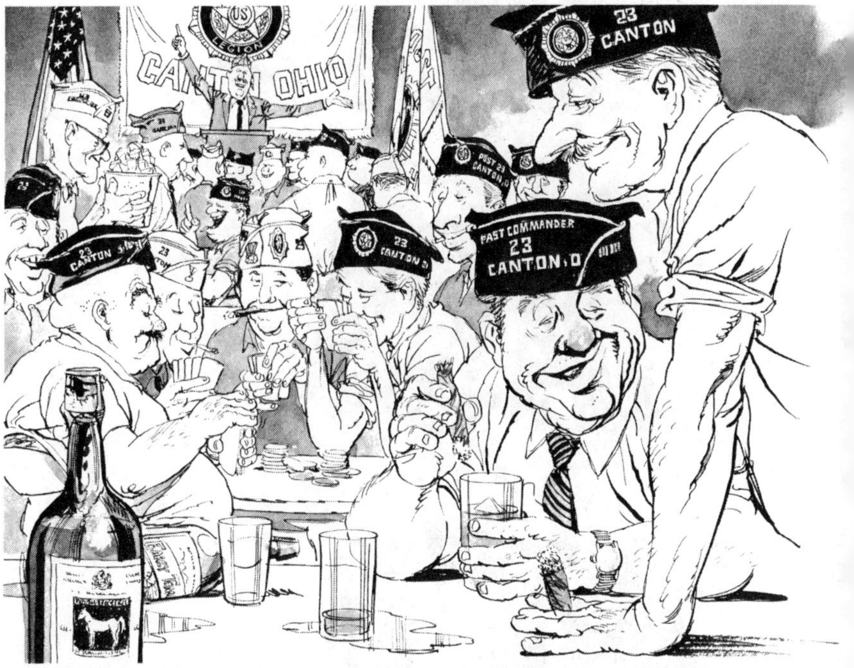
CANTON OHIO
LEGION
23 CANTON
PAST COMMANDER 23 CANTON, O

RALLY ROUND THE FLAG: American Legion Post #23, in Canton, Ohio, had a great Americanism rally Saturday night. Although scheduled keynote speaker "Chub" Freely couldn't make it because he's up on a drunken driving charge, and Hank Endicott is laid up with cirrhosis of the liver after his recent 19 day bourbon binge, the rally was still a great success. The theme of the rally was "Let's get pot out of our highschools before our kids ruin themselves."

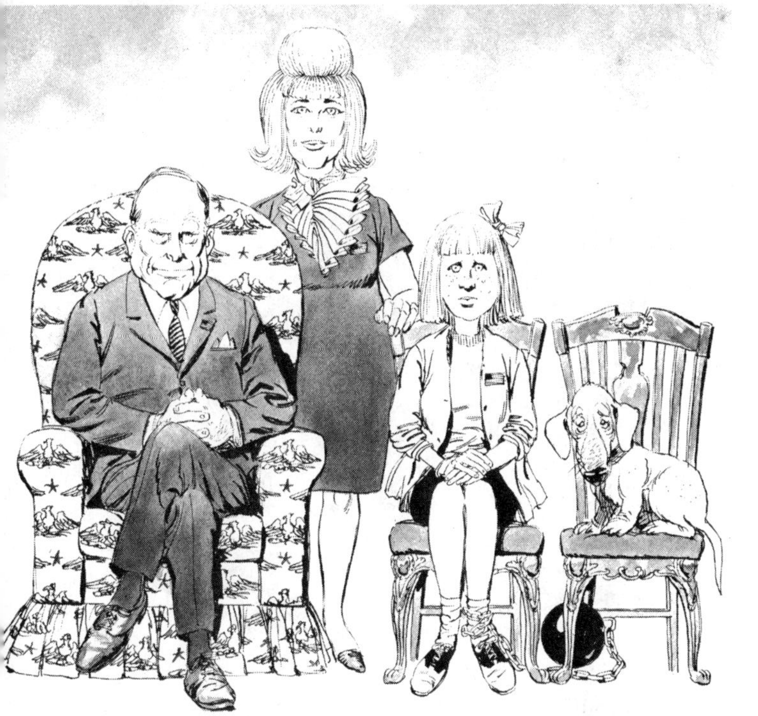

DDLE AMERICAN OF THE MONTH: Cheers to Henry Cotter and his wife lma, who are working side by side, building for the future by draw- from the past, like all Middle Americans. They are instilling the als they grew up with—Clean Living, Hard Work and Our Country, ght or Wrong—into their own children, with fantastic success. Cotters are (l. to r.): Henry, Wilma, their 15 year old daughter ncy, and Spiro. Their 12-year-old son Henry, Jr. wasn't available our staff photographer, having run away from home the week before.

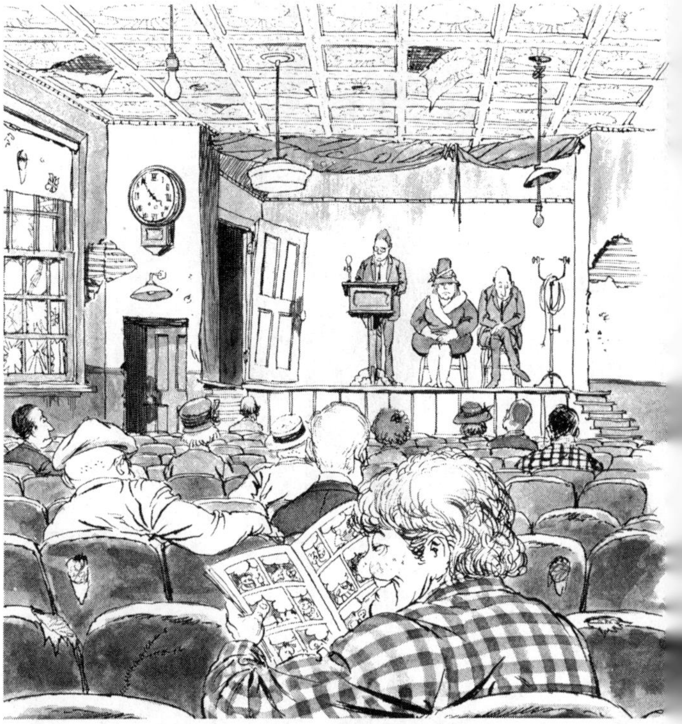

EXTREME DEDICATION: Our hats are off to the dedicated parents of School District #53 in Wilkes Barre, Pennsylvania. They have been holding regular meetings to try and determine ways to improve school conditions in their area. No solutions yet, but the group will meet again Thursday, right after they're expected to vote down the new school appropriations bond issue for the seventh time in over two years.

AUTO-SUGGESTION DEPT.

SPORTS CARS WE'D LIKE TO SEE

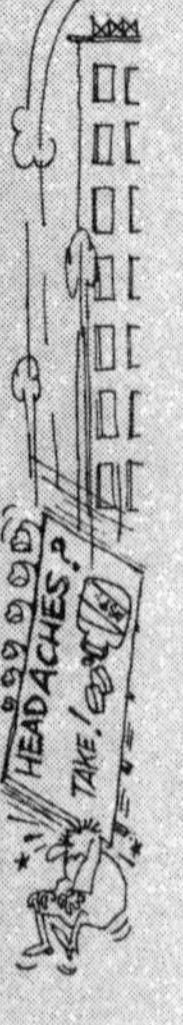
HEADACHES?

WRITER & ARTIST: BASIL WOLVERTON

THE DRAGGING DRAGSTER

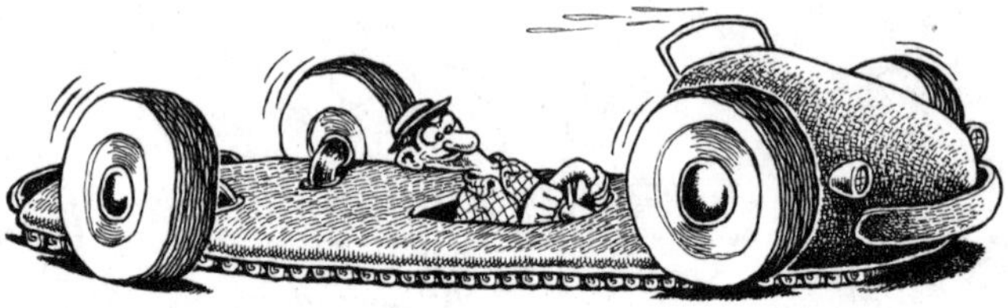

To most sports car enthusiasts, no beast is worth driving unless it is extremely low slung. Here is one design that is tops at hitting bottom. Flexible chassis slithers over ground on small rollers, causing onlookers to wonder just how low a driver can get. Not recommended for rocky roads.

THE STANLEY SCREAMER

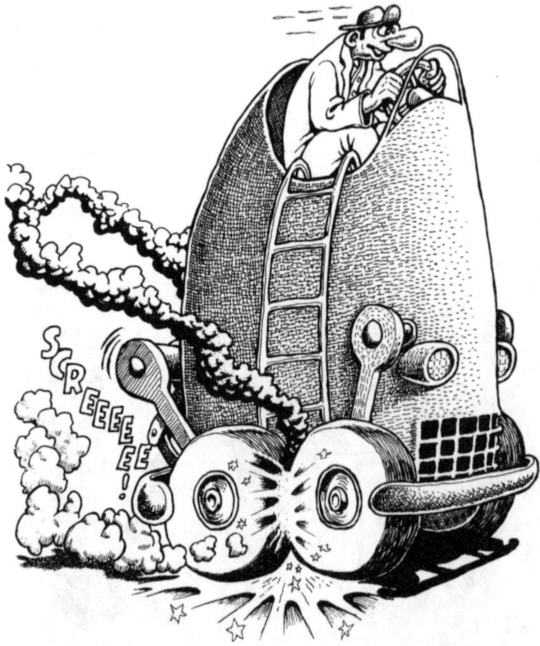
SCREEEEEEE!

Tire manufacturers will adore this innovation in design which produces, even in slow moving traffic, the shrieks and squeals that otherwise come from gunning and skidding sports cars at high speeds. Special pedal pushes back and front wheels together so they rub against each other. Odor of burning rubber, smoke, and ear-splitting screeches are thus produced, even while car is going ten miles an hour.

THE TERRIFIC TIRE TOTER

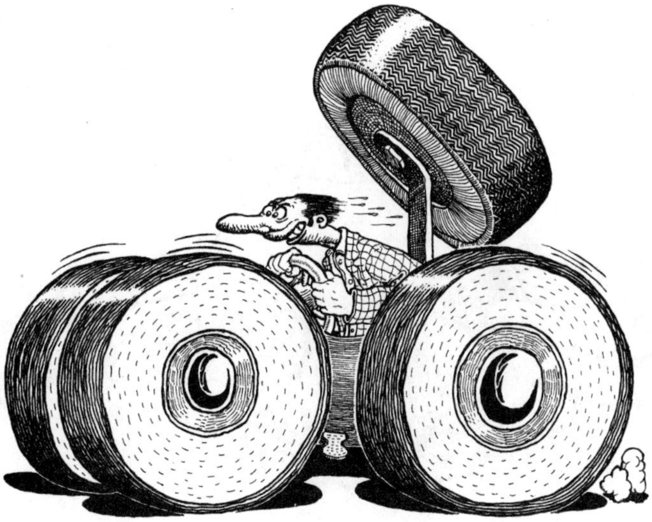

This design should be a sheer delight to those sports car enthusiasts who think mostly in terms of tires–big, wide, whirring tires. There are no distracting bumpers, fenders, etc. to hide these tires from full sight. Even the spare is in good view, because there's no room for it elsewhere.

THE BASHED-IN BOLTER

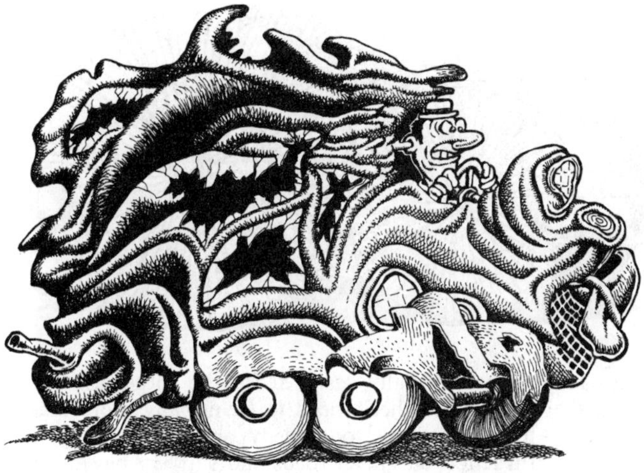

Comes direct from the factory looking like a wreck to give the impression that the driver is a hot-headed daredevil who better not be crossed. Just the thing for the timid sports car lover who wants to feel dangerous and powerful.

THE X-1 EXHAUSTER

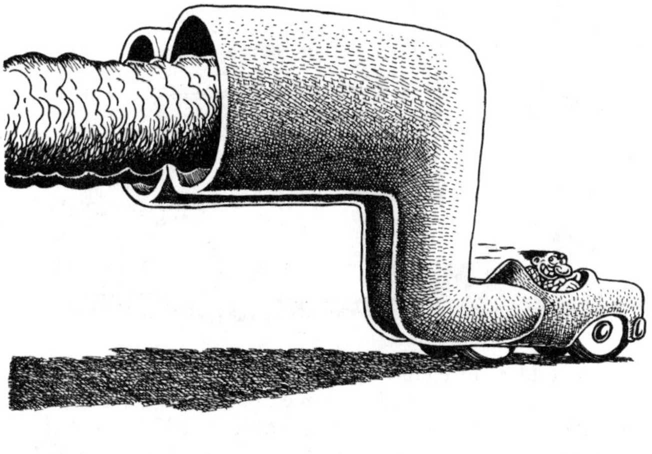

This model is designed to appeal to sports car buffs who feel that the size of the exhaust pipes together with the smoke and sounds that come from them should be emphasized. Smoke bombs and firecrackers from a special year's supply are automatically ignited every time the car is started.

THE CLASSY CLATTERER

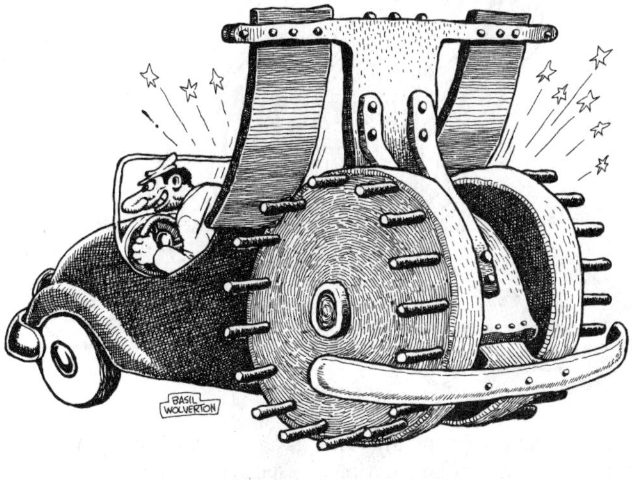
BASIL WOLVERTON

Since big sound and fury is necessary to many sports car buffs, here is the ultimate for them, based on the simple "spoke-clackers" that kids attach to the forks of their bicycles. In this model, two sheets of steel clang against heavy metal bars extending from the oversized rear wheels.

THE WIRE-SPOKE SPINNER

This model was especially designed for the enthusiast who feels that sports car wheels need to be nothing more than spokes. Although it isn't too speedy or smooth-riding, it has superb traction on gravel roads and slippery pavement.

THE LOFTY LURCHER

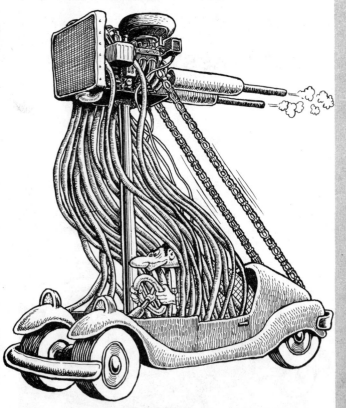

Service station attendants and garage mechanics will bust guts over this model, designed especially for drivers who believe that the power plant should be proudly displayed instead of being hidden under a hood. Drive is transferred via chain. Other functions, such as power brakes, ignition, power steering, lights, etc. present a problem in cables that is easily overcome by drivers with extra-long necks.

THE DENTLESS DASHER

To many sports car drivers, scratches and dents in their beloved machines are marks of shame. This model will not suffer such marks because it is ringed with jack hammers, any of which automatically goes into action when touched. However, design has one drawback. Driver himself must be careful when entering car to avoid getting dented in dome.

THE STOKER STENCHER

Because sudden accelerations, hard braking and long skids never seem to produce enough stench of burning rubber for the average sports car enthusiast, we designed this model. Equipped with a furnace from an antique coal-burning fire engine, it consumes old tires stuffed into it at intervals by the driver, who can now truthfully boast that it burns more rubber than any other sports car on the road. In the event that he runs out of old tires, the driver can always burn the tires that come with the car . . . or even his shoes.

SERMON ON THE AMOUNT DEPT.

ALTAR EGO

ARTIST: WALLACE WOOD WRITER: MARYLYN IPPOLITO

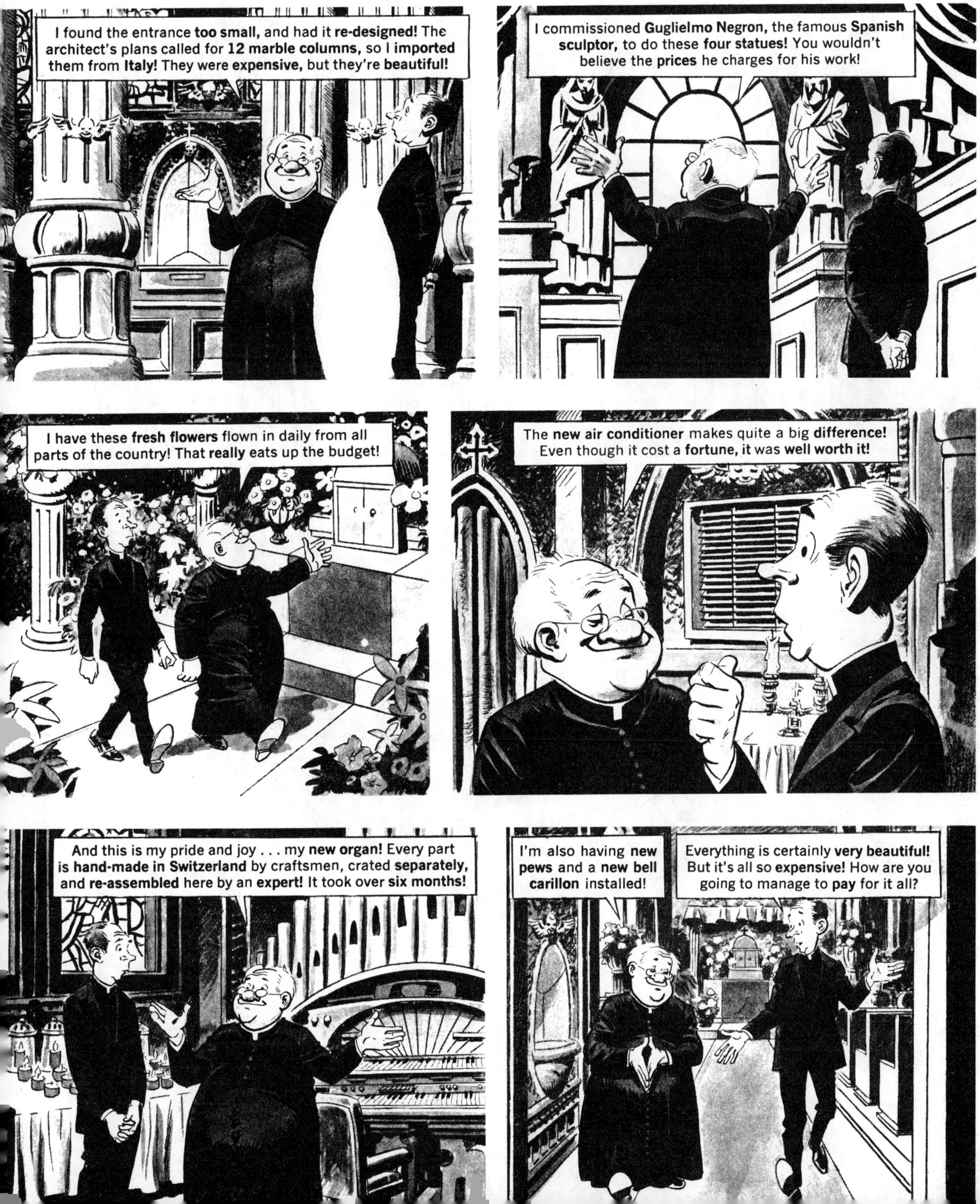
I found the entrance too small, and had it re-designed! The architect's plans called for 12 marble columns, so I imported them from Italy! They were expensive, but they're beautiful!
I commissioned Guglielmo Negron, the famous Spanish sculptor, to do these four statues! You wouldn't believe the prices he charges for his work!
I have these fresh flowers flown in daily from all parts of the country! That really eats up the budget!
The new air conditioner makes quite a big difference! Even though it cost a fortune, it was well worth it!
And this is my pride and joy . . . my new organ! Every part is hand-made in Switzerland by craftsmen, crated separately, and re-assembled here by an expert! It took over six months!
I'm also having new pews and a new bell carillon installed!
Everything is certainly very beautiful! But it's all so expensive! How are you going to manage to pay for it all?

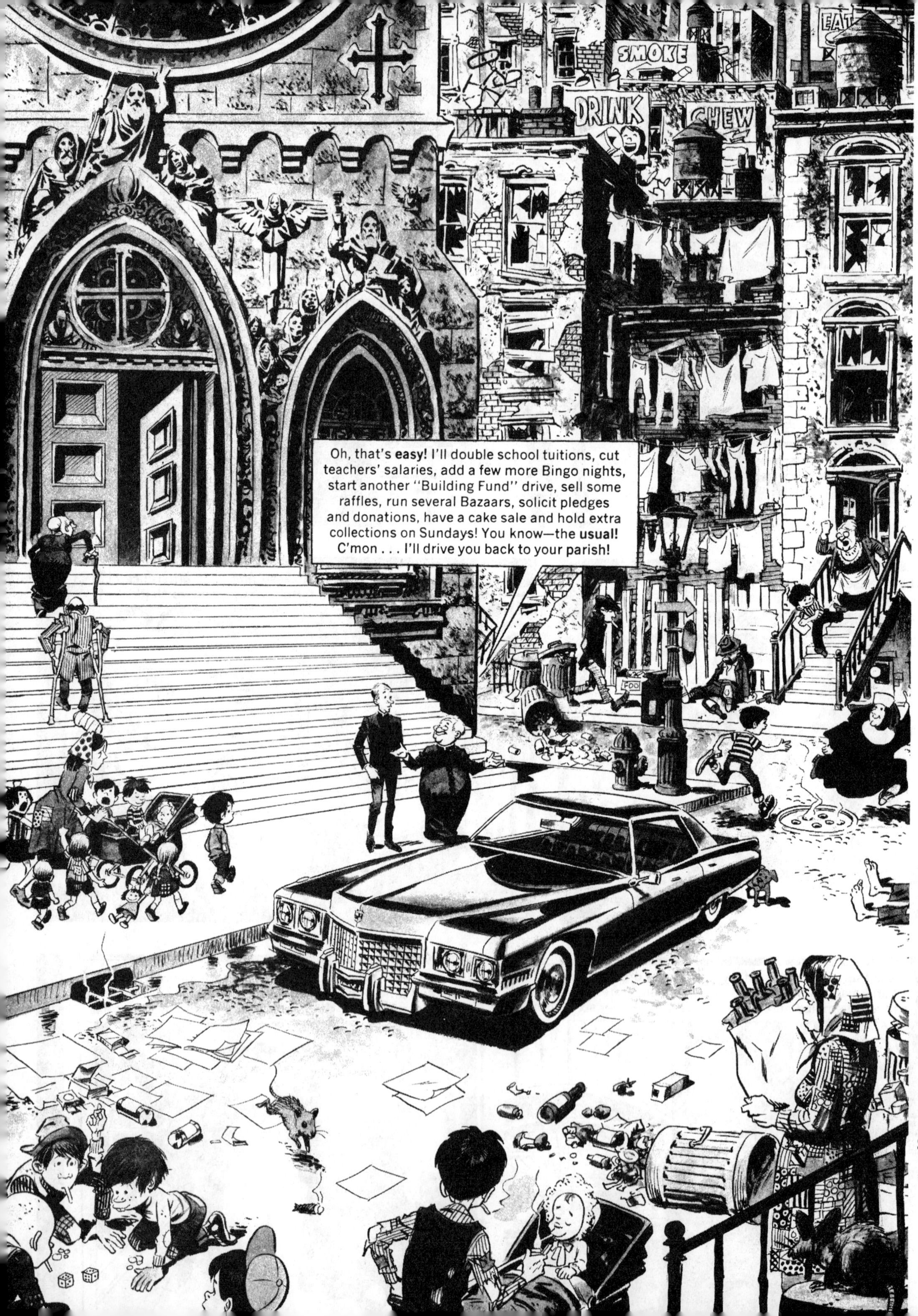
EAT
SMOKE
DRINK
CHEW
Oh, that's **easy!** I'll double school tuitions, cut teachers' salaries, add a few more Bingo nights, start another "Building Fund" drive, sell some raffles, run several Bazaars, solicit pledges and donations, have a cake sale and hold extra collections on Sundays! You know—the **usual!** C'mon . . . I'll drive you back to your parish!

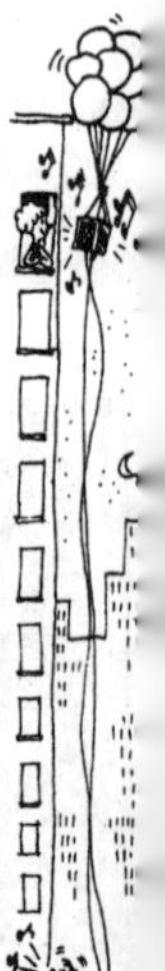

DON MARTIN DEPT. PART II

BACK IN THE OPERATING ROOM WITH DON MARTIN DURING A HEART TRANSPLANT

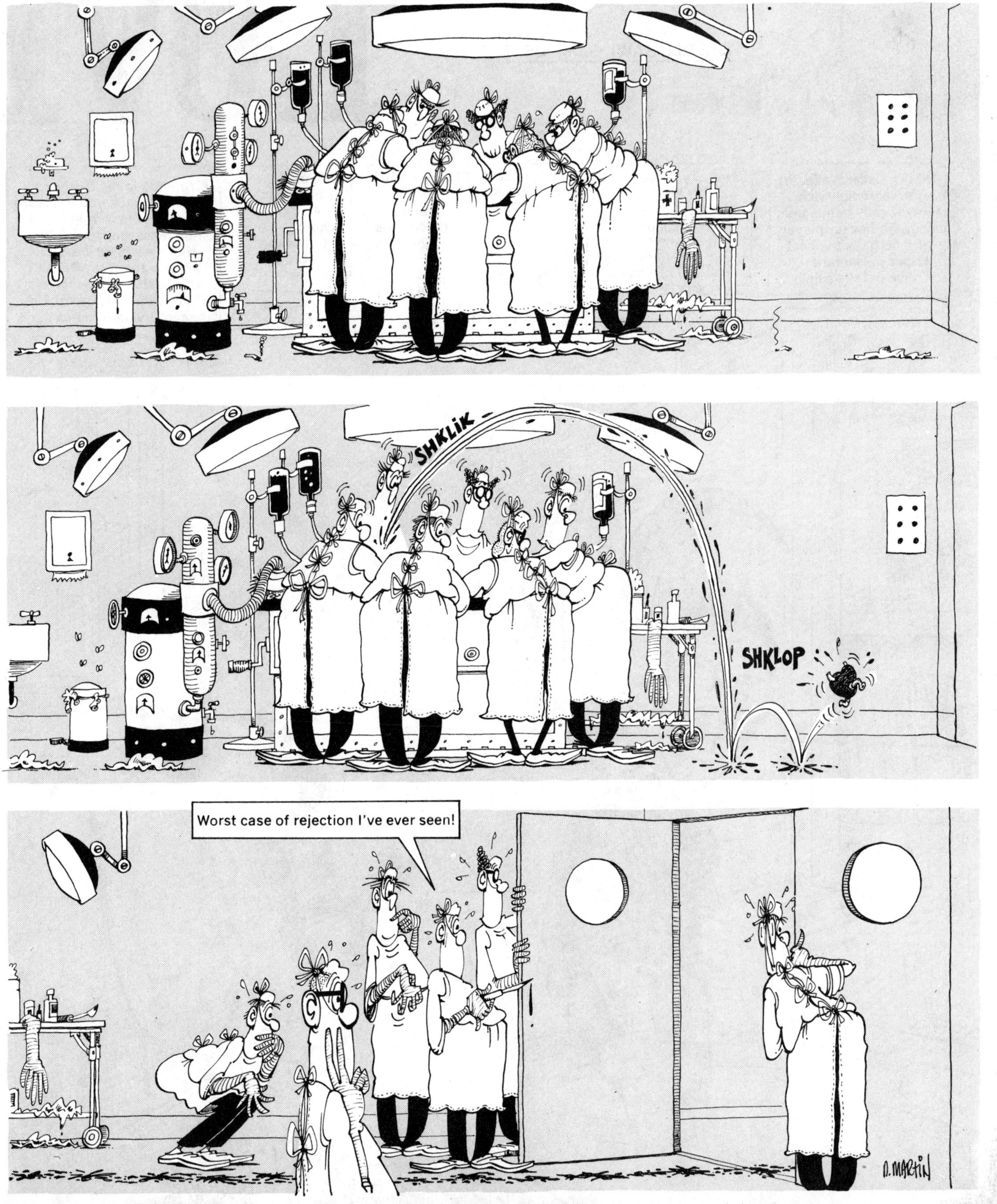
SHKLIK
SHKLOP
Worst case of rejection I've ever seen!
D. MARTIN

What can you say about a movie that actually shows two modern-day people **involved** with each other? You might say, **"That's strange!"**

What can you say about a movie that not only shows two people **involved** with each other, but also in **love?** You might say, **"That's unusual!"**

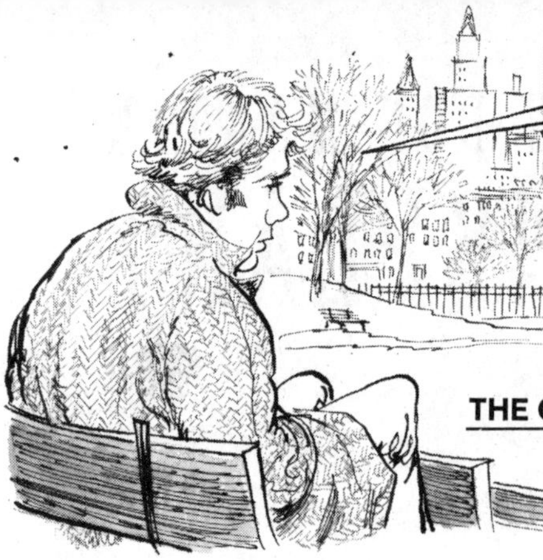

THE OLD BAWL GAME DEPT.

LOVE

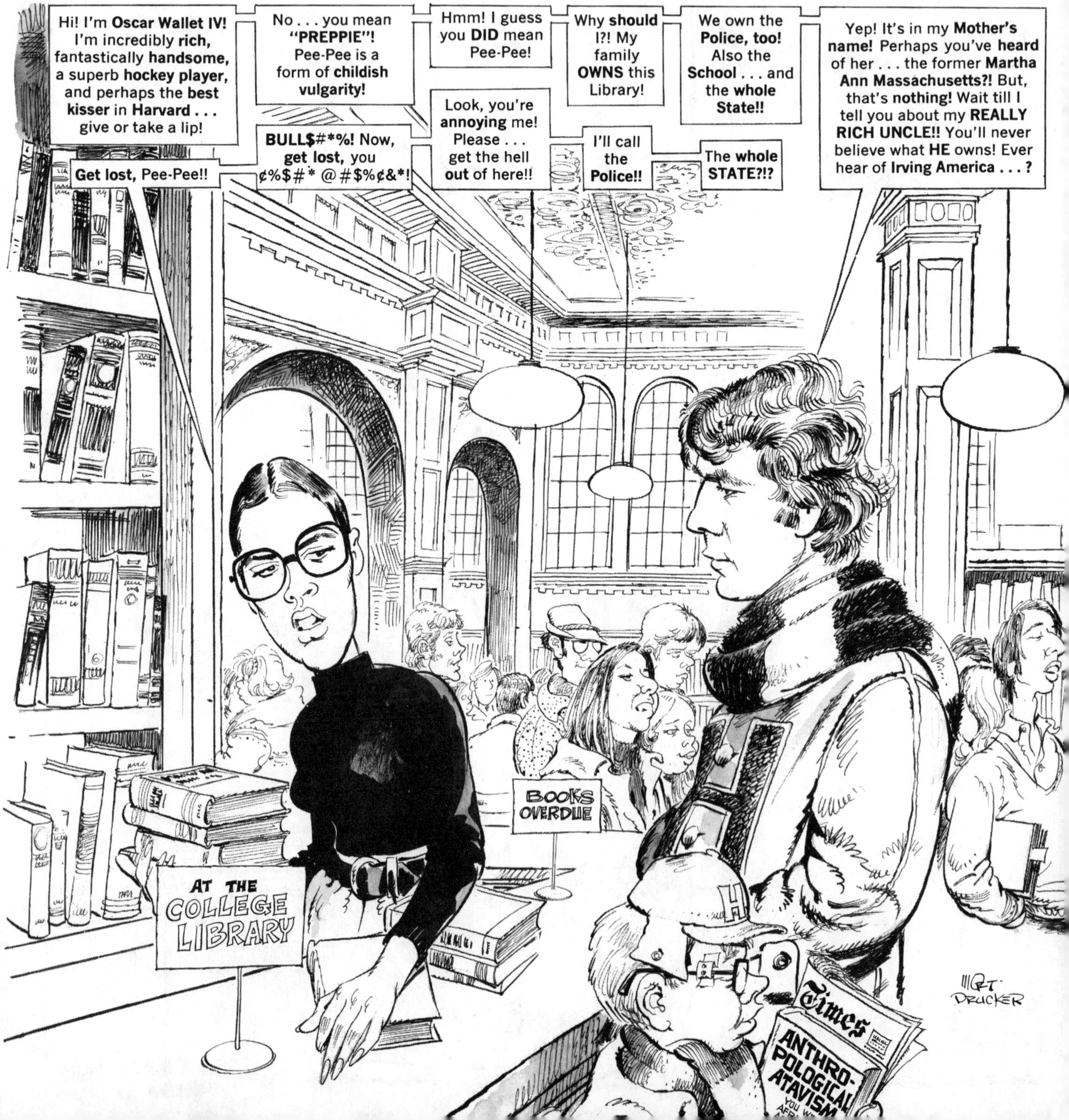
Hi! I'm Oscar Wallet IV! I'm incredibly rich, fantastically handsome, a superb hockey player, and perhaps the best kisser in Harvard . . . give or take a lip!
Get lost, Pee-Pee!!
No . . . you mean "PREPPIE"! Pee-Pee is a form of childish vulgarity!
BULL$#*%! Now, get lost, you ¢%$#* @#$%¢&*!
Hmm! I guess you DID mean Pee-Pee!
Look, you're annoying me! Please . . . get the hell out of here!!
Why should I?! My family OWNS this Library!
I'll call the Police!!
We own the Police, too! Also the School . . . and the whole State!!
The whole STATE?!?
Yep! It's in my Mother's name! Perhaps you've heard of her . . . the former Martha Ann Massachusetts?! But, that's nothing! Wait till I tell you about my REALLY RICH UNCLE!! You'll never believe what HE owns! Ever hear of Irving America . . . ?
BOOKS OVERDUE
AT THE COLLEGE LIBRARY
Times
ANTHRO-POLOGICAL ATAVISM
MORT DRUCKER

ell, then what do you say about a movie that, in this day and
e, not only shows two people **involved** with each other and in
ve, but also of **different sexes?** You might say, **"That's sick!"**

Okay, but please **bear** with me! Get out **25 boxes of Kleenex** and be prepared to **cry your eyes out!** You see, this is a . . . *sob* . . . *gulp* . . . *choke* . . .

R'S STORY

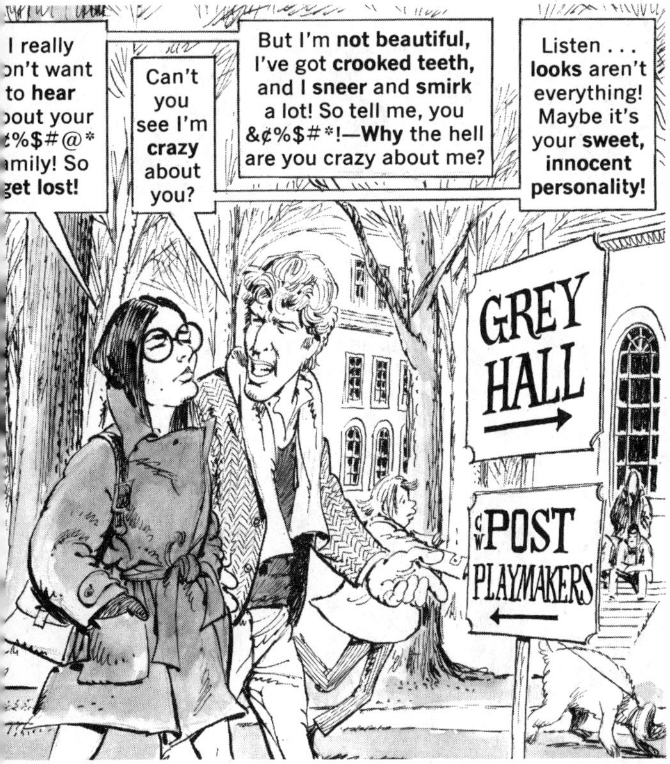

I really on't want to hear bout your ¢%$#@* amily! So get lost!
Can't you see I'm crazy about you?
But I'm not beautiful, I've got crooked teeth, and I sneer and smirk a lot! So tell me, you &¢%$#*!—Why the hell are you crazy about me?
Listen . . . looks aren't everything! Maybe it's your sweet, innocent personality!
GREY HALL
POST
PLAYMAKERS

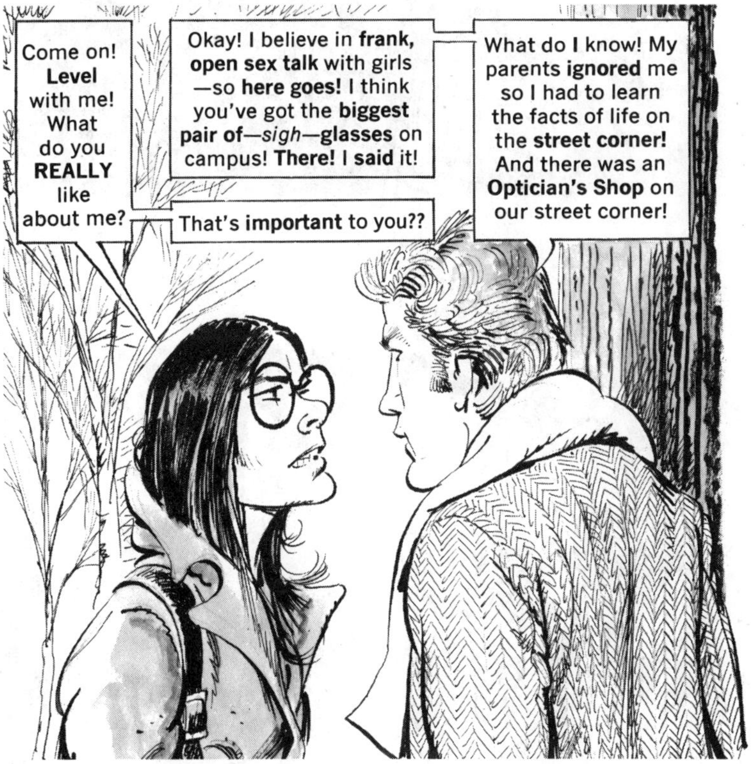

Come on! Level with me! What do you REALLY like about me?
Okay! I believe in frank, open sex talk with girls—so here goes! I think you've got the biggest pair of—sigh—glasses on campus! There! I said it!
That's important to you??
What do I know! My parents ignored me so I had to learn the facts of life on the street corner! And there was an Optician's Shop on our street corner!

ARTIST: MORT DRUCKER WRITER: LARRY SIEGEL

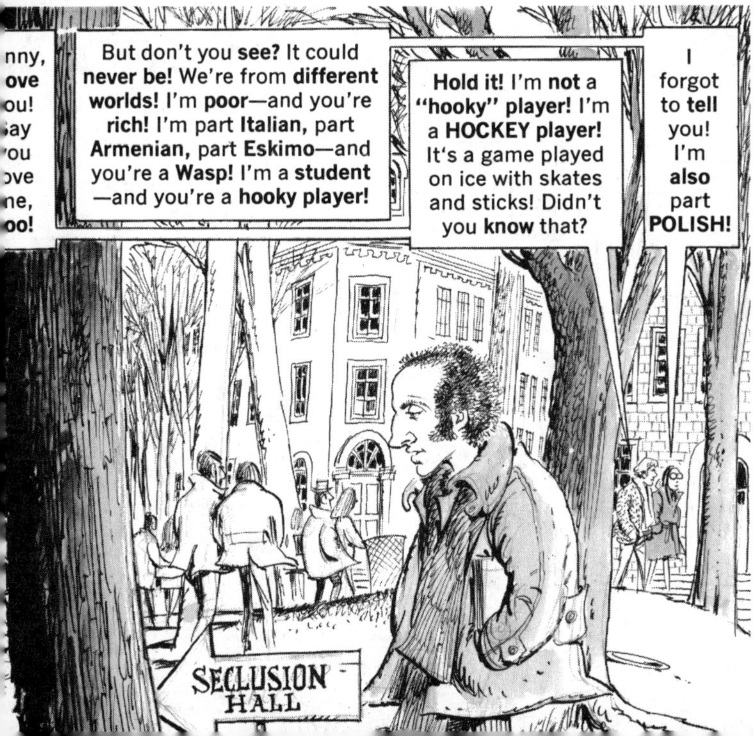

nny, ove ou! ay ou ove ne, oo!
But don't you see? It could never be! We're from different worlds! I'm poor—and you're rich! I'm part Italian, part Armenian, part Eskimo—and you're a Wasp! I'm a student—and you're a hooky player!
Hold it! I'm not a "hooky" player! I'm a HOCKEY player! It's a game played on ice with skates and sticks! Didn't you know that?
I forgot to tell you! I'm also part POLISH!
SECLUSION HALL

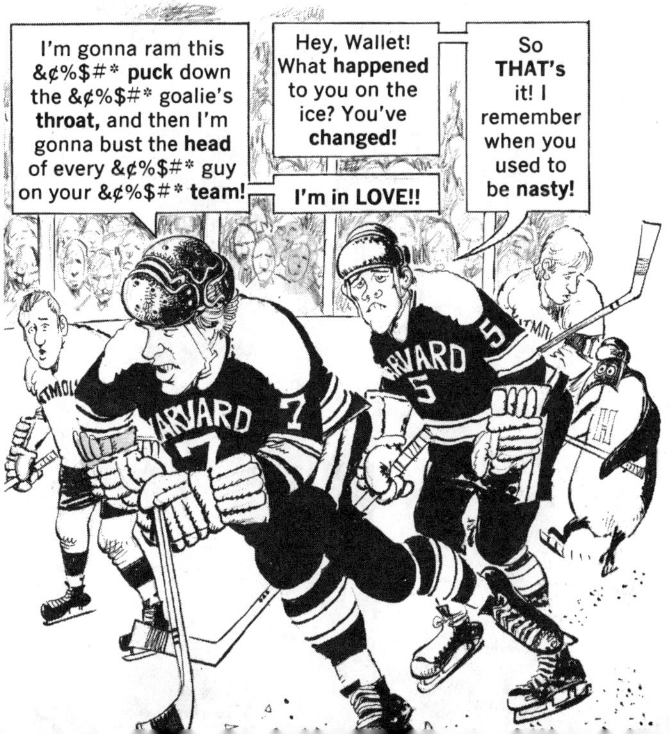

I'm gonna ram this &¢%$#* puck down the &¢%$#* goalie's throat, and then I'm gonna bust the head of every &¢%$#* guy on your &¢%$#* team!
Hey, Wallet! What happened to you on the ice? You've changed!
I'm in LOVE!!
So THAT's it! I remember when you used to be nasty!

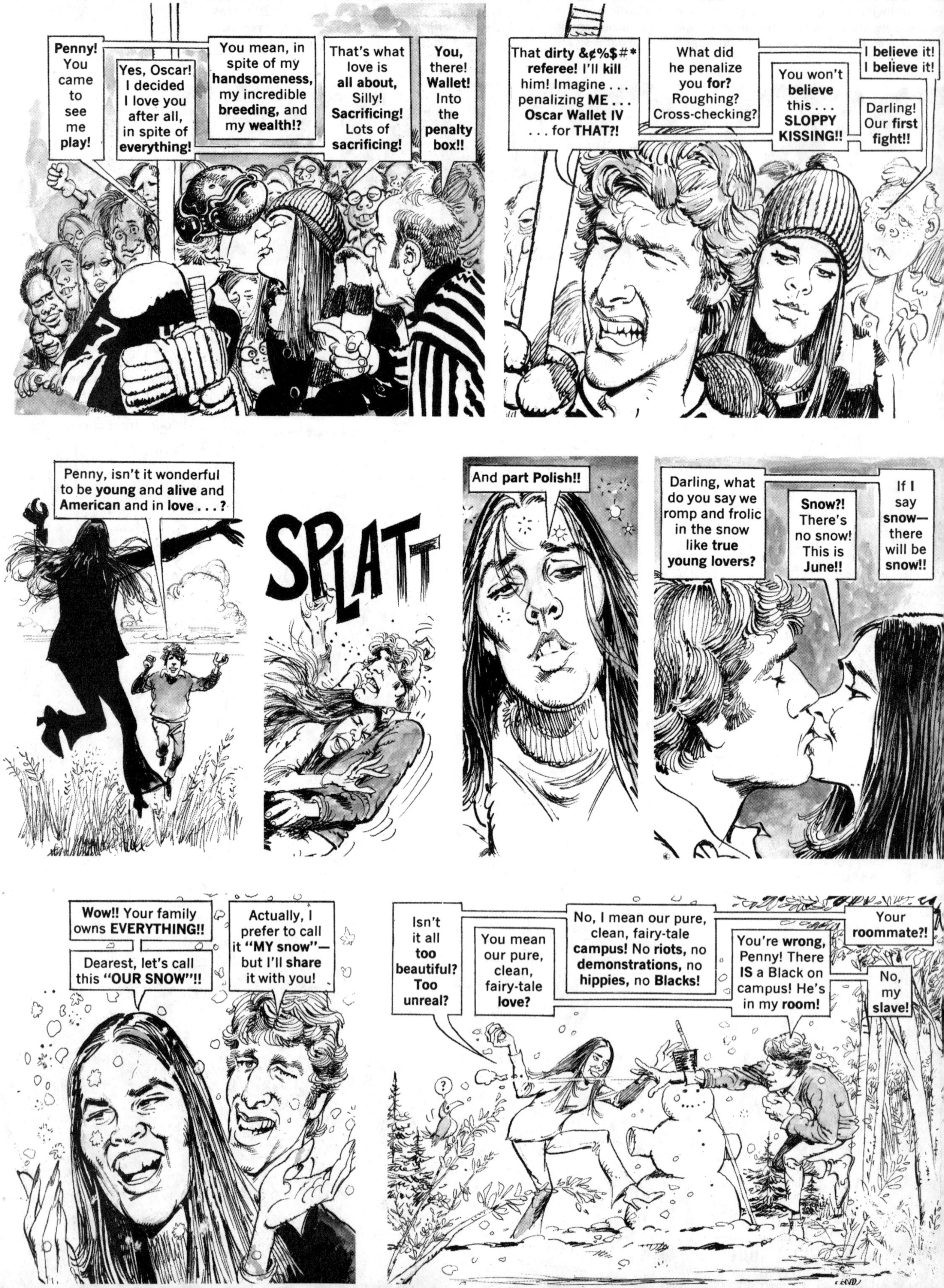
Penny! You came to see me play!
Yes, Oscar! I decided I love you after all, in spite of everything!
You mean, in spite of my handsomeness, my incredible breeding, and my wealth!?
That's what love is all about, Silly! Sacrificing! Lots of sacrificing!
You, there! Wallet! Into the penalty box!!
That dirty &¢%$#* referee! I'll kill him! Imagine . . . penalizing ME . . . Oscar Wallet IV . . . for THAT?!
What did he penalize you for? Roughing? Cross-checking?
You won't believe this . . . SLOPPY KISSING!!
I believe it! I believe it!
Darling! Our first fight!!
Penny, isn't it wonderful to be young and alive and American and in love . . . ?
SPLATT
And part Polish!!
Darling, what do you say we romp and frolic in the snow like true young lovers?
Snow?! There's no snow! This is June!!
If I say snow—there will be snow!!
Wow!! Your family owns EVERYTHING!!
Dearest, let's call this "OUR SNOW"!!
Actually, I prefer to call it "MY snow"—but I'll share it with you!
Isn't it all too beautiful? Too unreal?
You mean our pure, clean, fairy-tale love?
No, I mean our pure, clean, fairy-tale campus! No riots, no demonstrations, no hippies, no Blacks!
You're wrong, Penny! There IS a Black on campus! He's in my room!
Your roommate?!
No, my slave!
?

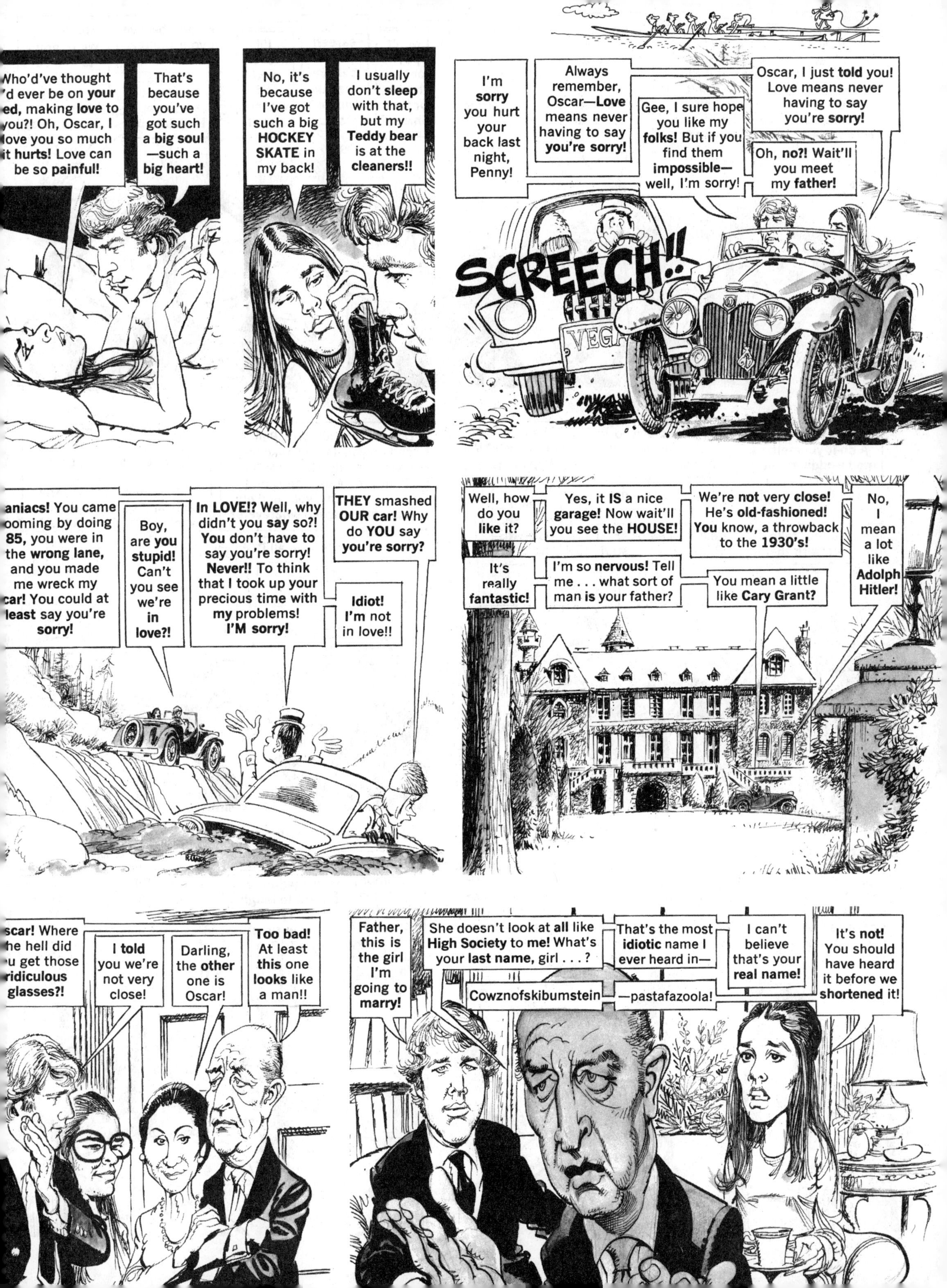

Who'd've thought 'd ever be on your ed, making love to you?! Oh, Oscar, I ove you so much it hurts! Love can be so painful!
That's because you've got such a big soul—such a big heart!
No, it's because I've got such a big HOCKEY SKATE in my back!
I usually don't sleep with that, but my Teddy bear is at the cleaners!!
I'm sorry you hurt your back last night, Penny!
Always remember, Oscar—Love means never having to say you're sorry!
Gee, I sure hope you like my folks! But if you find them impossible—well, I'm sorry!
Oscar, I just told you! Love means never having to say you're sorry!
Oh, no?! Wait'll you meet my father!
SCREECH!!
VEGA
aniacs! You came ooming by doing 85, you were in the wrong lane, and you made me wreck my car! You could at least say you're sorry!
Boy, are you stupid! Can't you see we're in love?!
In LOVE!? Well, why didn't you say so?! You don't have to say you're sorry! Never!! To think that I took up your precious time with my problems! I'M sorry!
THEY smashed OUR car! Why do YOU say you're sorry?
Idiot! I'm not in love!!
Well, how do you like it?
It's really fantastic!
Yes, it IS a nice garage! Now wait'll you see the HOUSE!
I'm so nervous! Tell me . . . what sort of man is your father?
We're not very close! He's old-fashioned! You know, a throwback to the 1930's!
You mean a little like Cary Grant?
No, I mean a lot like Adolph Hitler!
scar! Where he hell did u get those ridiculous glasses?!
I told you we're not very close!
Darling, the other one is Oscar!
Too bad! At least this one looks like a man!!
Father, this is the girl I'm going to marry!
She doesn't look at all like High Society to me! What's your last name, girl . . . ?
Cowznofskibumstein
That's the most idiotic name I ever heard in—
—pastafazoola!
I can't believe that's your real name!
It's not! You should have heard it before we shortened it!

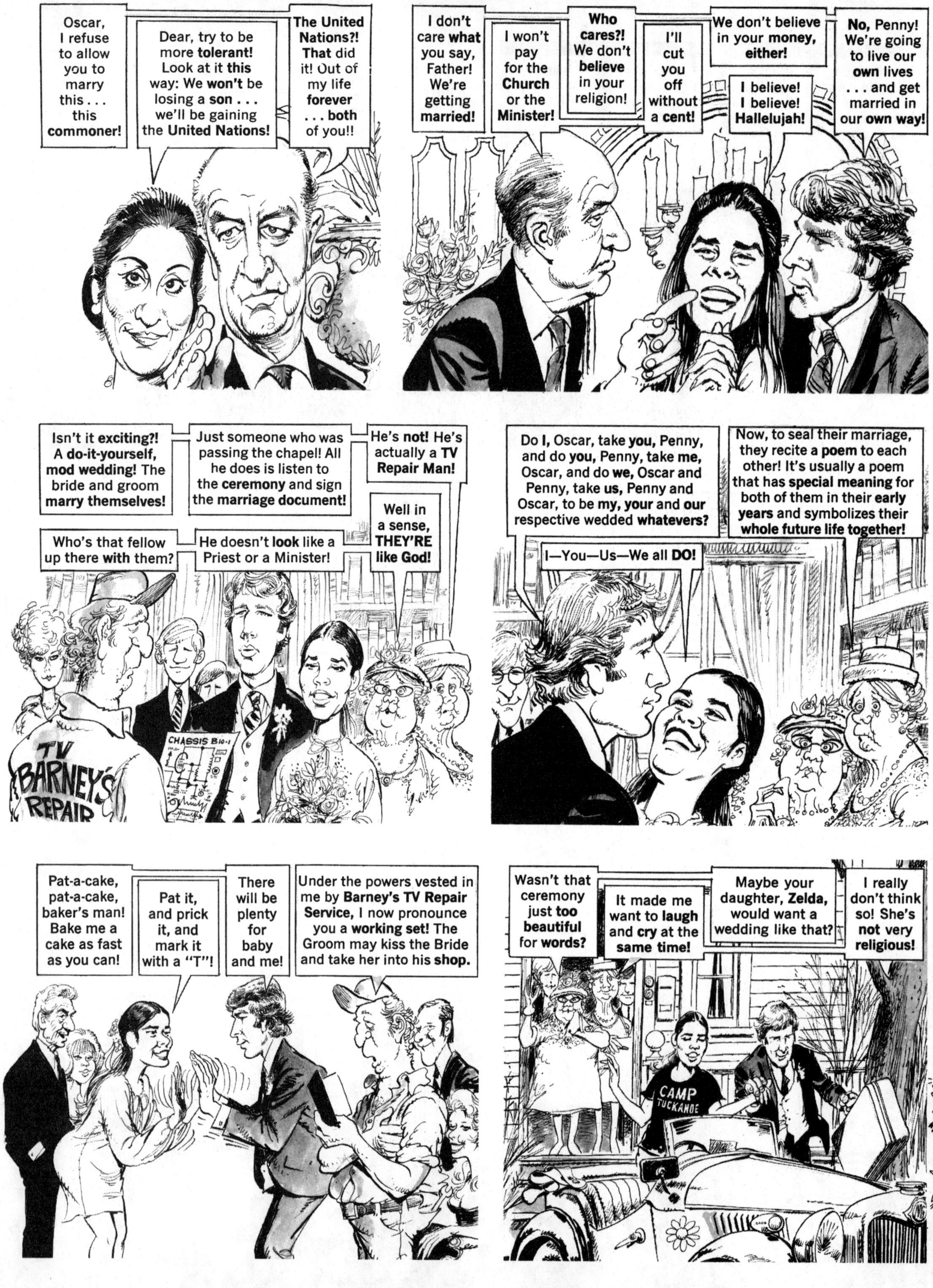

Oscar, I refuse to allow you to marry this . . . this **commoner!**
Dear, try to be more **tolerant!** Look at it **this** way: We **won't** be losing a **son . . .** we'll be gaining the **United Nations!**
The United Nations?! That did it! Out of my life **forever . . . both** of you!!
I don't care **what** you say, Father! We're getting **married!**
I won't pay for the **Church** or the **Minister!**
Who cares?! We don't **believe** in your religion!
I'll cut you off without **a cent!**
We don't believe in your **money, either!**
I believe! I believe! **Hallelujah!**
No, Penny! We're going to live our **own** lives . . . and get married in our **own way!**
Isn't it **exciting?!** A **do-it-yourself, mod wedding!** The bride and groom **marry themselves!**
Just someone who was passing the chapel! All he does is listen to the **ceremony** and sign the **marriage document!**
He's **not!** He's actually a **TV Repair Man!**
Who's that fellow up there **with** them?
He doesn't **look** like a Priest or a Minister!
Well in a sense, **THEY'RE like God!**
TV BARNEY'S REPAIR
CHASSIS B10-1
Do **I**, Oscar, take **you,** Penny, and do **you,** Penny, take **me,** Oscar, and do **we,** Oscar and Penny, take **us,** Penny and Oscar, to be **my, your** and **our** respective wedded **whatevers?**
Now, to seal their marriage, they recite a **poem** to each other! It's usually a poem that has **special meaning** for both of them in their **early years** and symbolizes their **whole future life together!**
I—You—Us—We all **DO!**
Pat-a-cake, pat-a-cake, baker's man! Bake me a cake as fast as you can!
Pat it, and prick it, and mark it with a "T"!
There will be plenty for baby and me!
Under the powers vested in me by **Barney's TV Repair Service,** I now pronounce you a **working set!** The Groom may kiss the Bride and take her into his **shop.**
Wasn't that ceremony just **too beautiful** for **words?**
It made me want to **laugh** and **cry** at the **same time!**
Maybe your daughter, **Zelda,** would want a wedding like that?
I really don't think so! She's **not** very **religious!**
CAMP TUCKAHOE

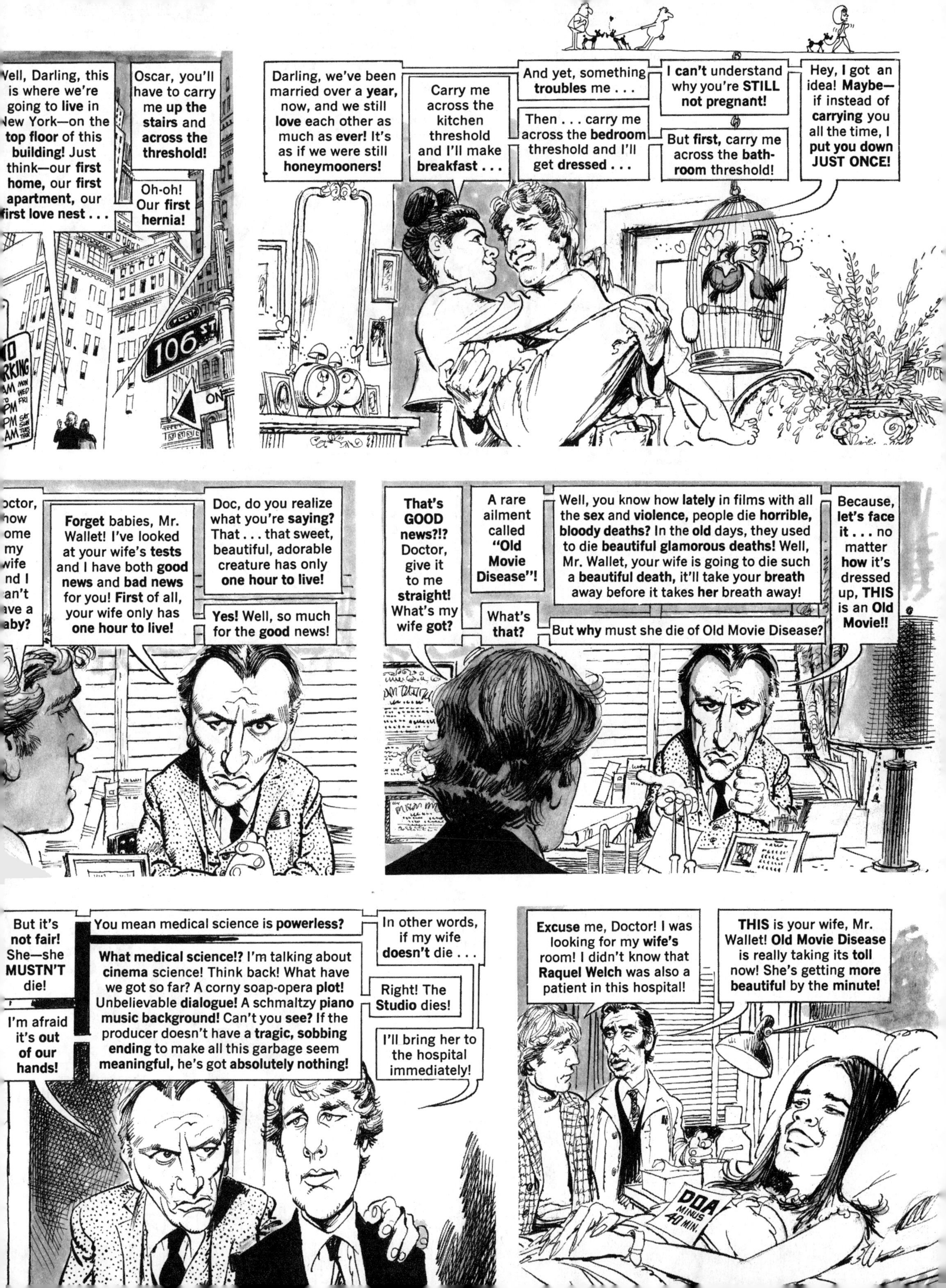
Vell, Darling, this is where we're going to live in lew York—on the top floor of this building! Just think—our first home, our first apartment, our irst love nest . . .
Oscar, you'll have to carry me up the stairs and across the threshold!
Oh-oh! Our first hernia!
106 ST
Darling, we've been married over a year, now, and we still love each other as much as ever! It's as if we were still honeymooners!
Carry me across the kitchen threshold and I'll make breakfast . . .
And yet, something troubles me . . .
Then . . . carry me across the bedroom threshold and I'll get dressed . . .
I can't understand why you're STILL not pregnant!
But first, carry me across the bathroom threshold!
Hey, I got an idea! Maybe— if instead of carrying you all the time, I put you down JUST ONCE!
octor, how ome my wife nd I an't ave a aby?
Forget babies, Mr. Wallet! I've looked at your wife's tests and I have both good news and bad news for you! First of all, your wife only has one hour to live!
Doc, do you realize what you're saying? That . . . that sweet, beautiful, adorable creature has only one hour to live!
Yes! Well, so much for the good news!
That's GOOD news?!? Doctor, give it to me straight! What's my wife got?
A rare ailment called "Old Movie Disease"!
What's that?
Well, you know how lately in films with all the sex and violence, people die horrible, bloody deaths? In the old days, they used to die beautiful glamorous deaths! Well, Mr. Wallet, your wife is going to die such a beautiful death, it'll take your breath away before it takes her breath away!
But why must she die of Old Movie Disease?
Because, let's face it . . . no matter how it's dressed up, THIS is an Old Movie!!
But it's not fair! She—she MUSTN'T die!
You mean medical science is powerless?
I'm afraid it's out of our hands!
What medical science!? I'm talking about cinema science! Think back! What have we got so far? A corny soap-opera plot! Unbelievable dialogue! A schmaltzy piano music background! Can't you see? If the producer doesn't have a tragic, sobbing ending to make all this garbage seem meaningful, he's got absolutely nothing!
In other words, if my wife doesn't die . . .
Right! The Studio dies!
I'll bring her to the hospital immediately!
Excuse me, Doctor! I was looking for my wife's room! I didn't know that Raquel Welch was also a patient in this hospital!
THIS is your wife, Mr. Wallet! Old Movie Disease is really taking its toll now! She's getting more beautiful by the minute!
DOA MINUS 40 MIN.

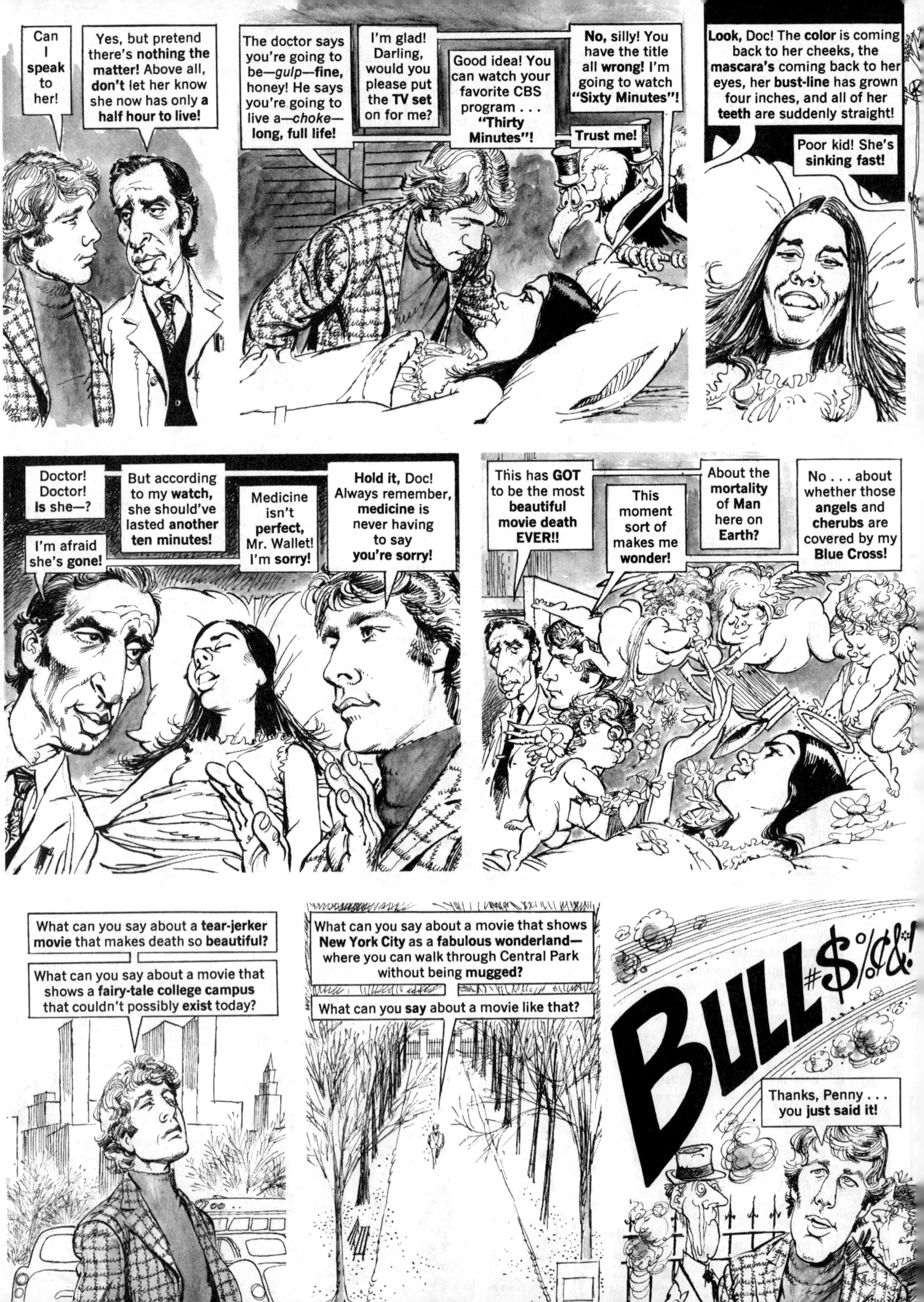
Can I speak to her!
Yes, but pretend there's nothing the matter! Above all, don't let her know she now has only a half hour to live!
The doctor says you're going to be—gulp—fine, honey! He says you're going to live a—choke—long, full life!
I'm glad! Darling, would you please put the TV set on for me?
Good idea! You can watch your favorite CBS program . . . "Thirty Minutes"!
No, silly! You have the title all wrong! I'm going to watch "Sixty Minutes"!
Trust me!
Look, Doc! The color is coming back to her cheeks, the mascara's coming back to her eyes, her bust-line has grown four inches, and all of her teeth are suddenly straight!
Poor kid! She's sinking fast!
Doctor! Doctor! Is she—?
I'm afraid she's gone!
But according to my watch, she should've lasted another ten minutes!
Medicine isn't perfect, Mr. Wallet! I'm sorry!
Hold it, Doc! Always remember, medicine is never having to say you're sorry!
This has GOT to be the most beautiful movie death EVER!!
This moment sort of makes me wonder!
About the mortality of Man here on Earth?
No . . . about whether those angels and cherubs are covered by my Blue Cross!
What can you say about a tear-jerker movie that makes death so beautiful?
What can you say about a movie that shows a fairy-tale college campus that couldn't possibly exist today?
What can you say about a movie that shows New York City as a fabulous wonderland—where you can walk through Central Park without being mugged?
What can you say about a movie like that?
BULL#$%¢&!
Thanks, Penny . . . you just said it!

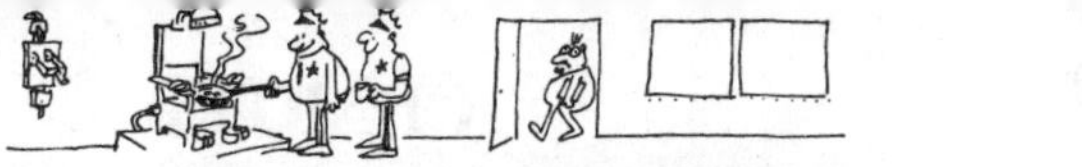

SHOW AND TELL DEPT.

Almost every day, the nation's newspapers carry nervous articles about the pros and cons of including (shh!) Sex Education in our schools. Since it's only a matter of time before the idea is universally accepted, MAD looks forward to the day when we will see honest and forthright textbooks on the subject . . . like for instance—

THE MAD SEX EDUCATION PRIMER

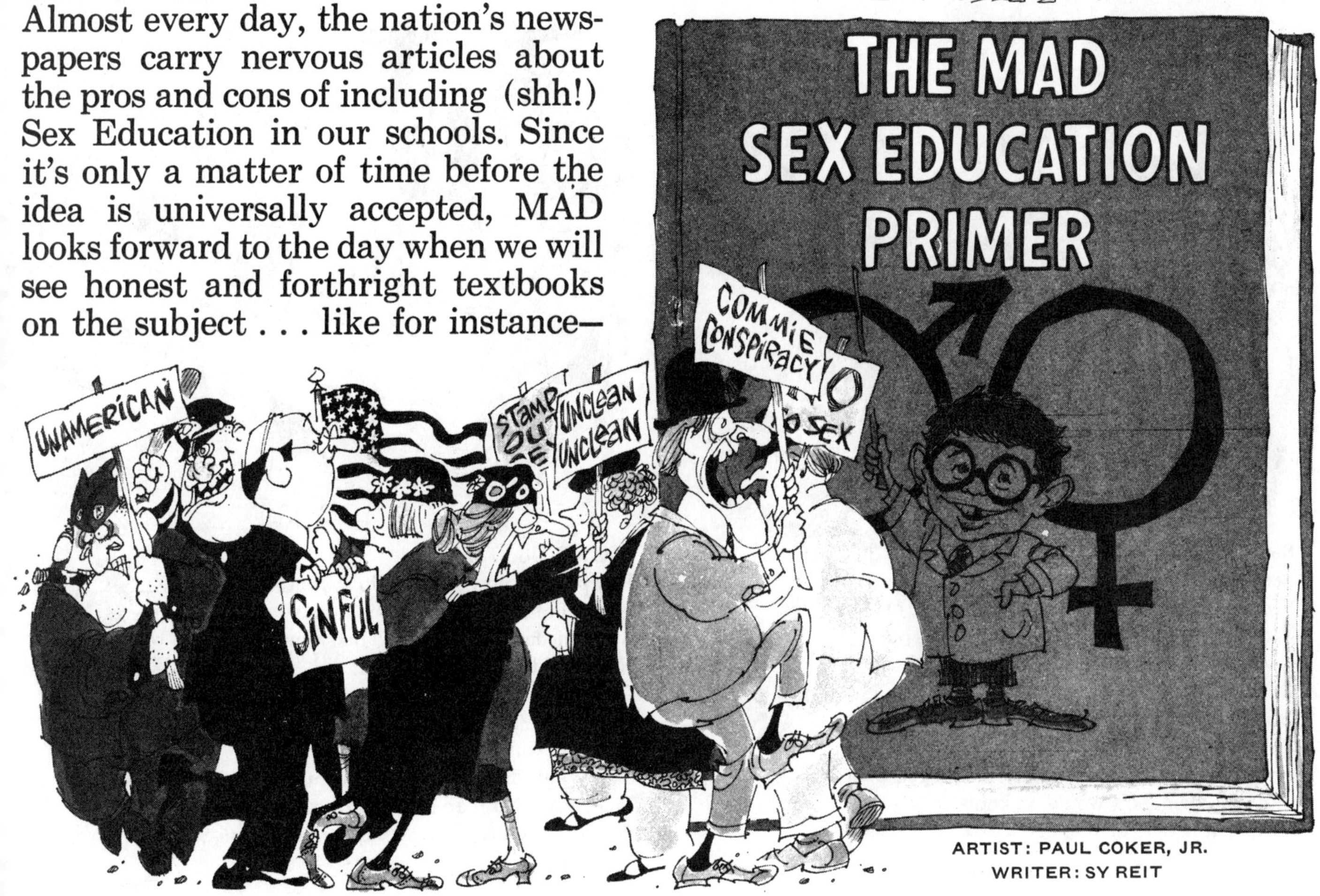

THE MAD SEX EDUCATION PRIMER
UNAMERICAN
UNCLEAN UNCLEAN
COMMIE CONSPIRACY
SINFUL

ARTIST: PAUL COKER, JR.
WRITER: SY REIT

CHAPTER 1.

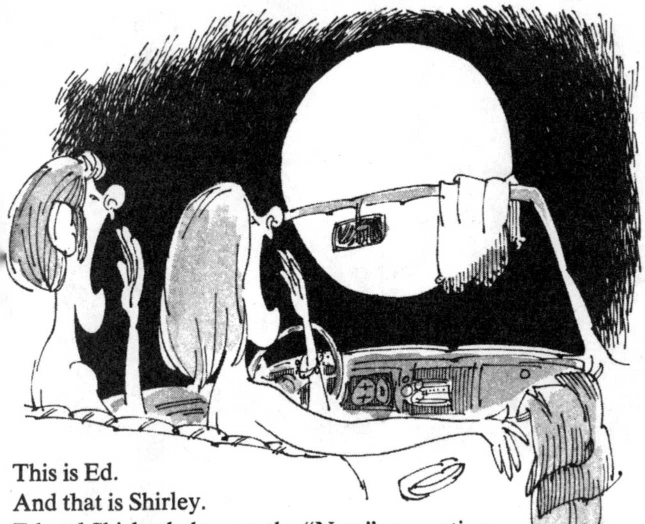

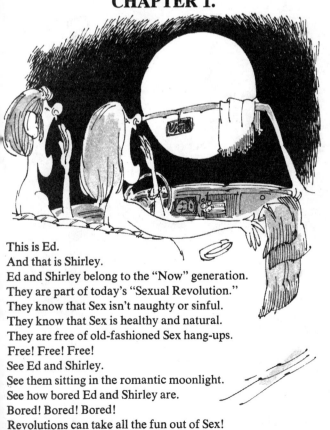

This is Ed.
And that is Shirley.
Ed and Shirley belong to the "Now" generation.
They are part of today's "Sexual Revolution."
They know that Sex isn't naughty or sinful.
They know that Sex is healthy and natural.
They are free of old-fashioned Sex hang-ups.
Free! Free! Free!
See Ed and Shirley.
See them sitting in the romantic moonlight.
See how bored Ed and Shirley are.
Bored! Bored! Bored!
Revolutions can take all the fun out of Sex!

CHAPTER 2.

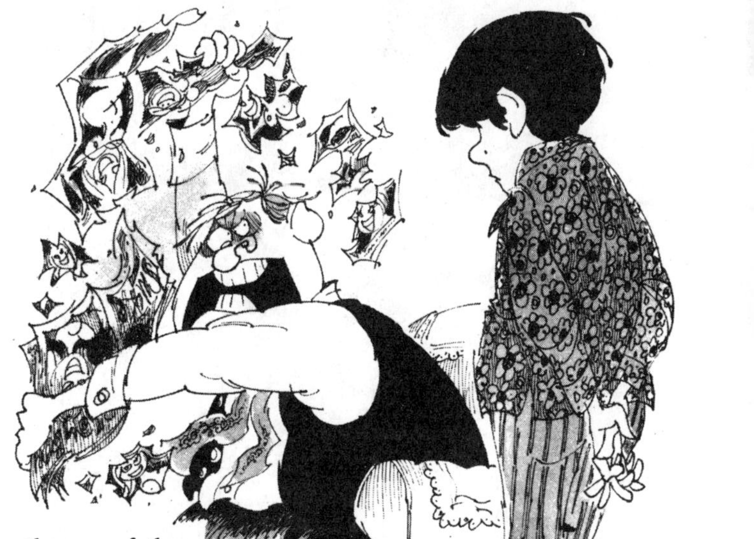

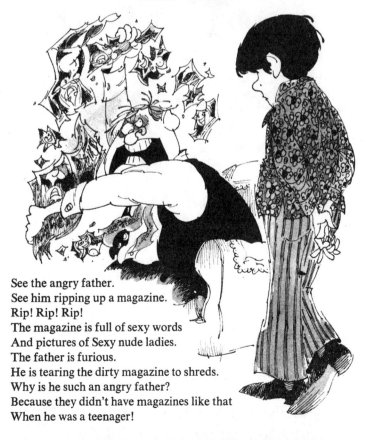

See the angry father.
See him ripping up a magazine.
Rip! Rip! Rip!
The magazine is full of sexy words
And pictures of Sexy nude ladies.
The father is furious.
He is tearing the dirty magazine to shreds.
Why is he such an angry father?
Because they didn't have magazines like that
When he was a teenager!

CHAPTER 3.

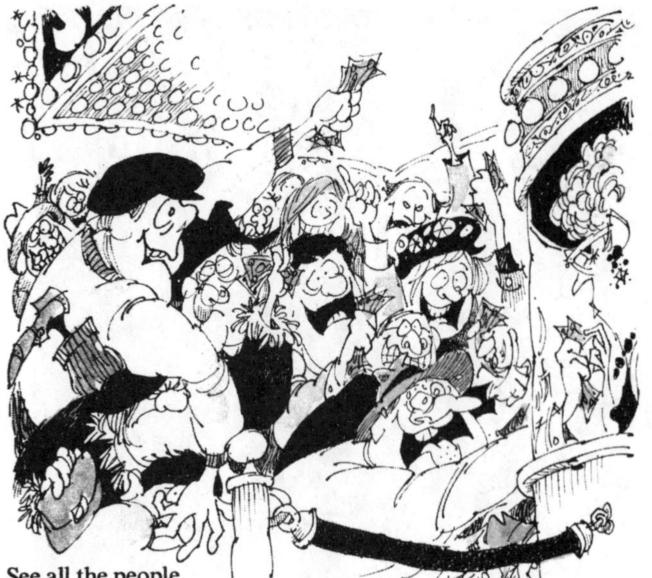

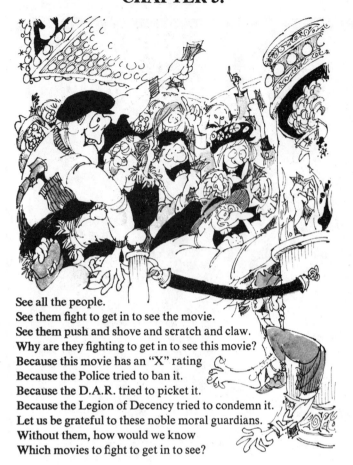

See all the people.
See them fight to get in to see the movie.
See them push and shove and scratch and claw.
Why are they fighting to get in to see this movie?
Because this movie has an "X" rating
Because the Police tried to ban it.
Because the D.A.R. tried to picket it.
Because the Legion of Decency tried to condemn it.
Let us be grateful to these noble moral guardians.
Without them, how would we know
Which movies to fight to get in to see?

CHAPTER 4.

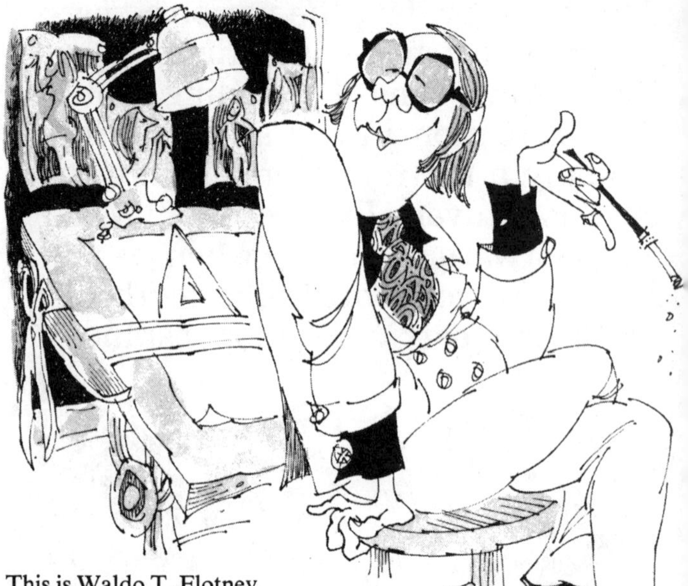

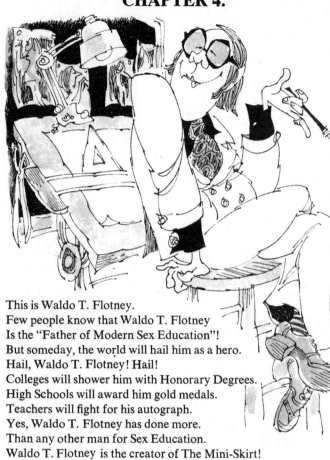

This is Waldo T. Flotney.
Few people know that Waldo T. Flotney
Is the "Father of Modern Sex Education"!
But someday, the world will hail him as a hero.
Hail, Waldo T. Flotney! Hail!
Colleges will shower him with Honorary Degrees.
High Schools will award him gold medals.
Teachers will fight for his autograph.
Yes, Waldo T. Flotney has done more.
Than any other man for Sex Education.
Waldo T. Flotney is the creator of The Mini-Skirt!

CHAPTER 5.

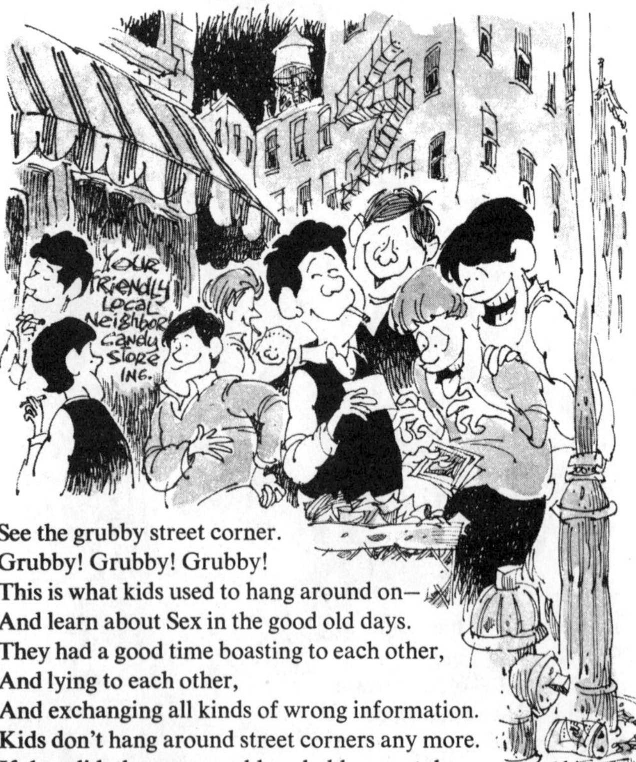
Your Friendly Local Neighbor Candy Store Inc.

See the grubby street corner.
Grubby! Grubby! Grubby!
This is what kids used to hang around on—
And learn about Sex in the good old days.
They had a good time boasting to each other,
And lying to each other,
And exchanging all kinds of wrong information.
Kids don't hang around street corners any more.
If they did, the cops would probably arrest them
For trying to start a riot.
Nope—
They don't make street corners like they used to!

CHAPTER 6.

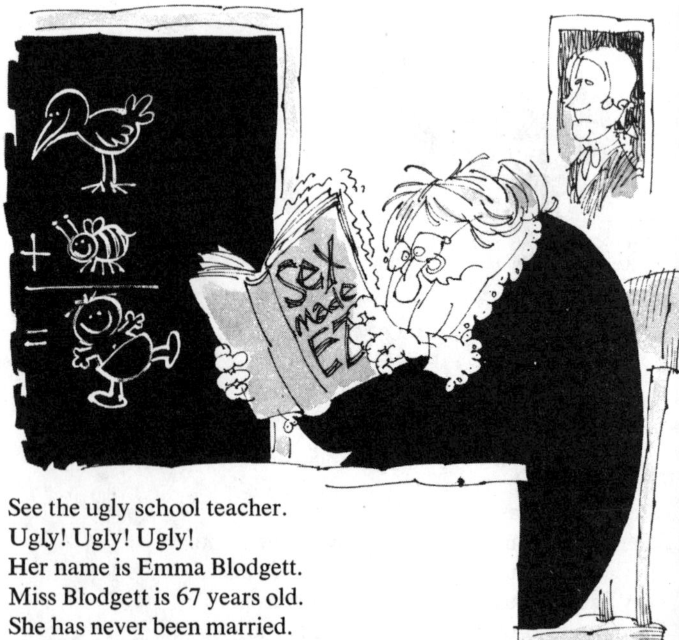
Sex made EZ

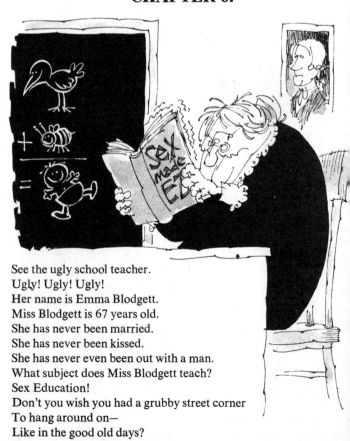

See the ugly school teacher.
Ugly! Ugly! Ugly!
Her name is Emma Blodgett.
Miss Blodgett is 67 years old.
She has never been married.
She has never been kissed.
She has never even been out with a man.
What subject does Miss Blodgett teach?
Sex Education!
Don't you wish you had a grubby street corner
To hang around on—
Like in the good old days?

CHAPTER 7.

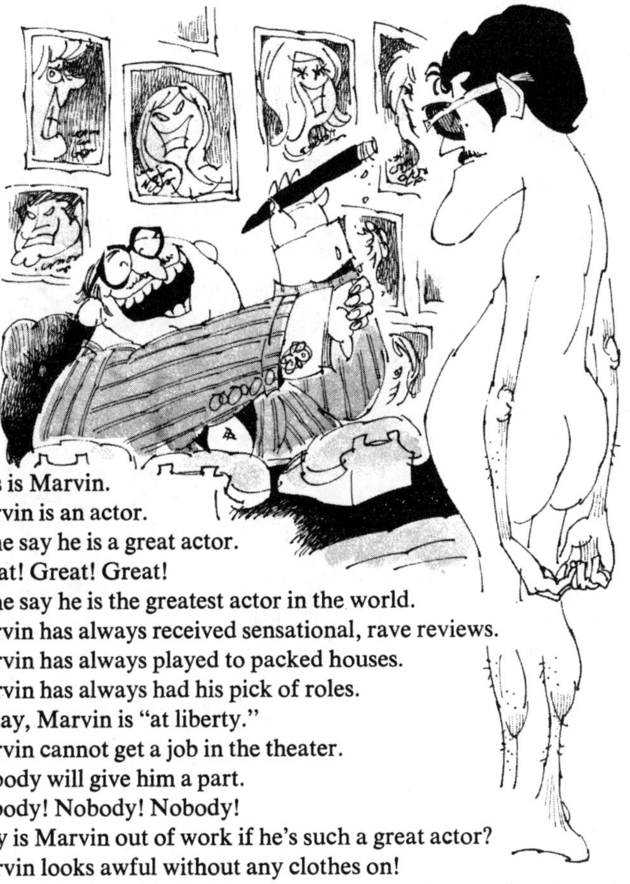

This is Marvin.
Marvin is an actor.
Some say he is a great actor.
Great! Great! Great!
Some say he is the greatest actor in the world.
Marvin has always received sensational, rave reviews.
Marvin has always played to packed houses.
Marvin has always had his pick of roles.
Today, Marvin is "at liberty."
Marvin cannot get a job in the theater.
Nobody will give him a part.
Nobody! Nobody! Nobody!
Why is Marvin out of work if he's such a great actor?
Marvin looks awful without any clothes on!

CHAPTER 8.

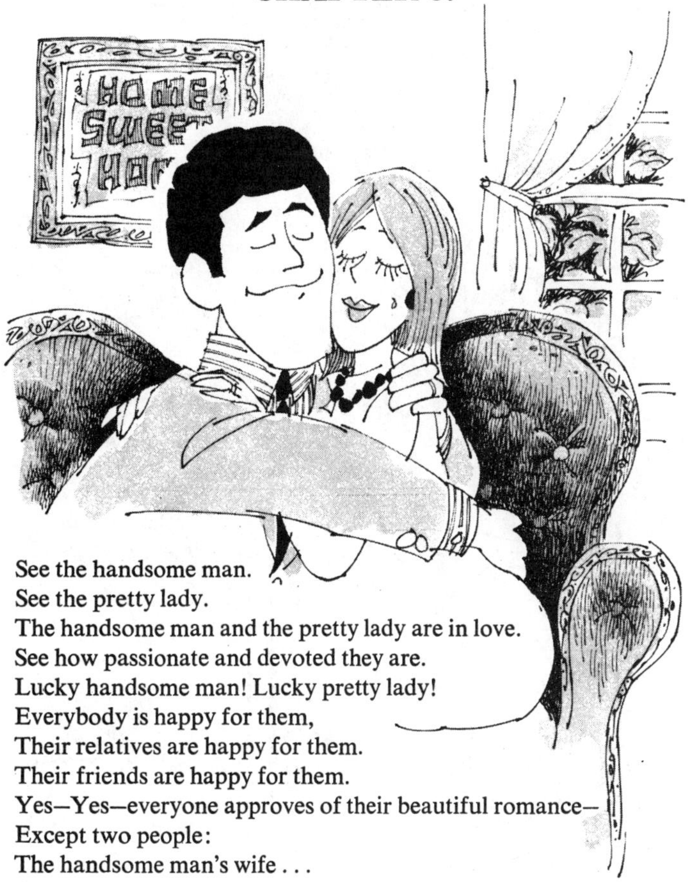
HOME
SWEET

See the handsome man.
See the pretty lady.
The handsome man and the pretty lady are in love.
See how passionate and devoted they are.
Lucky handsome man! Lucky pretty lady!
Everybody is happy for them,
Their relatives are happy for them.
Their friends are happy for them.
Yes–Yes–everyone approves of their beautiful romance–
Except two people:
The handsome man's wife . . .
And the pretty lady's husband!

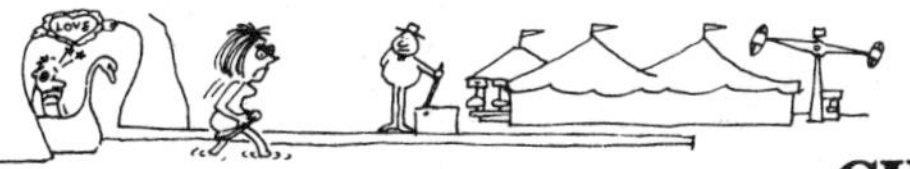

CHAPTER 9.

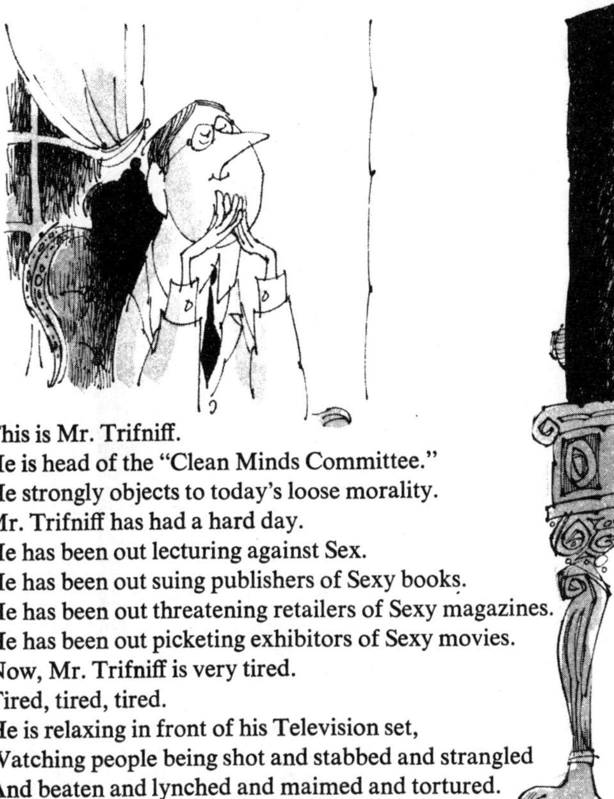

This is Mr. Trifniff.
He is head of the "Clean Minds Committee."
He strongly objects to today's loose morality.
Mr. Trifniff has had a hard day.
He has been out lecturing against Sex.
He has been out suing publishers of Sexy books.
He has been out threatening retailers of Sexy magazines.
He has been out picketing exhibitors of Sexy movies.
Now, Mr. Trifniff is very tired.
Tired, tired, tired.
He is relaxing in front of his Television set,
Watching people being shot and stabbed and strangled
And beaten and lynched and maimed and tortured.
Mr. Trifniff knows the difference
Between what is right . . . and what is wrong!

CHAPTER 10.

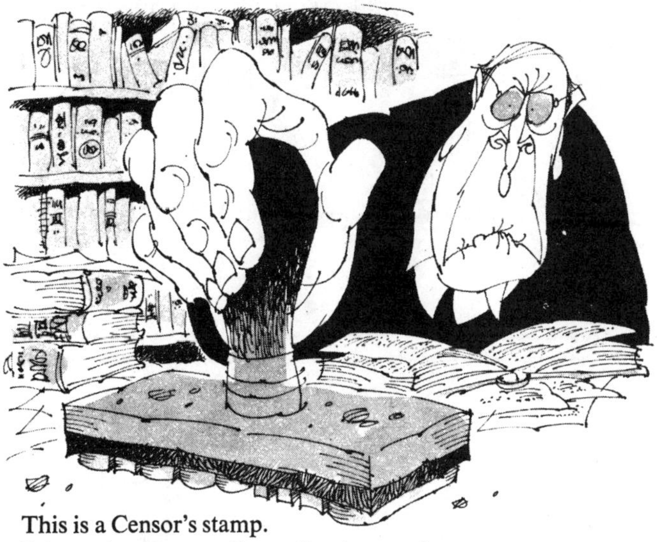

This is a Censor's stamp.
It is used to blot out dirty, offensive words
In books and magazines.
For example, it is used to blot out words like
CENSORED, and **CENSORED**,
Also **CENSORED**,
And especially **CENSORED**
But some dirty, offensive words are never censored.
Words like "wop" and "kike" and "Polack" and "nigger"!
Is it possible that our Censors
Are full of **CENSORED** ?

JOKE & DAGGER DEPT.

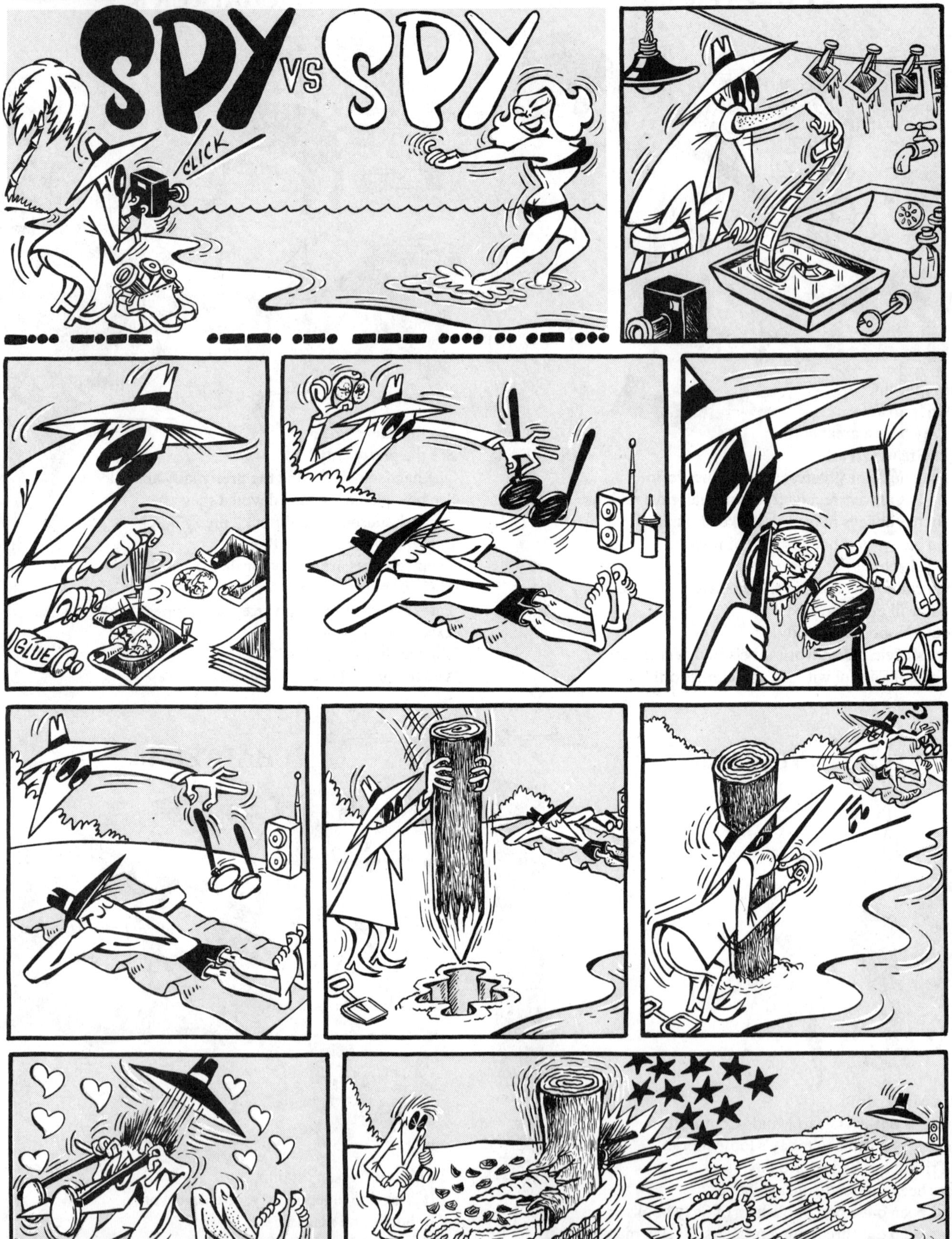
SPY VS SPY
CLICK
GLUE
Prohias.

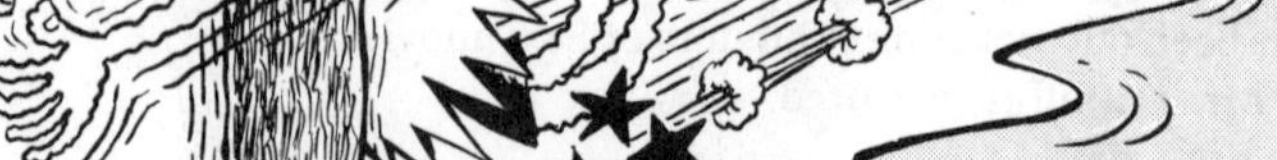

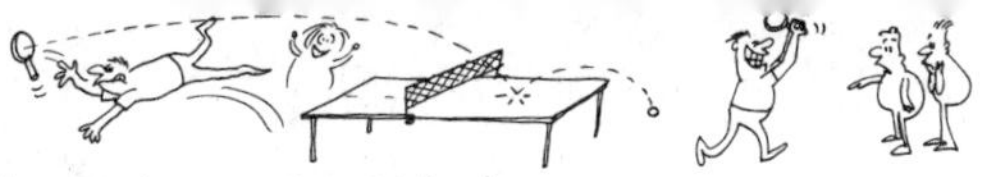

OPENED SESAME DEPT.

No one can fault the success of teaching children basic things in entertaining ways, and the television series "Sesame Street" does it better than most. Unfortunately, it helps little Johnny to read—but not between the lines! What we need is a television show that will prepare our youth for what <u>really</u> lies ahead, a program like

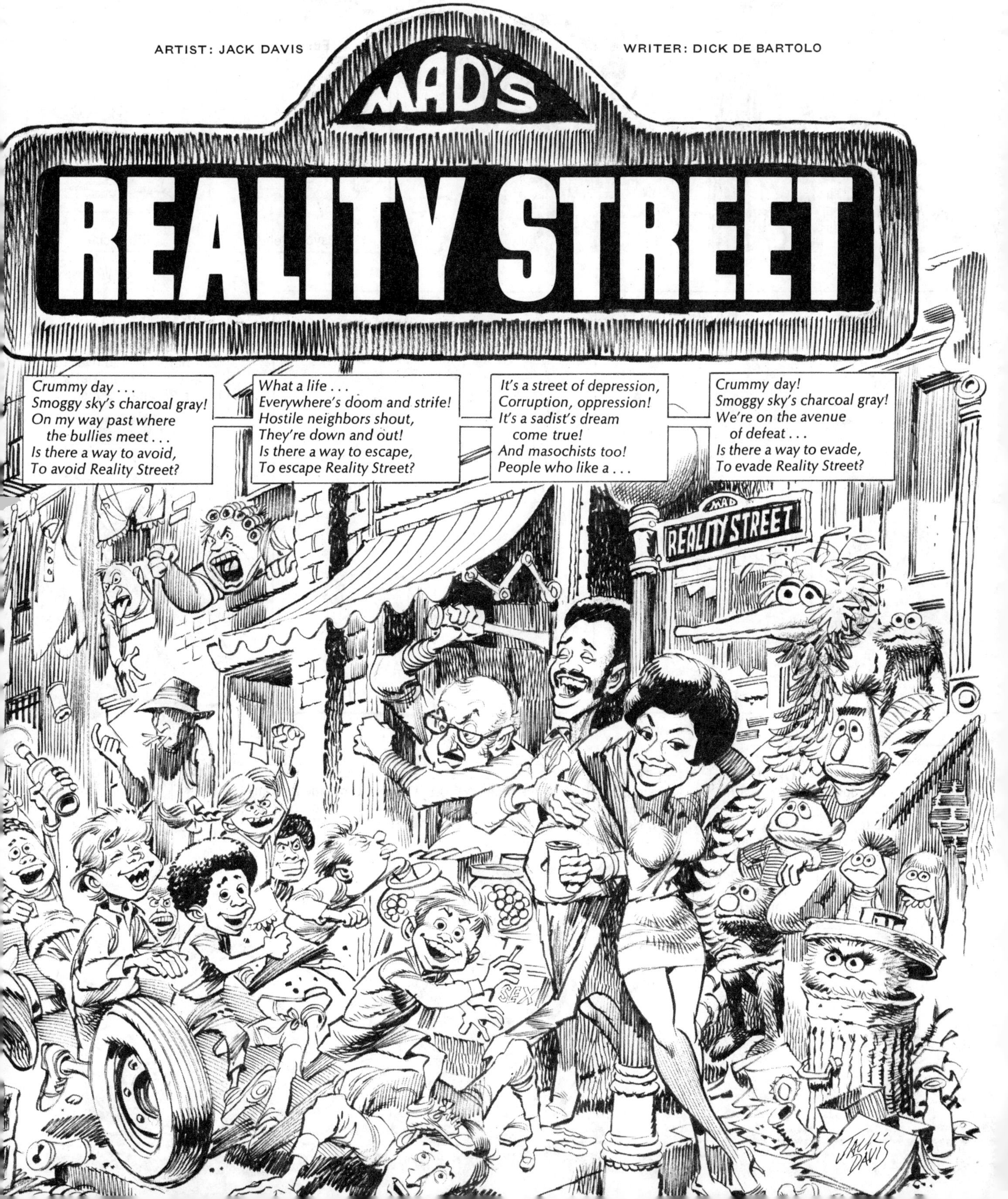

ARTIST: JACK DAVIS
WRITER: DICK DE BARTOLO
MAD'S
REALITY STREET
Crummy day . . . Smoggy sky's charcoal gray! On my way past where the bullies meet . . . Is there a way to avoid, To avoid Reality Street?
What a life . . . Everywhere's doom and strife! Hostile neighbors shout, They're down and out! Is there a way to escape, To escape Reality Street?
It's a street of depression, Corruption, oppression! It's a sadist's dream come true! And masochists too! People who like a . . .
Crummy day! Smoggy sky's charcoal gray! We're on the avenue of defeat . . . Is there a way to evade, To evade Reality Street?
MAD
REALITY STREET
SEX
JACK DAVIS

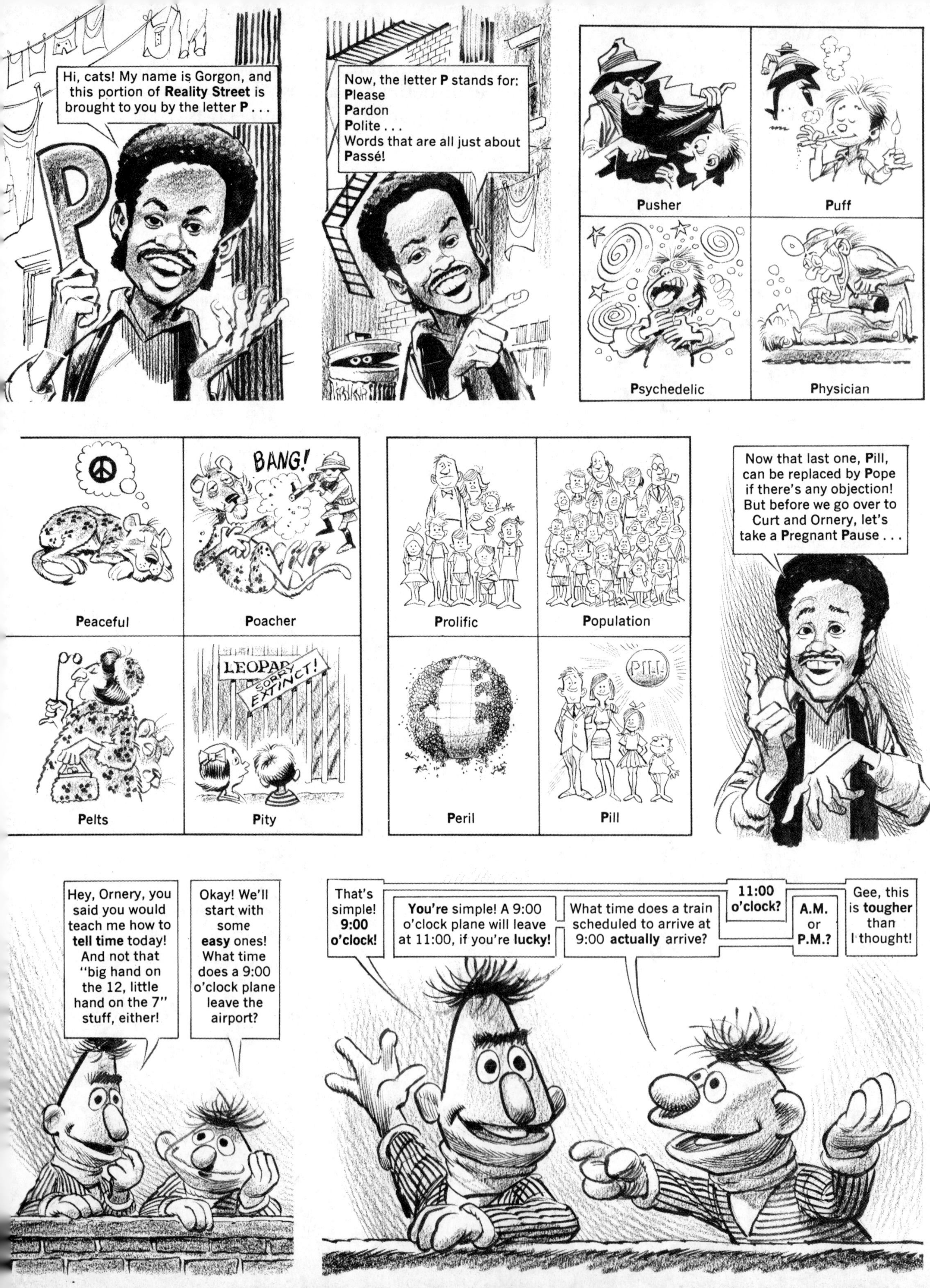

Hi, cats! My name is Gorgon, and this portion of **Reality Street** is brought to you by the letter **P** . . .
Now, the letter **P** stands for: **P**lease **P**ardon **P**olite . . . Words that are all just about **P**assé!
Pusher
Puff
Psychedelic
Physician
Peaceful
BANG!
Poacher
Pelts
LEOPAR
SORRY EXTINCT!
Pity
Prolific
Population
Peril
PILL
Pill
Now that last one, **P**ill, can be replaced by **P**ope if there's any objection! But before we go over to Curt and Ornery, let's take a **P**regnant **P**ause . . .
Hey, Ornery, you said you would teach me how to **tell time** today! And not that "big hand on the 12, little hand on the 7" stuff, either!
Okay! We'll start with some **easy** ones! What time does a 9:00 o'clock plane leave the airport?
That's simple! **9:00 o'clock!**
You're simple! A 9:00 o'clock plane will leave at 11:00, if you're **lucky!**
What time does a train scheduled to arrive at 9:00 **actually** arrive?
11:00 o'clock?
A.M. or **P.M.?**
Gee, this is **tougher** than I thought!

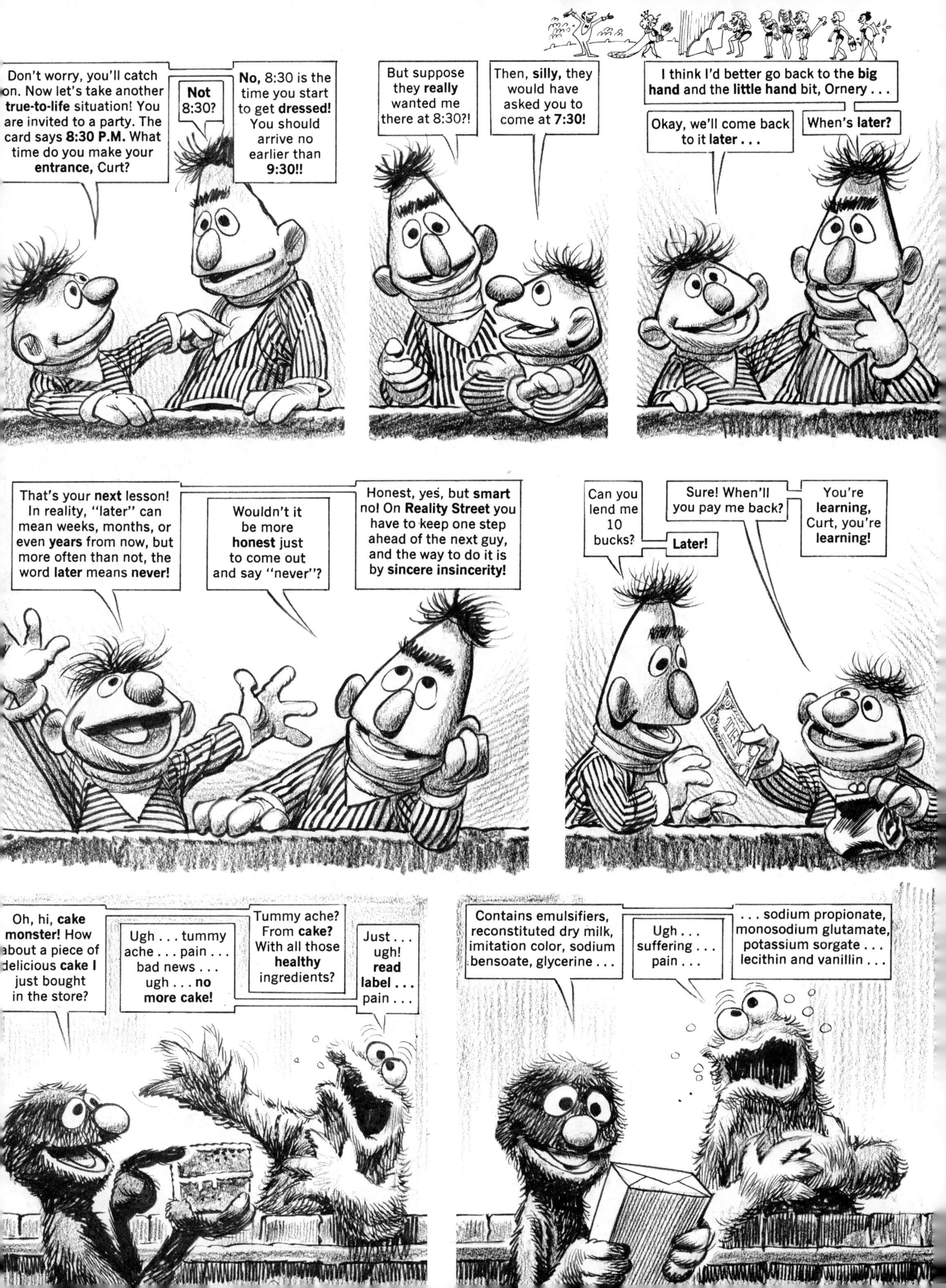

Don't worry, you'll catch on. Now let's take another true-to-life situation! You are invited to a party. The card says 8:30 P.M. What time do you make your entrance, Curt?
Not 8:30?
No, 8:30 is the time you start to get dressed! You should arrive no earlier than 9:30!!
But suppose they really wanted me there at 8:30?!
Then, silly, they would have asked you to come at 7:30!
I think I'd better go back to the big hand and the little hand bit, Ornery . . .
Okay, we'll come back to it later . . .
When's later?
That's your next lesson! In reality, "later" can mean weeks, months, or even years from now, but more often than not, the word later means never!
Wouldn't it be more honest just to come out and say "never"?
Honest, yes, but smart no! On Reality Street you have to keep one step ahead of the next guy, and the way to do it is by sincere insincerity!
Can you lend me 10 bucks?
Sure! When'll you pay me back?
Later!
You're learning, Curt, you're learning!
Oh, hi, cake monster! How about a piece of delicious cake I just bought in the store?
Ugh . . . tummy ache . . . pain . . . bad news . . . ugh . . . no more cake!
Tummy ache? From cake? With all those healthy ingredients?
Just . . . ugh! read label . . . pain . . .
Contains emulsifiers, reconstituted dry milk, imitation color, sodium bensoate, glycerine . . .
Ugh . . . suffering . . . pain . . .
. . . sodium propionate, monosodium glutamate, potassium sorgate . . . lecithin and vanillin . . .

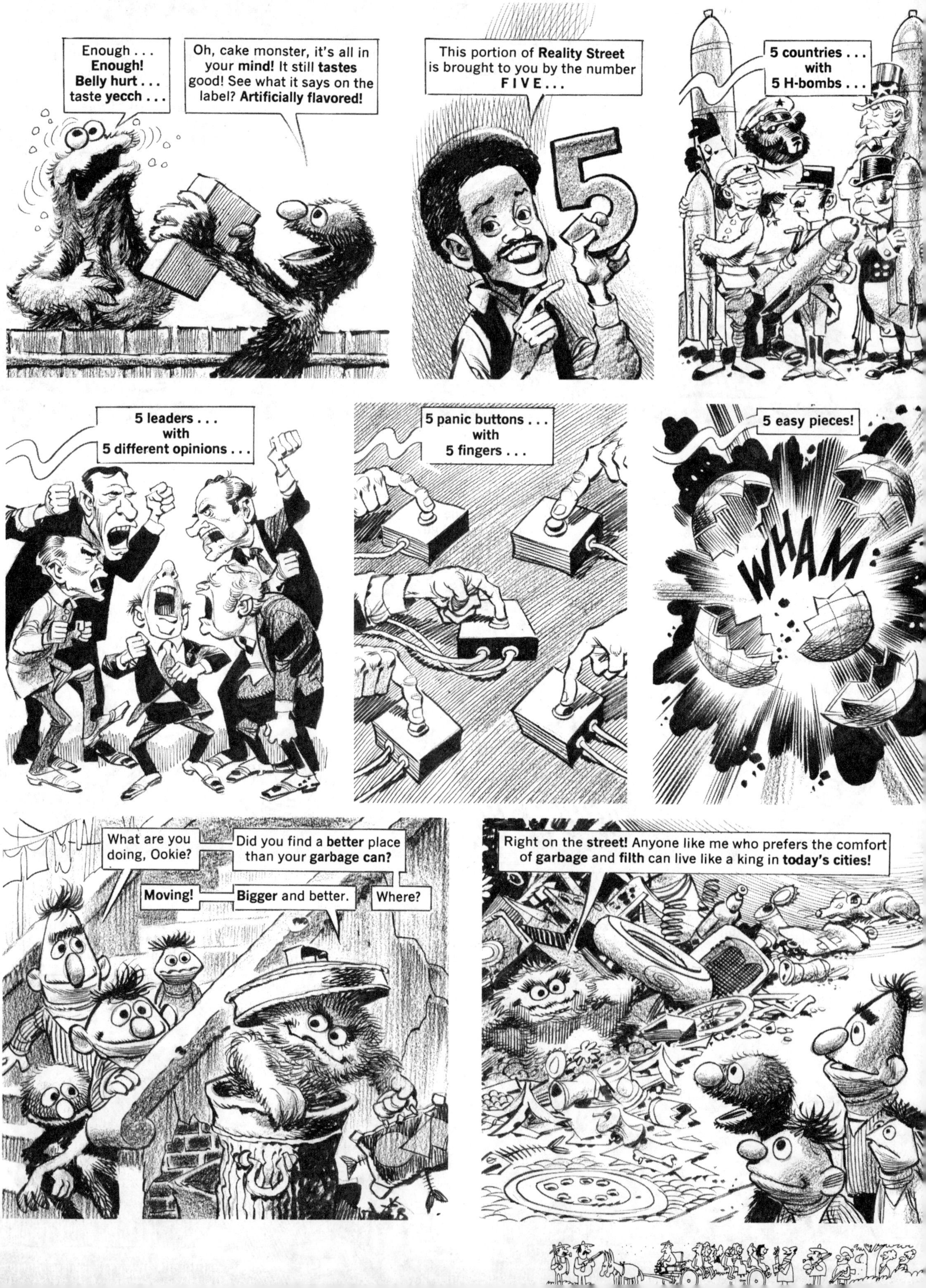
Enough . . . Enough! Belly hurt . . . taste yecch . . .
Oh, cake monster, it's all in your mind! It still tastes good! See what it says on the label? Artificially flavored!
This portion of Reality Street is brought to you by the number FIVE . . .
5
5 countries . . . with 5 H-bombs . . .
5 leaders . . . with 5 different opinions . . .
5 panic buttons . . . with 5 fingers . . .
5 easy pieces!
WHAM
What are you doing, Ookie?
Did you find a better place than your garbage can?
Moving!
Bigger and better.
Where?
Right on the street! Anyone like me who prefers the comfort of garbage and filth can live like a king in today's cities!

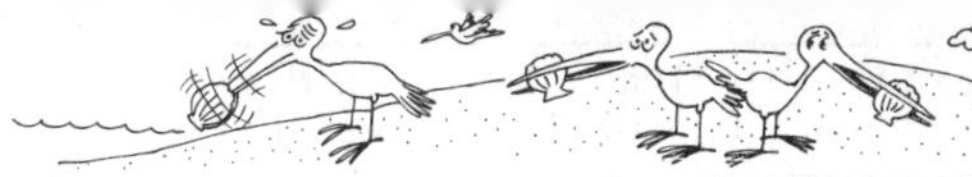

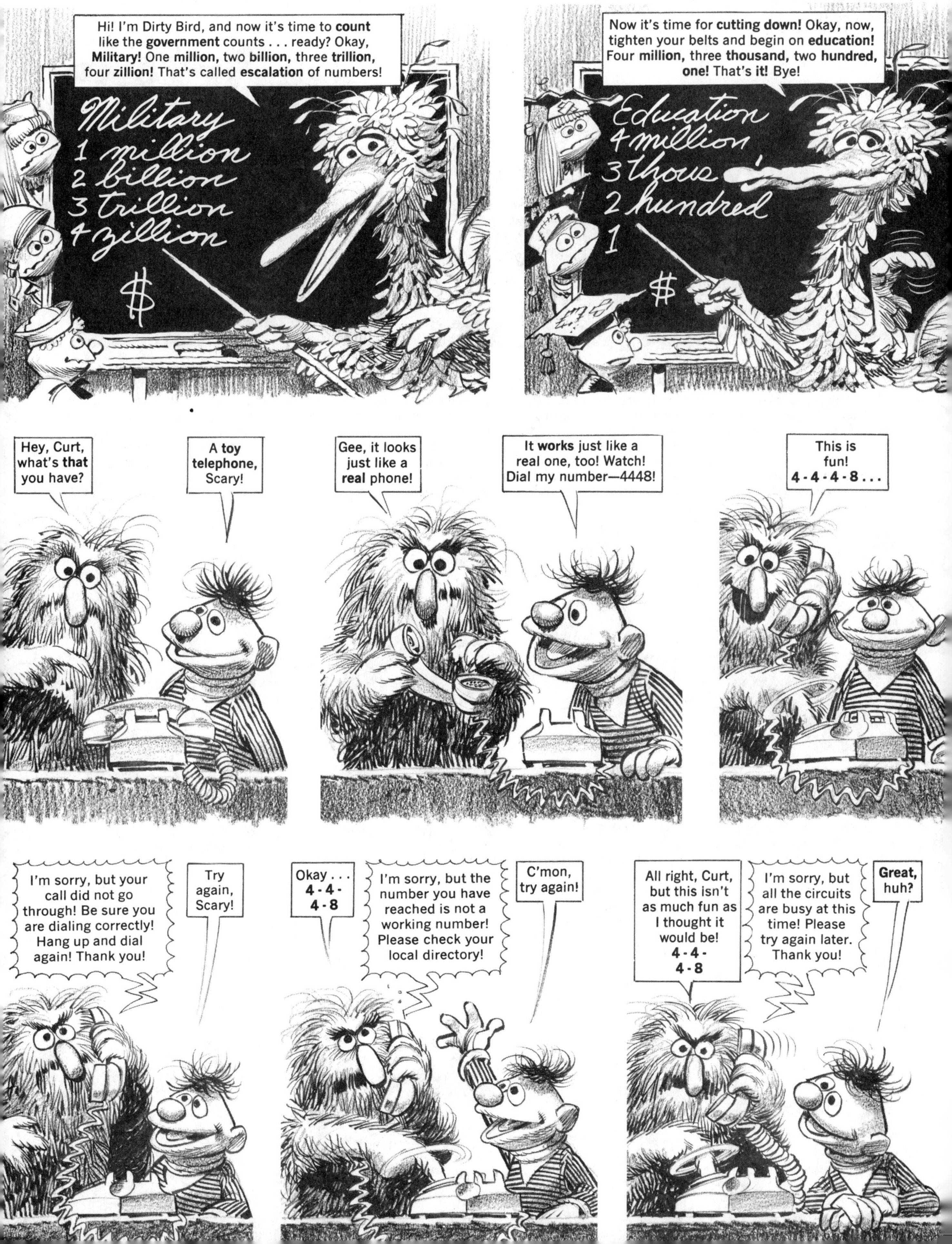
Hi! I'm Dirty Bird, and now it's time to **count** like the **government** counts . . . ready? Okay, **Military!** One **million,** two **billion,** three **trillion,** four **zillion!** That's called **escalation** of numbers!
Military
1 million
2 billion
3 trillion
4 zillion
$
Now it's time for **cutting down!** Okay, now, tighten your belts and begin on **education!** Four **million,** three **thousand,** two **hundred, one!** That's **it!** Bye!
Education
4 million
3 thous
2 hundred
1
$
Hey, Curt, what's **that** you have?
A **toy telephone,** Scary!
Gee, it looks just like a **real** phone!
It works just like a real one, too! Watch! Dial my number—4448!
This is fun! **4-4-4-8 . . .**
I'm sorry, but your call did not go through! Be sure you are dialing correctly! Hang up and dial again! Thank you!
Try again, Scary!
Okay . . . **4-4-4-8**
I'm sorry, but the number you have reached is not a working number! Please check your local directory!
C'mon, try again!
All right, Curt, but this isn't as much fun as I thought it would be! **4-4-4-8**
I'm sorry, but all the circuits are busy at this time! Please try again later. Thank you!
Great, huh?

Great? Why, I tried **3** times and couldn't get you **once!**

That's what makes this toy phone so **real!** If you **did** get me it would **spoil** everything!

Well, it looks like we've run out of time for today! But we'll be back tomorrow to bring you another . . .

Fat chance, buddy! We're here to knock this set down!

But you **can't do that!** This is **Reality Street,** especially constructed to show our young people about **life today!**

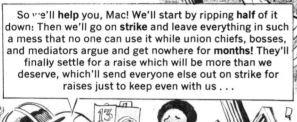

So we'll **help** you, Mac! We'll start by ripping **half** of it down! Then we'll go on **strike** and leave everything in such a mess that no one can use it while union chiefs, bosses, and mediators argue and get nowhere for **months!** They'll finally settle for a raise which will be more than we deserve, which'll send everyone else out on strike for raises just to keep even with us . . .

Of course, the strained power and transportation facilities will be strained even **more** in the whole process, and as inflation spirals **upwards,** more jobs will go **down the drain,** increasing unemployment, not to mention welfare costs. Taxes will go up to pay for it, naturally, while in Washington . . .

Enough! **Enough!** I get the point! But you still didn't tell me **why** they're taking **Reality Street** down! Do they need the space for a **library?** A **park?** A **hospital?**

Are you kidding? This site is being cleared for a new **munitions development plant!**

Get the picture, kiddies?

LITTLE BIGOT MAN DEPT.

Ever since Television began, situation comedies have been, more or less, the same. Now, all of a sudden, a new situation comedy has come along . . . and it's entirely different from the old-fashioned family fare. It doesn't deal with the same old stupid subjects involving idiotic, unbelievable characters. Instead, it concerns itself with relevant "now" subjects, involving even more idiotic unbelievable characters! Here, then, is MAD's version of . . .

GALL IN THE FAMILY FARE

This Week's Episode: "A Visit From A World War II Buddy"

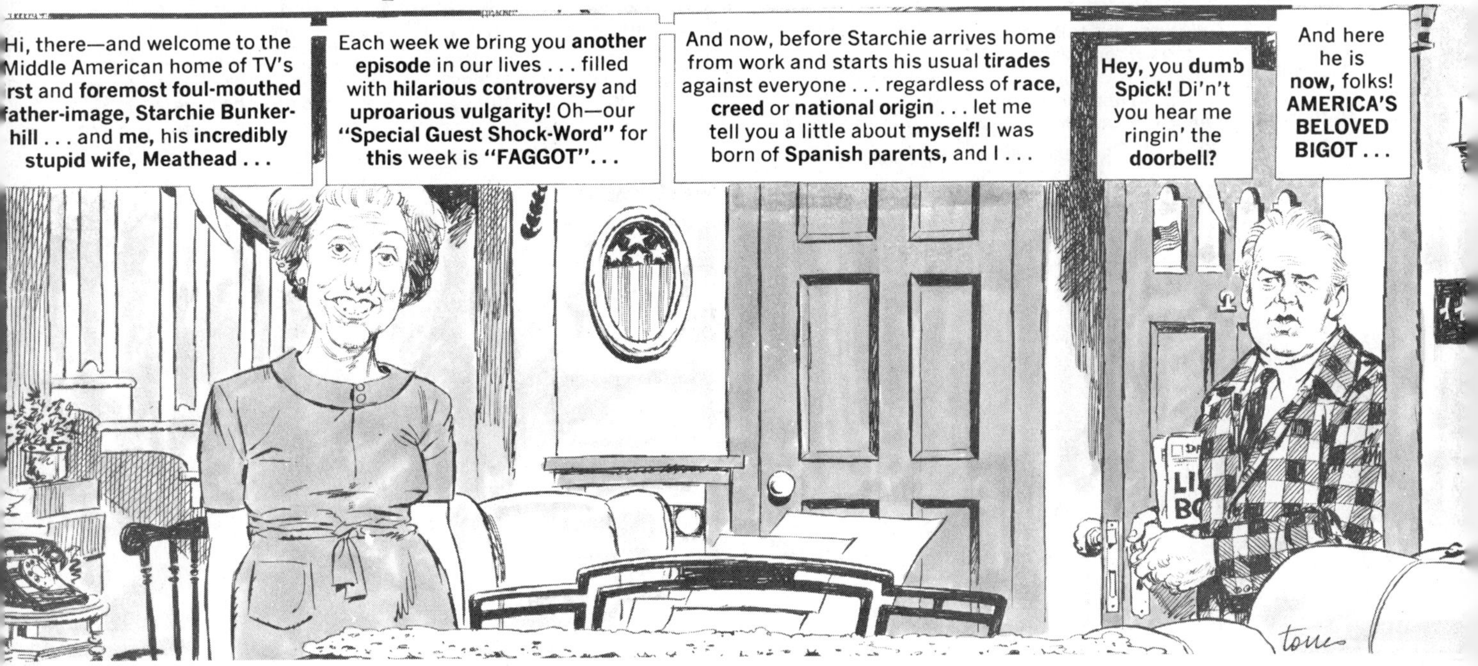
Hi, there—and welcome to the Middle American home of TV's rst and foremost foul-mouthed father-image, Starchie Bunker-hill . . . and me, his incredibly stupid wife, Meathead . . .
Each week we bring you another episode in our lives . . . filled with hilarious controversy and uproarious vulgarity! Oh—our "Special Guest Shock-Word" for this week is "FAGGOT". . .
And now, before Starchie arrives home from work and starts his usual tirades against everyone . . . regardless of race, creed or national origin . . . let me tell you a little about myself! I was born of Spanish parents, and I . . .
Hey, you dumb Spick! Di'n't you hear me ringin' the doorbell?
And here he is now, folks! AMERICA'S BELOVED BIGOT . . .
torres

ARTIST: ANGELO TORRES WRITER: LARRY SIEGEL

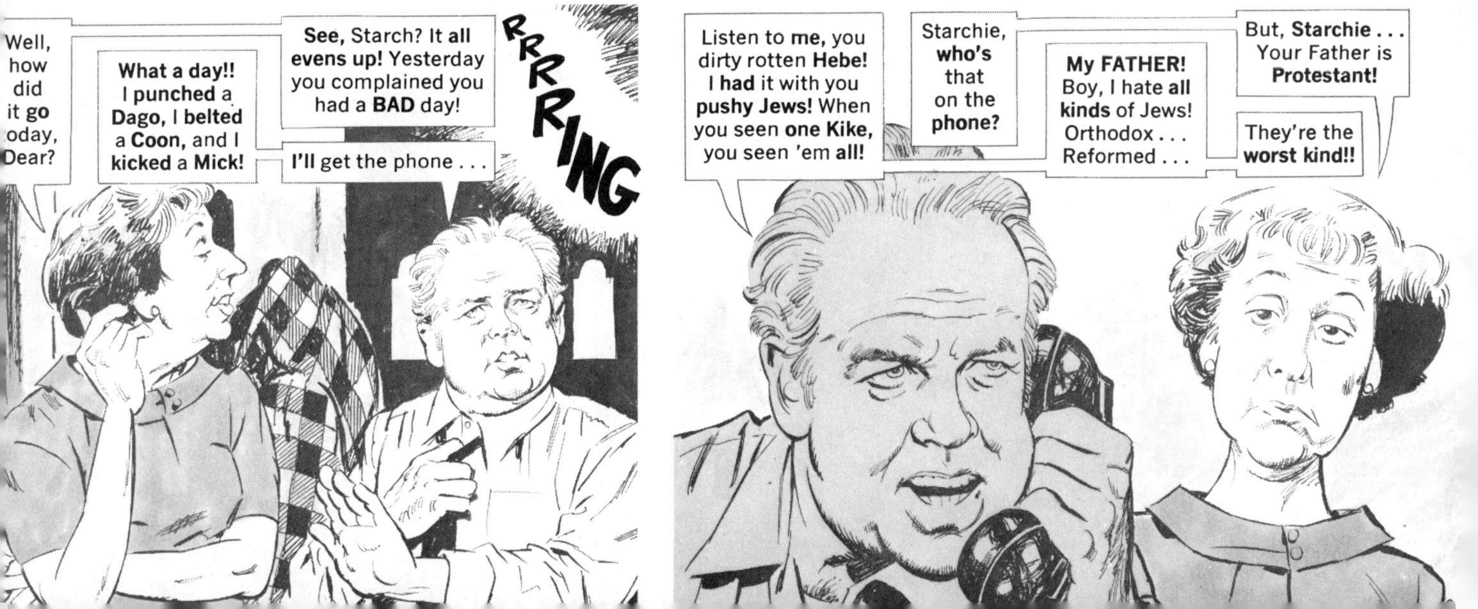
Well, how did it go oday, Dear?
What a day!! I punched a Dago, I belted a Coon, and I kicked a Mick!
See, Starch? It all evens up! Yesterday you complained you had a BAD day!
I'll get the phone . . .
RRRRING
Listen to me, you dirty rotten Hebe! I had it with you pushy Jews! When you seen one Kike, you seen 'em all!
Starchie, who's that on the phone?
My FATHER! Boy, I hate all kinds of Jews! Orthodox . . . Reformed . . .
But, Starchie . . . Your Father is Protestant!
They're the worst kind!!

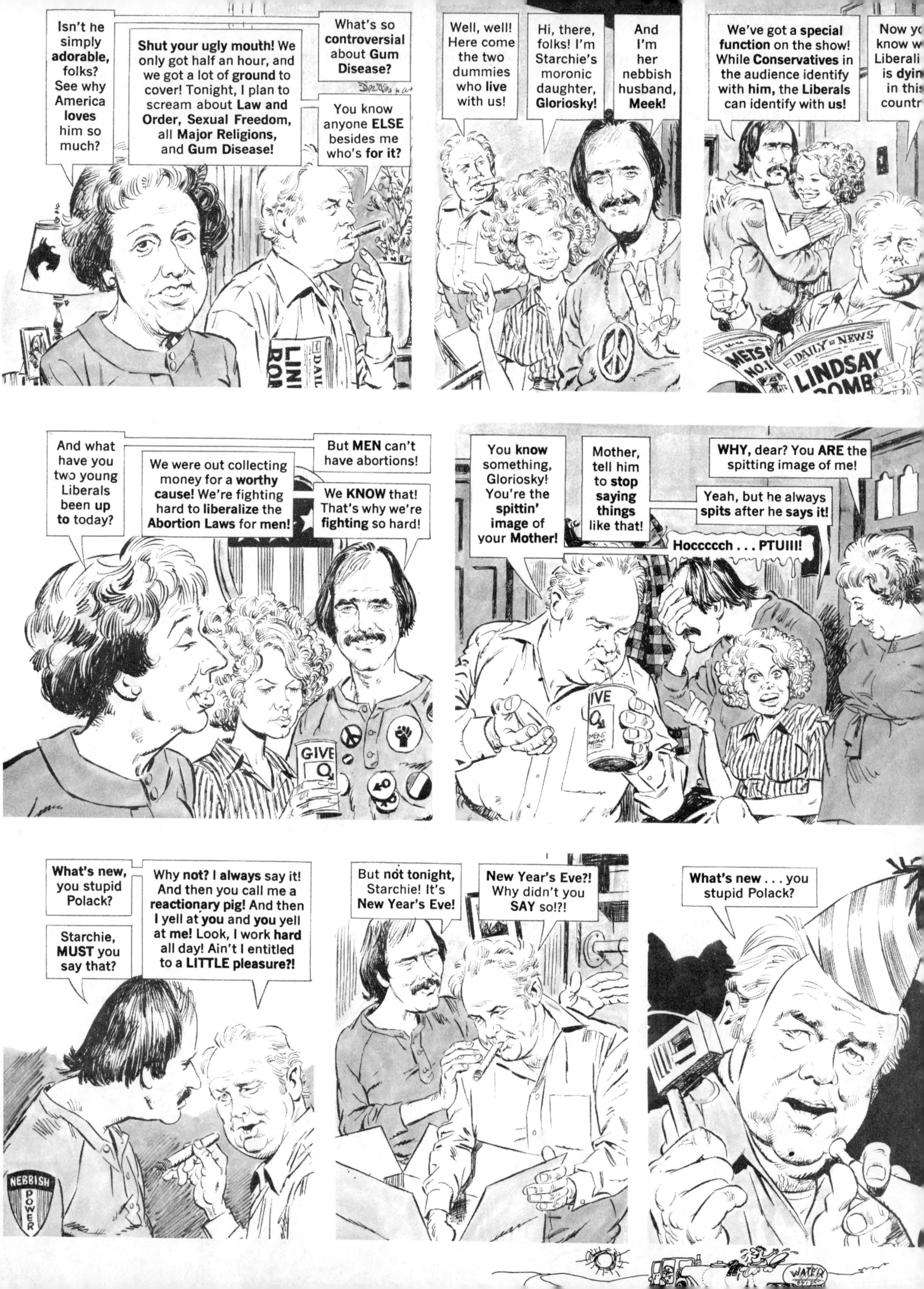
Isn't he simply adorable, folks? See why America loves him so much?
Shut your ugly mouth! We only got half an hour, and we got a lot of ground to cover! Tonight, I plan to scream about Law and Order, Sexual Freedom, all Major Religions, and Gum Disease!
What's so controversial about Gum Disease?
You know anyone ELSE besides me who's for it?
Well, well! Here come the two dummies who live with us!
Hi, there, folks! I'm Starchie's moronic daughter, Gloriosky!
And I'm her nebbish husband, Meek!
We've got a special function on the show! While Conservatives in the audience identify with him, the Liberals can identify with us!
DAILY NEWS
LINDSAY
And what have you two young Liberals been up to today?
We were out collecting money for a worthy cause! We're fighting hard to liberalize the Abortion Laws for men!
But MEN can't have abortions!
We KNOW that! That's why we're fighting so hard!
GIVE
You know something, Gloriosky! You're the spittin' image of your Mother!
Mother, tell him to stop saying things like that!
WHY, dear? You ARE the spitting image of me!
Yeah, but he always spits after he says it!
Hoccccch . . . PTUIII!
What's new, you stupid Polack?
Starchie, MUST you say that?
Why not? I always say it! And then you call me a reactionary pig! And then I yell at you and you yell at me! Look, I work hard all day! Ain't I entitled to a LITTLE pleasure?!
NEBBISH POWER
But not tonight, Starchie! It's New Year's Eve!
New Year's Eve?! Why didn't you SAY so!?!
What's new . . . you stupid Polack?

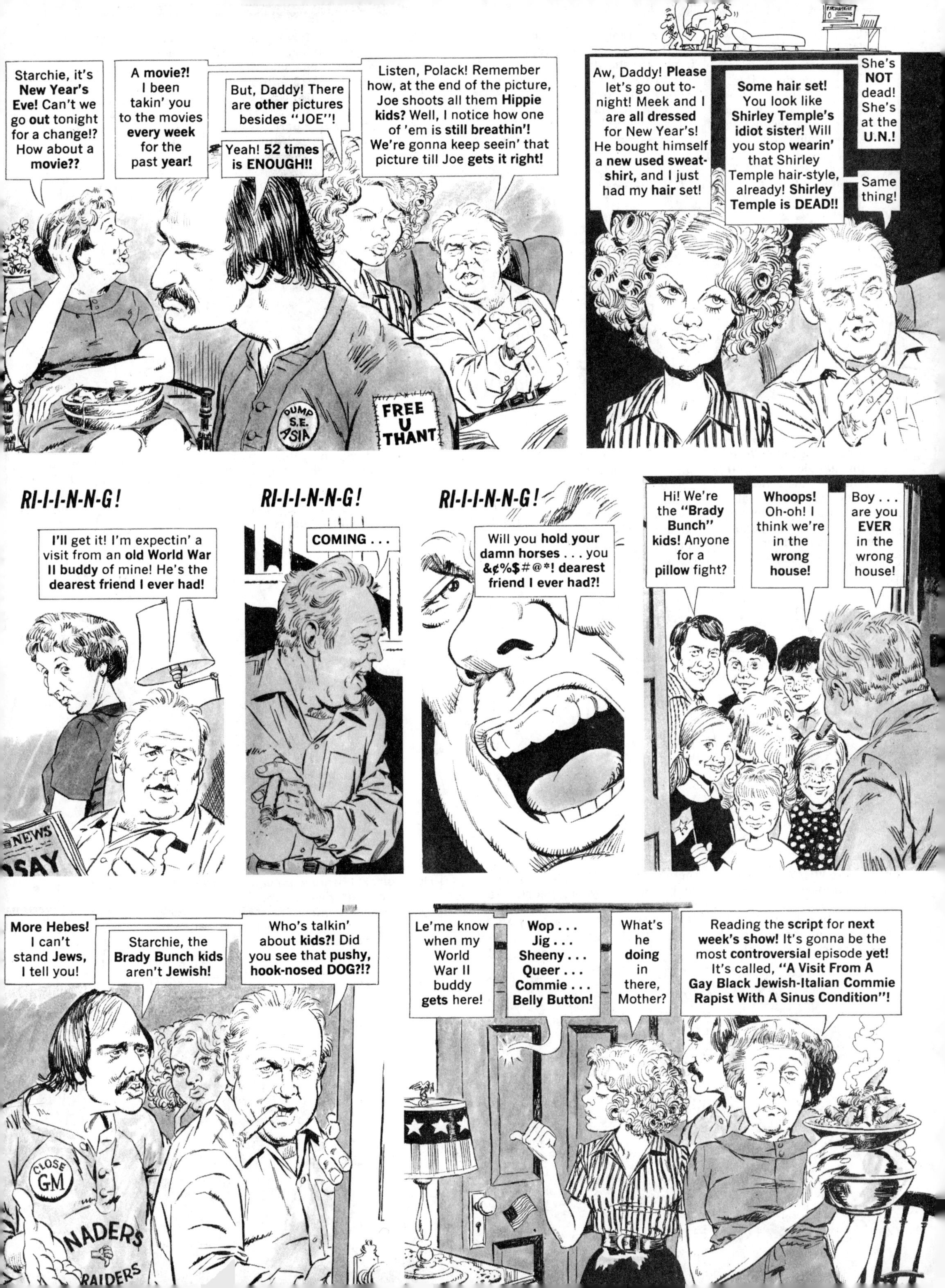
Starchie, it's New Year's Eve! Can't we go out tonight for a change!? How about a movie??
A movie?! I been takin' you to the movies every week for the past year!
But, Daddy! There are other pictures besides "JOE"!
Yeah! 52 times is ENOUGH!!
Listen, Polack! Remember how, at the end of the picture, Joe shoots all them Hippie kids? Well, I notice how one of 'em is still breathin'! We're gonna keep seein' that picture till Joe gets it right!
DUMP S.E. ASIA
FREE U THANT
Aw, Daddy! Please let's go out tonight! Meek and I are all dressed for New Year's! He bought himself a new used sweatshirt, and I just had my hair set!
Some hair set! You look like Shirley Temple's idiot sister! Will you stop wearin' that Shirley Temple hair-style, already! Shirley Temple is DEAD!!
She's NOT dead! She's at the U.N.!
Same thing!
RI-I-I-N-N-G!
I'll get it! I'm expectin' a visit from an old World War II buddy of mine! He's the dearest friend I ever had!
NEWS
RI-I-I-N-N-G!
COMING . . .
RI-I-I-N-N-G!
Will you hold your damn horses . . . you &¢%$#@*! dearest friend I ever had?!
Hi! We're the "Brady Bunch" kids! Anyone for a pillow fight?
Whoops! Oh-oh! I think we're in the wrong house!
Boy . . . are you EVER in the wrong house!
More Hebes! I can't stand Jews, I tell you!
Starchie, the Brady Bunch kids aren't Jewish!
Who's talkin' about kids?! Did you see that pushy, hook-nosed DOG?!?
CLOSE GM
NADERS RAIDERS
Le'me know when my World War II buddy gets here!
Wop . . . Jig . . . Sheeny . . . Queer . . . Commie . . . Belly Button!
What's he doing in there, Mother?
Reading the script for next week's show! It's gonna be the most controversial episode yet! It's called, "A Visit From A Gay Black Jewish-Italian Commie Rapist With A Sinus Condition"!

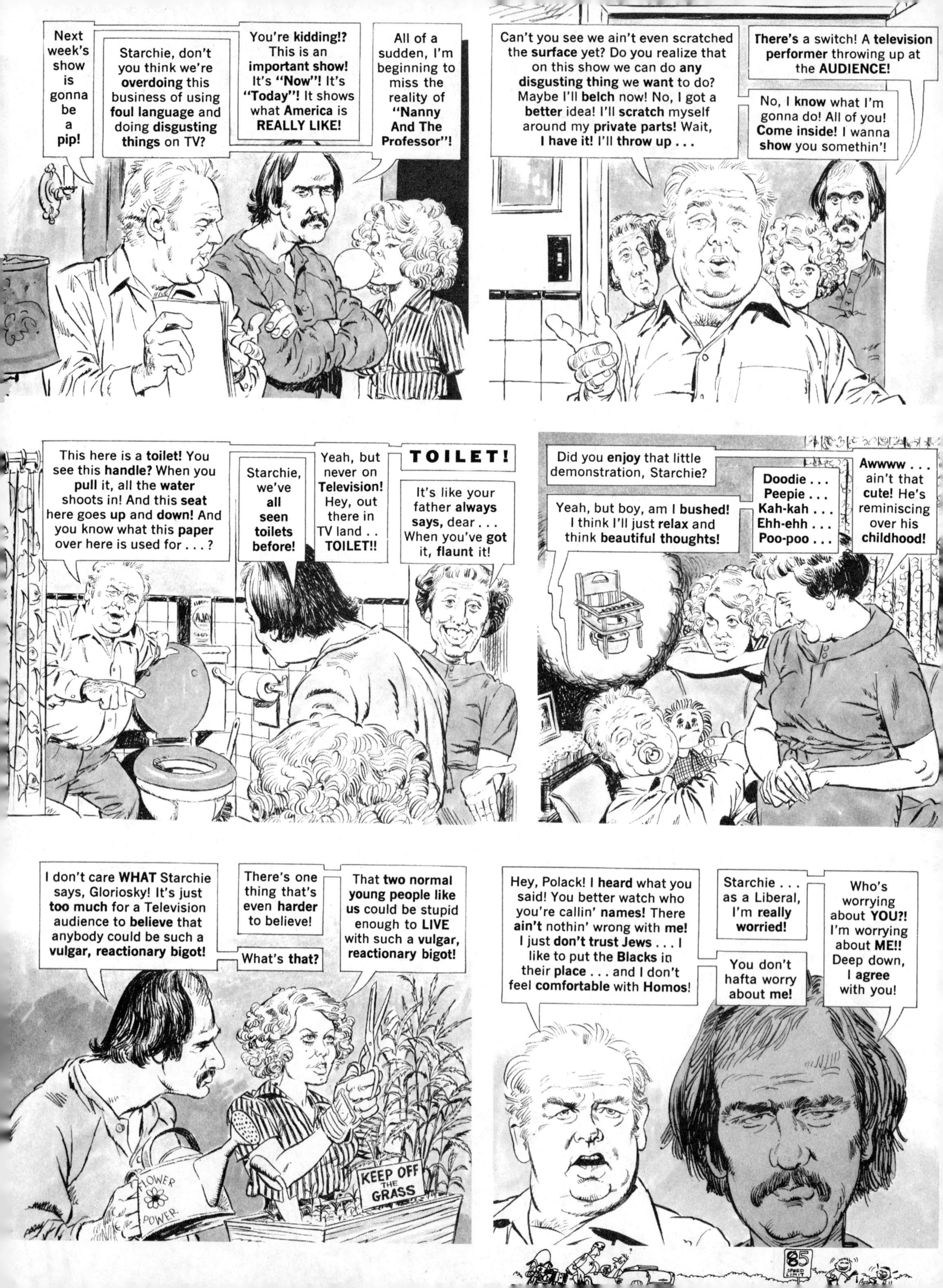

Next week's show is gonna be a pip!
Starchie, don't you think we're overdoing this business of using foul language and doing disgusting things on TV?
You're kidding!? This is an important show! It's "Now"! It's "Today"! It shows what America is REALLY LIKE!
All of a sudden, I'm beginning to miss the reality of "Nanny And The Professor"!
Can't you see we ain't even scratched the surface yet? Do you realize that on this show we can do any disgusting thing we want to do? Maybe I'll belch now! No, I got a better idea! I'll scratch myself around my private parts! Wait, I have it! I'll throw up . . .
There's a switch! A television performer throwing up at the AUDIENCE!
No, I know what I'm gonna do! All of you! Come inside! I wanna show you somethin'!
This here is a toilet! You see this handle? When you pull it, all the water shoots in! And this seat here goes up and down! And you know what this paper over here is used for . . . ?
Starchie, we've all seen toilets before!
Yeah, but never on Television! Hey, out there in TV land . . TOILET!!
TOILET!
It's like your father always says, dear . . . When you've got it, flaunt it!
Did you enjoy that little demonstration, Starchie?
Yeah, but boy, am I bushed! I think I'll just relax and think beautiful thoughts!
Doodie . . . Peepie . . . Kah-kah . . . Ehh-ehh . . . Poo-poo . . .
Awwww . . . ain't that cute! He's reminiscing over his childhood!
I don't care WHAT Starchie says, Gloriosky! It's just too much for a Television audience to believe that anybody could be such a vulgar, reactionary bigot!
There's one thing that's even harder to believe!
What's that?
That two normal young people like us could be stupid enough to LIVE with such a vulgar, reactionary bigot!
FLOWER POWER
KEEP OFF THE GRASS
Hey, Polack! I heard what you said! You better watch who you're callin' names! There ain't nothin' wrong with me! I just don't trust Jews . . . I like to put the Blacks in their place . . . and I don't feel comfortable with Homos!
Starchie . . . as a Liberal, I'm really worried!
You don't hafta worry about me!
Who's worrying about YOU?! I'm worrying about ME!! Deep down, I agree with you!
SPEED LIMIT

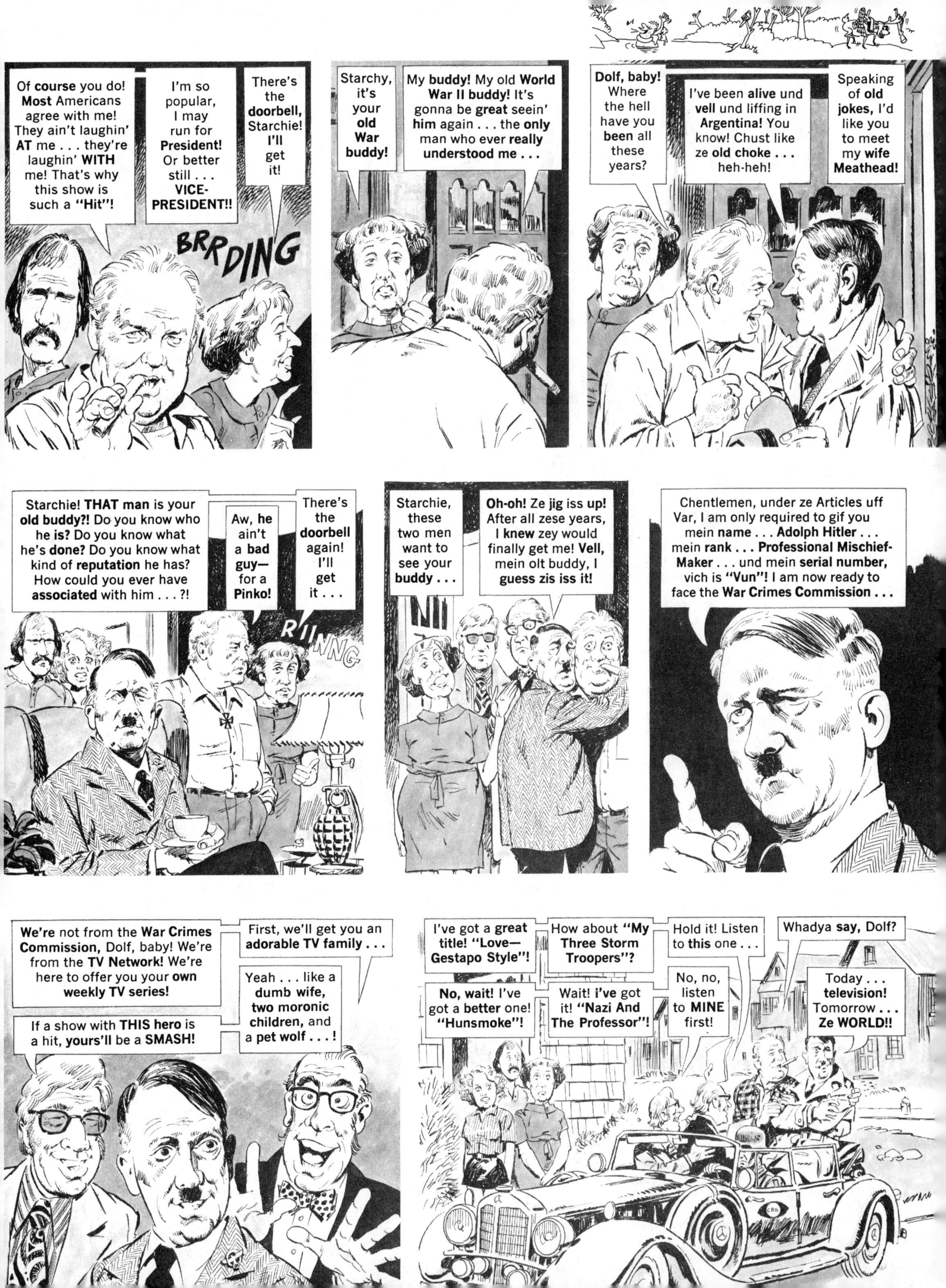
Of course you do! Most Americans agree with me! They ain't laughin' AT me . . . they're laughin' WITH me! That's why this show is such a "Hit"!
I'm so popular, I may run for President! Or better still . . . VICE-PRESIDENT!!
There's the doorbell, Starchie! I'll get it!
BRRDING
Starchy, it's your old War buddy!
My buddy! My old World War II buddy! It's gonna be great seein' him again . . . the only man who ever really understood me . . .
Dolf, baby! Where the hell have you been all these years?
I've been alive und vell und liffing in Argentina! You know! Chust like ze old choke . . . heh-heh!
Speaking of old jokes, I'd like you to meet my wife Meathead!
Starchie! THAT man is your old buddy?! Do you know who he is? Do you know what he's done? Do you know what kind of reputation he has? How could you ever have associated with him . . . ?!
Aw, he ain't a bad guy— for a Pinko!
There's the doorbell again! I'll get it . . .
RIINNG
Starchie, these two men want to see your buddy . . .
Oh-oh! Ze jig iss up! After all zese years, I knew zey would finally get me! Vell, mein olt buddy, I guess zis iss it!
Chentlemen, under ze Articles uff Var, I am only required to gif you mein name . . . Adolph Hitler . . . mein rank . . . Professional Mischief-Maker . . . und mein serial number, vich is "Vun"! I am now ready to face the War Crimes Commission . . .
We're not from the War Crimes Commission, Dolf, baby! We're from the TV Network! We're here to offer you your own weekly TV series!
If a show with THIS hero is a hit, yours'll be a SMASH!
First, we'll get you an adorable TV family . . .
Yeah . . . like a dumb wife, two moronic children, and a pet wolf . . . !
I've got a great title! "Love— Gestapo Style"!
No, wait! I've got a better one! "Hunsmoke"!
How about "My Three Storm Troopers"?
Wait! i've got it! "Nazi And The Professor"!
Hold it! Listen to this one . . .
No, no, listen to MINE first!
Whadya say, Dolf?
Today . . . television! Tomorrow . . . Ze WORLD!!

INSIDE-OUCH DEPT.

In many ways, the "Sexual Revolution" is just that—REVOLTING! But do

BEHIND THE SCENES AT A

ARTIST: PAUL COKER,

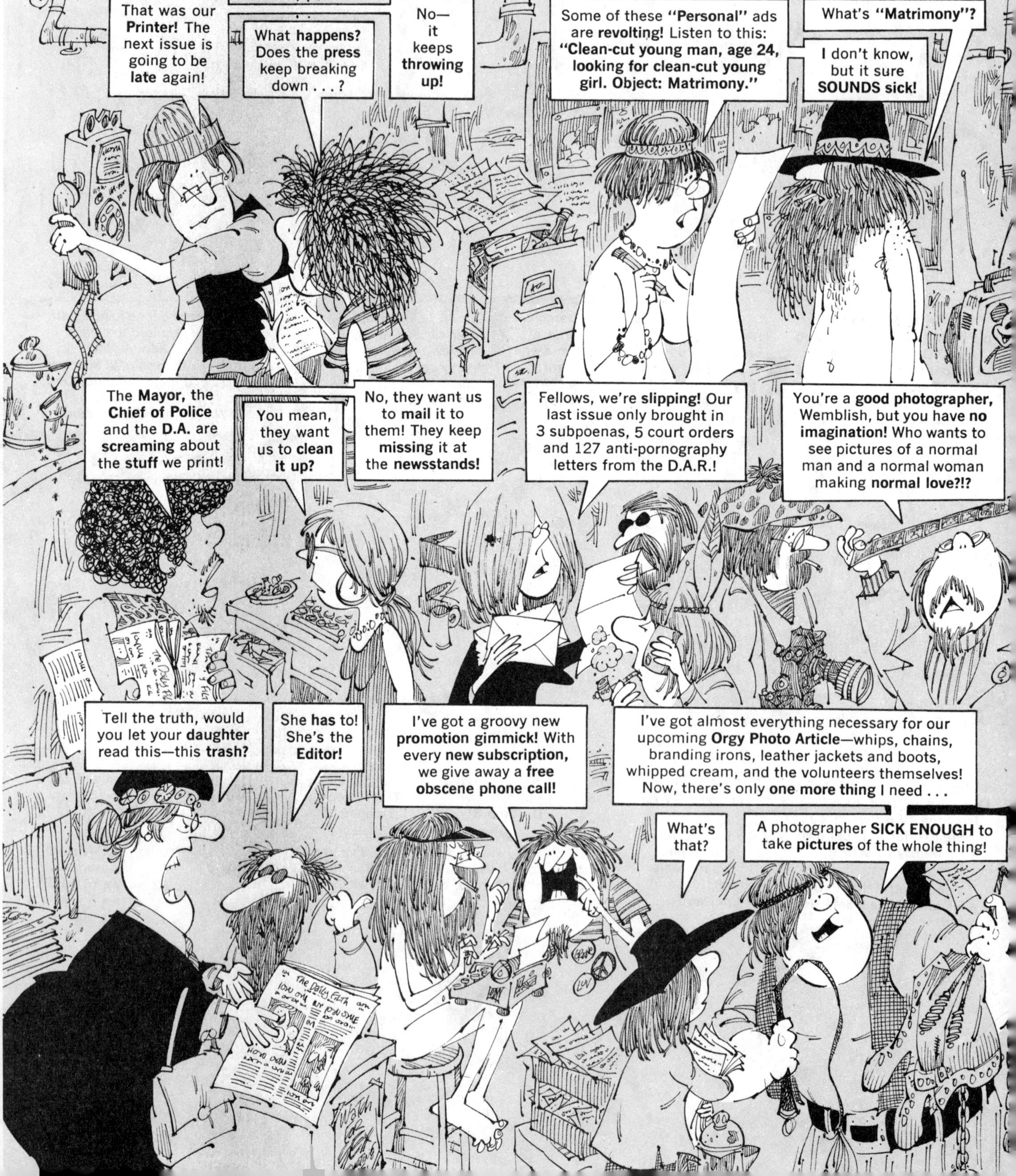

That was our Printer! The next issue is going to be late again!
What happens? Does the press keep breaking down . . . ?
No— it keeps throwing up!
Some of these "Personal" ads are revolting! Listen to this: "Clean-cut young man, age 24, looking for clean-cut young girl. Object: Matrimony."
What's "Matrimony"?
I don't know, but it sure SOUNDS sick!
The Mayor, the Chief of Police and the D.A. are screaming about the stuff we print!
You mean, they want us to clean it up?
No, they want us to mail it to them! They keep missing it at the newsstands!
Fellows, we're slipping! Our last issue only brought in 3 subpoenas, 5 court orders and 127 anti-pornography letters from the D.A.R.!
You're a good photographer, Wemblish, but you have no imagination! Who wants to see pictures of a normal man and a normal woman making normal love?!?
Tell the truth, would you let your daughter read this—this trash?
She has to! She's the Editor!
I've got a groovy new promotion gimmick! With every new subscription, we give away a free obscene phone call!
I've got almost everything necessary for our upcoming Orgy Photo Article—whips, chains, branding irons, leather jackets and boots, whipped cream, and the volunteers themselves! Now, there's only one more thing I need . . .
What's that?
A photographer SICK ENOUGH to take pictures of the whole thing!

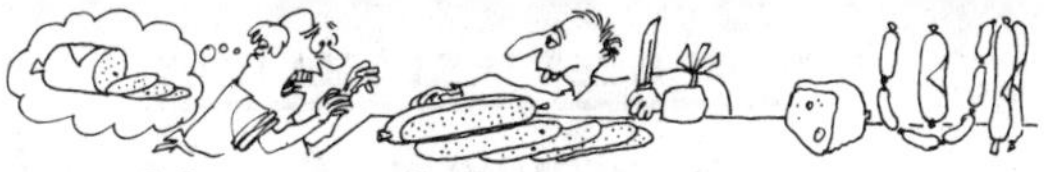

ake our word for it! See for yourself as MAD conducts this special tour

UNDERGROUND NEWSPAPER

RITER: SY REIT

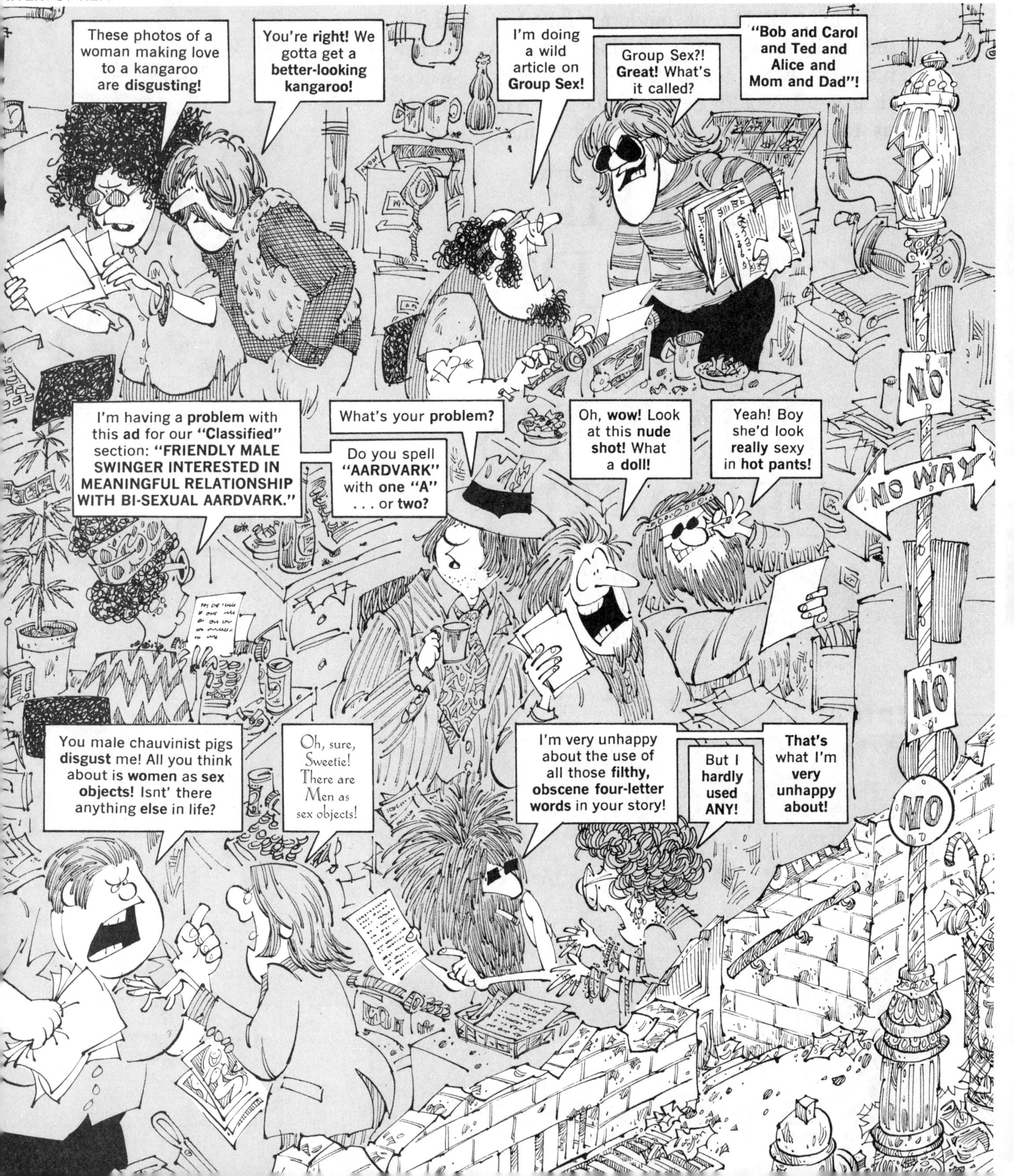

These photos of a woman making love to a kangaroo are **disgusting!**
You're **right!** We gotta get a **better-looking kangaroo!**
I'm doing a wild article on **Group Sex!**
Group Sex?! **Great!** What's it called?
"Bob and Carol and Ted and Alice and Mom and Dad"!
I'm having a **problem** with this **ad** for our **"Classified"** section: **"FRIENDLY MALE SWINGER INTERESTED IN MEANINGFUL RELATIONSHIP WITH BI-SEXUAL AARDVARK."**
What's your **problem?**
Do you spell **"AARDVARK"** with **one "A"** . . . or **two?**
Oh, **wow!** Look at this **nude shot!** What a **doll!**
Yeah! Boy she'd look **really** sexy in **hot pants!**
NO
NO WAY
You male chauvinist pigs **disgust** me! All you think about is **women as sex objects!** Isnt' there anything **else** in life?
Oh, sure, Sweetie! There are Men as sex objects!
I'm very unhappy about the use of all those **filthy, obscene four-letter words** in your story!
But I **hardly used ANY!**
That's what I'm **very unhappy about!**
NO
NO

"POP" GOES THE EASEL DEPT.

Look around in Art Galleries today, and what do you see? You see paintings of soup cans and Brillo boxes and incomprehensible blobs. Let's face it: If the great Masters of the past were alive today, they wouldn't stand a chance of success as serious painters. Their stuff just wouldn't sell in our modern Galleries. And so, they'd probably have to find work in another field of Art . . . like the Comic Strips, where their stuff would be appreciated. Which brings us to this article: Let's see what might happen

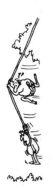

IF THE WORLD'S GREAT PAINTERS DREW THE COMICS

ARTIST: JACK RICKARD WRITER: FRANK JACOBS

MEDICAL LAFFS By Rembrandt

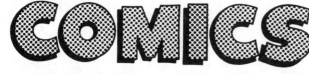

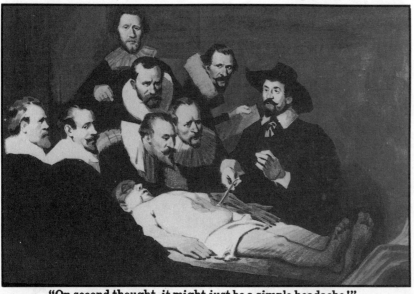

"On second thought, it might just be a simple headache!"

PRISSY PERCY

WE GOTTA LET PERCY PLAY IN OUR GAME TODAY!
WHY? HE'S SUCH A SISSY!

HARRIE & CARR

I'LL KILL THAT EZRA MULLET! I'LL MURDER HIM!
LAND'S SAKE HARRY! WHAT ARE YA FUSSIN ABOUT?

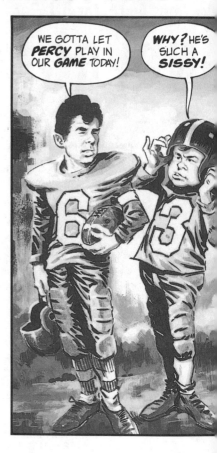

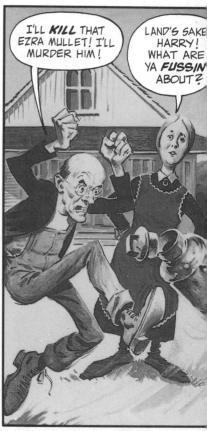

By Gainsborough

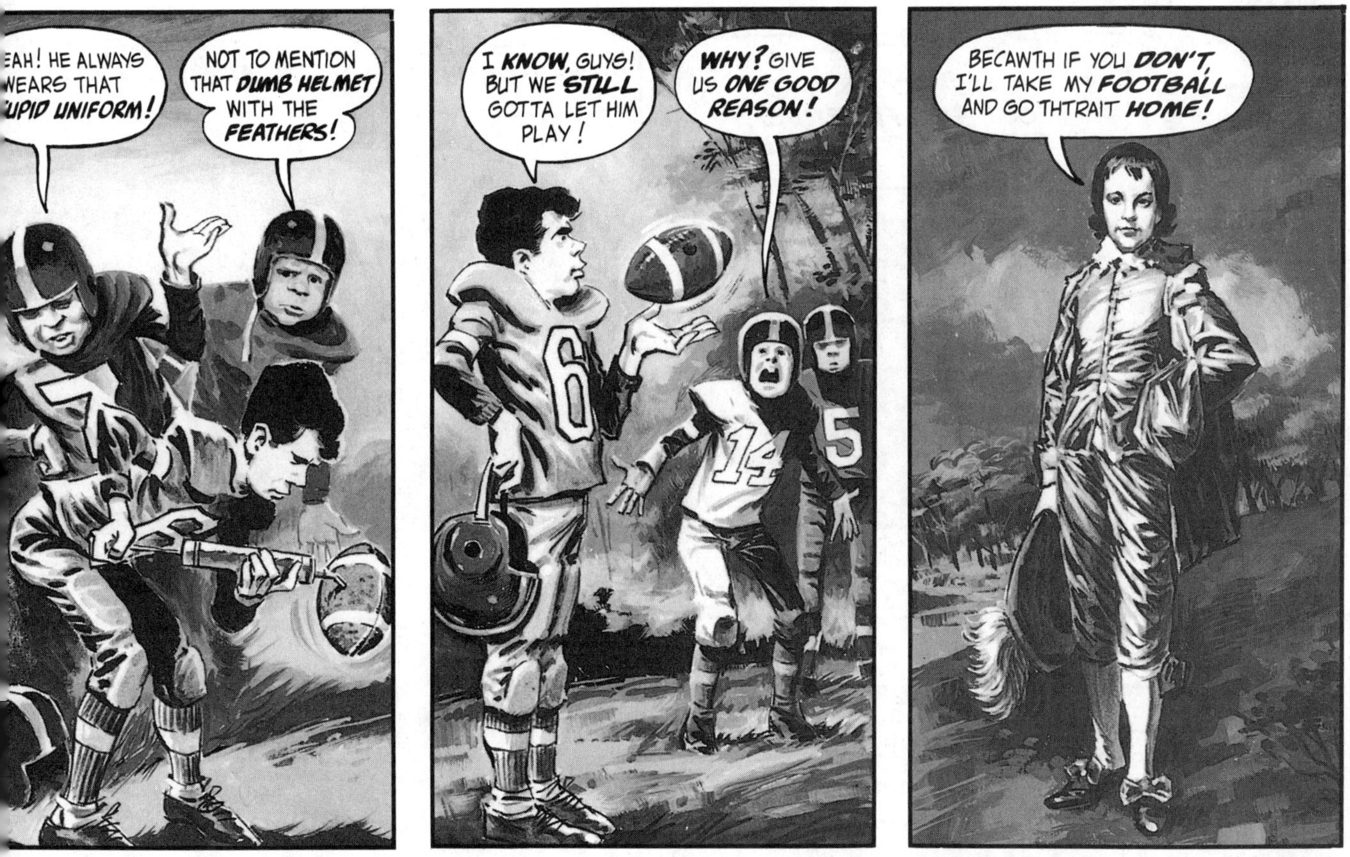
EAH! HE ALWAYS WEARS THAT UPID UNIFORM!
NOT TO MENTION THAT DUMB HELMET WITH THE FEATHERS!
I KNOW, GUYS! BUT WE STILL GOTTA LET HIM PLAY!
WHY? GIVE US ONE GOOD REASON!
BECAWTH IF YOU DON'T, I'LL TAKE MY FOOTBALL AND GO THTRAIT HOME!

By Grant Wood

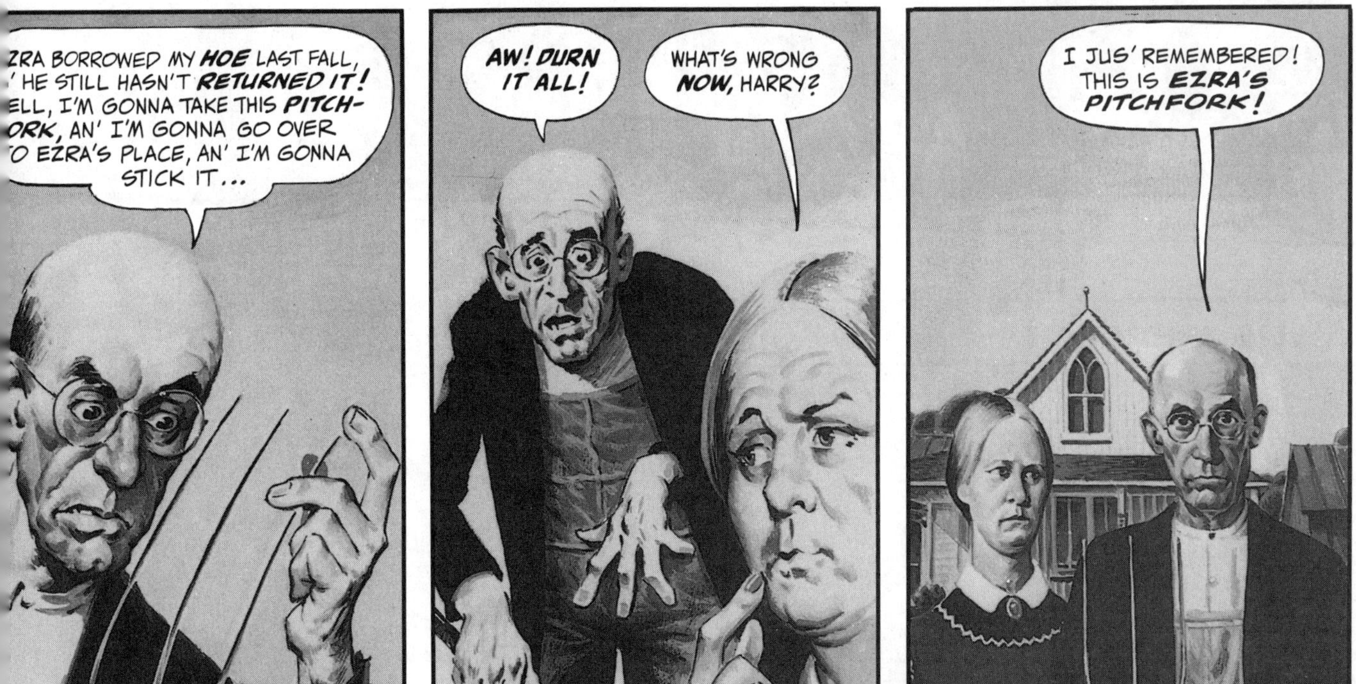
ZRA BORROWED MY HOE LAST FALL, ' HE STILL HASN'T RETURNED IT! ELL, I'M GONNA TAKE THIS PITCH-ORK, AN' I'M GONNA GO OVER O EZRA'S PLACE, AN' I'M GONNA STICK IT...
AW! DURN IT ALL!
WHAT'S WRONG NOW, HARRY?
I JUS' REMEMBERED! THIS IS EZRA'S PITCHFORK!

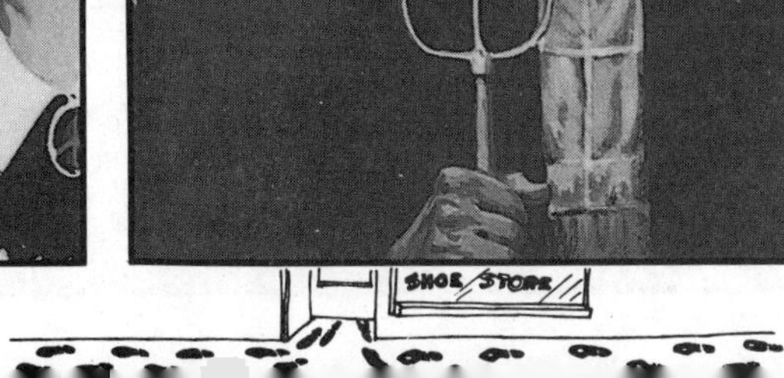
SHOE STORE

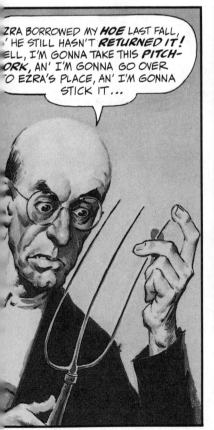

THOSE GIRLS By Millet

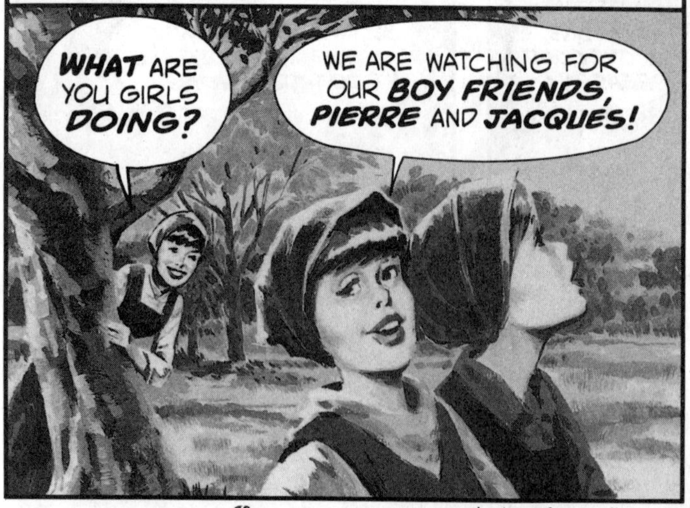
WHAT ARE YOU GIRLS DOING?
WE ARE WATCHING FOR OUR BOY FRIENDS, PIERRE AND JACQUES!

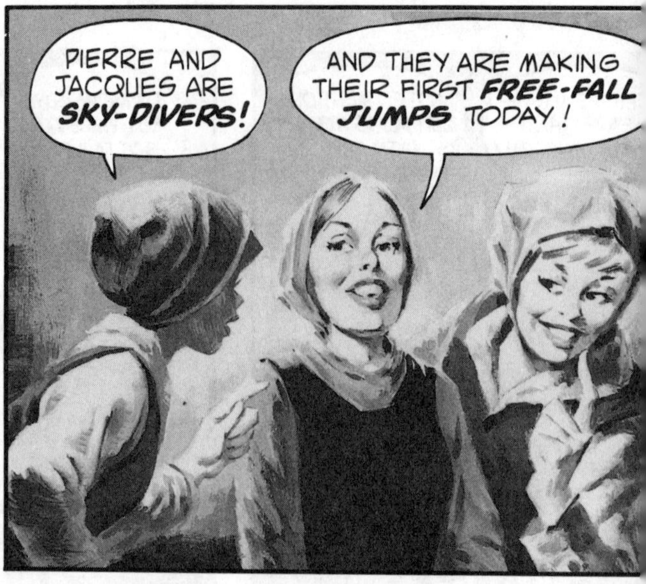
PIERRE AND JACQUES ARE SKY-DIVERS!
AND THEY ARE MAKING THEIR FIRST FREE-FALL JUMPS TODAY!

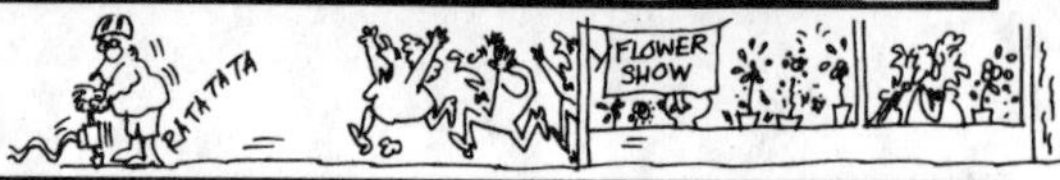
FLOWER SHOW

COOL CATS By Rousseau

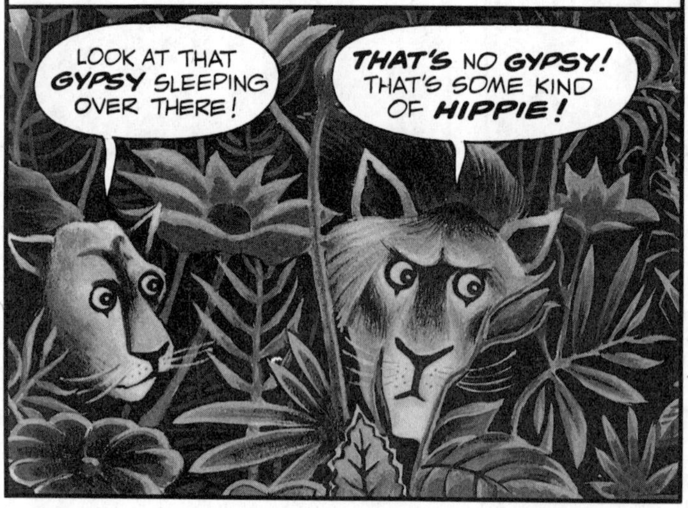
LOOK AT THAT GYPSY SLEEPING OVER THERE!
THAT'S NO GYPSY! THAT'S SOME KIND OF HIPPIE!

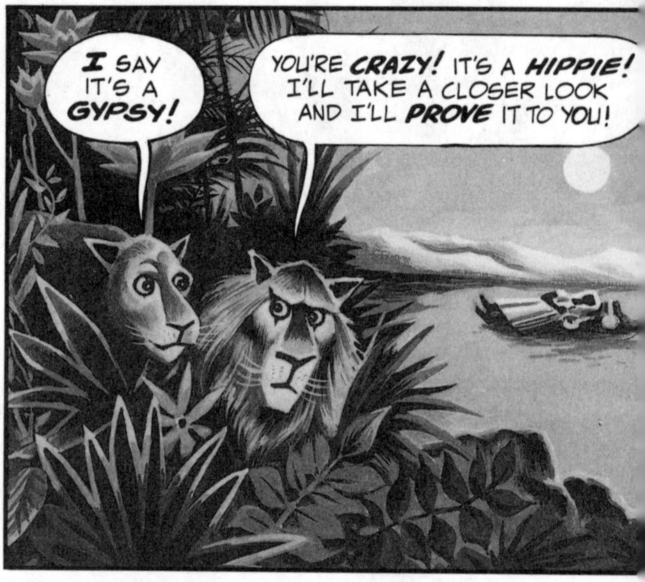
I SAY IT'S A GYPSY!
YOU'RE CRAZY! IT'S A HIPPIE! I'LL TAKE A CLOSER LOOK AND I'LL PROVE IT TO YOU!

TILLIE AND HER TV By Whistler

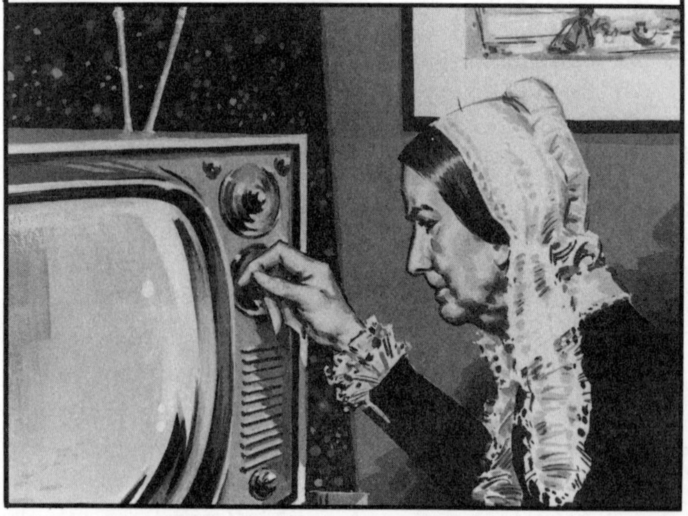

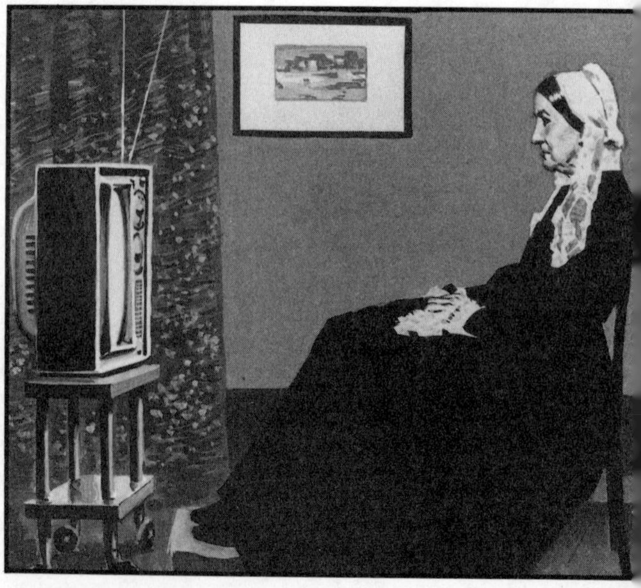

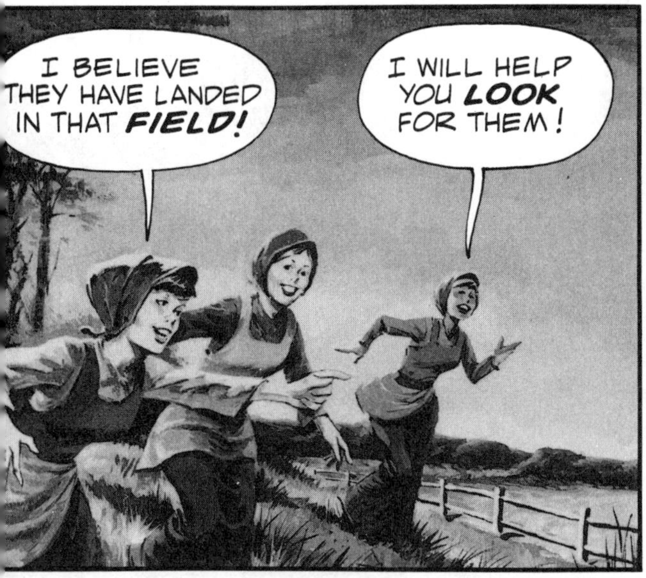
I BELIEVE THEY HAVE LANDED IN THAT FIELD!
I WILL HELP YOU LOOK FOR THEM!

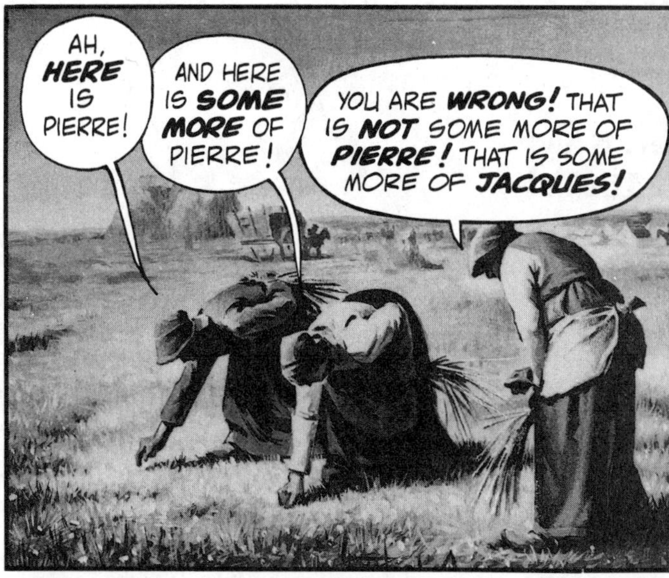
AH, HERE IS PIERRE!
AND HERE IS SOME MORE OF PIERRE!
YOU ARE WRONG! THAT IS NOT SOME MORE OF PIERRE! THAT IS SOME MORE OF JACQUES!

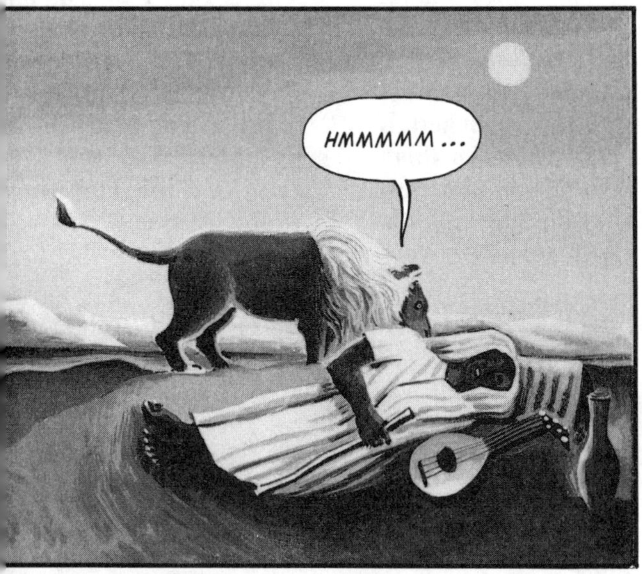
HMMMMM...

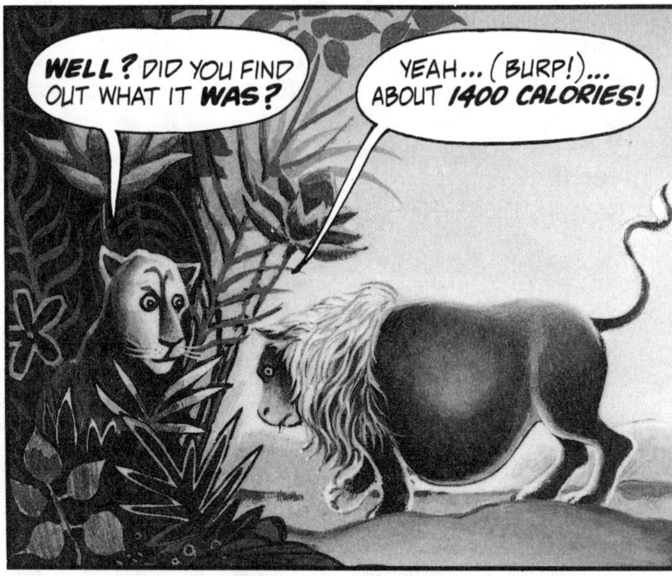
WELL? DID YOU FIND OUT WHAT IT WAS?
YEAH...(BURP!)... ABOUT 1400 CALORIES!

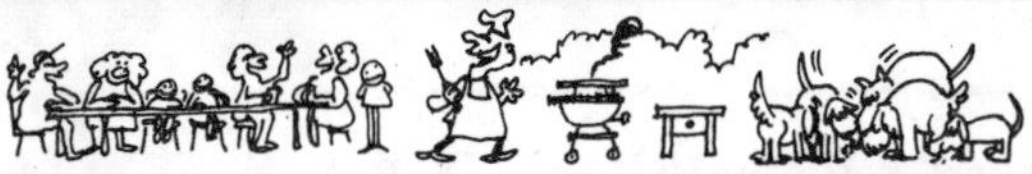

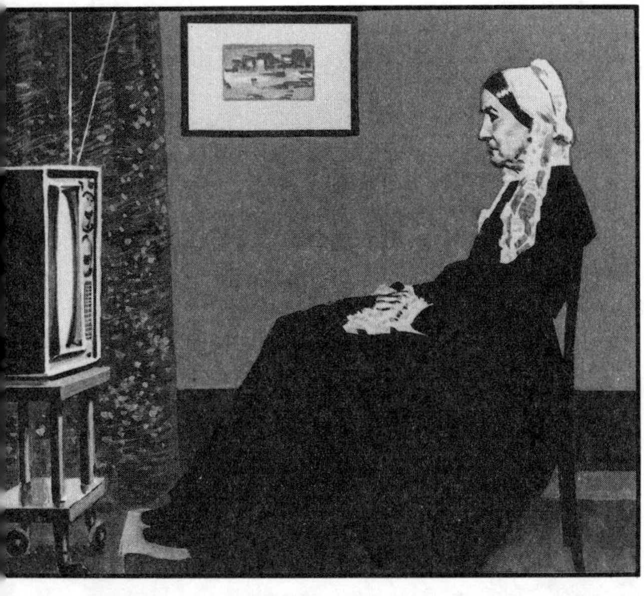

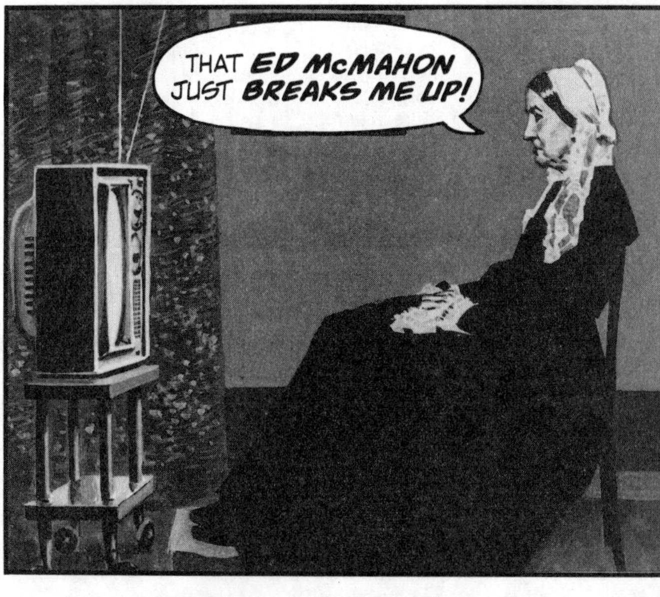
THAT ED McMAHON JUST BREAKS ME UP!

Hey, Gang! Tired of all the garbage they're showing on motion picture screens lately? Well, here's a "Family" film for a change! And now, meet the "Family":

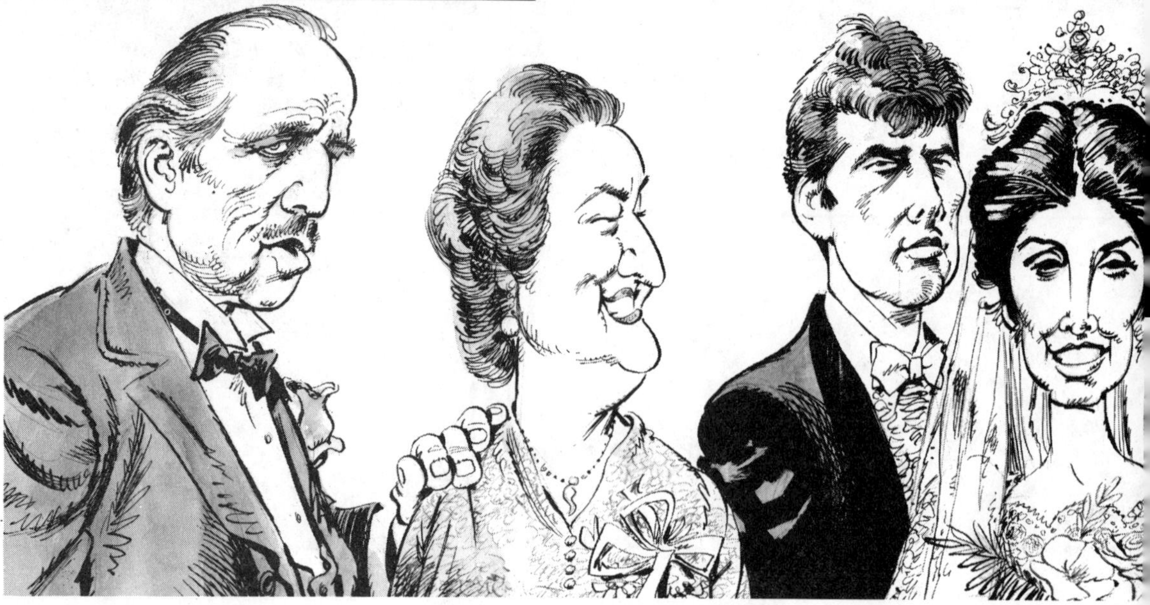

This is Don Vino Minestrone. Not too long ago, he was just a poor immigrant from Sicily. Now he's a leading racketeer, extortionist and killer. How did Don Vino get where he is today? By putting his faith in The American Way of Life.

Here's Mama Minestrone, a typical lovable Sicilian housewife. It seems like only yesterday at another wedding that Mama herself said, "I do!" Come to think of it, that was the last time she opened her mouth.

This is Don Vino's daugh Canny, and her bridegro Carly. Such a nice cou Everyone is saying that Vino is not really losin daughter. No, actually, this kind of Family, probably lose a Son-in-

And so, with such a strange family and such weird childr

THE ODD

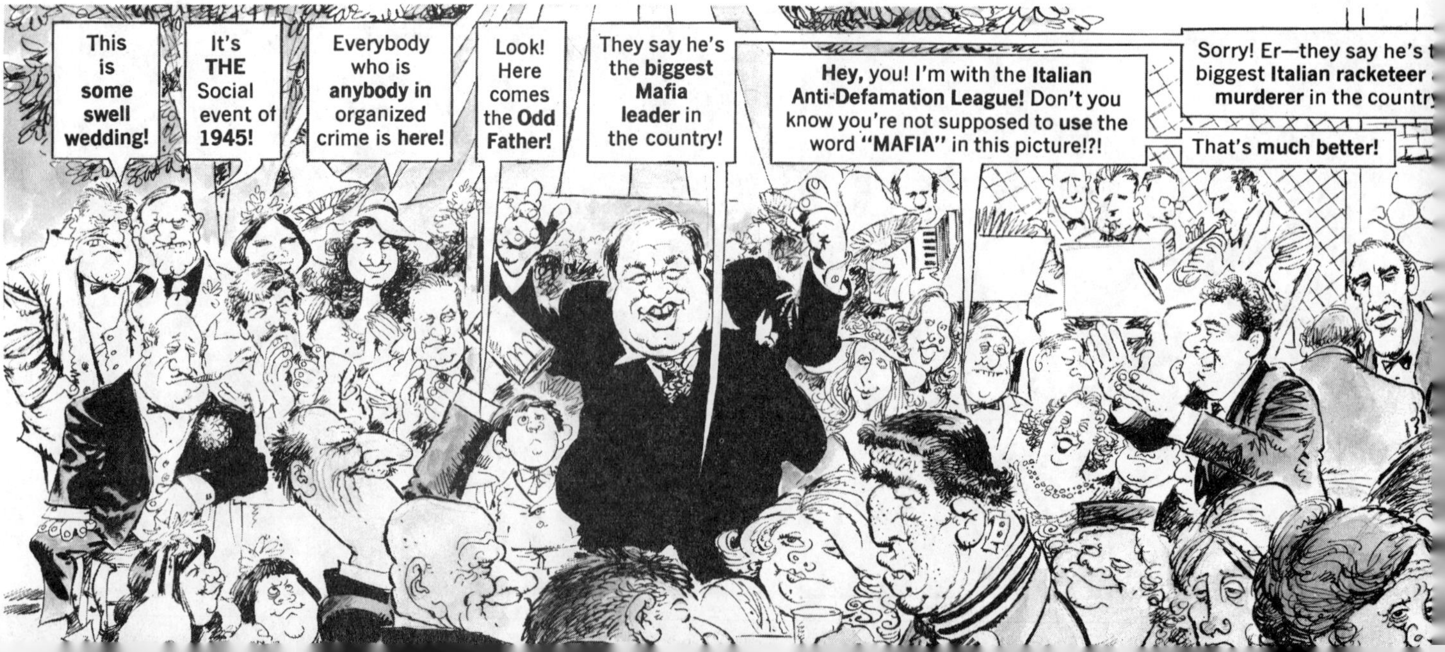
This is some swell wedding!
It's THE Social event of 1945!
Everybody who is anybody in organized crime is here!
Look! Here comes the Odd Father!
They say he's the biggest Mafia leader in the country!
Hey, you! I'm with the Italian Anti-Defamation League! Don't you know you're not supposed to use the word "MAFIA" in this picture!?!
Sorry! Er—they say he's t biggest Italian racketeer murderer in the countr
That's much better!

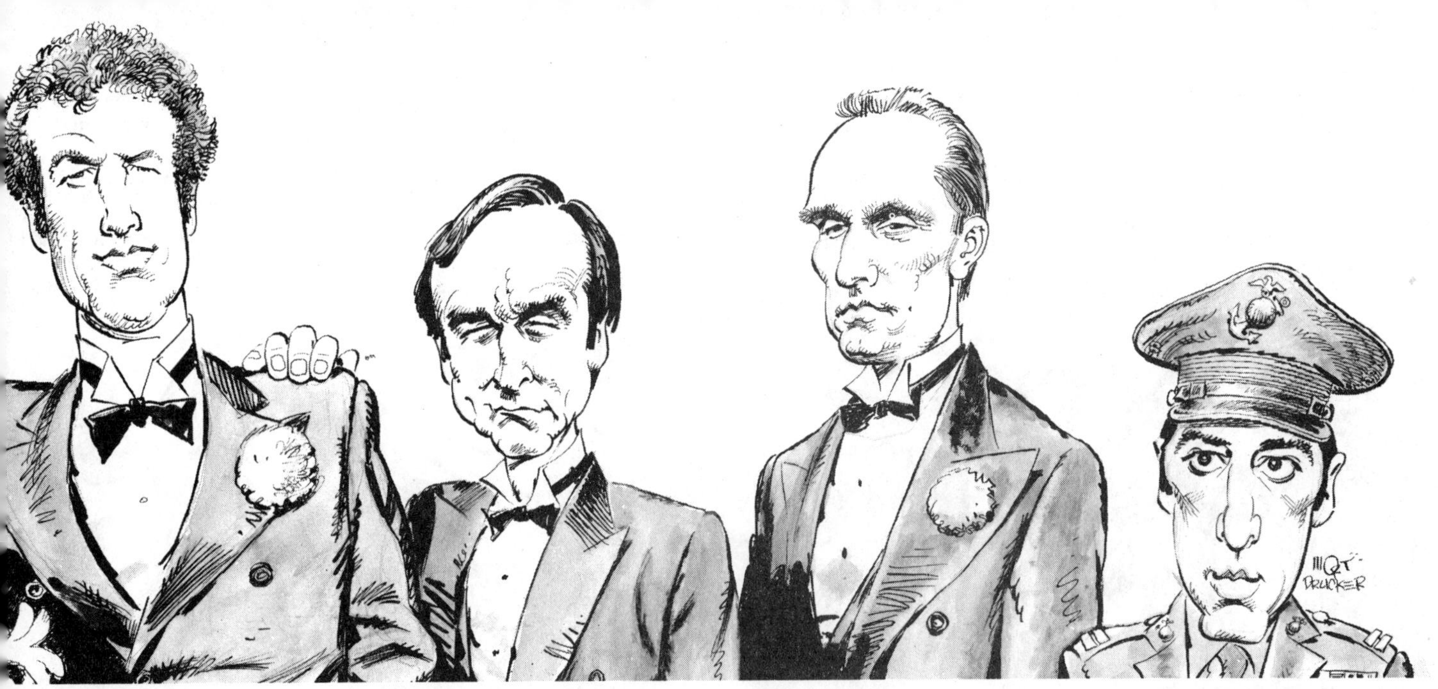

his is Sinny Minestrone, e Don's eldest son. He's xt in line, and it's only matter of time before he ts the Family business. hat is, of course, unless rival Family decides to ve him the business first.

This is the Don's second son, Freako. He's a sad, gentle soul. He cries at weddings and all kinds of Family crises. But he can also be a barrel of laughs. Just catch him at a funeral some time.

This is Tim Haven, the Don's adopted son. He's shrewd and smart. All his life, he dreamed of being a criminal lawyer. But he only finished half of his education —the "criminal" part.

And this is Micrin, the Don's youngest son. He's a college graduate, a veteran war hero, an honest law-abiding citizen —and a disgrace to the entire Family.

easy to see why Don Vino Minestrone is known as...

FATHER

ARTIST: MORT DRUCKER

WRITER: LARRY SIEGEL

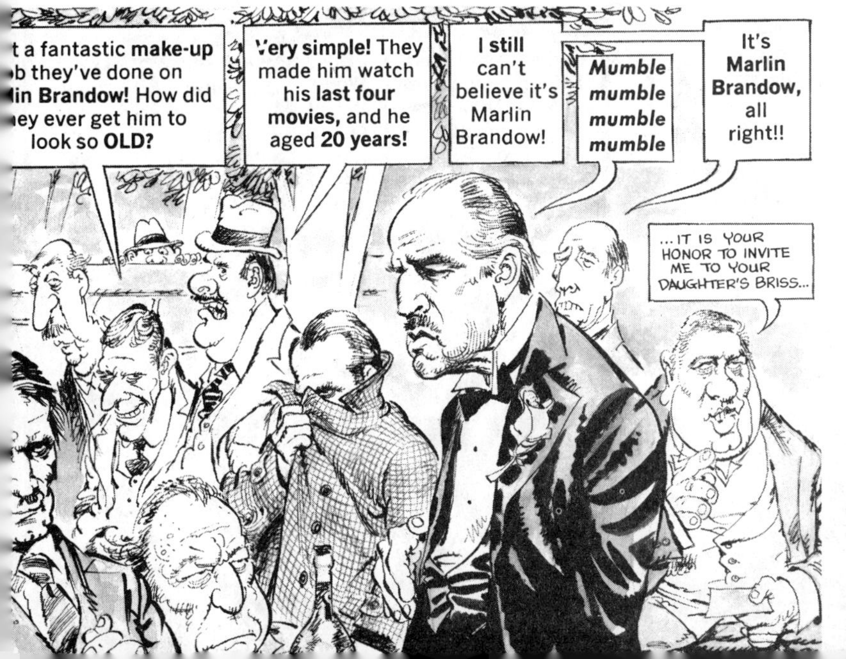

t a fantastic **make-up** b they've done on lin Brandow! How did ey ever get him to look so **OLD?**
Very simple! They made him watch his **last four movies,** and he aged **20 years!**
I still can't believe it's Marlin Brandow!
Mumble mumble mumble mumble
It's **Marlin Brandow,** all right!!
...IT IS YOUR HONOR TO INVITE ME TO YOUR DAUGHTER'S BRISS...

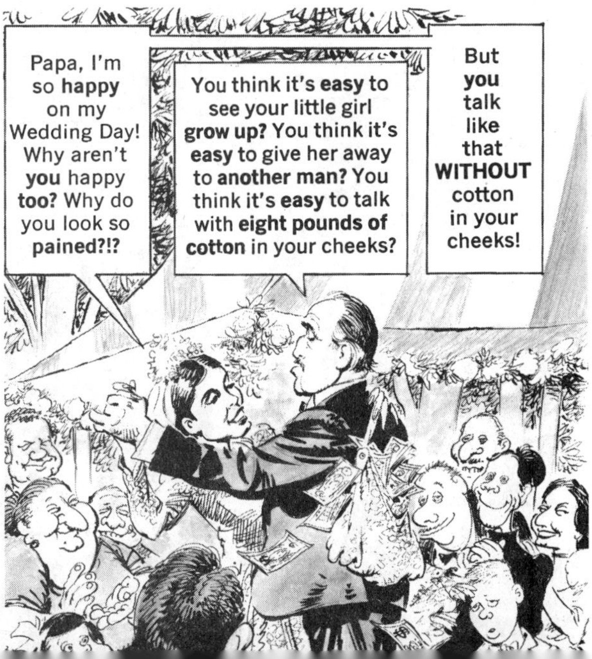

Papa, I'm so **happy** on my Wedding Day! Why aren't **you** happy **too?** Why do you look so **pained?!?**
You think it's **easy** to see your little girl **grow up?** You think it's **easy** to give her away to **another man?** You think it's **easy** to talk with **eight pounds of cotton** in your cheeks?
But **you** talk like that **WITHOUT** cotton in your cheeks!

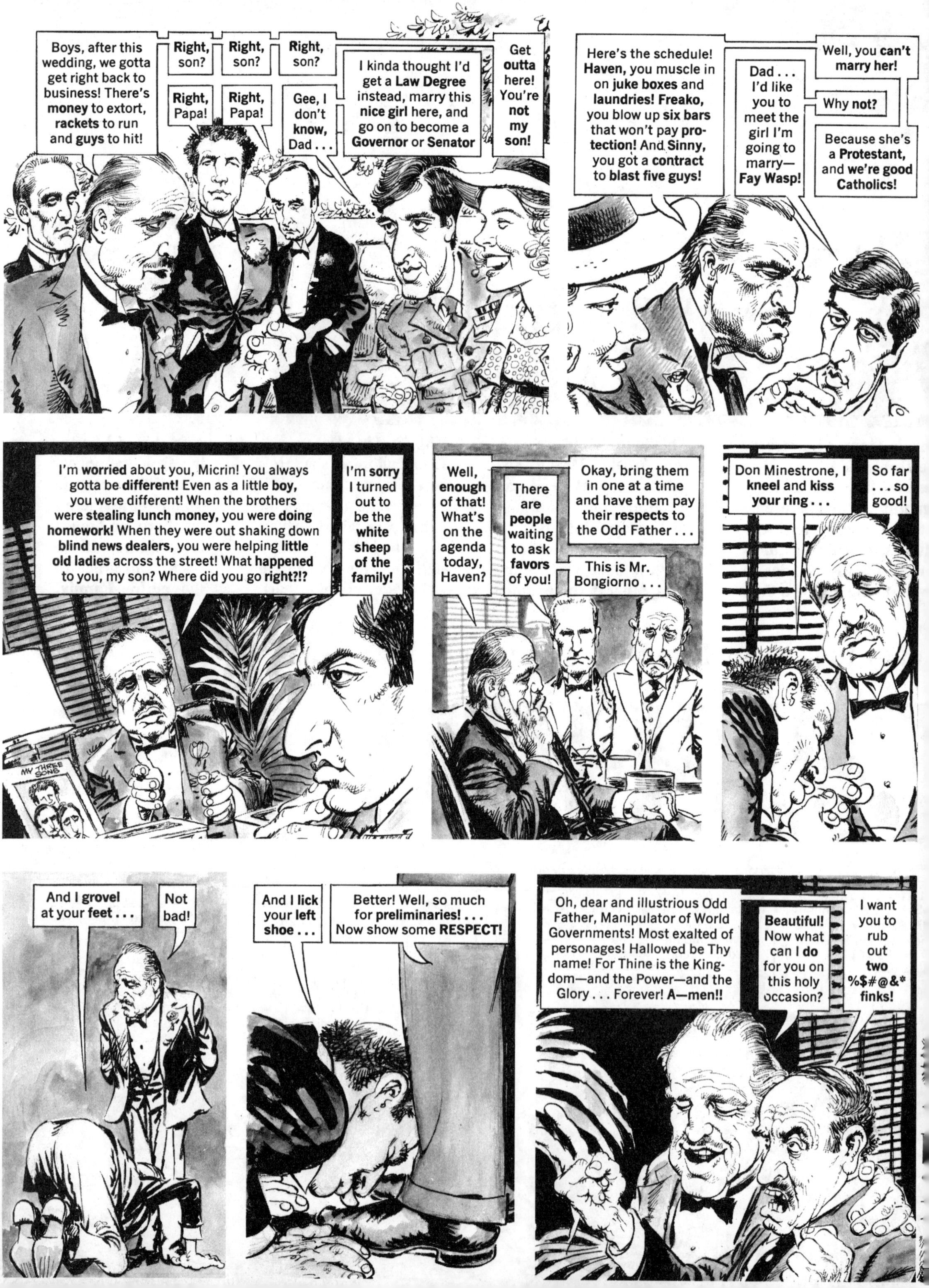
Boys, after this wedding, we gotta get right back to business! There's money to extort, rackets to run and guys to hit!
Right, son?
Right, son?
Right, son?
Right, Papa!
Right, Papa!
Gee, I don't know, Dad . . .
I kinda thought I'd get a Law Degree instead, marry this nice girl here, and go on to become a Governor or Senator
Get outta here! You're not my son!
Here's the schedule! Haven, you muscle in on juke boxes and laundries! Freako, you blow up six bars that won't pay protection! And Sinny, you got a contract to blast five guys!
Dad . . . I'd like you to meet the girl I'm going to marry— Fay Wasp!
Well, you can't marry her!
Why not?
Because she's a Protestant, and we're good Catholics!
I'm worried about you, Micrin! You always gotta be different! Even as a little boy, you were different! When the brothers were stealing lunch money, you were doing homework! When they were out shaking down blind news dealers, you were helping little old ladies across the street! What happened to you, my son? Where did you go right?!?
I'm sorry I turned out to be the white sheep of the family!
MY THREE SONS
Well, enough of that! What's on the agenda today, Haven?
There are people waiting to ask favors of you!
Okay, bring them in one at a time and have them pay their respects to the Odd Father . . .
This is Mr. Bongiorno . . .
Don Minestrone, I kneel and kiss your ring . . .
So far . . . so good!
And I grovel at your feet . . .
Not bad!
And I lick your left shoe . . .
Better! Well, so much for preliminaries! . . . Now show some RESPECT!
Oh, dear and illustrious Odd Father, Manipulator of World Governments! Most exalted of personages! Hallowed be Thy name! For Thine is the Kingdom—and the Power—and the Glory . . . Forever! A—men!!
Beautiful! Now what can I do for you on this holy occasion?
I want you to rub out two %$#@&* finks!

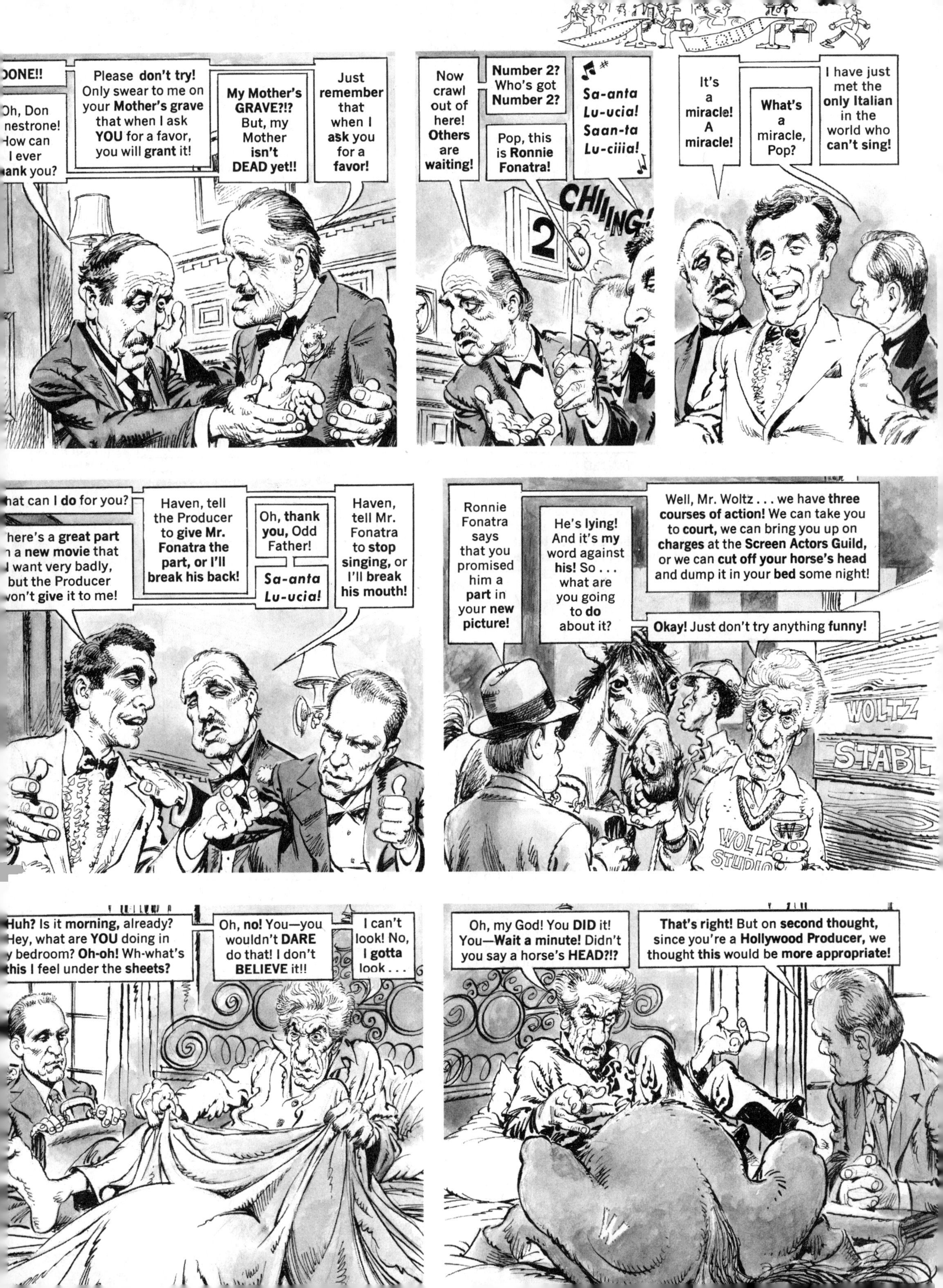

DONE!!
Oh, Don nestrone! How can I ever ank you?
Please don't try! Only swear to me on your Mother's grave that when I ask YOU for a favor, you will grant it!
My Mother's GRAVE?!? But, my Mother isn't DEAD yet!!
Just remember that when I ask you for a favor!
Now crawl out of here! Others are waiting!
Number 2? Who's got Number 2?
Pop, this is Ronnie Fonatra!
Sa-anta Lu-ucia! Saan-ta Lu-ciiia!
CHIIING!
2
It's a miracle! A miracle!
What's a miracle, Pop?
I have just met the only Italian in the world who can't sing!
hat can I do for you?
here's a great part n a new movie that I want very badly, but the Producer von't give it to me!
Haven, tell the Producer to give Mr. Fonatra the part, or I'll break his back!
Oh, thank you, Odd Father!
Sa-anta Lu-ucia!
Haven, tell Mr. Fonatra to stop singing, or I'll break his mouth!
Ronnie Fonatra says that you promised him a part in your new picture!
He's lying! And it's my word against his! So . . . what are you going to do about it?
Well, Mr. Woltz . . . we have three courses of action! We can take you to court, we can bring you up on charges at the Screen Actors Guild, or we can cut off your horse's head and dump it in your bed some night!
Okay! Just don't try anything funny!
WOLTZ
STABL
WOLTZ STUDIO
Huh? Is it morning, already? Hey, what are YOU doing in y bedroom? Oh-oh! Wh-what's this I feel under the sheets?
Oh, no! You—you wouldn't DARE do that! I don't BELIEVE it!!
I can't look! No, I gotta look . . .
Oh, my God! You DID it! You—Wait a minute! Didn't you say a horse's HEAD?!?
That's right! But on second thought, since you're a Hollywood Producer, we thought this would be more appropriate!

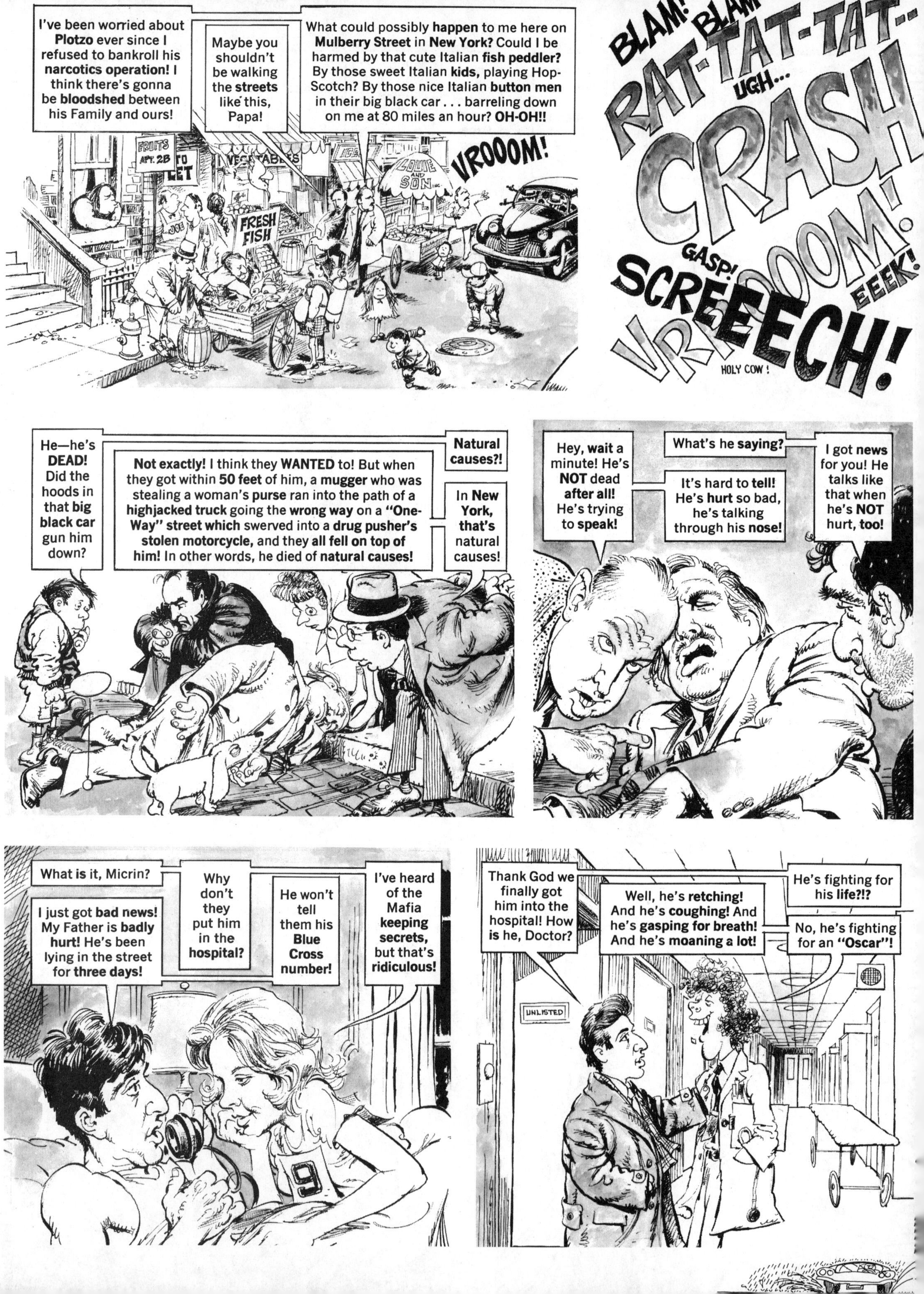
I've been worried about Plotzo ever since I refused to bankroll his narcotics operation! I think there's gonna be bloodshed between his Family and ours!
Maybe you shouldn't be walking the streets like this, Papa!
What could possibly happen to me here on Mulberry Street in New York? Could I be harmed by that cute Italian fish peddler? By those sweet Italian kids, playing Hop-Scotch? By those nice Italian button men in their big black car . . . barreling down on me at 80 miles an hour? OH-OH!!
FRUITS
APT. 2B
TO LET
VEGETABLES
JOE
FRESH FISH
LOUIE AND SON INC.
VROOOM!
BLAM! BLAM!
RAT-TAT-TAT...
UGH...
CRASH!
VROOOM!
GASP!
SCREEEECH!
EEEK!
HOLY COW!
He—he's DEAD! Did the hoods in that big black car gun him down?
Not exactly! I think they WANTED to! But when they got within 50 feet of him, a mugger who was stealing a woman's purse ran into the path of a highjacked truck going the wrong way on a "One-Way" street which swerved into a drug pusher's stolen motorcycle, and they all fell on top of him! In other words, he died of natural causes!
Natural causes?!
In New York, that's natural causes!
Hey, wait a minute! He's NOT dead after all! He's trying to speak!
What's he saying?
It's hard to tell! He's hurt so bad, he's talking through his nose!
I got news for you! He talks like that when he's NOT hurt, too!
What is it, Micrin?
I just got bad news! My Father is badly hurt! He's been lying in the street for three days!
Why don't they put him in the hospital?
He won't tell them his Blue Cross number!
I've heard of the Mafia keeping secrets, but that's ridiculous!
9
Thank God we finally got him into the hospital! How is he, Doctor?
Well, he's retching! And he's coughing! And he's gasping for breath! And he's moaning a lot!
He's fighting for his life?!?
No, he's fighting for an "Oscar"!
UNLISTED

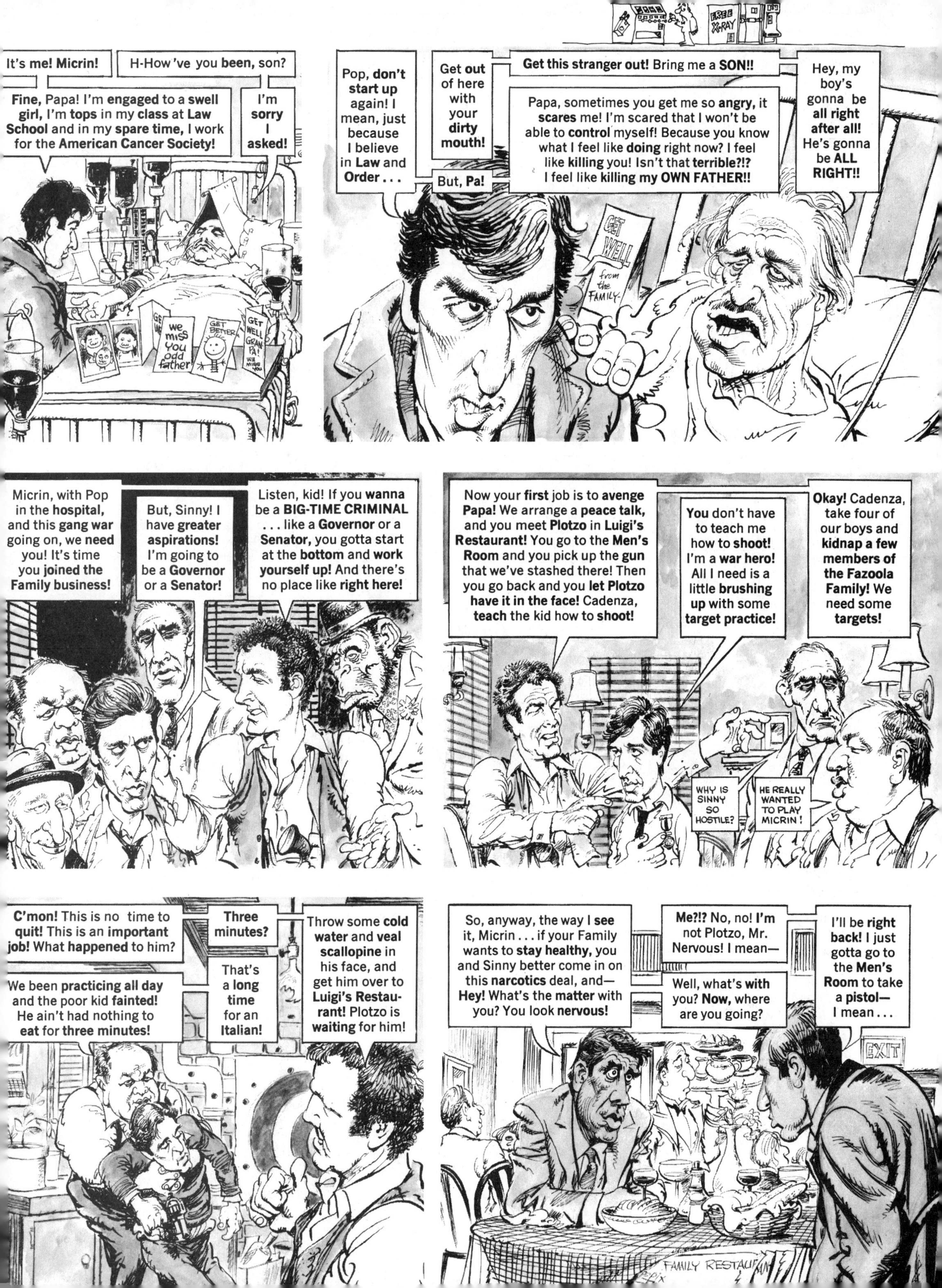
FREE X-RAY
It's **me! Micrin!**
H-How've you **been,** son?
Fine, Papa! I'm **engaged** to a **swell girl,** I'm **tops** in my **class** at **Law School** and in my **spare time,** I work for the **American Cancer Society!**
I'm **sorry** I **asked!**
we miss you odd father
GET BETTER
GET WELL GRAN-PA! WE MISS YOU
Pop, **don't start up** again! I mean, just because I believe in **Law** and **Order . . .**
Get **out** of here with your **dirty mouth!**
But, **Pa!**
Get this stranger out! Bring me a **SON!!**
Papa, sometimes you get me so **angry,** it **scares** me! I'm scared that I won't be able to **control** myself! Because you know what I feel like **doing** right now? I feel like **killing** you! Isn't that **terrible?!?** I feel like **killing my OWN FATHER!!**
Hey, my boy's gonna be **all right after all!** He's gonna be **ALL RIGHT!!**
GET WELL from the FAMILY
Micrin, with Pop in the **hospital,** and this **gang war** going on, we **need** you! It's time you **joined the Family business!**
But, Sinny! I have **greater aspirations!** I'm going to be a **Governor** or a **Senator!**
Listen, kid! If you **wanna** be a **BIG-TIME CRIMINAL . . .** like a **Governor** or a **Senator,** you gotta start at the **bottom** and **work yourself up!** And there's no place like **right here!**
Now your **first** job is to **avenge Papa!** We arrange a **peace talk,** and you meet **Plotzo** in **Luigi's Restaurant!** You go to the **Men's Room** and you pick up the **gun** that we've stashed there! Then you go back and you **let Plotzo have it in the face!** Cadenza, **teach** the kid how to **shoot!**
You don't have to teach me how to **shoot!** I'm a **war hero!** All I need is a little **brushing up** with some **target practice!**
Okay! Cadenza, take four of our boys and **kidnap a few members of the Fazoola Family!** We need some **targets!**
WHY IS SINNY SO HOSTILE?
HE REALLY WANTED TO PLAY MICRIN!
C'mon! This is no time to **quit!** This is an **important job!** What **happened** to him?
We been **practicing all day** and the poor kid **fainted!** He ain't had nothing to **eat** for **three minutes!**
Three minutes?
That's a **long time** for an **Italian!**
Throw some **cold water** and **veal scallopine** in his face, and get him over to **Luigi's Restaurant!** Plotzo is **waiting** for him!
So, anyway, the way I **see** it, Micrin . . . if your Family wants to **stay healthy,** you and Sinny better come in on this **narcotics** deal, and— **Hey!** What's the **matter** with you? You look **nervous!**
Me?!? No, no! **I'm** not Plotzo, Mr. Nervous! I mean—
Well, what's **with** you? **Now,** where are you going?
I'll be **right back!** I just gotta go to the **Men's Room** to take a **pistol—** I mean . . .
EXIT
FAMILY RESTAURANT

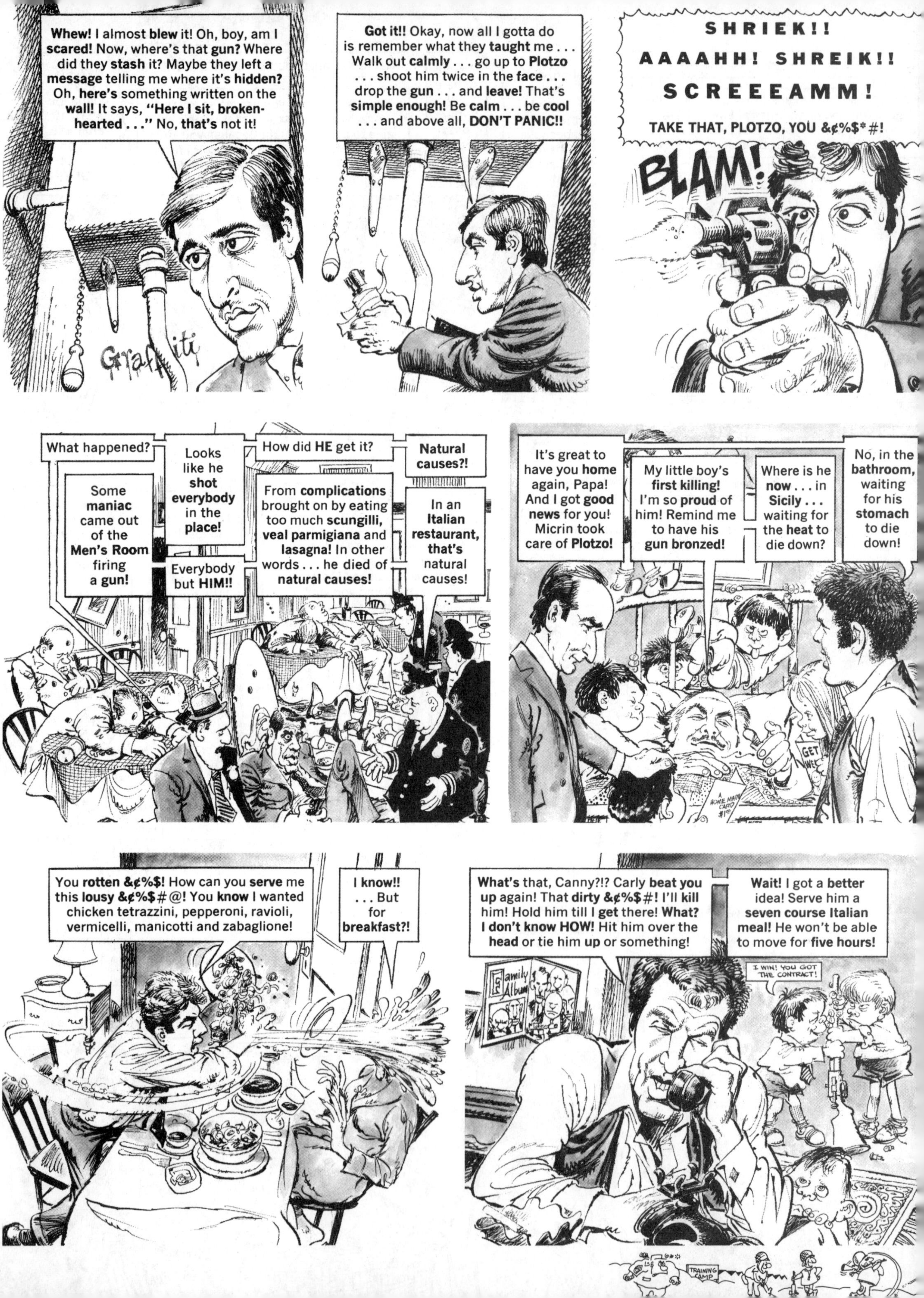
Whew! I almost blew it! Oh, boy, am I scared! Now, where's that gun? Where did they stash it? Maybe they left a message telling me where it's hidden? Oh, here's something written on the wall! It says, "Here I sit, broken-hearted . . ." No, that's not it!
Graffiti
Got it!! Okay, now all I gotta do is remember what they taught me . . . Walk out calmly . . . go up to Plotzo . . . shoot him twice in the face . . . drop the gun . . . and leave! That's simple enough! Be calm . . . be cool . . . and above all, DON'T PANIC!!
SHRIEK!! AAAAHH! SHREIK!! SCREEEAMM! TAKE THAT, PLOTZO, YOU &¢%$*#!
BLAM!
What happened?
Some maniac came out of the Men's Room firing a gun!
Looks like he shot everybody in the place!
Everybody but HIM!!
How did HE get it?
From complications brought on by eating too much scungilli, veal parmigiana and lasagna! In other words . . . he died of natural causes!
Natural causes?!
In an Italian restaurant, that's natural causes!
It's great to have you home again, Papa! And I got good news for you! Micrin took care of Plotzo!
My little boy's first killing! I'm so proud of him! Remind me to have his gun bronzed!
Where is he now . . . in Sicily . . . waiting for the heat to die down?
No, in the bathroom, waiting for his stomach to die down!
GET WE
You rotten &¢%$! How can you serve me this lousy &¢%$#@! You know I wanted chicken tetrazzini, pepperoni, ravioli, vermicelli, manicotti and zabaglione!
I know!! . . . But for breakfast?!
What's that, Canny?!? Carly beat you up again! That dirty &¢%$#! I'll kill him! Hold him till I get there! What? I don't know HOW! Hit him over the head or tie him up or something!
Wait! I got a better idea! Serve him a seven course Italian meal! He won't be able to move for five hours!
Family Album
I WIN! YOU GOT THE CONTRACT!
TRAINING CAMP

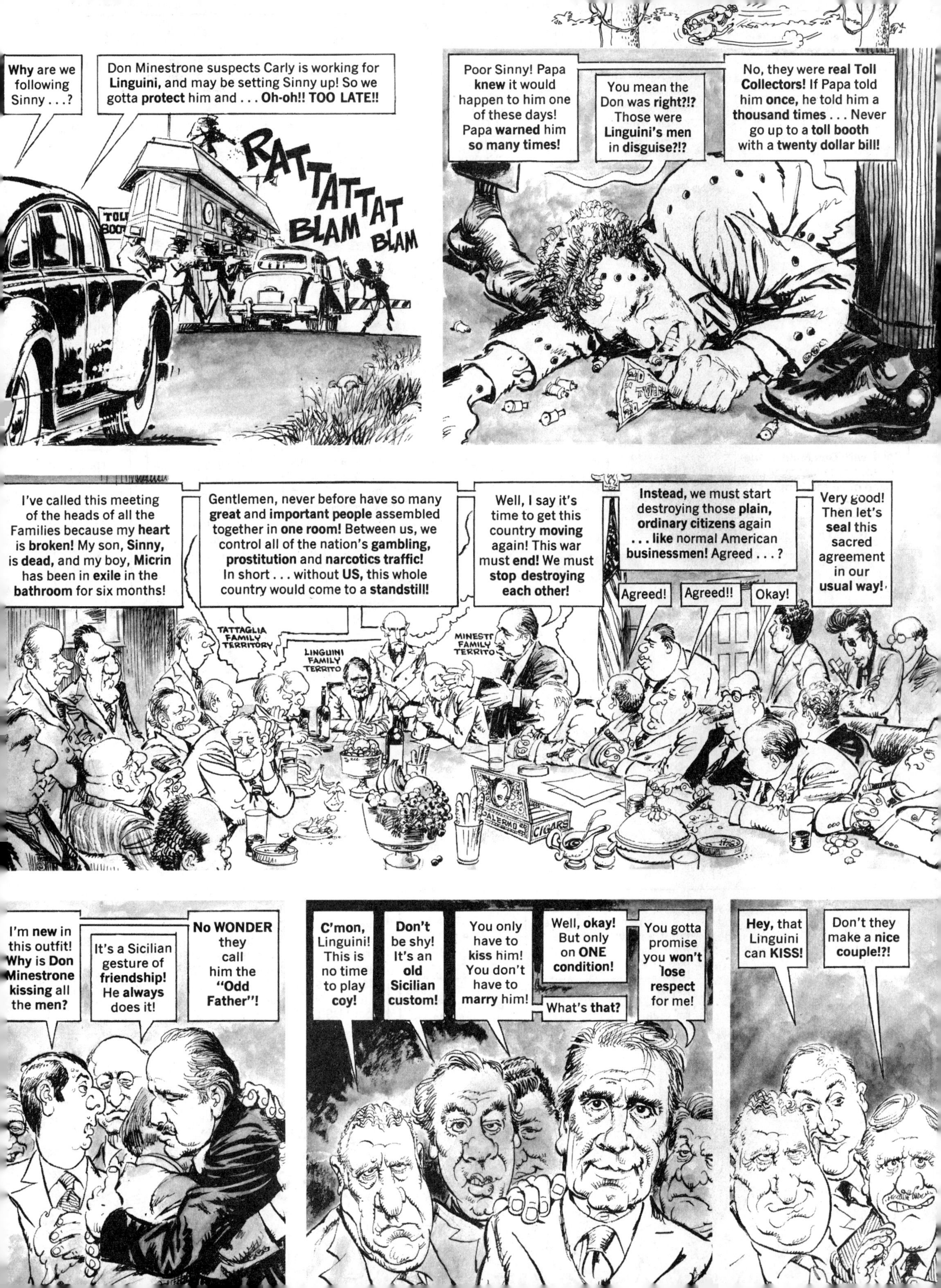

Why are we following Sinny . . .?
Don Minestrone suspects Carly is working for Linguini, and may be setting Sinny up! So we gotta protect him and . . . Oh-oh!! TOO LATE!!
RATTATTAT
BLAM
BLAM
Poor Sinny! Papa knew it would happen to him one of these days! Papa warned him so many times!
You mean the Don was right?!? Those were Linguini's men in disguise?!?
No, they were real Toll Collectors! If Papa told him once, he told him a thousand times . . . Never go up to a toll booth with a twenty dollar bill!
I've called this meeting of the heads of all the Families because my heart is broken! My son, Sinny, is dead, and my boy, Micrin has been in exile in the bathroom for six months!
Gentlemen, never before have so many great and important people assembled together in one room! Between us, we control all of the nation's gambling, prostitution and narcotics traffic! In short . . . without US, this whole country would come to a standstill!
Well, I say it's time to get this country moving again! This war must end! We must stop destroying each other!
Instead, we must start destroying those plain, ordinary citizens again . . . like normal American businessmen! Agreed . . . ?
Agreed!
Agreed!!
Okay!
Very good! Then let's seal this sacred agreement in our usual way!
TATTAGLIA FAMILY TERRITORY
LINGUINI FAMILY TERRITO
MINESTI FAMILY TERRITO
PALERMO CIGARS
I'm new in this outfit! Why is Don Minestrone kissing all the men?
It's a Sicilian gesture of friendship! He always does it!
No WONDER they call him the "Odd Father"!
C'mon, Linguini! This is no time to play coy!
Don't be shy! It's an old Sicilian custom!
You only have to kiss him! You don't have to marry him!
Well, okay! But only on ONE condition!
What's that?
You gotta promise you won't lose respect for me!
Hey, that Linguini can KISS!
Don't they make a nice couple!?!

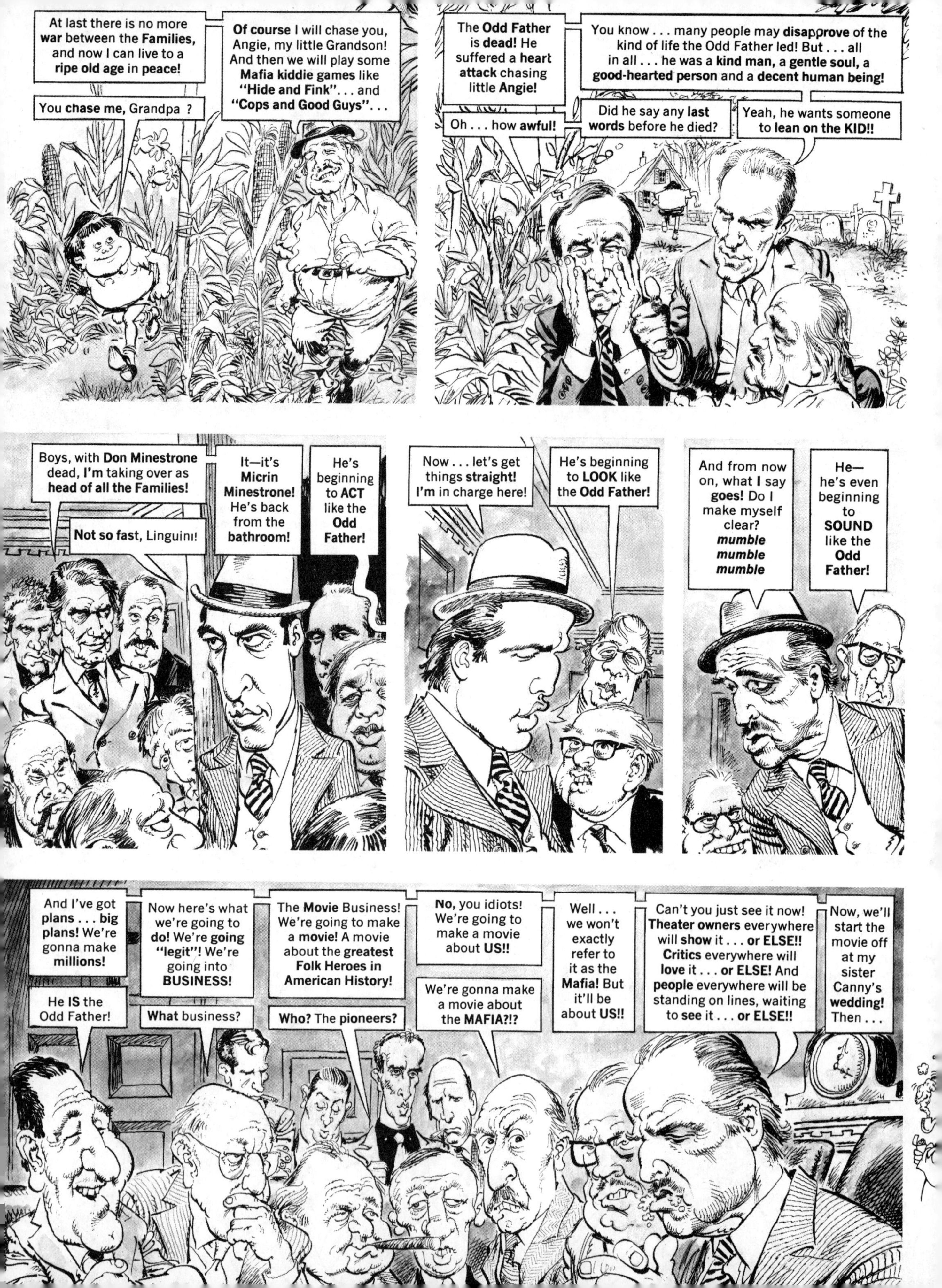
At last there is no more war between the Families, and now I can live to a ripe old age in peace!
You chase me, Grandpa ?
Of course I will chase you, Angie, my little Grandson! And then we will play some Mafia kiddie games like "Hide and Fink" . . . and "Cops and Good Guys" . . .
The Odd Father is dead! He suffered a heart attack chasing little Angie!
Oh . . . how awful!
You know . . . many people may disapprove of the kind of life the Odd Father led! But . . . all in all . . . he was a kind man, a gentle soul, a good-hearted person and a decent human being!
Did he say any last words before he died?
Yeah, he wants someone to lean on the KID!!
Boys, with Don Minestrone dead, I'm taking over as head of all the Families!
Not so fast, Linguini!
It—it's Micrin Minestrone! He's back from the bathroom!
He's beginning to ACT like the Odd Father!
Now . . . let's get things straight! I'm in charge here!
He's beginning to LOOK like the Odd Father!
And from now on, what I say goes! Do I make myself clear? mumble mumble mumble
He— he's even beginning to SOUND like the Odd Father!
And I've got plans . . . big plans! We're gonna make millions!
He IS the Odd Father!
Now here's what we're going to do! We're going "legit"! We're going into BUSINESS!
What business?
The Movie Business! We're going to make a movie! A movie about the greatest Folk Heroes in American History!
Who? The pioneers?
No, you idiots! We're going to make a movie about US!!
We're gonna make a movie about the MAFIA?!?
Well . . . we won't exactly refer to it as the Mafia! But it'll be about US!!
Can't you just see it now! Theater owners everywhere will show it . . . or ELSE!! Critics everywhere will love it . . . or ELSE! And people everywhere will be standing on lines, waiting to see it . . . or ELSE!!
Now, we'll start the movie off at my sister Canny's wedding! Then . . .

ONE DAY IN A CRASH-PAD

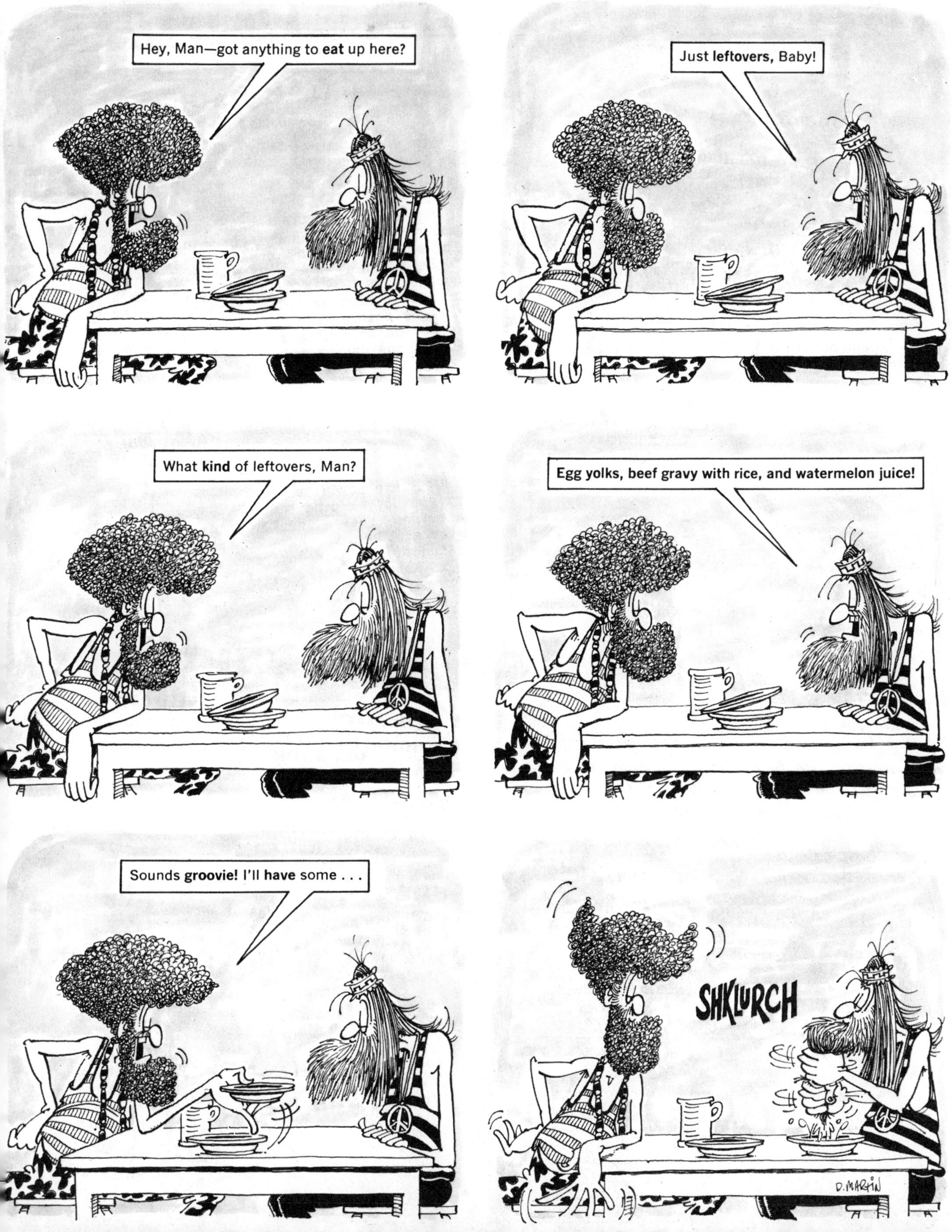
Hey, Man—got anything to eat up here?
Just leftovers, Baby!
What kind of leftovers, Man?
Egg yolks, beef gravy with rice, and watermelon juice!
Sounds groovie! I'll have some . . .
SHKLURCH
D. MARTIN

RECALLED FROM THE BACK POCKET DEPT.

Hey, muckraking fans! Here is a fictionalized "MAD" look at what we'd probably find if we were to make a thorough study of the contents of

RALPH NADER'S WALLET

Spector & Bobrick
Music Publishers
Brill Building
New York City

Dear Mr. Nader:—

We are in receipt of your recent letter.

As publishers of "In Your Merry Oldsmobile", we think you've gone out of your gourd, Man!

Your claim that this song is "unsafe" and should not be sung "at any speed" is, like, ridiculous! No doubt about it, Man, you are a "nut" and a "fanatic"!

Groovingly yours,
Sam Bobrick
Sam Bobrick
President

RALPH NADER
"The Nation's Conscience"
Washington, District of Columbia

Dear Mr. Bobrick:

I repeat my claim that your song is "unsafe" and should not be sung "at any speed"--as indeed ALL songs are unsafe and should not be sung at any speed--BY ROCK GROUPS! Rock Groups have a tendency to perform at extremely high decibles, this increasing the already intolerable "noise pollution" that is permeating our atmosphere and posing an increasing danger to our nation's consumers. So you see, I am not a "nut" or a "fanatic"!

Alertly yours,
Ralph Nader
Ralph Nader

P.S. I have conducted tests on the stationary you use, and have discovered that it is made from trees illegally cut from the Maine forests. Thus, you have contributed to the destruction of our environment. Next time I am in New York City, I will place you and your partner under a Citizen's Arrest!

R.N.

Mrs. Agatha Nader
135 Hamden Road
Winstead, Connecticut

Dear Ralph,

You were always my favorite nephew. I remember as a boy you were always polite, obedient and well-mannered. That is why it is hard for me to understand this sudden change in your behavior.

It was with all good intentions that I invited you to my dinner party last Friday evening. But instead of being grateful, you came and embarrassed me in front of all my guests.

First, you claimed that my fruit salad contained monosodium glutamate. And then you had the nerve to stand up and demand the recall of my meatloaf!

How dare you act in such a boorish manner!

This will not be forgotten, dear Nephew! I am seriously considering recycling you in my will!

Angrily,
Aunt Agatha

Slik, Imidge and Sellers
Public Relations Consultants
Washington, D.C.

Ralphie, Baby!

We're in luck!

We've just located another Men's Haberdasher with a limited supply of "ill-fitting suits".

We suggest that you go there immediately and buy three or four so that you can continue to project that "homespun"--"too-busy-to-care-about-clothes" image to the public.

Also, don't forget to pick up the usual "square" accessories...the 1957 style skinny ties, the drab wash-and-wear white shirts, and the ankle socks with the clocks on them.

Remember, the public digs the image of a simple man wearing ill-fitting clothes. Look what it's done for our last two Presidents!

Sincerely yours,
Budd E. Sellers
Bud E. Sellers

WRITER: ARNIE KOGE

IDENTIFICATION

NAME _Ralph Nader_
ADDRESS _Washington, D.C._
TELEPHONE _Tapped (Usually)_
MAKE OF AUTOMOBILE _Are You Kidding?!?_
OCCUPATION _Lawyer, Consumer Crusader, Ecologist, Recaller of Cars, Destroyer of Detergents, Busy-Body, and Long-Shot Presidential Candidate_

IN CASE OF EMERGENCY, NOTIFY
Me! I'm the only one the country can trust!

NOTES ON SPEECH BEFORE "MARKETING CONVENTION" PAGE 8

And so, let me conclude by saying that there is no excuse for carelessness and deceit.

Every corporation and every individual must be held responsible for his actions.

Too many people today attempt to get away with putting something over on the public for the sake of a buck.

Yes, the innocent consumer must be protected against carelessness, deceit, shoddy business practices, dishonest merchandising, tainted foods and

---

SEARS, ROEBUCK & CO.
Washington, D.C. Branch

Dear Customer:

MR. RALPH NADER. Acct.# 2-714-062-N

It was probably an oversight on your part, but your check number 573 dated 2/17/72 in the amount of $78.53 was returned to us by your bank for lack of sufficient funds.

Would you kindly correct this error by sending us a new check in the above amount and making sure that it does not bounce this time.

Thank you,
Ward Montgomery
Ward Montgomery,
Accounts Division

THE NATIONAL BROADCASTING COMPANY
NBC-TV STUDIOS
OLIVE STREET   BURBANK, CAL.

Dear Mr. Nader:

This time, you've gone too far!
We've been hearing about your investigations into television programs, but we didn't believe you were really serious.
First, you put down the <u>Galloping Gourmet</u> for violating the "Wholesome Meat Act of 1937". Then, you declared the <u>Partridge Family Bus</u> as "structurally unsafe." And then you shocked <u>Doris Day</u> by claiming her smile "contained cyclamates."
But now, you've gone beyond all reason with your latest attack. It is utterly ridiculous for you to demand that <u>Ironside</u> rotate the tires on his wheelchair every 13 weeks"!

Sincerely yours,
Cy Chermak
Cy Chermak
Executive Producer
<u>Ironsides</u>

Things To Do Today!

1. Investigate the NBA. Suspected of pumping polluted air into Basketballs.
2. Check Kosher Food Industry. Make sure they recall all Gefilte Swordfish.
3. Research "Safety In Prisons." Check to see that they install seat belts on <u>all</u> Electric Chairs.
4. Investigate reports that McDougle Hamburger Stands are recycling their leftovers as "Hashburgers."
5. Go to New York City and kick the G.M. building.
6. Then write obscene things on the Chrysler Building.
7. Then attend Old Timer's Day at Yankee Stadium and beat up Whitey Ford.
8. Sell the Edsel.

MATTER OVER MIND DEPT.

THE PROBLEM

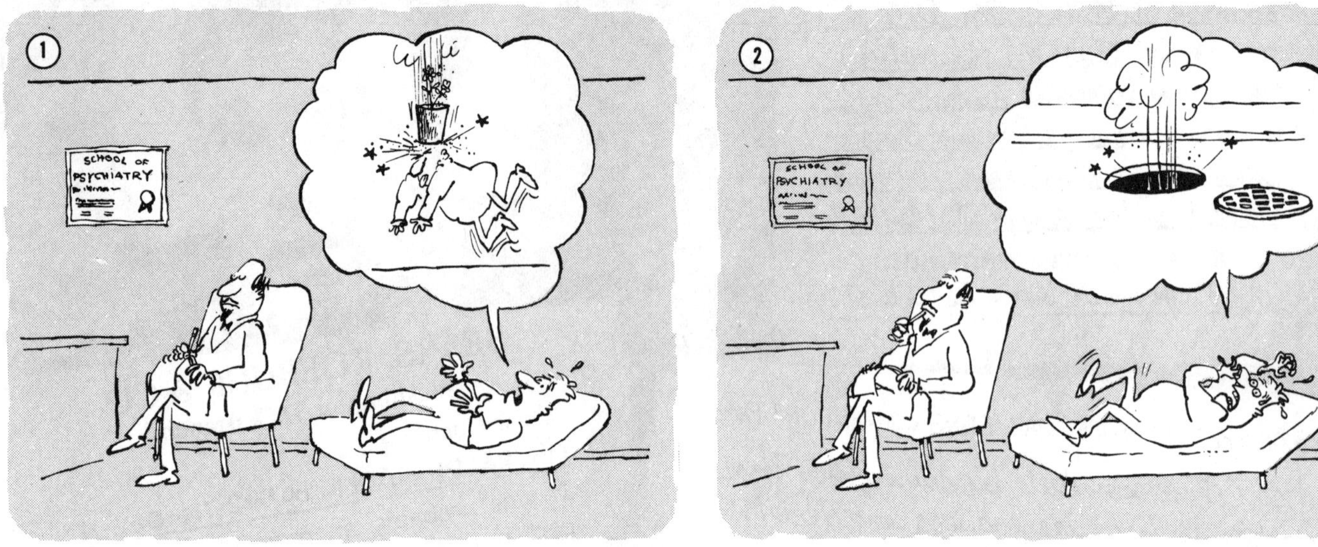
1
SCHOOL OF PSYCHIATRY
2
SCHOOL OF PSYCHIATRY

ARTIST & WRITER: SERGIO ARAGONES

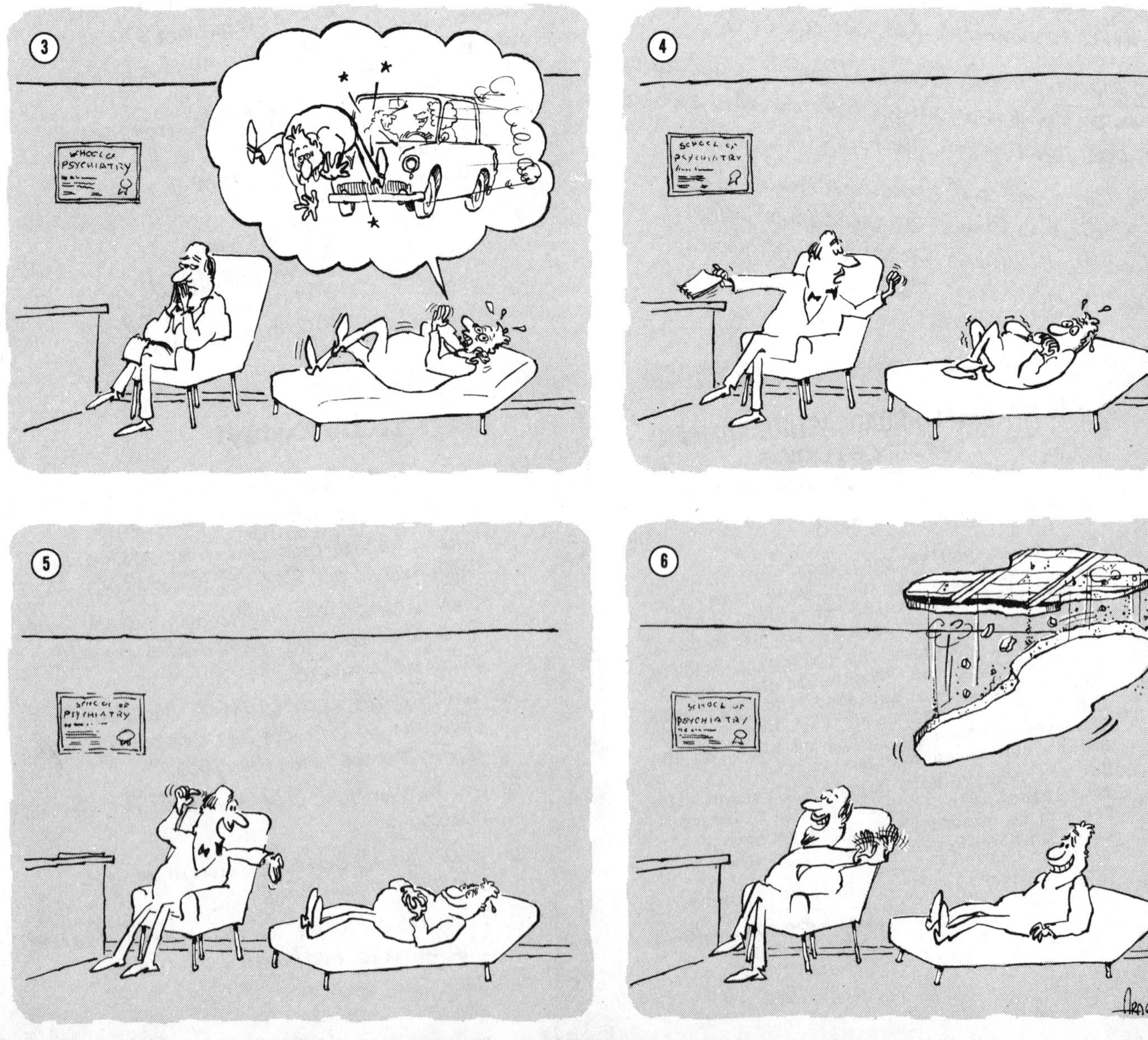
3
SCHOOL OF PSYCHIATRY
4
SCHOOL OF PSYCHIATRY
5
SCHOOL OF PSYCHIATRY
6
SCHOOL OF PSYCHIATRY
ARAGONES

Television may have an excuse for putting on all those unrealistic Medical Shows and unrealistic Police Shows and unrealistic Lawyer Shows and unrealistic Western Shows. After all, Television writers don't have any first-hand experience at being Doctors or Cops or Lawyers or Cowboys. But what's the alibi when Television puts on an unrealistic Comedy about Television? We're talking about the show that took that down-to-earth gal from the old "Dick Van Dyke Show," put her into an idiotic Television situation, and came up with the same old garbage...even though it was

THE MARY TAILOR-MADE SHOW

ARTIST: ANGELO TORRES WRITER: TOM KOCH

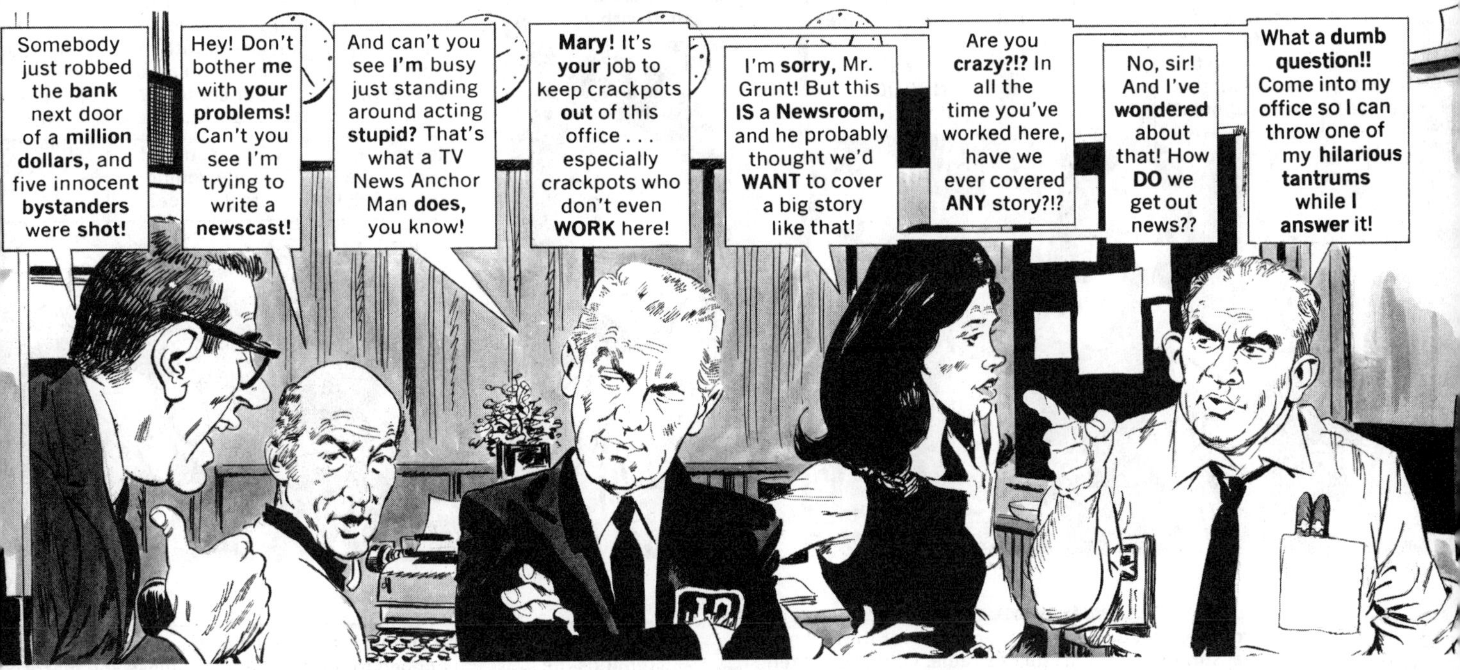
Somebody just robbed the **bank** next door of a **million dollars,** and five innocent **bystanders** were **shot!**
Hey! Don't bother **me** with **your problems!** Can't you see I'm trying to write a **newscast!**
And can't you see **I'm** busy just standing around acting **stupid?** That's what a TV News Anchor Man **does,** you know!
Mary! It's **your** job to keep crackpots **out** of this office . . . especially crackpots who don't even **WORK** here!
I'm **sorry,** Mr. Grunt! But this **IS** a **Newsroom,** and he probably thought we'd **WANT** to cover a big story like that!
Are you **crazy?!?** In all the time you've worked here, have we ever covered **ANY** story?!?
No, sir! And I've **wondered** about that! How **DO** we get out news??
What a **dumb question!!** Come into my office so I can throw one of my **hilarious tantrums** while I **answer** it!

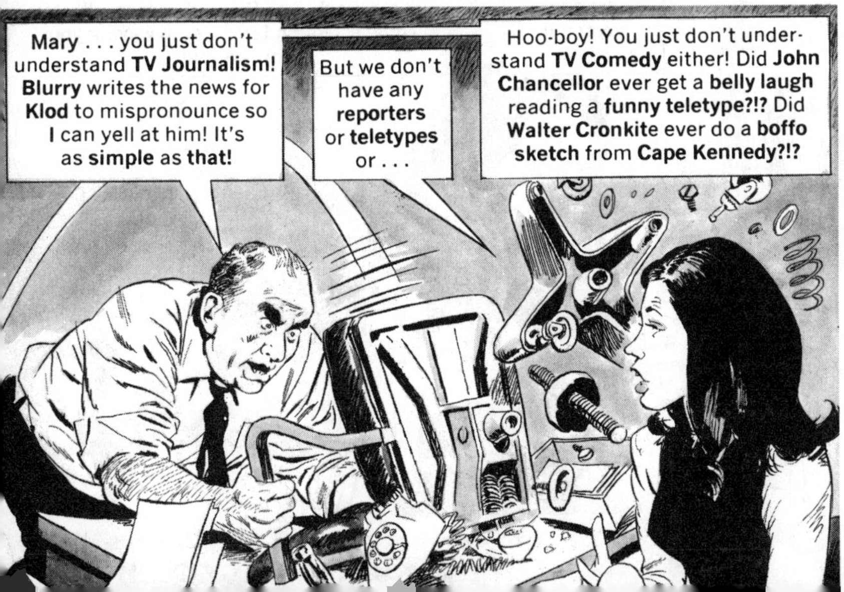
Mary . . . you just don't understand **TV Journalism! Blurry** writes the news for **Klod** to mispronounce so I can yell at him! It's as **simple** as **that!**
But we don't have any **reporters** or **teletypes** or . . .
Hoo-boy! You just don't understand **TV Comedy** either! Did **John Chancellor** ever get a **belly laugh** reading a **funny teletype?!?** Did **Walter Cronkite** ever do a **boffo sketch** from **Cape Kennedy?!?**

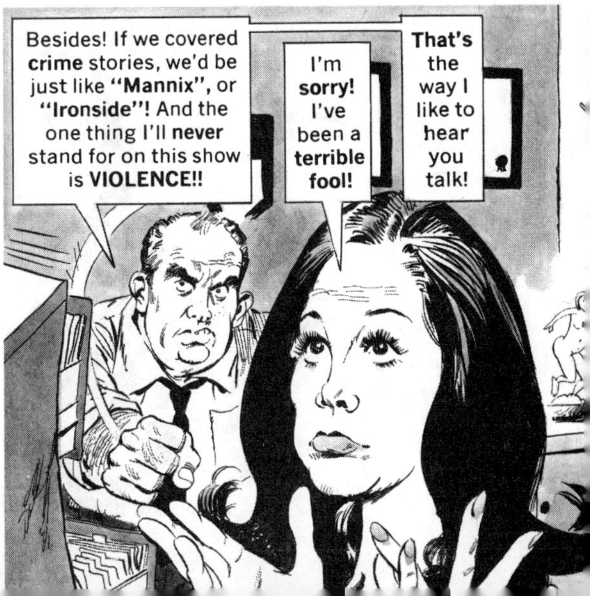
Besides! If we covered **crime** stories, we'd be just like **"Mannix"**, or **"Ironside"**! And the one thing I'll **never** stand for on this show is **VIOLENCE!!**
I'm **sorry!** I've been a **terrible fool!**
That's the way I like to hear you talk!

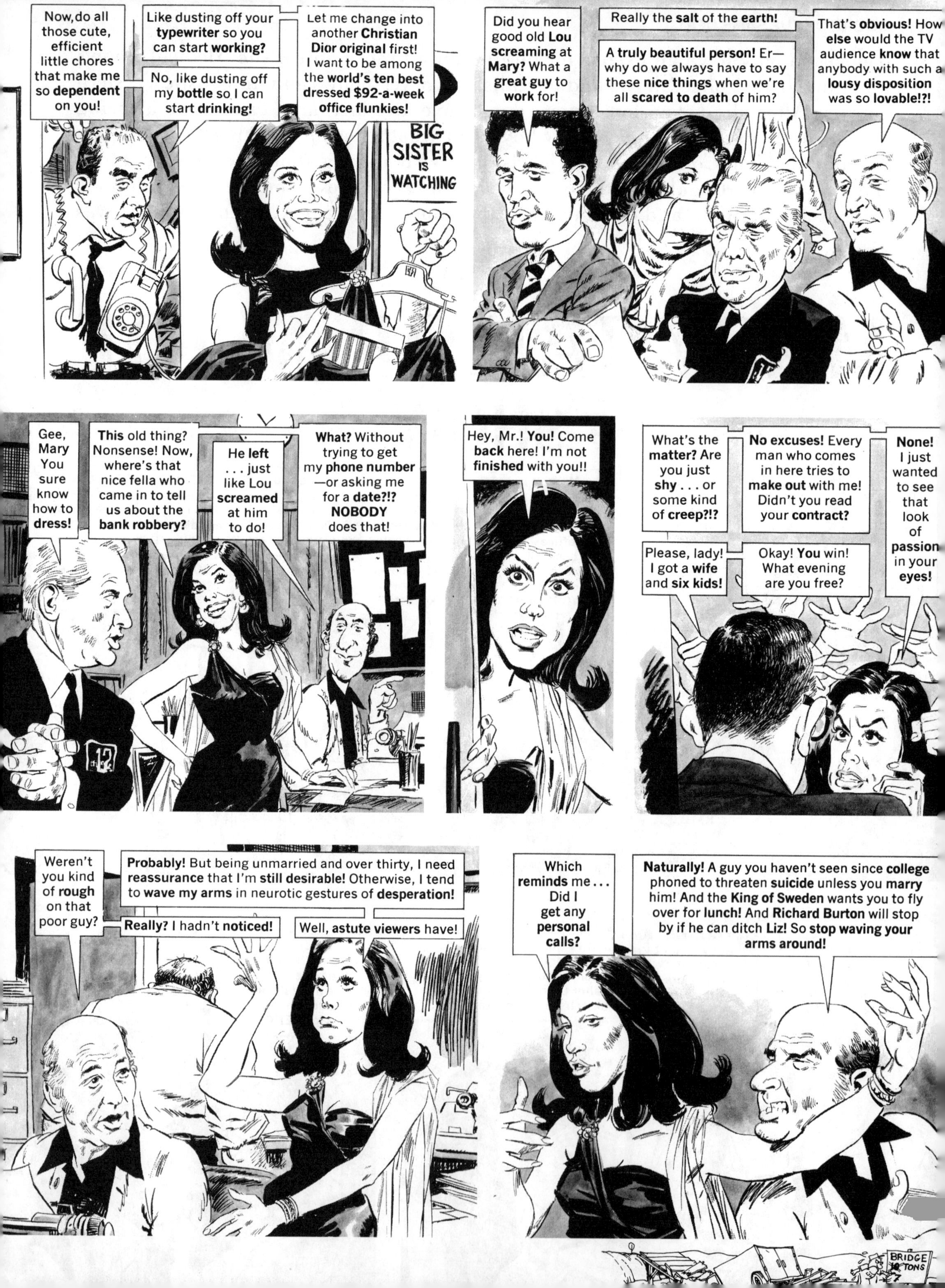

Now, do all those cute, efficient little chores that make me so dependent on you!
Like dusting off your typewriter so you can start working?
No, like dusting off my bottle so I can start drinking!
Let me change into another Christian Dior original first! I want to be among the world's ten best dressed $92-a-week office flunkies!
BIG SISTER IS WATCHING
Did you hear good old Lou screaming at Mary? What a great guy to work for!
Really the salt of the earth!
A truly beautiful person! Er—why do we always have to say these nice things when we're all scared to death of him?
That's obvious! How else would the TV audience know that anybody with such a lousy disposition was so lovable!?!
Gee, Mary You sure know how to dress!
This old thing? Nonsense! Now, where's that nice fella who came in to tell us about the bank robbery?
He left . . . just like Lou screamed at him to do!
What? Without trying to get my phone number—or asking me for a date?!? NOBODY does that!
Hey, Mr.! You! Come back here! I'm not finished with you!!
What's the matter? Are you just shy . . . or some kind of creep?!?
Please, lady! I got a wife and six kids!
No excuses! Every man who comes in here tries to make out with me! Didn't you read your contract?
Okay! You win! What evening are you free?
None! I just wanted to see that look of passion in your eyes!
Weren't you kind of rough on that poor guy?
Probably! But being unmarried and over thirty, I need reassurance that I'm still desirable! Otherwise, I tend to wave my arms in neurotic gestures of desperation!
Really? I hadn't noticed!
Well, astute viewers have!
Which reminds me . . . Did I get any personal calls?
Naturally! A guy you haven't seen since college phoned to threaten suicide unless you marry him! And the King of Sweden wants you to fly over for lunch! And Richard Burton will stop by if he can ditch Liz! So stop waving your arms around!
BRIDGE TONS

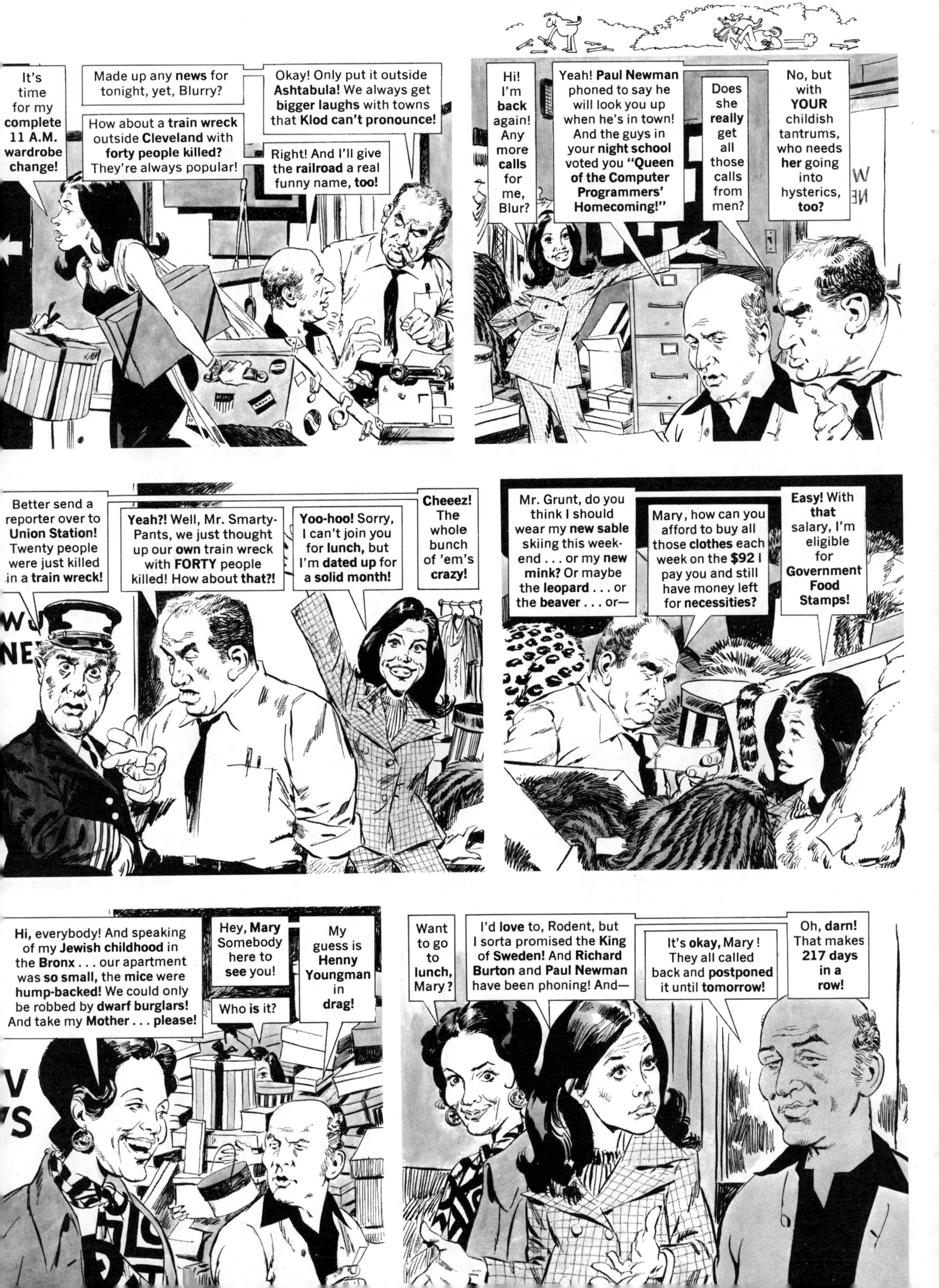

It's time for my complete 11 A.M. wardrobe change!
Made up any news for tonight, yet, Blurry?
How about a train wreck outside Cleveland with forty people killed? They're always popular!
Okay! Only put it outside Ashtabula! We always get bigger laughs with towns that Klod can't pronounce!
Right! And I'll give the railroad a real funny name, too!
Hi! I'm back again! Any more calls for me, Blur?
Yeah! Paul Newman phoned to say he will look you up when he's in town! And the guys in your night school voted you "Queen of the Computer Programmers' Homecoming!"
Does she really get all those calls from men?
No, but with YOUR childish tantrums, who needs her going into hysterics, too?
Better send a reporter over to Union Station! Twenty people were just killed in a train wreck!
Yeah?! Well, Mr. Smarty-Pants, we just thought up our own train wreck with FORTY people killed! How about that?!
Yoo-hoo! Sorry, I can't join you for lunch, but I'm dated up for a solid month!
Cheeez! The whole bunch of 'em's crazy!
Mr. Grunt, do you think I should wear my new sable skiing this week-end . . . or my new mink? Or maybe the leopard . . . or the beaver . . . or—
Mary, how can you afford to buy all those clothes each week on the $92 I pay you and still have money left for necessities?
Easy! With that salary, I'm eligible for Government Food Stamps!
Hi, everybody! And speaking of my Jewish childhood in the Bronx . . . our apartment was so small, the mice were hump-backed! We could only be robbed by dwarf burglars! And take my Mother . . . please!
Hey, Mary Somebody here to see you!
Who is it?
My guess is Henny Youngman in drag!
Want to go to lunch, Mary?
I'd love to, Rodent, but I sorta promised the King of Sweden! And Richard Burton and Paul Newman have been phoning! And—
It's okay, Mary! They all called back and postponed it until tomorrow!
Oh, darn! That makes 217 days in a row!

You don't have to pack a bag, Mary! We're only going downstairs to the coffee shop!
Well, you don't expect me to wear what I've got on for a whole hour, do you?
Mr. Grunt, meet my ugly friend, Rodent Droopstern! Notice how much less popular she is than me!
Hi! And speaking of my Jewish childhood in the Bronx, our idea of going to camp was sleeping on the fire escape for two weeks! We never heard of Cowboys and Indians! We played Slumlords and Tenants!
Pleased to meet yuh, Henny!
I don't care if people are staring! I just can't wear this same outfit for the whole trip down from the twelfth floor!
Hi, there! I'm Brute Trueblood, the new Sportscaster on the "Six O'clock News"!
Oh, wow! You're a MAN, aren't you?!?
Can't you tell?
Yeah! But if you believe this show's premise, I've never seen one up close before!
I'm here, now, fella! So you can stop boring yourself stiff talking to my homely friend!
Gasp! Why . . . you . . . you stepped out of a dream! You're sweeter than roses in May! A trip to the moon on gossamer wings!
Boy, it's lucky he reads his contract and boned up on Hit Parade "oldies"! If she started flapping her arms in this crowded elevator, somebody could get killed!
NIXON
Mary, why is your station the only one that never covers the news?
Go ask Mr. Grunt! He's still got two chairs left to smash up while he tells you!
What a sweet guy! Er—does he always strap new employees to the water cooler and give them twenty lashes?
No! When he's in a bad mood, he makes them hang by their thumbs from the sprinkler system!
Speaking of my Jewish childhood in the Bronx, what has four wheels and lies on its back? A dead bus! Where does a gorilla sleep? Any place it wants to!
I know I'm irresistible, but won't we attract attention holding hands like this?
Yes, but we'll attract even more attention if I let go and you begin that nutty arm-waving again

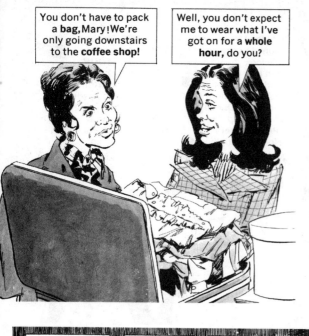

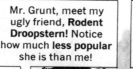

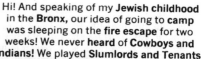

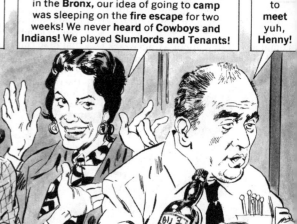

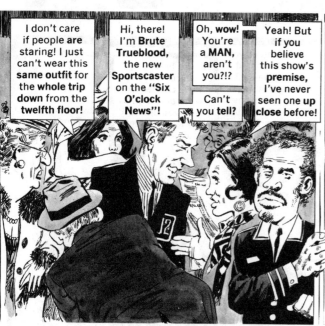

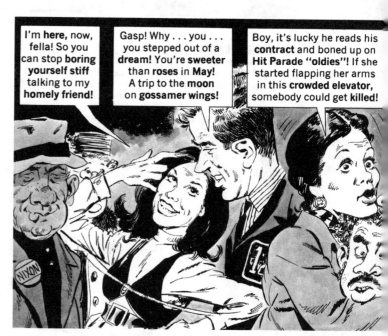

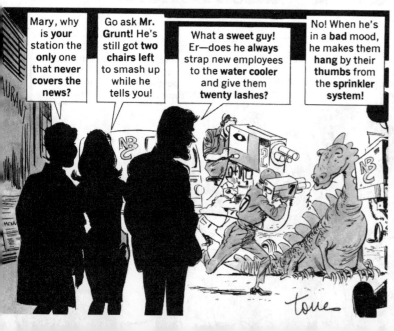

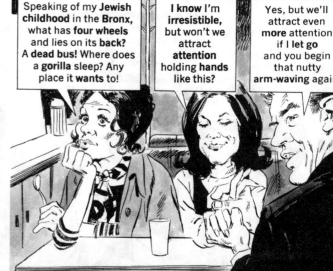

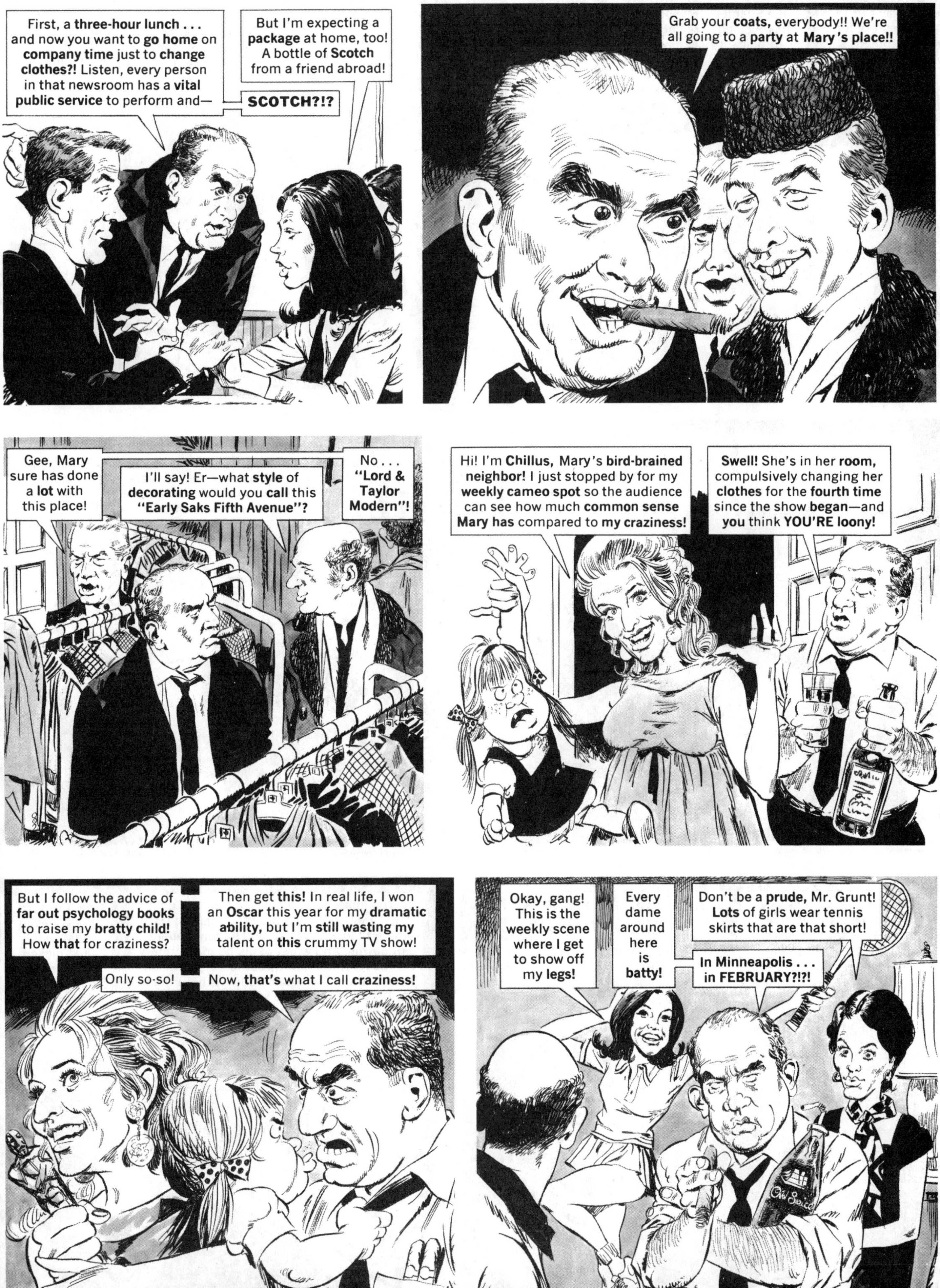
First, a three-hour lunch . . . and now you want to go home on company time just to change clothes?! Listen, every person in that newsroom has a vital public service to perform and—
But I'm expecting a package at home, too! A bottle of Scotch from a friend abroad!
SCOTCH?!?
Grab your coats, everybody!! We're all going to a party at Mary's place!!
Gee, Mary sure has done a lot with this place!
I'll say! Er—what style of decorating would you call this "Early Saks Fifth Avenue"?
No . . . "Lord & Taylor Modern"!
Hi! I'm Chillus, Mary's bird-brained neighbor! I just stopped by for my weekly cameo spot so the audience can see how much common sense Mary has compared to my craziness!
Swell! She's in her room, compulsively changing her clothes for the fourth time since the show began—and you think YOU'RE loony!
But I follow the advice of far out psychology books to raise my bratty child! How that for craziness?
Then get this! In real life, I won an Oscar this year for my dramatic ability, but I'm still wasting my talent on this crummy TV show!
Only so-so!
Now, that's what I call craziness!
Okay, gang! This is the weekly scene where I get to show off my legs!
Every dame around here is batty!
Don't be a prude, Mr. Grunt! Lots of girls wear tennis skirts that are that short!
In Minneapolis . . . in FEBRUARY?!?!

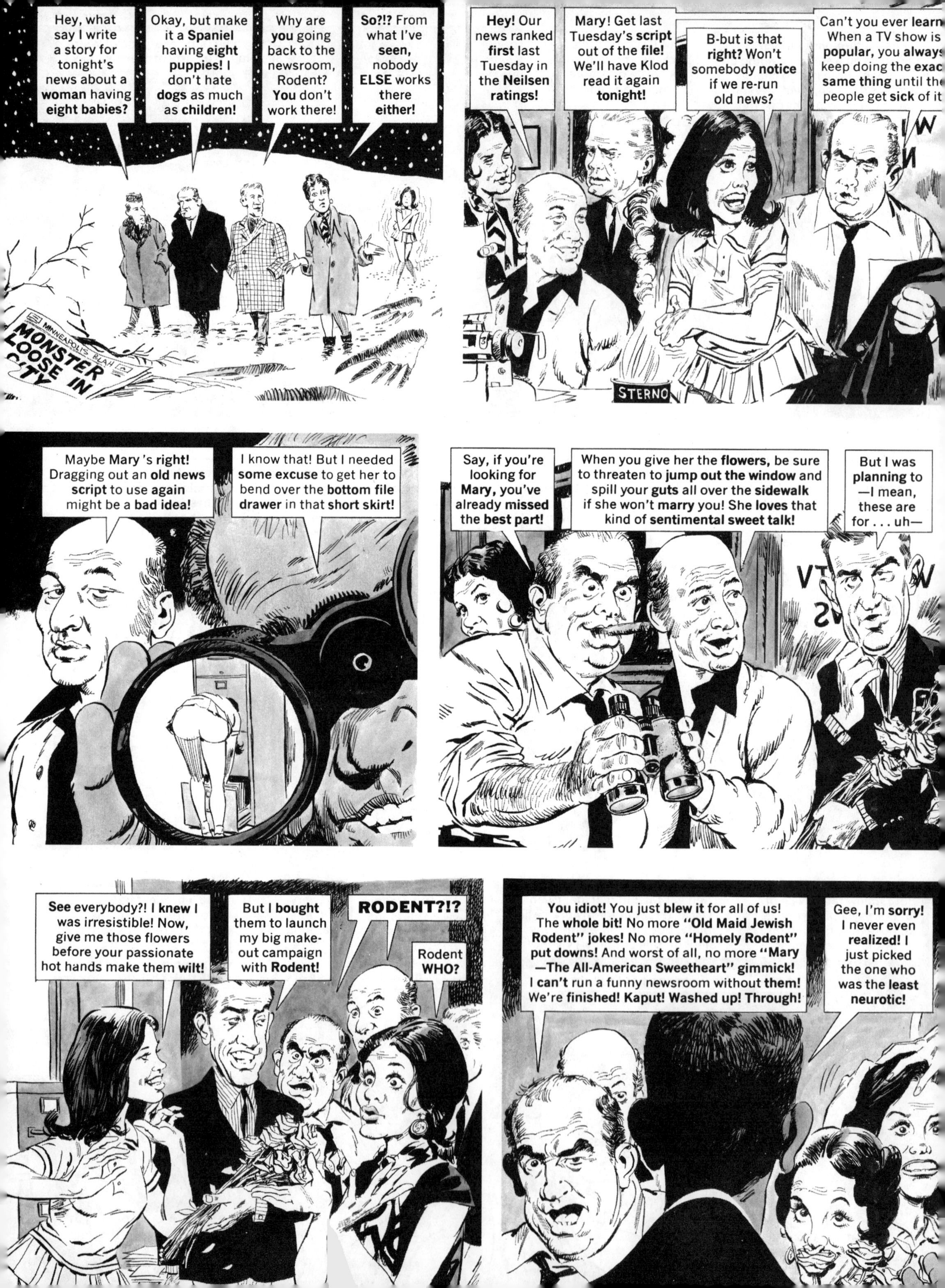
Hey, what say I write a story for tonight's news about a woman having eight babies?
Okay, but make it a Spaniel having eight puppies! I don't hate dogs as much as children!
Why are you going back to the newsroom, Rodent? You don't work there!
So?!? From what I've seen, nobody ELSE works there either!
MINNEAPOLIS BLAH
MONSTER LOOSE IN
Hey! Our news ranked first last Tuesday in the Neilsen ratings!
Mary! Get last Tuesday's script out of the file! We'll have Klod read it again tonight!
B-but is that right? Won't somebody notice if we re-run old news?
Can't you ever learn When a TV show is popular, you always keep doing the exac same thing until th people get sick of it
STERNO
Maybe Mary's right! Dragging out an old news script to use again might be a bad idea!
I know that! But I needed some excuse to get her to bend over the bottom file drawer in that short skirt!
Say, if you're looking for Mary, you've already missed the best part!
When you give her the flowers, be sure to threaten to jump out the window and spill your guts all over the sidewalk if she won't marry you! She loves that kind of sentimental sweet talk!
But I was planning to —I mean, these are for . . . uh—
See everybody?! I knew I was irresistible! Now, give me those flowers before your passionate hot hands make them wilt!
But I bought them to launch my big make-out campaign with Rodent!
RODENT?!?
Rodent WHO?
You idiot! You just blew it for all of us! The whole bit! No more "Old Maid Jewish Rodent" jokes! No more "Homely Rodent" put downs! And worst of all, no more "Mary—The All-American Sweetheart" gimmick! I can't run a funny newsroom without them! We're finished! Kaput! Washed up! Through!
Gee, I'm sorry! I never even realized! I just picked the one who was the least neurotic!

JOKE AND DAGGER DEPT.

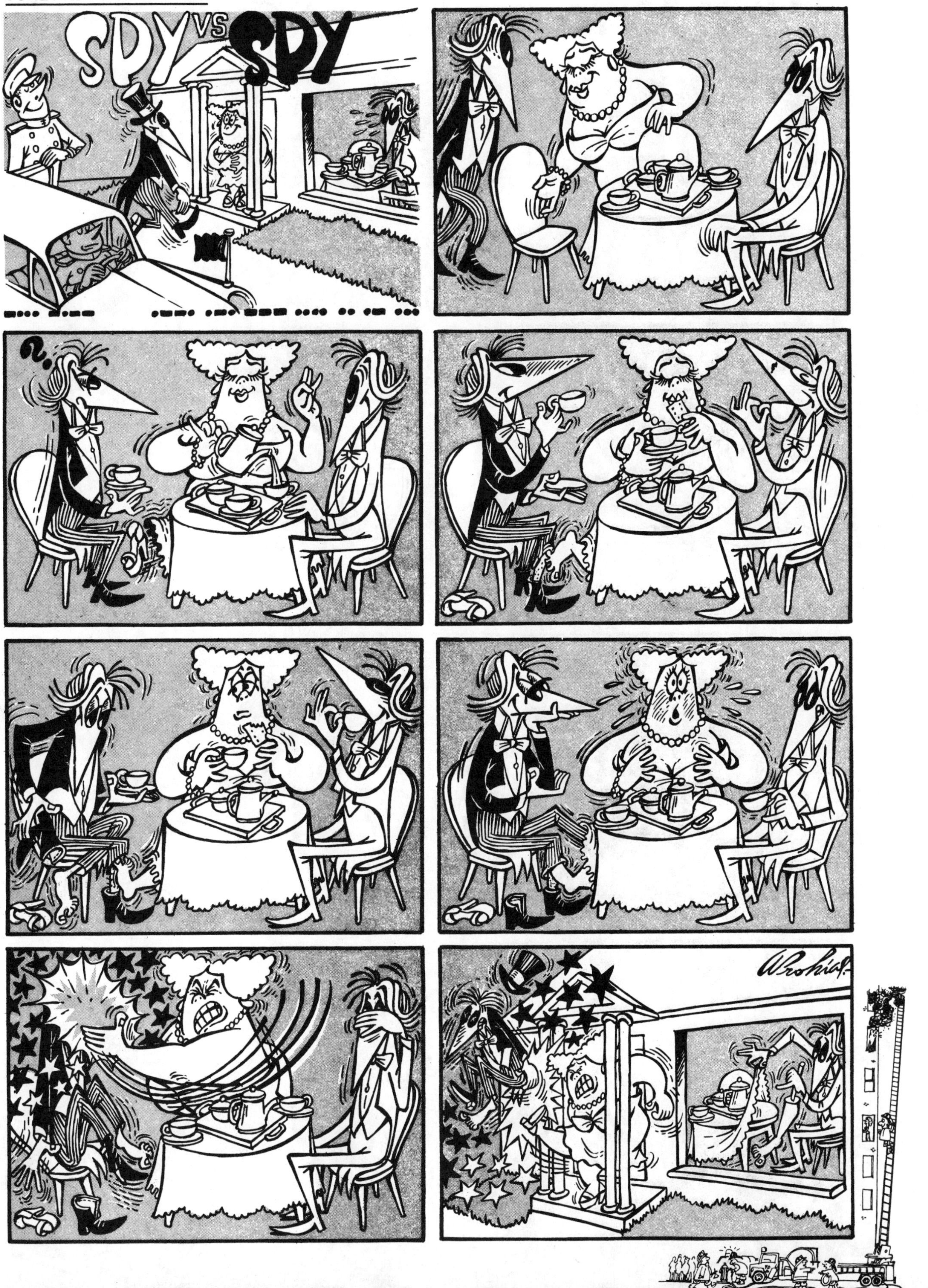
SPY vs SPY

WE GOT YOUR PENUMBRA DEPT.

Who Knows What Evils Lurk I

THE SHADOW

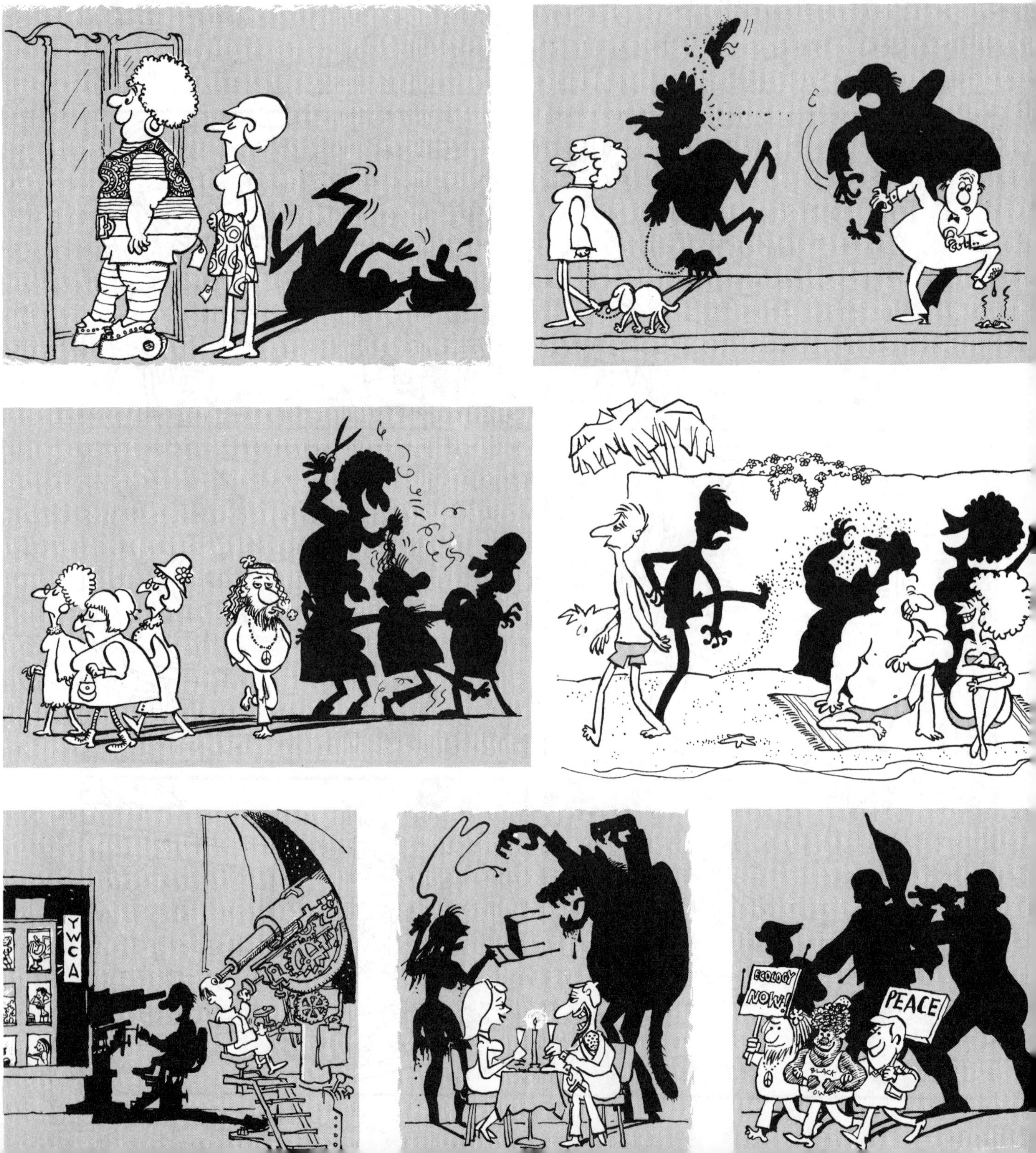
YWCA
ECOLOGY NOW!
PEACE

...he Hearts Of Men?

...KNOWS

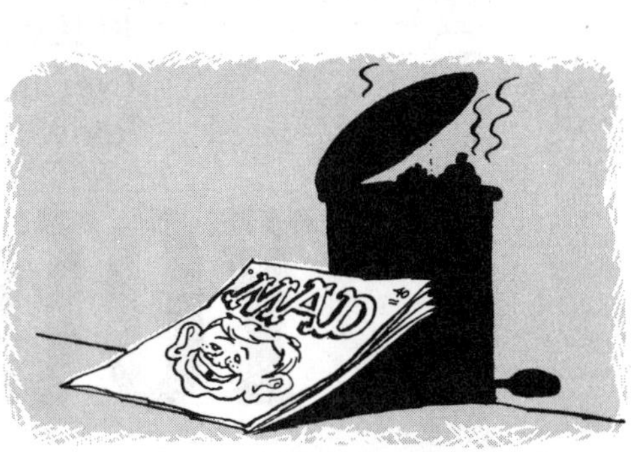
MAD

WRITER & ARTIST: SERGIO ARAGONES

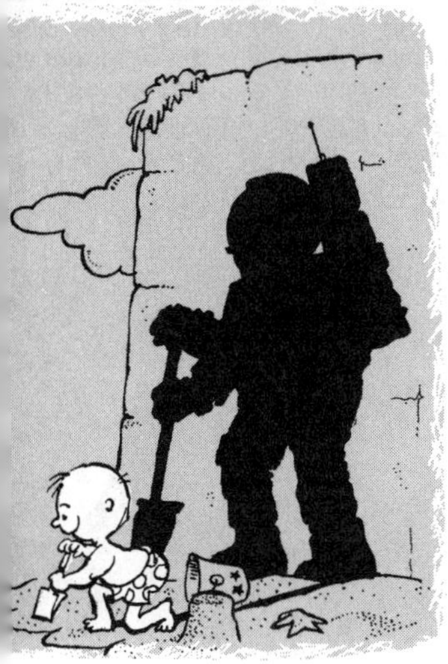

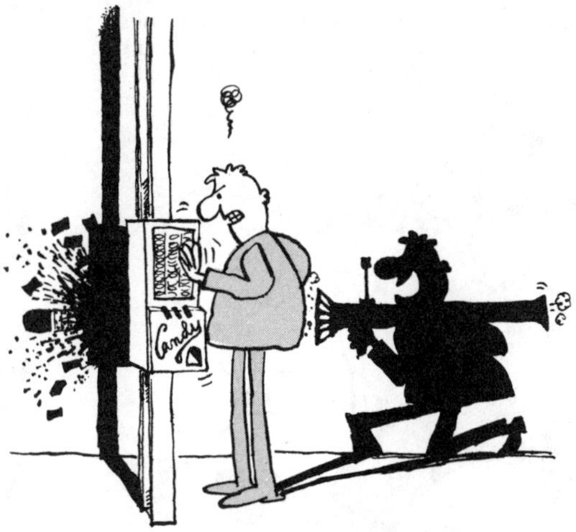
Candy

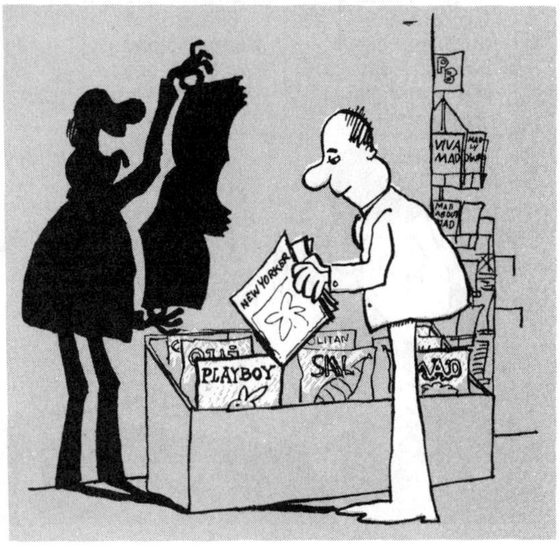
PB
VIVA MAD
NEW YORKER
PLAYBOY
SAL
MAD

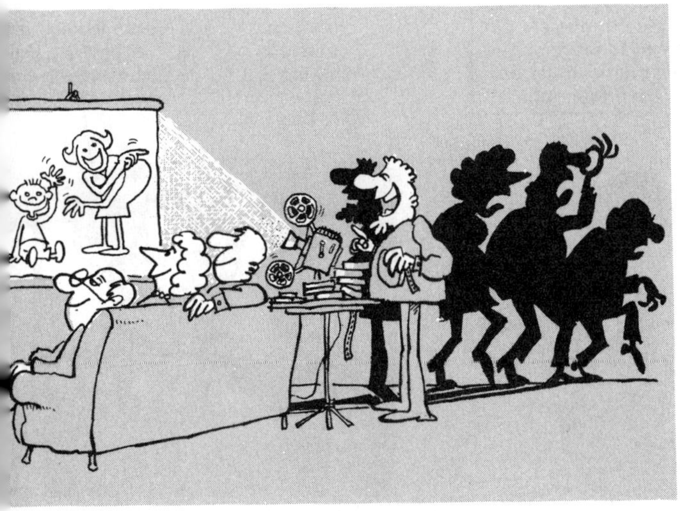

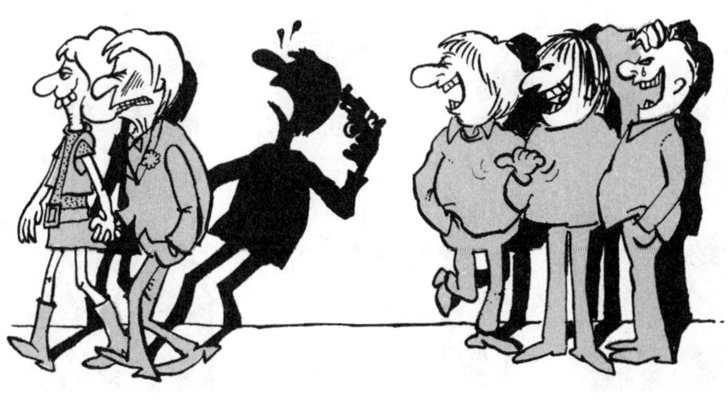

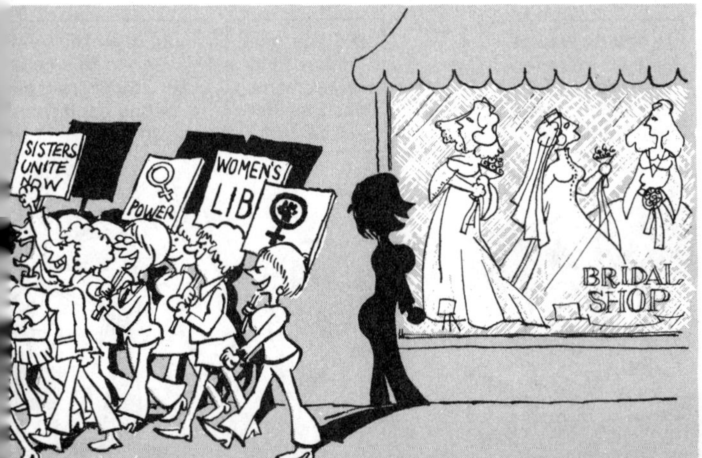
SISTERS UNITE NOW
POWER
WOMEN'S LIB
BRIDAL SHOP

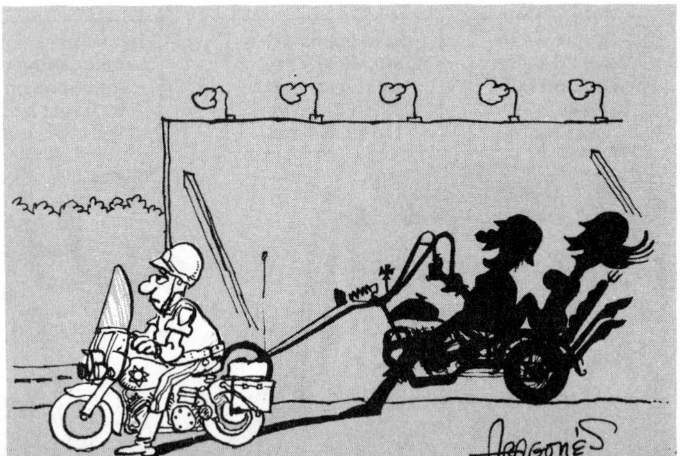
ARAGONÉS

IN THE IRE OF THE BEHOLDER DEPT.

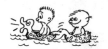

Ever meet a "Bigot"? Ever try to talk sense to him? If you have, then know it's a losing proposition. Because no matter what you say, he has

YOU NEVER CAN

ARTIST: PAUL COKER

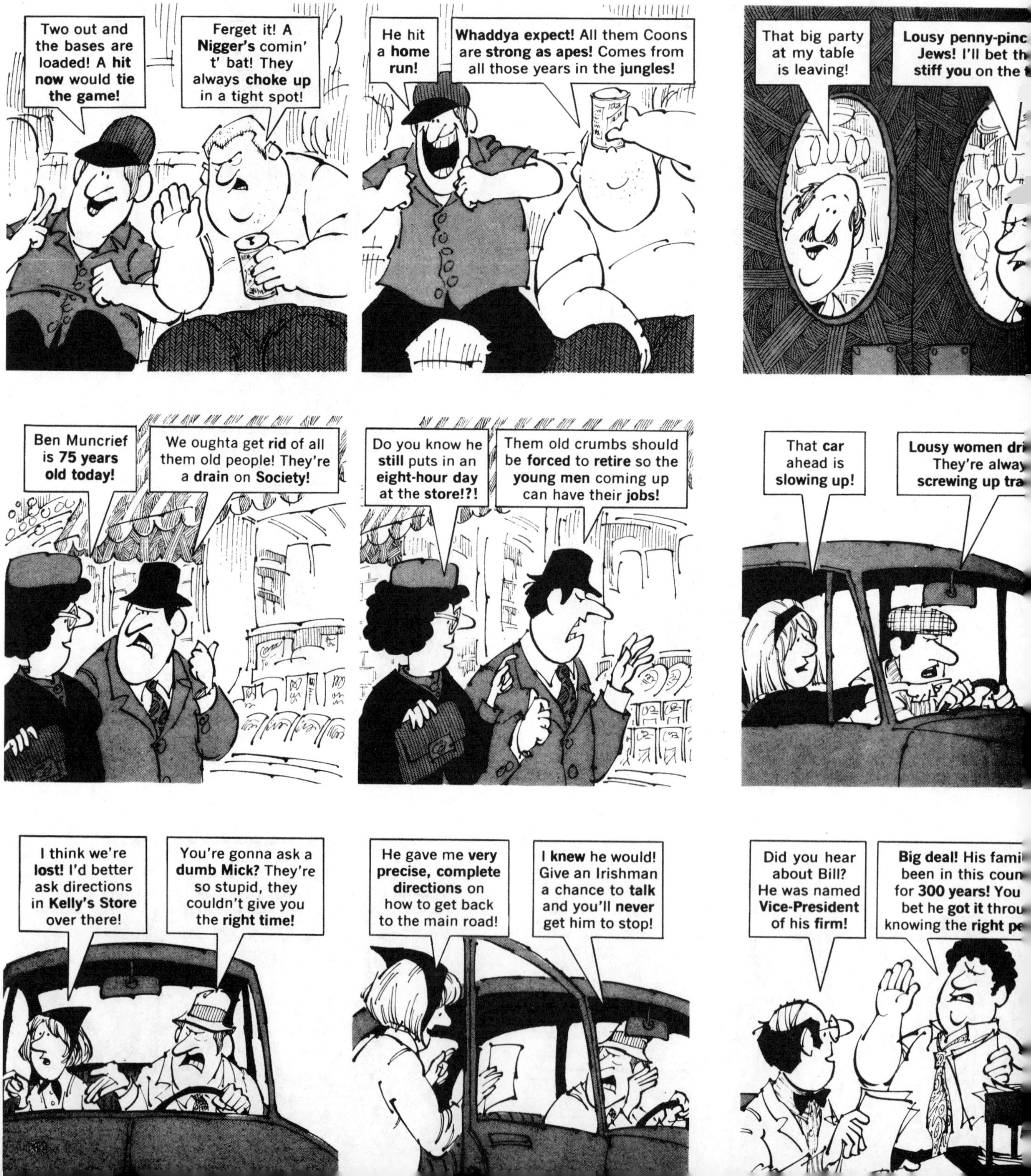

Two out and the bases are loaded! A hit now would tie the game!
Ferget it! A Nigger's comin' t' bat! They always choke up in a tight spot!
He hit a home run!
Whaddya expect! All them Coons are strong as apes! Comes from all those years in the jungles!
That big party at my table is leaving!
Lousy penny-pinc Jews! I'll bet th stiff you on the
Ben Muncrief is 75 years old today!
We oughta get rid of all them old people! They're a drain on Society!
Do you know he still puts in an eight-hour day at the store!?!
Them old crumbs should be forced to retire so the young men coming up can have their jobs!
That car ahead is slowing up!
Lousy women dri They're alway screwing up tra
I think we're lost! I'd better ask directions in Kelly's Store over there!
You're gonna ask a dumb Mick? They're so stupid, they couldn't give you the right time!
He gave me very precise, complete directions on how to get back to the main road!
I knew he would! Give an Irishman a chance to talk and you'll never get him to stop!
Did you hear about Bill? He was named Vice-President of his firm!
Big deal! His fami been in this coun for 300 years! You bet he got it throu knowing the right pe

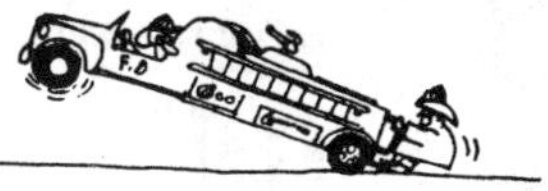

ver that supports his warped point of view. If you don't believe it, then
reading the following examples which clearly demonstrate exactly why...

N WITH A BIGOT!

TER: FRANK JACOBS

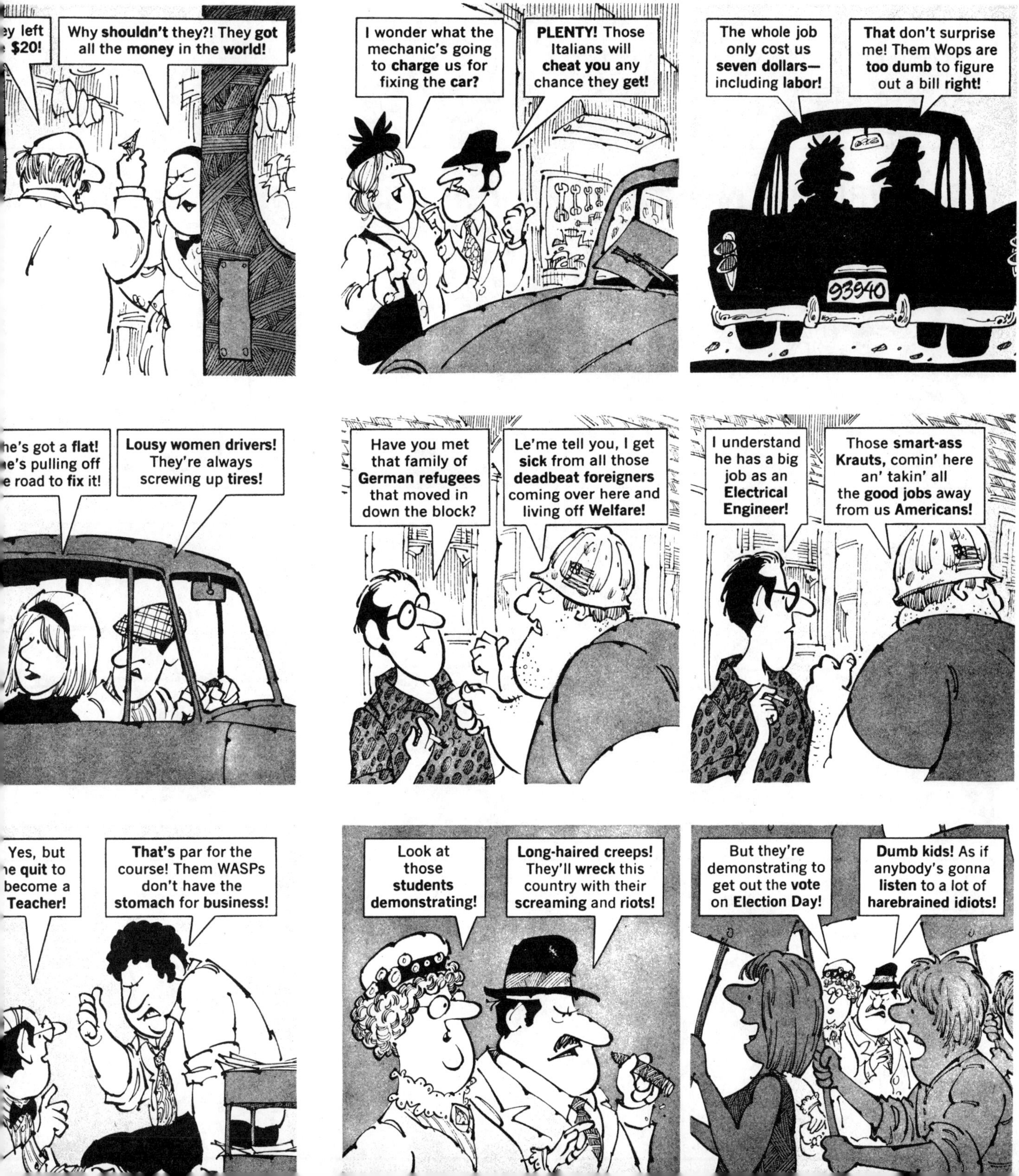

ey left
$20!
Why shouldn't they?! They got all the money in the world!
I wonder what the mechanic's going to charge us for fixing the car?
PLENTY! Those Italians will cheat you any chance they get!
The whole job only cost us seven dollars— including labor!
That don't surprise me! Them Wops are too dumb to figure out a bill right!
93940
he's got a flat!
e's pulling off
e road to fix it!
Lousy women drivers! They're always screwing up tires!
Have you met that family of German refugees that moved in down the block?
Le'me tell you, I get sick from all those deadbeat foreigners coming over here and living off Welfare!
I understand he has a big job as an Electrical Engineer!
Those smart-ass Krauts, comin' here an' takin' all the good jobs away from us Americans!
Yes, but
e quit to
become a
Teacher!
That's par for the course! Them WASPs don't have the stomach for business!
Look at those students demonstrating!
Long-haired creeps! They'll wreck this country with their screaming and riots!
But they're demonstrating to get out the vote on Election Day!
Dumb kids! As if anybody's gonna listen to a lot of harebrained idiots!

DON MARTIN DEPT. PART II

ONE DAY ON A TRANSCONTINENTAL JET

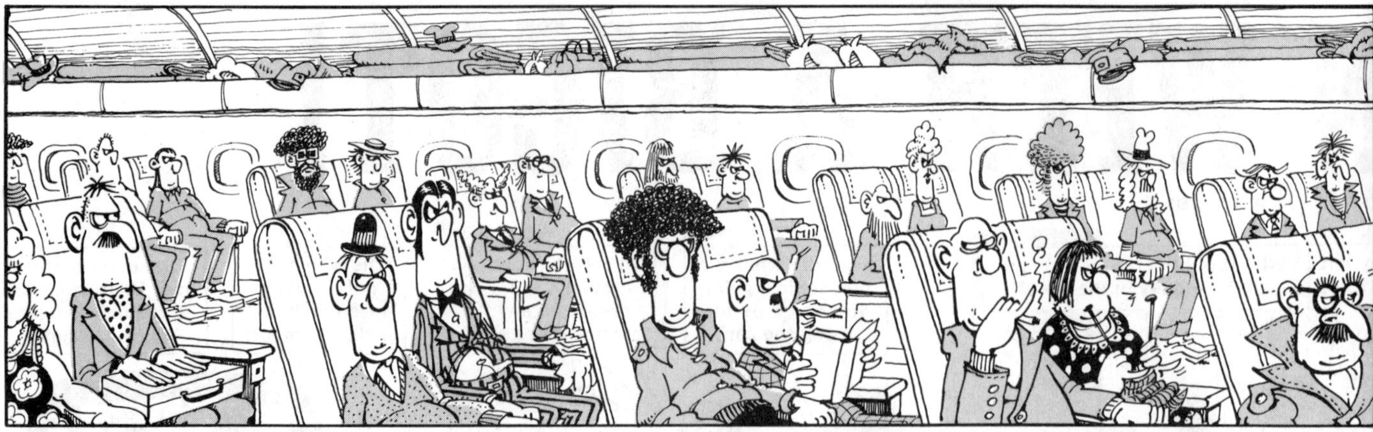

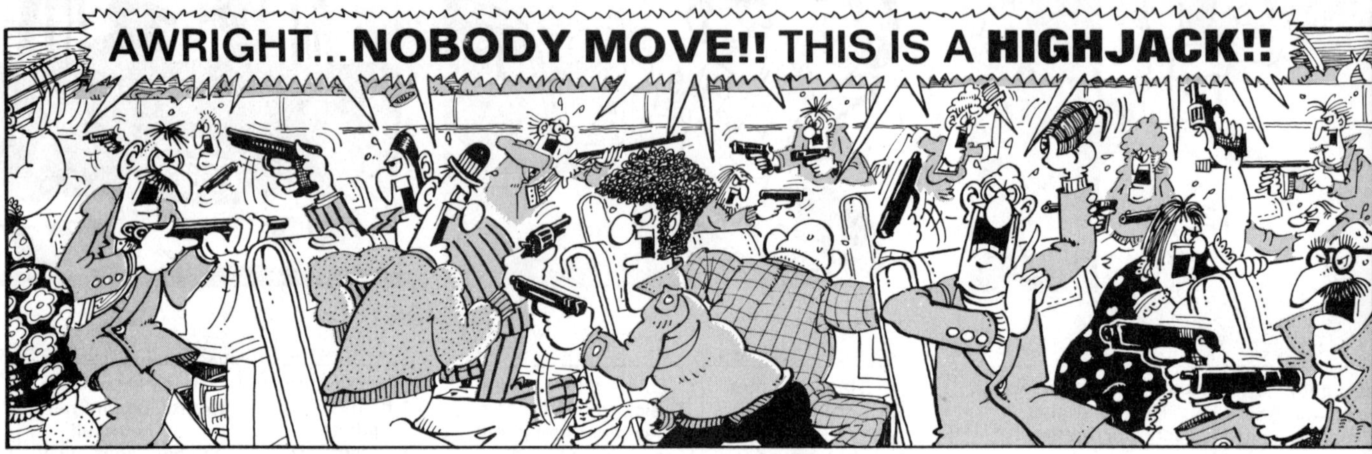
AWRIGHT...NOBODY MOVE!! THIS IS A HIGHJACK!!

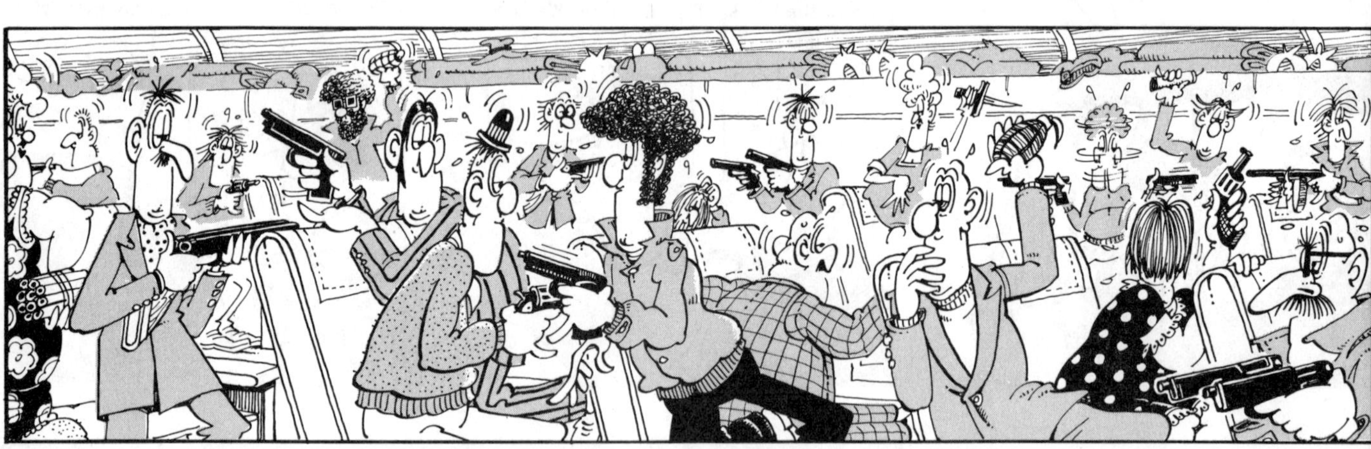

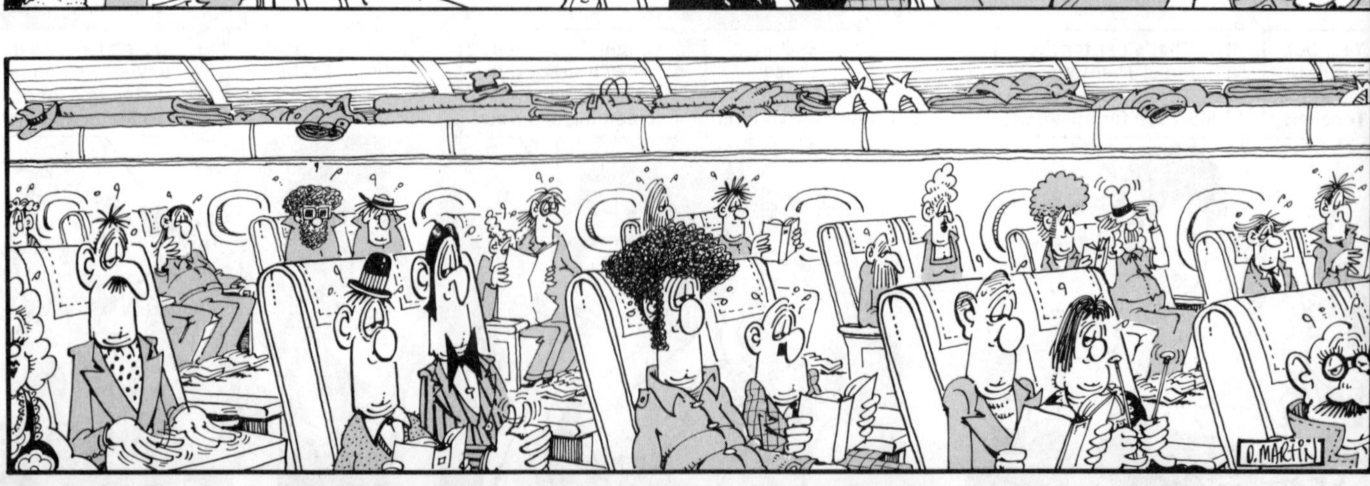
D. MARTIN

Early 1974: A botched burglary, dating back a year and a half, of the Democratic National Committee's office in Washington's Watergate apartment and office complex has since been linked to a chain of command that leads all the way to President Richard M. Nixon. Investigators have just determined that an eighteen-and-a-half-minute gap in the so-called Watergate tapes was a deliberate erasure. A severe gas crisis has led to long lines at the pump, with waits of up to six hours. An "odd-even" plan has been adopted in some states: drivers with odd-numbered license plates may purchase gas only on odd-numbered days, those with even-numbered plates on even-numbered days. The top three records on the pop charts are "You're Sixteen" by Ringo Starr, "Show and Tell" by Al Wilson, and "The Way We Were" by Barbra Streisand. And continuing to grin idiotically from America's newsstands is *MAD* cover boy, Alfred E. Neuman.

The cover of *MAD*'s 166th issue (April 1974), showing the traditional raised middle finger "salute," caused such controversy that letters of apology, signed by publisher Bill Gaines and editor Al Feldstein, had to be sent out to irate wholesalers, newsdealers, and readers.

"The Big Con" cover of issue #171 (December 1974, illustrated by Norman Mingo) juxtaposes Richard Nixon's and Spiro Agnew's political shenanigans with the characters played by Robert Redford and Paul Newman in the feature film *The Sting*. As a result of his being hopelessly entangled in the Watergate scandal and facing possible impeachment proceedings, Nixon resigned from the presidency on August 8, 1974, becoming the first president to do so. His exit was in line with Vice President Spiro Agnew's, who had previously left his office in disgrace on a charge of income tax evasion. Gerald Ford, whom Nixon had appointed as Vice President after Agnew's departure, assumed the office of president upon Nixon's resignation. The piece on "Our Floundering Fathers," illustrated by Jack Rickard and written by Al Jaffee, is yet another jab at Richard Nixon. Curiously, *MAD* did no satires aimed directly at the Watergate debacle itself; Watergate was so much a part of the zeitgeist of the early seventies that little setup was needed to place a satirical piece in the context of the scandal. *MAD*'s Watergate-related pieces were aimed slightly to one side or the other, hitting on the character flaws of Nixon and his cronies rather than the actual facts of the Watergate break-in and subsequent cover-up.

The United States celebrated its bicentennial in 1976, and *MAD* commemorated the occasion with the cover of issue #181 (March 1976), showing a rather unusually rendered visage of George Washington (actually done by Norman Mingo, but unsigned so as not to interfere with the cover's gag).

The "rabbit out of a hat" cover of issue #182 (April 1976) was painted by successful illustrator and advertising artist Bob Jones. It was Jones who had rendered the original Esso "Tiger in My Tank" ads some ten years before, an ad campaign that *MAD* parodied at the time with "I Just Put a Gas Station Attendant in <u>My</u> Tank!" (collected in *MAD About the Sixties*).

Movie- and TV-related covers in this section include *MAD* "tributes" to *Jaws* (#180, January 1976), *Star Trek* (#186, October 1976), and *Happy Days* (#187, December 1976). The *Jaws* parody cover was painted for *MAD* by the artist responsible for the original one-sheet theatrical poster for the film, Morton Kuntzler (who signed the *MAD* piece with the pseudonym "Mutz" so as not to harm his professional reputation).

Women's Liberation was a relatively new and hot topic in the seventies; two one-pagers on the subject are in this section: "Ms. Liberty," with another pseudonymous painting by Morton Kuntzler, and "<u>I</u> Want, Too," a beautifully rendered Norman Mingo send-up of the original James Montgomery Flagg Army recruitment poster. Oddly enough, there is a *MAD* connection even to the Women's Liberation movement: on the editorial staff of original *MAD* creator Harvey Kurtzman's early sixties humor magazine *HELP!* was a pre-feminist Gloria Steinem.

"The Modern-Day Carpetbaggers" is a comment on the OPEC nations' embargo on selling oil to the U.S., which resulted in the gas crisis. *MAD* staffers appearing in costume as the Arab carpetbaggers are editor Nick Meglin, art director Lenny Brenner, and sometime *MAD* artist/writer Arnoldo Franchioni. It is worth noting that by the seventies *MAD* was doing fewer and fewer parodies of Madison Avenue's advertising campaigns, running instead either humorous pieces that also made political and/or social statements (like the aforementioned "Ms. Liberty" or "The Modern-Day Carpetbaggers") or straight gag-driven material (like the "Pinocchio/Scenes We'd Like to See" page by Jack Rickard and Don Edwing at the beginning of this section). The Madison Avenue takeoffs *MAD* did run, however, were no less biting: the "Let Your Fingers Do the Walk . . ." one-pager in this section takes the long-running Yellow Pages ad to its illogical (and gross-but-funny) conclusion.

"M*A*S*H*UGA" is *MAD*'s look at the TV version of *M*A*S*H*, the highly popular comedy series that ran on CBS from 1972 to 1983. Based on the Robert Altman film of the same name and set during the Korean war, *M*A*S*H* was rarely out of the top ten during its eleven-year run. The final episode, aired on February 28, 1983, was a national "event" and was seen by the largest single viewing audience in television history. "M*A*S*H*UGA," written by Stan Hart and drawn by Angelo Torres, appeared in issue #166 (April 1974) before the first of many cast changes on the show. The "Crapper John" character caricatures actor Wayne Rogers, who left the show in 1975, as did McLean Stevenson, shown here as "Col. Bleak."

Dave Berg's "The Lighter Side of . . ." was introduced in 1961 and rapidly became a readers' favorite. The "Lighter Side" in this section is a "Berg's eye view" of the energy crisis, which affected not only people's driving habits but also electricity use and coal-oil consumption for heating. As was typical by the seventies, Berg draws himself in the feature (in the panels at the bottom of the second page). Another readers' favorite, Don Martin, had by the seventies become as famous for his "sound effects" as he had for his drawing. The Martin-devised word "*THWAK*" in "One Day on a Tennis Court" is a particularly vivid example.

"American Confetti" spoofs *American Graffiti*, the second feature film by writer/director George Lucas. The film starred Ron Howard (who was best known at the time for his role as Opie on the *Andy Griffith Show*), Richard Dreyfuss (in an early role), and Harrison Ford, who would become a permanent member of Lucas's stable of preferred actors. "American Confetti" was written and drawn by two of *MAD*'s best film parodists, Larry Siegel and Mort Drucker. Siegel's surprise ending to the parody is nothing less than brilliant. Drucker had a strong connection to the piece from the outset, for he had illustrated the one-sheet movie poster for *American Graffiti*'s original theatrical release. Other

movie parodies in this section by the crack Siegel/Drucker team include "The Ecchorcist" (spoofing William Peter Blatty's screen adaptation of his book *The Exorcist*), "Jaw'd" (parodying director Steven Spielberg's first monster hit — so to speak — *Jaws*), and "Gall of the President's Men" (taking off on the film version of Bob Woodward and Carl Bernstein's book *All the President's Men*, starring Dustin Hoffman and Robert Redford).

Sprinkled throughout this book are prime examples of the long-running "SPY vs SPY" feature, created and drawn by Cuban-born artist Antonio Prohias. The pieces selected for inclusion here not only represent funny gags, but are also beautifully rendered examples that showcase Prohias's formidable talents as a cartoon stylist.

"Crappy Days" is, of course, *MAD*'s version of the hit TV sitcom *Happy Days*. The *Happy Days* series was inspired by (but not based upon) George Lucas's *American Graffiti*; actor Ron Howard appears and plays a similar role in both. The series was originally designed to be a starring vehicle for Howard, but the Fonzie character (played by Henry Winkler) quickly became the breakout star of the show. At the show's height of popularity, Winkler was getting thousands of fan letters a day. In 1980, no less than the Smithsonian Institution announced that it had acquired the Fonz's leather jacket for permanent display. *MAD*'s version, expertly realized by artist Angelo Torres and writer Arnie Kogen, deals with just this shift of star power on the show — replete with a *MAD* twist ending, naturally.

"One Cuckoo Flew Over the Rest" is *MAD*'s send-up of *One Flew Over the Cuckoo's Nest*, the film version of the book written by a pre-Merry Pranksters Ken Kesey. The film starred Jack Nicholson, who by the mid-seventies had become a ubiquitous film actor. *Cuckoo's Nest*'s kooky-looking cast of actors and its insane asylum setting provided unusually ample subject matter for Mort Drucker to caricature and for Dick DeBartolo to satirize. Consequently, Drucker and DeBartolo's version of this offbeat film remains a high point among *MAD*'s film spoofs.

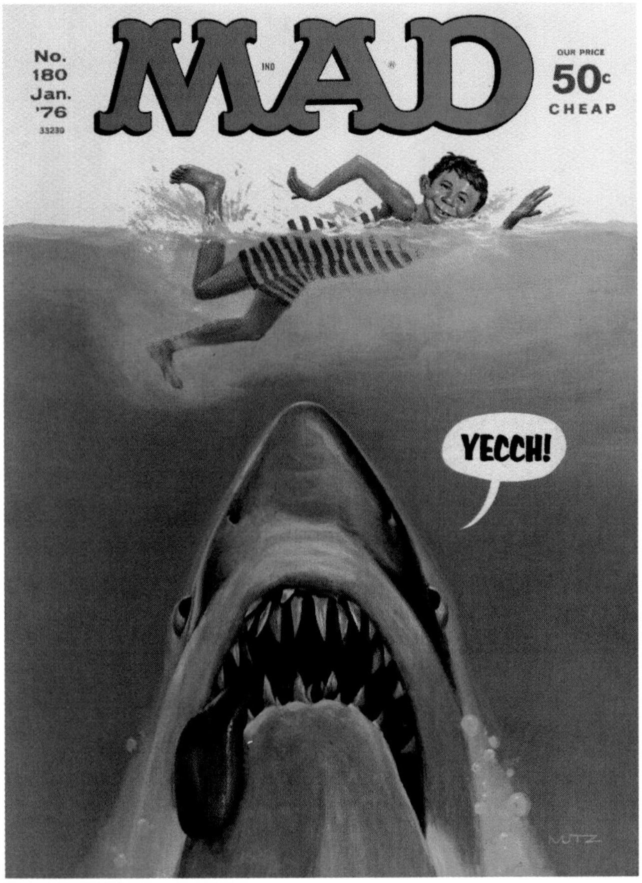
No.
180
Jan.
'76
33230
MAD
OUR PRICE
50c
CHEAP
YECCH!

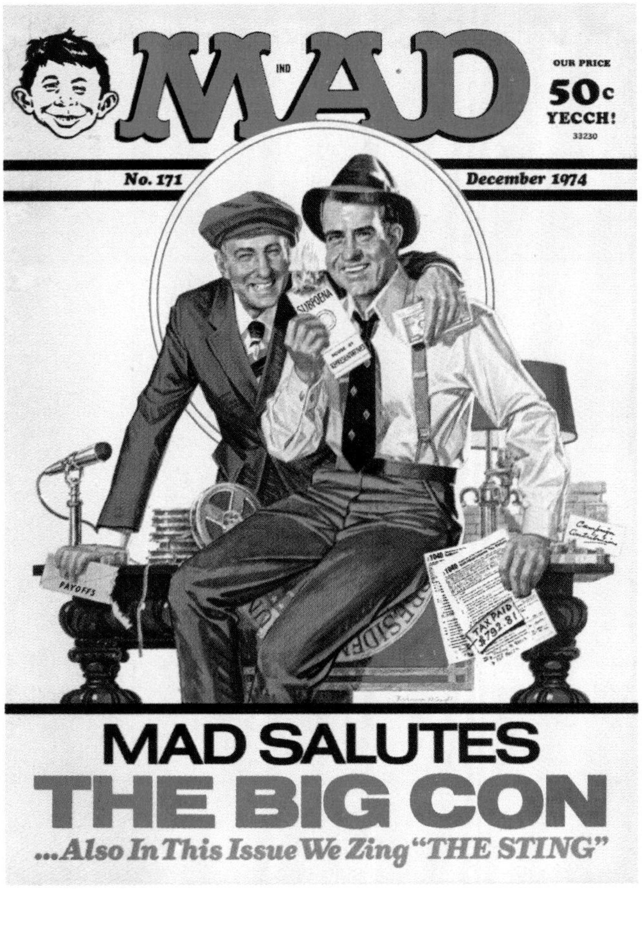
MAD
OUR PRICE
50c
YECCH!
33230
No. 171
December 1974
SUBPOENA
PAYOFFS
TAX PAID
MAD SALUTES
THE BIG CON
...Also In This Issue We Zing "THE STING"

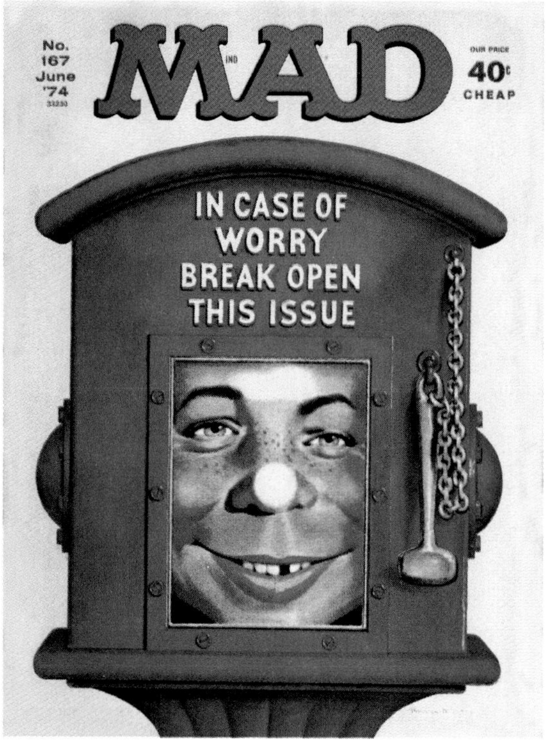
No.
167
June
'74
MAD
OUR PRICE
40¢
CHEAP
IN CASE OF
WORRY
BREAK OPEN
THIS ISSUE
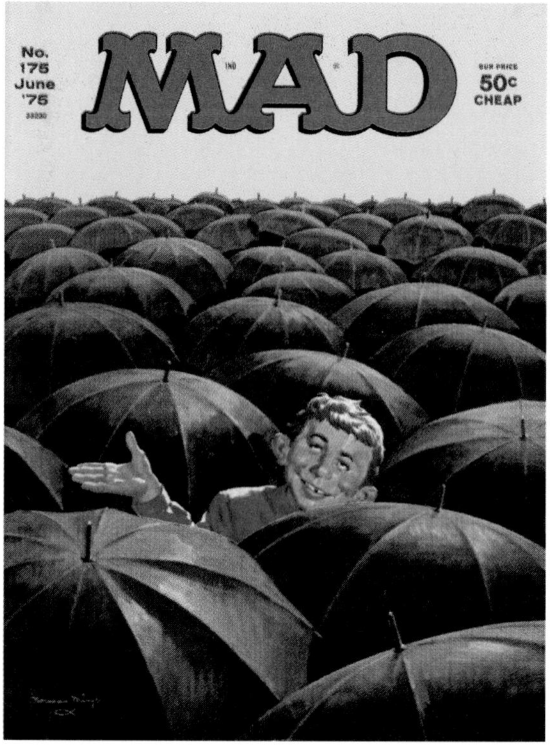
No.
175
June
'75
MAD
OUR PRICE
50¢
CHEAP
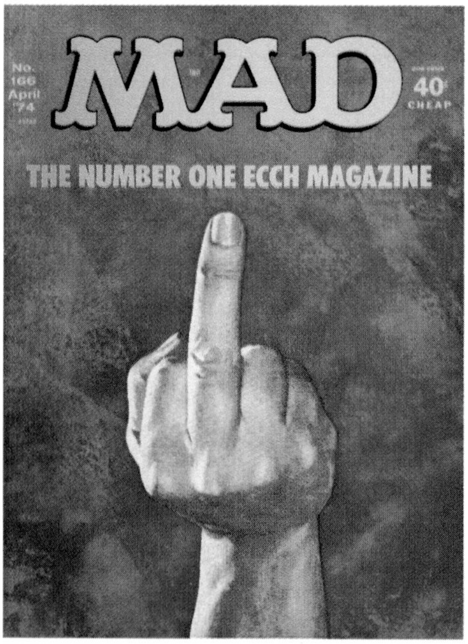
No.
166
April
'74
MAD
40¢
CHEAP
THE NUMBER ONE ECCH MAGAZINE
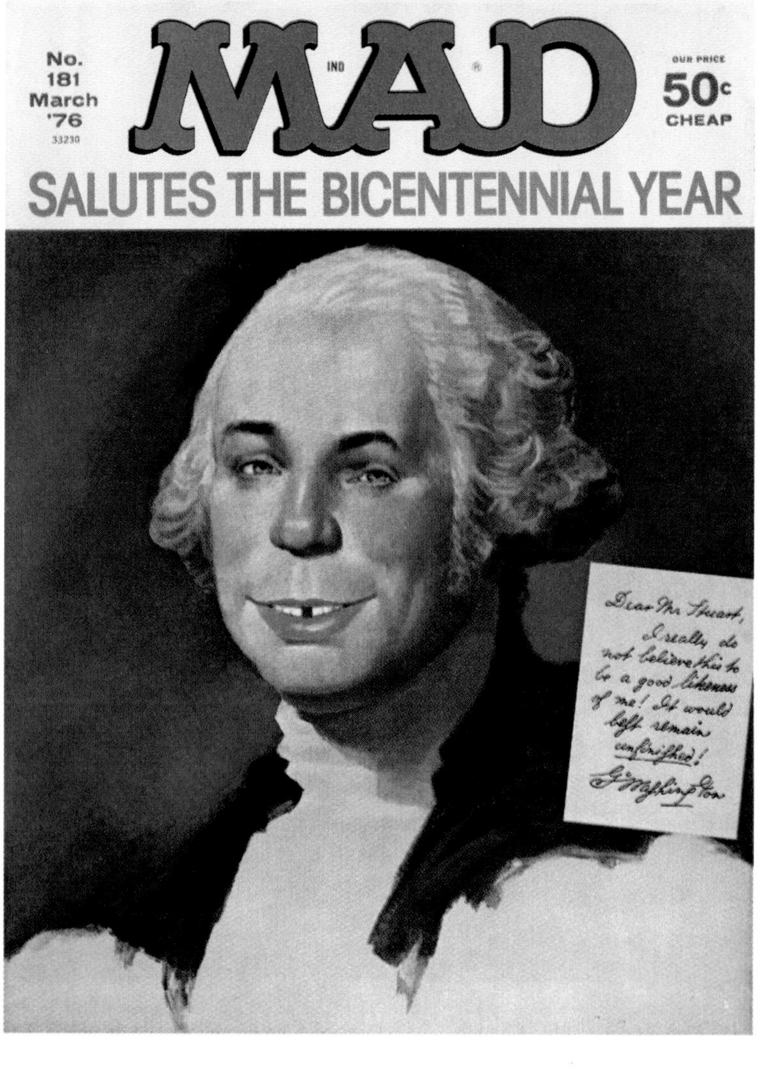
No.
181
March
'76
33230
MAD
OUR PRICE
50¢
CHEAP
SALUTES THE BICENTENNIAL YEAR
Dear Mr. Stuart,
I really do not believe this to be a good likeness of me! It would best remain unfinished!
G. Washington

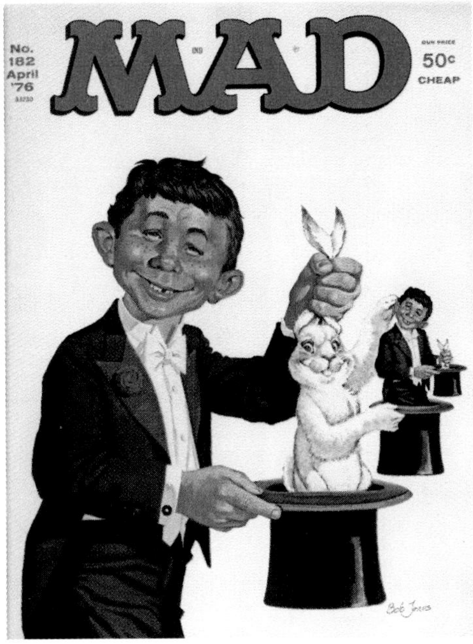
No. 182 April '76 33230
MAD
IND
OUR PRICE 50¢ CHEAP

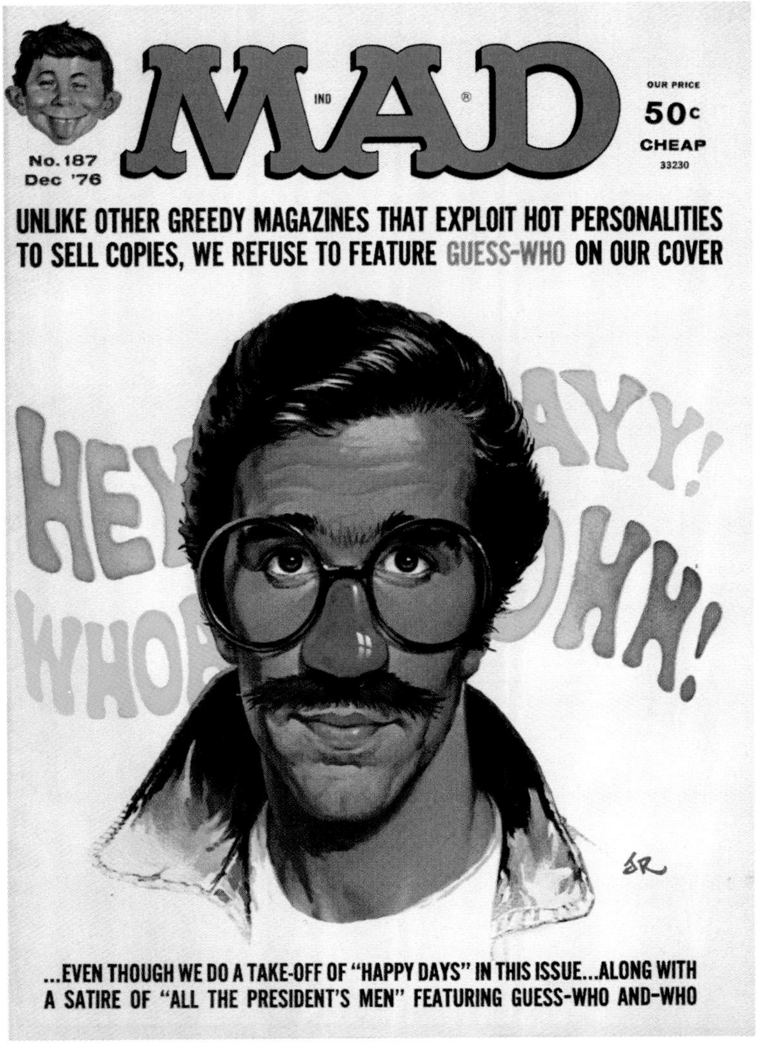
MAD
IND
No. 187 Dec '76
OUR PRICE 50¢ CHEAP 33230
UNLIKE OTHER GREEDY MAGAZINES THAT EXPLOIT HOT PERSONALITIES TO SELL COPIES, WE REFUSE TO FEATURE GUESS-WHO ON OUR COVER
...EVEN THOUGH WE DO A TAKE-OFF OF "HAPPY DAYS" IN THIS ISSUE...ALONG WITH A SATIRE OF "ALL THE PRESIDENT'S MEN" FEATURING GUESS-WHO AND-WHO

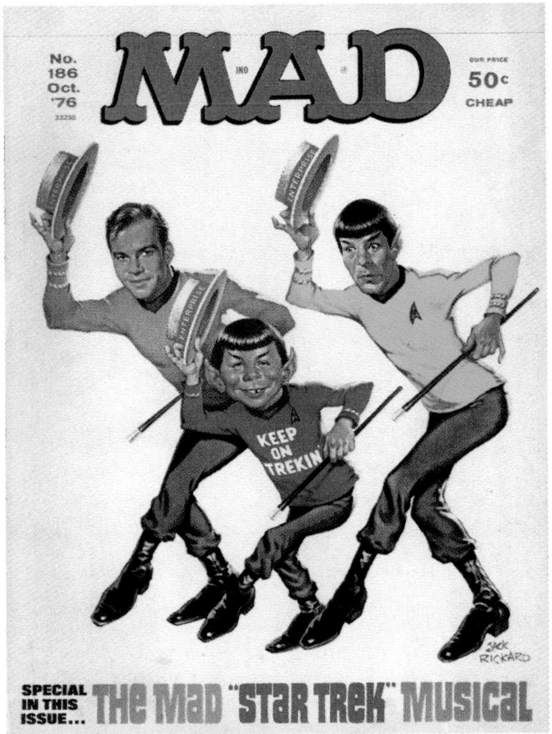
No. 186 Oct. '76 33230
MAD
IND
OUR PRICE 50¢ CHEAP
KEEP ON TREKIN
JACK RICKARD
SPECIAL IN THIS ISSUE... THE MAD "STAR TREK" MUSICAL

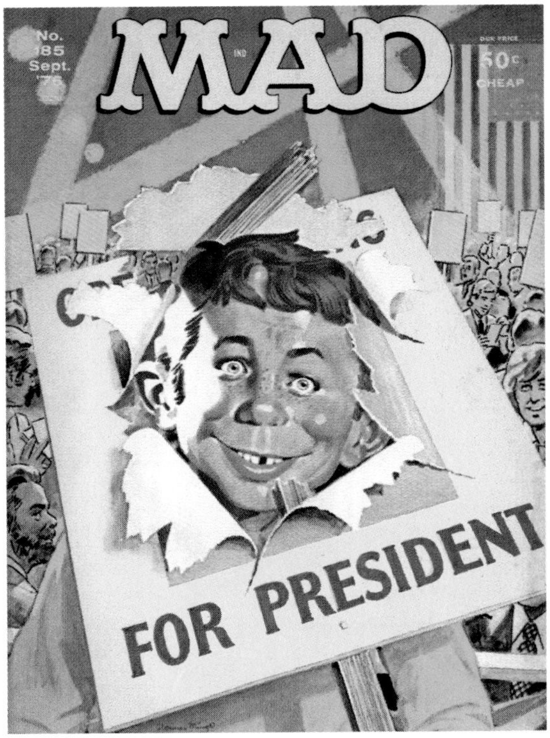
No. 185 Sept. '76
MAD
IND
OUR PRICE 50¢ CHEAP
FOR PRESIDENT

Scenes We'd Like To See

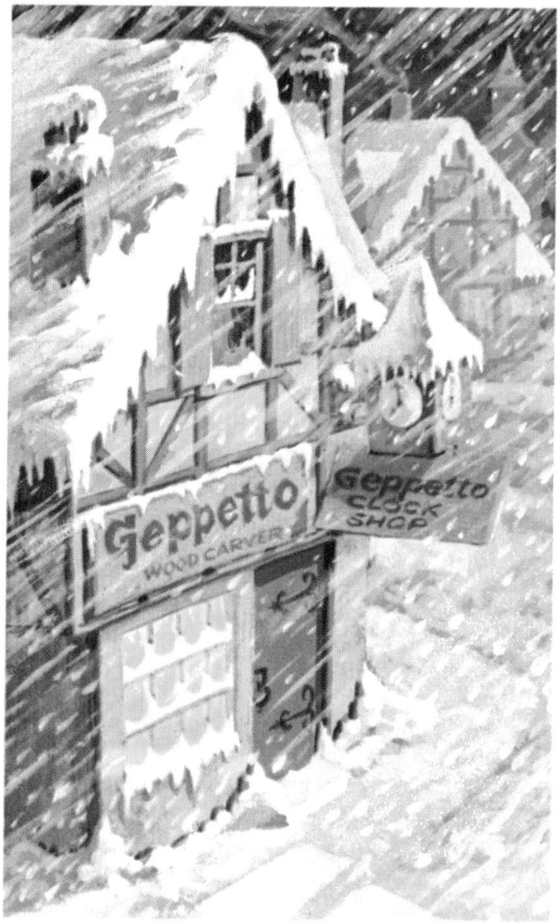
Geppetto
WOOD CARVER
Geppetto
CLOCK
SHOP

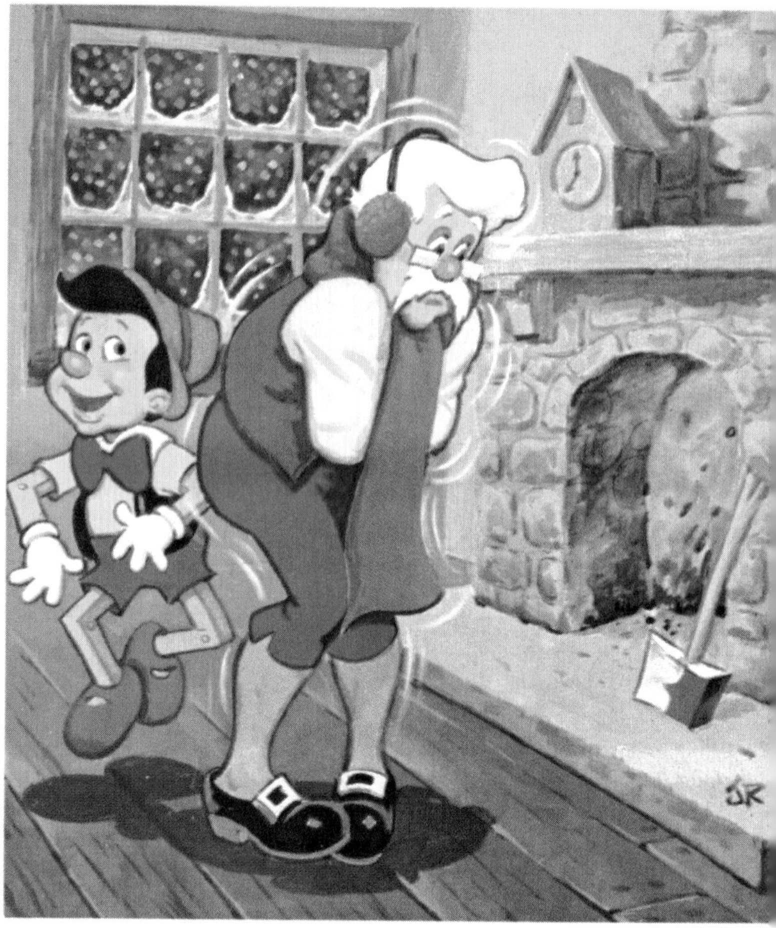

ARTIST: JACK RICKARD WRITER: DON EDWING

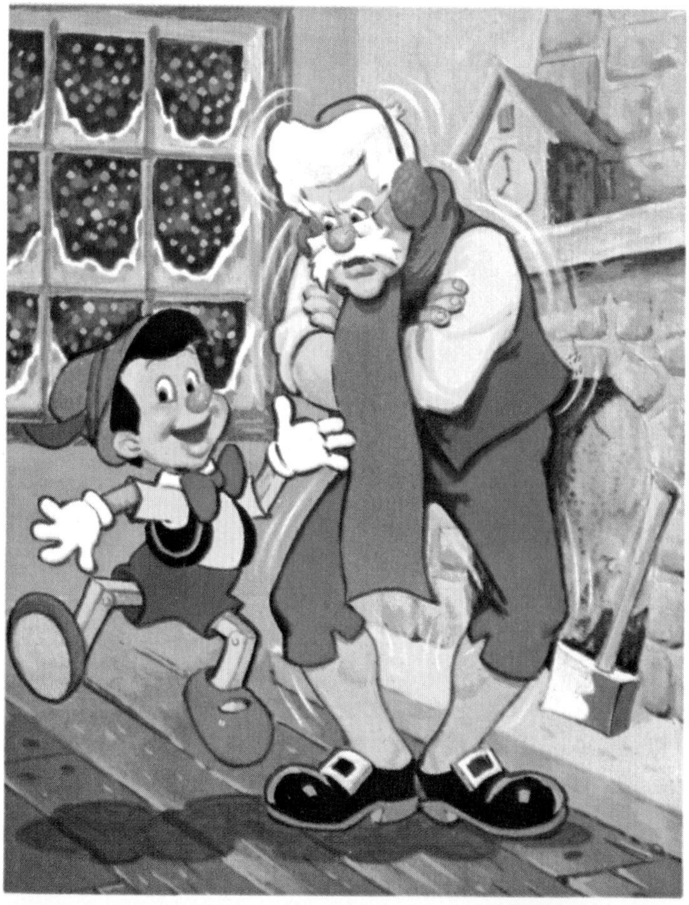

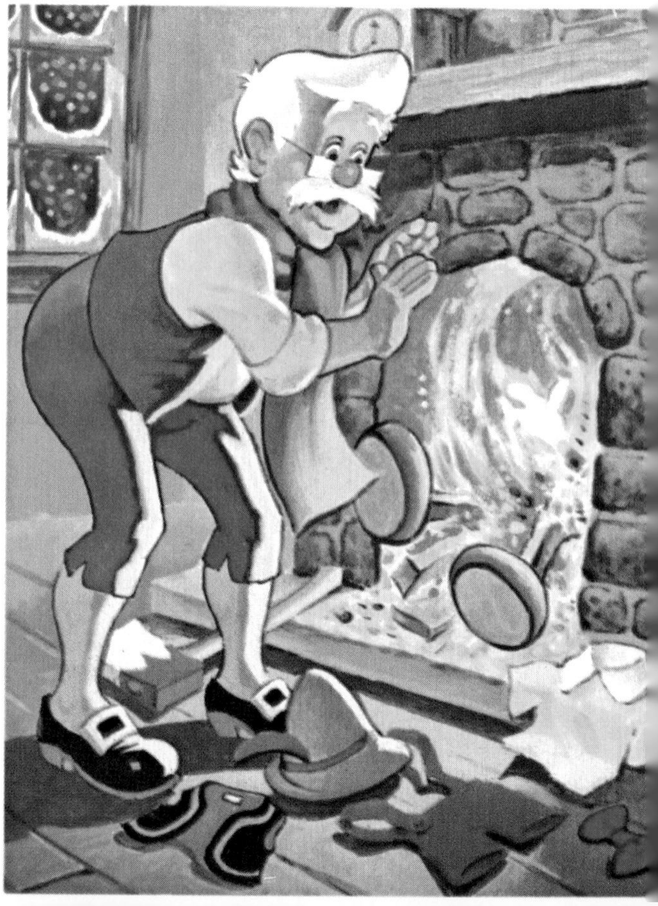

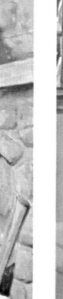

OUR FLOUNDERING FATHERS

"SCENES FROM CHILDHOOD" SERIES—No. 37

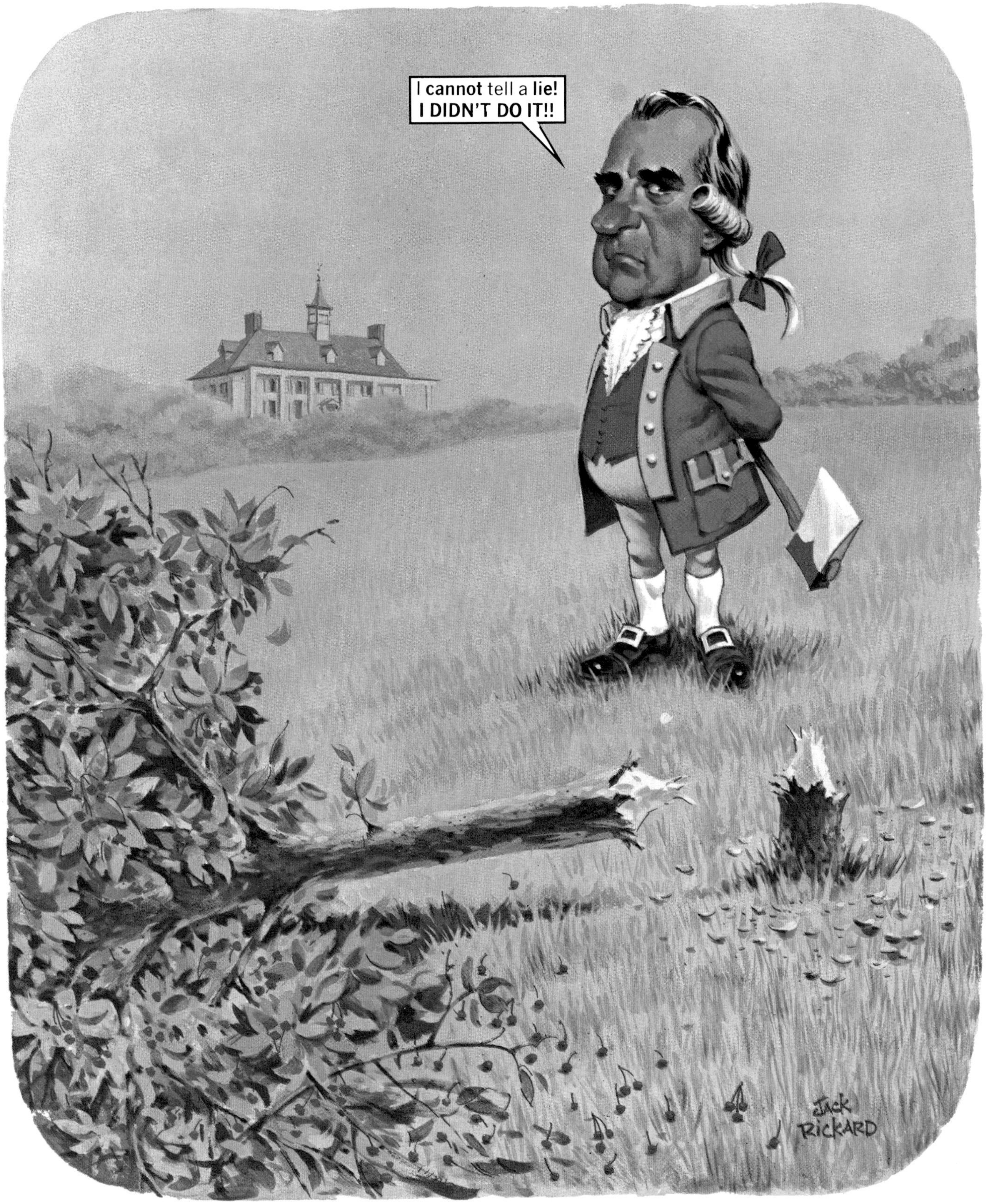

I cannot tell a lie!
I DIDN'T DO IT!!
JACK RICKARD

ARTIST: JACK RICKARD

ANOTHER MAD MOMENT FROM HISTORY

WRITER: AL JAFFEE

A MAD MEDICAL REPORT

NAME: Uncle Sam   **ADDRESS: U.S.A.**
AGE: 198   OCCUPATION: National Symbol

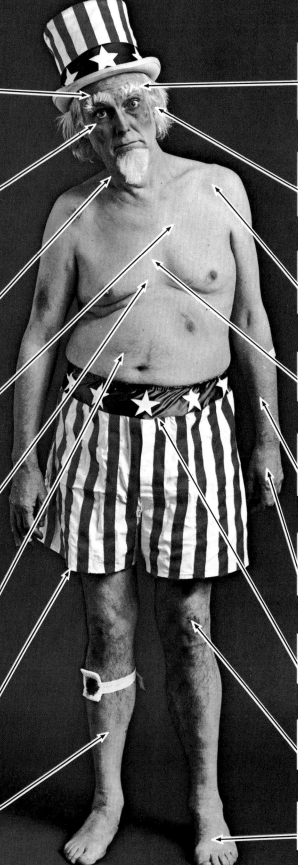

HEAD
Subject suffers chronic headaches of increasing drug abuses, rising crime and urban blight, worsened by the pressures of civil strife.

EYES
Fuzzy vision prevents the subject from focusing on his short-range problems. Also prevents subject from perceiving long-range goals.

NECK
Red in some areas, stiff in most, preventing subject from accepting good advice from his Right or Left.

HEART
Shrinking in size, and hardening, thus weakening his entire system. Fortunately, subject is blessed with a very strong Constitution.

LUNGS
Gasps and wheezes indicate subject is suffering from trade imbalance, as his intake exceeds his output.

STOMACH
Turned, by evidence of corruption and graft on all levels, resulting in occasional internal upheavals.

BUTTOCKS
Bruised and sore from kicks and beatings delivered by nations once considered to be subject's allies.

LEGS
Appear to be atrophied. Patient is unable to keep stride with rapid pace of his overseas competitors.

BRAIN
Signs of severe damage caused by corruption at the top. Possibility of a dangerous major stroke exists unless drastic surgery undertaken.

EARS
Apparent loss of hearing. Subject seems deaf to needs of the economy and pleas of the under-privileged.

SHOULDERS
Sagging from years of carrying the rest of the world. Now weakened to point of being unable to carry self.

CHEST
Partially caved in, indicating the possibility of a future depression.

MUSCLE
Severe deterioration and softening of muscle of subject is obvious, due to a lack of National Purpose.

HANDS
A creeping paralysis is apparent, preventing the subject from grasping his role in a changing world.

INTESTINAL TRACT
Clogged with bureaucratic waste, causing overall sluggish behavior.

KNEES
Fortunately, in good shape, since subject may be forced to his soon.

FEET
Arches collapsing. Feet unable to bear weight of over-inflated body.

WHAT SIMPLE PASTIME IS [F]AST BECOMING [A] LUXURY THAT [M]ANY AMERICANS [C]AN NO LONGER AFFORD?

HERE WE GO WITH ANOTHER RIDICULOUS

MAD FOLD-IN

The United States is one of the most beautiful and bountiful nations on earth. And yet, the way the cost of living is climbing, there are a lot of simple pleasures that many Americans will have to start doing without. To discover one popular pastime that is quickly becoming impossibly expensive, fold in page as shown.

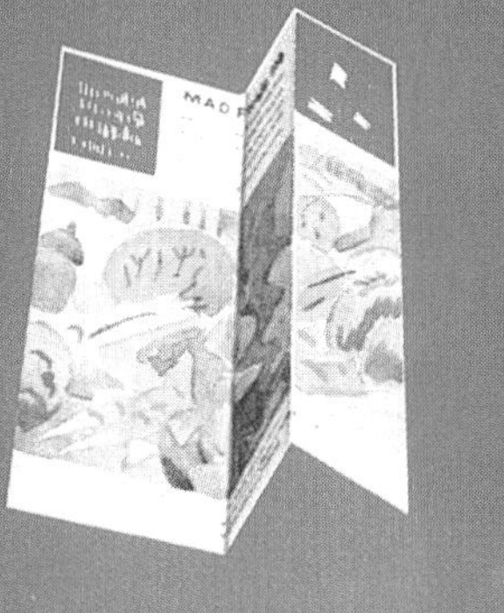

MAD

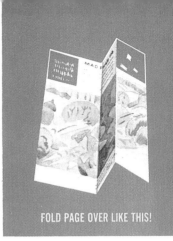

FOLD PAGE OVER LIKE THIS!

A▶ FOLD THIS SECTION OVER LEFT ◀B FOLD BACK SO "A" MEETS "B"

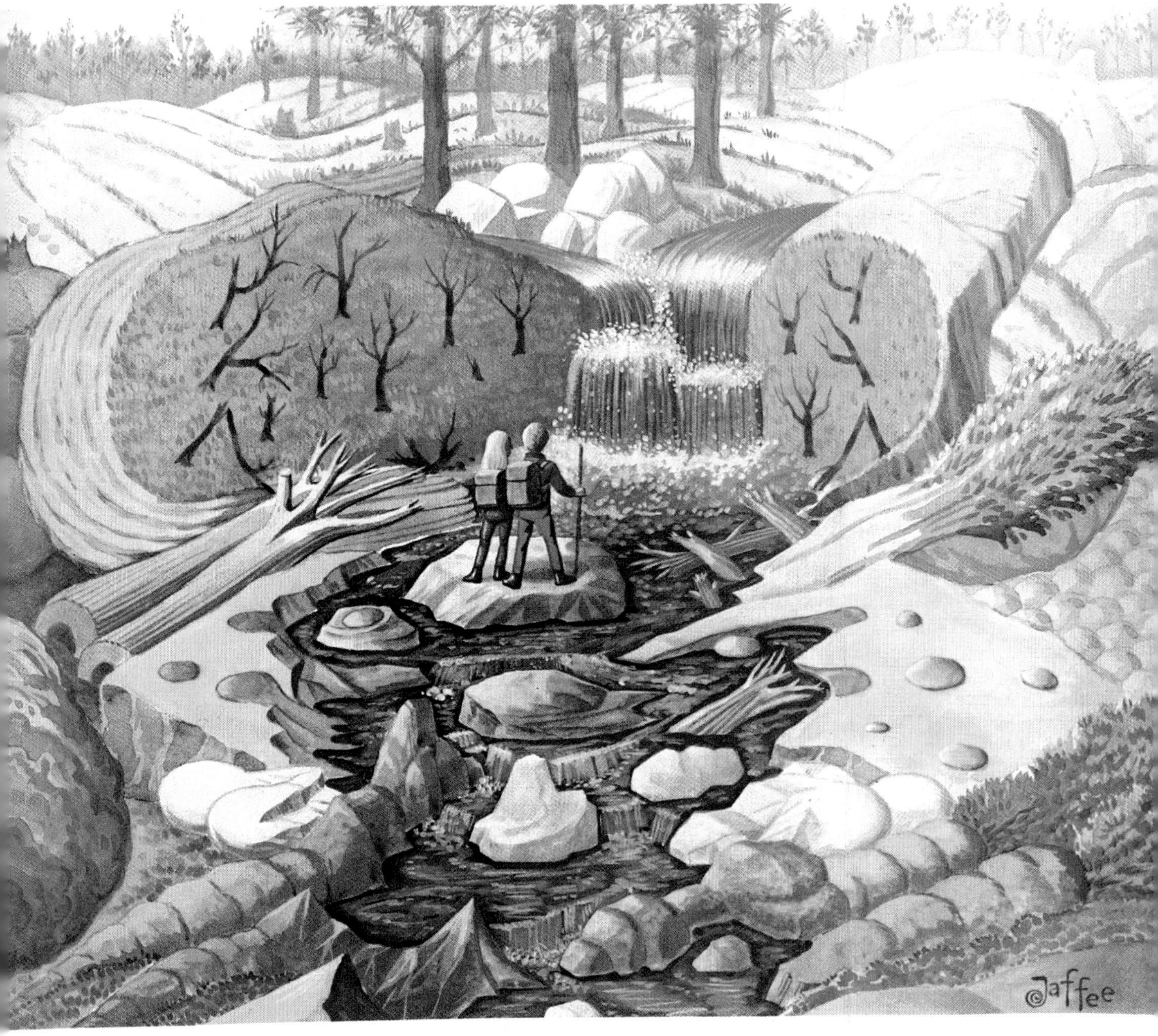

Jaffee

AMERICA AFFORDS MANY DIVERSE PLEASURES TO EACH CITIZEN. BUT INCREASING COSTS ARE STARTING TO MAKE SOME LUXURIES IMPOSSIBLE TO ENJOY

[A]RTIST & WRITER:
AL JAFFEE

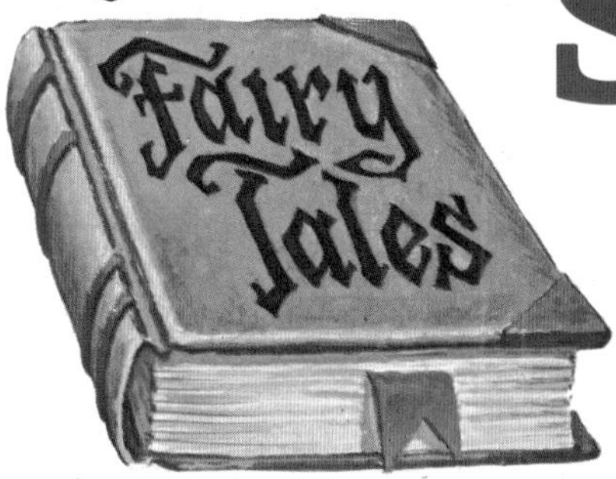
Fairy Tales

MORE SCENES WE'D LIKE TO SEE

(THE FROG PRINCE)

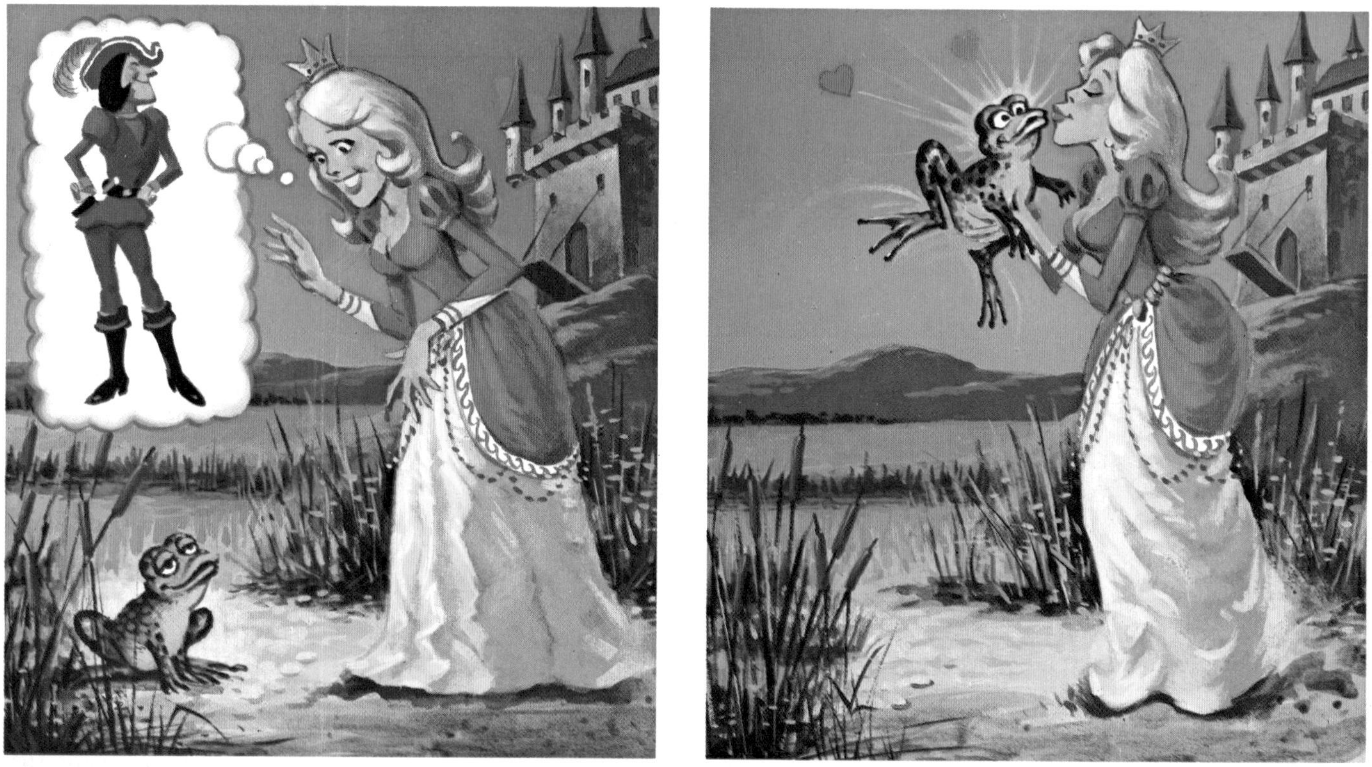

ARTIST: JACK RICKARD WRITER: SERGIO ARAGONES

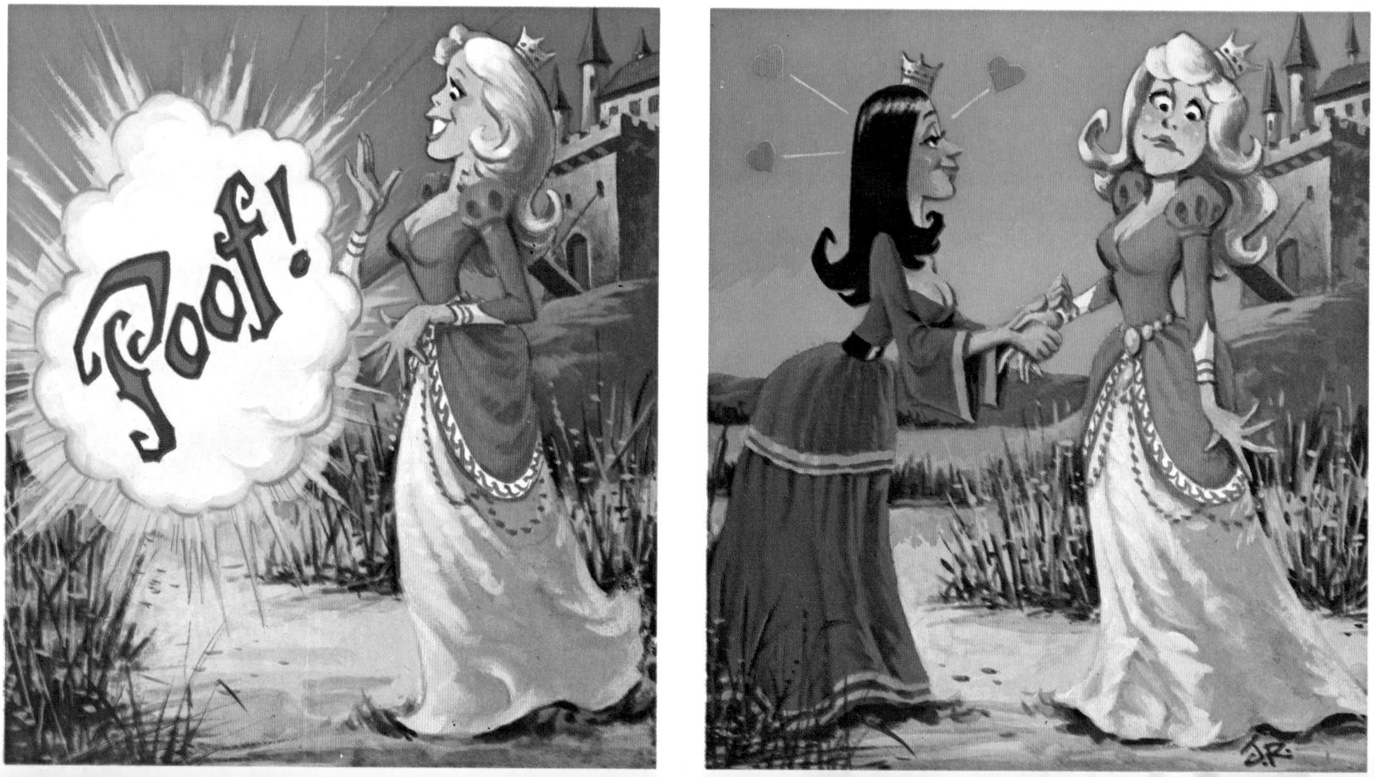
Poof!

Ms. LIBERTY

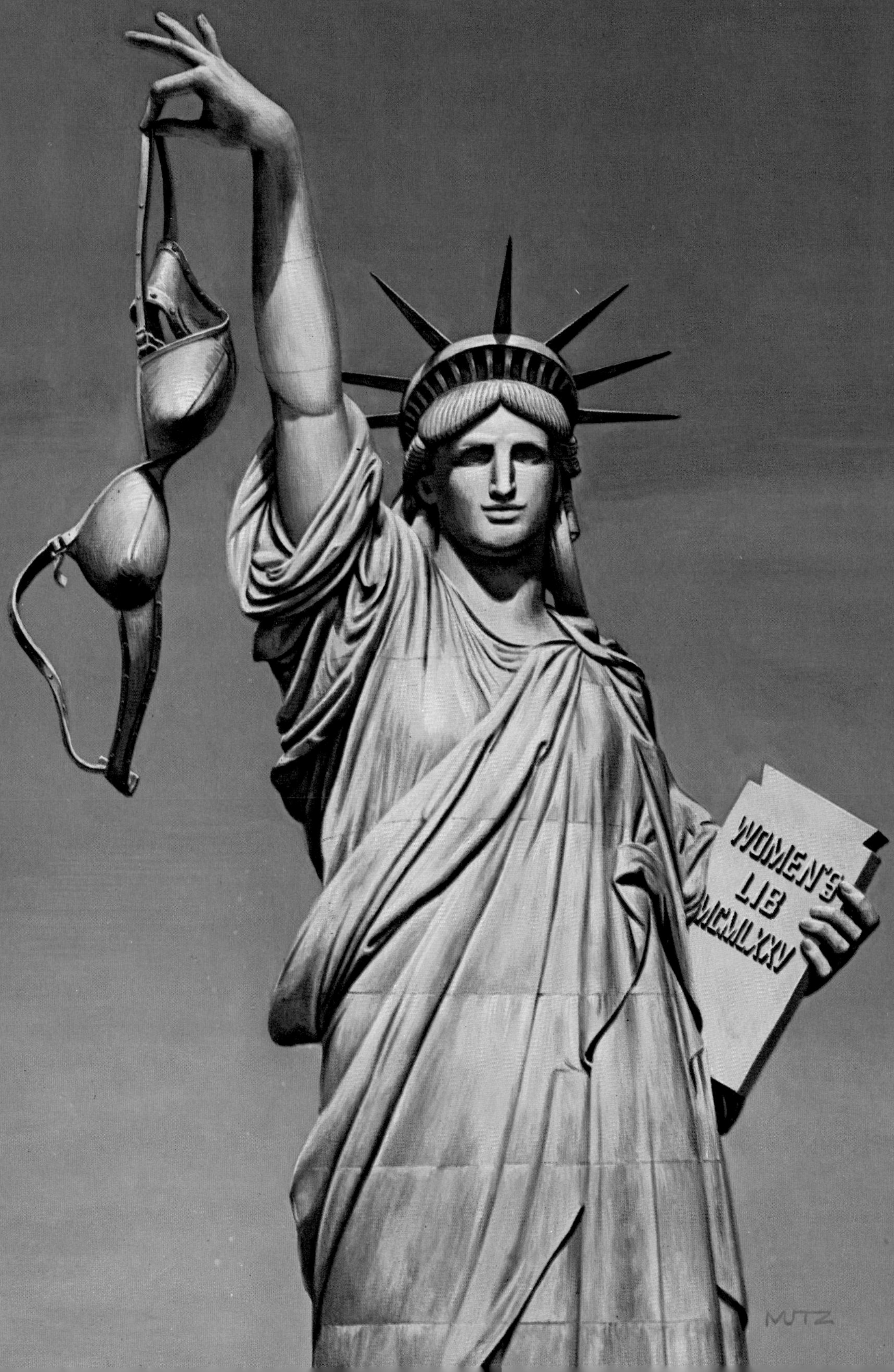
WOMEN'S
LIB
MCMLXXV
MUTZ

ANOTHER MAD MINI-POSTER

ARTIST: MUTZ IDEA: AL JAFFEE

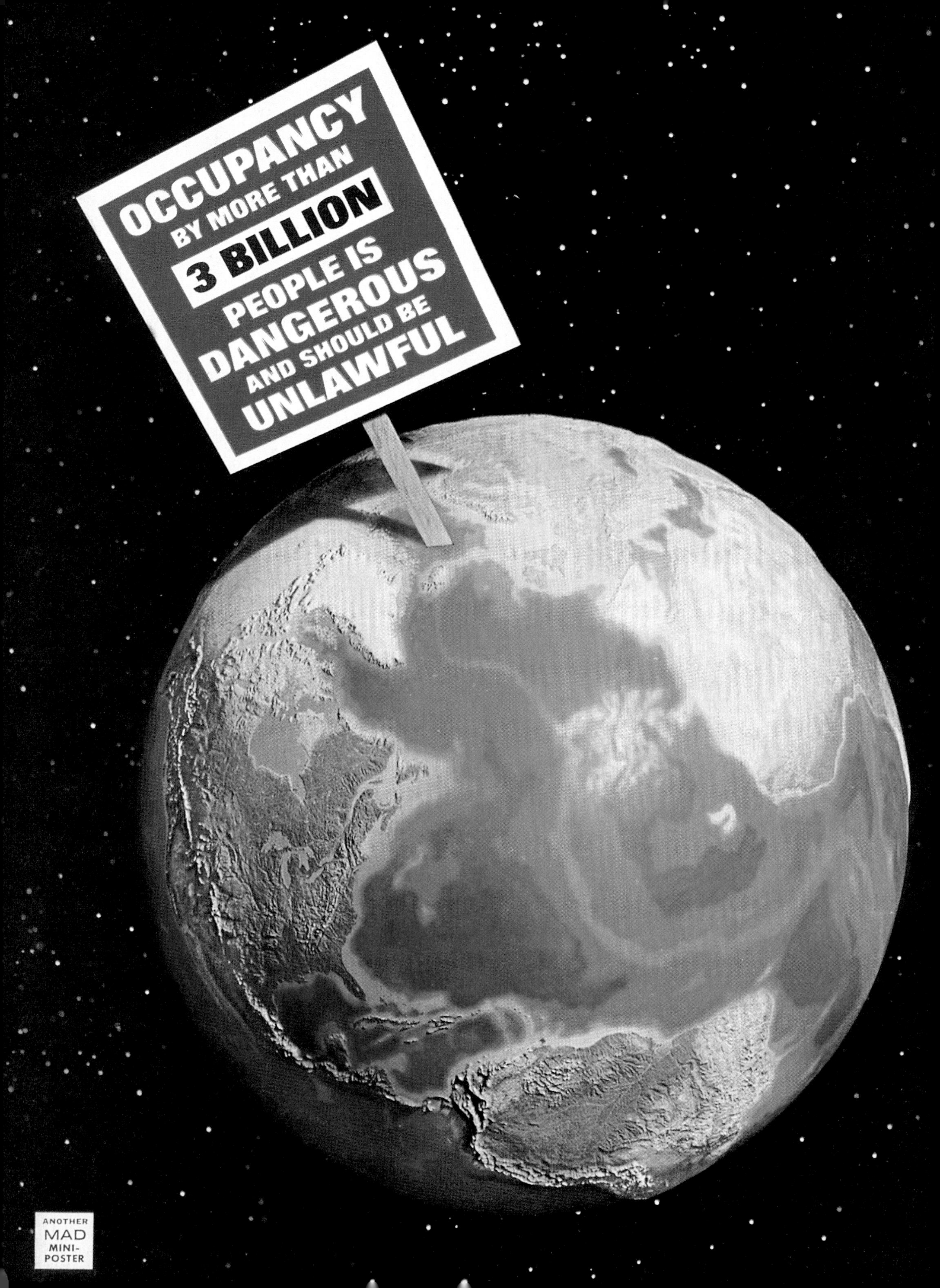
OCCUPANCY
BY MORE THAN
3 BILLION
PEOPLE IS
DANGEROUS
AND SHOULD BE
UNLAWFUL

ANOTHER MAD MINI-POSTER

THE MODERN-DAY CARPETBAGGERS

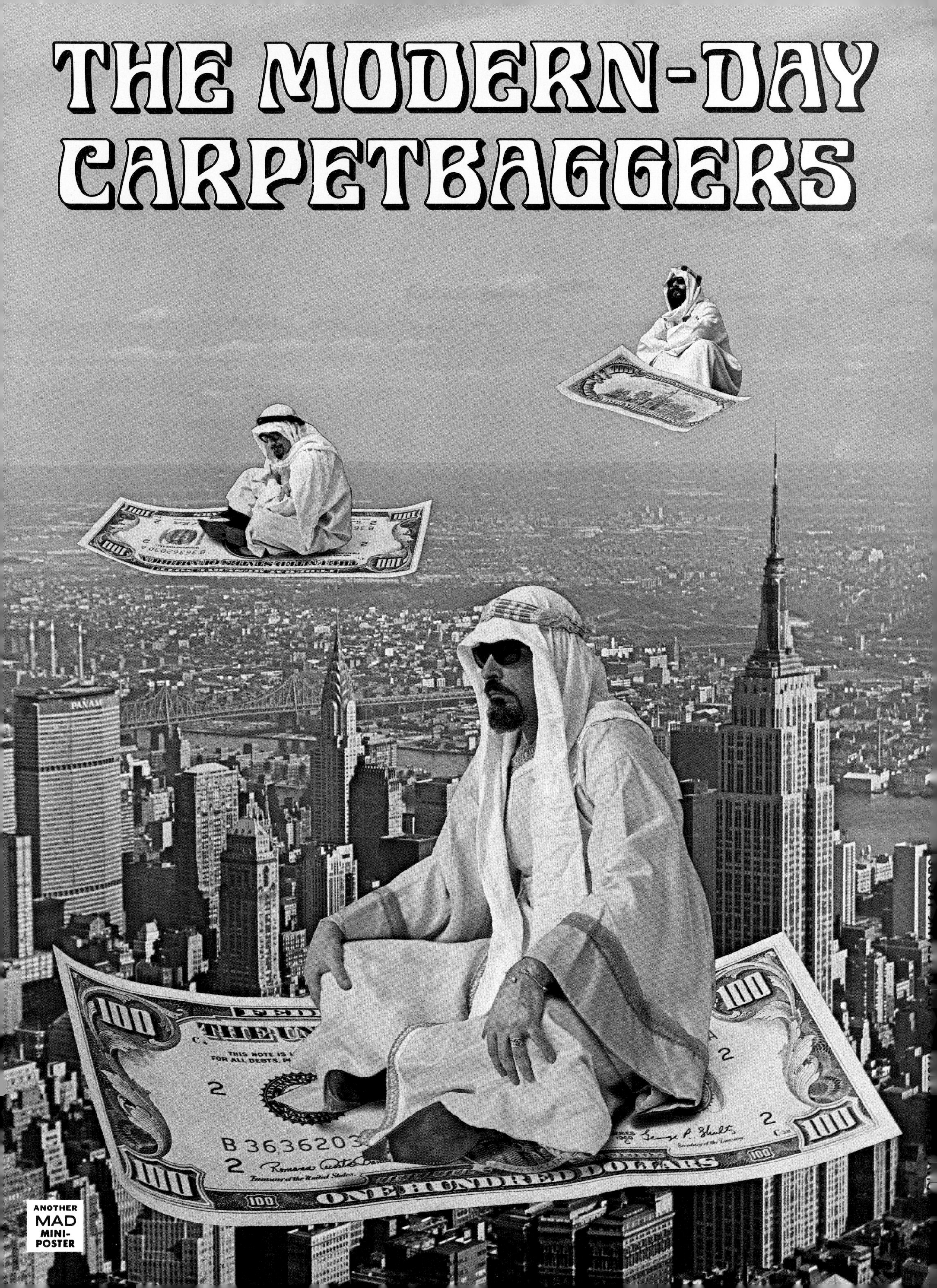

100
THIS NOTE IS
FOR ALL DEBTS,
B 3636203
ONE HUNDRED DOLLARS
ANOTHER MAD MINI-POSTER

ANOTHER
MAD
MINI-
POSTER

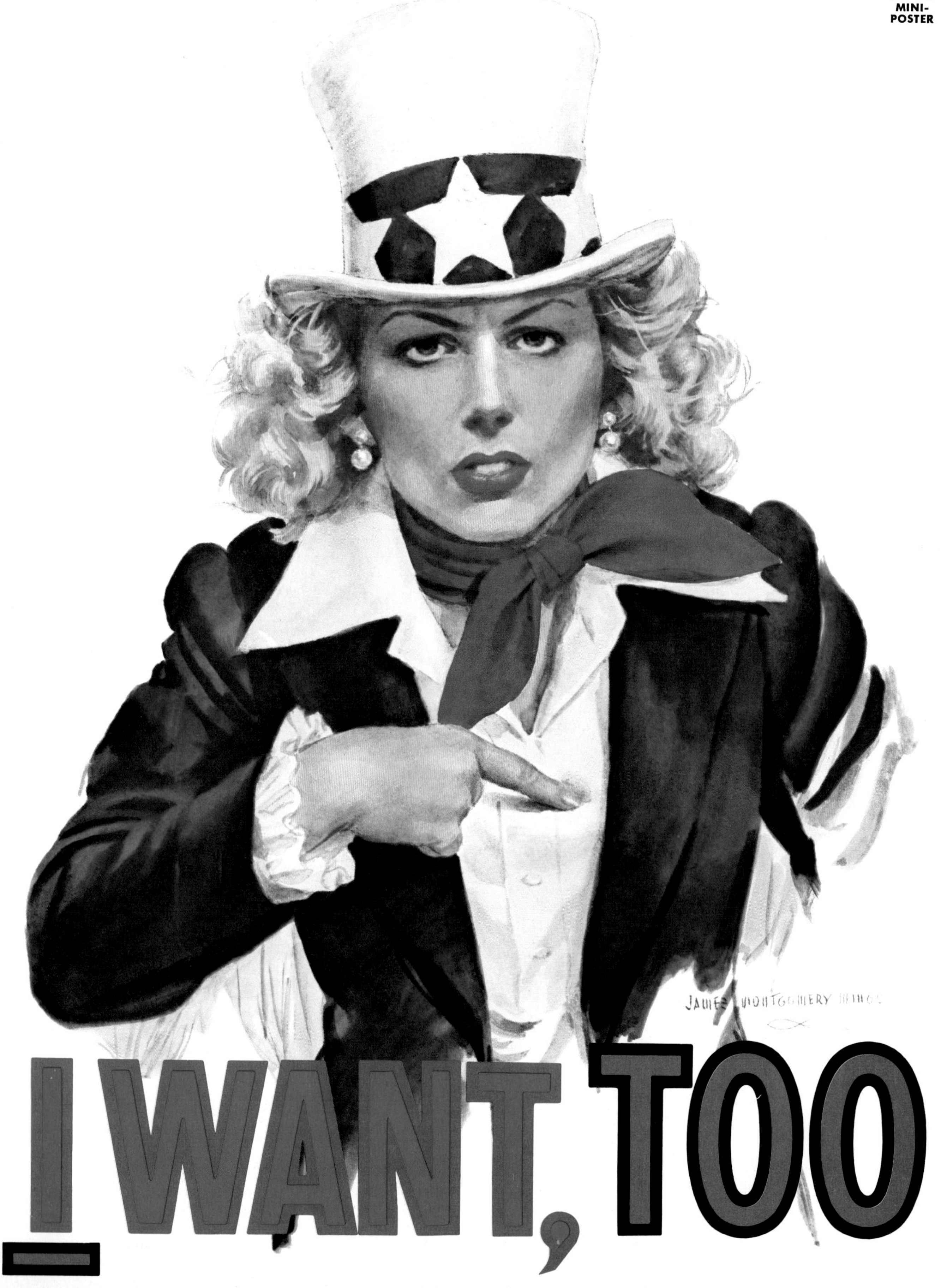
I WANT, TOO

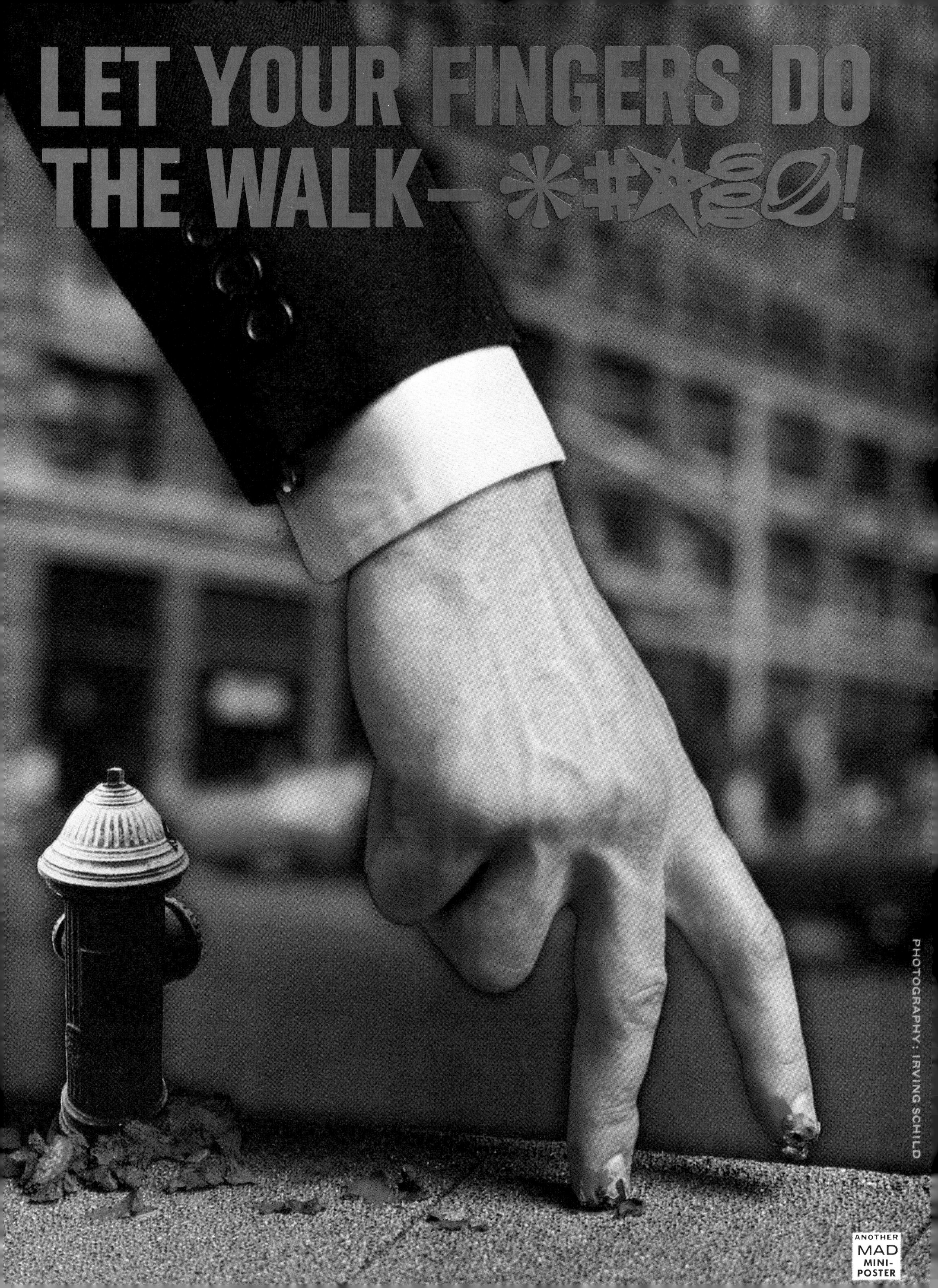
LET YOUR FINGERS DO
THE WALK—*#★@Ø!
PHOTOGRAPHY: IRVING SCHILD
ANOTHER MAD MINI-POSTER

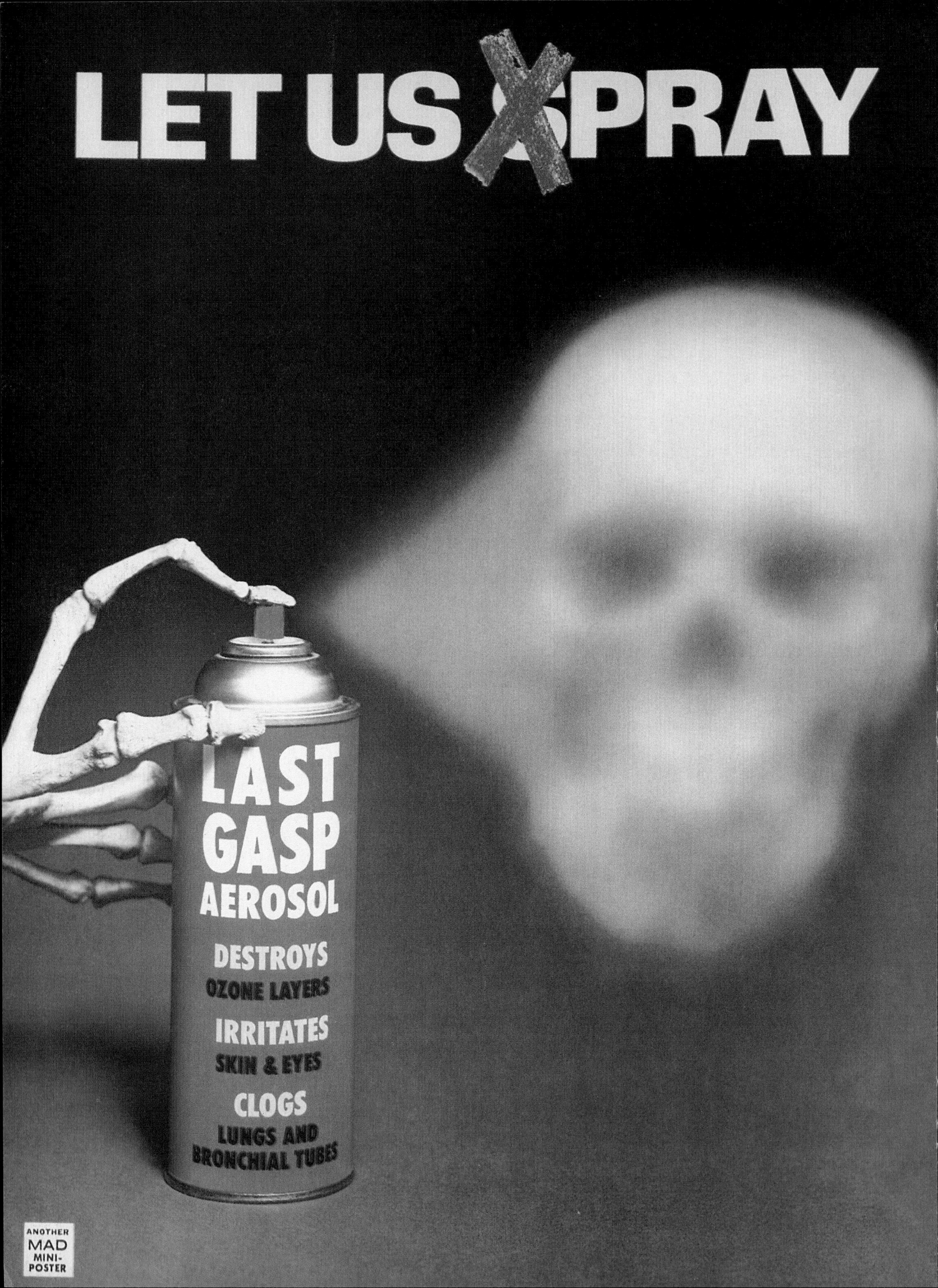

LET US SPRAY
LAST GASP AEROSOL
DESTROYS OZONE LAYERS
IRRITATES SKIN & EYES
CLOGS LUNGS AND BRONCHIAL TUBES
ANOTHER MAD MINI-POSTER

PATRONS OF THE ODDS DEPT.

Remember not too long ago, when we were taught that "War is Hell"? Well, maybe we were taught wrong. Because for the second year in a row, there's a show on the tube that seems to prove —not that "War is Hell!"—but that "War is A Hell-Of-A-Lot-Of-Fun!" Which, when you think about it, is a sickeningly idiotic idea, in any language. In French, it's "Fou," in Spanish, it's "Loco," in Italian, it's "Pazzo," in German, it's "Ferrucht" and in Yiddish, it's . . .

M*A*S*H*UGA

ARTIST: ANGELO TORRES WRITER: STAN HART

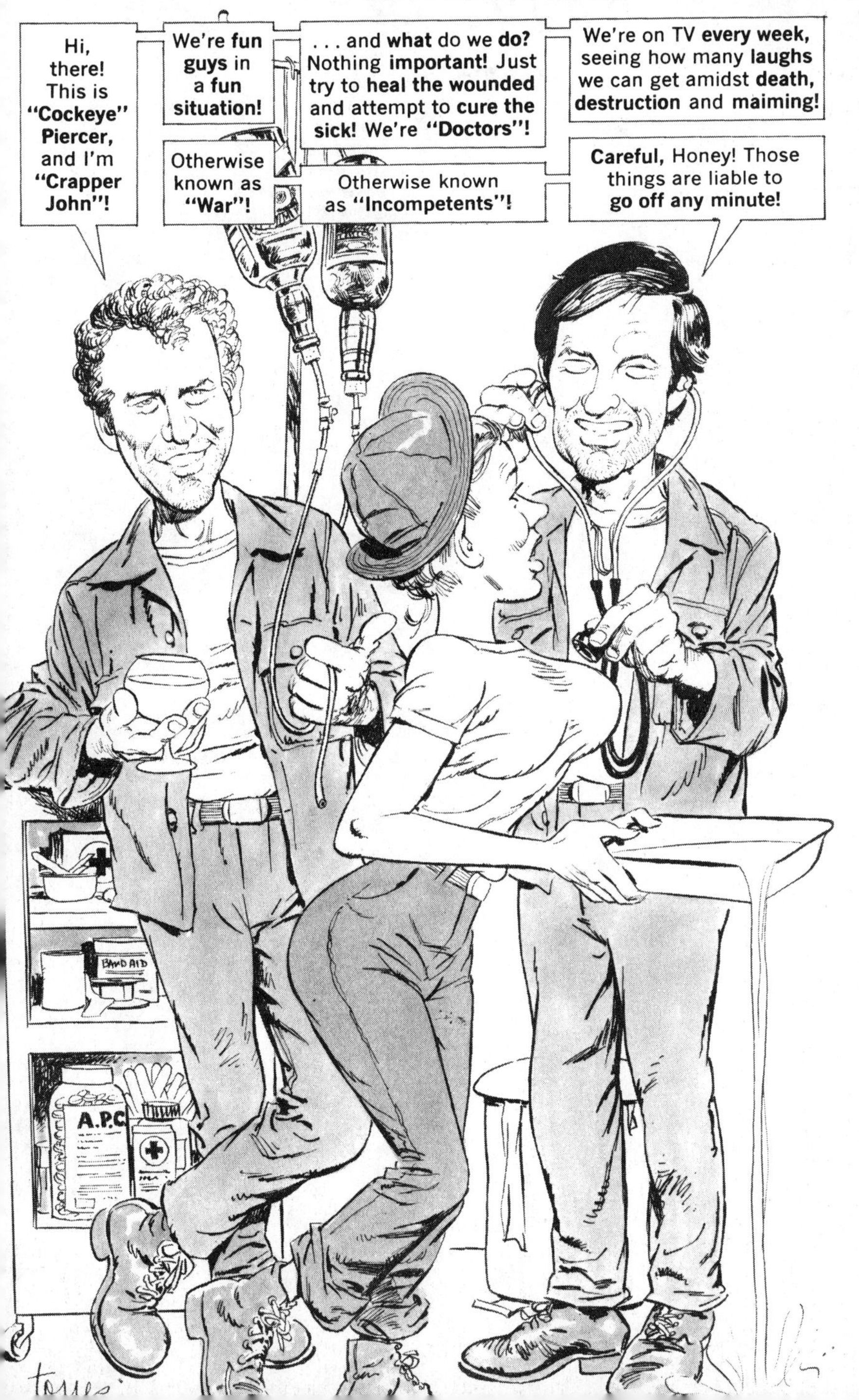
Hi, there! This is "Cockeye" Piercer, and I'm "Crapper John"!
We're fun guys in a fun situation!
. . . and what do we do? Nothing important! Just try to heal the wounded and attempt to cure the sick! We're "Doctors"!
We're on TV every week, seeing how many laughs we can get amidst death, destruction and maiming!
Otherwise known as "War"!
Otherwise known as "Incompetents"!
Careful, Honey! Those things are liable to go off any minute!
BAND AID
A.P.C.
torres

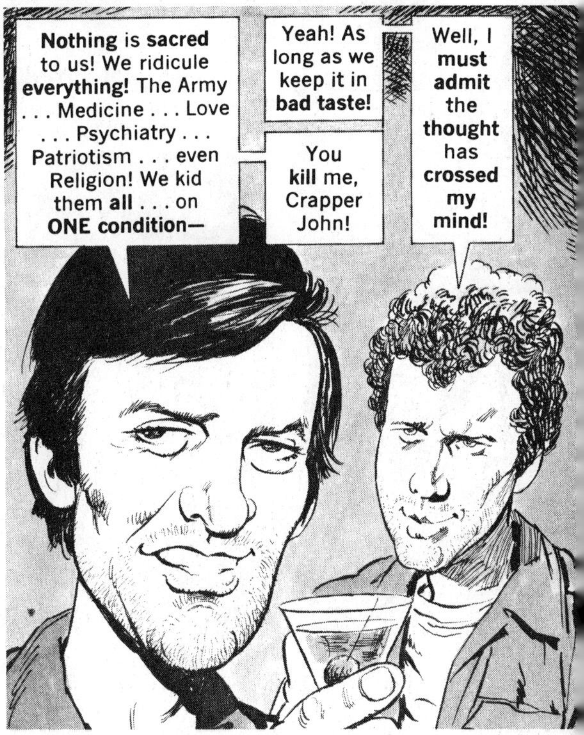
Nothing is sacred to us! We ridicule everything! The Army . . . Medicine . . . Love . . . Psychiatry . . . Patriotism . . . even Religion! We kid them all . . . on ONE condition—
Yeah! As long as we keep it in bad taste!
You kill me, Crapper John!
Well, I must admit the thought has crossed my mind!

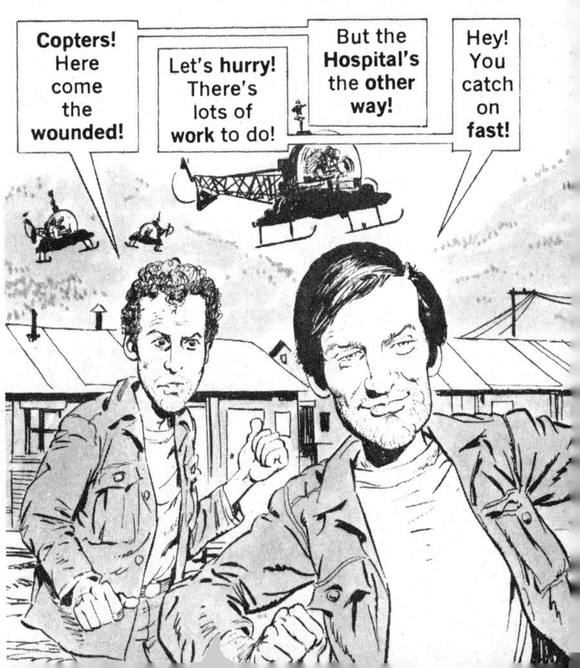
Copters! Here come the wounded!
Let's hurry! There's lots of work to do!
But the Hospital's the other way!
Hey! You catch on fast!

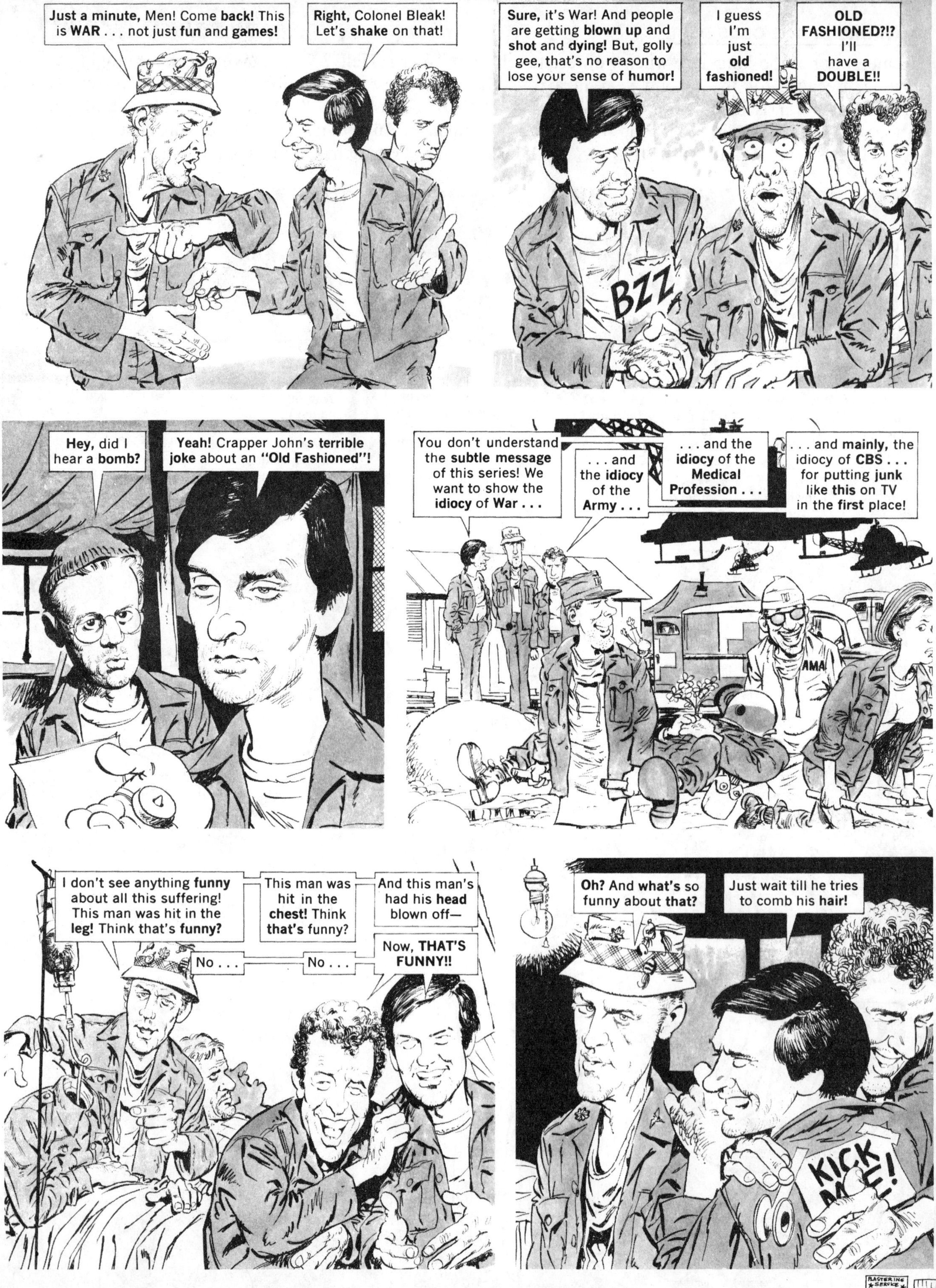
Just a minute, Men! Come back! This is WAR . . . not just fun and games!
Right, Colonel Bleak! Let's shake on that!
Sure, it's War! And people are getting blown up and shot and dying! But, golly gee, that's no reason to lose your sense of humor!
BZZ
I guess I'm just old fashioned!
OLD FASHIONED?!? I'll have a DOUBLE!!
Hey, did I hear a bomb?
Yeah! Crapper John's terrible joke about an "Old Fashioned"!
You don't understand the subtle message of this series! We want to show the idiocy of War . . .
. . . and the idiocy of the Army . . .
. . . and the idiocy of the Medical Profession . . .
. . . and mainly, the idiocy of CBS . . . for putting junk like this on TV in the first place!
AMA
I don't see anything funny about all this suffering! This man was hit in the leg! Think that's funny?
No . . .
This man was hit in the chest! Think that's funny?
No . . .
And this man's had his head blown off—
Now, THAT'S FUNNY!!
Oh? And what's so funny about that?
Just wait till he tries to comb his hair!
KICK ME!

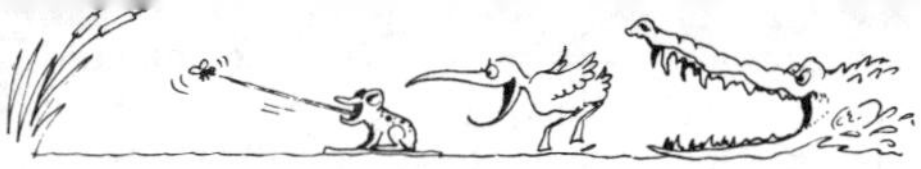

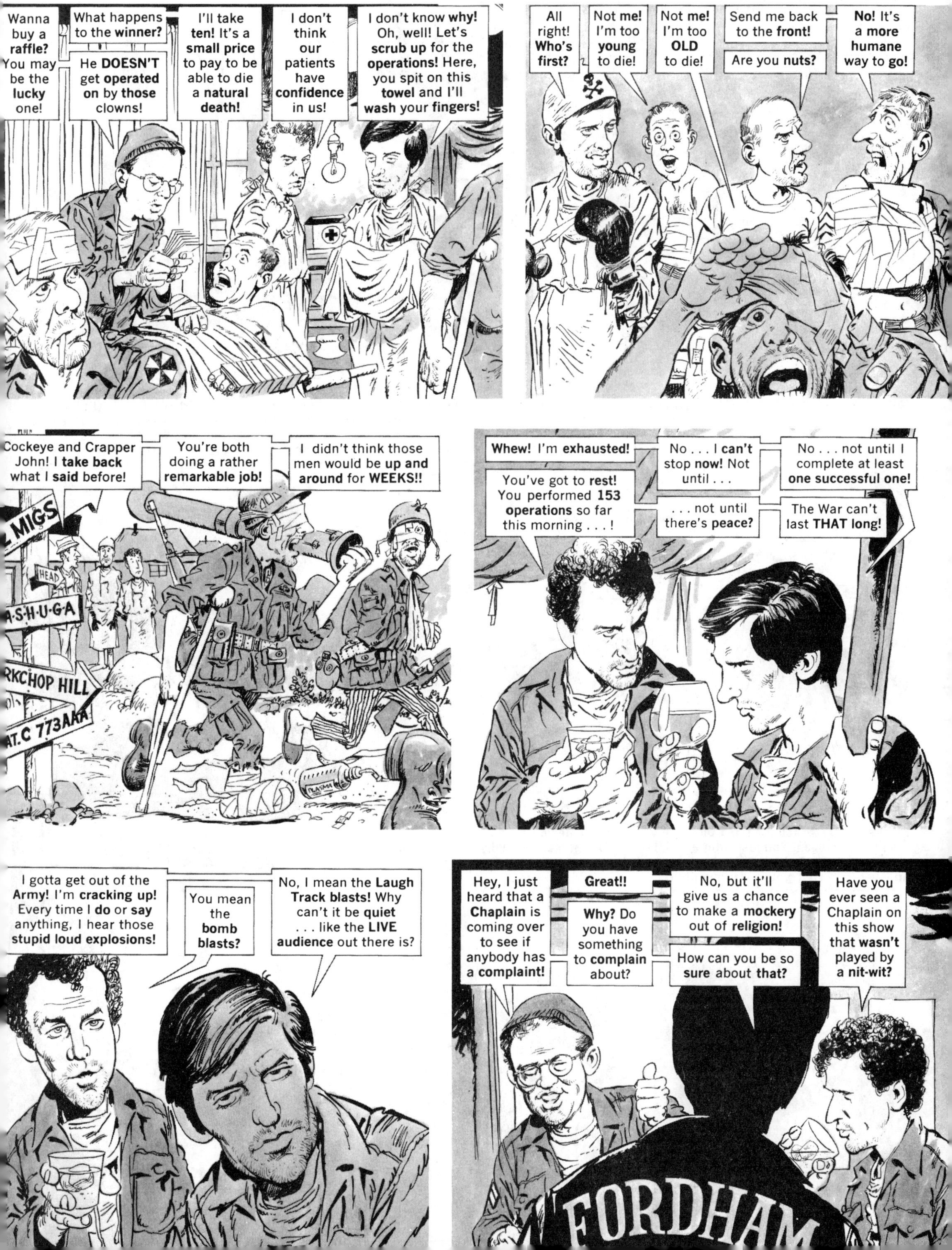

Wanna buy a raffle? You may be the lucky one!
What happens to the winner?
He DOESN'T get operated on by those clowns!
I'll take ten! It's a small price to pay to be able to die a natural death!
I don't think our patients have confidence in us!
I don't know why! Oh, well! Let's scrub up for the operations! Here, you spit on this towel and I'll wash your fingers!
All right! Who's first?
Not me! I'm too young to die!
Not me! I'm too OLD to die!
Send me back to the front!
Are you nuts?
No! It's a more humane way to go!
Cockeye and Crapper John! I take back what I said before!
You're both doing a rather remarkable job!
I didn't think those men would be up and around for WEEKS!!
MIGS
HEAD
A-S-H-U-G-A
RKCHOP HILL
AT.C 773AAA
PLASMA
Whew! I'm exhausted!
You've got to rest! You performed 153 operations so far this morning . . . !
No . . . I can't stop now! Not until . . .
No . . . not until I complete at least one successful one!
. . . not until there's peace?
The War can't last THAT long!
I gotta get out of the Army! I'm cracking up! Every time I do or say anything, I hear those stupid loud explosions!
You mean the bomb blasts?
No, I mean the Laugh Track blasts! Why can't it be quiet . . . like the LIVE audience out there is?
Hey, I just heard that a Chaplain is coming over to see if anybody has a complaint!
Great!!
Why? Do you have something to complain about?
No, but it'll give us a chance to make a mockery out of religion!
How can you be so sure about that?
Have you ever seen a Chaplain on this show that wasn't played by a nit-wit?
FORDHAM

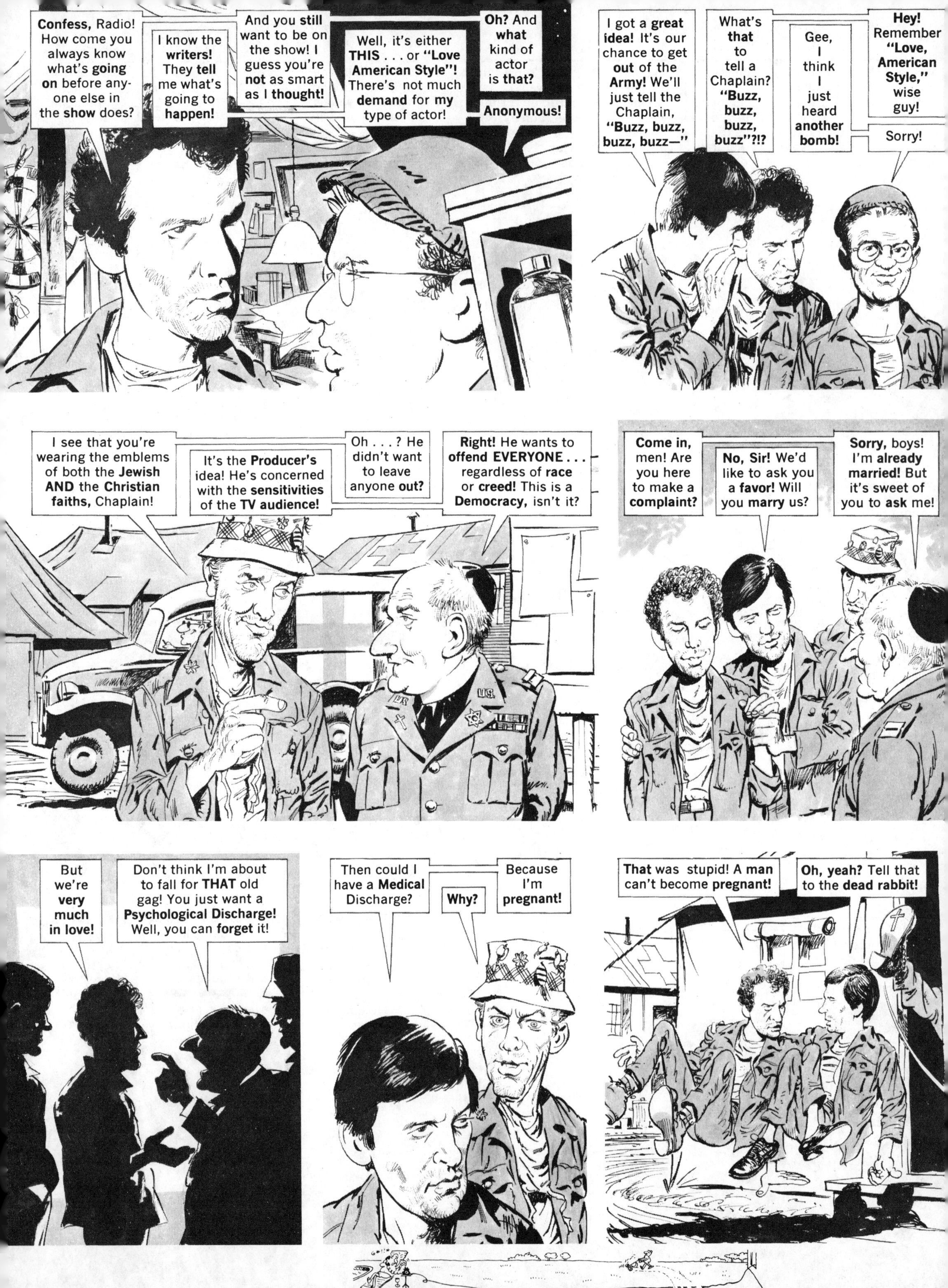
Confess, Radio! How come you always know what's going on before any-one else in the show does?
I know the writers! They tell me what's going to happen!
And you still want to be on the show! I guess you're not as smart as I thought!
Well, it's either THIS . . . or "Love American Style"! There's not much demand for my type of actor!
Oh? And what kind of actor is that?
Anonymous!
I got a great idea! It's our chance to get out of the Army! We'll just tell the Chaplain, "Buzz, buzz, buzz, buzz—"
What's that to tell a Chaplain? "Buzz, buzz, buzz, buzz"?!?
Gee, I think I just heard another bomb!
Hey! Remember "Love, American Style," wise guy!
Sorry!
I see that you're wearing the emblems of both the Jewish AND the Christian faiths, Chaplain!
It's the Producer's idea! He's concerned with the sensitivities of the TV audience!
Oh . . . ? He didn't want to leave anyone out?
Right! He wants to offend EVERYONE . . . regardless of race or creed! This is a Democracy, isn't it?
Come in, men! Are you here to make a complaint?
No, Sir! We'd like to ask you a favor! Will you marry us?
Sorry, boys! I'm already married! But it's sweet of you to ask me!
But we're very much in love!
Don't think I'm about to fall for THAT old gag! You just want a Psychological Discharge! Well, you can forget it!
Then could I have a Medical Discharge?
Why?
Because I'm pregnant!
That was stupid! A man can't become pregnant!
Oh, yeah? Tell that to the dead rabbit!

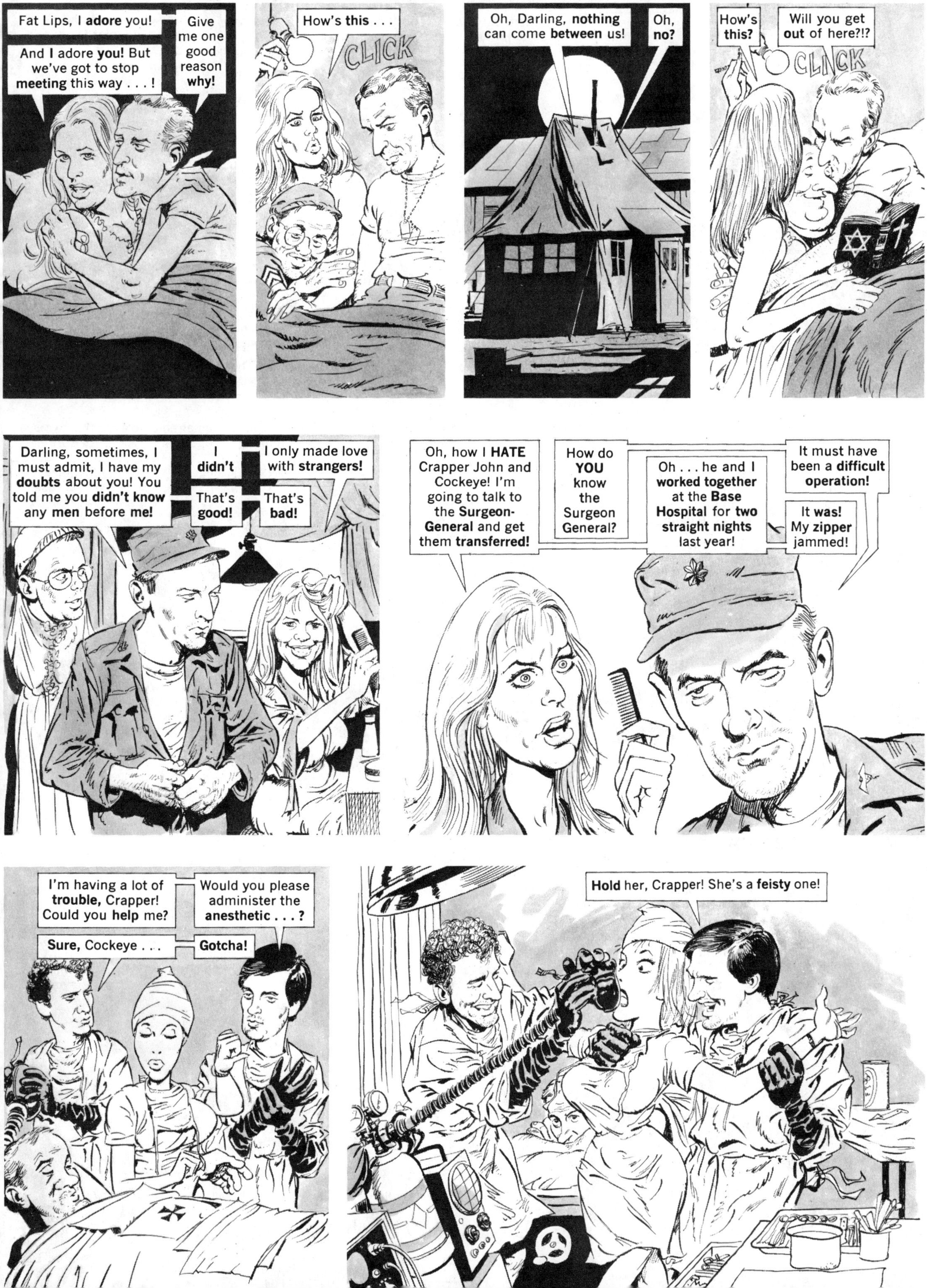

Fat Lips, I adore you!
And I adore you! But we've got to stop meeting this way . . . !
Give me one good reason why!
How's this . . .
CLICK
Oh, Darling, nothing can come between us!
Oh, no?
How's this?
Will you get out of here?!?
CLICK
Darling, sometimes, I must admit, I have my doubts about you! You told me you didn't know any men before me!
I didn't
I only made love with strangers!
That's good!
That's bad!
Oh, how I HATE Crapper John and Cockeye! I'm going to talk to the Surgeon-General and get them transferred!
How do YOU know the Surgeon General?
Oh . . . he and I worked together at the Base Hospital for two straight nights last year!
It must have been a difficult operation!
It was! My zipper jammed!
I'm having a lot of trouble, Crapper! Could you help me?
Would you please administer the anesthetic . . . ?
Sure, Cockeye . . .
Gotcha!
Hold her, Crapper! She's a feisty one!

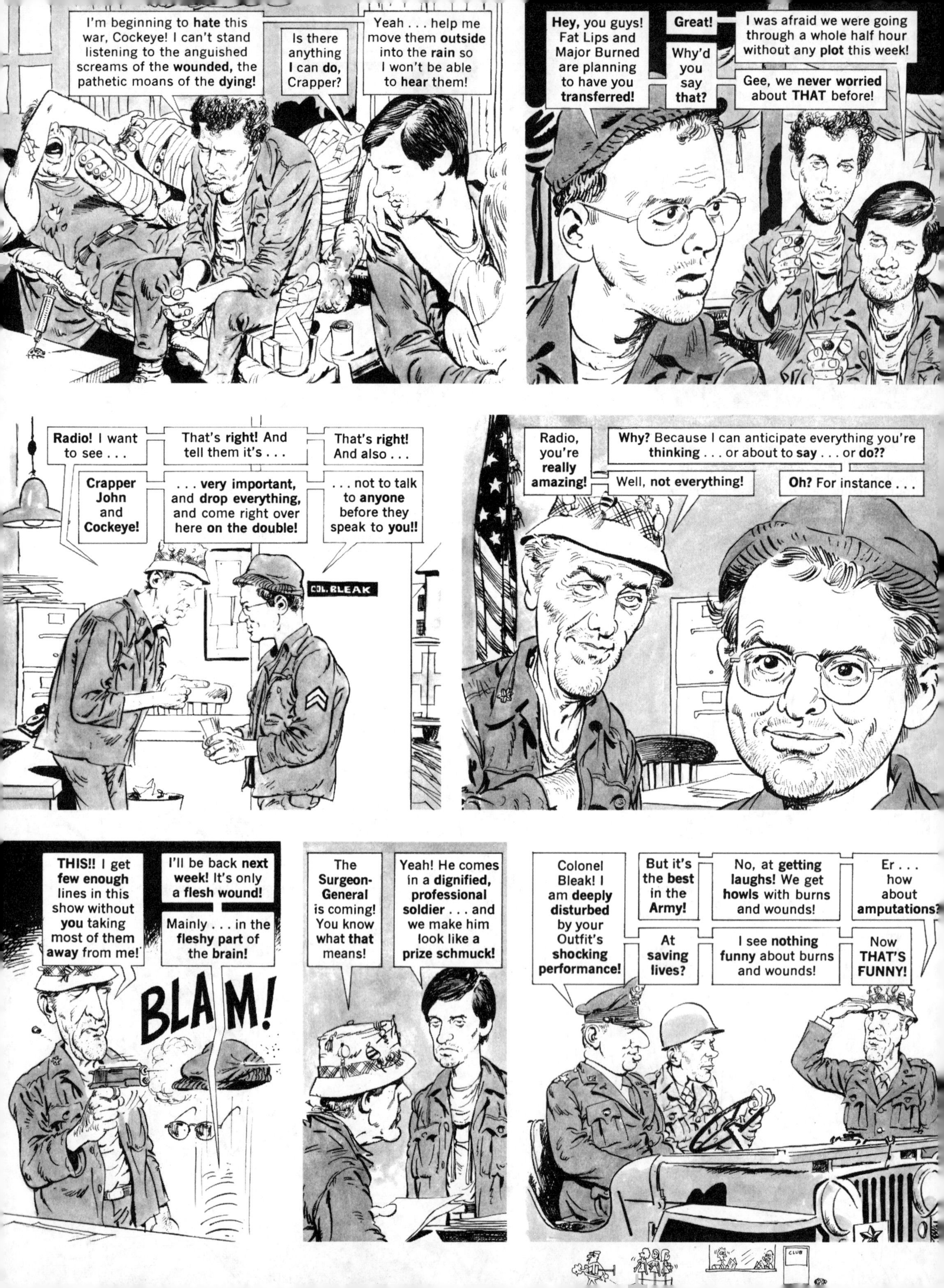

I'm beginning to hate this war, Cockeye! I can't stand listening to the anguished screams of the wounded, the pathetic moans of the dying!
Is there anything I can do, Crapper?
Yeah . . . help me move them outside into the rain so I won't be able to hear them!
Hey, you guys! Fat Lips and Major Burned are planning to have you transferred!
Great!
I was afraid we were going through a whole half hour without any plot this week!
Why'd you say that?
Gee, we never worried about THAT before!
Radio! I want to see . . .
That's right! And tell them it's . . .
That's right! And also . . .
Crapper John and Cockeye!
. . . very important, and drop everything, and come right over here on the double!
. . . not to talk to anyone before they speak to you!!
COL. BLEAK
Radio, you're really amazing!
Why? Because I can anticipate everything you're thinking . . . or about to say . . . or do??
Well, not everything!
Oh? For instance . . .
THIS!! I get few enough lines in this show without you taking most of them away from me!
I'll be back next week! It's only a flesh wound!
Mainly . . . in the fleshy part of the brain!
BLAM!
The Surgeon-General is coming! You know what that means!
Yeah! He comes in a dignified, professional soldier . . . and we make him look like a prize schmuck!
Colonel Bleak! I am deeply disturbed by your Outfit's shocking performance!
But it's the best in the Army!
No, at getting laughs! We get howls with burns and wounds!
Er . . . how about amputations?
At saving lives?
I see nothing funny about burns and wounds!
Now THAT'S FUNNY!
CLUB

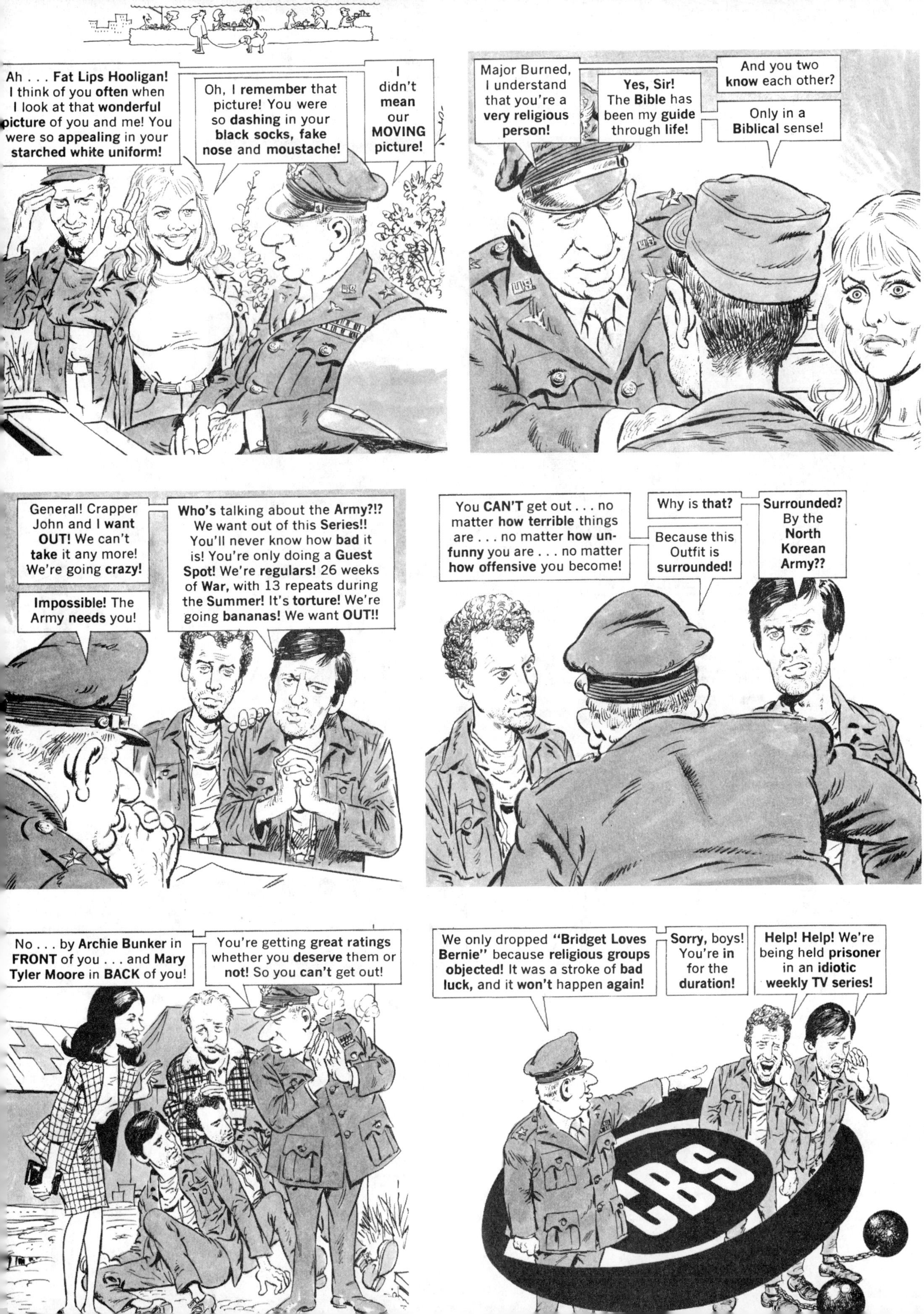
Ah . . . Fat Lips Hooligan! I think of you often when I look at that wonderful picture of you and me! You were so appealing in your starched white uniform!
Oh, I remember that picture! You were so dashing in your black socks, fake nose and moustache!
I didn't mean our MOVING picture!
Major Burned, I understand that you're a very religious person!
Yes, Sir! The Bible has been my guide through life!
And you two know each other?
Only in a Biblical sense!
General! Crapper John and I want OUT! We can't take it any more! We're going crazy!
Impossible! The Army needs you!
Who's talking about the Army?!? We want out of this Series!! You'll never know how bad it is! You're only doing a Guest Spot! We're regulars! 26 weeks of War, with 13 repeats during the Summer! It's torture! We're going bananas! We want OUT!!
You CAN'T get out . . . no matter how terrible things are . . . no matter how un-funny you are . . . no matter how offensive you become!
Why is that?
Because this Outfit is surrounded!
Surrounded? By the North Korean Army??
No . . . by Archie Bunker in FRONT of you . . . and Mary Tyler Moore in BACK of you!
You're getting great ratings whether you deserve them or not! So you can't get out!
We only dropped "Bridget Loves Bernie" because religious groups objected! It was a stroke of bad luck, and it won't happen again!
Sorry, boys! You're in for the duration!
Help! Help! We're being held prisoner in an idiotic weekly TV series!
CBS

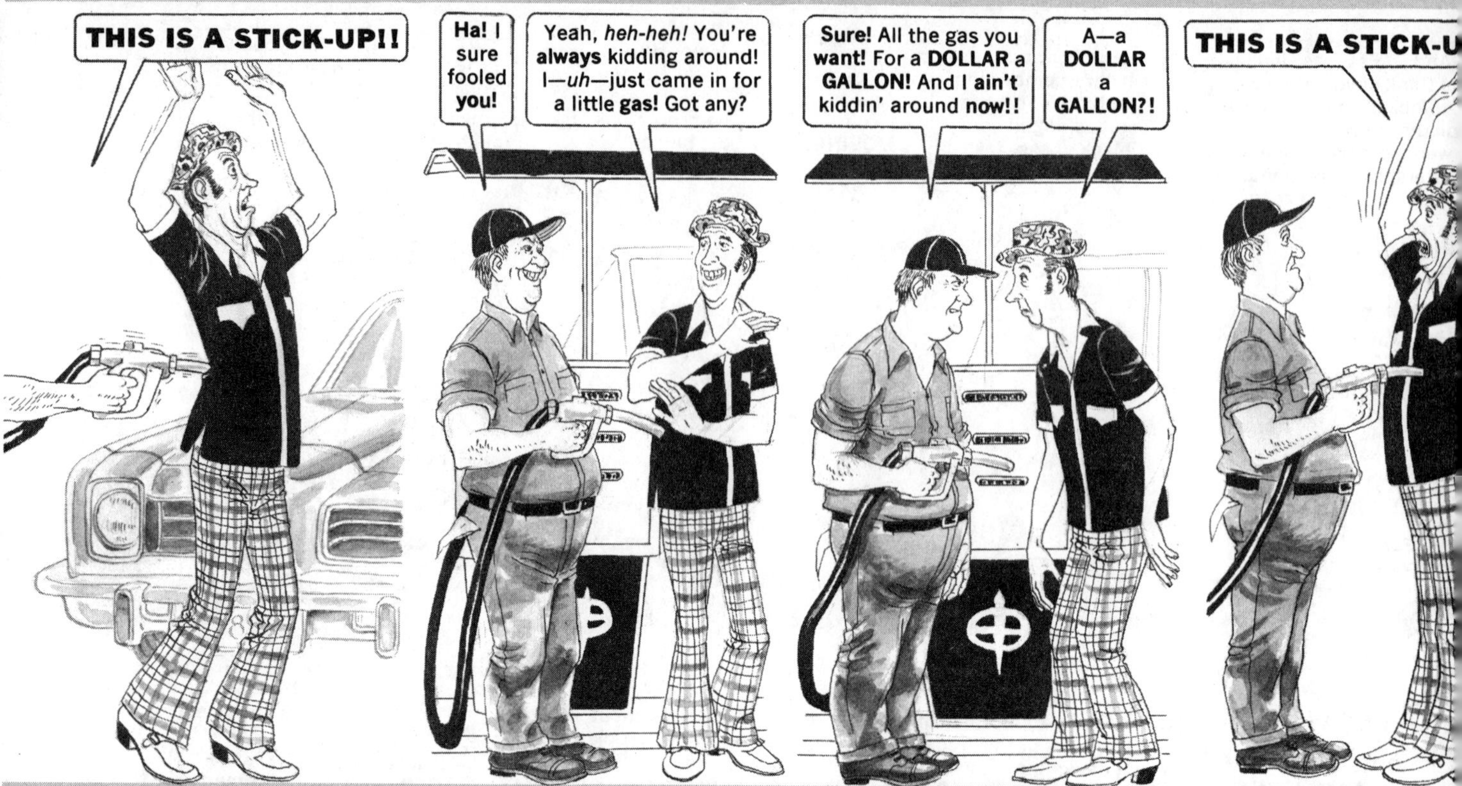

THIS IS A STICK-UP!!
Ha! I sure fooled you!
Yeah, heh-heh! You're always kidding around! I—uh—just came in for a little gas! Got any?
Sure! All the gas you want! For a DOLLAR a GALLON! And I ain't kiddin' around now!!
A—a DOLLAR a GALLON?!
THIS IS A STICK-U

BERG'S-EYE VIEW DEPT.

THE LIGHTER SIDE OF...

THE E

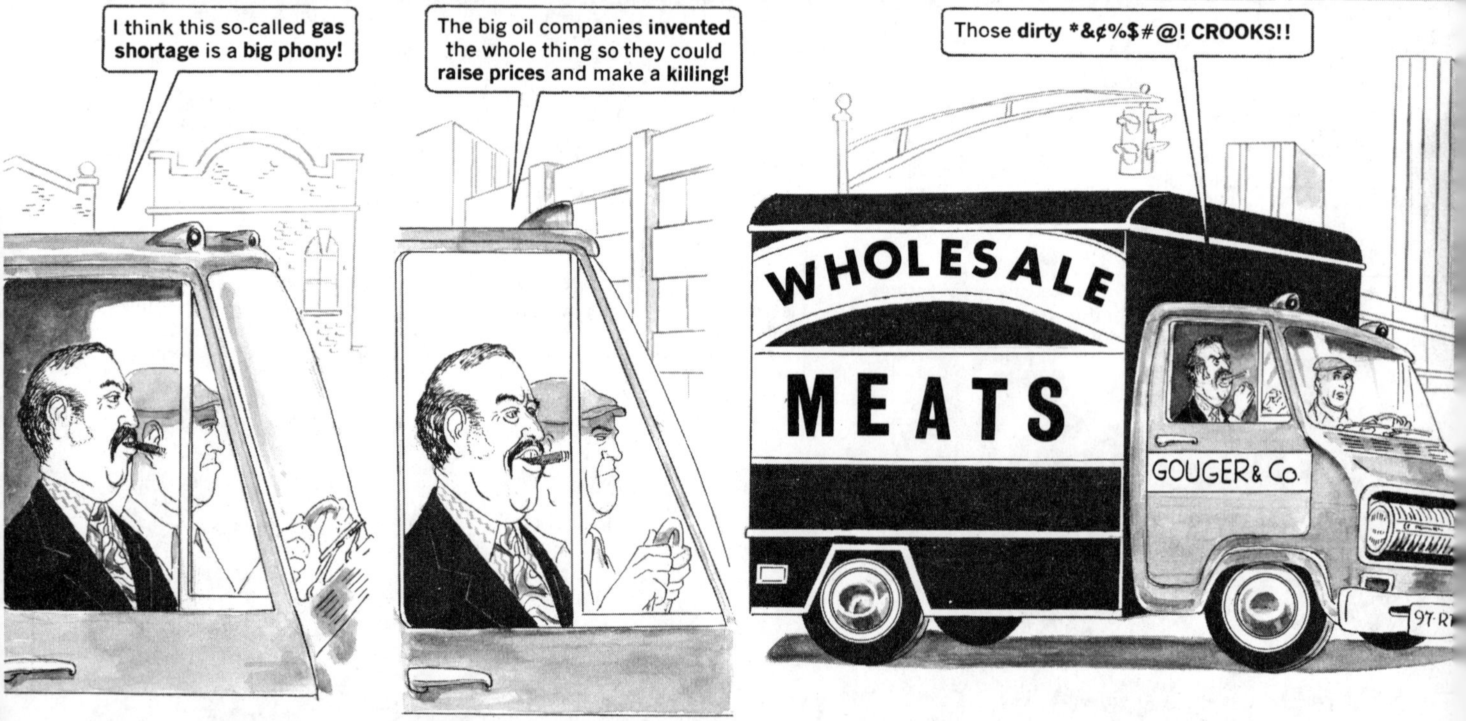

I think this so-called gas shortage is a big phony!
The big oil companies invented the whole thing so they could raise prices and make a killing!
Those dirty *&¢%$#@! CROOKS!!
WHOLESALE
MEATS
GOUGER & Co.

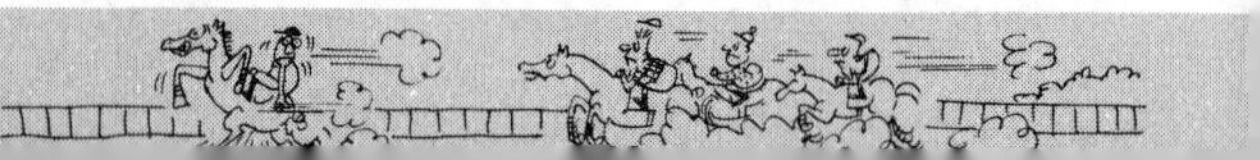

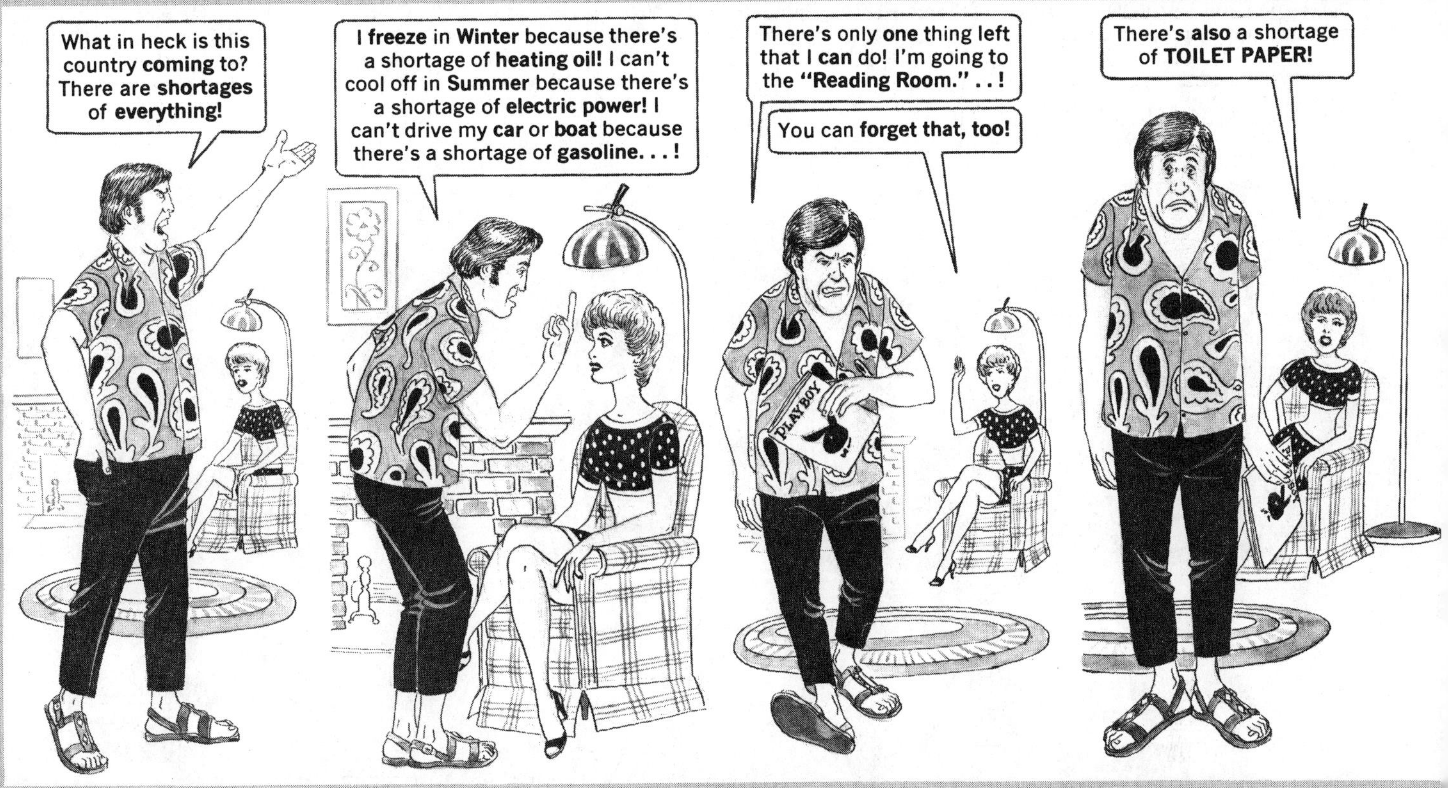
What in heck is this country coming to? There are shortages of everything!
I freeze in Winter because there's a shortage of heating oil! I can't cool off in Summer because there's a shortage of electric power! I can't drive my car or boat because there's a shortage of gasoline. . . !
There's only one thing left that I can do! I'm going to the "Reading Room." . . !
You can forget that, too!
PLAYBOY
There's also a shortage of TOILET PAPER!

ERGY CRISIS

ARTIST & WRITER: DAVE BERG

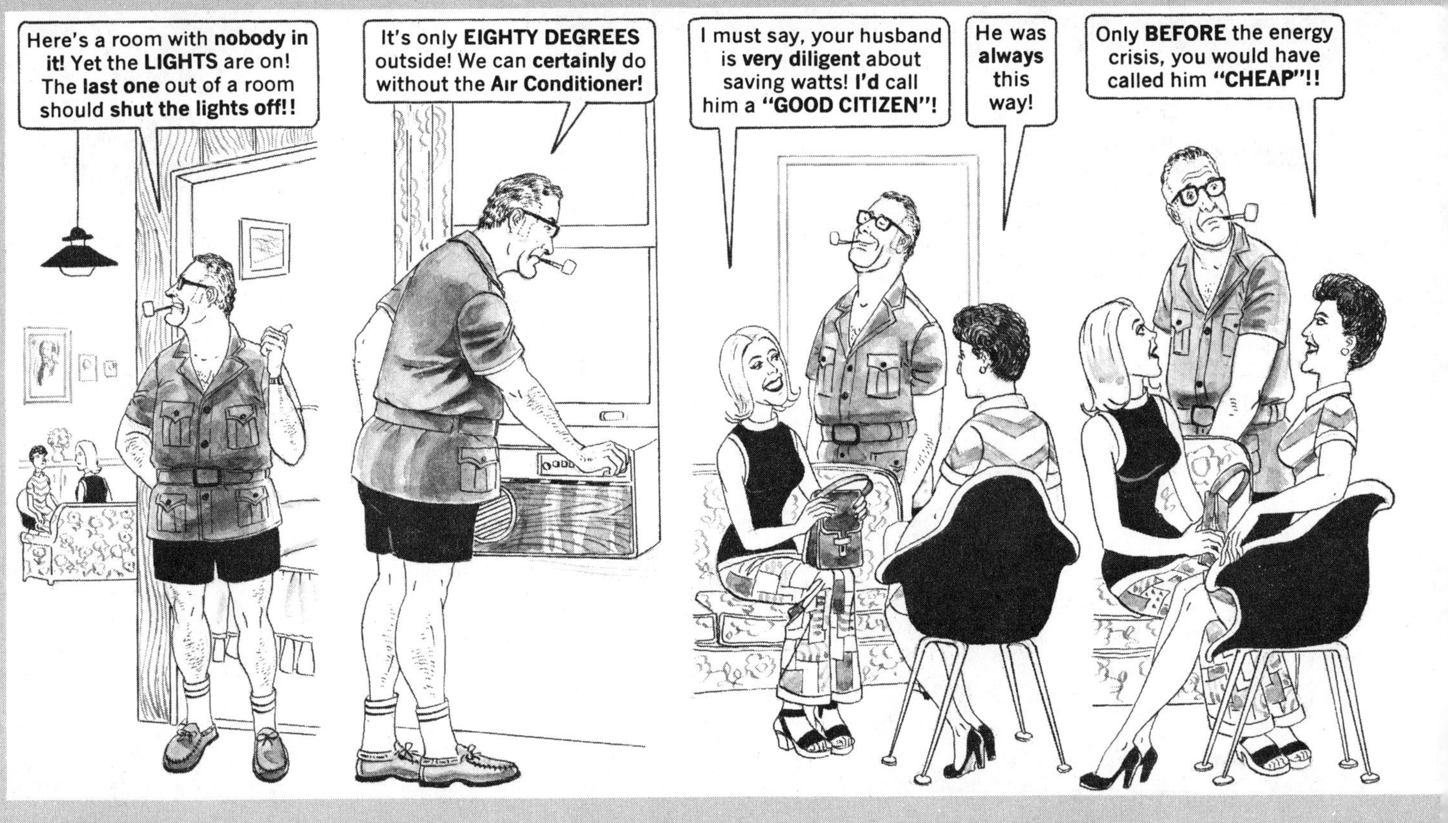
Here's a room with nobody in it! Yet the LIGHTS are on! The last one out of a room should shut the lights off!!
It's only EIGHTY DEGREES outside! We can certainly do without the Air Conditioner!
I must say, your husband is very diligent about saving watts! I'd call him a "GOOD CITIZEN"!
He was always this way!
Only BEFORE the energy crisis, you would have called him "CHEAP"!!

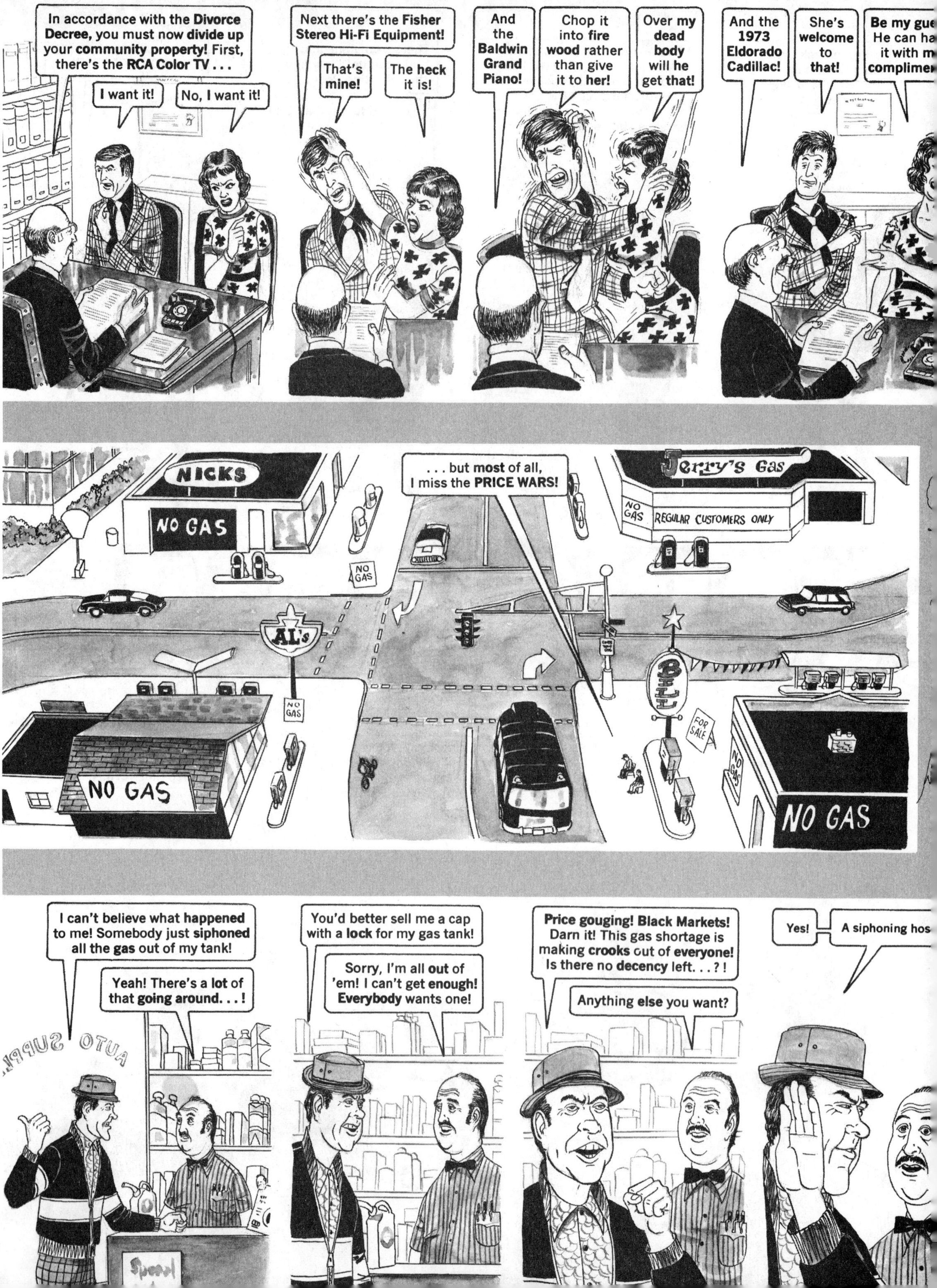
In accordance with the **Divorce Decree,** you must now **divide up** your **community property!** First, there's the **RCA Color TV . . .**
I want it!
No, I want it!
Next there's the **Fisher Stereo Hi-Fi Equipment!**
That's **mine!**
The heck it is!
And the **Baldwin Grand Piano!**
Chop it into **fire wood** rather than give it to **her!**
Over my **dead body** will he get **that!**
And the **1973 Eldorado Cadillac!**
She's **welcome** to **that!**
Be my gue
He can ha
it with m
complime
NICKS
NO GAS
. . . but **most** of all, I miss the **PRICE WARS!**
Jerry's Gas
NO GAS
REGULAR CUSTOMERS ONLY
NO GAS
AL's
NO GAS
NO GAS
BELL
FOR SALE
NO GAS
NO GAS
I can't believe what **happened** to me! Somebody just **siphoned** all the **gas** out of my tank!
Yeah! There's a **lot** of that **going around. . . !**
AUTO SUPPL
You'd better sell me a cap with a **lock** for my gas tank!
Sorry, I'm all **out** of 'em! I can't get **enough! Everybody** wants one!
Price gouging! Black Markets! Darn it! This gas shortage is making **crooks** out of **everyone!** Is there no **decency** left. . . ? !
Anything **else** you want?
Yes!
A siphoning hos

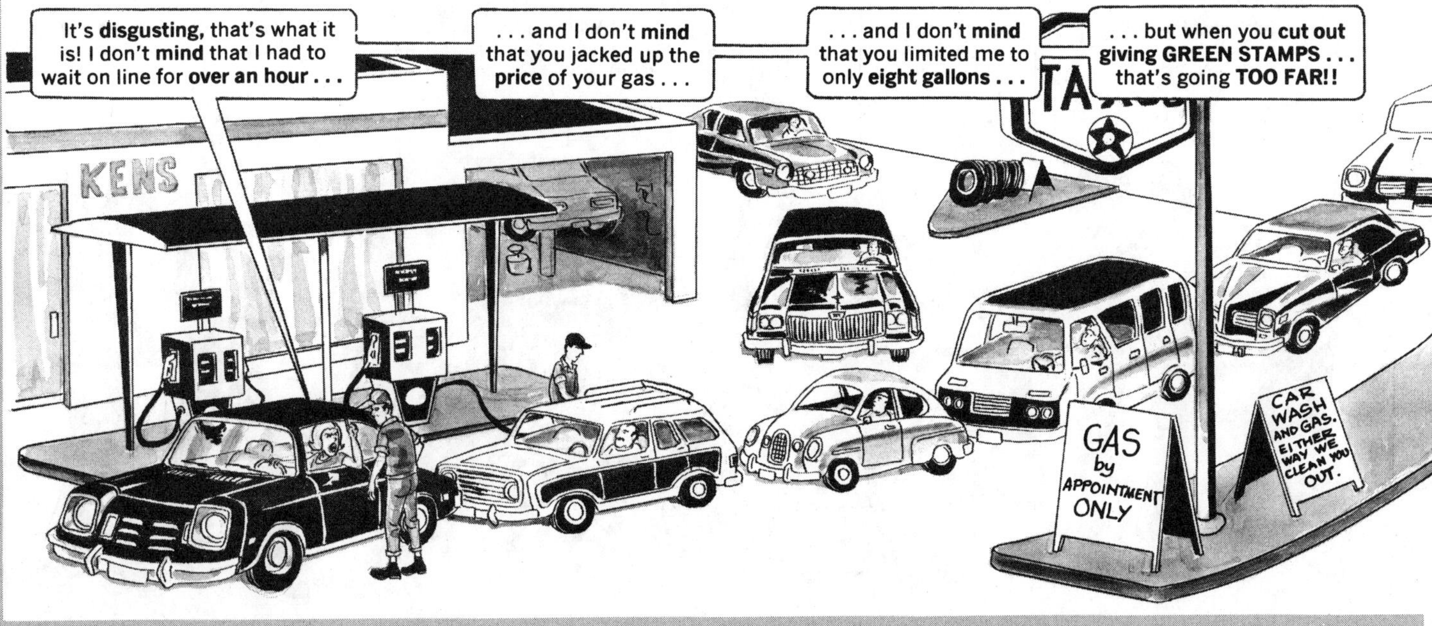
It's **disgusting**, that's what it is! I don't **mind** that I had to wait on line for **over an hour . . .**
. . . and I don't **mind** that you jacked up the **price** of your gas . . .
. . . and I don't **mind** that you limited me to only **eight gallons . . .**
. . . but when you **cut out giving GREEN STAMPS . . .** that's going **TOO FAR!!**
KENS
GAS by APPOINTMENT ONLY
CAR WASH AND GAS. EITHER WAY WE CLEAN YOU OUT.

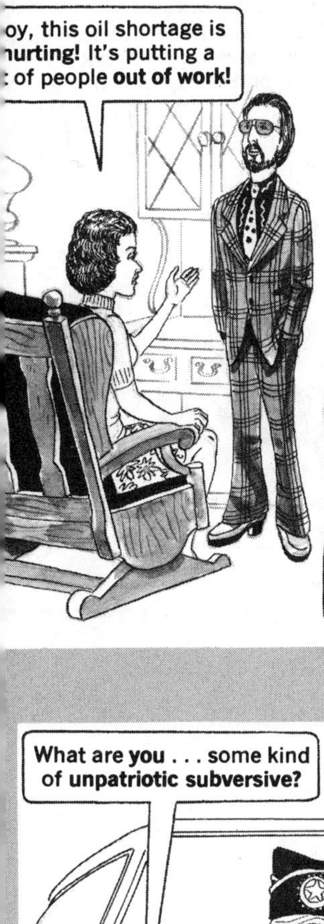
oy, this oil shortage is hurting! It's putting a of people **out of work!**

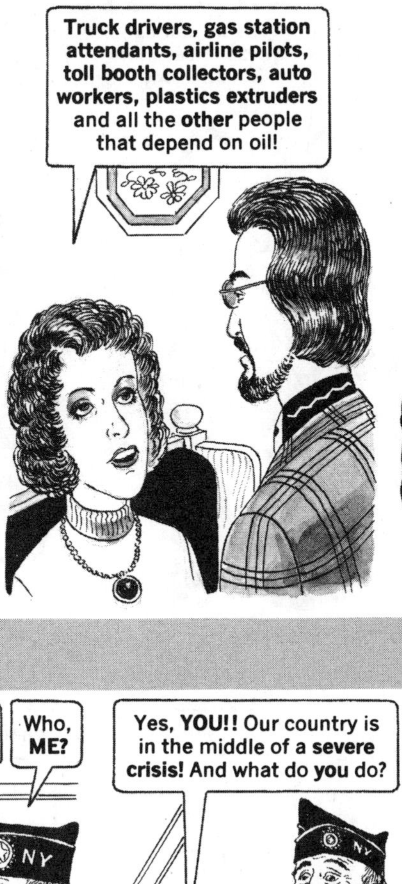
Truck drivers, gas station attendants, airline pilots, toll booth collectors, auto workers, plastics extruders and all the **other** people that depend on oil!

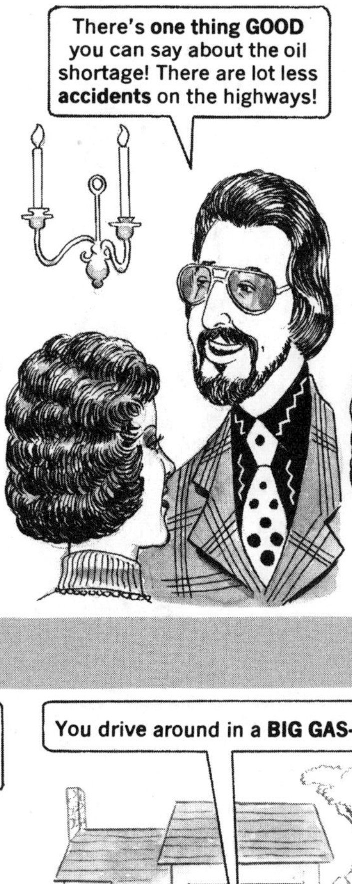
There's **one thing GOOD** you can say about the oil shortage! There are lot less **accidents** on the highways!

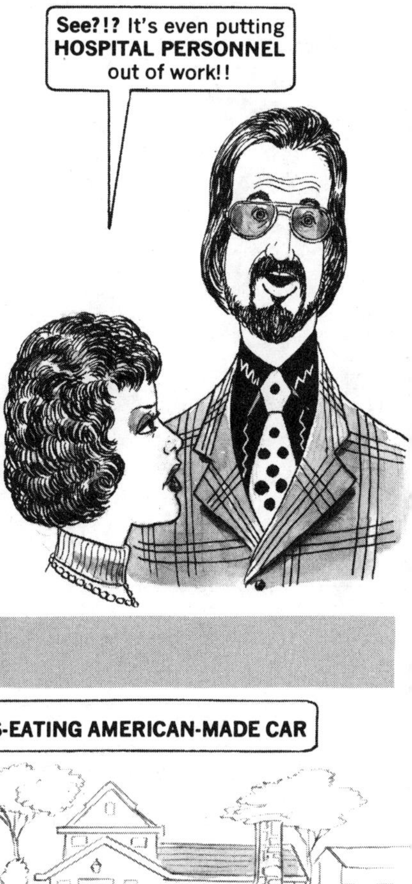
See?!? It's even putting **HOSPITAL PERSONNEL** out of work!!

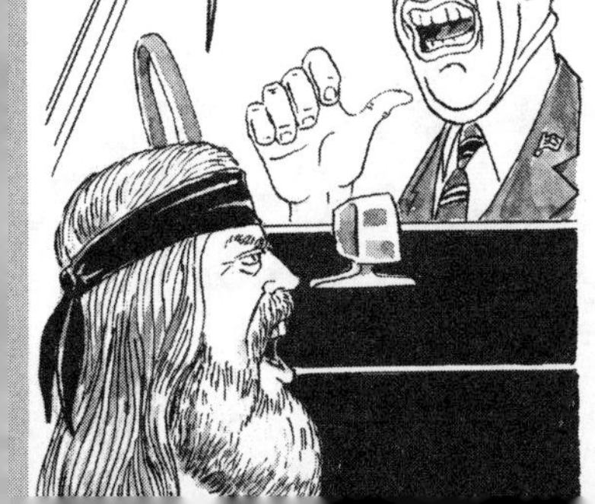
What are **you** . . . some kind of **unpatriotic subversive?**
Who, **ME?**
NY

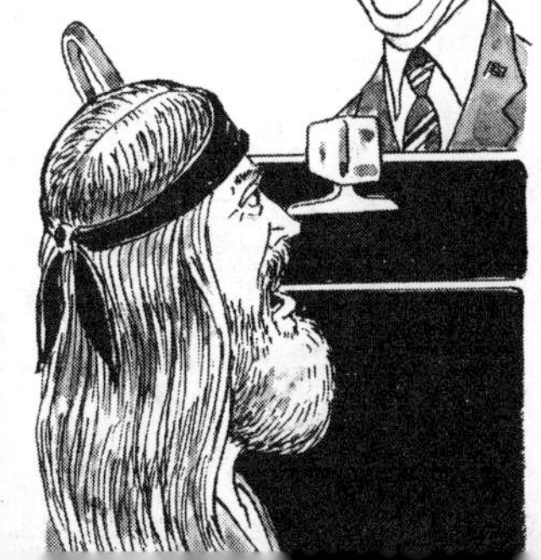
Yes, **YOU!!** Our country is in the middle of a **severe crisis!** And what do **you** do?
NY

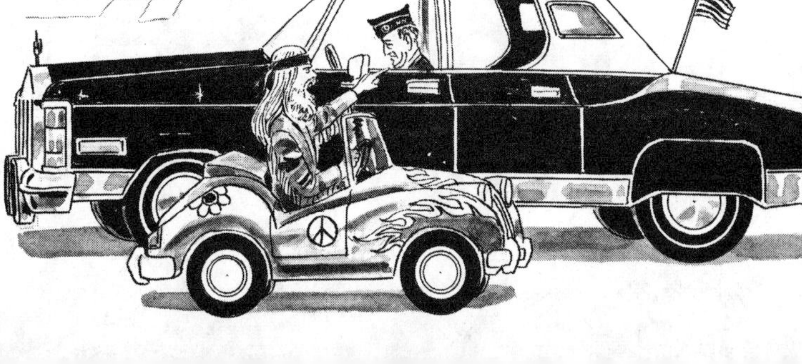
You drive around in a **BIG GAS-EATING AMERICAN-MADE CAR**

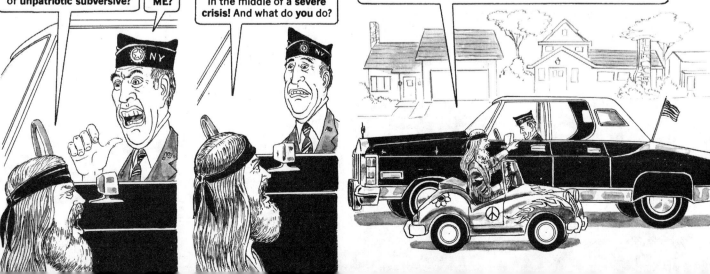

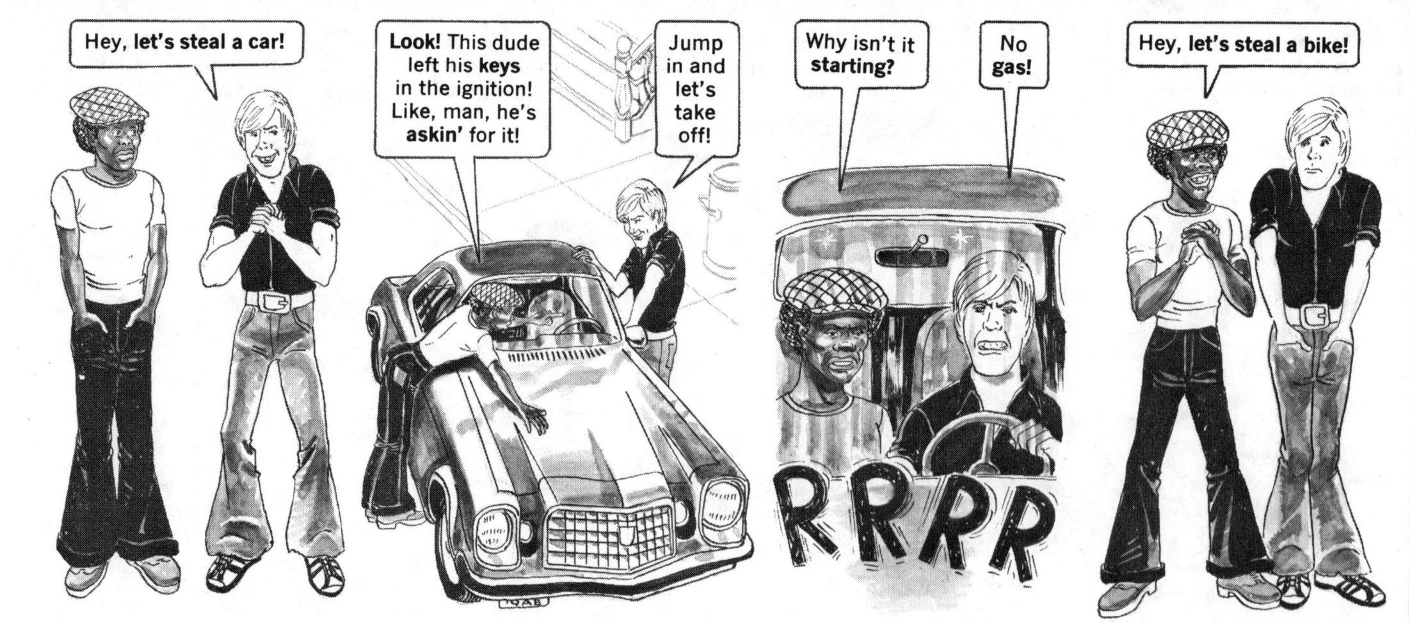
Hey, **let's steal a car!**
Look! This dude left his **keys** in the ignition! Like, man, he's **askin'** for it!
Jump in and let's take off!
Why isn't it **starting?**
No **gas!**
RRRR
Hey, **let's steal a bike!**

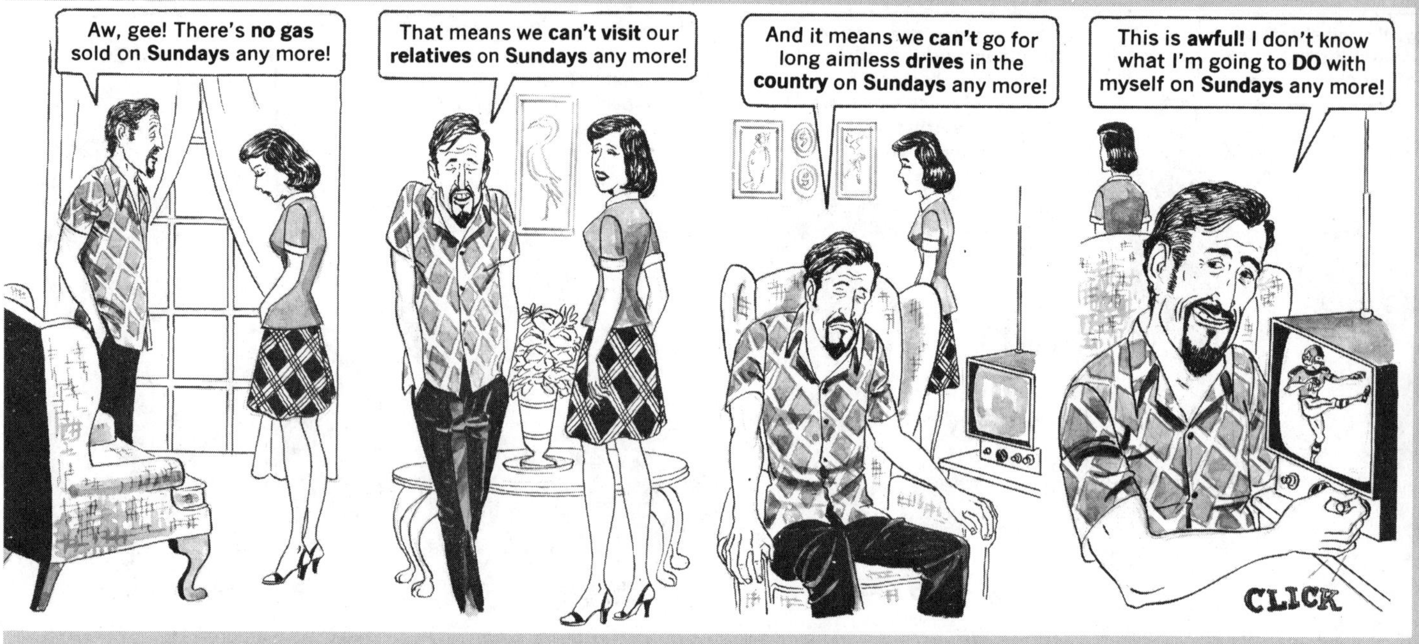
Aw, gee! There's **no gas** sold on **Sundays** any more!
That means we **can't visit** our **relatives** on **Sundays** any more!
And it means we **can't** go for long aimless **drives** in the **country** on **Sundays** any more!
This is **awful!** I don't know what I'm going to **DO** with myself on **Sundays** any more!
CLICK

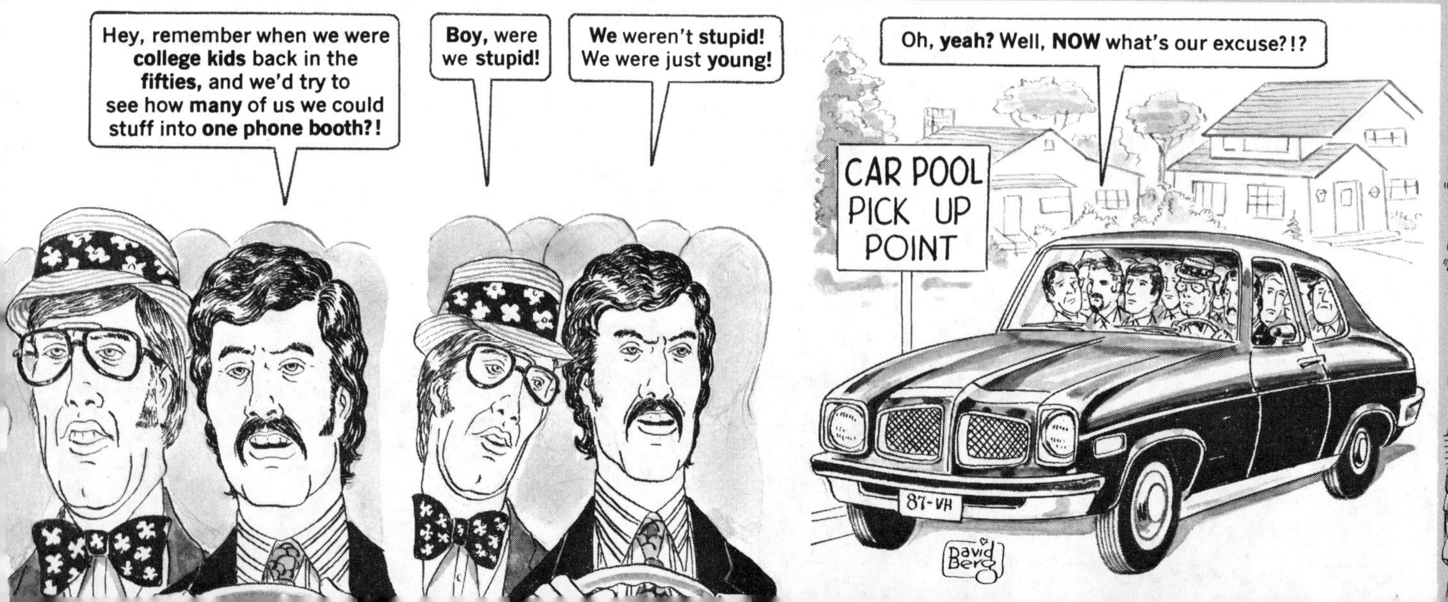
Hey, remember when we were **college kids** back in the **fifties**, and we'd try to see how **many** of us we could stuff into **one phone booth?!**
Boy, were we **stupid!**
We weren't **stupid!** We were just **young!**
Oh, **yeah?** Well, **NOW** what's our excuse?!?
CAR POOL PICK UP POINT
87-VH
David Berg

DON MARTIN DEPT. PART III

ONE DAY ON A TENNIS COURT

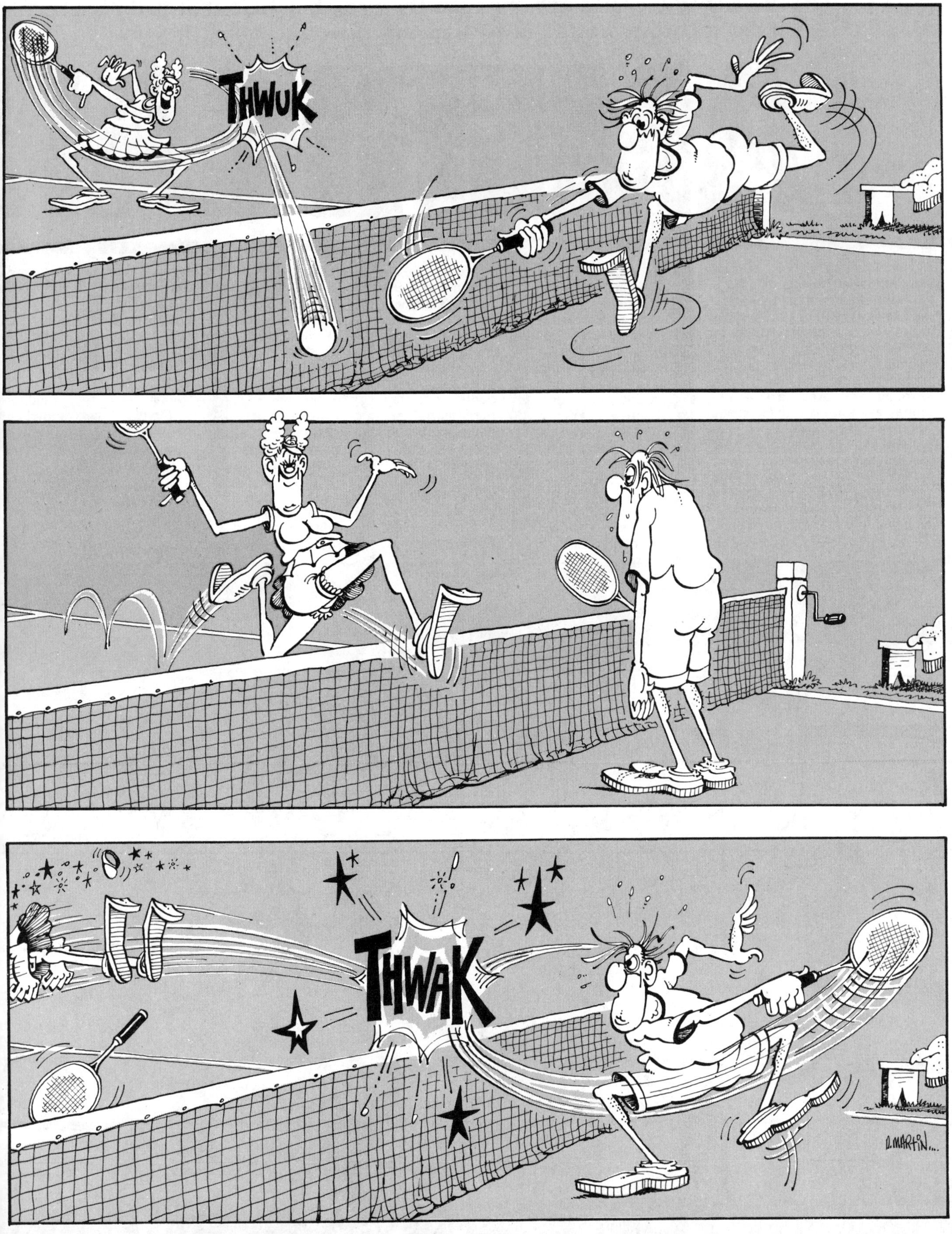
THWUK
THWAK
D. MARTIN...

THERE'S GOLD IN OLDIES DEPT.

What's been just about the biggest thing going in the movies for the pa couple of years? Nostalgia, right? The film-makers took us back to the 192 in "The Boy Friend", to the '30's in "Paper Moon", to the '40's in "Summer '42", and to the '50's in "The Last Picture Show". So that just about uses all the important nostalgia decades, and now on to other things, right? Wror

AMERICAN

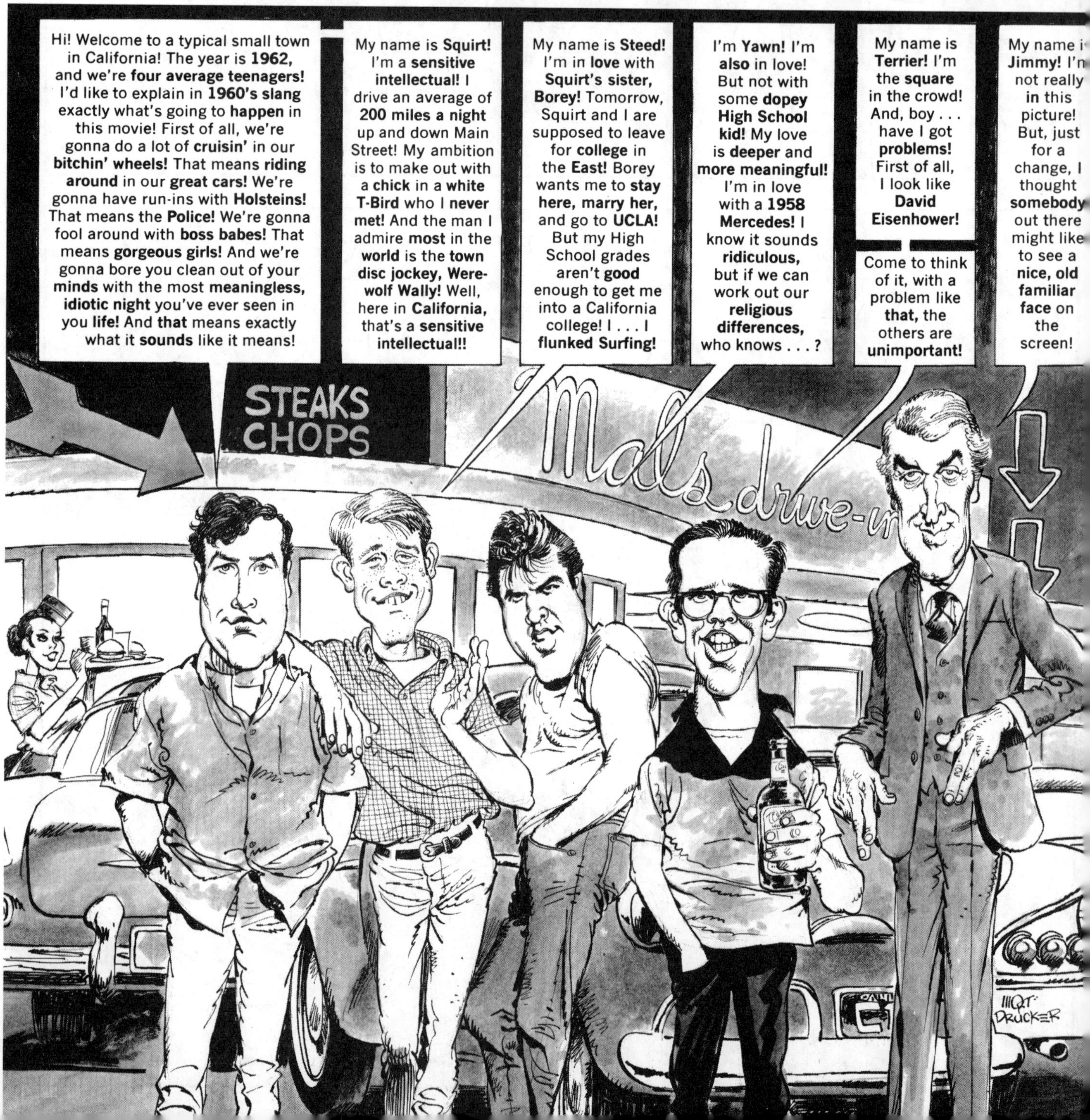
Hi! Welcome to a typical small town in California! The year is 1962, and we're four average teenagers! I'd like to explain in 1960's slang exactly what's going to happen in this movie! First of all, we're gonna do a lot of cruisin' in our bitchin' wheels! That means riding around in our great cars! We're gonna have run-ins with Holsteins! That means the Police! We're gonna fool around with boss babes! That means gorgeous girls! And we're gonna bore you clean out of your minds with the most meaningless, idiotic night you've ever seen in you life! And that means exactly what it sounds like it means!
My name is Squirt! I'm a sensitive intellectual! I drive an average of 200 miles a night up and down Main Street! My ambition is to make out with a chick in a white T-Bird who I never met! And the man I admire most in the world is the town disc jockey, Were-wolf Wally! Well, here in California, that's a sensitive intellectual!!
My name is Steed! I'm in love with Squirt's sister, Borey! Tomorrow, Squirt and I are supposed to leave for college in the East! Borey wants me to stay here, marry her, and go to UCLA! But my High School grades aren't good enough to get me into a California college! I . . . I flunked Surfing!
I'm Yawn! I'm also in love! But not with some dopey High School kid! My love is deeper and more meaningful! I'm in love with a 1958 Mercedes! I know it sounds ridiculous, but if we can work out our religious differences, who knows . . . ?
My name is Terrier! I'm the square in the crowd! And, boy . . . have I got problems! First of all, I look like David Eisenhower!
Come to think of it, with a problem like that, the others are unimportant!
My name i Jimmy! I'n not really in this picture! But, just for a change, I thought somebody out there might like to see a nice, old familiar face on the screen!
STEAKS CHOPS
Mel's drive-in
DRUCKER

:me producer has just discovered another decade! What else? The 1960's! ay, all you nostalgic 12-year-olds out there, it's time now to go back to the)aring Sixties" and reminisce over your glorious past—just a few minutes). So bring out the banners, fall into line, and get ready to march in one more :rade down "Memory Lane, U.S.A."...while we here at MAD start tossing

CONFETTI

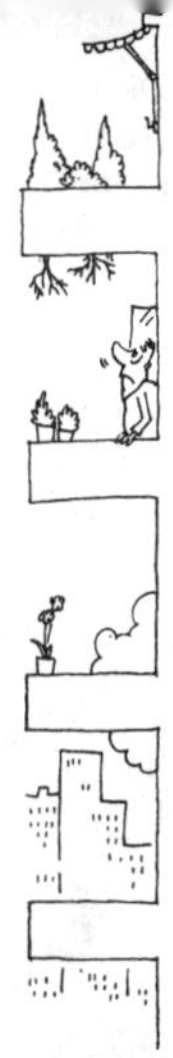

ARTIST:
MORT DRUCKER

WRITER:
LARRY SIEGEL

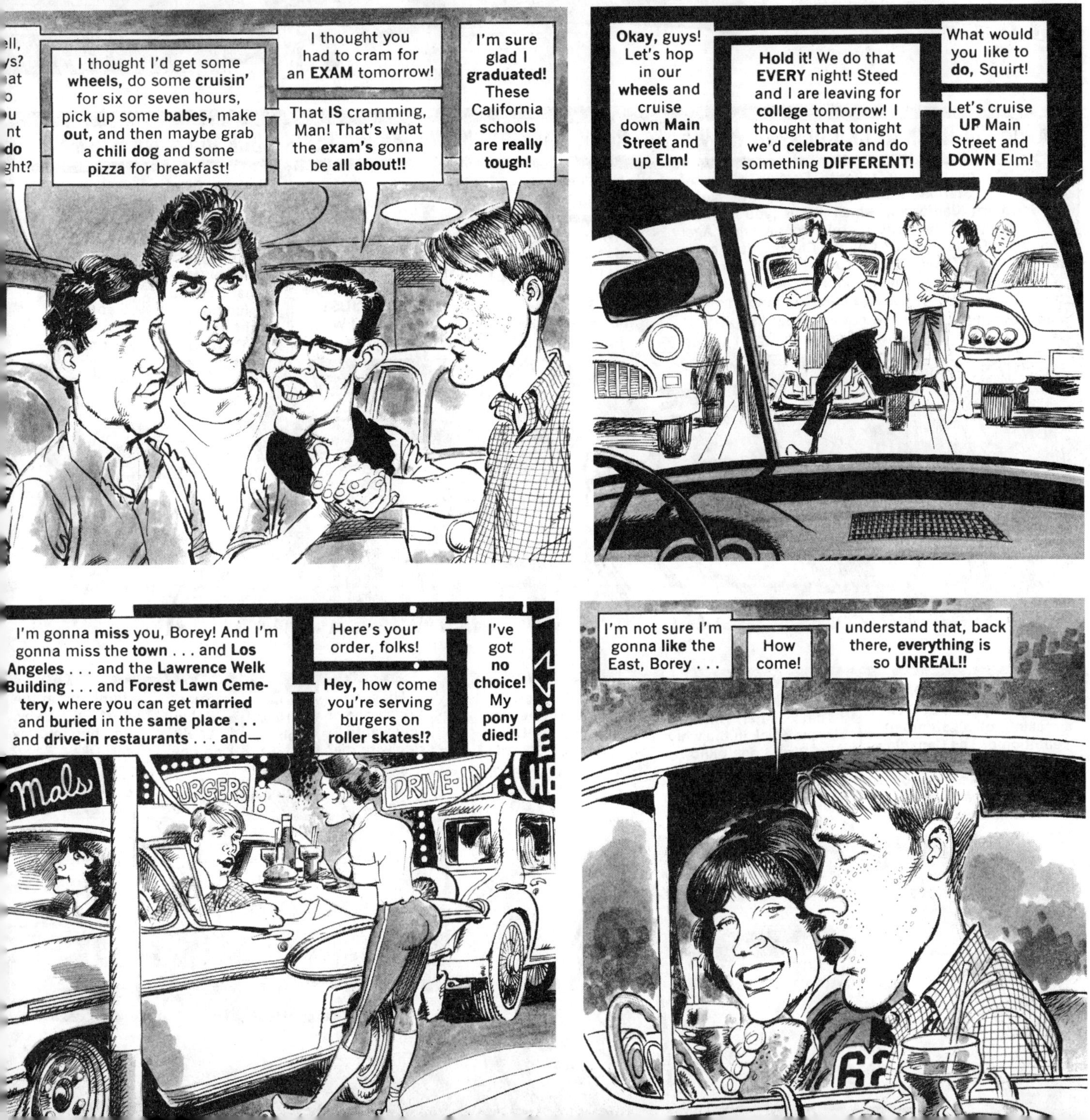
I thought I'd get some wheels, do some cruisin' for six or seven hours, pick up some babes, make out, and then maybe grab a chili dog and some pizza for breakfast!
I thought you had to cram for an EXAM tomorrow!
That IS cramming, Man! That's what the exam's gonna be all about!!
I'm sure glad I graduated! These California schools are really tough!
Okay, guys! Let's hop in our wheels and cruise down Main Street and up Elm!
Hold it! We do that EVERY night! Steed and I are leaving for college tomorrow! I thought that tonight we'd celebrate and do something DIFFERENT!
What would you like to do, Squirt!
Let's cruise UP Main Street and DOWN Elm!
I'm gonna miss you, Borey! And I'm gonna miss the town . . . and Los Angeles . . . and the Lawrence Welk Building . . . and Forest Lawn Cemetery, where you can get married and buried in the same place . . . and drive-in restaurants . . . and—
Here's your order, folks!
Hey, how come you're serving burgers on roller skates!?
I've got no choice! My pony died!
Mals
BURGERS
DRIVE-IN
I'm not sure I'm gonna like the East, Borey . . .
How come!
I understand that, back there, everything is so UNREAL!!
62

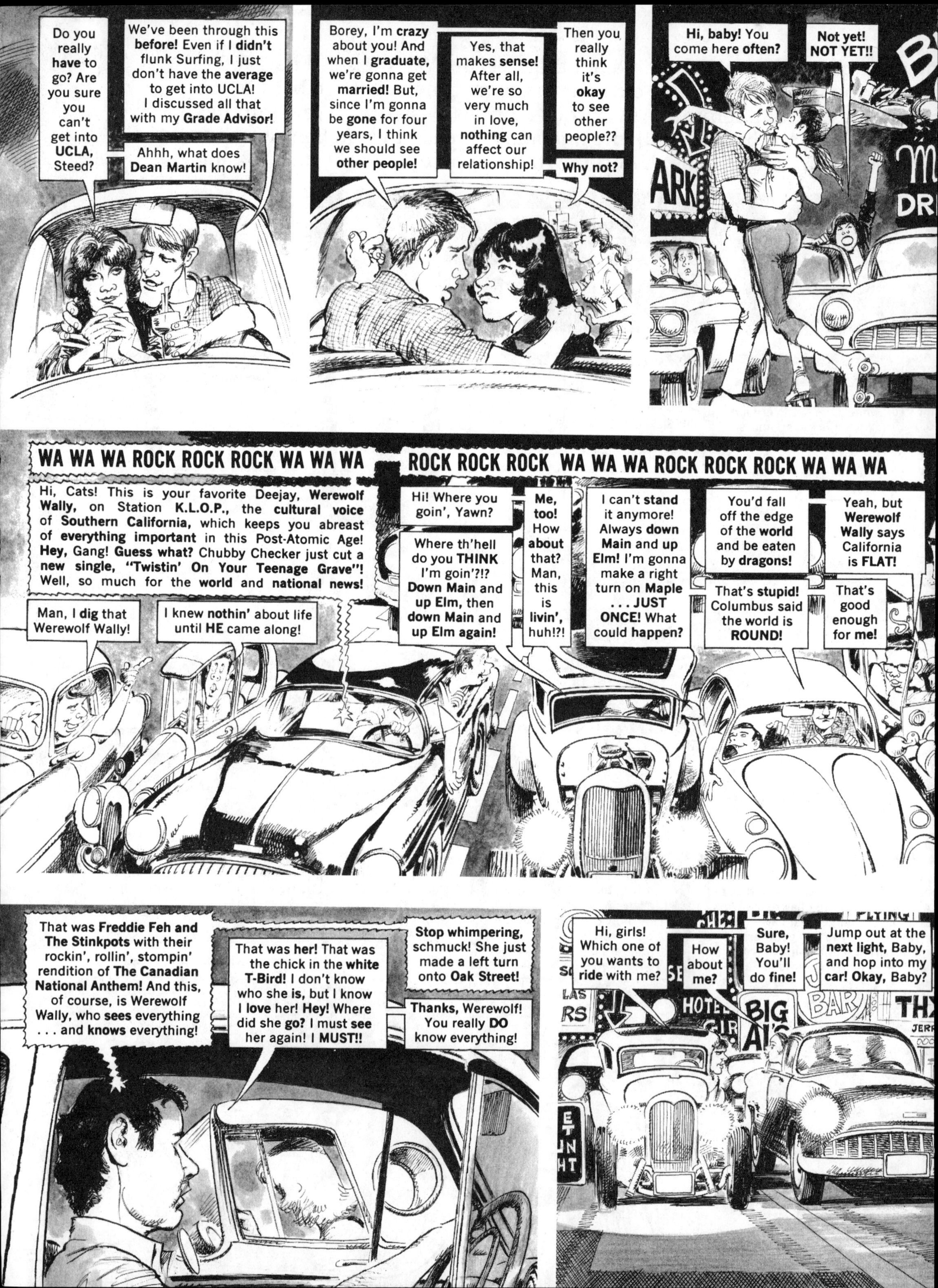
Do you really have to go? Are you sure you can't get into UCLA, Steed?
We've been through this before! Even if I didn't flunk Surfing, I just don't have the average to get into UCLA! I discussed all that with my Grade Advisor!
Ahhh, what does Dean Martin know!
Borey, I'm crazy about you! And when I graduate, we're gonna get married! But, since I'm gonna be gone for four years, I think we should see other people!
Yes, that makes sense! After all, we're so very much in love, nothing can affect our relationship!
Then you really think it's okay to see other people??
Why not?
Hi, baby! You come here often?
Not yet! NOT YET!!
WA WA WA ROCK ROCK ROCK WA WA WA
ROCK ROCK ROCK WA WA WA ROCK ROCK ROCK WA WA WA
Hi, Cats! This is your favorite Deejay, Werewolf Wally, on Station K.L.O.P., the cultural voice of Southern California, which keeps you abreast of everything important in this Post-Atomic Age! Hey, Gang! Guess what? Chubby Checker just cut a new single, "Twistin' On Your Teenage Grave"! Well, so much for the world and national news!
Man, I dig that Werewolf Wally!
I knew nothin' about life until HE came along!
Hi! Where you goin', Yawn?
Where th'hell do you THINK I'm goin'?!? Down Main and up Elm, then down Main and up Elm again!
Me, too! How about that? Man, this is livin', huh!?!
I can't stand it anymore! Always down Main and up Elm! I'm gonna make a right turn on Maple . . . JUST ONCE! What could happen?
You'd fall off the edge of the world and be eaten by dragons!
Yeah, but Werewolf Wally says California is FLAT!
That's stupid! Columbus said the world is ROUND!
That's good enough for me!
That was Freddie Feh and The Stinkpots with their rockin', rollin', stompin' rendition of The Canadian National Anthem! And this, of course, is Werewolf Wally, who sees everything . . . and knows everything!
That was her! That was the chick in the white T-Bird! I don't know who she is, but I know I love her! Hey! Where did she go? I must see her again! I MUST!!
Stop whimpering, schmuck! She just made a left turn onto Oak Street!
Thanks, Werewolf! You really DO know everything!
Hi, girls! Which one of you wants to ride with me?
How about me?
Sure, Baby! You'll do fine!
Jump out at the next light, Baby, and hop into my car! Okay, Baby?
HOTEL
BIG AL'S
BAR

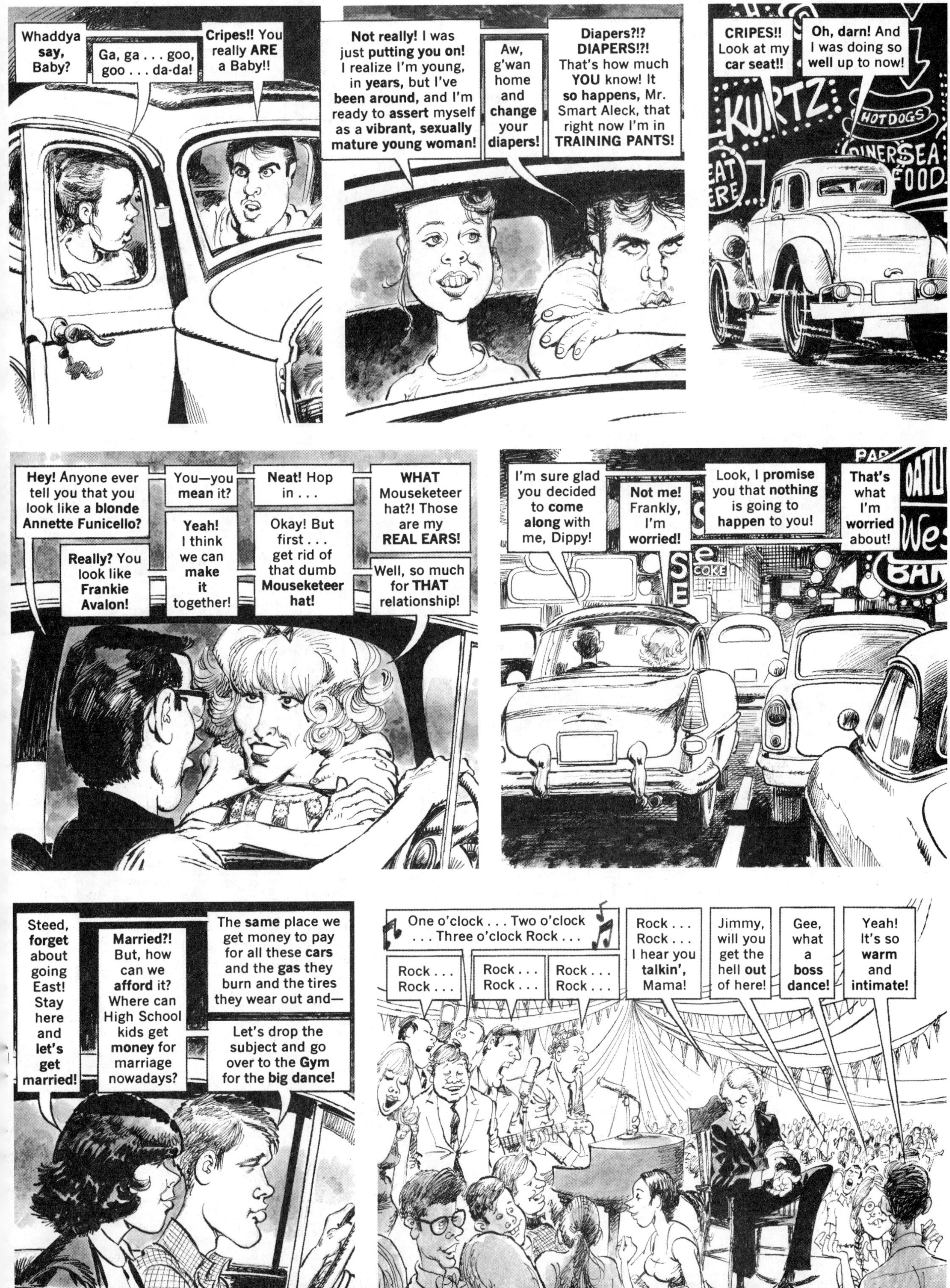
Whaddya say, Baby?
Ga, ga . . . goo, goo . . . da-da!
Cripes!! You really ARE a Baby!!
Not really! I was just putting you on! I realize I'm young, in years, but I've been around, and I'm ready to assert myself as a vibrant, sexually mature young woman!
Aw, g'wan home and change your diapers!
Diapers?!? DIAPERS!?! That's how much YOU know! It so happens, Mr. Smart Aleck, that right now I'm in TRAINING PANTS!
CRIPES!! Look at my car seat!!
Oh, darn! And I was doing so well up to now!
KURTZ
HOTDOGS
DINER
SEA FOOD
Hey! Anyone ever tell you that you look like a blonde Annette Funicello?
Really? You look like Frankie Avalon!
You—you mean it?
Yeah! I think we can make it together!
Neat! Hop in . . .
Okay! But first . . . get rid of that dumb Mouseketeer hat!
WHAT Mouseketeer hat?! Those are my REAL EARS!
Well, so much for THAT relationship!
I'm sure glad you decided to come along with me, Dippy!
Not me! Frankly, I'm worried!
Look, I promise you that nothing is going to happen to you!
That's what I'm worried about!
Steed, forget about going East! Stay here and let's get married!
Married?! But, how can we afford it? Where can High School kids get money for marriage nowadays?
The same place we get money to pay for all these cars and the gas they burn and the tires they wear out and—
Let's drop the subject and go over to the Gym for the big dance!
One o'clock . . . Two o'clock . . . Three o'clock Rock . . .
Rock . . . Rock . . .
Rock . . . Rock . . .
Rock . . . Rock . . .
Rock . . . Rock . . . I hear you talkin', Mama!
Jimmy, will you get the hell out of here!
Gee, what a boss dance!
Yeah! It's so warm and intimate!

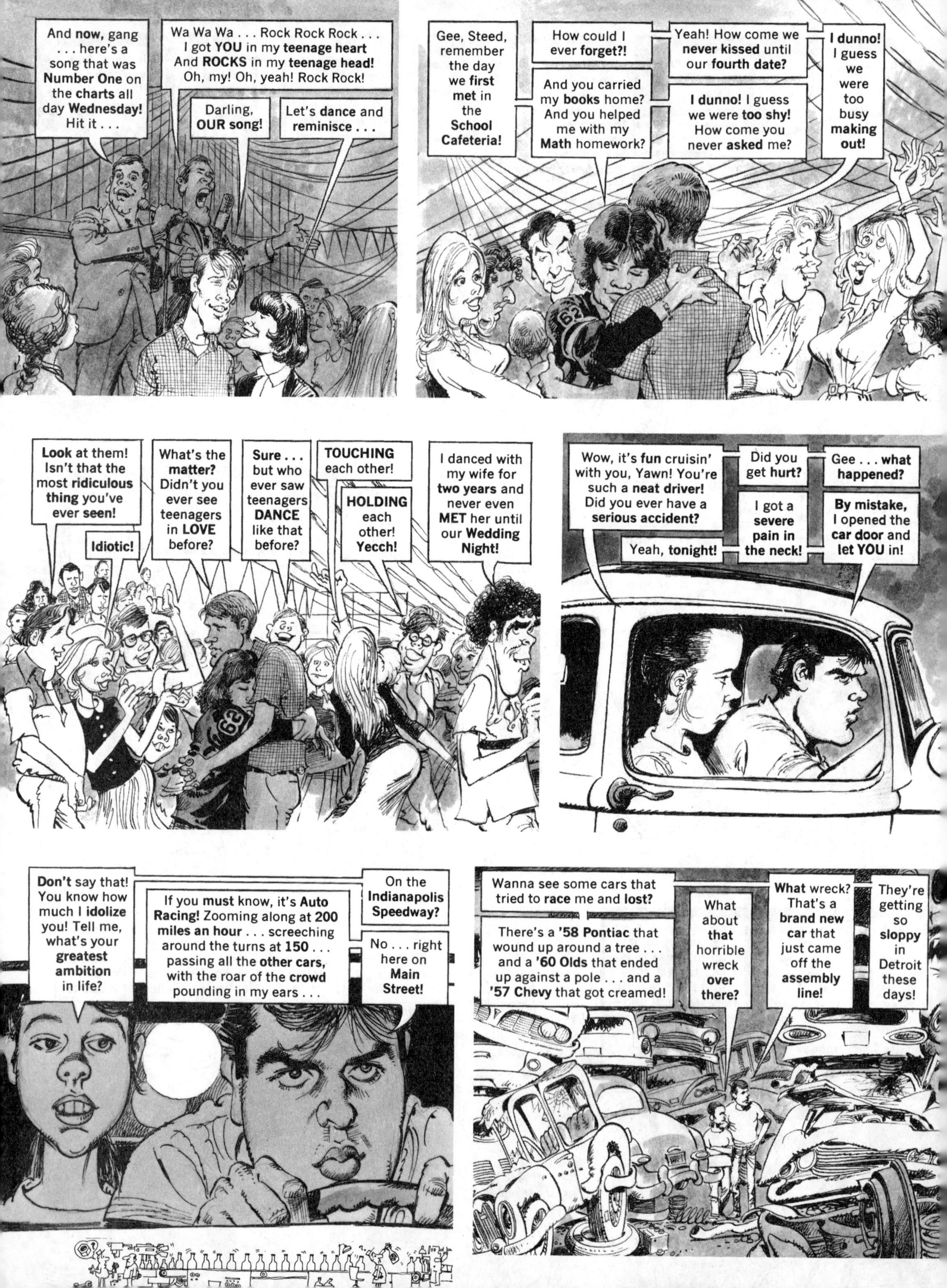

And now, gang . . . here's a song that was Number One on the charts all day Wednesday! Hit it . . .
Wa Wa Wa . . . Rock Rock Rock . . . I got YOU in my teenage heart And ROCKS in my teenage head! Oh, my! Oh, yeah! Rock Rock!
Darling, OUR song!
Let's dance and reminisce . . .
Gee, Steed, remember the day we first met in the School Cafeteria!
How could I ever forget?!
And you carried my books home? And you helped me with my Math homework?
Yeah! How come we never kissed until our fourth date?
I dunno! I guess we were too shy! How come you never asked me?
I dunno! I guess we were too busy making out!
Look at them! Isn't that the most ridiculous thing you've ever seen!
Idiotic!
What's the matter? Didn't you ever see teenagers in LOVE before?
Sure . . . but who ever saw teenagers DANCE like that before?
TOUCHING each other!
HOLDING each other! Yecch!
I danced with my wife for two years and never even MET her until our Wedding Night!
Wow, it's fun cruisin' with you, Yawn! You're such a neat driver! Did you ever have a serious accident?
Yeah, tonight!
Did you get hurt?
I got a severe pain in the neck!
Gee . . . what happened?
By mistake, I opened the car door and let YOU in!
Don't say that! You know how much I idolize you! Tell me, what's your greatest ambition in life?
If you must know, it's Auto Racing! Zooming along at 200 miles an hour . . . screeching around the turns at 150 . . . passing all the other cars, with the roar of the crowd pounding in my ears . . .
On the Indianapolis Speedway?
No . . . right here on Main Street!
Wanna see some cars that tried to race me and lost?
There's a '58 Pontiac that wound up around a tree . . . and a '60 Olds that ended up against a pole . . . and a '57 Chevy that got creamed!
What about that horrible wreck over there?
What wreck? That's a brand new car that just came off the assembly line!
They're getting so sloppy in Detroit these days!

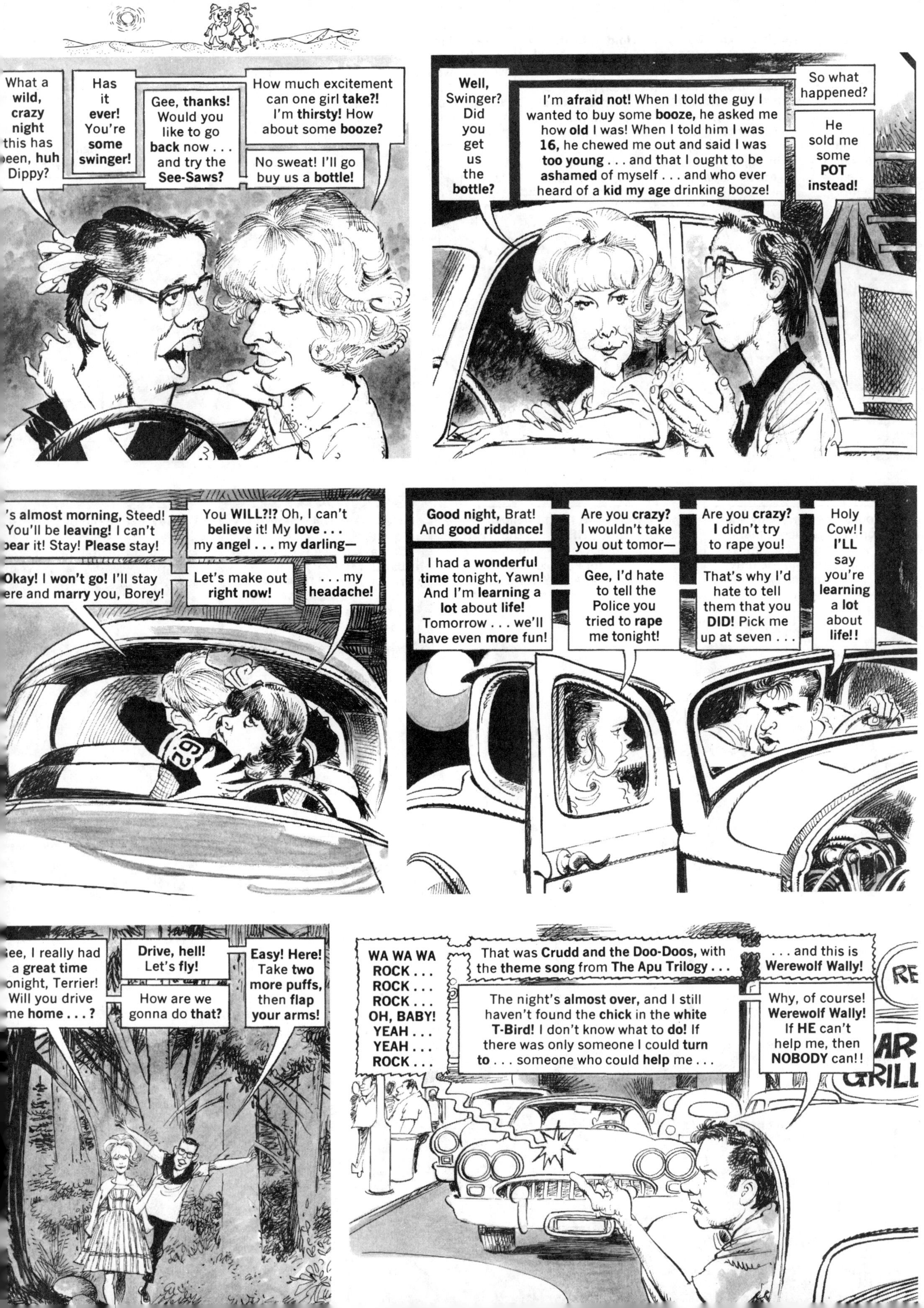

What a wild, crazy night this has een, huh Dippy?
Has it ever! You're some swinger!
Gee, thanks! Would you like to go back now . . . and try the See-Saws?
How much excitement can one girl take?! I'm thirsty! How about some booze?
No sweat! I'll go buy us a bottle!
Well, Swinger? Did you get us the bottle?
I'm afraid not! When I told the guy I wanted to buy some booze, he asked me how old I was! When I told him I was 16, he chewed me out and said I was too young . . . and that I ought to be ashamed of myself . . . and who ever heard of a kid my age drinking booze!
So what happened?
He sold me some POT instead!
's almost morning, Steed! You'll be leaving! I can't ear it! Stay! Please stay!
You WILL?!? Oh, I can't believe it! My love . . . my angel . . . my darling—
Okay! I won't go! I'll stay ere and marry you, Borey!
Let's make out right now!
. . . my headache!
Good night, Brat! And good riddance!
I had a wonderful time tonight, Yawn! And I'm learning a lot about life! Tomorrow . . . we'll have even more fun!
Are you crazy? I wouldn't take you out tomor—
Gee, I'd hate to tell the Police you tried to rape me tonight!
Are you crazy? I didn't try to rape you!
That's why I'd hate to tell them that you DID! Pick me up at seven . . .
Holy Cow!! I'LL say you're learning a lot about life!!
ee, I really had a great time tonight, Terrier! Will you drive me home . . . ?
Drive, hell! Let's fly!
How are we gonna do that?
Easy! Here! Take two more puffs, then flap your arms!
WA WA WA ROCK . . . ROCK . . . ROCK . . . OH, BABY! YEAH . . . YEAH . . . ROCK . . .
That was Crudd and the Doo-Doos, with the theme song from The Apu Trilogy . . .
. . . and this is Werewolf Wally!
The night's almost over, and I still haven't found the chick in the white T-Bird! I don't know what to do! If there was only someone I could turn to . . . someone who could help me . . .
Why, of course! Werewolf Wally! If HE can't help me, then NOBODY can!!
GRILL

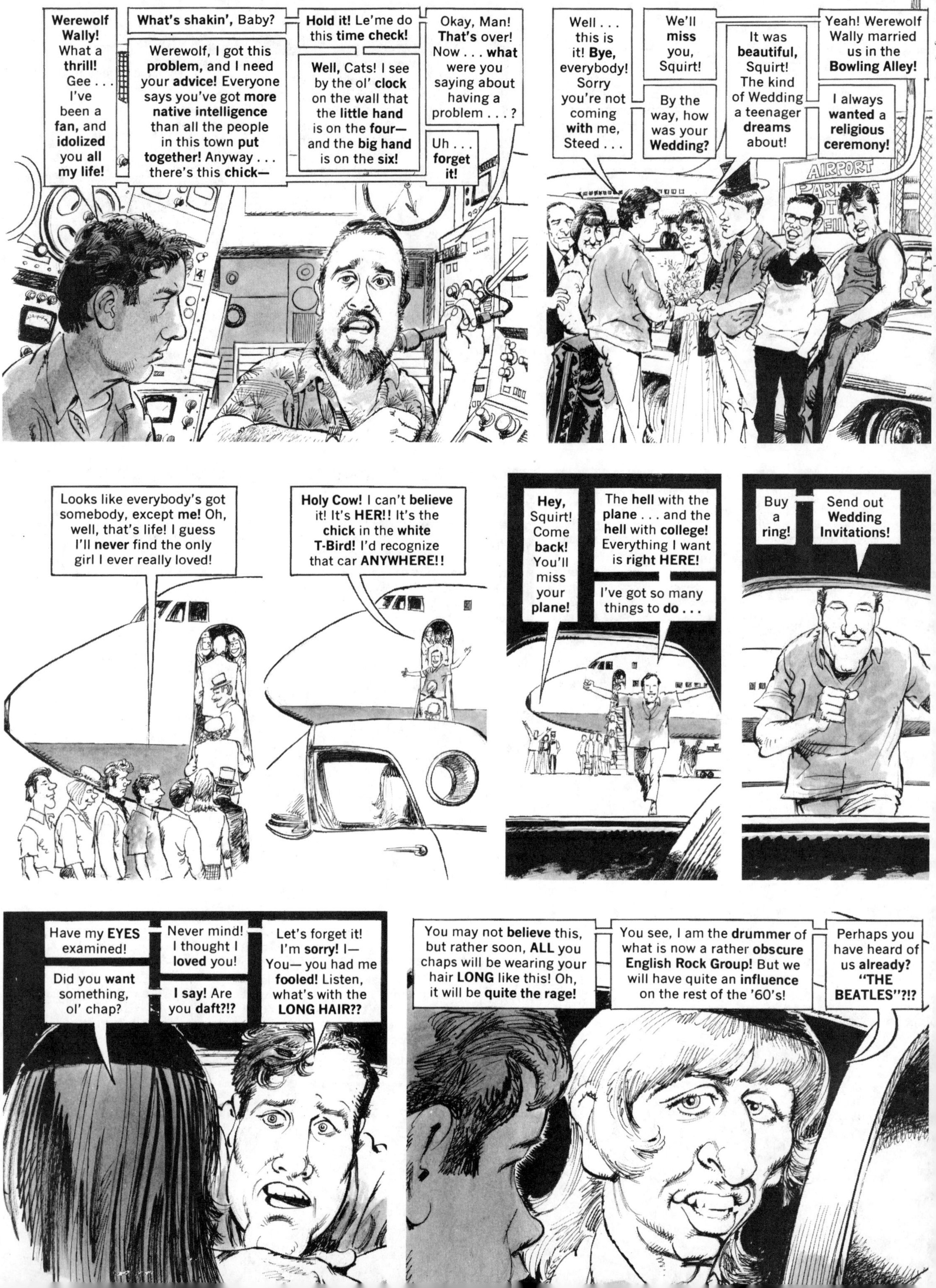
Werewolf Wally! What a thrill! Gee . . . I've been a fan, and idolized you all my life!
What's shakin', Baby?
Werewolf, I got this problem, and I need your advice! Everyone says you've got more native intelligence than all the people in this town put together! Anyway . . . there's this chick—
Hold it! Le'me do this time check!
Well, Cats! I see by the ol' clock on the wall that the little hand is on the four— and the big hand is on the six!
Okay, Man! That's over! Now . . . what were you saying about having a problem . . . ?
Uh . . . forget it!
Well . . . this is it! Bye, everybody! Sorry you're not coming with me, Steed . . .
We'll miss you, Squirt!
By the way, how was your Wedding?
It was beautiful, Squirt! The kind of Wedding a teenager dreams about!
Yeah! Werewolf Wally married us in the Bowling Alley!
I always wanted a religious ceremony!
AIRPORT
Looks like everybody's got somebody, except me! Oh, well, that's life! I guess I'll never find the only girl I ever really loved!
Holy Cow! I can't believe it! It's HER!! It's the chick in the white T-Bird! I'd recognize that car ANYWHERE!!
Hey, Squirt! Come back! You'll miss your plane!
The hell with the plane . . . and the hell with college! Everything I want is right HERE!
I've got so many things to do . . .
Buy a ring!
Send out Wedding Invitations!
Have my EYES examined!
Never mind! I thought I loved you!
Did you want something, ol' chap?
I say! Are you daft?!?
Let's forget it! I'm sorry! I— You— you had me fooled! Listen, what's with the LONG HAIR??
You may not believe this, but rather soon, ALL you chaps will be wearing your hair LONG like this! Oh, it will be quite the rage!
You see, I am the drummer of what is now a rather obscure English Rock Group! But we will have quite an influence on the rest of the '60's!
Perhaps you have heard of us already? "THE BEATLES"?!?

JOKE AND DAGGER DEPT.

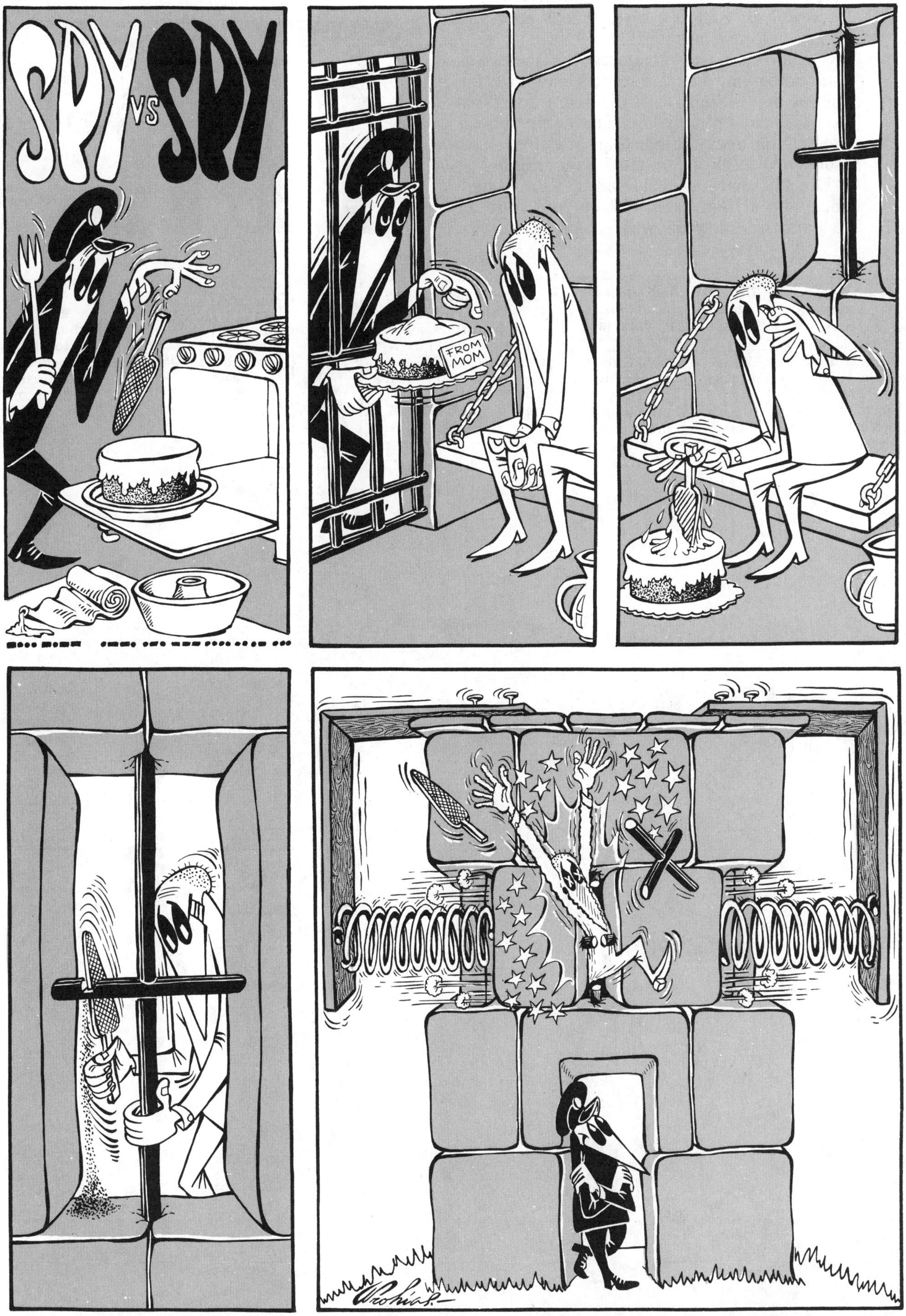
SPY vs SPY
FROM MOM

BETWEEN THE DEVIL AND THE HOLY SEE DEPT.

Remember the good old days when Hollywood used to make horror movies about vampires, werewolves, zombies, seventy foot apes and other assorted monsters? Let's face it, they were all disgusting creatures, but there was still something kinda harmless and loveable about them. Well, those days are gone forever. Today's film makers have come up with something *really* disgusting. Yessiree, you screamed at "Frankenstein," you shrieked at "Dracula" and you shuddered at "King Kong," but take it from us . . . those guys were all a bunch of pussycats when compared to . . .

THE

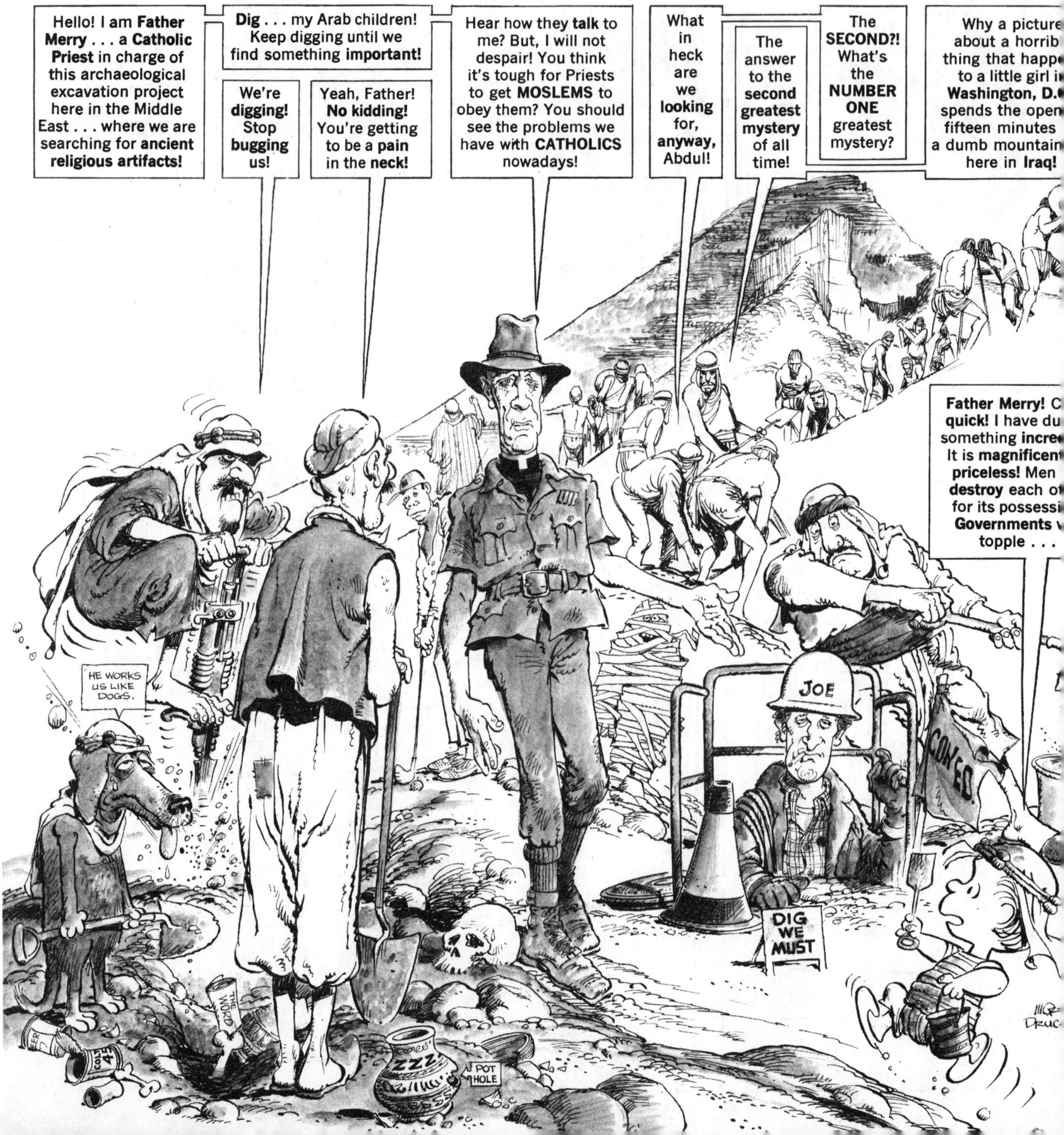

Hello! I am Father Merry . . . a Catholic Priest in charge of this archaeological excavation project here in the Middle East . . . where we are searching for ancient religious artifacts!
Dig . . . my Arab children! Keep digging until we find something important!
We're digging! Stop bugging us!
Yeah, Father! No kidding! You're getting to be a pain in the neck!
Hear how they talk to me? But, I will not despair! You think it's tough for Priests to get MOSLEMS to obey them? You should see the problems we have with CATHOLICS nowadays!
What in heck are we looking for, anyway, Abdul!
The answer to the second greatest mystery of all time!
The SECOND?! What's the NUMBER ONE greatest mystery?
Why a picture about a horrib thing that happe to a little girl i Washington, D. spends the open fifteen minutes a dumb mountain here in Iraq!
Father Merry! C quick! I have du something incre It is magnificent priceless! Men destroy each o for its possessi Governments topple . . .
HE WORKS US LIKE DOGS.
JOE
CON ED
DIG WE MUST
POT HOLE
THE WORD
ZZZ

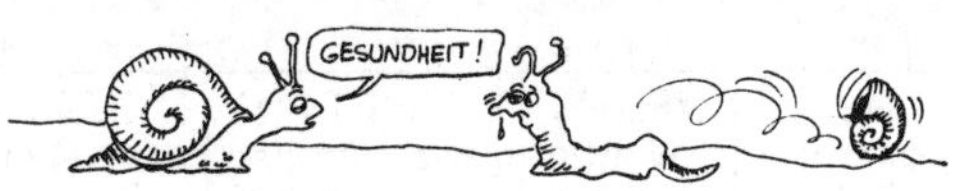
GESUNDHEIT!

CCHORCIST

ARTIST: MORT DRUCKER WRITER: LARRY SIEGEL

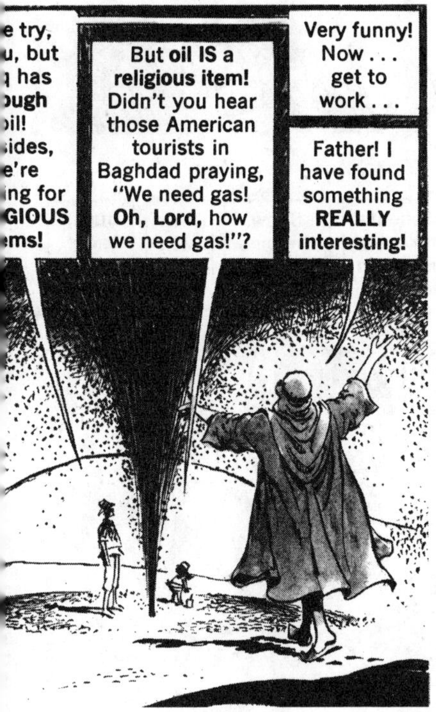
e try, u, but has ough oil! ides, e're ng for GIOUS ems!
But oil IS a religious item! Didn't you hear those American tourists in Baghdad praying, "We need gas! Oh, Lord, how we need gas!"?
Very funny! Now . . . get to work . . .
Father! I have found something REALLY interesting!

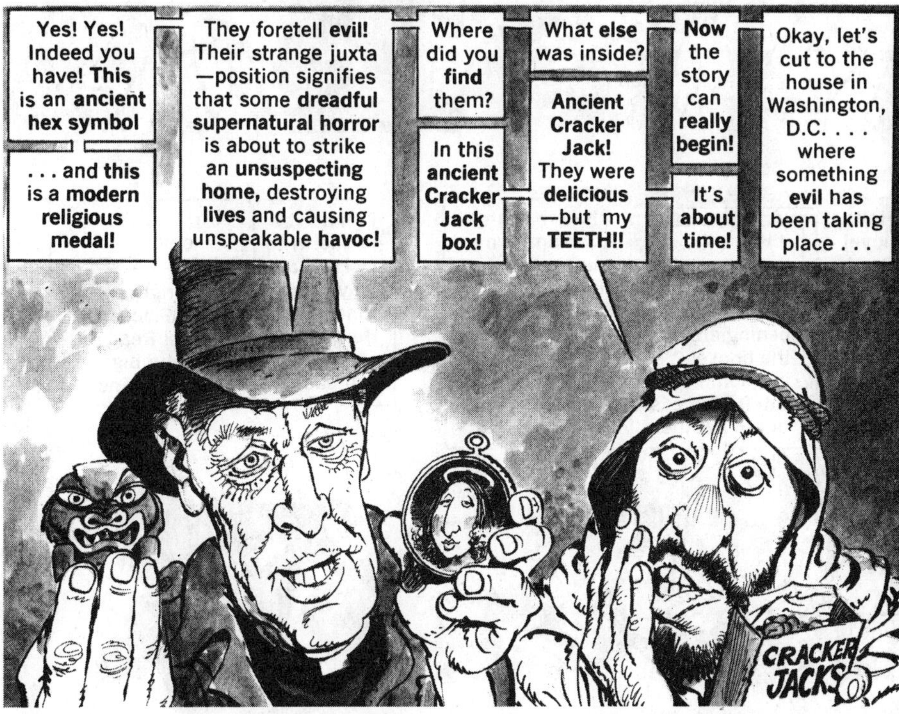
Yes! Yes! Indeed you have! This is an ancient hex symbol
. . . and this is a modern religious medal!
They foretell evil! Their strange juxta—position signifies that some dreadful supernatural horror is about to strike an unsuspecting home, destroying lives and causing unspeakable havoc!
Where did you find them?
In this ancient Cracker Jack box!
What else was inside?
Ancient Cracker Jack! They were delicious—but my TEETH!!
Now the story can really begin!
It's about time!
Okay, let's cut to the house in Washington, D.C. . . . where something evil has been taking place . . .
CRACKER JACKS

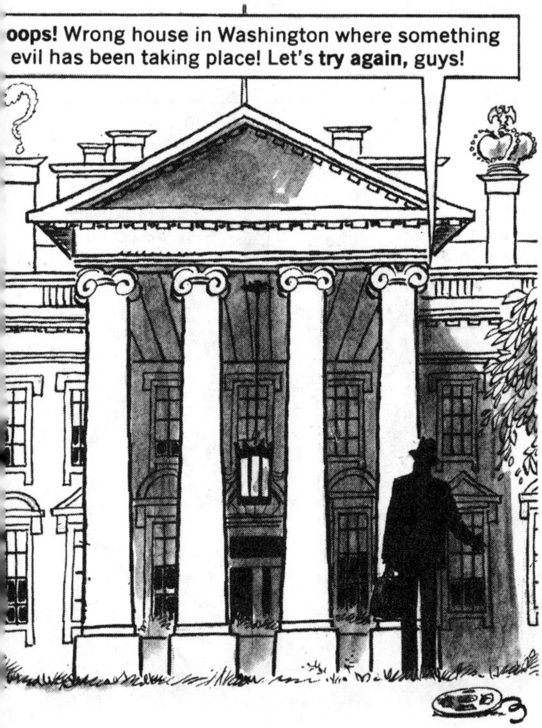
oops! Wrong house in Washington where something evil has been taking place! Let's try again, guys!

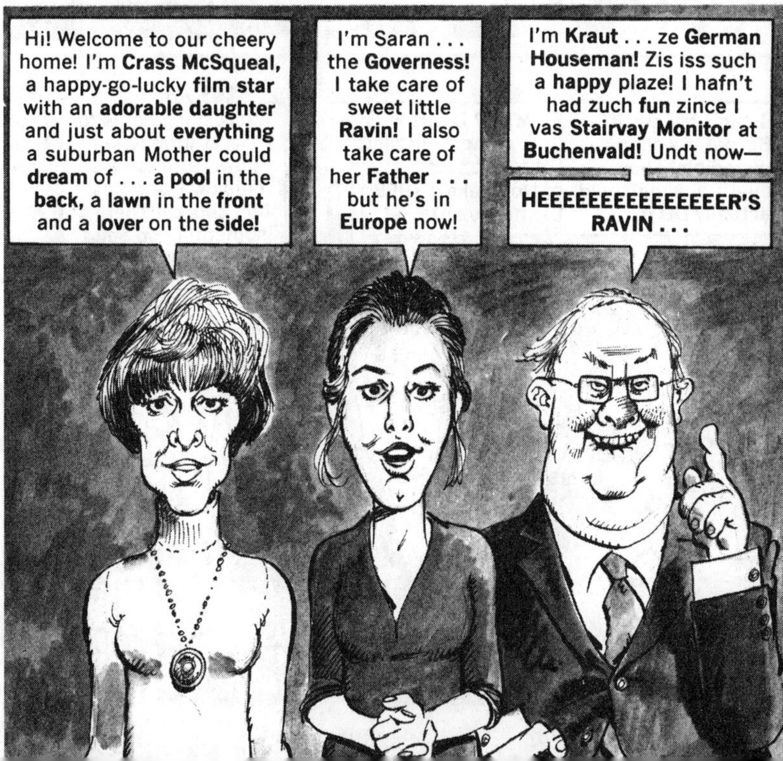
Hi! Welcome to our cheery home! I'm Crass McSqueal, a happy-go-lucky film star with an adorable daughter and just about everything a suburban Mother could dream of . . . a pool in the back, a lawn in the front and a lover on the side!
I'm Saran . . . the Governess! I take care of sweet little Ravin! I also take care of her Father . . . but he's in Europe now!
I'm Kraut . . . ze German Houseman! Zis iss such a happy plaze! I hafn't had zuch fun zince I vas Stairvay Monitor at Buchenvald! Undt now—
HEEEEEEEEEEEEEER'S RAVIN . . .

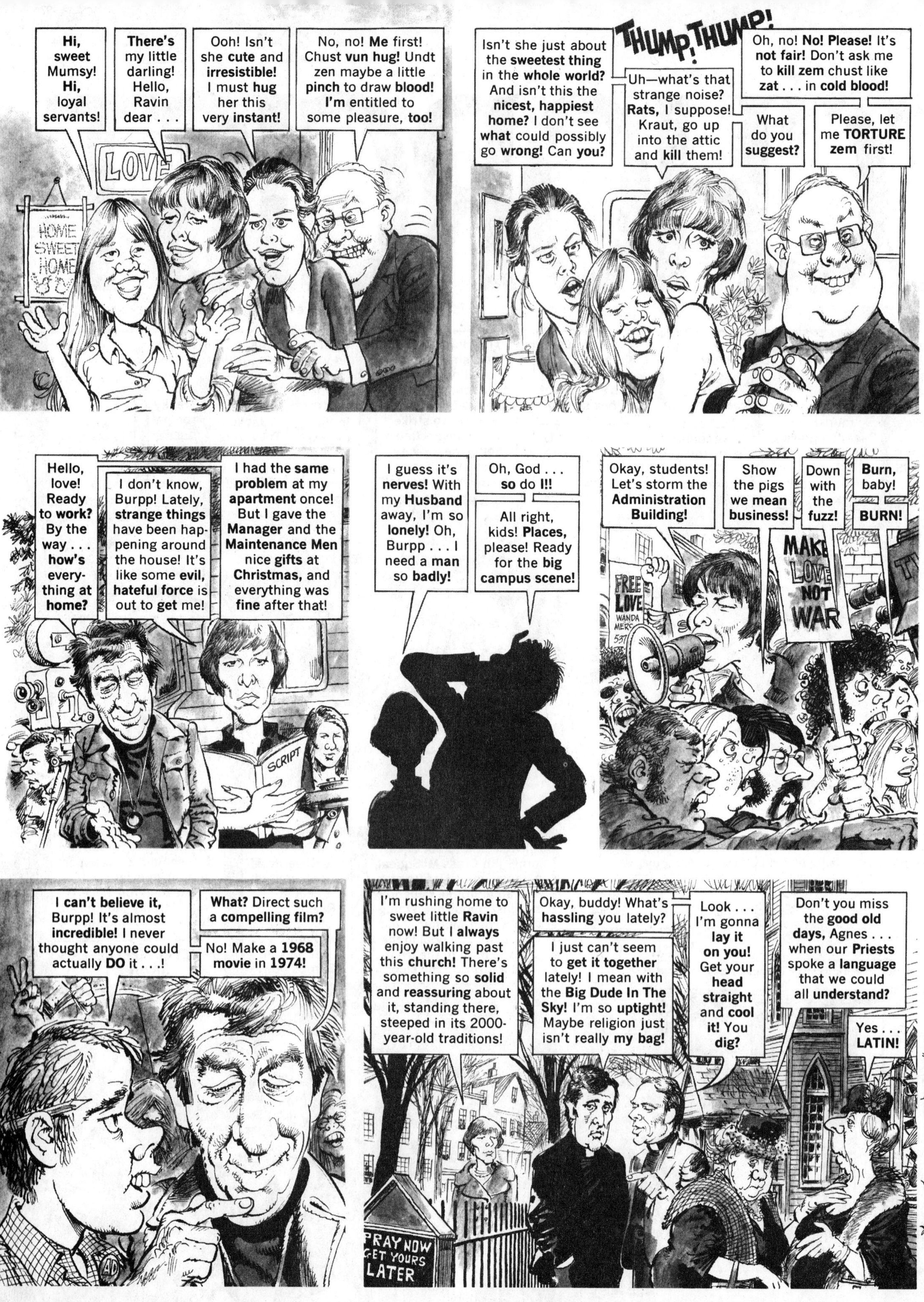
Hi, sweet Mumsy! Hi, loyal servants!
There's my little darling! Hello, Ravin dear . . .
Ooh! Isn't she cute and irresistible! I must hug her this very instant!
No, no! Me first! Chust vun hug! Undt zen maybe a little pinch to draw blood! I'm entitled to some pleasure, too!
LOVE
HOME SWEET HOME
Isn't she just about the sweetest thing in the whole world? And isn't this the nicest, happiest home? I don't see what could possibly go wrong! Can you?
THUMP! THUMP!
Uh—what's that strange noise? Rats, I suppose! Kraut, go up into the attic and kill them!
Oh, no! No! Please! It's not fair! Don't ask me to kill zem chust like zat . . . in cold blood!
What do you suggest?
Please, let me TORTURE zem first!
Hello, love! Ready to work? By the way . . . how's everything at home?
I don't know, Burpp! Lately, strange things have been happening around the house! It's like some evil, hateful force is out to get me!
I had the same problem at my apartment once! But I gave the Manager and the Maintenance Men nice gifts at Christmas, and everything was fine after that!
SCRIPT
I guess it's nerves! With my Husband away, I'm so lonely! Oh, Burpp . . . I need a man so badly!
Oh, God . . . so do I!!
All right, kids! Places, please! Ready for the big campus scene!
Okay, students! Let's storm the Administration Building!
Show the pigs we mean business!
Down with the fuzz!
Burn, baby!
BURN!
MAKE LOVE NOT WAR
FREE LOVE
I can't believe it, Burpp! It's almost incredible! I never thought anyone could actually DO it . . .!
What? Direct such a compelling film?
No! Make a 1968 movie in 1974!
I'm rushing home to sweet little Ravin now! But I always enjoy walking past this church! There's something so solid and reassuring about it, standing there, steeped in its 2000-year-old traditions!
Okay, buddy! What's hassling you lately?
I just can't seem to get it together lately! I mean with the Big Dude In The Sky! I'm so uptight! Maybe religion just isn't really my bag!
Look . . . I'm gonna lay it on you! Get your head straight and cool it! You dig?
Don't you miss the good old days, Agnes . . . when our Priests spoke a language that we could all understand?
Yes . . . LATIN!
PRAY NOW GET YOURS LATER

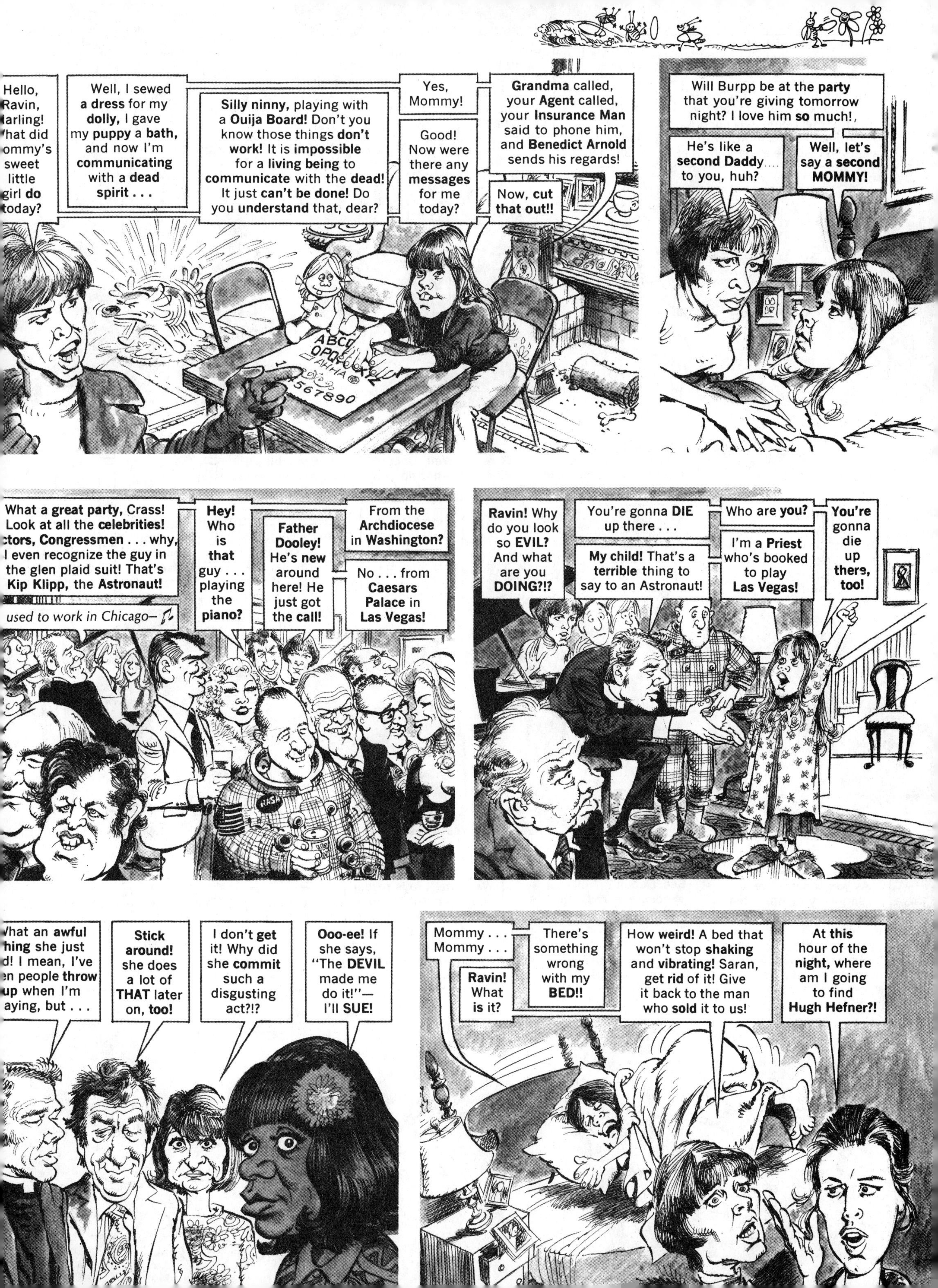

Hello, Ravin, arling! 'hat did ommy's sweet little girl do today?
Well, I sewed a dress for my dolly, I gave my puppy a bath, and now I'm communicating with a dead spirit . . .
Silly ninny, playing with a Ouija Board! Don't you know those things don't work! It is impossible for a living being to communicate with the dead! It just can't be done! Do you understand that, dear?
Yes, Mommy!
Good! Now were there any messages for me today?
Grandma called, your Agent called, your Insurance Man said to phone him, and Benedict Arnold sends his regards!
Now, cut that out!!
ABCD
OPQ
1234567890
Will Burpp be at the party that you're giving tomorrow night? I love him so much!,
He's like a second Daddy. . . . to you, huh?
Well, let's say a second MOMMY!
What a great party, Crass! Look at all the celebrities! ctors, Congressmen . . . why, I even recognize the guy in the glen plaid suit! That's Kip Klipp, the Astronaut!
used to work in Chicago—
Hey! Who is that guy . . . playing the piano?
Father Dooley! He's new around here! He just got the call!
From the Archdiocese in Washington?
No . . . from Caesars Palace in Las Vegas!
NASA
Ravin! Why do you look so EVIL? And what are you DOING?!?
You're gonna DIE up there . . .
My child! That's a terrible thing to say to an Astronaut!
Who are you?
I'm a Priest who's booked to play Las Vegas!
You're gonna die up there, too!
'hat an awful hing she just d! I mean, I've en people throw up when I'm aying, but . . .
Stick around! she does a lot of THAT later on, too!
I don't get it! Why did she commit such a disgusting act?!?
Ooo-ee! If she says, "The DEVIL made me do it!"— I'll SUE!
Mommy . . . Mommy . . .
Ravin! What is it?
There's something wrong with my BED!!
How weird! A bed that won't stop shaking and vibrating! Saran, get rid of it! Give it back to the man who sold it to us!
At this hour of the night, where am I going to find Hugh Hefner?!

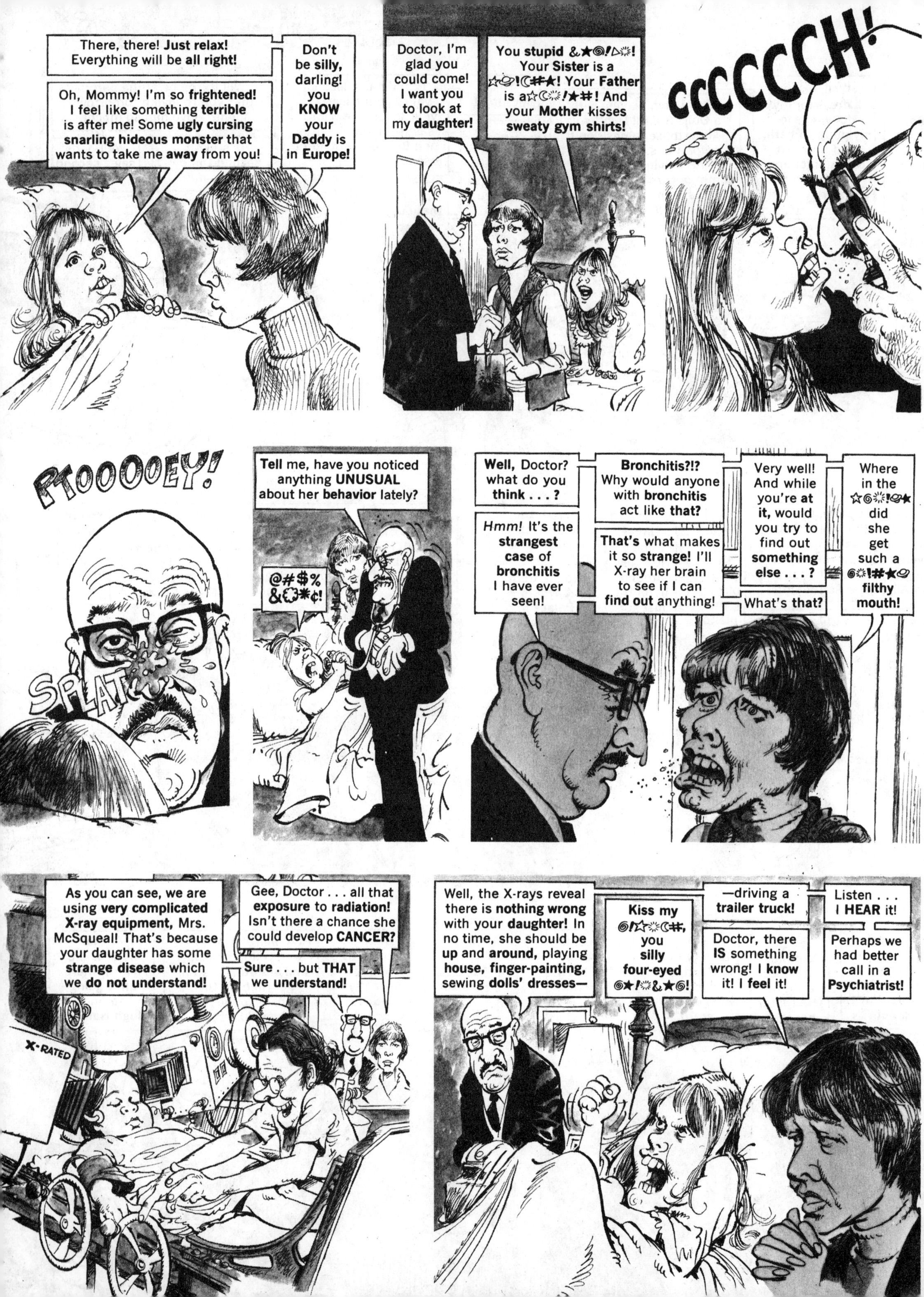
There, there! Just relax! Everything will be **all right!**
Oh, Mommy! I'm so **frightened!** I feel like something **terrible** is after me! Some **ugly cursing snarling hideous monster** that wants to take me **away** from you!
Don't be **silly,** darling! you **KNOW** your **Daddy** is in **Europe!**
Doctor, I'm glad you could come! I want you to look at my **daughter!**
You **stupid** &★@!△☼! Your **Sister** is a ☆♋!☾#★! Your **Father** is a☆☾☼!★#! And your **Mother** kisses **sweaty gym shirts!**
CCCCCCH!
PTOOOOEY!
SPLAT
Tell me, have you noticed anything **UNUSUAL** about her **behavior** lately?
@#$% &☼*¢!
Well, Doctor? what do you **think . . . ?**
Hmm! It's the **strangest case** of **bronchitis** I have ever seen!
Bronchitis?!? Why would anyone with **bronchitis** act like **that?**
That's what makes it so **strange!** I'll X-ray her brain to see if I can **find out** anything!
Very well! And while you're **at it,** would you try to find out **something else . . . ?**
What's **that?**
Where in the ☆@☼!♋★ did she get such a @☼!#★♋ **filthy mouth!**
As you can see, we are using **very complicated X-ray equipment,** Mrs. McSqueal! That's because your daughter has some **strange disease** which we **do not understand!**
Gee, Doctor . . . all that **exposure** to **radiation!** Isn't there a chance she could develop **CANCER?**
Sure . . . but **THAT** we **understand!**
X-RATED
Well, the X-rays reveal there is **nothing wrong** with your **daughter!** In no time, she should be **up** and **around,** playing **house, finger-painting,** sewing **dolls' dresses—**
Kiss my @!☆☼☾#, **you silly four-eyed** @★!☼&★@!
—driving a **trailer truck!**
Doctor, there **IS** something wrong! I **know** it! I **feel** it!
Listen . . . I **HEAR** it!
Perhaps we had better call in a **Psychiatrist!**

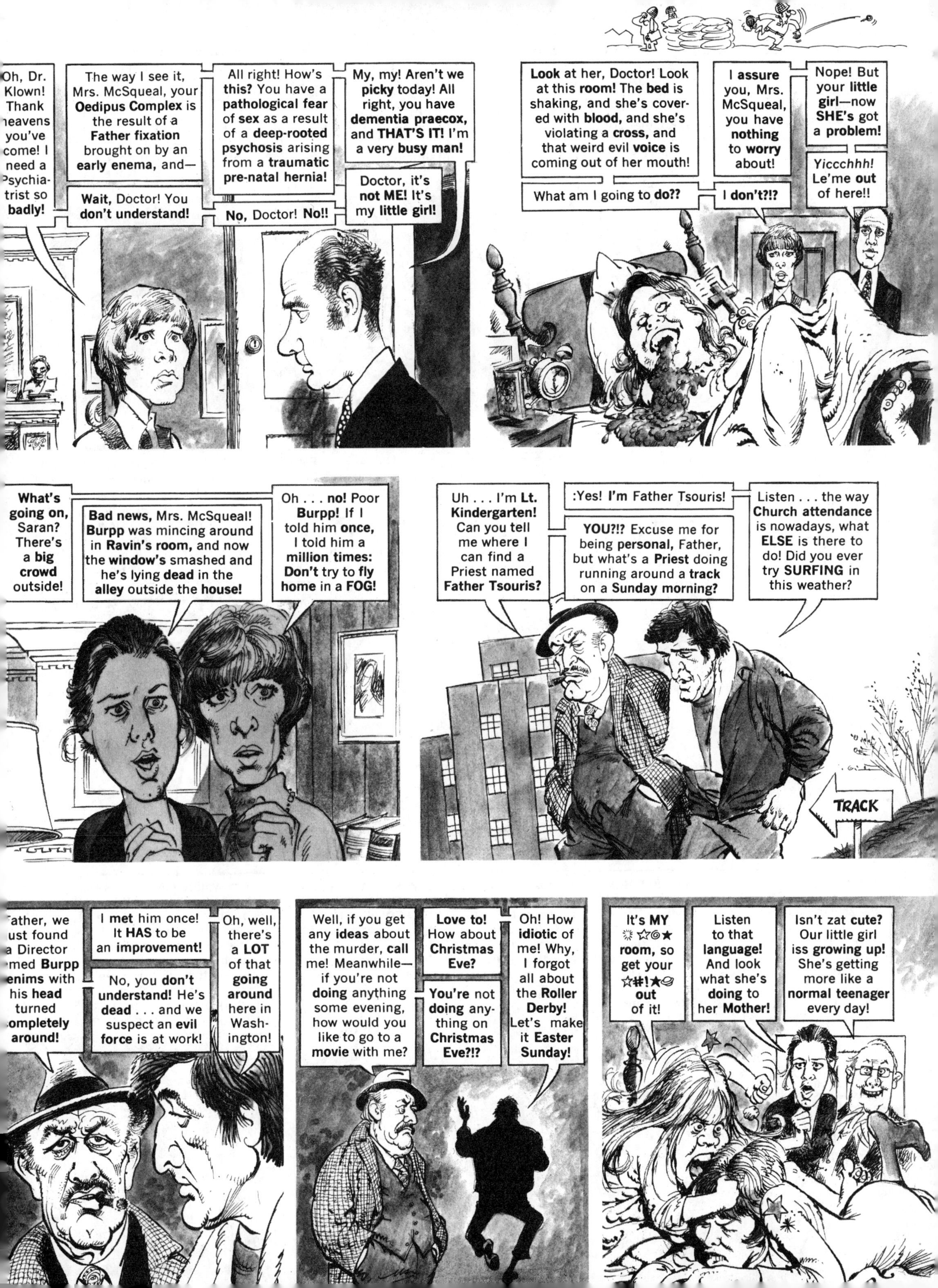

Oh, Dr. Klown! Thank eavens you've come! I need a sychia-trist so badly!
The way I see it, Mrs. McSqueal, your Oedipus Complex is the result of a Father fixation brought on by an early enema, and—
Wait, Doctor! You don't understand!
All right! How's this? You have a pathological fear of sex as a result of a deep-rooted psychosis arising from a traumatic pre-natal hernia!
No, Doctor! No!!
My, my! Aren't we picky today! All right, you have dementia praecox, and THAT'S IT! I'm a very busy man!
Doctor, it's not ME! It's my little girl!
Look at her, Doctor! Look at this room! The bed is shaking, and she's cover-ed with blood, and she's violating a cross, and that weird evil voice is coming out of her mouth!
What am I going to do??
I assure you, Mrs. McSqueal, you have nothing to worry about!
I don't?!?
Nope! But your little girl—now SHE's got a problem!
Yiccchhh! Le'me out of here!!
What's going on, Saran? There's a big crowd outside!
Bad news, Mrs. McSqueal! Burpp was mincing around in Ravin's room, and now the window's smashed and he's lying dead in the alley outside the house!
Oh . . . no! Poor Burpp! If I told him once, I told him a million times: Don't try to fly home in a FOG!
Uh . . . I'm Lt. Kindergarten! Can you tell me where I can find a Priest named Father Tsouris?
:Yes! I'm Father Tsouris!
YOU?!? Excuse me for being personal, Father, but what's a Priest doing running around a track on a Sunday morning?
Listen . . . the way Church attendance is nowadays, what ELSE is there to do! Did you ever try SURFING in this weather?
TRACK
ather, we ust found a Director med Burpp enims with his head turned ompletely around!
I met him once! It HAS to be an improvement!
No, you don't understand! He's dead . . . and we suspect an evil force is at work!
Oh, well, there's a LOT of that going around here in Wash-ington!
Well, if you get any ideas about the murder, call me! Meanwhile—if you're not doing anything some evening, how would you like to go to a movie with me?
Love to! How about Christmas Eve?
You're not doing any-thing on Christmas Eve?!?
Oh! How idiotic of me! Why, I forgot all about the Roller Derby! Let's make it Easter Sunday!
It's MY ☼☆@★ room, so get your ☆#!★@ out of it!
Listen to that language! And look what she's doing to her Mother!
Isn't zat cute? Our little girl iss growing up! She's getting more like a normal teenager every day!

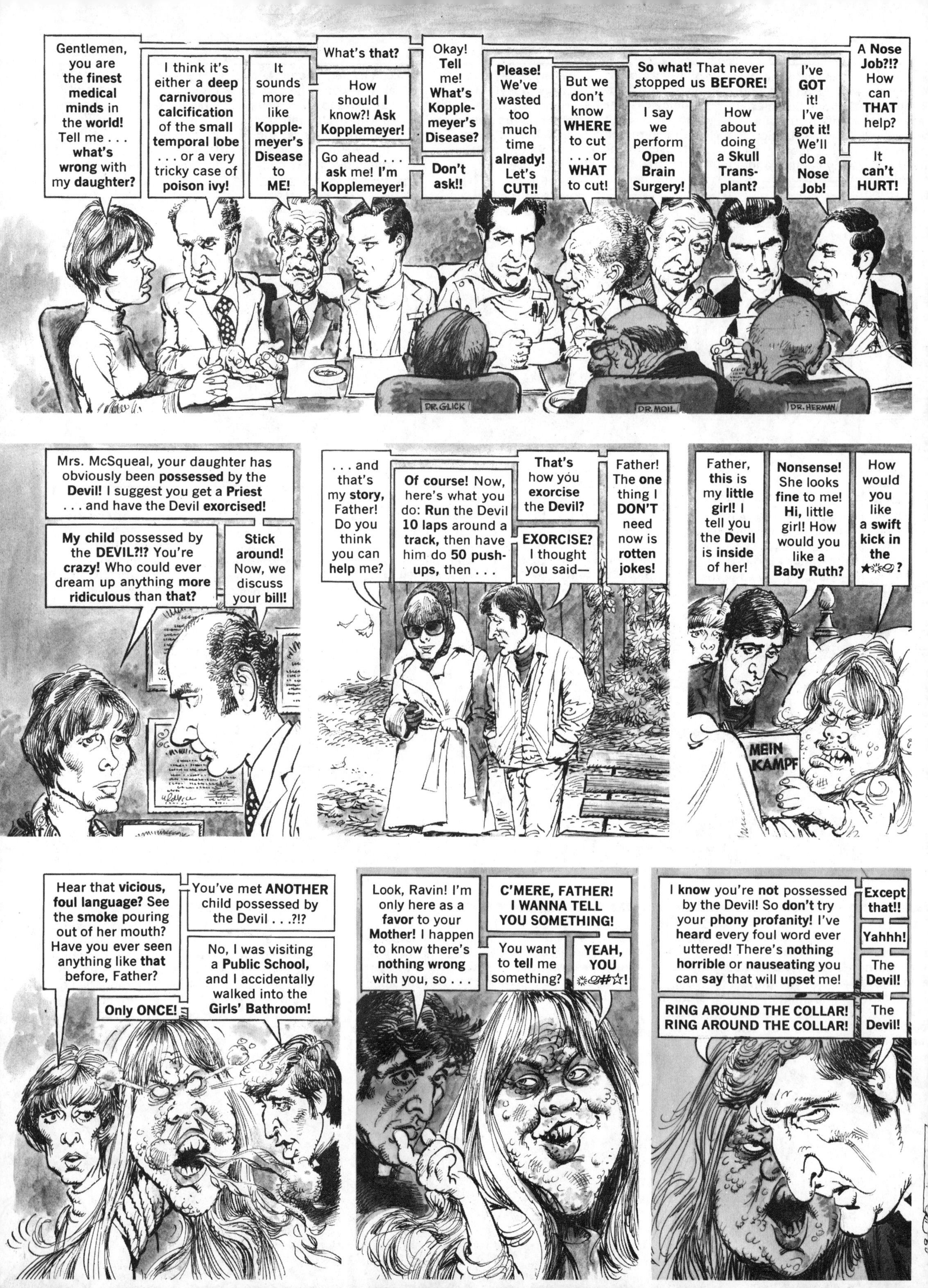

Gentlemen, you are the finest medical minds in the world! Tell me . . . what's wrong with my daughter?
I think it's either a deep carnivorous calcification of the small temporal lobe . . . or a very tricky case of poison ivy!
It sounds more like Kopplemeyer's Disease to ME!
What's that?
How should I know?! Ask Kopplemeyer!
Go ahead . . . ask me! I'm Kopplemeyer!
Okay! Tell me! What's Kopplemeyer's Disease?
Don't ask!!
Please! We've wasted too much time already! Let's CUT!!
But we don't know WHERE to cut . . . or WHAT to cut!
So what! That never stopped us BEFORE!
I say we perform Open Brain Surgery!
How about doing a Skull Transplant?
I've GOT it! I've got it! We'll do a Nose Job!
A Nose Job?!? How can THAT help?
It can't HURT!
DR. GLICK
DR. MOIL
DR. HERMAN
Mrs. McSqueal, your daughter has obviously been possessed by the Devil! I suggest you get a Priest . . . and have the Devil exorcised!
My child possessed by the DEVIL?!? You're crazy! Who could ever dream up anything more ridiculous than that?
Stick around! Now, we discuss your bill!
. . . and that's my story, Father! Do you think you can help me?
Of course! Now, here's what you do: Run the Devil 10 laps around a track, then have him do 50 push-ups, then . . .
That's how you exorcise the Devil?
EXORCISE? I thought you said—
Father! The one thing I DON'T need now is rotten jokes!
Father, this is my little girl! I tell you the Devil is inside of her!
Nonsense! She looks fine to me! Hi, little girl! How would you like a Baby Ruth?
How would you like a swift kick in the ★☼@?
MEIN KAMPF
Hear that vicious, foul language? See the smoke pouring out of her mouth? Have you ever seen anything like that before, Father?
Only ONCE!
You've met ANOTHER child possessed by the Devil . . .?!?
No, I was visiting a Public School, and I accidentally walked into the Girls' Bathroom!
Look, Ravin! I'm only here as a favor to your Mother! I happen to know there's nothing wrong with you, so . . .
C'MERE, FATHER! I WANNA TELL YOU SOMETHING!
You want to tell me something?
YEAH, YOU ☼@#☆!
I know you're not possessed by the Devil! So don't try your phony profanity! I've heard every foul word ever uttered! There's nothing horrible or nauseating you can say that will upset me!
Except that!!
Yahhh!
The Devil!
RING AROUND THE COLLAR! RING AROUND THE COLLAR!
The Devil!

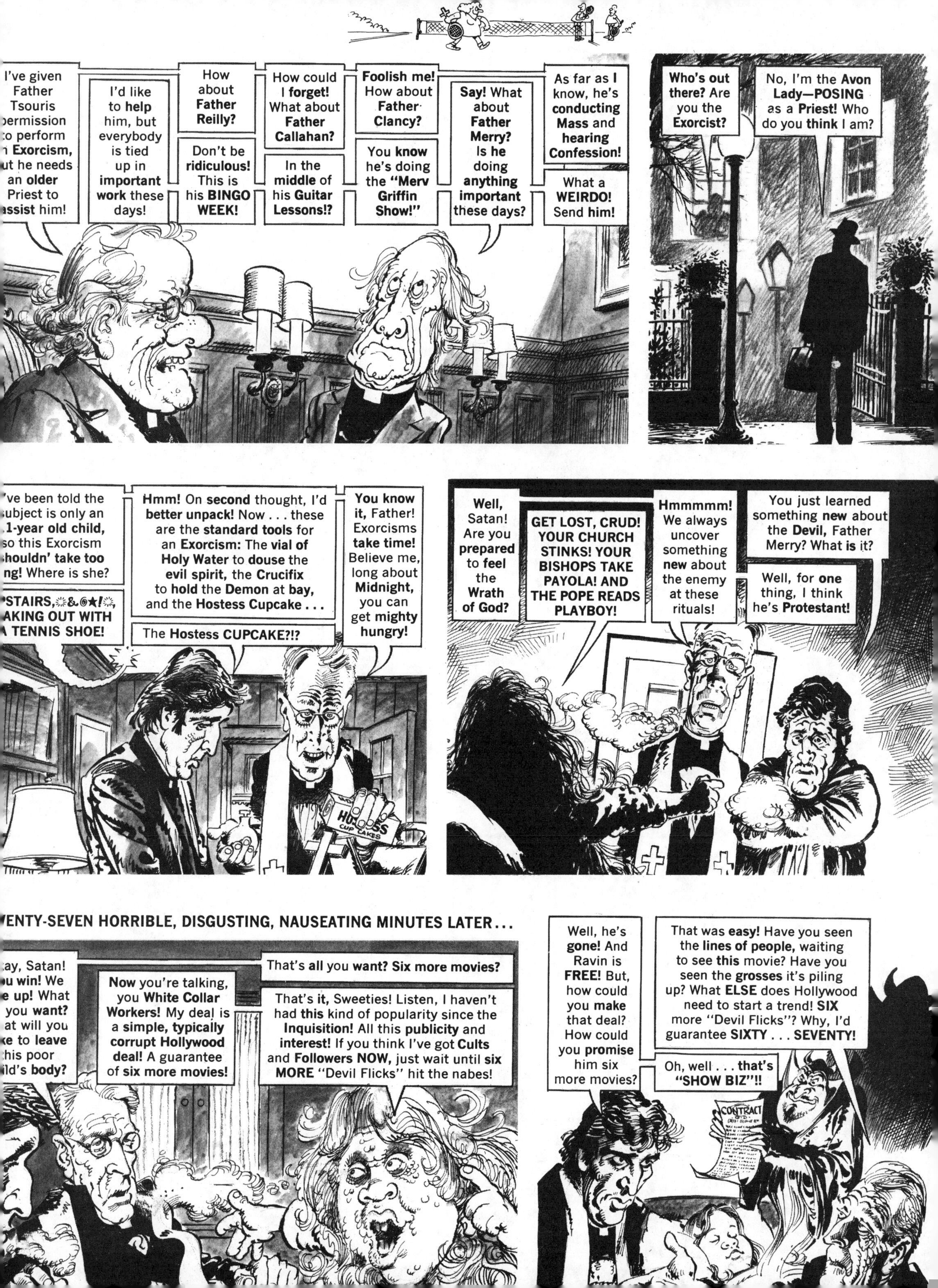

I've given Father Tsouris ermission o perform n Exorcism, ut he needs an older Priest to ssist him!
I'd like to help him, but everybody is tied up in important work these days!
How about Father Reilly?
Don't be ridiculous! This is his BINGO WEEK!
How could I forget! What about Father Callahan?
In the middle of his Guitar Lessons!?
Foolish me! How about Father Clancy?
You know he's doing the "Merv Griffin Show!"
Say! What about Father Merry? Is he doing anything important these days?
As far as I know, he's conducting Mass and hearing Confession!
What a WEIRDO! Send him!
Who's out there? Are you the Exorcist?
No, I'm the Avon Lady—POSING as a Priest! Who do you think I am?
've been told the ubject is only an 1-year old child, so this Exorcism houldn' take too ng! Where is she?
PSTAIRS, ☼&@★!☼, AKING OUT WITH A TENNIS SHOE!
Hmm! On second thought, I'd better unpack! Now . . . these are the standard tools for an Exorcism: The vial of Holy Water to douse the evil spirit, the Crucifix to hold the Demon at bay, and the Hostess Cupcake . . .
The Hostess CUPCAKE?!?
You know it, Father! Exorcisms take time! Believe me, long about Midnight, you can get mighty hungry!
HOSTESS CUP CAKES
Well, Satan! Are you prepared to feel the Wrath of God?
GET LOST, CRUD! YOUR CHURCH STINKS! YOUR BISHOPS TAKE PAYOLA! AND THE POPE READS PLAYBOY!
Hmmmmm! We always uncover something new about the enemy at these rituals!
You just learned something new about the Devil, Father Merry? What is it?
Well, for one thing, I think he's Protestant!
ENTY-SEVEN HORRIBLE, DISGUSTING, NAUSEATING MINUTES LATER . . .
ay, Satan! u win! We e up! What you want? at will you ke to leave his poor ld's body?
Now you're talking, you White Collar Workers! My deal is a simple, typically corrupt Hollywood deal! A guarantee of six more movies!
That's all you want? Six more movies?
That's it, Sweeties! Listen, I haven't had this kind of popularity since the Inquisition! All this publicity and interest! If you think I've got Cults and Followers NOW, just wait until six MORE "Devil Flicks" hit the nabes!
Well, he's gone! And Ravin is FREE! But, how could you make that deal? How could you promise him six more movies?
That was easy! Have you seen the lines of people, waiting to see this movie? Have you seen the grosses it's piling up? What ELSE does Hollywood need to start a trend! SIX more "Devil Flicks"? Why, I'd guarantee SIXTY . . . SEVENTY!
Oh, well . . . that's "SHOW BIZ"!!
CONTRACT

NARROW-MINDED DEPT.

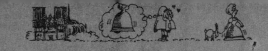

A SECOND MAD COLLECTIO

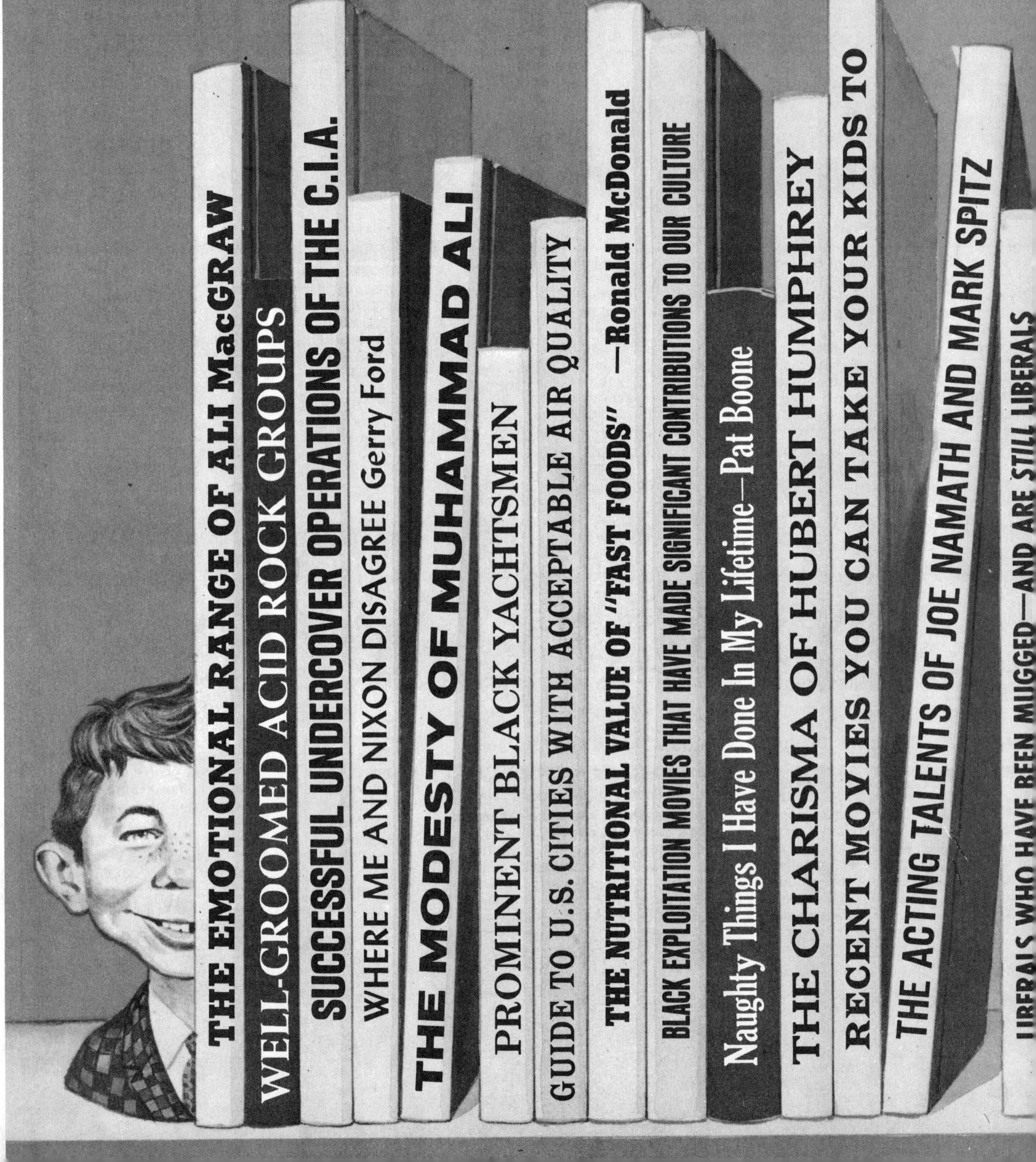

THE EMOTIONAL RANGE OF ALI MacGRAW
WELL-GROOMED ACID ROCK GROUPS
SUCCESSFUL UNDERCOVER OPERATIONS OF THE C.I.A.
WHERE ME AND NIXON DISAGREE Gerry Ford
THE MODESTY OF MUHAMMAD ALI
PROMINENT BLACK YACHTSMEN
GUIDE TO U.S. CITIES WITH ACCEPTABLE AIR QUALITY
THE NUTRITIONAL VALUE OF "FAST FOODS" —Ronald McDonald
BLACK EXPLOITATION MOVIES THAT HAVE MADE SIGNIFICANT CONTRIBUTIONS TO OUR CULTURE
Naughty Things I Have Done In My Lifetime—Pat Boone
THE CHARISMA OF HUBERT HUMPHREY
RECENT MOVIES YOU CAN TAKE YOUR KIDS TO
THE ACTING TALENTS OF JOE NAMATH AND MARK SPITZ
LIBERALS WHO HAVE BEEN MUGGED—AND ARE STILL LIBERALS

OF EXTREMELY THIN BOOKS

WRITER: ARNIE KOGEN

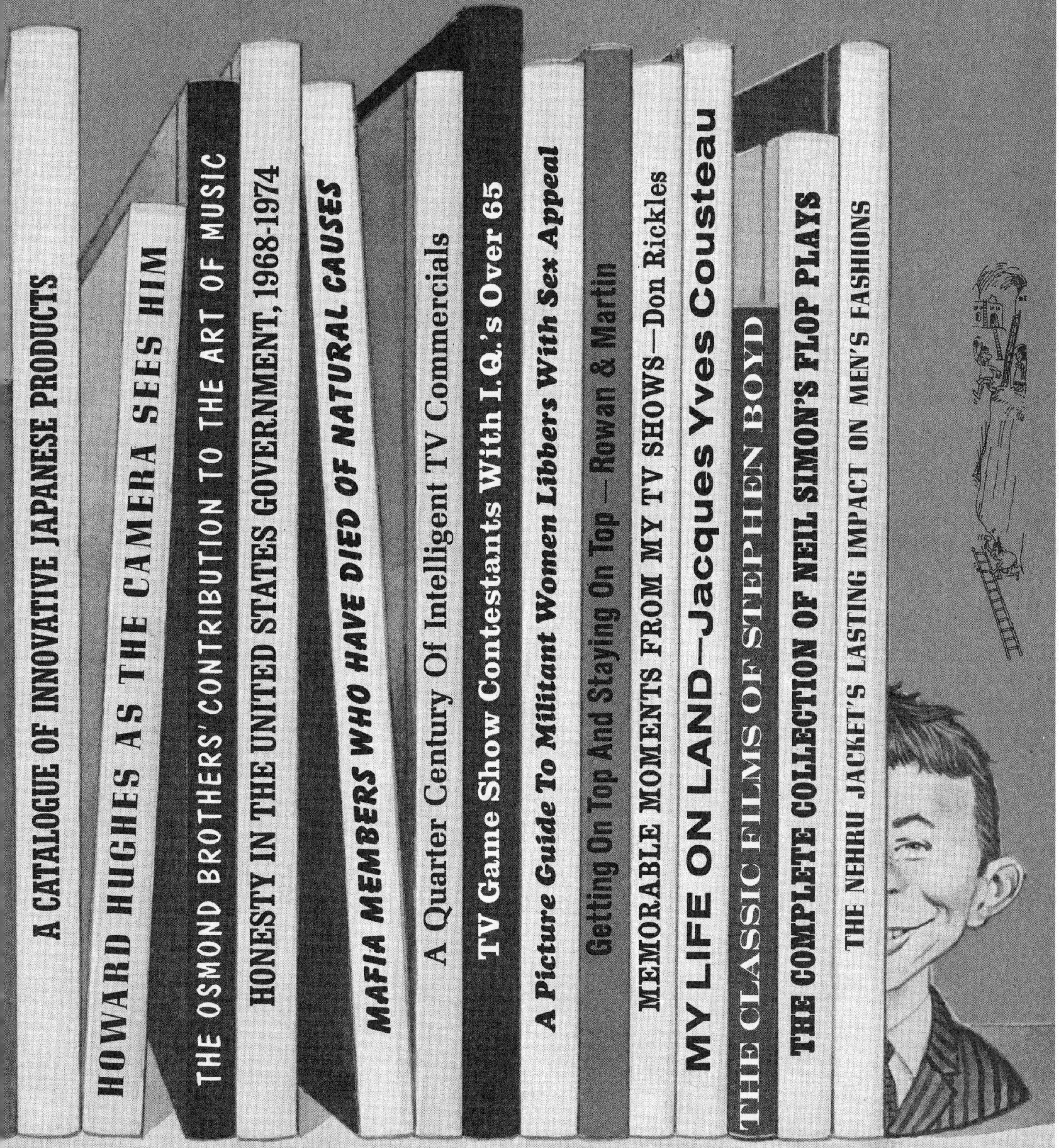
A CATALOGUE OF INNOVATIVE JAPANESE PRODUCTS
HOWARD HUGHES AS THE CAMERA SEES HIM
THE OSMOND BROTHERS' CONTRIBUTION TO THE ART OF MUSIC
HONESTY IN THE UNITED STATES GOVERNMENT, 1968-1974
MAFIA MEMBERS WHO HAVE DIED OF NATURAL CAUSES
A Quarter Century Of Intelligent TV Commercials
TV Game Show Contestants With I.Q.'s Over 65
A Picture Guide To Militant Women Libbers With Sex Appeal
Getting On Top And Staying On Top — Rowan & Martin
MEMORABLE MOMENTS FROM MY TV SHOWS—Don Rickles
MY LIFE ON LAND—Jacques Yves Cousteau
THE CLASSIC FILMS OF STEPHEN BOYD
THE COMPLETE COLLECTION OF NEIL SIMON'S FLOP PLAYS
THE NEHRU JACKET'S LASTING IMPACT ON MEN'S FASHIONS

PLAYING IT FOR SHARK VALUE DEPT.

There's a sick new trend in movies! It started with "Airport", continued with "Towering Inferno", sunk to a low with "Earthquake" and has now reached the depths with the movie that's REALLY packing 'em in, the one about a giant shark that terrorizes a summer community! Yep, it's obvious that people get their kicks out of seeing other people die . . . in every horrible way possible, which includes being . . .

JA

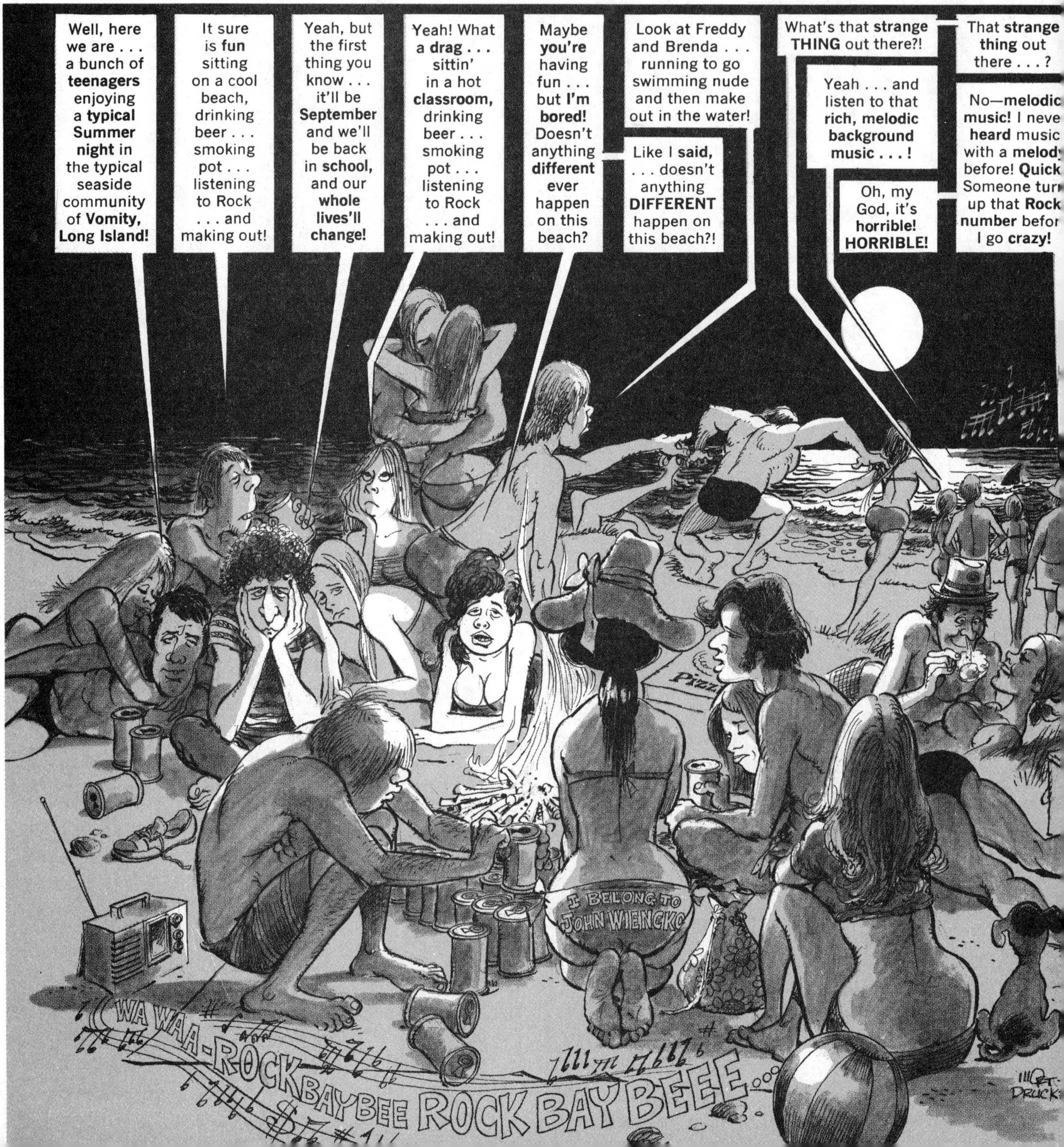

Well, here we are . . . a bunch of teenagers enjoying a typical Summer night in the typical seaside community of Vomity, Long Island!
It sure is fun sitting on a cool beach, drinking beer . . . smoking pot . . . listening to Rock . . . and making out!
Yeah, but the first thing you know . . . it'll be September and we'll be back in school, and our whole lives'll change!
Yeah! What a drag . . . sittin' in a hot classroom, drinking beer . . . smoking pot . . . listening to Rock . . . and making out!
Maybe you're having fun . . . but I'm bored! Doesn't anything different ever happen on this beach?
Look at Freddy and Brenda . . . running to go swimming nude and then make out in the water!
Like I said, . . . doesn't anything DIFFERENT happen on this beach?!
What's that strange THING out there?!
That strange thing out there . . . ?
Yeah . . . and listen to that rich, melodic background music . . . !
Oh, my God, it's horrible! HORRIBLE!
No—melodic music! I neve heard music with a melod before! Quick Someone tur up that Rock number befor I go crazy!
I BELONG TO JOHN WIENCKO
WA WAA-ROCK BAYBEE ROCK BAYBEEE...

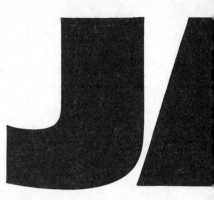

W'D

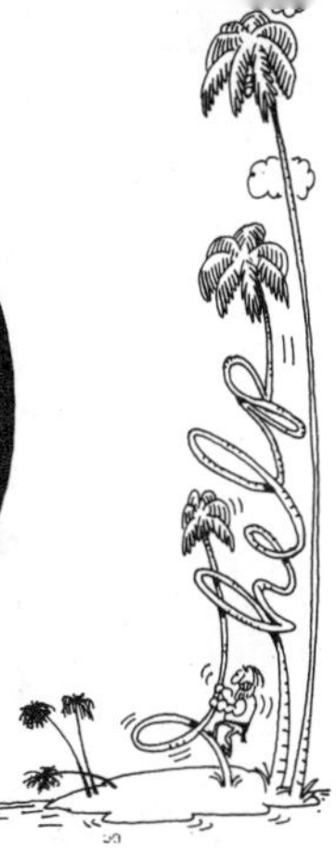

ARTIST: MORT DRUCKER WRITER: LARRY SIEGEL

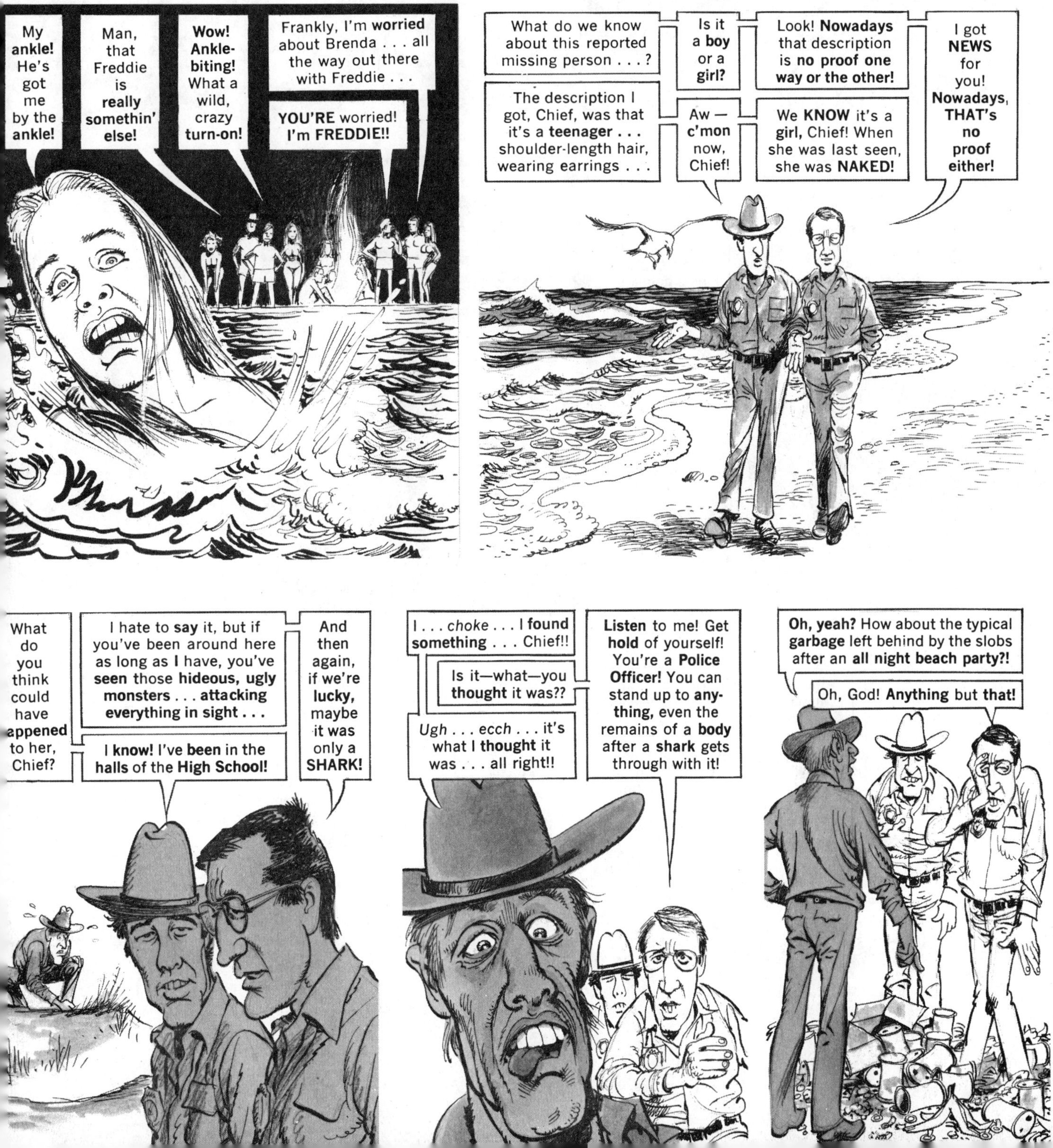
My ankle! He's got me by the ankle!
Man, that Freddie is really somethin' else!
Wow! Ankle-biting! What a wild, crazy turn-on!
Frankly, I'm worried about Brenda . . . all the way out there with Freddie . . .
YOU'RE worried! I'm FREDDIE!!
What do we know about this reported missing person . . . ?
The description I got, Chief, was that it's a teenager . . . shoulder-length hair, wearing earrings . . .
Is it a boy or a girl?
Aw — c'mon now, Chief!
Look! Nowadays that description is no proof one way or the other!
We KNOW it's a girl, Chief! When she was last seen, she was NAKED!
I got NEWS for you! Nowadays, THAT's no proof either!
What do you think could have appened to her, Chief?
I hate to say it, but if you've been around here as long as I have, you've seen those hideous, ugly monsters . . . attacking everything in sight . . .
I know! I've been in the halls of the High School!
And then again, if we're lucky, maybe it was only a SHARK!
I . . . choke . . . I found something . . . Chief!!
Is it—what—you thought it was??
Ugh . . . ecch . . . it's what I thought it was . . . all right!!
Listen to me! Get hold of yourself! You're a Police Officer! You can stand up to anything, even the remains of a body after a shark gets through with it!
Oh, yeah? How about the typical garbage left behind by the slobs after an all night beach party?!
Oh, God! Anything but that!

Uggh! Melon rinds and banana peels!

Blaah! Anchovy pizza scraps and scungili!

Pyuch! Peanut butter sandwiches and —

What do you think **you're** doing, Chief Brooding?!?

The remains of a **girl** were found, Mayor Vault! She must have been eaten by a **shark**! We can't allow any **people** in the water!

Are you **insane?!** Close our beaches with **July 4th** a week away?! That's when we do all our **business** around here! **Forget** about that shark and **take down that sign!**

Forget about it?! Do you realize what **horror** you may be subjecting people to on this beach? Have you no **conscience**? Particularly on **Independence Day**, when Americans celebrate their precious, hard-earned **freedom** by blowing off their **arms** and **legs** with **fire-crackers**, and **driving drunkenly** down our nation's **highways** . . .

Con to thir of i I'll tak dow the sign

NO SWIMMING ON THIS BEACH By Order of Vomity P.D. INCORPORATED TOWNSHIP OF VO POPULATION 3,012½

How come we're all **enjoying** ourselves, and the Chief of Police has to **work**?

They say a mysterious thing is endangering the beach, and he's **protecting** all of us!

It must be **tough** looking through those glasses hours on end!

What dedication! I'm sure that whatever he's **looking** for, he's going to **GET it!**

Not unless somebody tells his **WIFE!!**

Well, Schmendricks, so far . . . so good!

That's **great!** No sign of the **shark**?

No sign of her Husba

What happened?

All of a sudden I heard this **rich melodic music**, and then this **kid** started **screaming** and . . . ugh . . . it was just **awful** . . . !

Yecch! All that **blood** and **gore** and **torn limbs!** You know what **this** means, don't you, Chief . . . ?

Right! There goes the picture's **"G"** rating! But a **"PG"** will **still** pull in the kids . . . !

What about that **line** in the **ads** that says, **"May Be Too Intense For Younger Children"?** Won't that **hurt** us?

Are you **kidding?!?** That's like trying to scare **ants** away from a **picnic** by pouring **sugar** on the ground!

I've called this meeting of you key townspeople because there is a **silly rumor** going around that an **alleged shark** has **allegedly killed two alleged people**! We will now have the **Coroner's** report! Er . . . where is the Coroner?

He's **dead!**

WHAT?! How did it happen?

The alle shark off his allege head! A his alle arms a legs . .

Very well! The meeting is open to suggestions! Would anyone like to speak . . .?

AAARRRGH!

SHRIEK!

YEOW!

SCREEEECHHH

Does Captain Squint **always** do **disgusting things** like that for attention?

No . . . he usually just **belches!**

Now, listen to **me**, Matey . . . and **listen good!** I'm the **only** Sea Captain around here who can **CATCH** that mother, and **you know it!** But it's gonna cost you **ten thousand dollars!**

Take it . . . or **leave it!** And the more you **wait**, the more it's gonna **cost** you! And if you don't **like** my offer, **you** and this **whole** ☆✪☀!☀✦✪☀ town can go #★✦☀&✪★!!

We'll **think** about it, **Captain Squint!**

Does he actually make a living as a **Sea Captain?**

Not really! He **moonlights** on the **side!**

What's his **other** job?

He works for **The Welcome Wagon!**

We're in **trouble**, Schmendricks! The Mayor is still not sold on the **shark** story, and I'm not sure I trust **Squint!** Isn't there **ANYONE** who can **help** us?!?

Hi, there! **I'd** like to help! My name is **Clod Hopper**, and I'm a **brilliant young Scientist!** I know **ALL ABOUT** sharks! God, but they're **beautiful creatures!** Do you know that I once made **LOVE** to a shark?! I mean . . . **this** one really turned me on, and—

What?!? How could **ANYONE** make love to a **shark!!**

Very carefully!

Hmmm! I notice—as I scientifically examine the remains of this victim—that the thorax and the upper anatomy in general, particularly the sternum and scapula, have been **severely traumatized**, and that the metatarsal bones on the severed foot that I hold in my hand have been **nearly obliterated** . . .

Uh-huh . . . Uh-huh . . . **quite interesting!** Now . . . after **assimilating** all this, there is **one thing** I'd like to **say** as a **Scholar** . . . and as a **Scientist** . . .

What's that . . .?

YECCCH!

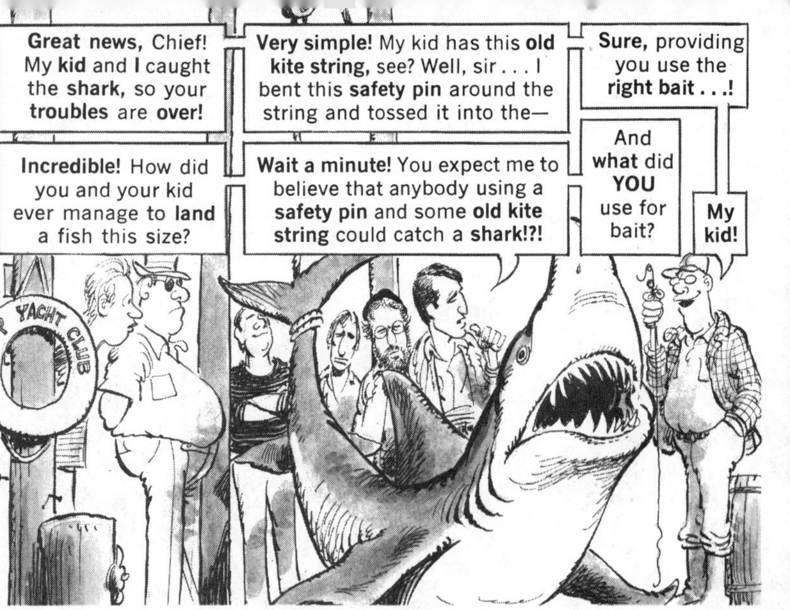
Great news, Chief! My kid and I caught the shark, so your troubles are over!
Incredible! How did you and your kid ever manage to land a fish this size?
Very simple! My kid has this old kite string, see? Well, sir . . . I bent this safety pin around the string and tossed it into the—
Wait a minute! You expect me to believe that anybody using a safety pin and some old kite string could catch a shark!?!
Sure, providing you use the right bait . . .!
And what did YOU use for bait?
My kid!
VOMITY YACHT CLUB

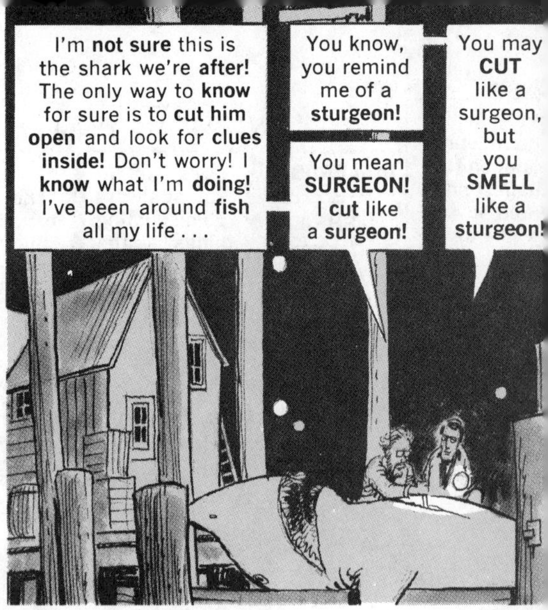
I'm not sure this is the shark we're after! The only way to know for sure is to cut him open and look for clues inside! Don't worry! I know what I'm doing! I've been around fish all my life . . .
You know, you remind me of a sturgeon!
You mean SURGEON! I cut like a surgeon!
You may CUT like a surgeon, but you SMELL like a sturgeon!

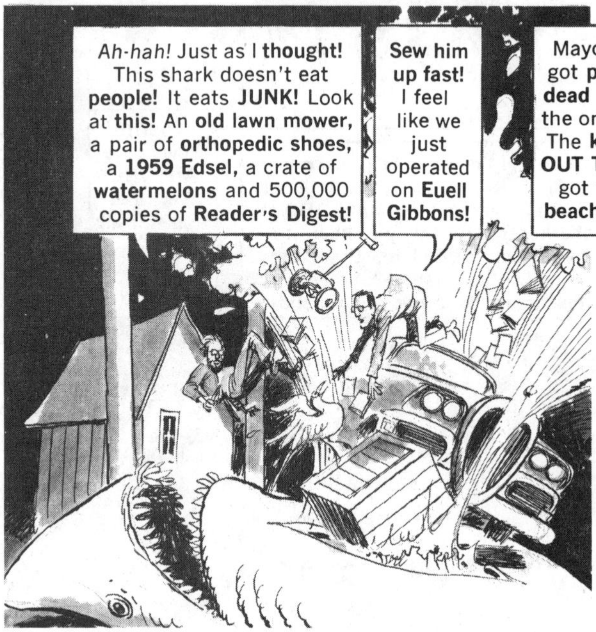
Ah-hah! Just as I thought! This shark doesn't eat people! It eats JUNK! Look at this! An old lawn mower, a pair of orthopedic shoes, a 1959 Edsel, a crate of watermelons and 500,000 copies of Reader's Digest!
Sew him up fast! I feel like we just operated on Euell Gibbons!

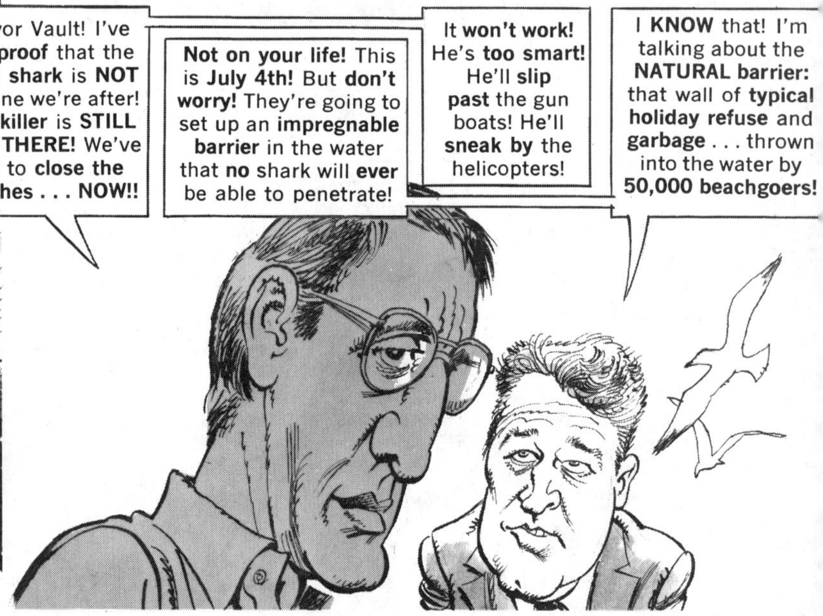
Mayor Vault! I've got proof that the dead shark is NOT the one we're after! The killer is STILL OUT THERE! We've got to close the beaches . . . NOW!!
Not on your life! This is July 4th! But don't worry! They're going to set up an impregnable barrier in the water that no shark will ever be able to penetrate!
It won't work! He's too smart! He'll slip past the gun boats! He'll sneak by the helicopters!
I KNOW that! I'm talking about the NATURAL barrier: that wall of typical holiday refuse and garbage . . . thrown into the water by 50,000 beachgoers!

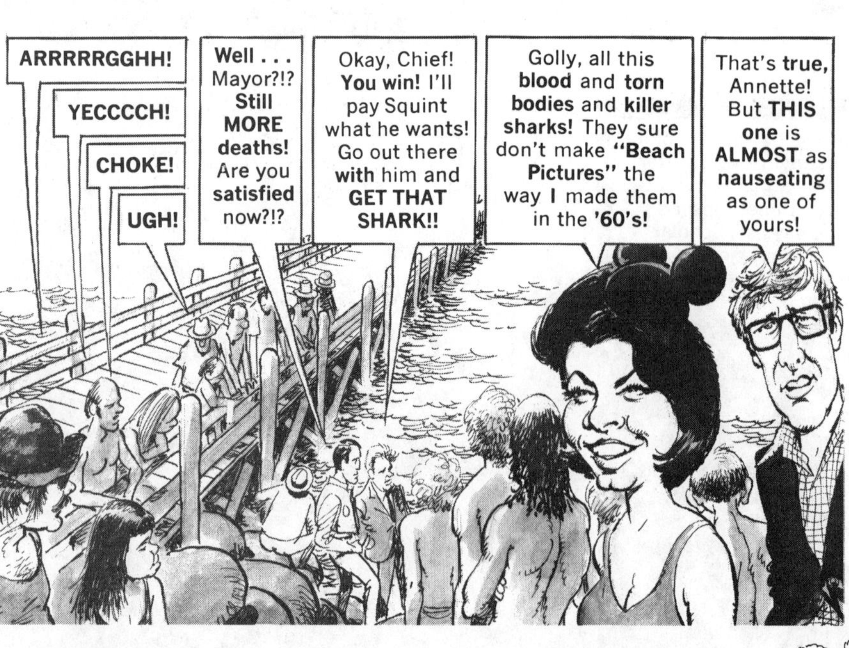
ARRRRRGGHH!
YECCCCH!
CHOKE!
UGH!
Well . . . Mayor?!? Still MORE deaths! Are you satisfied now?!?
Okay, Chief! You win! I'll pay Squint what he wants! Go out there with him and GET THAT SHARK!!
Golly, all this blood and torn bodies and killer sharks! They sure don't make "Beach Pictures" the way I made them in the '60's!
That's true, Annette! But THIS one is ALMOST as nauseating as one of yours!

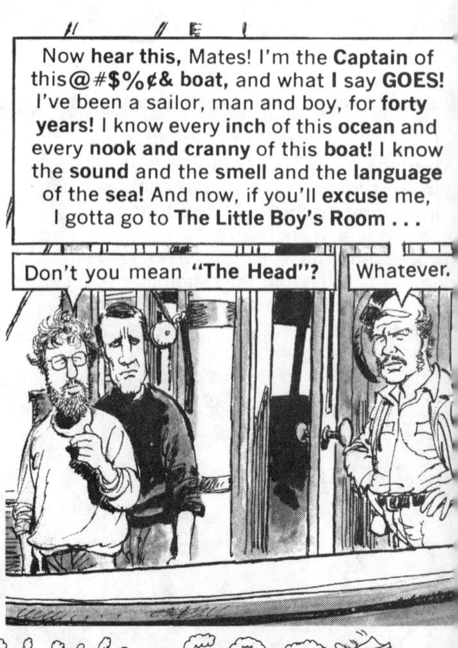
Now hear this, Mates! I'm the Captain of this@#$%¢& boat, and what I say GOES! I've been a sailor, man and boy, for forty years! I know every inch of this ocean and every nook and cranny of this boat! I know the sound and the smell and the language of the sea! And now, if you'll excuse me, I gotta go to The Little Boy's Room . . .
Don't you mean "The Head"?
Whatever.

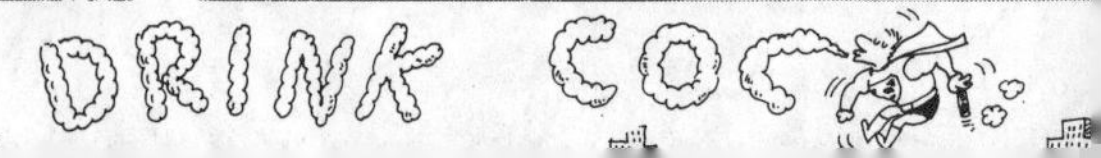
DRINK CO

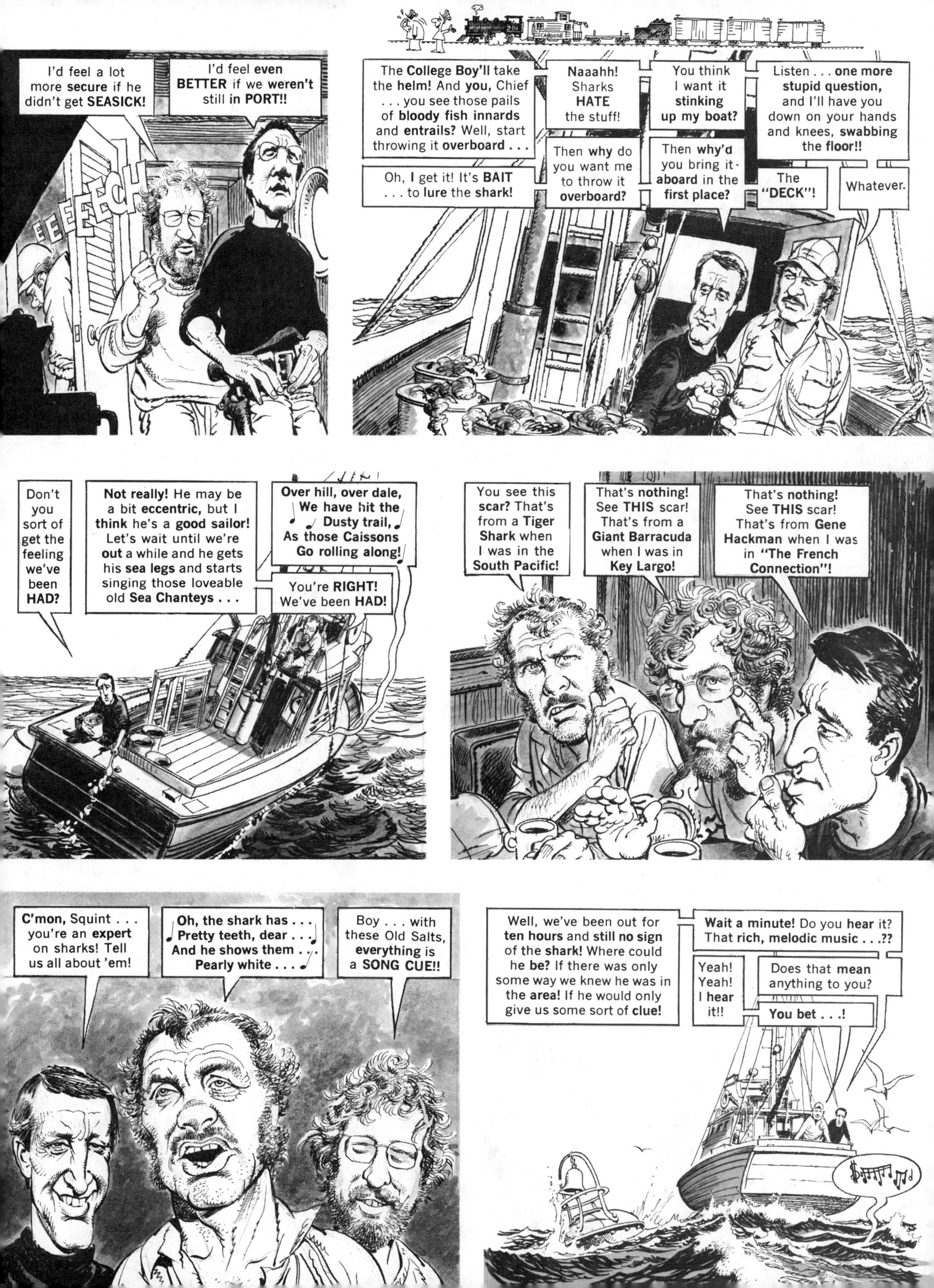

I'd feel a lot more secure if he didn't get SEASICK!
I'd feel even BETTER if we weren't still in PORT!!
EEEEECH
The College Boy'll take the helm! And you, Chief . . . you see those pails of bloody fish innards and entrails? Well, start throwing it overboard . . .
Oh, I get it! It's BAIT . . . to lure the shark!
Naaahh! Sharks HATE the stuff!
Then why do you want me to throw it overboard?
You think I want it stinking up my boat?
Then why'd you bring it aboard in the first place?
Listen . . . one more stupid question, and I'll have you down on your hands and knees, swabbing the floor!!
The "DECK"!
Whatever.
Don't you sort of get the feeling we've been HAD?
Not really! He may be a bit eccentric, but I think he's a good sailor! Let's wait until we're out a while and he gets his sea legs and starts singing those loveable old Sea Chanteys . . .
Over hill, over dale, We have hit the Dusty trail, As those Caissons Go rolling along!
You're RIGHT! We've been HAD!
You see this scar? That's from a Tiger Shark when I was in the South Pacific!
That's nothing! See THIS scar! That's from a Giant Barracuda when I was in Key Largo!
That's nothing! See THIS scar! That's from Gene Hackman when I was in "The French Connection"!
C'mon, Squint . . . you're an expert on sharks! Tell us all about 'em!
Oh, the shark has . . . Pretty teeth, dear . . . And he shows them . . . Pearly white . . .
Boy . . . with these Old Salts, everything is a SONG CUE!!
Well, we've been out for ten hours and still no sign of the shark! Where could he be? If there was only some way we knew he was in the area! If he would only give us some sort of clue!
Wait a minute! Do you hear it? That rich, melodic music . . .??
Yeah! Yeah! I hear it!!
Does that mean anything to you?
You bet . . .!

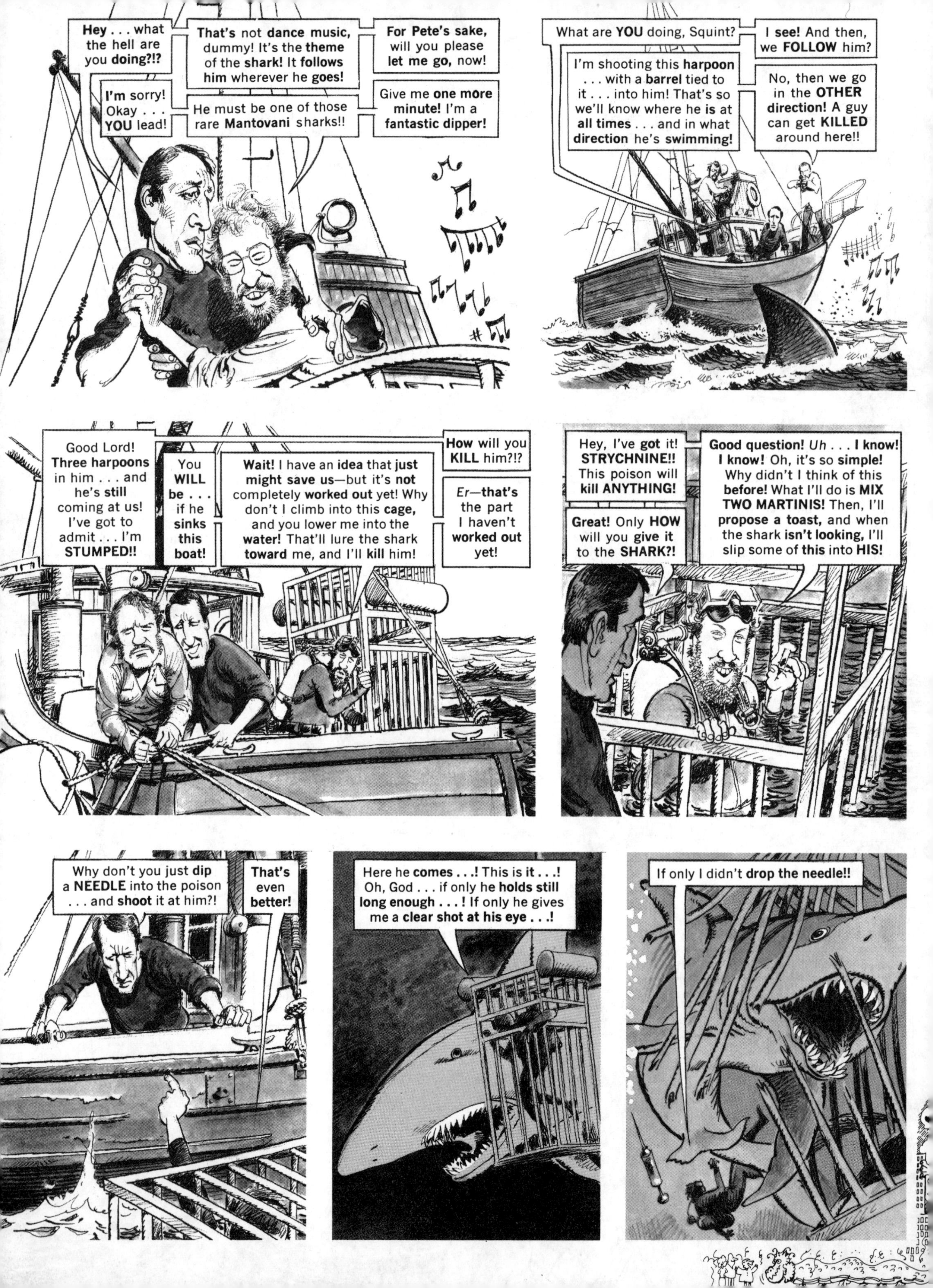
Hey . . . what the hell are you doing?!?
That's not dance music, dummy! It's the theme of the shark! It follows him wherever he goes!
For Pete's sake, will you please let me go, now!
I'm sorry! Okay . . . YOU lead!
He must be one of those rare Mantovani sharks!!
Give me one more minute! I'm a fantastic dipper!
What are YOU doing, Squint?
I'm shooting this harpoon . . . with a barrel tied to it . . . into him! That's so we'll know where he is at all times . . . and in what direction he's swimming!
I see! And then, we FOLLOW him?
No, then we go in the OTHER direction! A guy can get KILLED around here!!
Good Lord! Three harpoons in him . . . and he's still coming at us! I've got to admit . . . I'm STUMPED!!
You WILL be . . . if he sinks this boat!
Wait! I have an idea that just might save us—but it's not completely worked out yet! Why don't I climb into this cage, and you lower me into the water! That'll lure the shark toward me, and I'll kill him!
How will you KILL him?!?
Er—that's the part I haven't worked out yet!
Hey, I've got it! STRYCHNINE!! This poison will kill ANYTHING!
Great! Only HOW will you give it to the SHARK?!
Good question! Uh . . . I know! I know! Oh, it's so simple! Why didn't I think of this before! What I'll do is MIX TWO MARTINIS! Then, I'll propose a toast, and when the shark isn't looking, I'll slip some of this into HIS!
Why don't you just dip a NEEDLE into the poison . . . and shoot it at him?!
That's even better!
Here he comes . . .! This is it . . .! Oh, God . . . if only he holds still long enough . . .! If only he gives me a clear shot at his eye . . .!
If only I didn't drop the needle!!

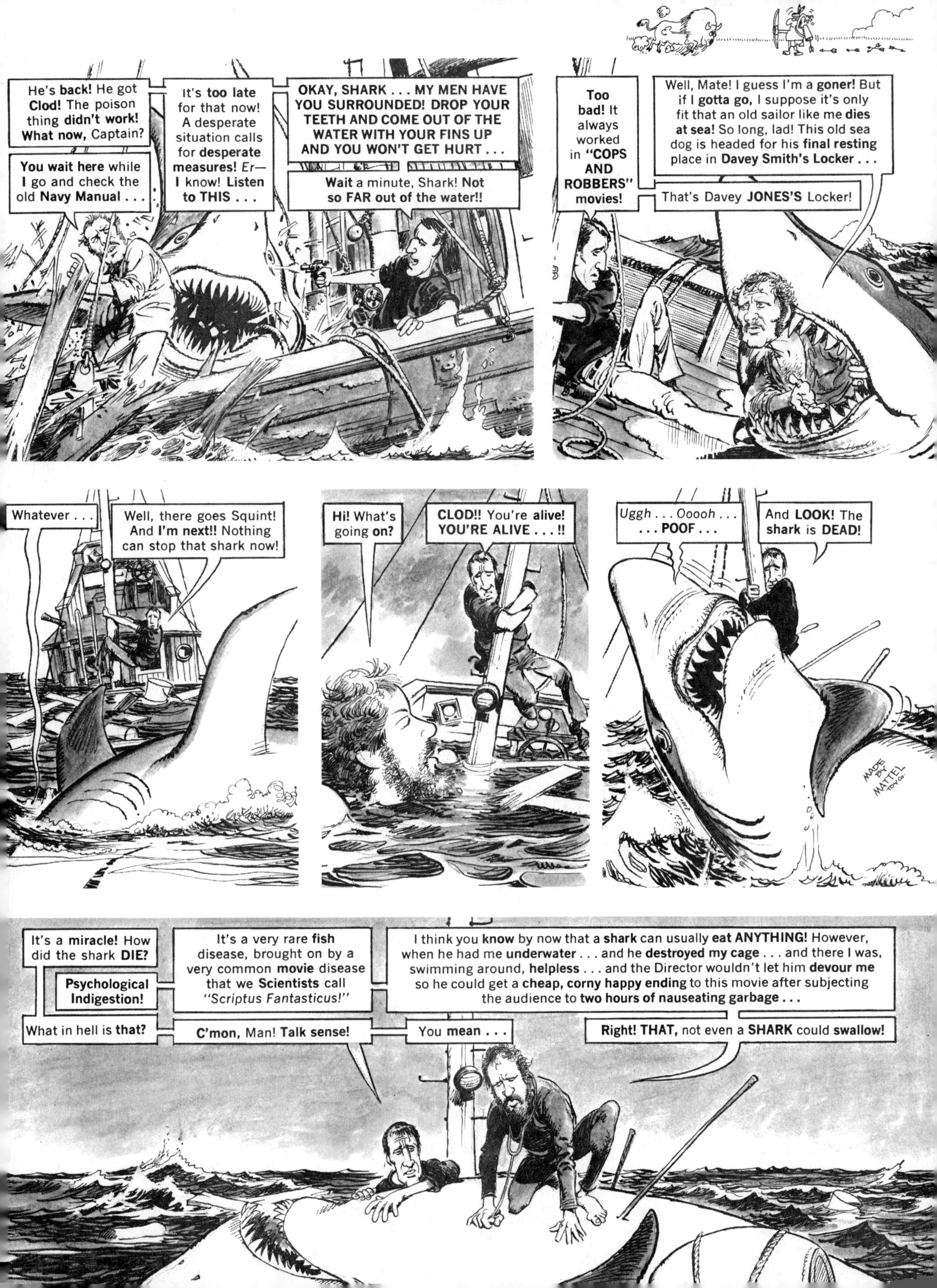
He's back! He got Clod! The poison thing didn't work! What now, Captain?
You wait here while I go and check the old Navy Manual . . .
It's too late for that now! A desperate situation calls for desperate measures! Er— I know! Listen to THIS . . .
OKAY, SHARK . . . MY MEN HAVE YOU SURROUNDED! DROP YOUR TEETH AND COME OUT OF THE WATER WITH YOUR FINS UP AND YOU WON'T GET HURT . . .
Wait a minute, Shark! Not so FAR out of the water!!
Too bad! It always worked in "COPS AND ROBBERS" movies!
Well, Mate! I guess I'm a goner! But if I gotta go, I suppose it's only fit that an old sailor like me dies at sea! So long, lad! This old sea dog is headed for his final resting place in Davey Smith's Locker . . .
That's Davey JONES'S Locker!
Whatever . . .
Well, there goes Squint! And I'm next!! Nothing can stop that shark now!
Hi! What's going on?
CLOD!! You're alive! YOU'RE ALIVE . . . !!
Uggh . . . Ooooh . . . . . . POOF . . .
And LOOK! The shark is DEAD!
MADE BY MATTEL TOY CO.
It's a miracle! How did the shark DIE?
Psychological Indigestion!
What in hell is that?
It's a very rare fish disease, brought on by a very common movie disease that we Scientists call "Scriptus Fantasticus!"
C'mon, Man! Talk sense!
I think you know by now that a shark can usually eat ANYTHING! However, when he had me underwater . . . and he destroyed my cage . . . and there I was, swimming around, helpless . . . and the Director wouldn't let him devour me so he could get a cheap, corny happy ending to this movie after subjecting the audience to two hours of nauseating garbage . . .
You mean . . .
Right! THAT, not even a SHARK could swallow!

NEUMANCLATURE DEPT.

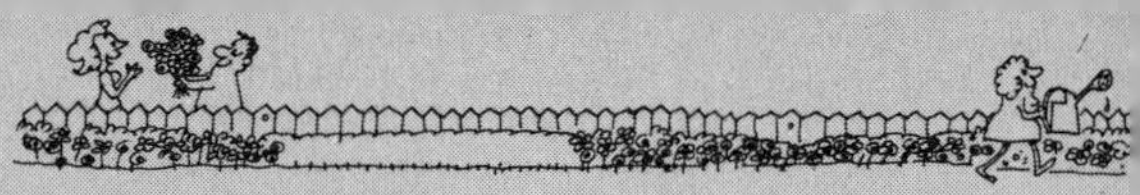

Dozens of the words we use today come from the names of real people. For instance, "sandwich" is named after the Earl of Sandwich, "bloomer" after Amelia Bloomer, and "zeppelin" after Count Ferdinand von Zeppelin. You never know when someone's name is going to become part of our language and get in the dictionary, but there are a lot of celebrities today who have a good chance. In fact, MAD believes it's time that Noah Webster immortalized these current-day big-shots, namely with these...

ADDITIONS TO THE DICTIONARY

WRITER: FRANK JACOBS

516

welk

abzug

abzug ('ab-zug) *n.* **:** a violent eruption, such as from a volcano. (*Run for your lives or the* abzug *will get us!*)

agnew ('ag-nū) *v.i.* **:** to turn out differently than expected; to boomerang. (*The ball* agnewed *and hit him in the face.*)

ali (äl-'ē) *adj.* **:** made of clay.

brando ('bran-dō) *v.i.* **:** to speak incoherently; to mumble. (*Who can understand him, the way he* brandos!)

[1]**buckley** ('buk-lē) *v.i.* **:** to make a succession of right turns until one returns to his original position.

[2]**buckley** *adj.* **:** intellectual to the point of being incomprehensible.

carson ('kar-sun) *n.* **:** a glib huckster. **syn.** griffin, cavett, bishop (*obs.*).

chiang (che-äng) *n.* **:** a small, broken fragment of antique china.

[1]**cosell** (kō-'sel) *v.i.* **:** to infuriate an audience by speaking in a tiresome manner. (*He* coselled *until twelve million viewers turned off their sets in disgust.*)

[2]**cosell** *n.* **:** an inflammation of the mouth. (*"I thought it might be strep, but it's only a* cosell," *the doctor said.*)

eagleton ('ē-gul-tun) *n.* **:** anything supported one thousand per cent.

faisal ('fī-zul) *n.* **:** an energy crisis. (*We can't turn on the lights, baby, because of the* faisal.)

fischer ('fish-ur) *n.* **:** a victory without a winner.

[1]**fonda** ('fon-duh) *n.* **:** a parent bewildered by the generation gap.

[2]**fonda** *v.i.* **:** to take a wild ride, esp. on a motorcycle.

[3]**fonda** *n.* **1:** a peace chant intoned by North Vietnamese in times of war. **2:** a war chant intoned by North Vietnamese in times of peace.

friedan (fri-'dan) *adj.* **:** unresponsive to the needs of man. (*His marriage, alas, was* friedan *and doomed.*)

getty ('get-ē) see **onassis.**

hughes (huz) *n? adj?* meaning obscure.

humphrey ('hum-frē) *v.i.* **:** to speak in a single breath a sentence of more than fifty words covering six or more topics. (*He* humphreyed, *but, as usual, no one listened.*)

irving ('ir-ving) *n.* **1:** a tall tale. **2:** a cliff-hanger.

kunstler ('kunst-lur) *n.* **:** a mouthpiece for blowing one's horn.

leary ('li·u·rē) *n.* **:** an unidentifiable flying object. (*It's a* leary," *the navigator said, "and it's gaining on us."*)

lindsay ('lin-zē) *v.i.* **:** to party-hop.

liz (liz) *adj.* **:** split; severed; disconnected.

lovelace ('luv-lās) *n.* a union of two or more people; an unlimited partnership.

mao (mȧo) *n.* a Chinese staple, usually consumed with rice. (*An hour after having our* mao, *we were hungry again.*)

[1]**neuman** ('nü-mun) *n.* **:** an expected disaster.

[2]**neuman** *adj.* **:** nothing. (*It was a* neuman *year.*)

[3]**neuman** *v.i.* to worry. (*What? Me* neuman?)

nixon ('nik-sun) *n.* **1:** a busted football play. **2:** an illness lasting six years. (*"You must let the* nixon *run its course," the doctor said.*)

onassis (ō-'nas-is) *n.* **:** an ancient unit of wealth, five of which equal one getty.

plimpton ('plimp-tun) *v.t.* **:** to imitate poorly something done expertly. (*I thought he was action, but all he could do was* plimpton.)

puzo ('pū-zō) *n.* an offer impossible to refuse. (*The shotgun in his face told him it was a* puzo.)

rainier (ran-'yā) *adj.* **:** ruling with grace.

redgrave ('red-grāv) *n.* **:** any species of English bird exhibiting peculiar mating habits.

riggs (rigs) *n.* **1:** a female impersonator. **2:** an old pretender to the throne of a king. (*The court bowed to the* riggs, *but the king did not.*)

roth (rȯth) *n.* **:** a four-letter word.

sadat (sȧ-'dȧt) *n.* **:** a hot wind of the desert, which blows hard but goes nowhere. (*Get back on your camels; it's only a* sadat.)

schulz (shulz) *adj.* **:** describing someone who works for peanuts.

spitz (spits) *v.i.* **:** to worship one's self. (*While others prayed to God, he* spitzed.)

spock (spok) *interj.* **:** the cry of a spoiled child. (*One more* spock *and you can say bye-bye to "Sesame Street."*)

susskind ('sus-kīnd) *n.* **:** a liberal dose difficult to swallow.

tim (tim) *n.* **1:** a male camp follower. **2:** a female camp follower.

unitas (ü-'nīt-us) *n.* **:** a colt put out to pasture.

wayne (wān) *adj.* **:** saddle-sore.

welch (welch) *n.* **:** a well-stocked chest. (*Her* welch *would sustain her through the winter.*)

welk (welk) *.adj.* **:** rockless. (*Everywhere we looked it was* welk *and flat.*)

THE FATUOUS FIFTIES DEPT.

Have you noticed that people seem to get disgustingly nostalgic about things they weren't really very crazy about in the first place? Like the 50's? We figure that any decade that had the Korean War, the Edsel, Senator Joseph McCarthy, Davy Crockett hats, the Hula-Hoop and Pat Boone wearing fruit boots can't be ALL GOOD! And yet, the hottest show on TV these days is about this very bland, very silly decade where the biggest problem seemed to be *who* was making out with *whom*, and how fast your *face* would clear up. So, okay nerds. Go put on your blue suede shoes, your pedal pushers, your ankle slave bracelets and your leather jackets and get yourselves arrested for committing an idiocy while reading

CRAPPY DAYS

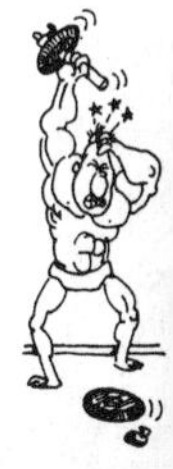

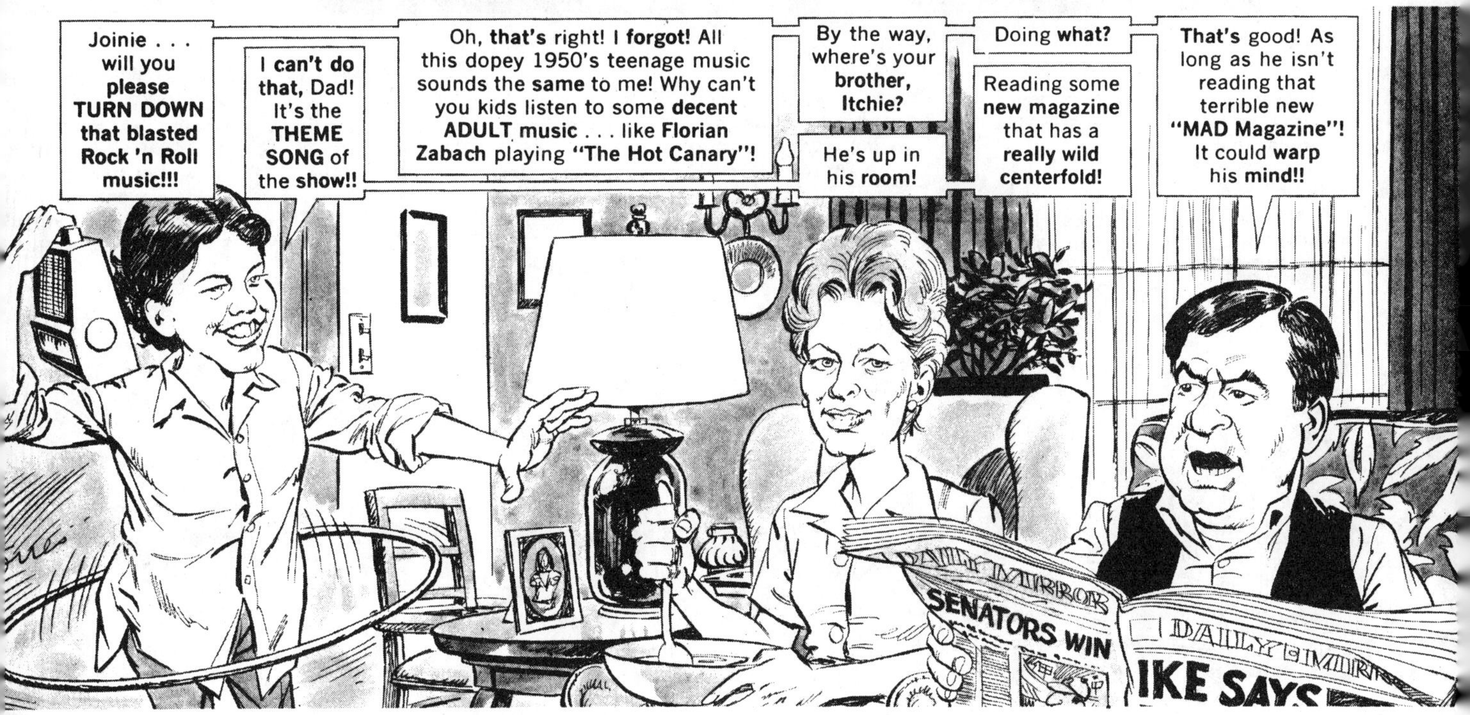

Joinie . . . will you please TURN DOWN that blasted Rock 'n Roll music!!!
I can't do that, Dad! It's the THEME SONG of the show!!
Oh, that's right! I forgot! All this dopey 1950's teenage music sounds the same to me! Why can't you kids listen to some decent ADULT music . . . like Florian Zabach playing "The Hot Canary"!
By the way, where's your brother, Itchie?
He's up in his room!
Doing what?
Reading some new magazine that has a really wild centerfold!
That's good! As long as he isn't reading that terrible new "MAD Magazine"! It could warp his mind!!
DAILY MIRROR
SENATORS WIN
IKE SAYS

ARTIST: ANGELO TORRES WRITER: ARNIE KOGEN

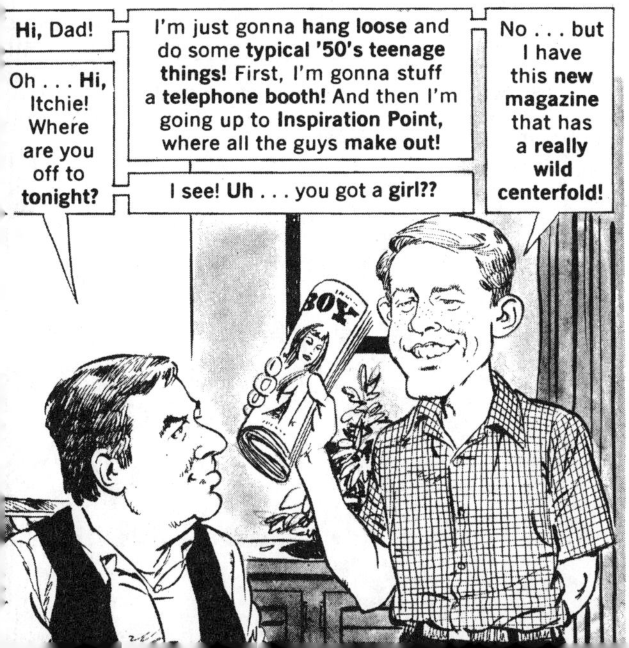

Hi, Dad!
Oh . . . Hi, Itchie! Where are you off to tonight?
I'm just gonna hang loose and do some typical '50's teenage things! First, I'm gonna stuff a telephone booth! And then I'm going up to Inspiration Point, where all the guys make out!
I see! Uh . . . you got a girl??
No . . . but I have this new magazine that has a really wild centerfold!
BOY

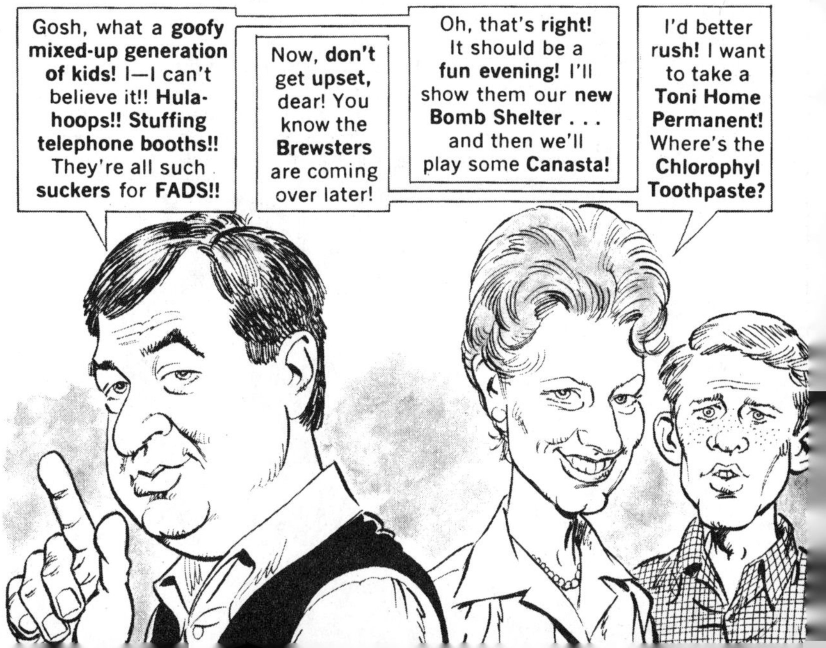

Gosh, what a goofy mixed-up generation of kids! I—I can't believe it!! Hula-hoops!! Stuffing telephone booths!! They're all such suckers for FADS!!
Now, don't get upset, dear! You know the Brewsters are coming over later!
Oh, that's right! It should be a fun evening! I'll show them our new Bomb Shelter . . . and then we'll play some Canasta!
I'd better rush! I want to take a Toni Home Permanent! Where's the Chlorophyl Toothpaste?

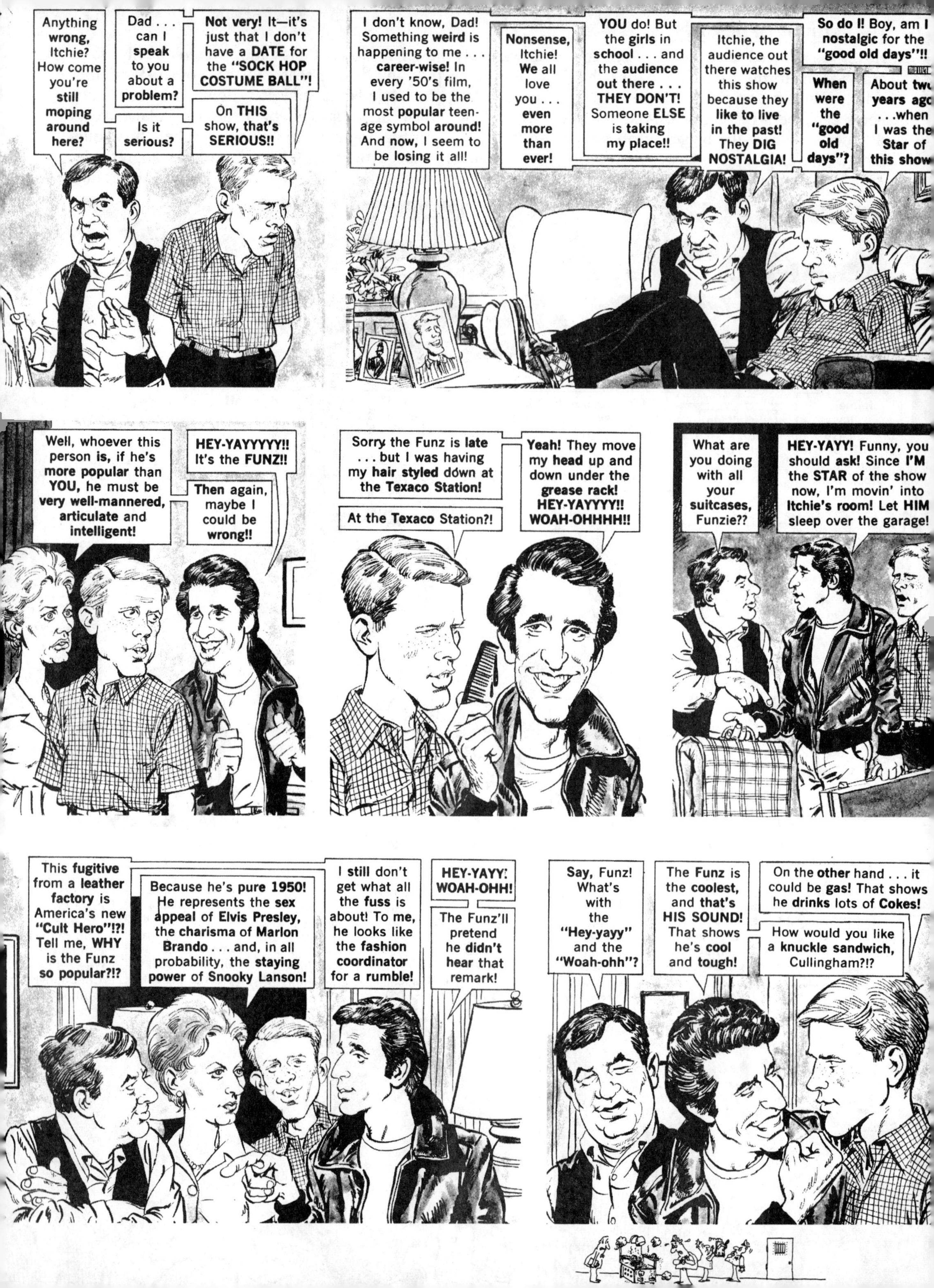
Anything wrong, Itchie? How come you're still moping around here?
Dad . . . can I speak to you about a problem?
Is it serious?
Not very! It—it's just that I don't have a DATE for the "SOCK HOP COSTUME BALL"!
On THIS show, that's SERIOUS!!
I don't know, Dad! Something weird is happening to me . . . career-wise! In every '50's film, I used to be the most popular teen-age symbol around! And now, I seem to be losing it all!
Nonsense, Itchie! We all love you . . . even more than ever!
YOU do! But the girls in school . . . and the audience out there . . . THEY DON'T! Someone ELSE is taking my place!!
Itchie, the audience out there watches this show because they like to live in the past! They DIG NOSTALGIA!
So do I! Boy, am I nostalgic for the "good old days"!!
When were the "good old days"?
About tw years ag . . .when I was the Star of this show
Well, whoever this person is, if he's more popular than YOU, he must be very well-mannered, articulate and intelligent!
HEY-YAYYYYY!! It's the FUNZ!!
Then again, maybe I could be wrong!!
Sorry the Funz is late . . . but I was having my hair styled down at the Texaco Station!
At the Texaco Station?!
Yeah! They move my head up and down under the grease rack! HEY-YAYYYY!! WOAH-OHHHH!!
What are you doing with all your suitcases, Funzie??
HEY-YAYY! Funny, you should ask! Since I'M the STAR of the show now, I'm movin' into Itchie's room! Let HIM sleep over the garage!
This fugitive from a leather factory is America's new "Cult Hero"!?! Tell me, WHY is the Funz so popular?!?
Because he's pure 1950! He represents the sex appeal of Elvis Presley, the charisma of Marlon Brando . . . and, in all probability, the staying power of Snooky Lanson!
I still don't get what all the fuss is about! To me, he looks like the fashion coordinator for a rumble!
HEY-YAYY! WOAH-OHH!
The Funz'll pretend he didn't hear that remark!
Say, Funz! What's with the "Hey-yayy" and the "Woah-ohh"?
The Funz is the coolest, and that's HIS SOUND! That shows he's cool and tough!
On the other hand . . . it could be gas! That shows he drinks lots of Cokes!
How would you like a knuckle sandwich, Cullingham?!?

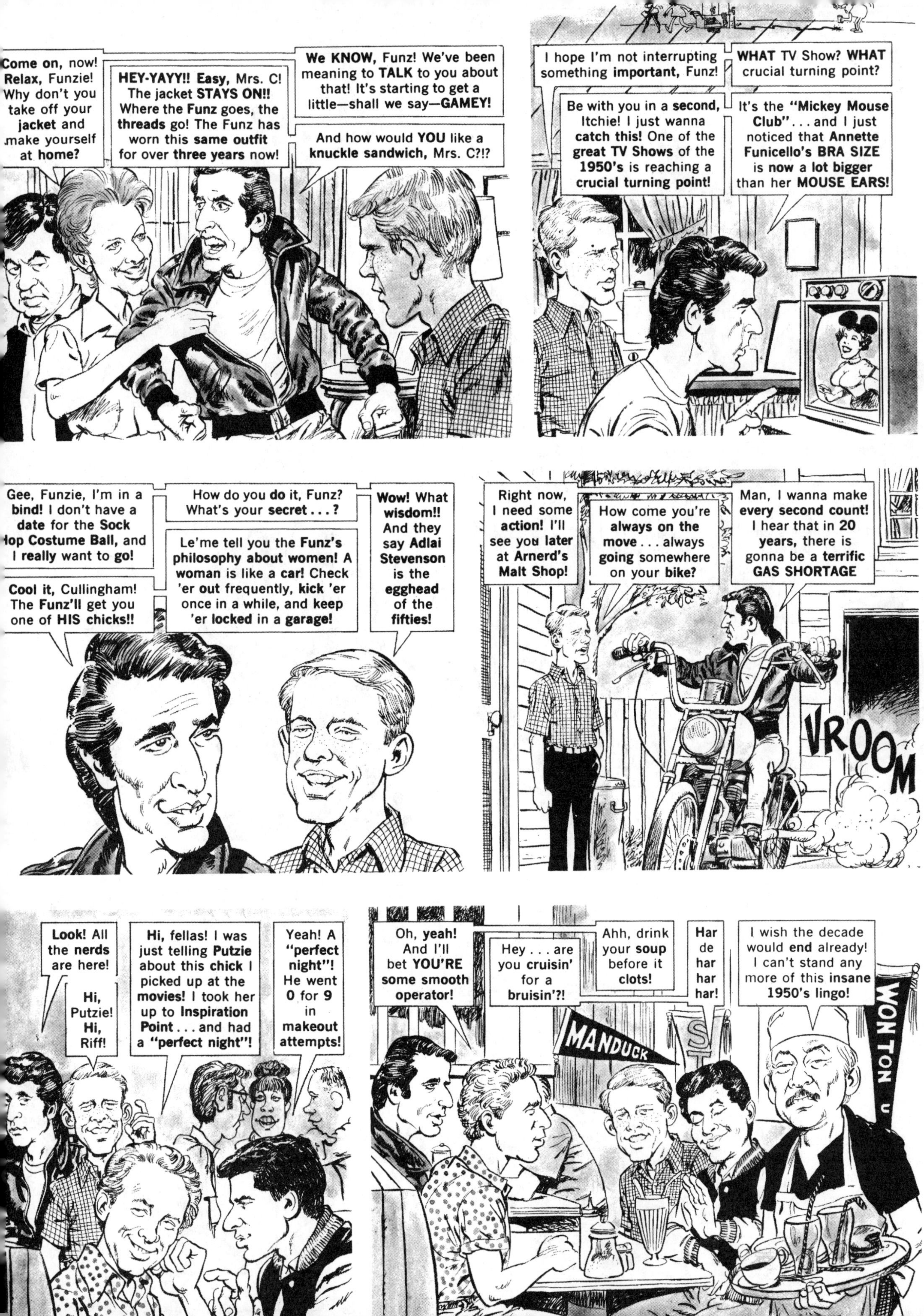

Come on, now! Relax, Funzie! Why don't you take off your jacket and make yourself at home?
HEY-YAYY!! Easy, Mrs. C! The jacket STAYS ON!! Where the Funz goes, the threads go! The Funz has worn this same outfit for over three years now!
We KNOW, Funz! We've been meaning to TALK to you about that! It's starting to get a little—shall we say—GAMEY!
And how would YOU like a knuckle sandwich, Mrs. C?!?
I hope I'm not interrupting something important, Funz!
Be with you in a second, Itchie! I just wanna catch this! One of the great TV Shows of the 1950's is reaching a crucial turning point!
WHAT TV Show? WHAT crucial turning point?
It's the "Mickey Mouse Club" . . . and I just noticed that Annette Funicello's BRA SIZE is now a lot bigger than her MOUSE EARS!
Gee, Funzie, I'm in a bind! I don't have a date for the Sock Hop Costume Ball, and I really want to go!
Cool it, Cullingham! The Funz'll get you one of HIS chicks!!
How do you do it, Funz? What's your secret . . . ?
Le'me tell you the Funz's philosophy about women! A woman is like a car! Check 'er out frequently, kick 'er once in a while, and keep 'er locked in a garage!
Wow! What wisdom!! And they say Adlai Stevenson is the egghead of the fifties!
Right now, I need some action! I'll see you later at Arnerd's Malt Shop!
How come you're always on the move . . . always going somewhere on your bike?
Man, I wanna make every second count! I hear that in 20 years, there is gonna be a terrific GAS SHORTAGE
VROOM
Look! All the nerds are here!
Hi, Putzie! Hi, Riff!
Hi, fellas! I was just telling Putzie about this chick I picked up at the movies! I took her up to Inspiration Point . . . and had a "perfect night"!
Yeah! A "perfect night"! He went 0 for 9 in makeout attempts!
Oh, yeah! And I'll bet YOU'RE some smooth operator!
Hey . . . are you cruisin' for a bruisin'?!
Ahh, drink your soup before it clots!
Har de har har har!
I wish the decade would end already! I can't stand any more of this insane 1950's lingo!
MANDUCK
WON TON

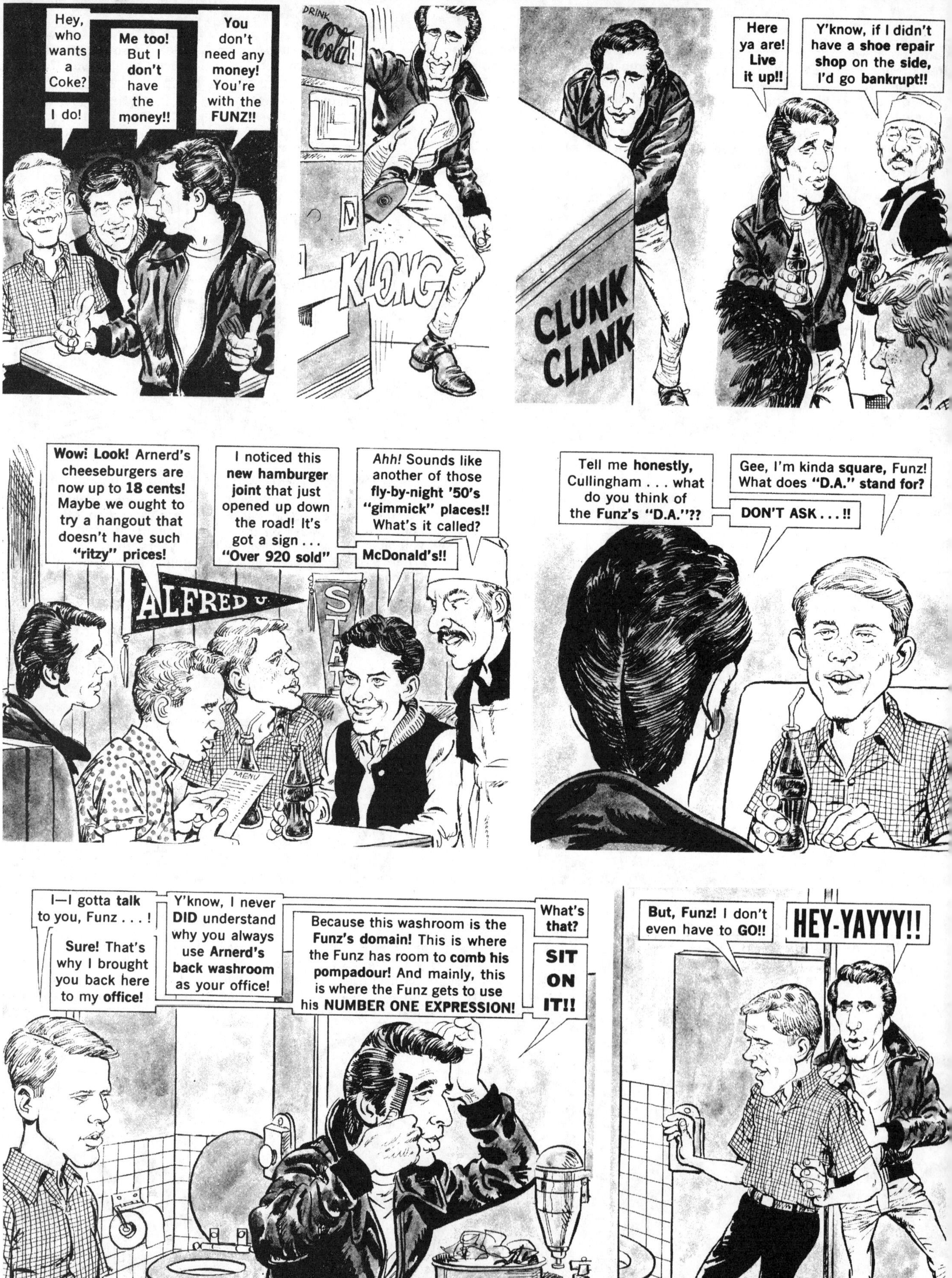
Hey, who wants a Coke?
I do!
Me too! But I don't have the money!!
You don't need any money! You're with the FUNZ!!
DRINK Coca-Cola
KLONG
CLUNK CLANK
Here ya are! Live it up!!
Y'know, if I didn't have a shoe repair shop on the side, I'd go bankrupt!!
Wow! Look! Arnerd's cheeseburgers are now up to 18 cents! Maybe we ought to try a hangout that doesn't have such "ritzy" prices!
I noticed this new hamburger joint that just opened up down the road! It's got a sign . . .
"Over 920 sold"
Ahh! Sounds like another of those fly-by-night '50's "gimmick" places!! What's it called?
McDonald's!!
ALFRED U
STAT
MENU
Tell me honestly, Cullingham . . . what do you think of the Funz's "D.A."??
Gee, I'm kinda square, Funz! What does "D.A." stand for?
DON'T ASK . . . !!
I—I gotta talk to you, Funz . . . !
Sure! That's why I brought you back here to my office!
Y'know, I never DID understand why you always use Arnerd's back washroom as your office!
Because this washroom is the Funz's domain! This is where the Funz has room to comb his pompadour! And mainly, this is where the Funz gets to use his NUMBER ONE EXPRESSION!
What's that?
SIT ON IT!!
But, Funz! I don't even have to GO!!
HEY-YAYYY!!

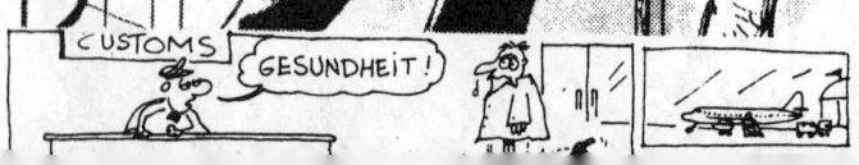
CUSTOMS
GESUNDHEIT!

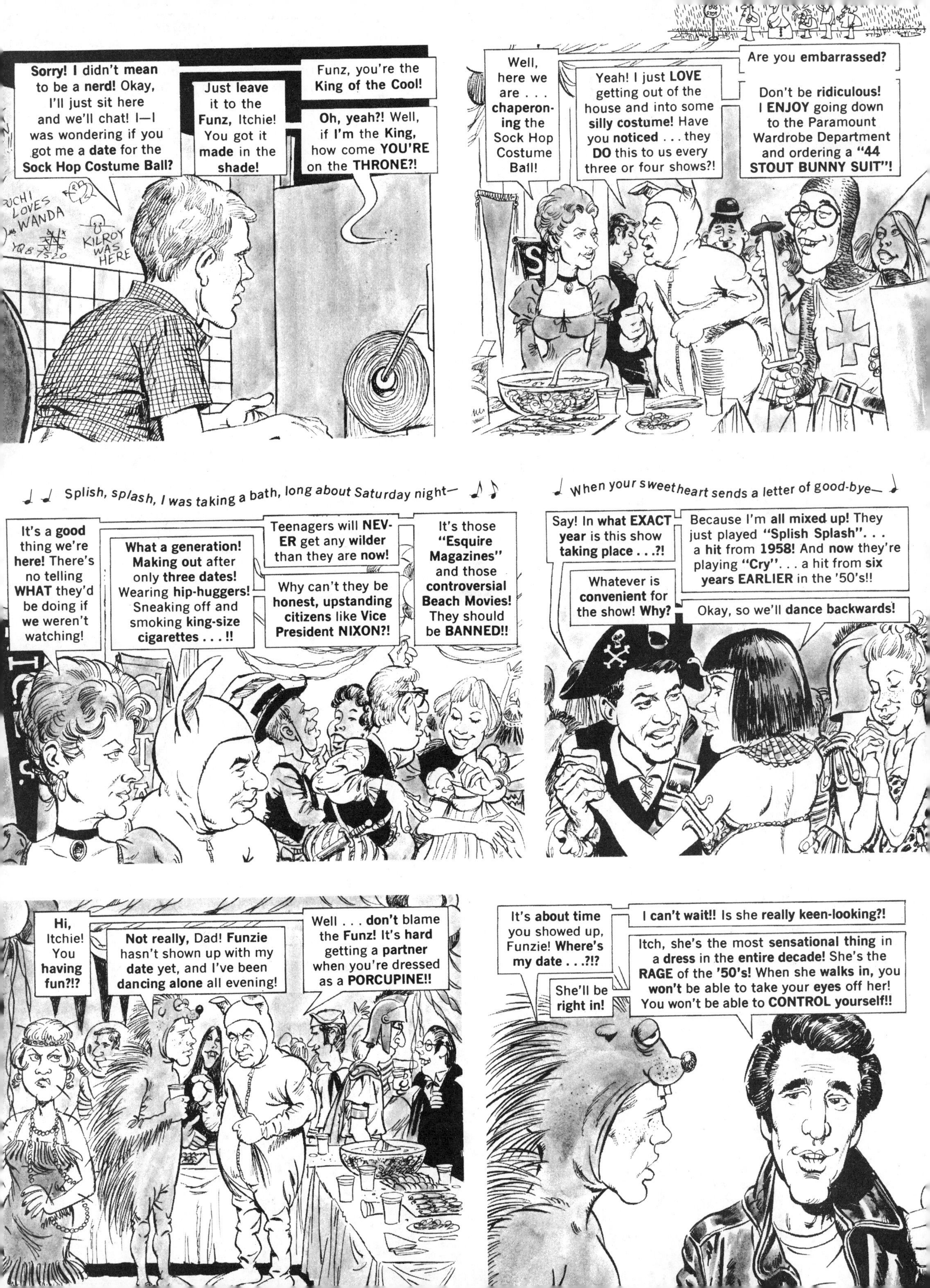

Sorry! I didn't mean to be a nerd! Okay, I'll just sit here and we'll chat! I—I was wondering if you got me a date for the Sock Hop Costume Ball?
Just leave it to the Funz, Itchie! You got it made in the shade!
Funz, you're the King of the Cool!
Oh, yeah?! Well, if I'm the King, how come YOU'RE on the THRONE?!
LOVES WANDA
KILROY WAS HERE
Well, here we are . . . chaperoning the Sock Hop Costume Ball!
Yeah! I just LOVE getting out of the house and into some silly costume! Have you noticed . . . they DO this to us every three or four shows?!
Are you embarrassed?
Don't be ridiculous! I ENJOY going down to the Paramount Wardrobe Department and ordering a "44 STOUT BUNNY SUIT"!
Splish, splash, I was taking a bath, long about Saturday night—
It's a good thing we're here! There's no telling WHAT they'd be doing if we weren't watching!
What a generation! Making out after only three dates! Wearing hip-huggers! Sneaking off and smoking king-size cigarettes . . . !!
Teenagers will NEVER get any wilder than they are now!
Why can't they be honest, upstanding citizens like Vice President NIXON?!
It's those "Esquire Magazines" and those controversial Beach Movies! They should be BANNED!!
When your sweetheart sends a letter of good-bye—
Say! In what EXACT year is this show taking place . . .?!
Because I'm all mixed up! They just played "Splish Splash". . . a hit from 1958! And now they're playing "Cry" . . . a hit from six years EARLIER in the '50's!!
Whatever is convenient for the show! Why?
Okay, so we'll dance backwards!
Hi, Itchie! You having fun?!?
Not really, Dad! Funzie hasn't shown up with my date yet, and I've been dancing alone all evening!
Well . . . don't blame the Funz! It's hard getting a partner when you're dressed as a PORCUPINE!!
It's about time you showed up, Funzie! Where's my date . . .?!?
I can't wait!! Is she really keen-looking?!
She'll be right in!
Itch, she's the most sensational thing in a dress in the entire decade! She's the RAGE of the '50's! When she walks in, you won't be able to take your eyes off her! You won't be able to CONTROL yourself!!

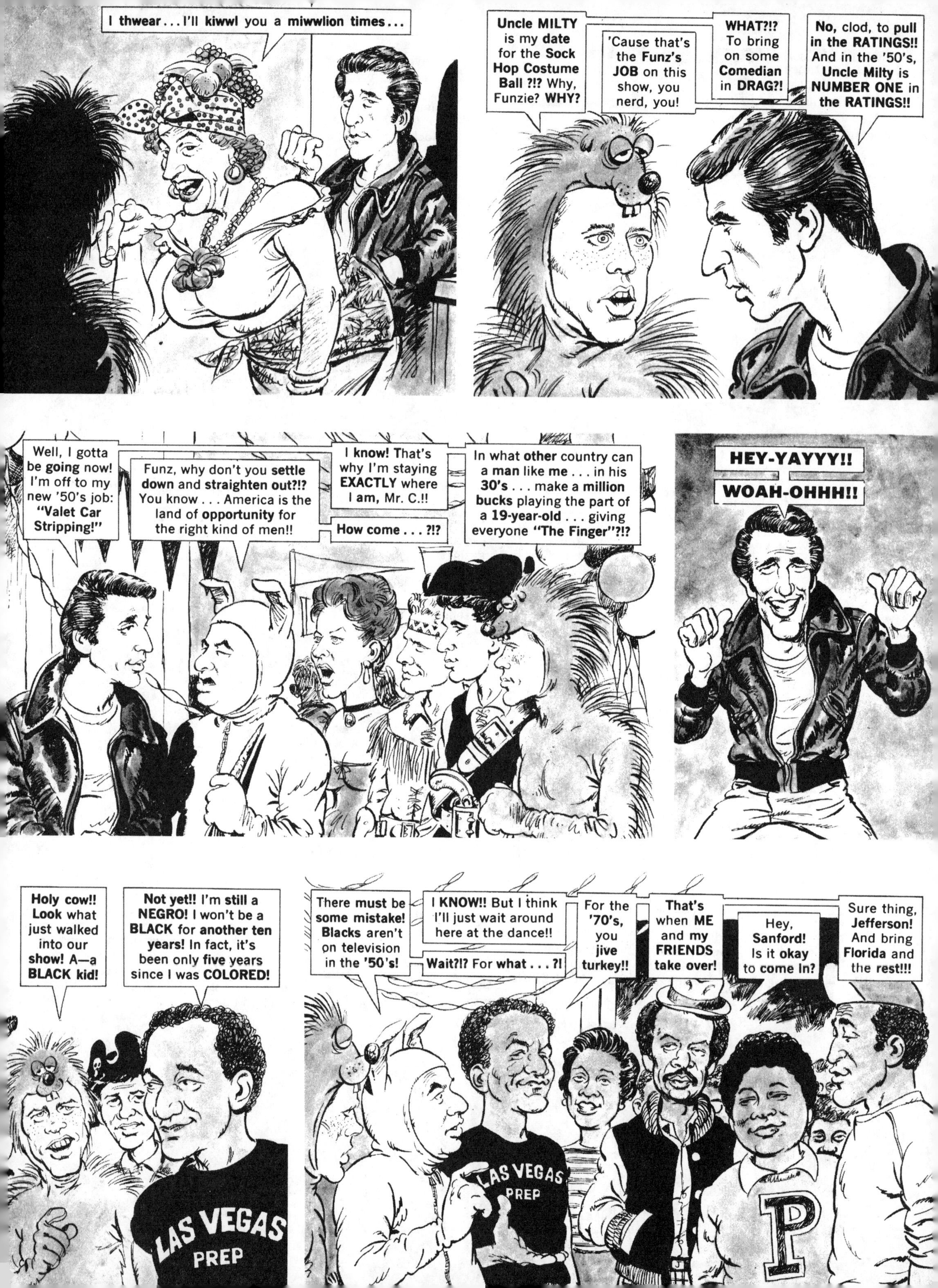
I thwear . . . I'll kiwwl you a miwwlion times . . .
Uncle MILTY is my date for the Sock Hop Costume Ball ?!? Why, Funzie? WHY?
'Cause that's the Funz's JOB on this show, you nerd, you!
WHAT?!? To bring on some Comedian in DRAG?!
No, clod, to pull in the RATINGS!! And in the '50's, Uncle Milty is NUMBER ONE in the RATINGS!!
Well, I gotta be going now! I'm off to my new '50's job: "Valet Car Stripping!"
Funz, why don't you settle down and straighten out?!? You know . . . America is the land of opportunity for the right kind of men!!
I know! That's why I'm staying EXACTLY where I am, Mr. C.!!
How come . . . ?!?
In what other country can a man like me . . . in his 30's . . . make a million bucks playing the part of a 19-year-old . . . giving everyone "The Finger"?!?
HEY-YAYYY!!
WOAH-OHHH!!
Holy cow!! Look what just walked into our show! A—a BLACK kid!
Not yet!! I'm still a NEGRO! I won't be a BLACK for another ten years! In fact, it's been only five years since I was COLORED!
LAS VEGAS PREP
There must be some mistake! Blacks aren't on television in the '50's!
I KNOW!! But I think I'll just wait around here at the dance!!
Wait?!? For what . . . ?!
For the '70's, you jive turkey!!
That's when ME and my FRIENDS take over!
Hey, Sanford! Is it okay to come In?
Sure thing, Jefferson! And bring Florida and the rest!!!
LAS VEGAS PREP

JOKE AND DAGGER DEPT.

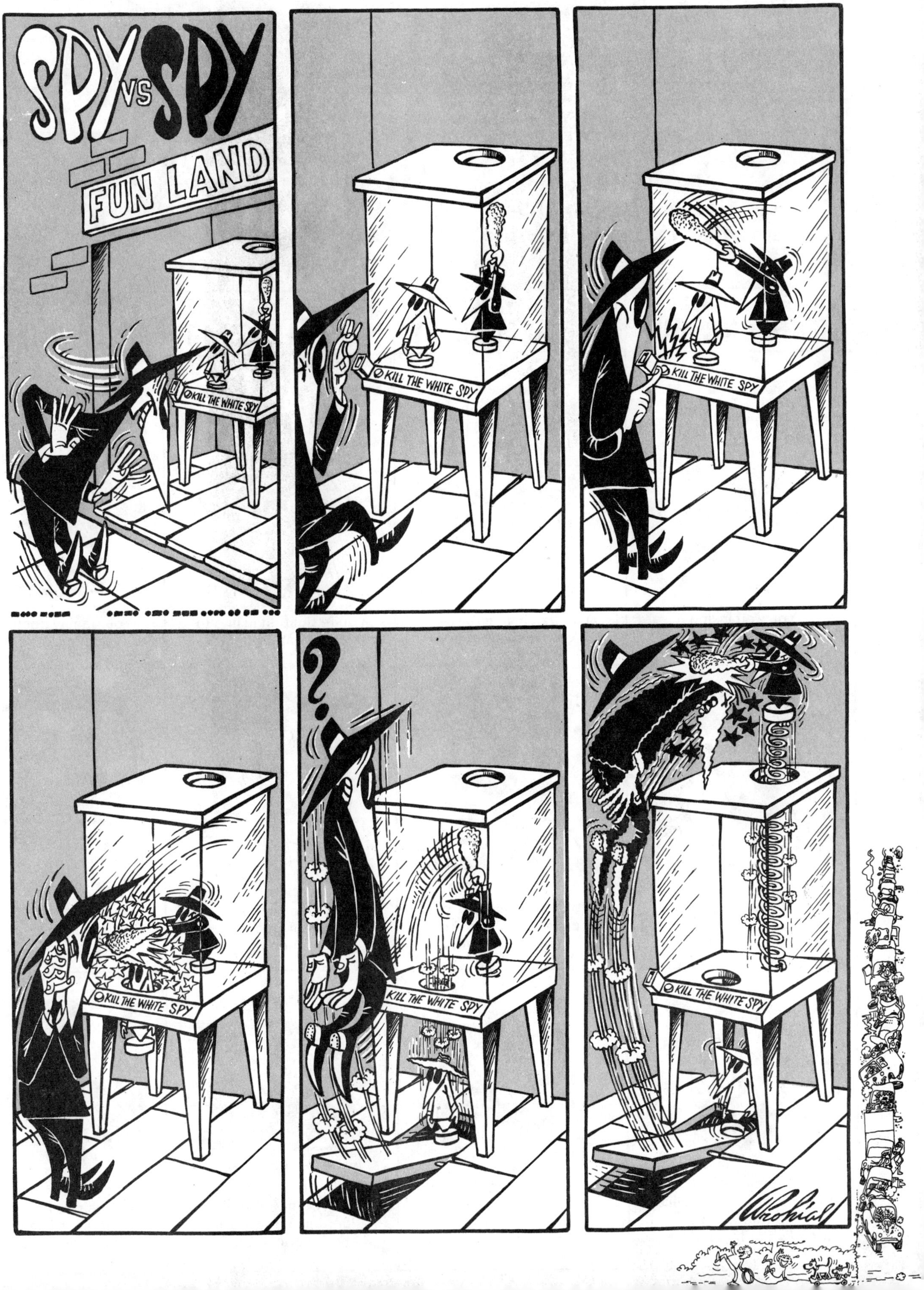
SPY vs SPY
FUN LAND
KILL THE WHITE SPY
KILL THE WHITE SPY
KILL THE WHITE SPY
KILL THE WHITE SPY
KILL THE WHITE SPY
KILL THE WHITE SPY
Prohias

STATUS QUOTIENTS DEPT.

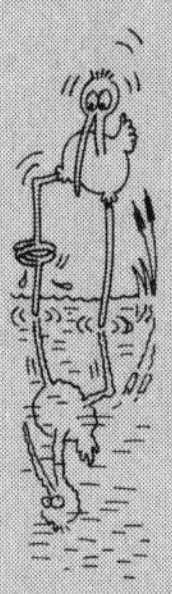

There are people who say that the American Class System is dying out... that America is becoming a "Classless Society." To those people, we say, "Forget it!" The Class System lives, and to help you distinguish who falls into what category, here's

A MAD GU
AMERICA

WHEN YOU'RE DOWN AND OUT	WHEN YOU'RE JUST GETTING BY	WHEN YOU'RE MAKING IT	WHEN YOU'RE ON TOP OF THE HEA
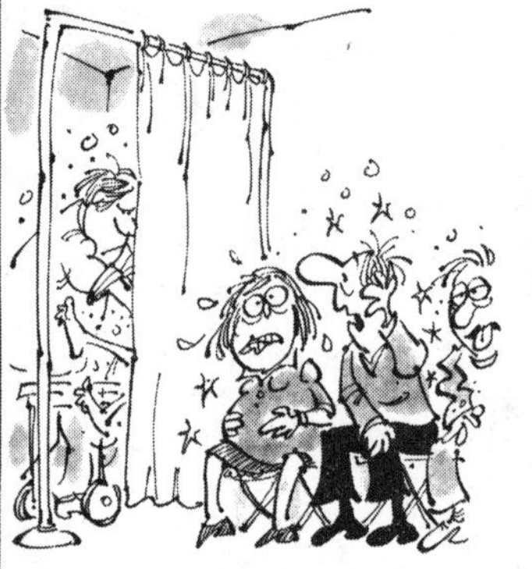 You wait in line at the clinic.	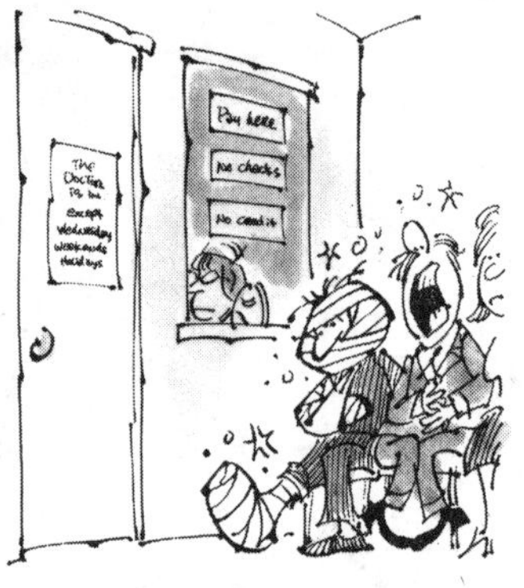 Pay here No checks No credit You wait in line to see your family doctor.	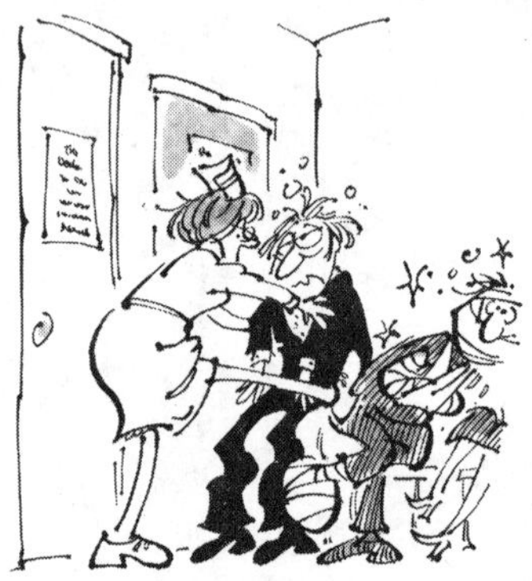 You're put first in line to see your family doctor.	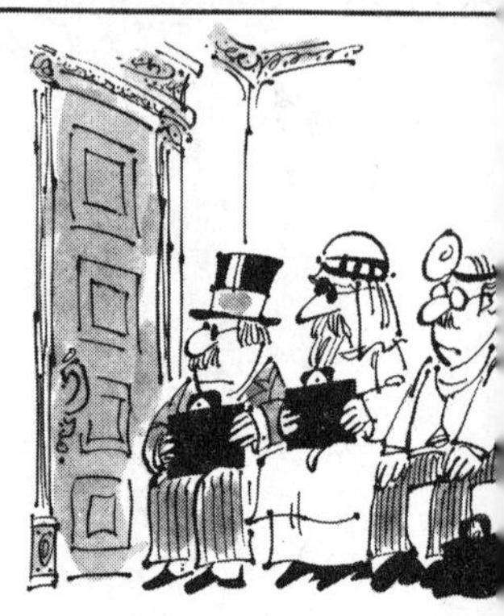 Your family doctor waits in line to see you.
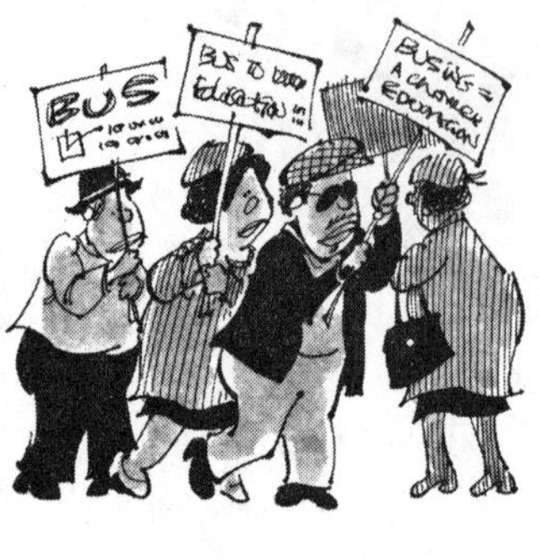 BUS You're for Busing because you figure that any change in schools has got to help.	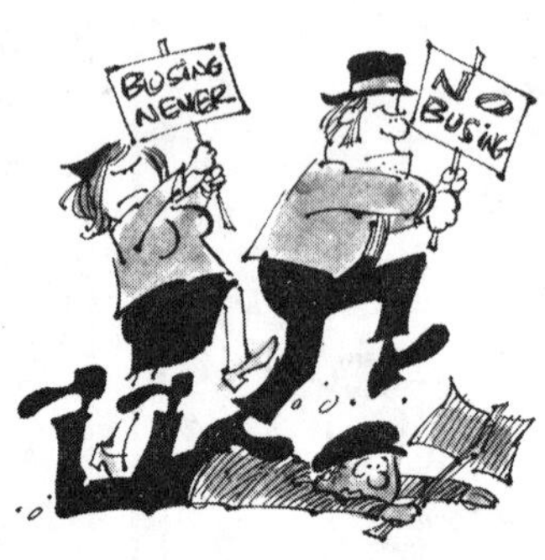 BUSING NEVER NO BUSING You're against Busing because the Down-And-Outers are for it.	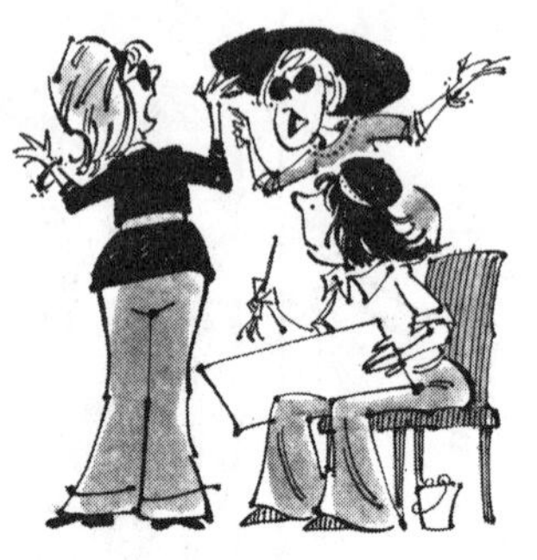 You take whatever view of Busing is fashionable.	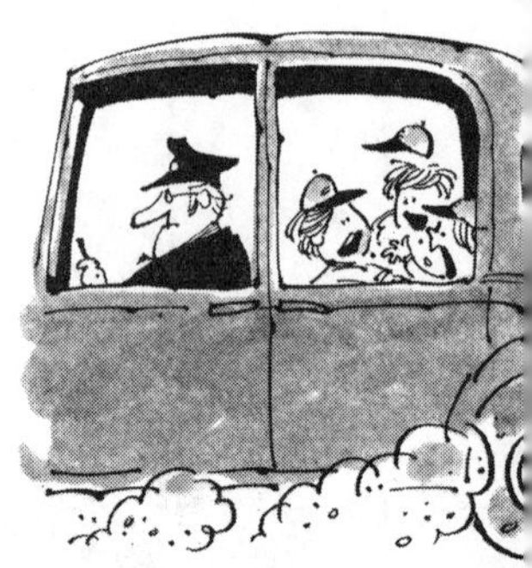 You're not for or against Busing, since your kids go to private schools anyway.
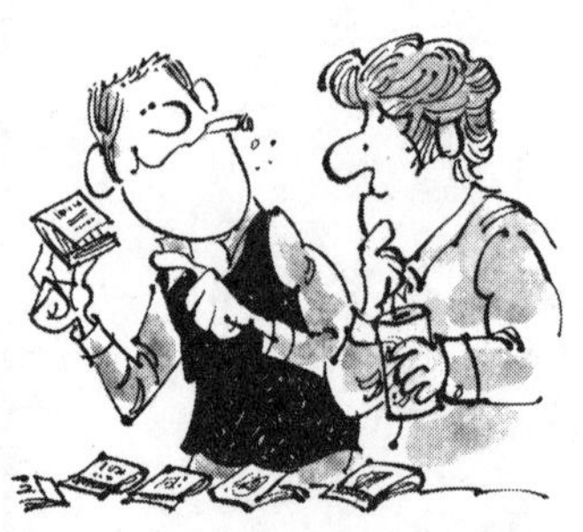 You collect matchbook covers from far-away places like The Trenton Holiday Inn and Al's Bar In Sandusky.	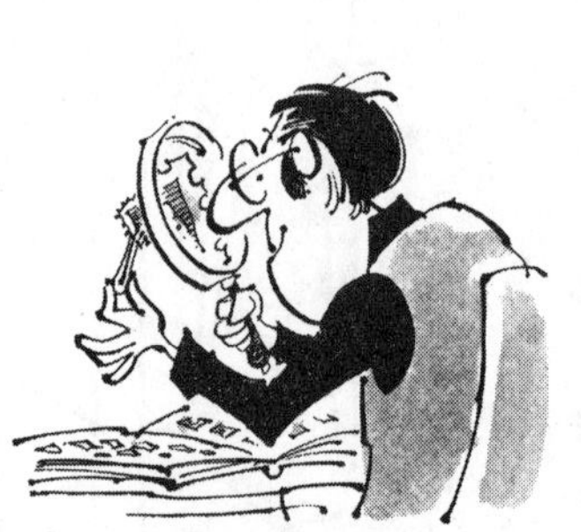 You collect stamps from exotic countries like Outer Mongolia and Tierra del Fuego.	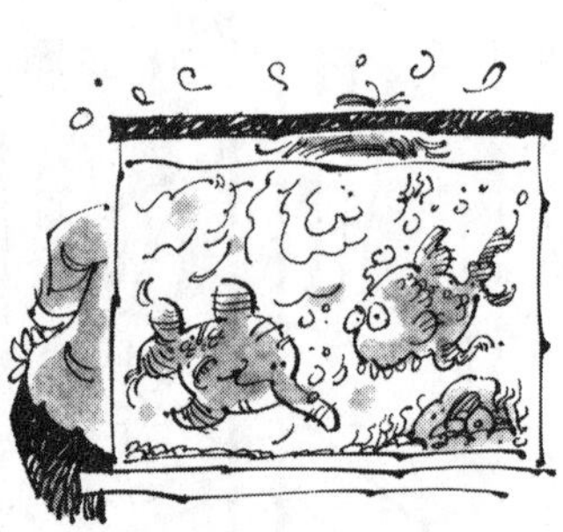 You collect tropical fish from South-Sea paradises like Tahiti and American Samoa.	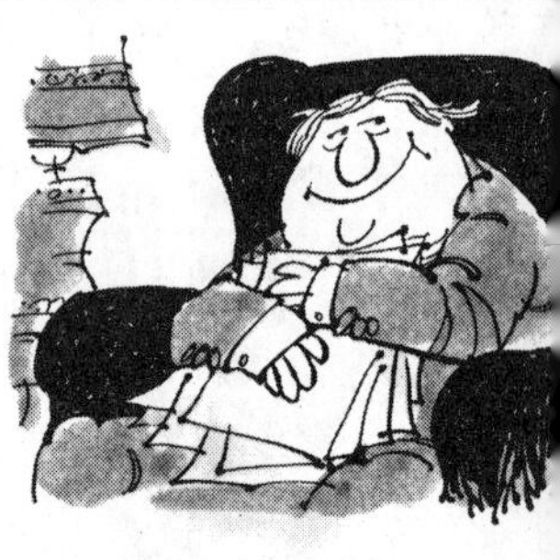 You collect common stock certificates from dull old companies like General Motors and U.S. Steel.

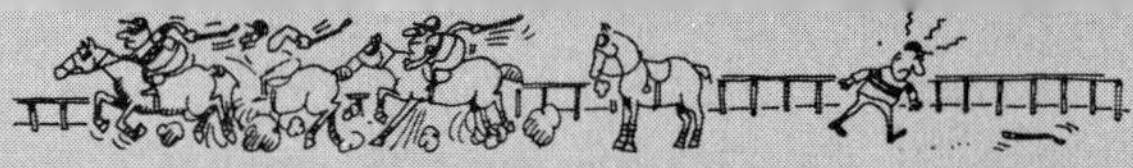

DE TO THE MODERN N CLASS SYSTEM

ARTIST: PAUL COKER, JR. WRITER: FRANK JACOBS IDEA BY: MARYLIN D'AMICO

WHEN YOU'RE DOWN AND OUT	WHEN YOU'RE JUST GETTING BY	WHEN YOU'RE MAKING IT	WHEN YOU'RE ON TOP OF THE HEAP
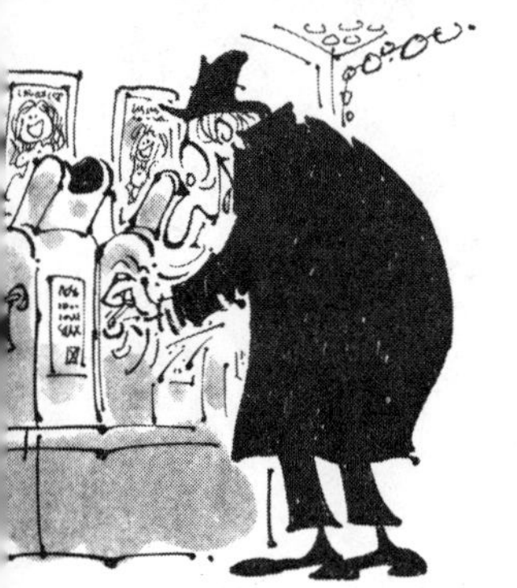 You peep at X-rated movies in penny arcades.	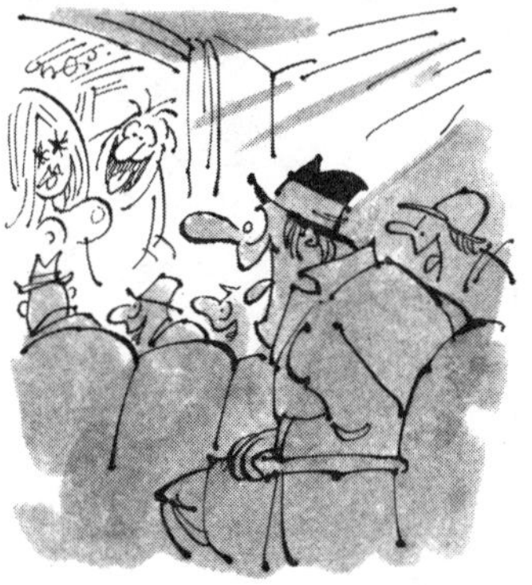 You watch X-rated movies in theaters.	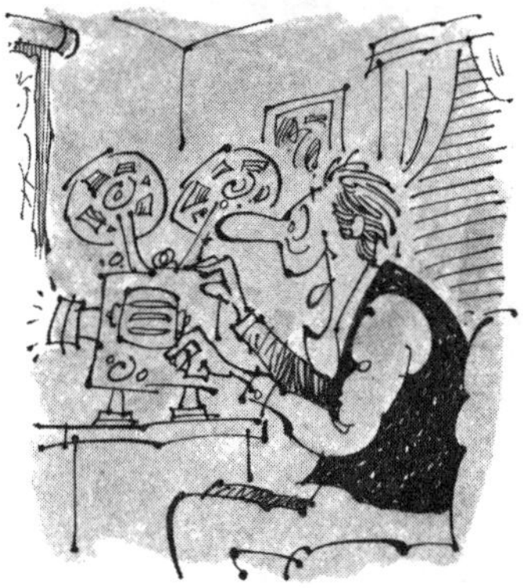 You rent X-rated movies and show them at home.	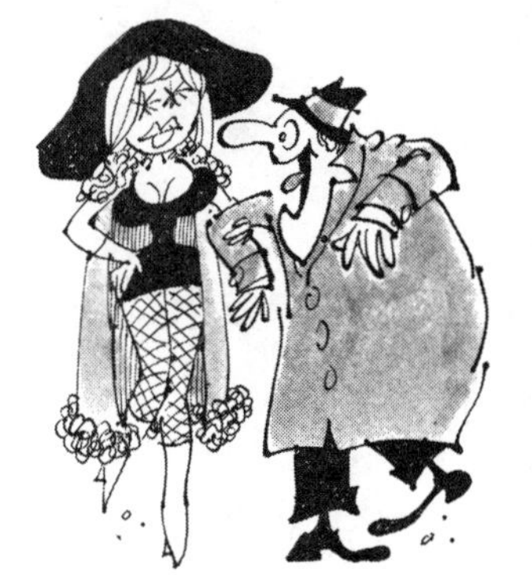 You date the star.
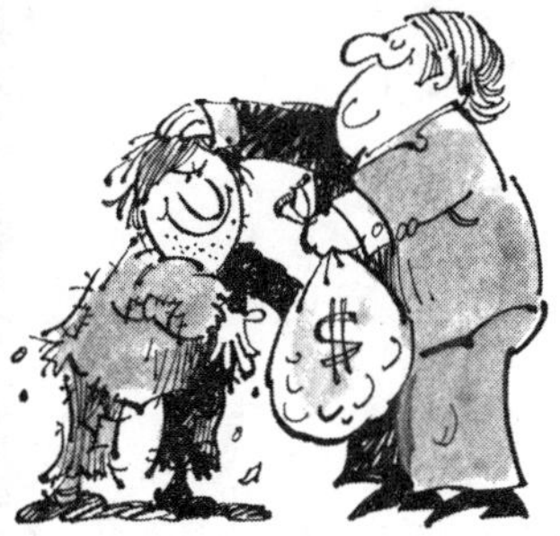 You vote for the politician who promises to increase Welfare.	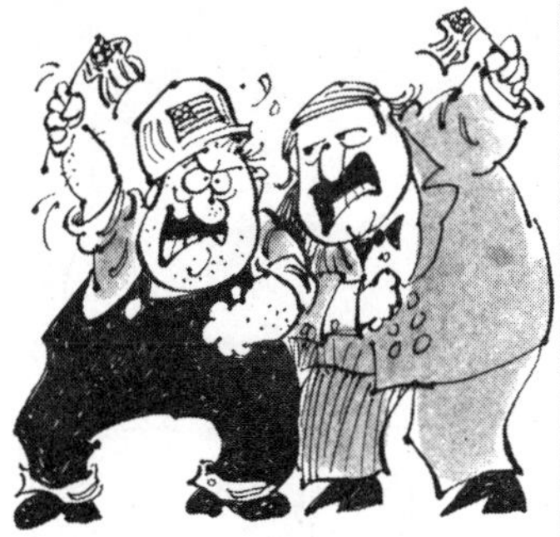 You vote for the politician who promises to preserve neighborhoods.	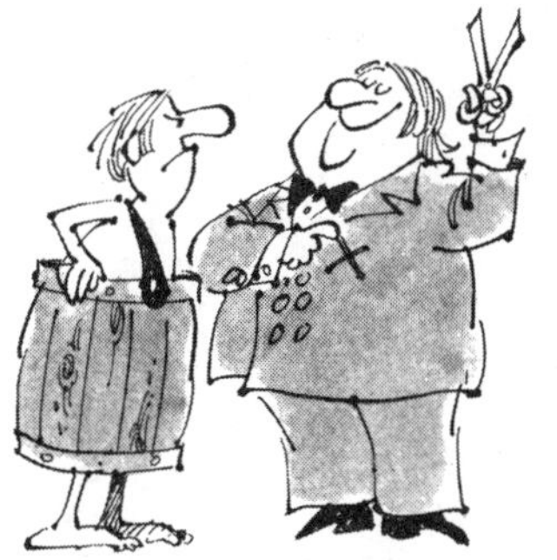 You vote for the politician who promises to lower taxes.	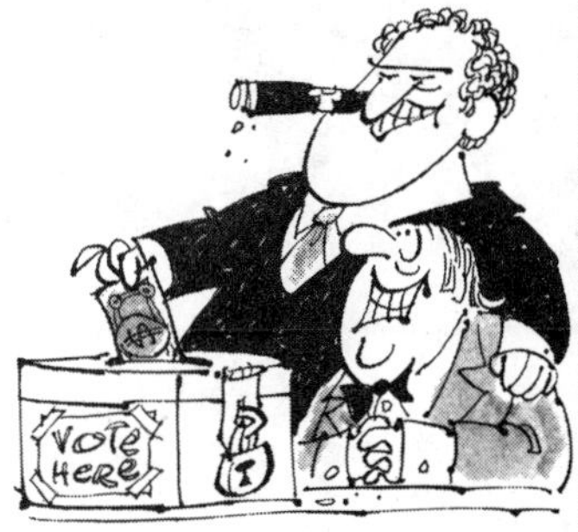VOTE HERE You vote for the politician you own.
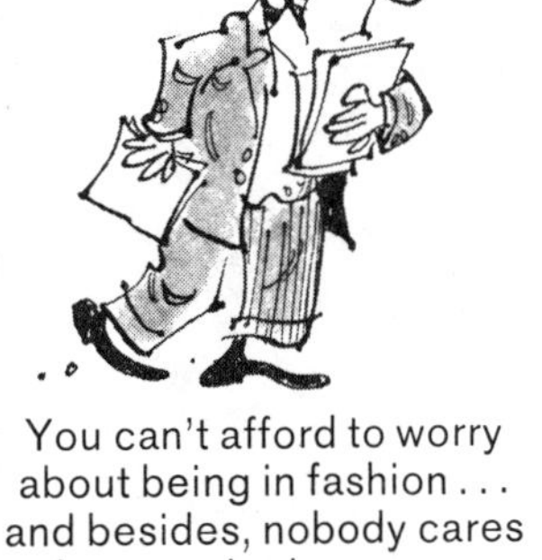 You can't afford to worry about being in fashion . . . and besides, nobody cares how you look anyway.	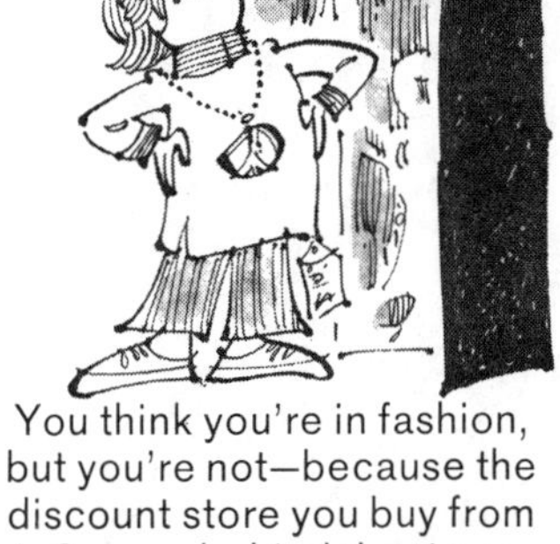 You think you're in fashion, but you're not—because the discount store you buy from is 3 years behind the times.	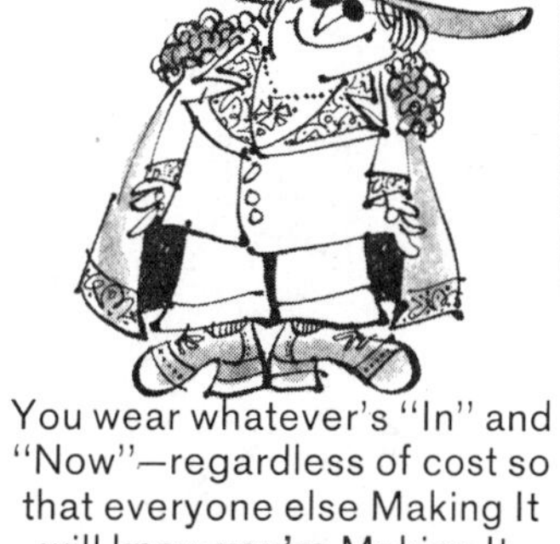 You wear whatever's "In" and "Now"—regardless of cost so that everyone else Making It will know **you're** Making It.	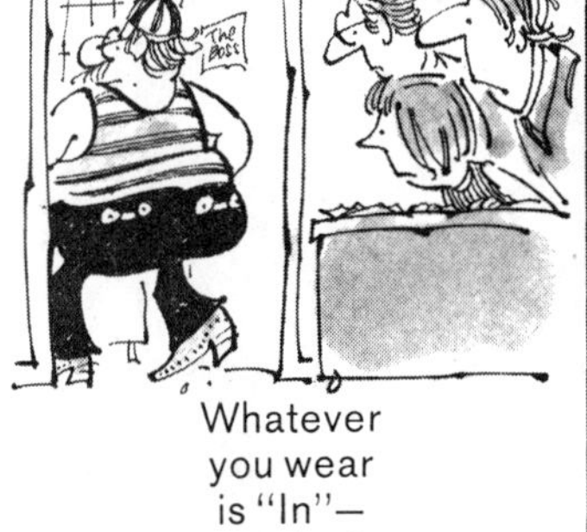 Whatever you wear is "In"— **or else!**

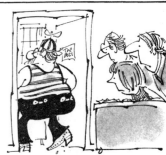

LOONEY BINGE DEPT.

HERE WE GO WITH OUR VERSION OF THE RECENT SMASH-HIT-MOVIE ABOU

ONE CUCKOO FL

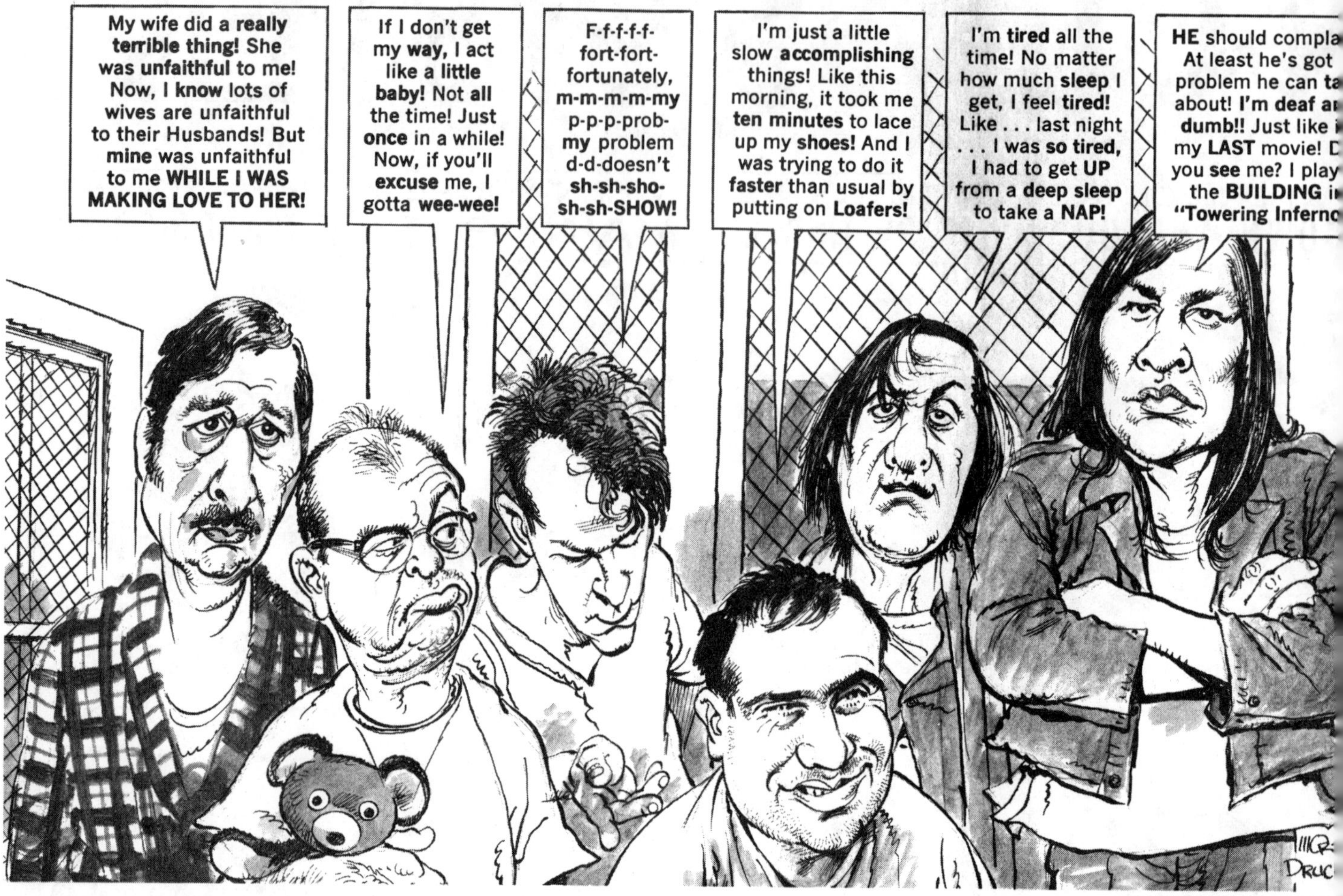

My wife did a really terrible thing! She was unfaithful to me! Now, I know lots of wives are unfaithful to their Husbands! But mine was unfaithful to me WHILE I WAS MAKING LOVE TO HER!
If I don't get my way, I act like a little baby! Not all the time! Just once in a while! Now, if you'll excuse me, I gotta wee-wee!
F-f-f-f-f- fort-fort- fortunately, m-m-m-m-my p-p-p-prob- my problem d-d-doesn't sh-sh-sho- sh-sh-SHOW!
I'm just a little slow accomplishing things! Like this morning, it took me ten minutes to lace up my shoes! And I was trying to do it faster than usual by putting on Loafers!
I'm tired all the time! No matter how much sleep I get, I feel tired! Like . . . last night . . . I was so tired, I had to get UP from a deep sleep to take a NAP!
HE should compla At least he's got problem he can ta about! I'm deaf a dumb!! Just like my LAST movie! D you see me? I play the BUILDING i "Towering Inferno

ARTIST: MORT DRUC

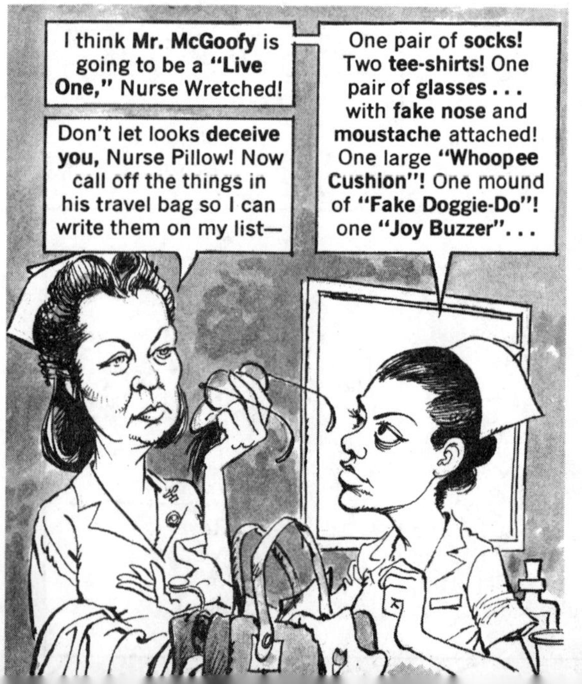

I think Mr. McGoofy is going to be a "Live One," Nurse Wretched!
Don't let looks deceive you, Nurse Pillow! Now call off the things in his travel bag so I can write them on my list—
One pair of socks! Two tee-shirts! One pair of glasses . . . with fake nose and moustache attached! One large "Whoopee Cushion"! One mound of "Fake Doggie-Do"! one "Joy Buzzer". . .

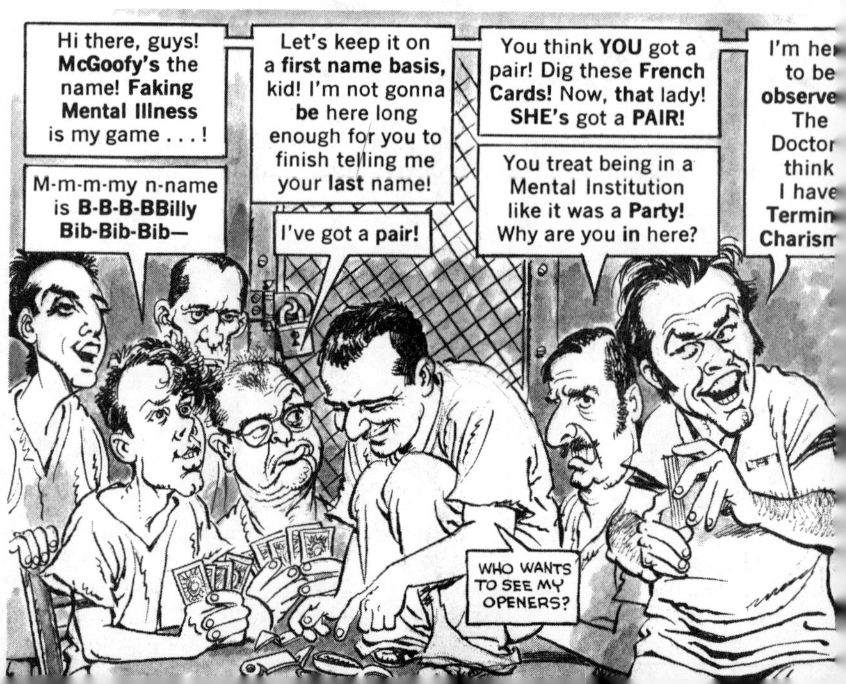

Hi there, guys! McGoofy's the name! Faking Mental Illness is my game . . . !
M-m-m-my n-name is B-B-B-BBilly Bib-Bib-Bib—
Let's keep it on a first name basis, kid! I'm not gonna be here long enough for you to finish telling me your last name!
I've got a pair!
You think YOU got a pair! Dig these French Cards! Now, that lady! SHE's got a PAIR!
You treat being in a Mental Institution like it was a Party! Why are you in here?
I'm he to be observe The Doctor think I have Termin Charism
WHO WANTS TO SEE MY OPENERS?

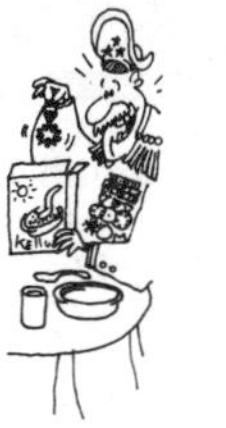

UBLE-MAKER AMONG THE INSANE! NO, IT'S NOT RALPH NADER! IT'S . . .

V OVER THE REST

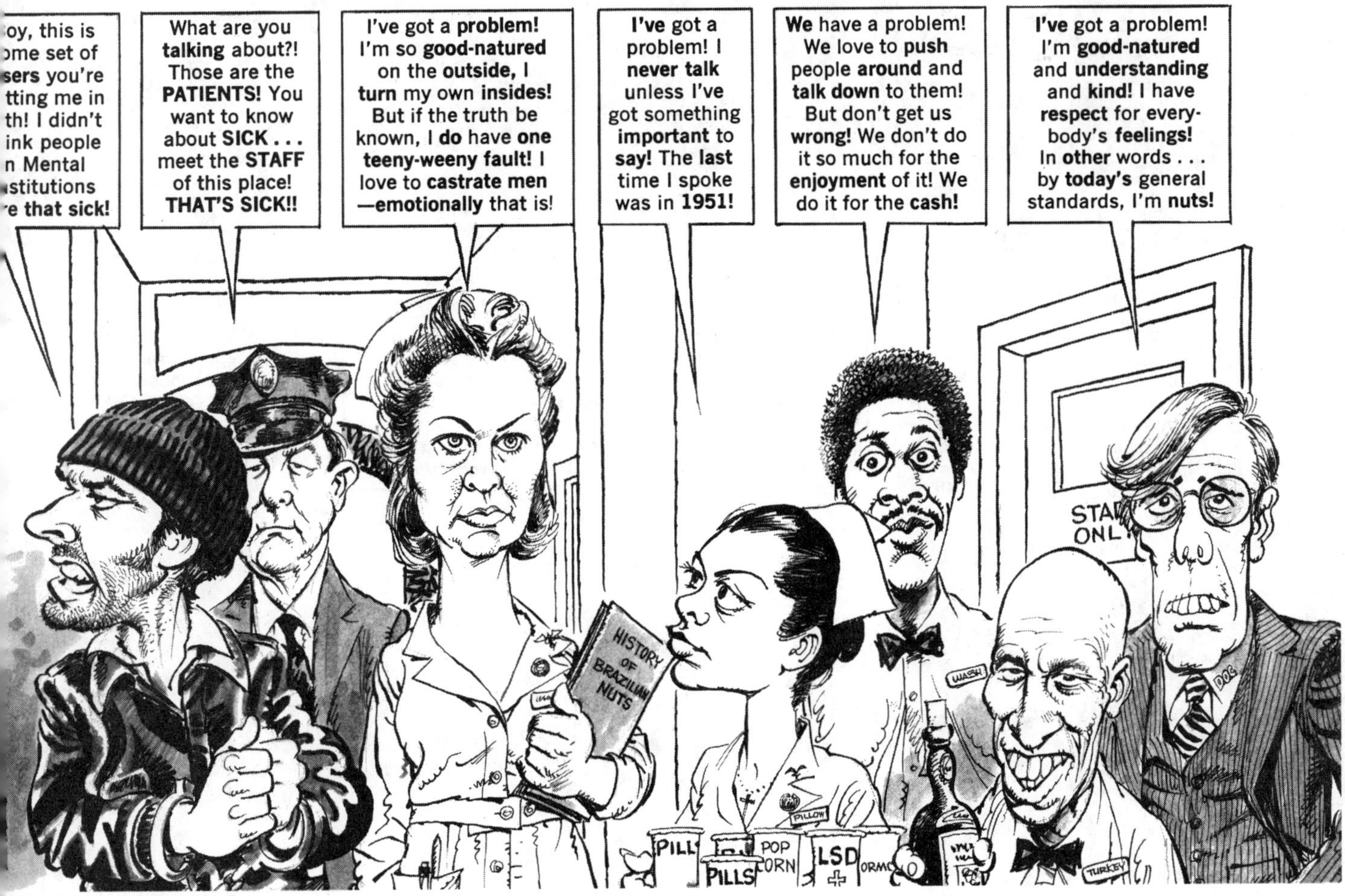

oy, this is ome set of sers you're tting me in th! I didn't ink people n Mental stitutions e that sick!
What are you talking about?! Those are the PATIENTS! You want to know about SICK . . . meet the STAFF of this place! THAT'S SICK!!
I've got a problem! I'm so good-natured on the outside, I turn my own insides! But if the truth be known, I do have one teeny-weeny fault! I love to castrate men —emotionally that is!
HISTORY OF BRAZILIAN NUTS
I've got a problem! I never talk unless I've got something important to say! The last time I spoke was in 1951!
We have a problem! We love to push people around and talk down to them! But don't get us wrong! We don't do it so much for the enjoyment of it! We do it for the cash!
I've got a problem! I'm good-natured and understanding and kind! I have respect for everybody's feelings! In other words . . . by today's general standards, I'm nuts!
STAF ONL
PILLS
POP CORN
LSD
PILLOW
WASH
TURKEY
DOC

TER: DICK DE BARTOLO

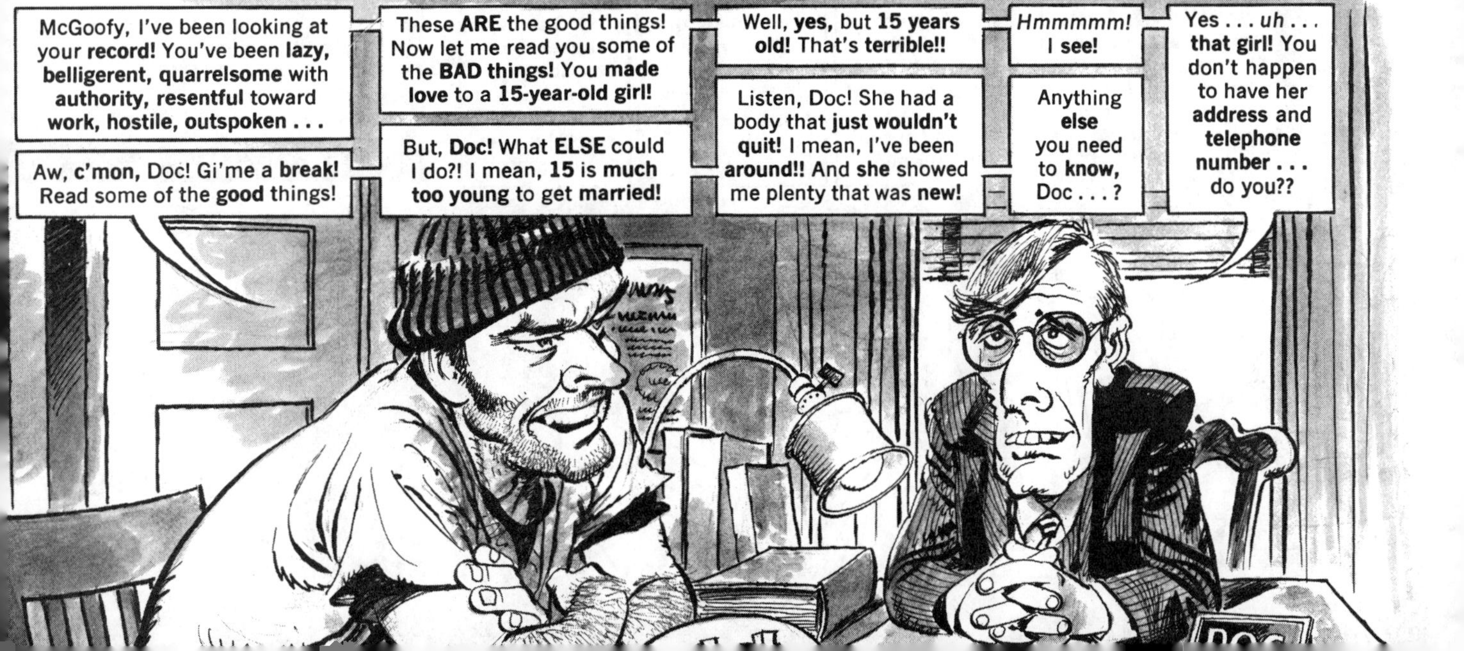

McGoofy, I've been looking at your record! You've been lazy, belligerent, quarrelsome with authority, resentful toward work, hostile, outspoken . . .
Aw, c'mon, Doc! Gi'me a break! Read some of the good things!
These ARE the good things! Now let me read you some of the BAD things! You made love to a 15-year-old girl!
But, Doc! What ELSE could I do?! I mean, 15 is much too young to get married!
Well, yes, but 15 years old! That's terrible!!
Listen, Doc! She had a body that just wouldn't quit! I mean, I've been around!! And she showed me plenty that was new!
Hmmmmm! I see!
Anything else you need to know, Doc . . . ?
Yes . . . uh . . . that girl! You don't happen to have her address and telephone number . . . do you??

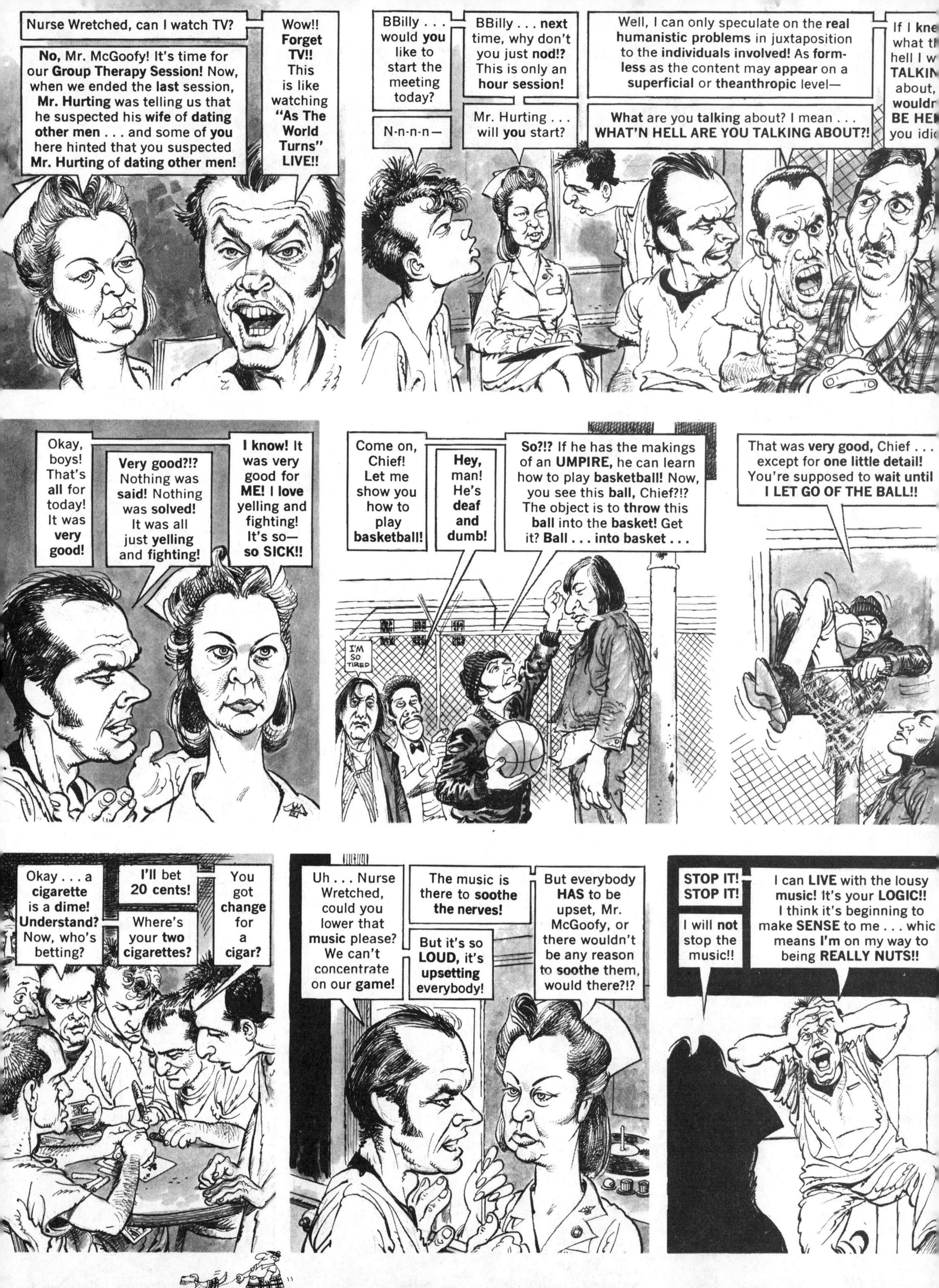

Nurse Wretched, can I watch TV?
No, Mr. McGoofy! It's time for our Group Therapy Session! Now, when we ended the last session, Mr. Hurting was telling us that he suspected his wife of dating other men . . . and some of you here hinted that you suspected Mr. Hurting of dating other men!
Wow!! Forget TV!! This is like watching "As The World Turns" LIVE!!
BBilly . . . would you like to start the meeting today?
N-n-n-n—
BBilly . . . next time, why don't you just nod!? This is only an hour session!
Mr. Hurting . . . will you start?
Well, I can only speculate on the real humanistic problems in juxtaposition to the individuals involved! As formless as the content may appear on a superficial or theanthropic level—
What are you talking about? I mean . . . WHAT'N HELL ARE YOU TALKING ABOUT?!
If I kne what th hell I w TALKIN about, BE HE you idi
Okay, boys! That's all for today! It was very good!
Very good?!? Nothing was said! Nothing was solved! It was all just yelling and fighting!
I know! It was very good for ME! I love yelling and fighting! It's so— so SICK!!
Come on, Chief! Let me show you how to play basketball!
Hey, man! He's deaf and dumb!
So?!? If he has the makings of an UMPIRE, he can learn how to play basketball! Now, you see this ball, Chief?!? The object is to throw this ball into the basket! Get it? Ball . . . into basket . . .
I'M SO TIRED
That was very good, Chief . . . except for one little detail! You're supposed to wait until I LET GO OF THE BALL!!
Okay . . . a cigarette is a dime! Understand? Now, who's betting?
I'll bet 20 cents!
Where's your two cigarettes?
You got change for a cigar?
Uh . . . Nurse Wretched, could you lower that music please? We can't concentrate on our game!
The music is there to soothe the nerves!
But it's so LOUD, it's upsetting everybody!
But everybody HAS to be upset, Mr. McGoofy, or there wouldn't be any reason to soothe them, would there?!?
STOP IT! STOP IT!
I will not stop the music!!
I can LIVE with the lousy music! It's your LOGIC!! I think it's beginning to make SENSE to me . . . whic means I'm on my way to being REALLY NUTS!!

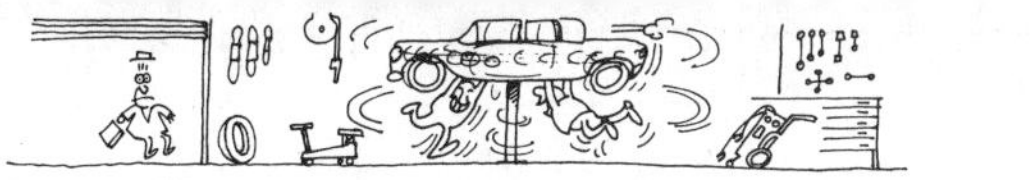

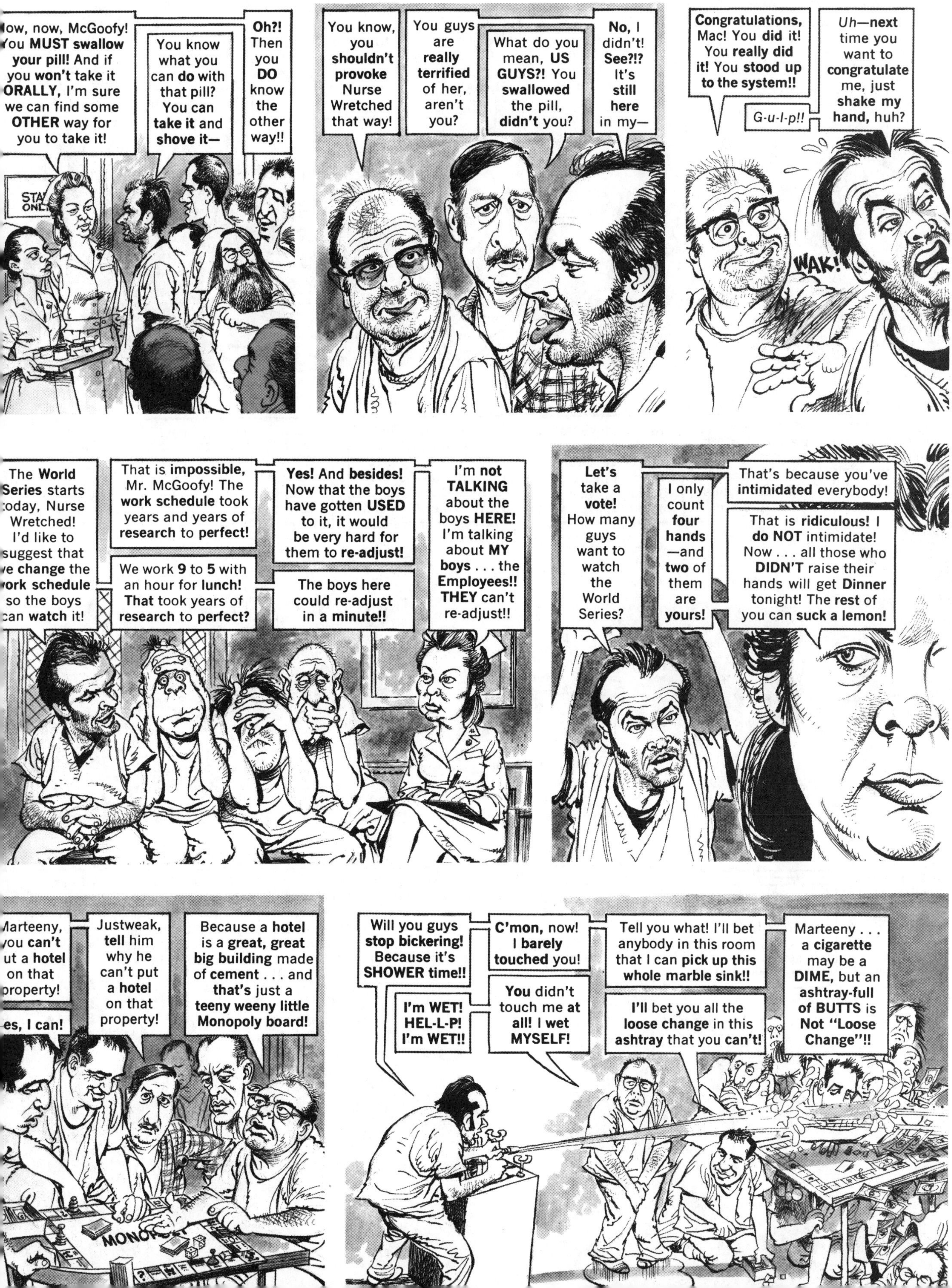

ow, now, McGoofy! 'ou MUST swallow your pill! And if you won't take it ORALLY, I'm sure we can find some OTHER way for you to take it!
You know what you can do with that pill? You can take it and shove it—
Oh?! Then you DO know the other way!!
STA ONL
You know, you shouldn't provoke Nurse Wretched that way!
You guys are really terrified of her, aren't you?
What do you mean, US GUYS?! You swallowed the pill, didn't you?
No, I didn't! See?!? It's still here in my—
Congratulations, Mac! You did it! You really did it! You stood up to the system!!
WAK!
G-u-l-p!!
Uh—next time you want to congratulate me, just shake my hand, huh?
The World Series starts oday, Nurse Wretched! I'd like to suggest that e change the ork schedule so the boys an watch it!
That is impossible, Mr. McGoofy! The work schedule took years and years of research to perfect!
We work 9 to 5 with an hour for lunch! That took years of research to perfect?
Yes! And besides! Now that the boys have gotten USED to it, it would be very hard for them to re-adjust!
The boys here could re-adjust in a minute!!
I'm not TALKING about the boys HERE! I'm talking about MY boys . . . the Employees!! THEY can't re-adjust!!
Let's take a vote! How many guys want to watch the World Series?
I only count four hands —and two of them are yours!
That's because you've intimidated everybody!
That is ridiculous! I do NOT intimidate! Now . . . all those who DIDN'T raise their hands will get Dinner tonight! The rest of you can suck a lemon!
Marteeny, 'ou can't ut a hotel on that roperty!
es, I can!
Justweak, tell him why he can't put a hotel on that property!
Because a hotel is a great, great big building made of cement . . . and that's just a teeny weeny little Monopoly board!
MONO
Will you guys stop bickering! Because it's SHOWER time!!
I'm WET! HEL-L-P! I'm WET!!
C'mon, now! I barely touched you!
You didn't touch me at all! I wet MYSELF!
Tell you what! I'll bet anybody in this room that I can pick up this whole marble sink!!
I'll bet you all the loose change in this ashtray that you can't!
Marteeny . . . a cigarette may be a DIME, but an ashtray-full of BUTTS is Not "Loose Change"!!

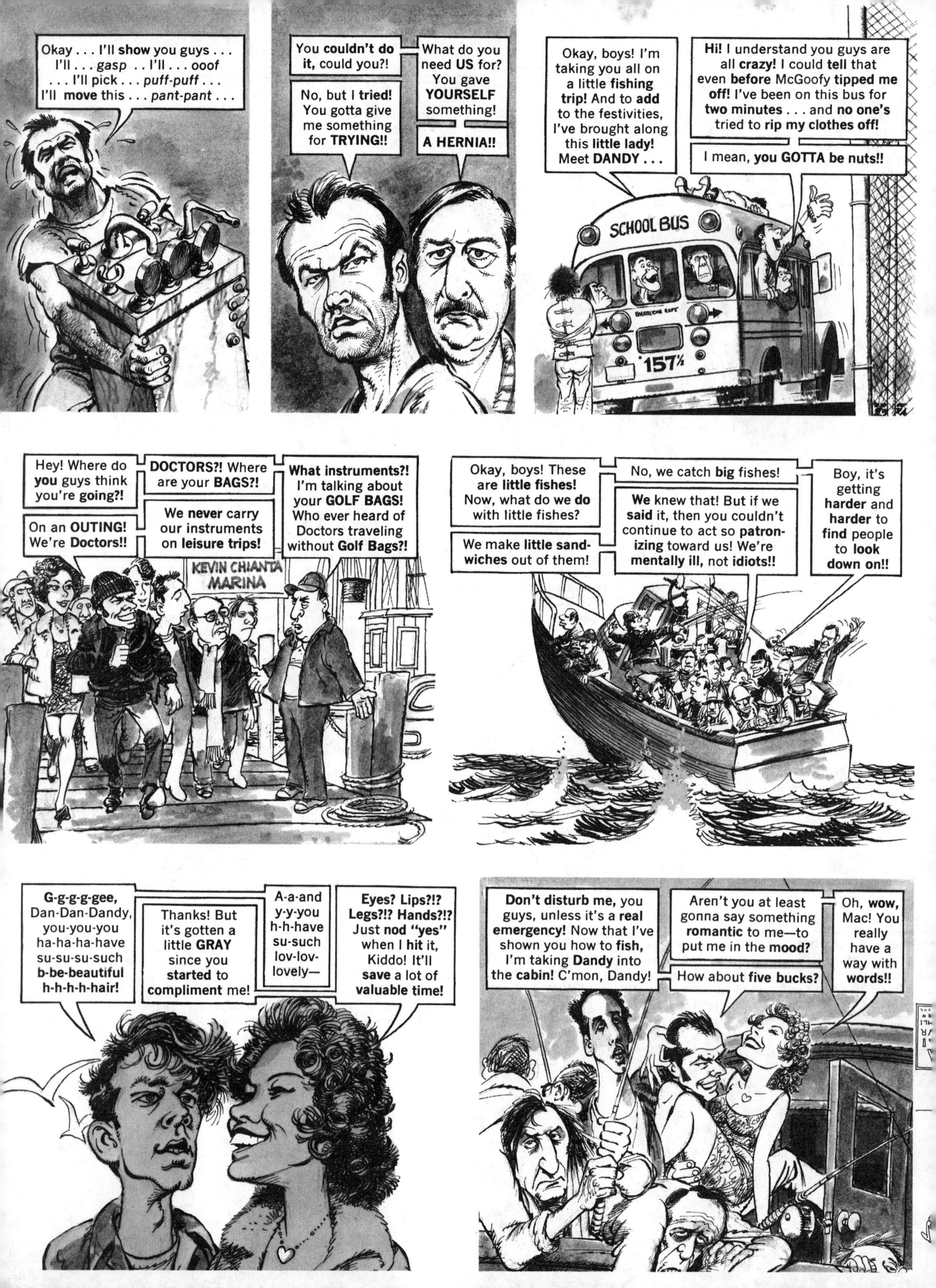
Okay . . . I'll show you guys . . . I'll . . . gasp . . I'll . . . ooof . . . I'll pick . . . puff-puff . . . I'll move this . . . pant-pant . . .
You couldn't do it, could you?!
No, but I tried! You gotta give me something for TRYING!!
What do you need US for? You gave YOURSELF something!
A HERNIA!!
Okay, boys! I'm taking you all on a little fishing trip! And to add to the festivities, I've brought along this little lady! Meet DANDY . . .
Hi! I understand you guys are all crazy! I could tell that even before McGoofy tipped me off! I've been on this bus for two minutes . . . and no one's tried to rip my clothes off!
I mean, you GOTTA be nuts!!
SCHOOL BUS
157½
Hey! Where do you guys think you're going?!
On an OUTING! We're Doctors!!
DOCTORS?! Where are your BAGS?!
We never carry our instruments on leisure trips!
What instruments?! I'm talking about your GOLF BAGS! Who ever heard of Doctors traveling without Golf Bags?!
KEVIN CHIANTA MARINA
Okay, boys! These are little fishes! Now, what do we do with little fishes?
We make little sandwiches out of them!
No, we catch big fishes!
We knew that! But if we said it, then you couldn't continue to act so patronizing toward us! We're mentally ill, not idiots!!
Boy, it's getting harder and harder to find people to look down on!!
G-g-g-gee, Dan-Dan-Dandy, you-you-you ha-ha-ha-have su-su-su-such b-be-beautiful h-h-h-h-hair!
Thanks! But it's gotten a little GRAY since you started to compliment me!
A-a-and y-y-you h-h-have su-such lov-lov-lovely—
Eyes? Lips?!? Legs?!? Hands?!? Just nod "yes" when I hit it, Kiddo! It'll save a lot of valuable time!
Don't disturb me, you guys, unless it's a real emergency! Now that I've shown you how to fish, I'm taking Dandy into the cabin! C'mon, Dandy!
Aren't you at least gonna say something romantic to me—to put me in the mood?
How about five bucks?
Oh, wow, Mac! You really have a way with words!!

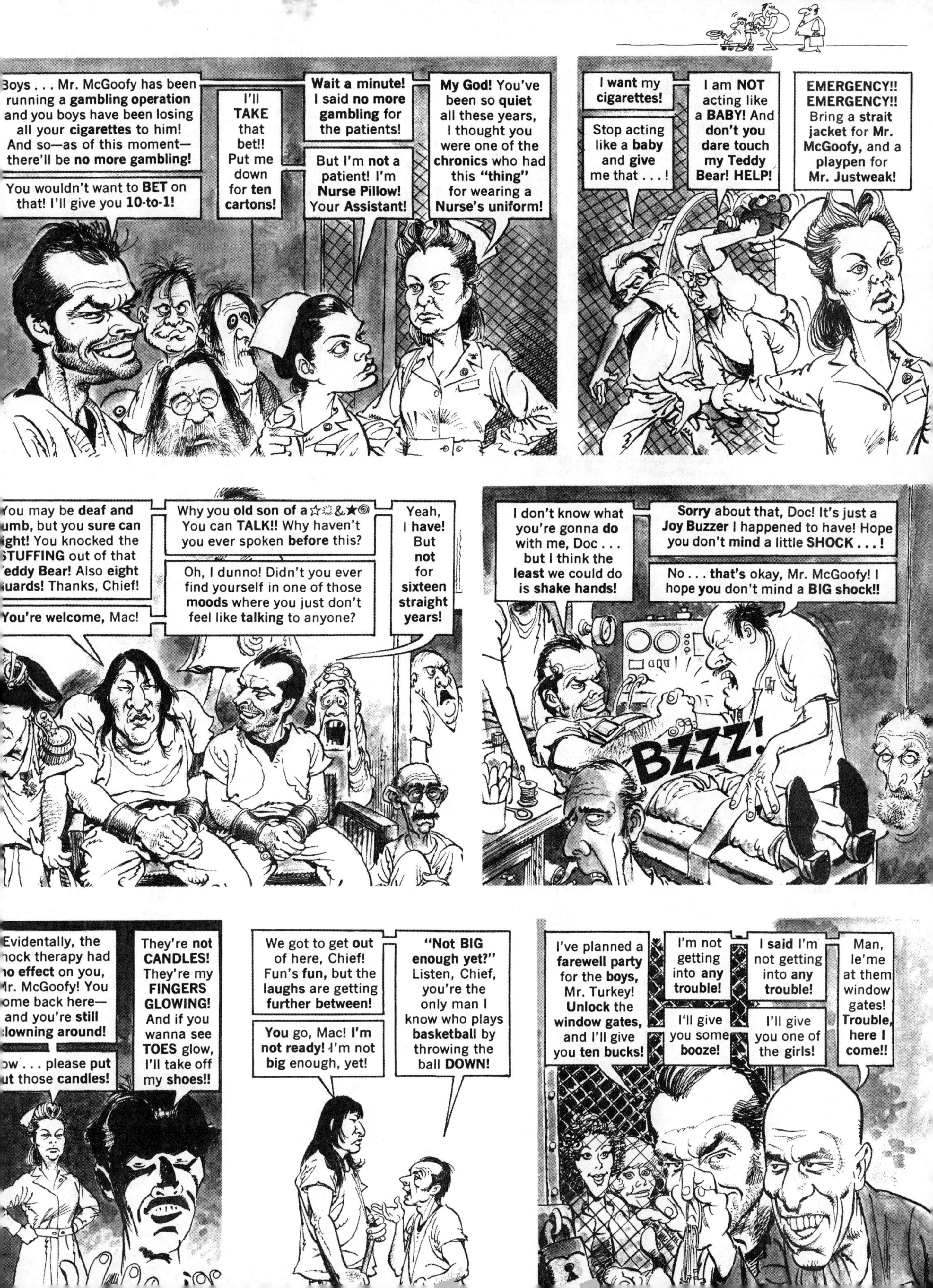
oys . . . Mr. McGoofy has been running a gambling operation and you boys have been losing all your cigarettes to him! And so—as of this moment—there'll be no more gambling!
You wouldn't want to BET on that! I'll give you 10-to-1!
I'll TAKE that bet!! Put me down for ten cartons!
Wait a minute! I said no more gambling for the patients!
But I'm not a patient! I'm Nurse Pillow! Your Assistant!
My God! You've been so quiet all these years, I thought you were one of the chronics who had this "thing" for wearing a Nurse's uniform!
I want my cigarettes!
Stop acting like a baby and give me that . . . !
I am NOT acting like a BABY! And don't you dare touch my Teddy Bear! HELP!
EMERGENCY!! EMERGENCY!! Bring a strait jacket for Mr. McGoofy, and a playpen for Mr. Justweak!
ou may be deaf and umb, but you sure can ight! You knocked the STUFFING out of that eddy Bear! Also eight uards! Thanks, Chief!
You're welcome, Mac!
Why you old son of a ☆⁂&★◎ You can TALK!! Why haven't you ever spoken before this?
Oh, I dunno! Didn't you ever find yourself in one of those moods where you just don't feel like talking to anyone?
Yeah, I have! But not for sixteen straight years!
I don't know what you're gonna do with me, Doc . . . but I think the least we could do is shake hands!
Sorry about that, Doc! It's just a Joy Buzzer I happened to have! Hope you don't mind a little SHOCK . . . !
No . . . that's okay, Mr. McGoofy! I hope you don't mind a BIG shock!!
BZZZ!
Evidentally, the hock therapy had o effect on you, Mr. McGoofy! You ome back here— and you're still lowning around!
ow . . . please put ut those candles!
They're not CANDLES! They're my FINGERS GLOWING! And if you wanna see TOES glow, I'll take off my shoes!!
We got to get out of here, Chief! Fun's fun, but the laughs are getting further between!
You go, Mac! I'm not ready! I'm not big enough, yet!
"Not BIG enough yet?" Listen, Chief, you're the only man I know who plays basketball by throwing the ball DOWN!
I've planned a farewell party for the boys, Mr. Turkey! Unlock the window gates, and I'll give you ten bucks!
I'm not getting into any trouble!
I'll give you some booze!
I said I'm not getting into any trouble!
I'll give you one of the girls!
Man, le'me at them window gates! Trouble, here I come!!

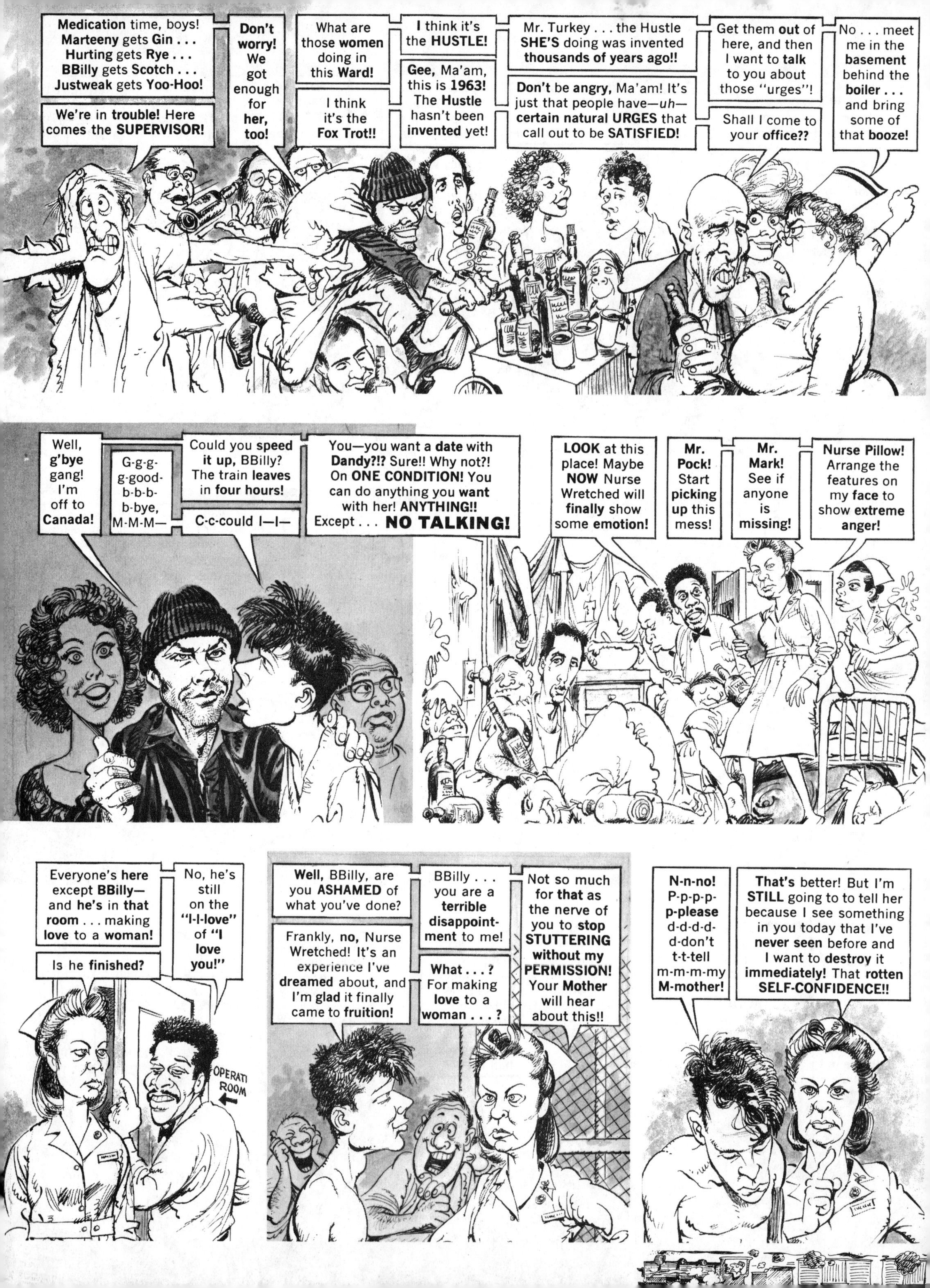

Medication time, boys! Marteeny gets Gin . . . Hurting gets Rye . . . BBilly gets Scotch . . . Justweak gets Yoo-Hoo!
We're in trouble! Here comes the SUPERVISOR!
Don't worry! We got enough for her, too!
What are those women doing in this Ward!
I think it's the HUSTLE!
I think it's the Fox Trot!!
Gee, Ma'am, this is 1963! The Hustle hasn't been invented yet!
Mr. Turkey . . . the Hustle SHE'S doing was invented thousands of years ago!!
Don't be angry, Ma'am! It's just that people have—uh—certain natural URGES that call out to be SATISFIED!
Get them out of here, and then I want to talk to you about those "urges"!
Shall I come to your office??
No . . . meet me in the basement behind the boiler . . . and bring some of that booze!
Well, g'bye gang! I'm off to Canada!
G-g-g-g-good-b-b-b-b-bye, M-M-M—
Could you speed it up, BBilly? The train leaves in four hours!
C-c-could I—I—
You—you want a date with Dandy?!? Sure!! Why not?! On ONE CONDITION! You can do anything you want with her! ANYTHING!! Except . . . NO TALKING!
LOOK at this place! Maybe NOW Nurse Wretched will finally show some emotion!
Mr. Pock! Start picking up this mess!
Mr. Mark! See if anyone is missing!
Nurse Pillow! Arrange the features on my face to show extreme anger!
Everyone's here except BBilly—and he's in that room . . . making love to a woman!
No, he's still on the "I-I-love" of "I love you!"
Is he finished?
OPERATI ROOM
Well, BBilly, are you ASHAMED of what you've done?
Frankly, no, Nurse Wretched! It's an experience I've dreamed about, and I'm glad it finally came to fruition!
BBilly . . . you are a terrible disappointment to me!
What . . . ? For making love to a woman . . . ?
Not so much for that as the nerve of you to stop STUTTERING without my PERMISSION! Your Mother will hear about this!!
N-n-no! P-p-p-p-p-please d-d-d-d-d-don't t-t-tell m-m-m-my M-mother!
That's better! But I'm STILL going to to tell her because I see something in you today that I've never seen before and I want to destroy it immediately! That rotten SELF-CONFIDENCE!!

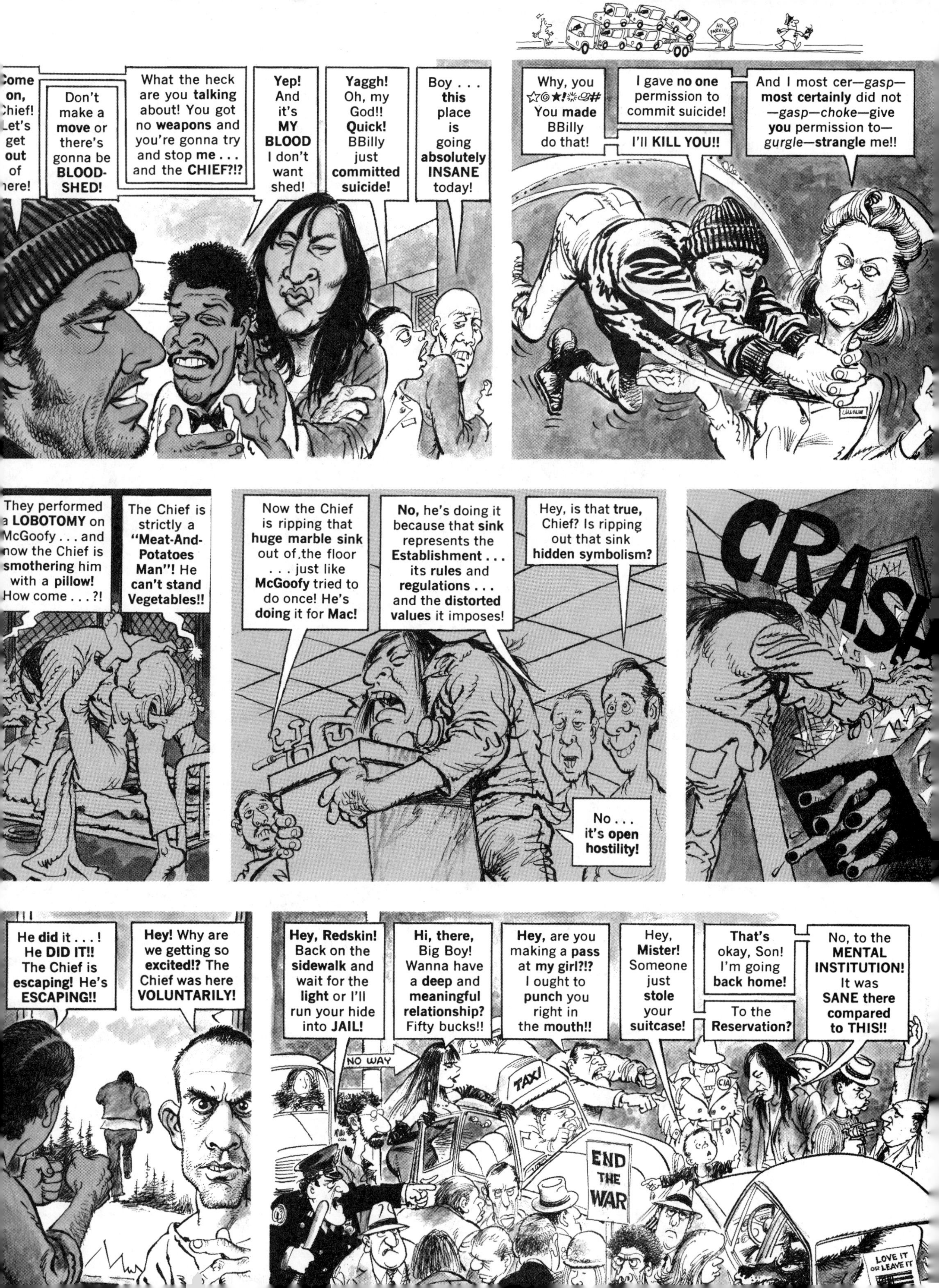

NO PARKING
Come on, Chief! Let's get out of here!
Don't make a move or there's gonna be BLOOD-SHED!
What the heck are you talking about! You got no weapons and you're gonna try and stop me . . . and the CHIEF?!?
Yep! And it's MY BLOOD I don't want shed!
Yaggh! Oh, my God!! Quick! BBilly just committed suicide!
Boy . . . this place is going absolutely INSANE today!
Why, you ☆◎★!☼@# You made BBilly do that!
I gave no one permission to commit suicide!
I'll KILL YOU!!
And I most cer—*gasp*— most certainly did not —*gasp*—*choke*—give you permission to— *gurgle*—strangle me!!
They performed a LOBOTOMY on McGoofy . . . and now the Chief is smothering him with a pillow! How come . . . ?!
The Chief is strictly a "Meat-And-Potatoes Man"! He can't stand Vegetables!!
Now the Chief is ripping that huge marble sink out of the floor . . . just like McGoofy tried to do once! He's doing it for Mac!
No, he's doing it because that sink represents the Establishment . . . its rules and regulations . . . and the distorted values it imposes!
Hey, is that true, Chief? Is ripping out that sink hidden symbolism?
No . . . it's open hostility!
CRASH
He did it . . . ! He DID IT!! The Chief is escaping! He's ESCAPING!!
Hey! Why are we getting so excited!? The Chief was here VOLUNTARILY!
Hey, Redskin! Back on the sidewalk and wait for the light or I'll run your hide into JAIL!
Hi, there, Big Boy! Wanna have a deep and meaningful relationship? Fifty bucks!!
Hey, are you making a pass at my girl?!? I ought to punch you right in the mouth!!
Hey, Mister! Someone just stole your suitcase!
That's okay, Son! I'm going back home!
To the Reservation?
No, to the MENTAL INSTITUTION! It was SANE there compared to THIS!!
NO WAY
TAXI
CIA
END THE WAR
LOVE IT OR LEAVE IT

WASHINGTON POST-MORTEM DEPT.

For more than four years, we've all read about "Watergate" in newspapers, we've watched it on television, we've heard about it on radio and we've read about it in best-seller books! Now, before it becomes a TV Series with a different law-breaker indicted every week (and no need for Summer re-runs because there's plenty of crooks to go around for years!), here's MAD's version of the smash-hit "WATERGATE MOVIE"! The time is 1972, the place is Washington, D.C., and we are about to discover the unmitigated . . .

GALL
PRES

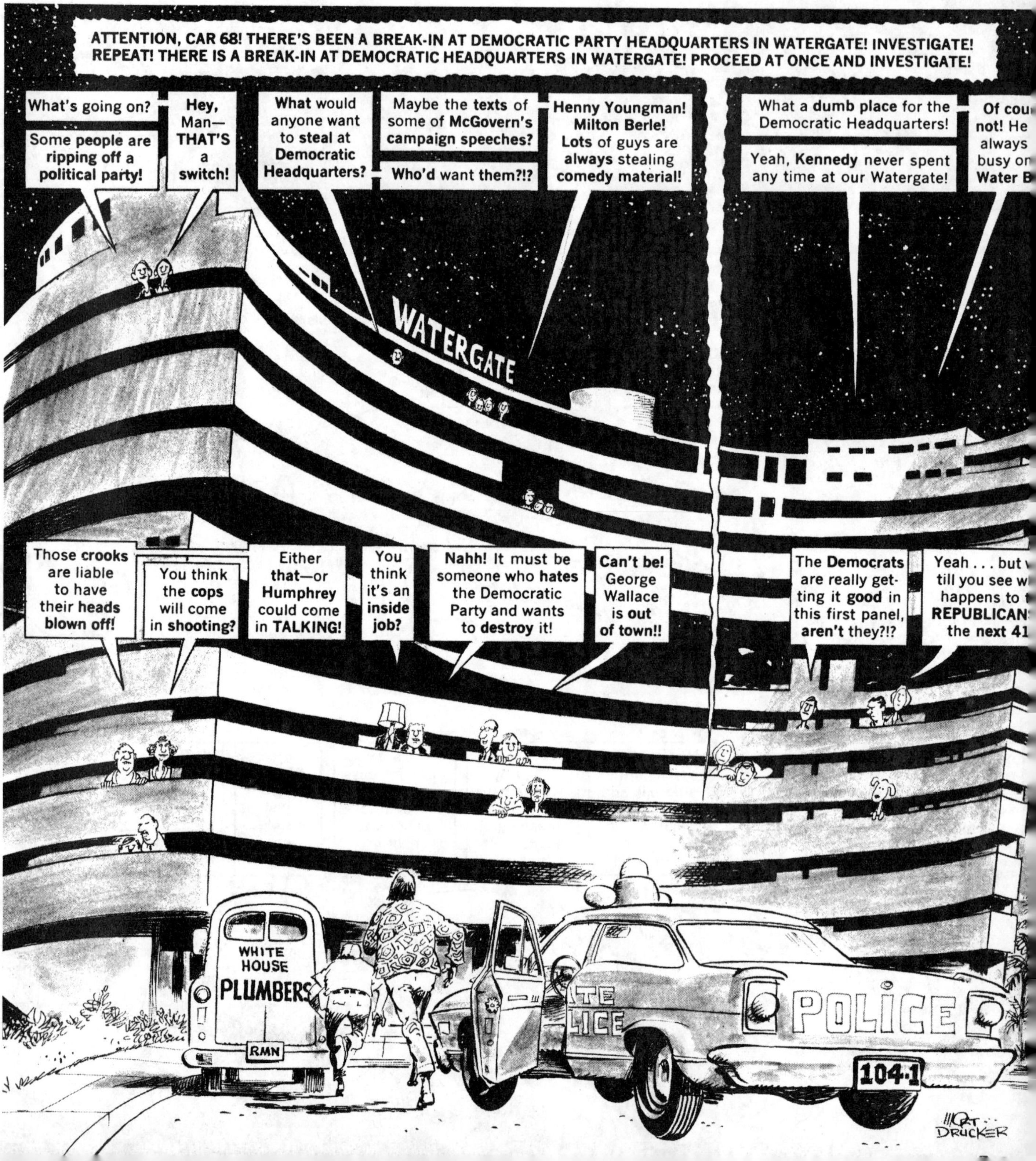

ATTENTION, CAR 68! THERE'S BEEN A BREAK-IN AT DEMOCRATIC PARTY HEADQUARTERS IN WATERGATE! INVESTIGATE! REPEAT! THERE IS A BREAK-IN AT DEMOCRATIC HEADQUARTERS IN WATERGATE! PROCEED AT ONCE AND INVESTIGATE!
What's going on?
Some people are ripping off a political party!
Hey, Man— THAT'S a switch!
What would anyone want to steal at Democratic Headquarters?
Maybe the texts of some of McGovern's campaign speeches?
Who'd want them?!?
Henny Youngman! Milton Berle! Lots of guys are always stealing comedy material!
What a dumb place for the Democratic Headquarters!
Yeah, Kennedy never spent any time at our Watergate!
Of cou not! He always busy on Water B
WATERGATE
Those crooks are liable to have their heads blown off!
You think the cops will come in shooting?
Either that—or Humphrey could come in TALKING!
You think it's an inside job?
Nahh! It must be someone who hates the Democratic Party and wants to destroy it!
Can't be! George Wallace is out of town!!
The Democrats are really getting it good in this first panel, aren't they?!?
Yeah . . . but till you see w happens to t REPUBLICAN the next 41
WHITE HOUSE PLUMBERS
RMN
POLICE
104-1
MORT DRUCKER

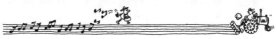

OF THE
DENT'S MEN

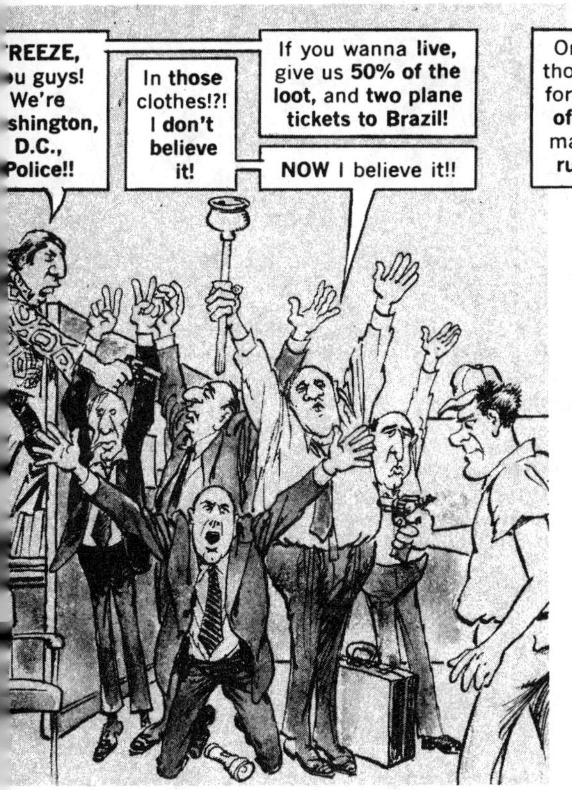
REEZE, u guys! We're shington, D.C., Police!!
In those clothes!?! I don't believe it!
If you wanna live, give us 50% of the loot, and two plane tickets to Brazil!
NOW I believe it!!

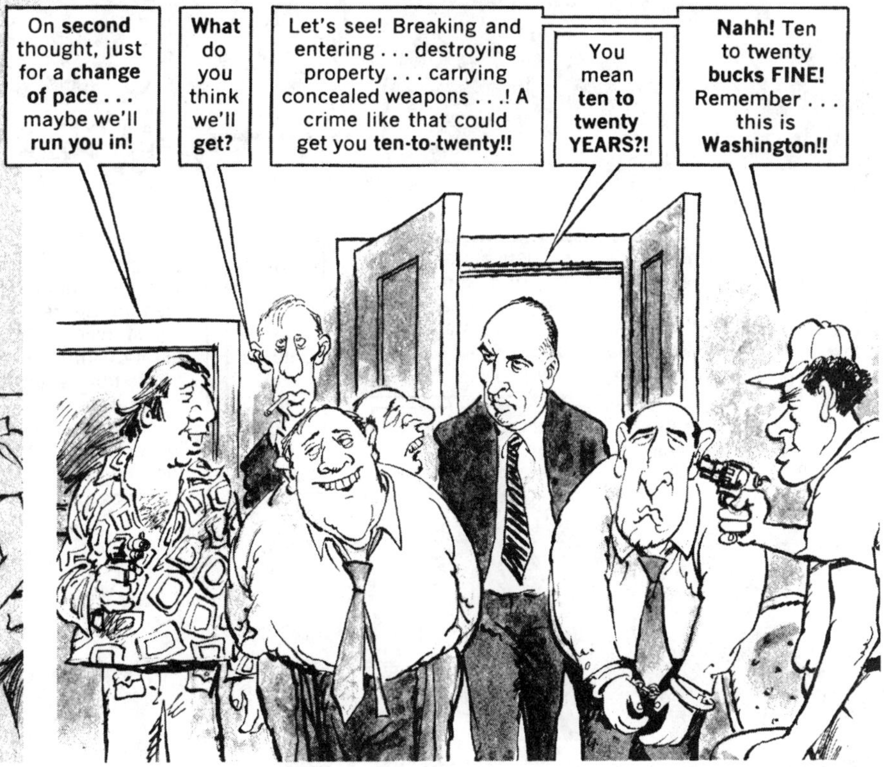
On second thought, just for a change of pace . . . maybe we'll run you in!
What do you think we'll get?
Let's see! Breaking and entering . . . destroying property . . . carrying concealed weapons . . .! A crime like that could get you ten-to-twenty!!
You mean ten to twenty YEARS?!
Nahh! Ten to twenty bucks FINE! Remember . . . this is Washington!!

ARTIST: MORT DRUCKER WRITER: LARRY SIEGEL

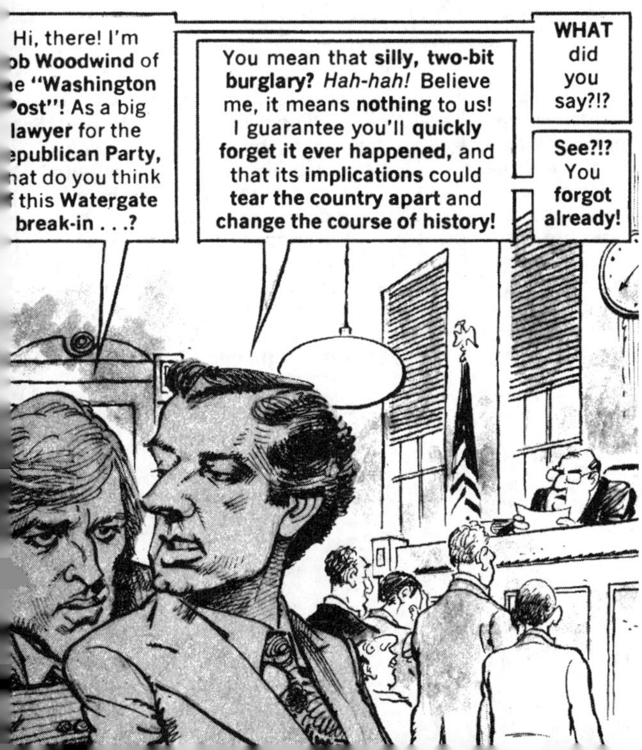
Hi, there! I'm ob Woodwind of e "Washington ost"! As a big lawyer for the epublican Party, hat do you think this Watergate break-in . . .?
You mean that silly, two-bit burglary? Hah-hah! Believe me, it means nothing to us! I guarantee you'll quickly forget it ever happened, and that its implications could tear the country apart and change the course of history!
WHAT did you say?!?
See?!? You forgot already!

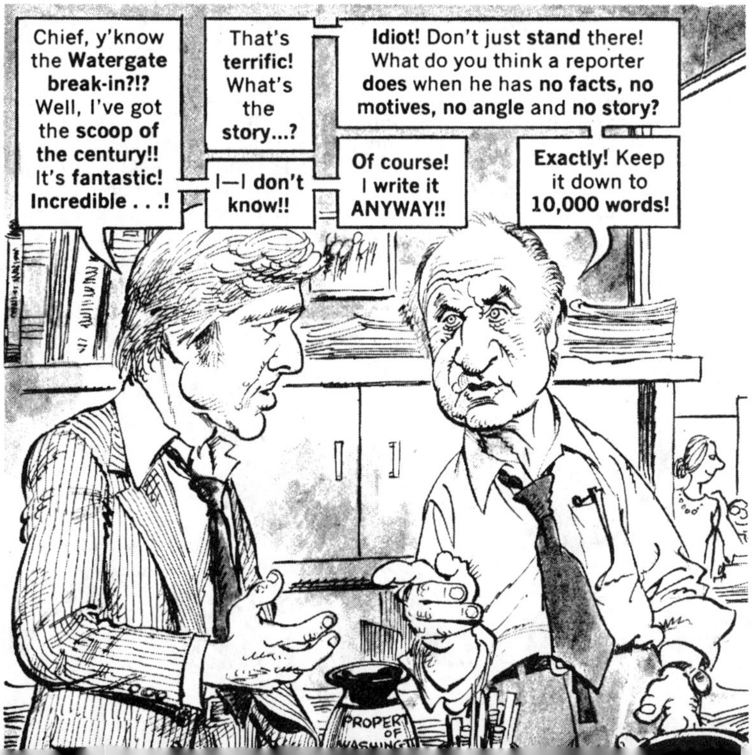
Chief, y'know the Watergate break-in?!? Well, I've got the scoop of the century!! It's fantastic! Incredible . . .!
That's terrific! What's the story...?
I—I don't know!!
Idiot! Don't just stand there! What do you think a reporter does when he has no facts, no motives, no angle and no story?
Of course! I write it ANYWAY!!
Exactly! Keep it down to 10,000 words!

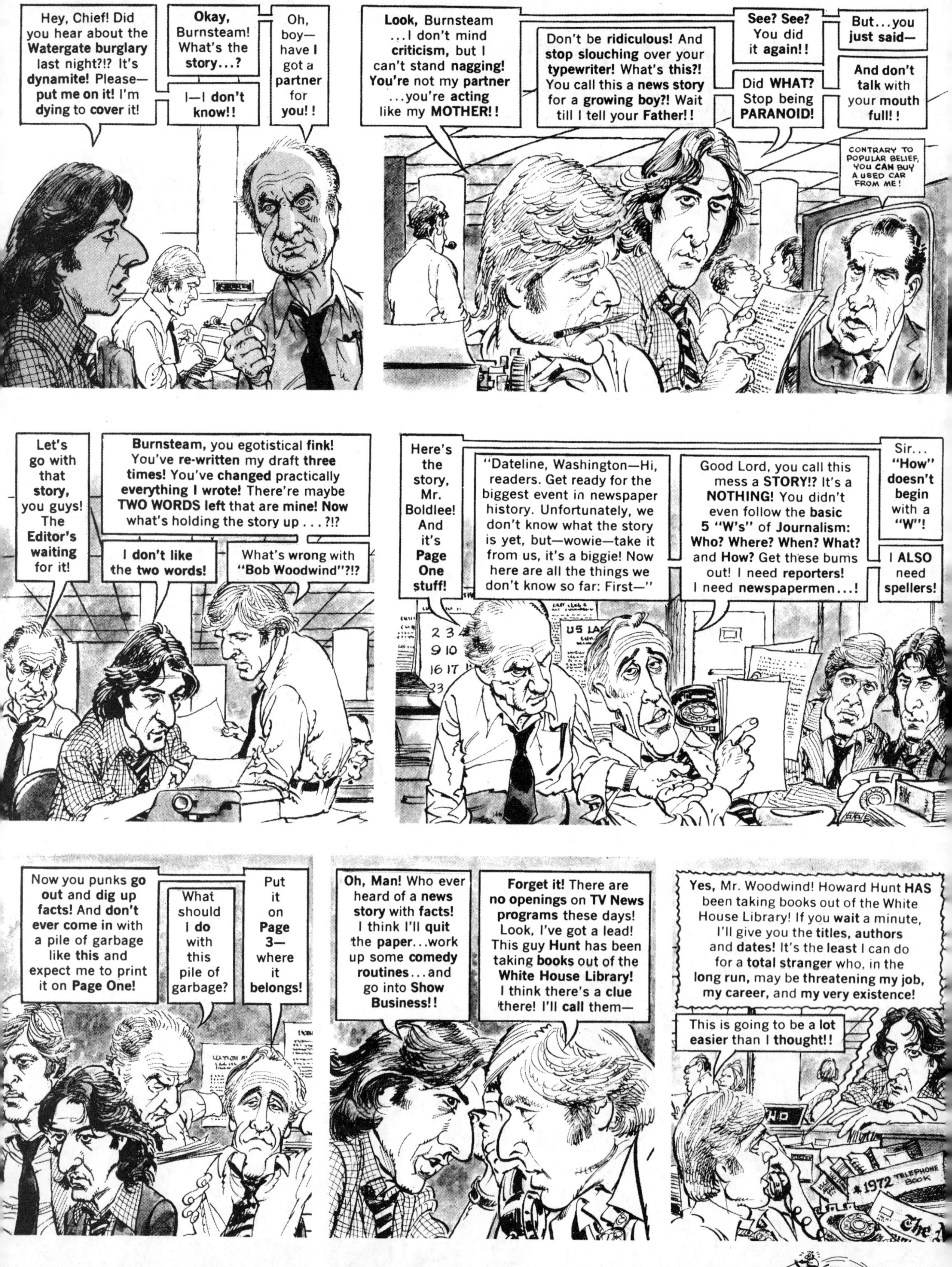

Hey, Chief! Did you hear about the Watergate burglary last night?!? It's dynamite! Please—put me on it! I'm dying to cover it!
Okay, Burnsteam! What's the story...?
I—I don't know!!
Oh, boy—have I got a partner for you!!
Look, Burnsteam ...I don't mind criticism, but I can't stand nagging! You're not my partner ...you're acting like my MOTHER!!
Don't be ridiculous! And stop slouching over your typewriter! What's this?! You call this a news story for a growing boy?! Wait till I tell your Father!!
See? See? You did it again!!
Did WHAT? Stop being PARANOID!
But...you just said—
And don't talk with your mouth full!!
CONTRARY TO POPULAR BELIEF, YOU CAN BUY A USED CAR FROM ME!
Let's go with that story, you guys! The Editor's waiting for it!
Burnsteam, you egotistical fink! You've re-written my draft three times! You've changed practically everything I wrote! There're maybe TWO WORDS left that are mine! Now what's holding the story up . . . ?!?
I don't like the two words!
What's wrong with "Bob Woodwind"?!?
Here's the story, Mr. Boldlee! And it's Page One stuff!
"Dateline, Washington—Hi, readers. Get ready for the biggest event in newspaper history. Unfortunately, we don't know what the story is yet, but—wowie—take it from us, it's a biggie! Now here are all the things we don't know so far: First—"
Good Lord, you call this mess a STORY!? It's a NOTHING! You didn't even follow the basic 5 "W's" of Journalism: Who? Where? When? What? and How? Get these bums out! I need reporters! I need newspapermen...!
Sir... "How" doesn't begin with a "W"!
I ALSO need spellers!
Now you punks go out and dig up facts! And don't ever come in with a pile of garbage like this and expect me to print it on Page One!
What should I do with this pile of garbage?
Put it on Page 3—where it belongs!
Oh, Man! Who ever heard of a news story with facts! I think I'll quit the paper...work up some comedy routines...and go into Show Business!!
Forget it! There are no openings on TV News programs these days! Look, I've got a lead! This guy Hunt has been taking books out of the White House Library! I think there's a clue there! I'll call them—
Yes, Mr. Woodwind! Howard Hunt HAS been taking books out of the White House Library! If you wait a minute, I'll give you the titles, authors and dates! It's the least I can do for a total stranger who, in the long run, may be threatening my job, my career, and my very existence!
This is going to be a lot easier than I thought!!
1972 TELEPHONE BOOK

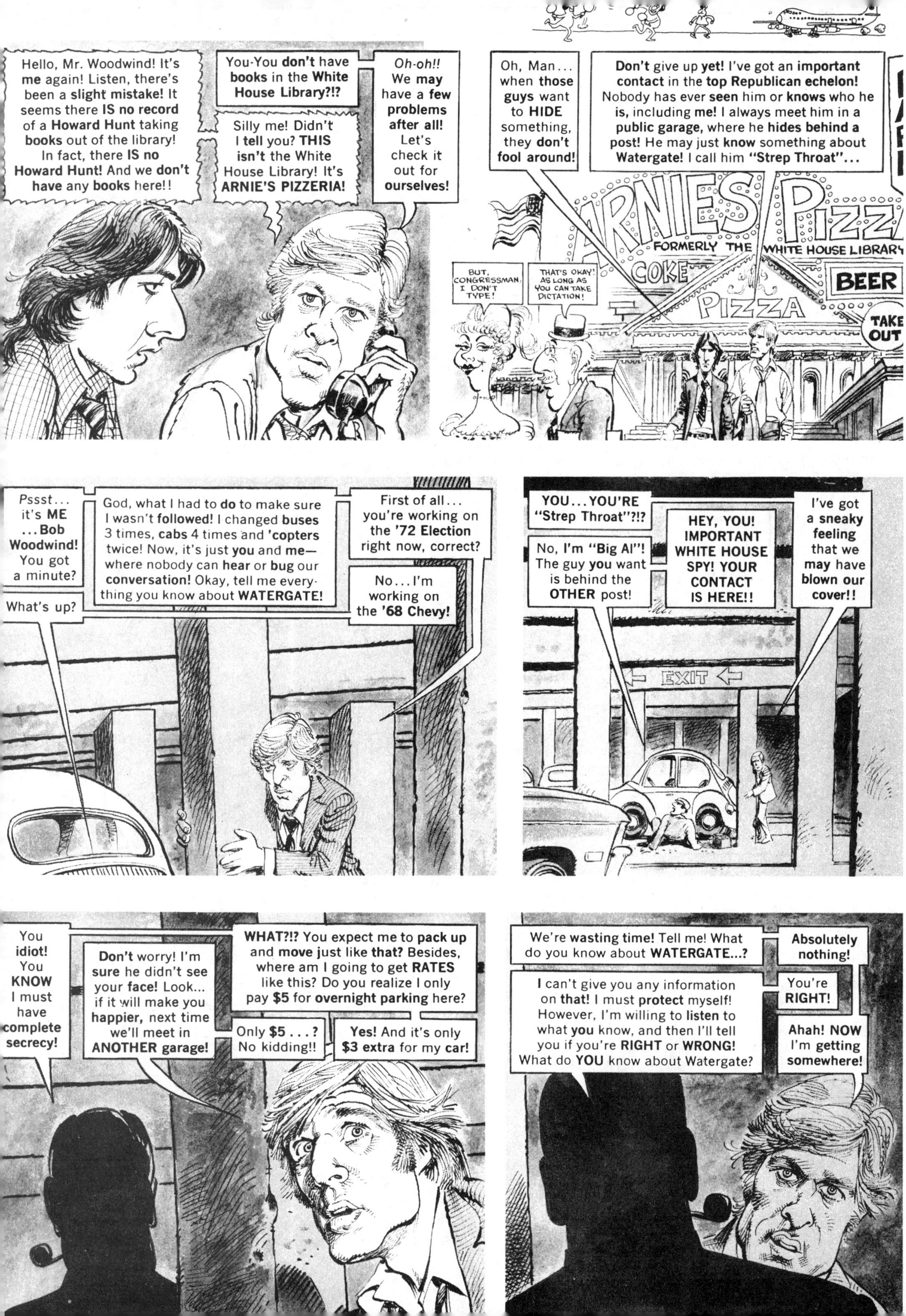
Hello, Mr. Woodwind! It's me again! Listen, there's been a slight mistake! It seems there IS no record of a Howard Hunt taking books out of the library! In fact, there IS no Howard Hunt! And we don't have any books here!!
You-You don't have books in the White House Library?!?
Silly me! Didn't I tell you? THIS isn't the White House Library! It's ARNIE'S PIZZERIA!
Oh-oh!! We may have a few problems after all! Let's check it out for ourselves!
Oh, Man... when those guys want to HIDE something, they don't fool around!
Don't give up yet! I've got an important contact in the top Republican echelon! Nobody has ever seen him or knows who he is, including me! I always meet him in a public garage, where he hides behind a post! He may just know something about Watergate! I call him "Strep Throat"...
ARNIES PIZZA
FORMERLY THE WHITE HOUSE LIBRARY
COKE
BEER
PIZZA
TAKE OUT
BUT, CONGRESSMAN, I DON'T TYPE!
THAT'S OKAY! AS LONG AS YOU CAN TAKE DICTATION!
Pssst... it's ME ...Bob Woodwind! You got a minute?
What's up?
God, what I had to do to make sure I wasn't followed! I changed buses 3 times, cabs 4 times and 'copters twice! Now, it's just you and me—where nobody can hear or bug our conversation! Okay, tell me everything you know about WATERGATE!
First of all... you're working on the '72 Election right now, correct?
No... I'm working on the '68 Chevy!
YOU... YOU'RE "Strep Throat"?!?
No, I'm "Big Al"! The guy you want is behind the OTHER post!
HEY, YOU! IMPORTANT WHITE HOUSE SPY! YOUR CONTACT IS HERE!!
I've got a sneaky feeling that we may have blown our cover!!
EXIT
You idiot! You KNOW I must have complete secrecy!
Don't worry! I'm sure he didn't see your face! Look... if it will make you happier, next time we'll meet in ANOTHER garage!
WHAT?!? You expect me to pack up and move just like that? Besides, where am I going to get RATES like this? Do you realize I only pay $5 for overnight parking here?
Only $5...? No kidding!!
Yes! And it's only $3 extra for my car!
We're wasting time! Tell me! What do you know about WATERGATE...?
Absolutely nothing!
I can't give you any information on that! I must protect myself! However, I'm willing to listen to what you know, and then I'll tell you if you're RIGHT or WRONG! What do YOU know about Watergate?
You're RIGHT!
Ahah! NOW I'm getting somewhere!

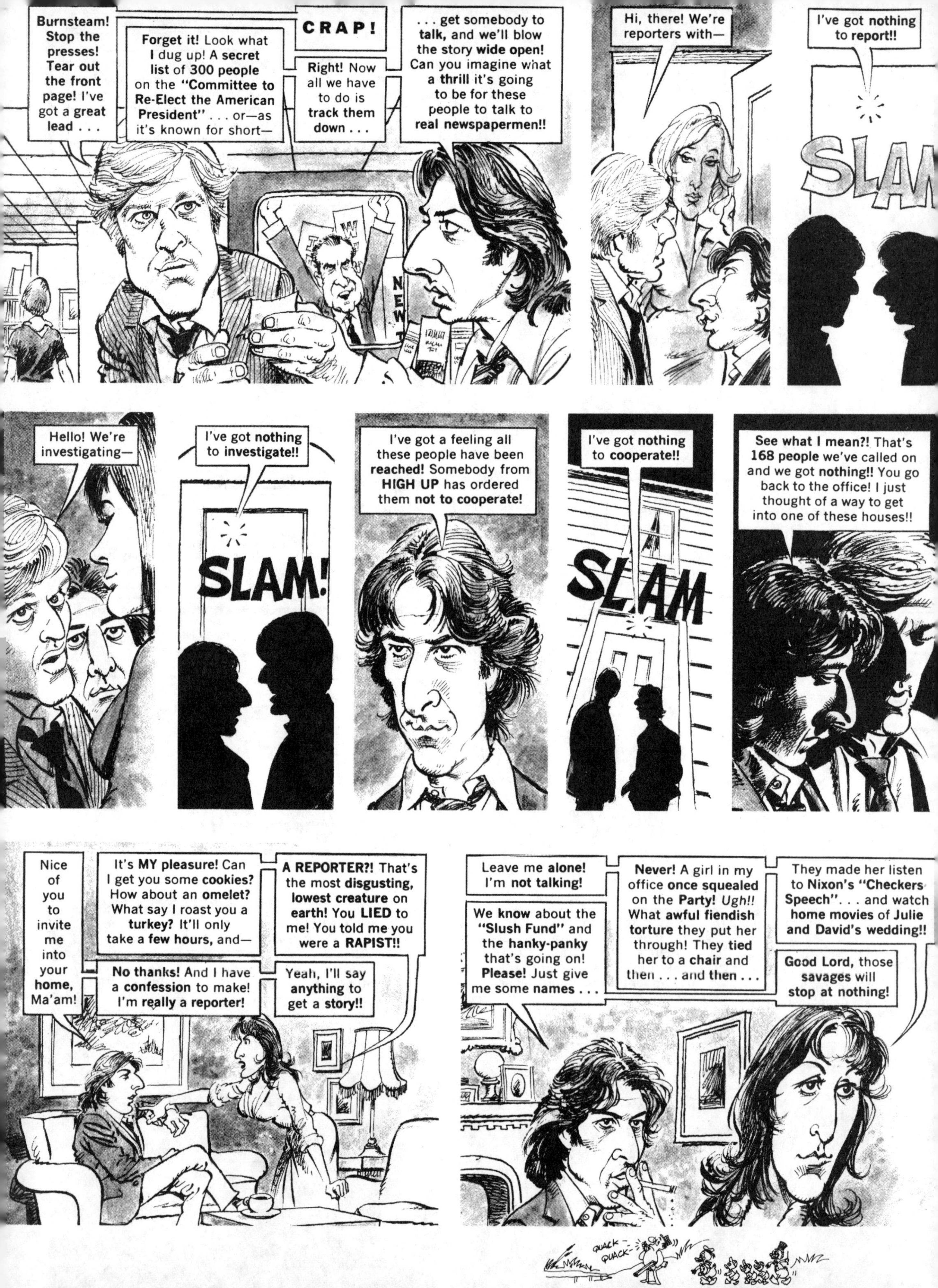

Burnsteam! Stop the presses! Tear out the front page! I've got a great lead . . .
Forget it! Look what I dug up! A secret list of 300 people on the "Committee to Re-Elect the American President" . . . or—as it's known for short—
CRAP!
Right! Now all we have to do is track them down . . .
. . . get somebody to talk, and we'll blow the story wide open! Can you imagine what a thrill it's going to be for these people to talk to real newspapermen!!
Hi, there! We're reporters with—
I've got nothing to report!!
SLAM
Hello! We're investigating—
I've got nothing to investigate!!
SLAM!
I've got a feeling all these people have been reached! Somebody from HIGH UP has ordered them not to cooperate!
I've got nothing to cooperate!!
SLAM
See what I mean?! That's 168 people we've called on and we got nothing!! You go back to the office! I just thought of a way to get into one of these houses!!
Nice of you to invite me into your home, Ma'am!
It's MY pleasure! Can I get you some cookies? How about an omelet? What say I roast you a turkey? It'll only take a few hours, and—
No thanks! And I have a confession to make! I'm really a reporter!
A REPORTER?! That's the most disgusting, lowest creature on earth! You LIED to me! You told me you were a RAPIST!!
Yeah, I'll say anything to get a story!!
Leave me alone! I'm not talking!
We know about the "Slush Fund" and the hanky-panky that's going on! Please! Just give me some names . . .
Never! A girl in my office once squealed on the Party! Ugh!! What awful fiendish torture they put her through! They tied her to a chair and then . . . and then . . .
They made her listen to Nixon's "Checkers Speech". . . and watch home movies of Julie and David's wedding!!
Good Lord, those savages will stop at nothing!
QUACK-QUACK

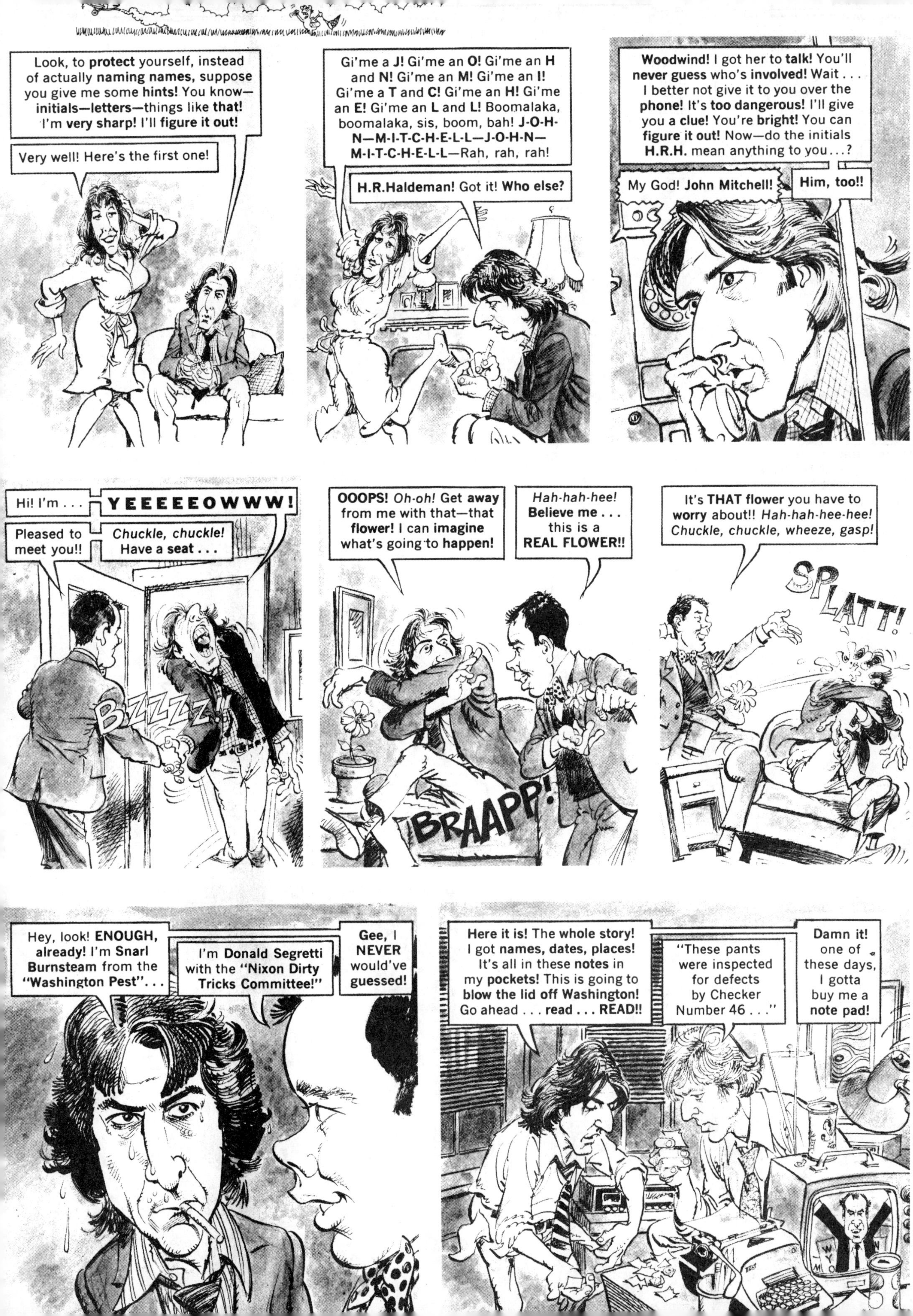

Look, to **protect** yourself, instead of actually **naming names,** suppose you give me some **hints!** You know—**initials—letters**—things like **that!** I'm **very sharp!** I'll **figure it out!**
Very well! Here's the first one!
Gi'me a **J!** Gi'me an **O!** Gi'me an **H** and **N!** Gi'me an **M!** Gi'me an **I!** Gi'me a **T** and **C!** Gi'me an **H!** Gi'me an **E!** Gi'me an **L** and **L!** Boomalaka, boomalaka, sis, boom, bah! **J-O-H-N—M-I-T-C-H-E-L-L—J-O-H-N—M-I-T-C-H-E-L-L**—Rah, rah, rah!
H.R.Haldeman! Got it! **Who else?**
Woodwind! I got her to **talk!** You'll **never guess** who's **involved!** Wait . . . I better not give it to you over the **phone!** It's **too dangerous!** I'll give you **a clue!** You're **bright!** You can **figure it out!** Now—do the initials **H.R.H.** mean anything to you . . .?
My God! **John Mitchell!**
Him, too!!
Hi! I'm . . .
YEEEEEOWWW!
Pleased to meet you!!
Chuckle, chuckle! Have a **seat . . .**
BZZZZZ!
OOOPS! *Oh-oh!* Get **away** from me with that—that **flower!** I can **imagine** what's going to **happen!**
Hah-hah-hee! **Believe me . . .** this is a **REAL FLOWER!!**
BRAAPP!
It's **THAT flower** you have to **worry** about!! *Hah-hah-hee-hee! Chuckle, chuckle, wheeze, gasp!*
SPLATT!
Hey, look! **ENOUGH,** already! I'm **Snarl Burnsteam** from the **"Washington Pest"** . . .
I'm **Donald Segretti** with the **"Nixon Dirty Tricks Committee!"**
Gee, I **NEVER** would've **guessed!**
Here it is! The whole story! I got **names, dates, places!** It's all in these **notes** in my **pockets!** This is going to **blow the lid off Washington!** Go ahead . . . **read . . . READ!!**
"These pants were inspected for defects by Checker Number 46 . . ."
Damn it! one of these days, I gotta buy me a **note pad!**

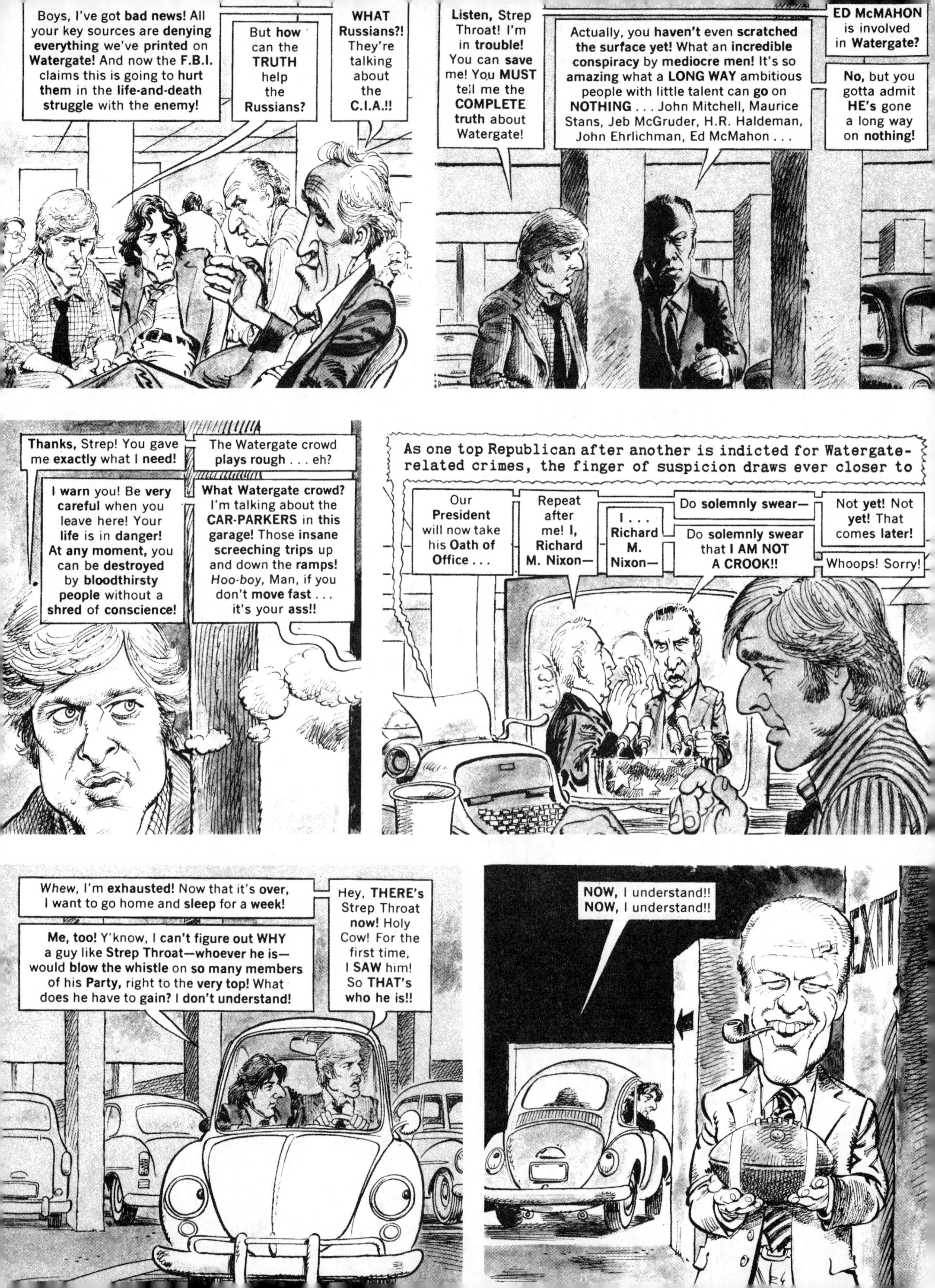
Boys, I've got bad news! All your key sources are denying everything we've printed on Watergate! And now the F.B.I. claims this is going to hurt them in the life-and-death struggle with the enemy!
But how can the TRUTH help the Russians?
WHAT Russians?! They're talking about the C.I.A.!!
Listen, Strep Throat! I'm in trouble! You can save me! You MUST tell me the COMPLETE truth about Watergate!
Actually, you haven't even scratched the surface yet! What an incredible conspiracy by mediocre men! It's so amazing what a LONG WAY ambitious people with little talent can go on NOTHING . . . John Mitchell, Maurice Stans, Jeb McGruder, H.R. Haldeman, John Ehrlichman, Ed McMahon . . .
ED McMAHON is involved in Watergate?
No, but you gotta admit HE's gone a long way on nothing!
Thanks, Strep! You gave me exactly what I need!
The Watergate crowd plays rough . . . eh?
I warn you! Be very careful when you leave here! Your life is in danger! At any moment, you can be destroyed by bloodthirsty people without a shred of conscience!
What Watergate crowd? I'm talking about the CAR-PARKERS in this garage! Those insane screeching trips up and down the ramps! Hoo-boy, Man, if you don't move fast . . . it's your ass!!
As one top Republican after another is indicted for Watergate-related crimes, the finger of suspicion draws ever closer to
Our President will now take his Oath of Office . . .
Repeat after me! I, Richard M. Nixon—
I . . . Richard M. Nixon—
Do solemnly swear—
Do solemnly swear that I AM NOT A CROOK!!
Not yet! Not yet! That comes later!
Whoops! Sorry!
Whew, I'm exhausted! Now that it's over, I want to go home and sleep for a week!
Me, too! Y'know, I can't figure out WHY a guy like Strep Throat—whoever he is—would blow the whistle on so many members of his Party, right to the very top! What does he have to gain? I don't understand!
Hey, THERE's Strep Throat now! Holy Cow! For the first time, I SAW him! So THAT's who he is!!
NOW, I understand!! NOW, I understand!!
EXIT

January 1977: A peanut farmer from Georgia, Jimmy Carter, is inaugurated as president after narrowly beating Gerald Ford in the November election. Ford, who had been appointed to the office by Richard Nixon before he stepped down, in turn becomes the first incumbent president to lose an election since Herbert Hoover in 1932. At the top of *Billboard*'s charts are "I Wish," by Stevie Wonder, "Car Wash," by Rose Royce, and "You Make Me Feel Like Dancing," by Leo Sayer. A new fad is sweeping the nation: the CB (citizens band) radio. The device was originally adopted by truckers, but now seemingly everyone is getting into the act, adopting strange-sounding monikers and uttering CB lingo like "ten-four, good buddy!" And continuing with tradition, the *MAD*-men stumble ever onward.

As feature films in the seventies raked in record numbers of box-office greenbacks, *MAD* responded by running more and more covers taking off on hit movies. The cover of issue #194 (October 1977) is an homage to Sylvester Stallone's blockbuster film *Rocky* (*MAD*'s parody of the film, "Rockhead," by writer Stan Hart and artist Mort Drucker, appears later in this section). George Lucas's *Star Wars*, by far the seventies box-office champ, gets the *MAD* treatment on the cover of issue #196 (January 1978). With the second Star Wars film nearly three years away, *MAD* invented their own *Star Wars* sequel on the cover and interior of issue #203 (December 1978): "The *MAD Star Wars* Musical."

Other big-box-office films parodied on *MAD*'s covers appearing in this section are *Close Encounters of the Third Kind* (#200, July 1978), *Saturday Night Fever* (#201, September 1978), *Grease* (#205, March 1979), and *Superman: The Movie* (#208, July 1979). These covers were done by Jack Rickard, who became *MAD*'s main cover artist when Norman Mingo began slowing down his output for the magazine. Mingo, who passed away on May 8, 1980, at the age of eighty-four, had been associated with the publication on and off (but mostly on) since 1956. Because of his highly regarded work for *MAD*, Norman Mingo had become enough of a pop cultural hero to rate a long obituary (with photo) in the July 10, 1980, issue of *Rolling Stone* magazine. His last *MAD* cover, which appears in this section, is found on issue #211 (December 1979).

Movies weren't the only focus of *MAD*'s covers at the time; TV series were skewered as well. Appearing here are *MAD* "nods" to *Welcome Back, Kotter* (#189,

March 1977) and *Charlie's Angels* (#193, September 1977), both rendered by Jack Rickard. Also seeded among the movie- and TV-related covers were both topical and more gag-oriented ones.

Issue #198's cover (April 1978) refers to the mandatory adoption of the "universal price code" (UPC) at the beginning of 1978. All magazines published in the United States were required from this point onward (whether they liked it or not) to have the UPC symbol on the front cover, which could then be read by an infrared scanner at the checkout counter. Characteristically, *MAD* made the symbol the butt of a joke on virtually every cover from then on.

President Jimmy Carter made the cover of issue #197 (March 1978), looking a lot like an older (but not wiser) Alfred E. Neuman. Another dubious salute to Carter, "He's sure heavy, Voters . . . he's m' brother!" (#209, September 1979), refers to the president's embarrassment over his redneck brother Billy's antics, which included public drunkenness and vulgarity, all of which were dutifully reported upon in the media.

The King of Rock 'n' Roll, Elvis Presley, died at his Graceland estate on August 16, 1977, and immediately became more marketable than ever, a fact addressed by Al Jaffee in the first "Fold-In" in this section. Jaffee's second "Fold-In" appearing here is, given the state of the world today, remarkably prophetic.

The one and only time the "What—Me Worry?" kid got worried appears here in the *MAD* mini-poster "Yes . . . me worry!," a comment on the March 28, 1979, accident at the Three Mile Island nuclear power plant, which caused a partial meltdown of its core (#210, October 1979). Officials at the time, of course, maintained that not much radiation was released outside the plant, but "not much" was too much even for Alfred E. Neuman, and for a lot of the general population as well.

"Welcome Back, Klodder" sends up the Gabe Kaplan TV vehicle *Welcome Back, Kotter*, which ran on ABC from 1975 to 1979. The series was created by Kaplan and was based upon his real-life experiences as a Brooklyn high school student. The show made a star of John Travolta ("Vinnie Barbarino"), who graduated into making such feature films as *Carrie* and *Saturday Night Fever* even as he was appearing on the series. As for Kaplan, he counted as one of his major influences the legendary comedian Groucho Marx, and after *Kotter* he even appeared for a time as Groucho in a one-man show of his own devising.

Polish jokes were all the rage for a while in the seventies, perhaps because of Archie Bunker's relentless carping about his "meathead" Polish son-in-law on *All in the Family*. "American Jokes They're Telling in Poland," written by Frank Jacobs and illustrated by Paul Coker, Jr., is an ingenious turn of the tables. Other Jacobs-written articles in this section include "When You're Poor . . . and . . . When You're Rich" (illustrated by Jack Davis), and "The White House Follies of 1977" (illustrated by Mort Drucker), a "musical" examination of the Carter administration.

Charlie's Angels was yet another hit TV series from bazillionaire producer Aaron Spelling. Starring Kate Jackson, Farrah Fawcett, and Jaclyn Smith as young, sexy police academy graduates working as detectives, the show made an overnight sensation of one of its three Angels, Farrah Fawcett. Farrah's appeal to women was based largely upon her long, flowing blond locks, which became a widely imitated hairstyle. Her appeal to men was based largely upon a swimsuit poster that was an enticing showcase of her curvaceous anatomy. Not surprisingly, millions of the posters were sold. *MAD*'s take on the show, "Churlie's Angles" (#193, September 1977), gives voice to what most of us knew but didn't want to admit: the only reason anyone watched the series was to see the three beautiful young women in various revealing outfits, a fact the show's producers counted on and played to the hilt.

For many people, the world changed forever after the May 25, 1977, opening of the George Lucas film *Star Wars*. Only the third feature film to be directed by Lucas, the movie grossed $193,500,000 at the box office and had a *Star Wars*–crazy public queuing up at theaters, seemingly in competition to see how many times they could attend repeat performances of the film while it was still in its original theatrical release. Science fiction and fantasy, which had traditionally been the province of low-budget B movies, were suddenly big business, with studios falling over themselves to option suitable SF and fantasy-oriented scripts. *MAD*'s version, "Star Roars" (#196, January 1978, but actually on the newsstands several months before), was written by Larry Siegel and Dick DeBartolo and illustrated by Harry North. Englishman North was recruited from the pages of the British edition of *MAD*; *MAD*'s American editors noticed him there and were impressed enough to hire him to work on the U.S. edition.

The success of *Star Wars* paved the way for another film that would prove to be a hit at the box office, 1978's *Superman: The Movie*. Hiring a then-unknown Christopher Reeve for the leading role, the producers hedged their bets by securing legendary actor Marlon Brando to play Superman's father, Jor-El. *MAD*'s spoof, by Drucker and Siegel, was entitled "Superduperman" (#208, July 1979). This was not the first time the title was used, however; *MAD* first parodied the Superman comic book in a feature also called "Superduperman" (#4, April–May 1953). That early lampoon was an immediate hit and is widely credited with helping to push the fledgling publication toward profitability. ("Superduperman" and other comic-book parodies will appear in *MAD About the Fifties*, coming next year to a bookstore near you.)

Saturday Night Fever is the 1977 film that vaulted John Travolta into superstar status while at the same time fanning disco music's flame to red hot. The soundtrack album, which contained songs written for the film by the Bee Gees and other artists, sold a whopping 11 million copies in the U.S. alone. Considering the career Travolta had in the several years following, the ending of *MAD*'s parody of the movie, "Saturday Night Feeble" (by Mort Drucker and Arnie Kogen), proved to be remarkably clairvoyant. A related piece, "A *MAD* Look at Discos" (#201, September 1978), was illustrated by Harry North and written by Dick DeBartolo, who was more than familiar with the subject.

John Ficarra, who began freelance writing for *MAD* in the late seventies, joined the magazine's staff as an associate editor in the fall of 1980. In 1985, after the retirement of longtime *MAD* editor Al Feldstein, Ficarra assumed the role of coeditor (with Nick Meglin). Appearing in this section is John's very first *MAD* sale, "*MAD*'s Table of Little-Known and Very Useless Weights, Measures & Distances," from *MAD* #210 (October 1979, illustrated by Bob Clarke).

Ending this section is *MAD*'s spoof of the TV show that made comedian Robin Williams a household name, *Mork and Mindy*. *MAD*'s version, entitled "Shmork & Windy," appeared in *MAD* #209, September 1979. The series was spun off from an episode of *Happy Days* that featured Williams as an alien from the planet Ork who attempts to kidnap Richie (Ron Howard). The spinoff was an instant hit and ran from fall 1978 to summer 1982.

As we conclude our guided tour of the "Me Decade," a thought strikes: with all of the insanity in the world, it is strangely comforting to know that there is a magazine whose only agenda is to skewer pretension, illuminate hypocrisy, remind us not to believe everything we see or read, and to make us laugh in the process. Unfortunately, the name of the magazine I'm referring to escapes me for the moment, but you probably know the one I mean. In the meanwhile, may the farce be with you!

— Grant Geissman

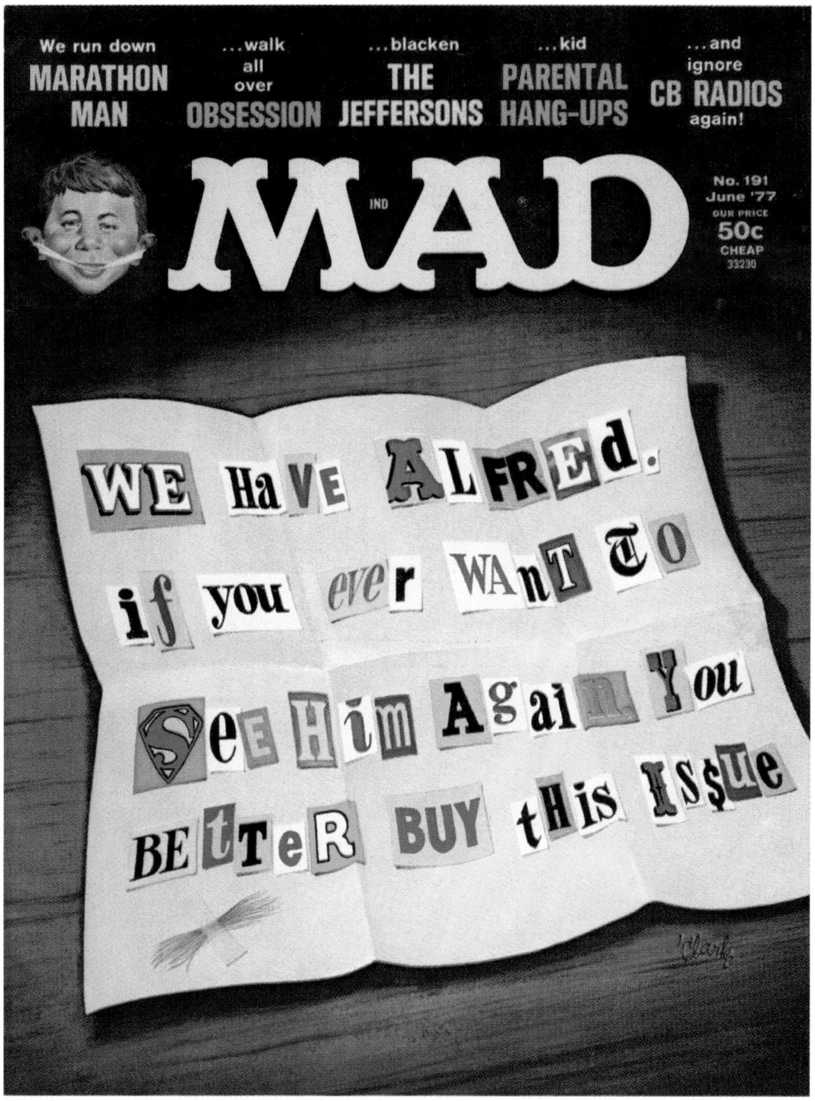
We run down MARATHON MAN
...walk all over OBSESSION
...blacken THE JEFFERSONS
...kid PARENTAL HANG-UPS
...and ignore CB RADIOS again!
MAD
No. 191
June '77
OUR PRICE
50c
CHEAP
33230
WE HaVE ALFREd.
if you ever WAnT To
SeE Him Again You
BETTeR BUY tHis I$$ue
Clark

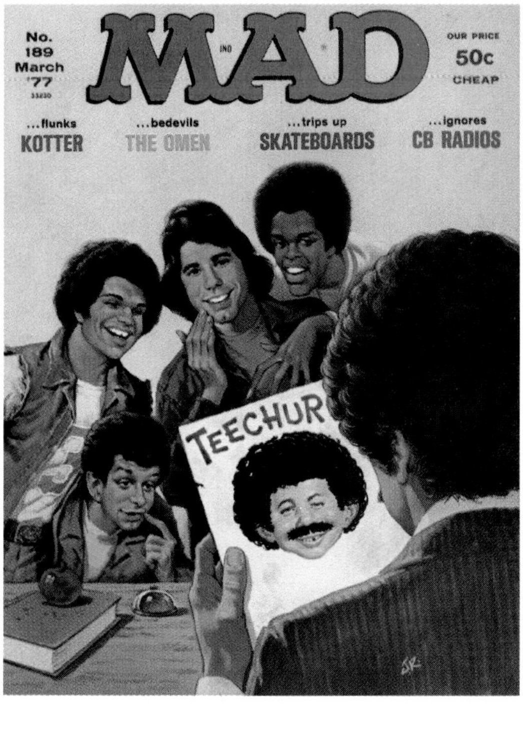
No. 189
March '77
MAD
OUR PRICE
50c
CHEAP
...flunks KOTTER
...bedevils THE OMEN
...trips up SKATEBOARDS
...ignores CB RADIOS
TEECHUR

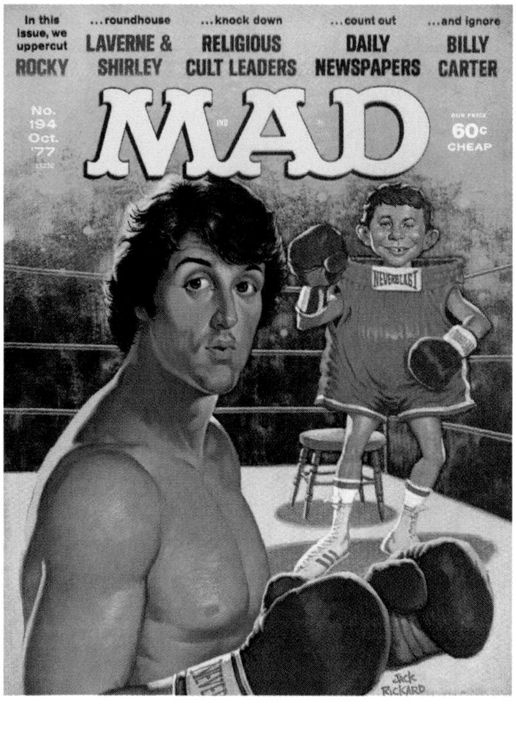
In this issue, we uppercut ROCKY
...roundhouse LAVERNE & SHIRLEY
...knock down RELIGIOUS CULT LEADERS
...count out DAILY NEWSPAPERS
...and ignore BILLY CARTER
No. 194
Oct. '77
MAD
OUR PRICE
60c
CHEAP
NEVERBLAST
JACK RICKARD

We zap... STAR WARS
...slap THREE'S COMPANY
...scrap PUBLIC SERVICES
...flap MODERN HIGH SCHOOLS
...and rap RECENT BEST-SELLERS
No. 196 Jan. '78
MAD
OUR PRICE 60¢ CHEAP
JACK RICKARD

SPECIAL IN THIS ISSUE
THE MAD" STAR WARS" MUSICAL
No. 203 Dec. '78
MAD
OUR PRICE 60¢ CHEAP
JACK RICKARD
EXCLUSIVE: SCIENTISTS RELEASE FIRST COMPUTER-WRITTEN JOKE

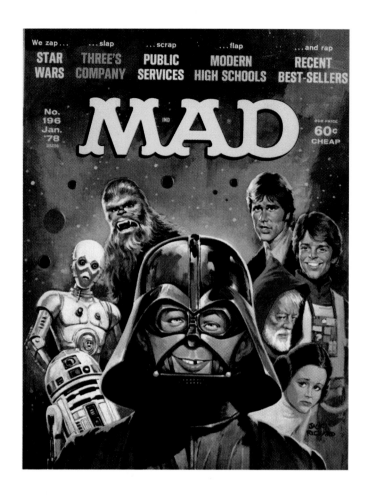

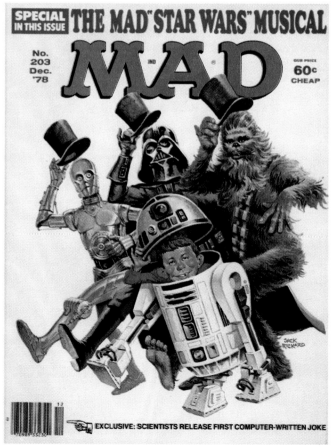

We burn up... "SATURDAY NIGHT FEVER"

...scorch TEENAGE TACTICS

...broil BUFFET SUPPERS

...roast DISCO JOINTS

...and incinerate "EIGHT IS ENOUGH"

No. 201 Sept. '78

MAD

IND ®

OUR PRICE 60¢ CHEAP

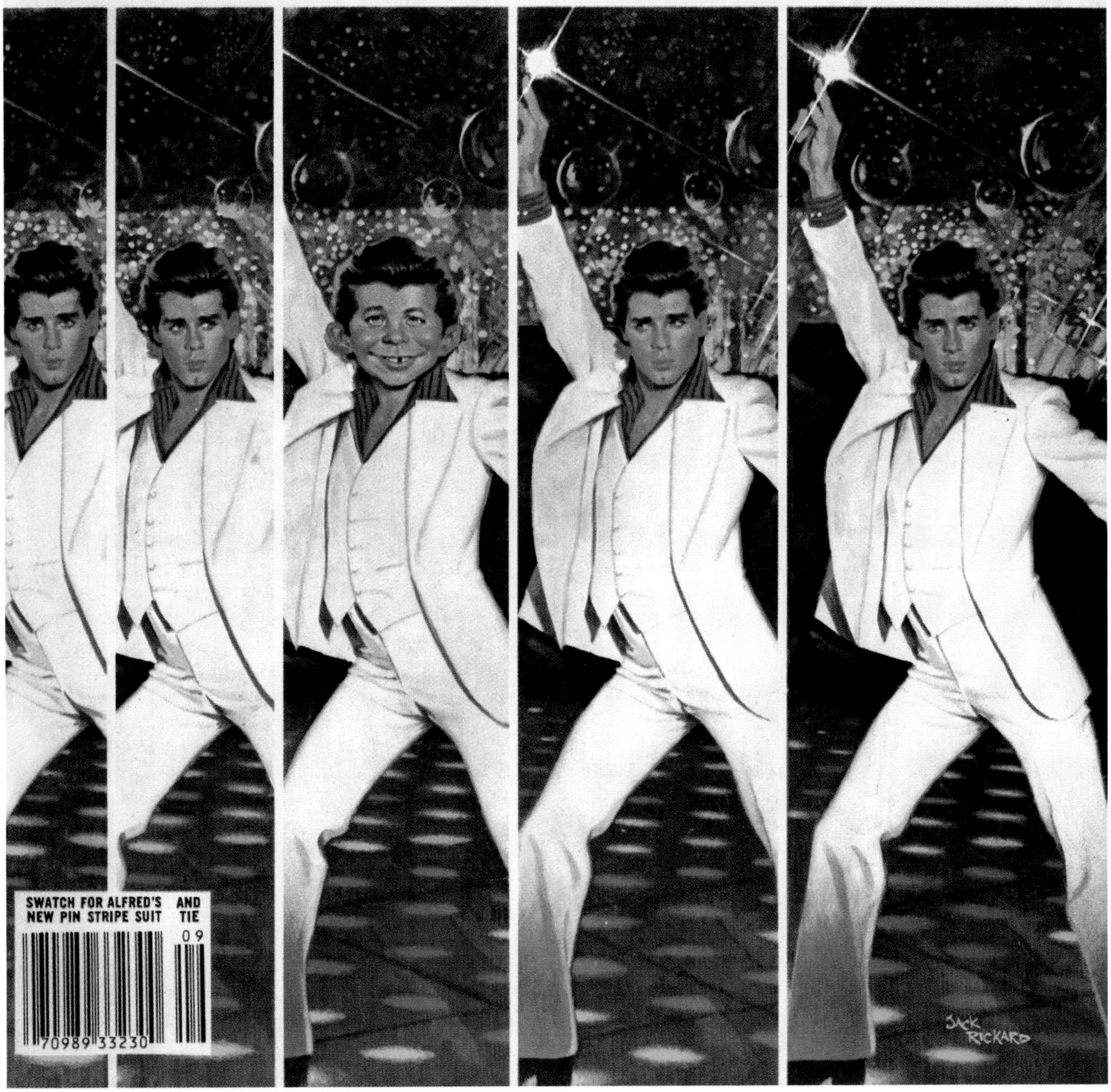

SWATCH FOR ALFRED'S NEW PIN STRIPE SUIT
AND TIE
09
70989 33230
JACK RICKARD

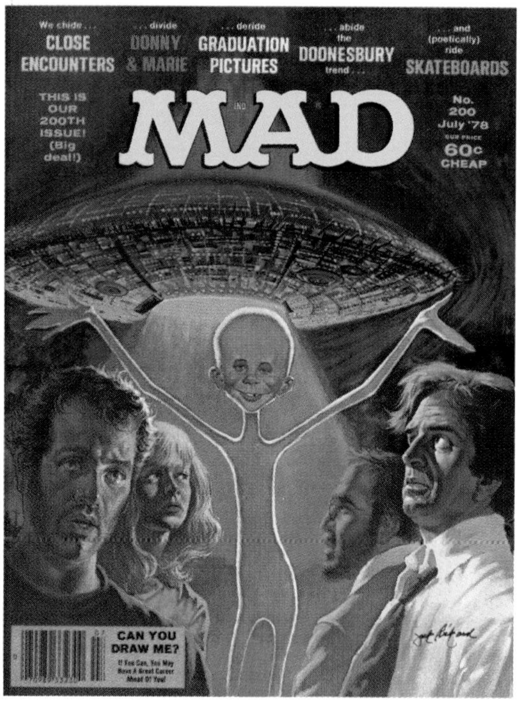
We chide . . . CLOSE ENCOUNTERS
. . . divide DONNY & MARIE
. . . deride GRADUATION PICTURES
. . . abide the DOONESBURY trend . . .
. . . and (poetically) ride SKATEBOARDS
THIS IS OUR 200TH ISSUE! (Big deal!)
MAD
No. 200 July '78
OUR PRICE 60¢ CHEAP
CAN YOU DRAW ME?
If You Can, You May Have A Great Career Ahead Of You!

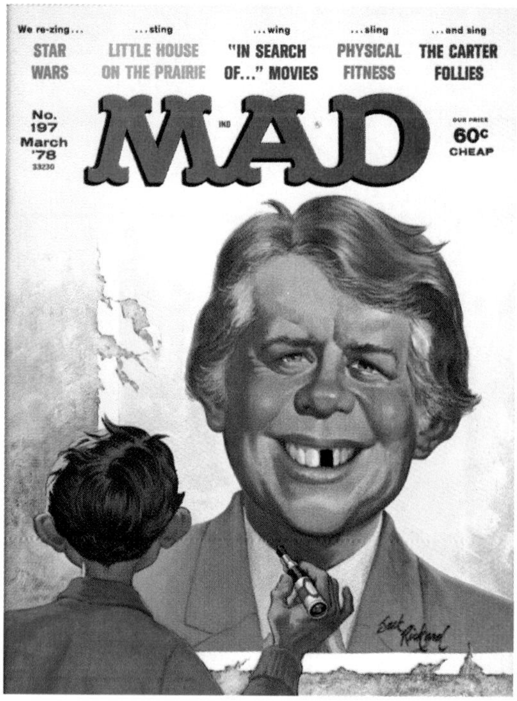
We re-zing . . . STAR WARS
. . . sting LITTLE HOUSE ON THE PRAIRIE
. . . wing "IN SEARCH OF…" MOVIES
. . . sling PHYSICAL FITNESS
. . . and sing THE CARTER FOLLIES
No. 197 March '78
33230
MAD
OUR PRICE 60¢ CHEAP

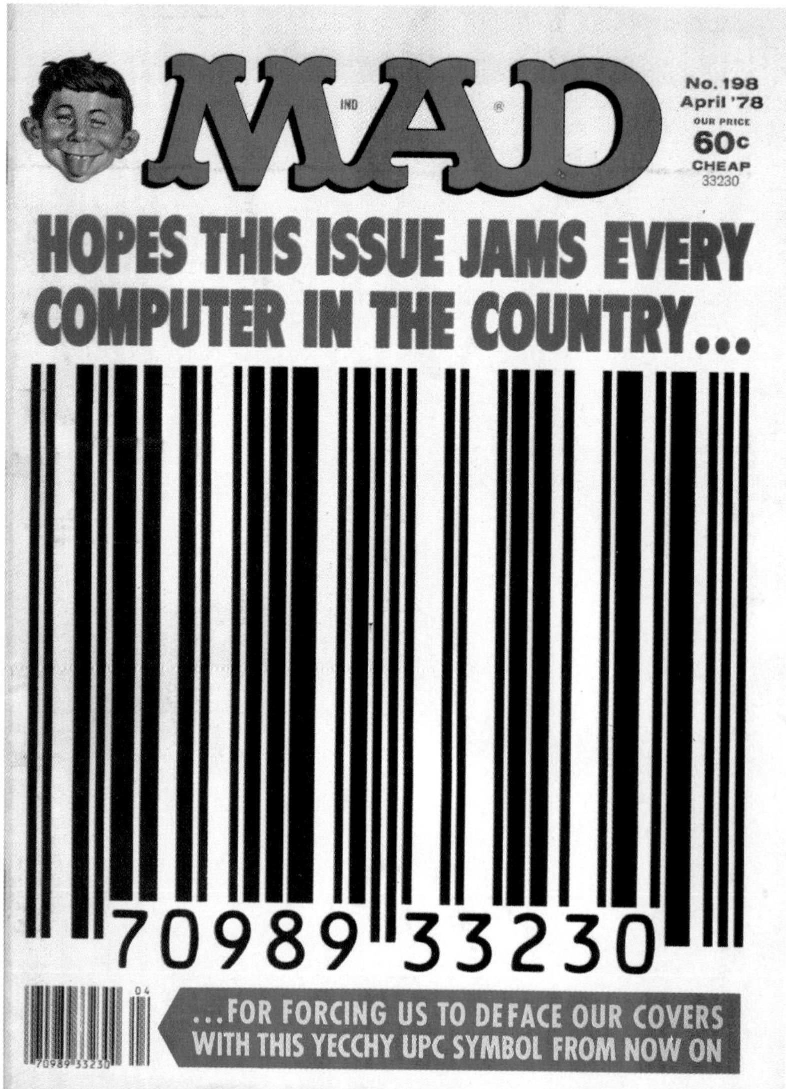
MAD
No. 198 April '78
OUR PRICE 60¢ CHEAP
33230
HOPES THIS ISSUE JAMS EVERY COMPUTER IN THE COUNTRY...
70989 33230
...FOR FORCING US TO DEFACE OUR COVERS WITH THIS YECCHY UPC SYMBOL FROM NOW ON

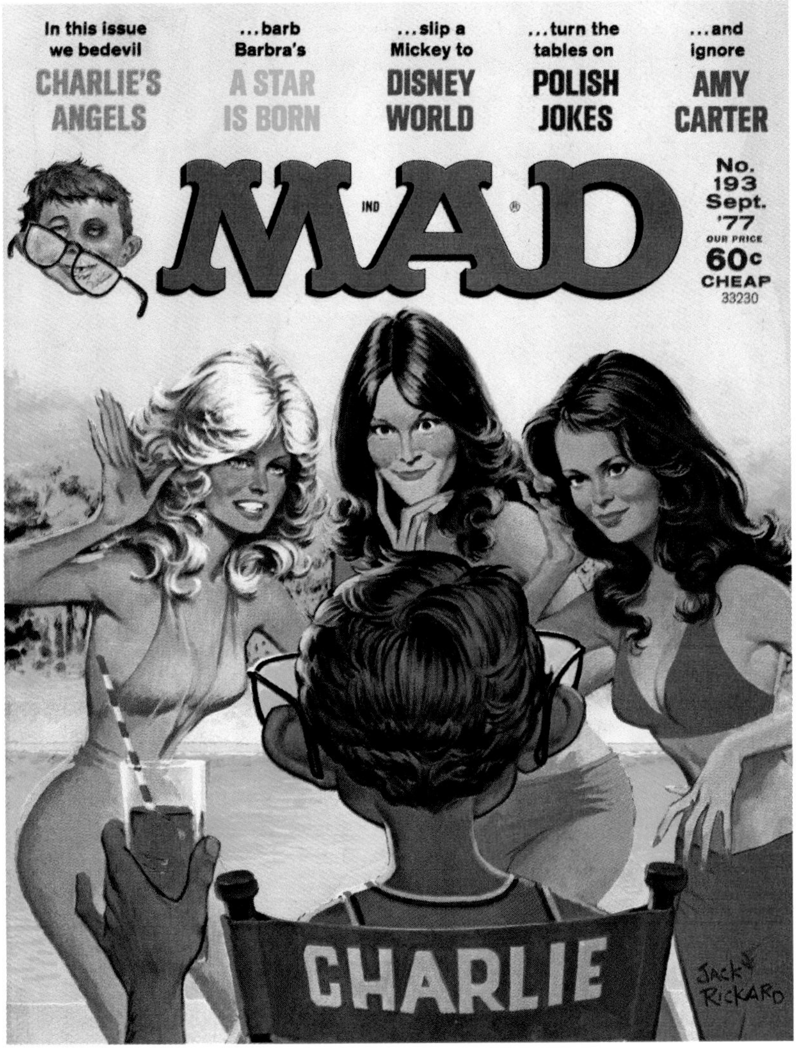
In this issue we bedevil CHARLIE'S ANGELS
...barb Barbra's A STAR IS BORN
...slip a Mickey to DISNEY WORLD
...turn the tables on POLISH JOKES
...and ignore AMY CARTER
MAD
No. 193 Sept. '77
OUR PRICE 60¢ CHEAP
33230
CHARLIE
JACK RICKARD

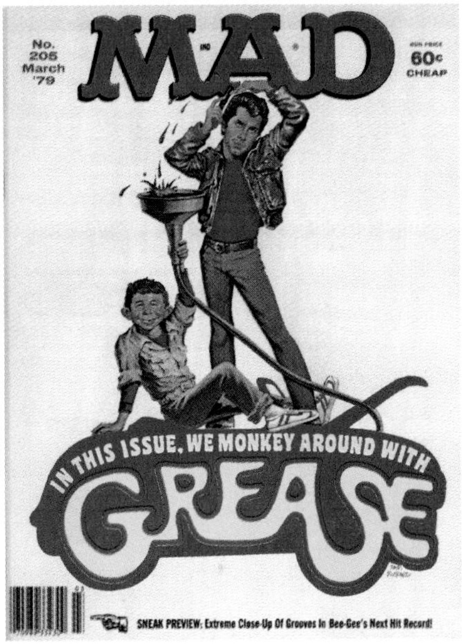
No. 205 March '79
MAD
60¢ CHEAP
IN THIS ISSUE, WE MONKEY AROUND WITH
GREASE
SNEAK PREVIEW: Extreme Close-Up Of Grooves In Bee-Gee's Next Hit Record!

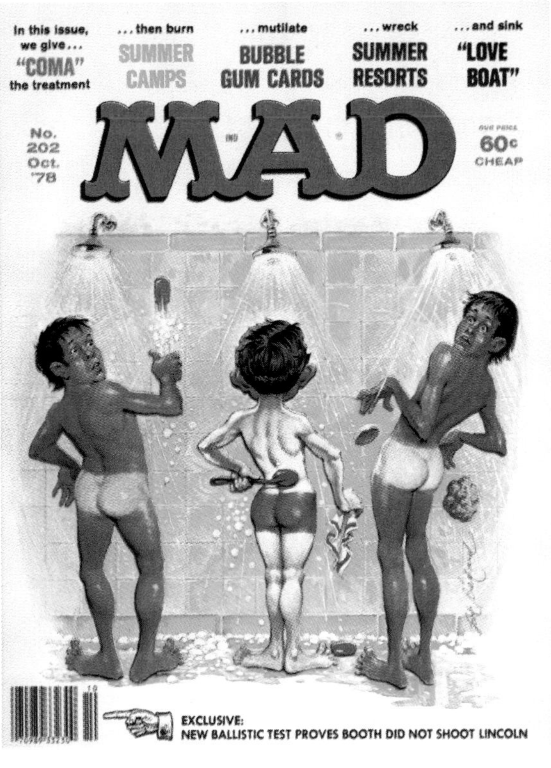
In this issue, we give... "COMA" the treatment
...then burn SUMMER CAMPS
...mutilate BUBBLE GUM CARDS
...wreck SUMMER RESORTS
...and sink "LOVE BOAT"
No. 202 Oct. '78
MAD
OUR PRICE 60¢ CHEAP
EXCLUSIVE:
NEW BALLISTIC TEST PROVES BOOTH DID NOT SHOOT LINCOLN

Look! In this issue! It's a bird! It's a bomb! It's... "SUPERMAN"
It's a waste of space! It's... "BATTLESTAR GALACTICA"
It's a bunch of crooks! It's... LAWYERS & REPAIRMEN
It's a slice of life! It's... THE MEN'S RAZOR RACE
And it's a pack of lies! It's... TV RATING SYSTEMS
No. 208 July '79
MAD
IND
OUR PRICE 60¢ CHEAP
SUPER BARF BAG
NEW POSTAGE STAMP COMMEMORATING 50 YEARS OF POLLUTED WATERFALLS
RICKARD

No. 211 Dec. '79
MAD
IND
OUR PRICE 75¢ CHEAP
K
EXCLUSIVE: SPECTROGRAM REVEALS NO GASOLINE ON MARS, EITHER!

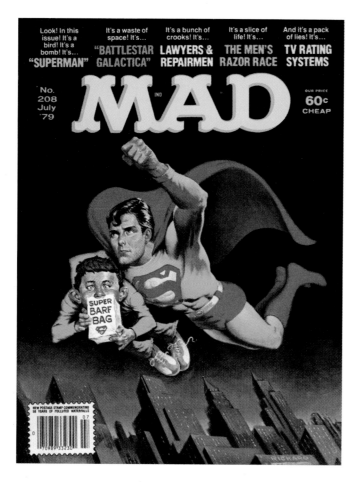

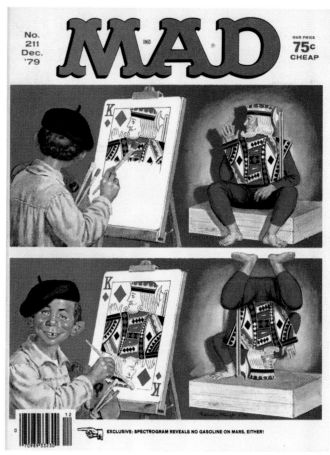

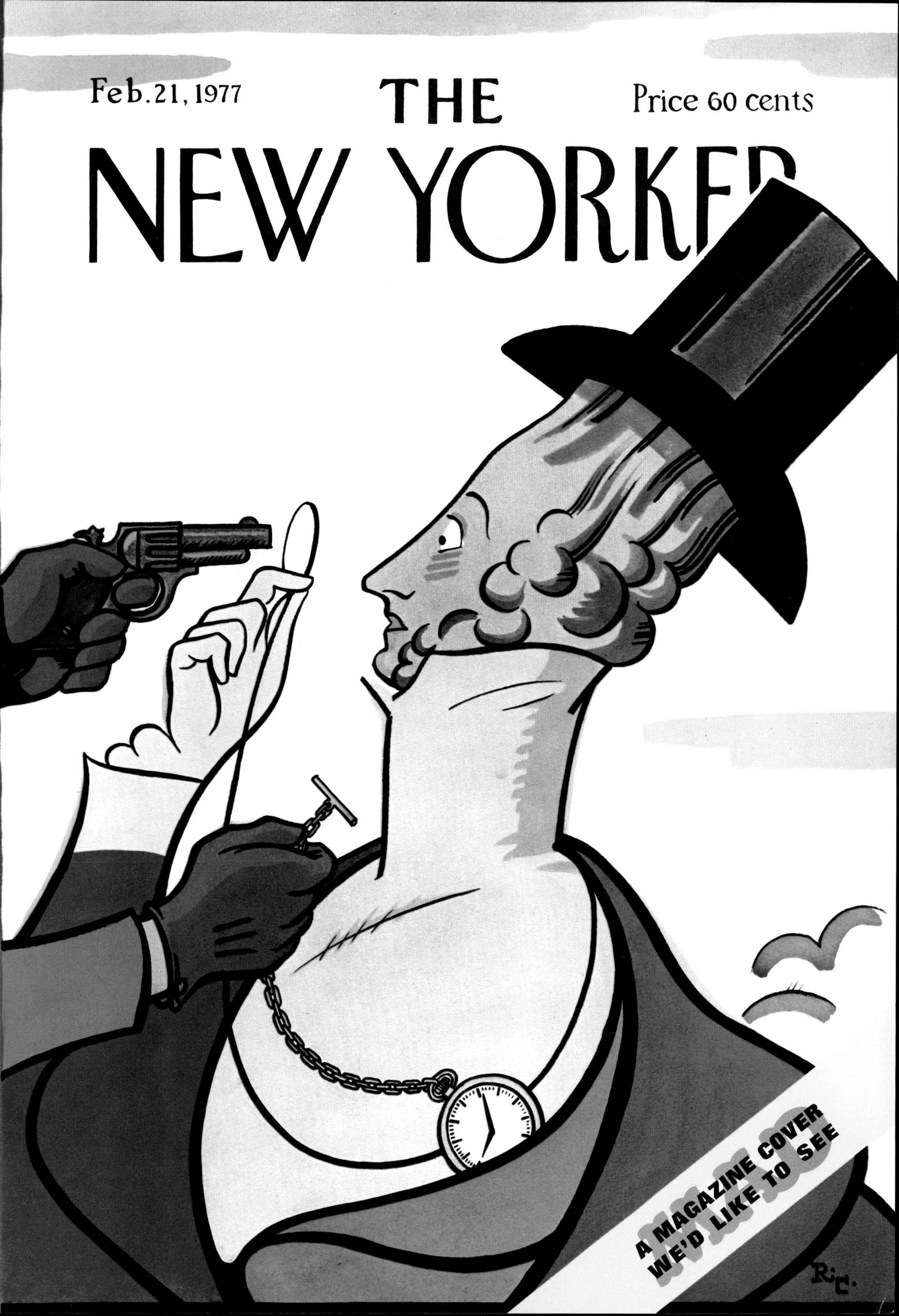
Feb. 21, 1977
THE
NEW YORKE
Price 60 cents
A MAGAZINE COVER WE'D LIKE TO SEE
MAD
Ric.

MAD SALUTES THE AUTOMOBILE INDUSTRY

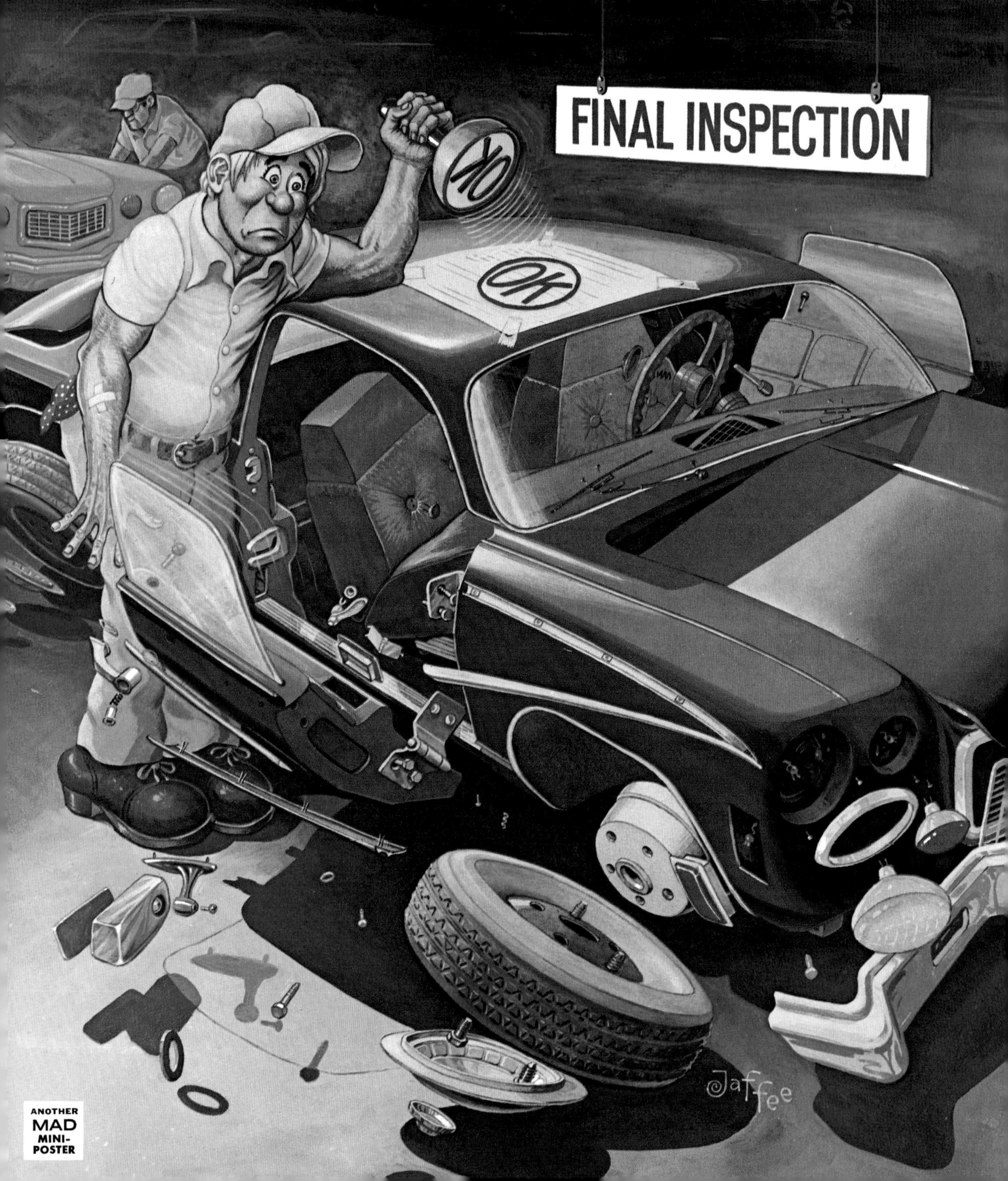
FINAL INSPECTION
OK
OK
Jaffee
ANOTHER MAD MINI-POSTER

ONE NIGHT IN THE CITY

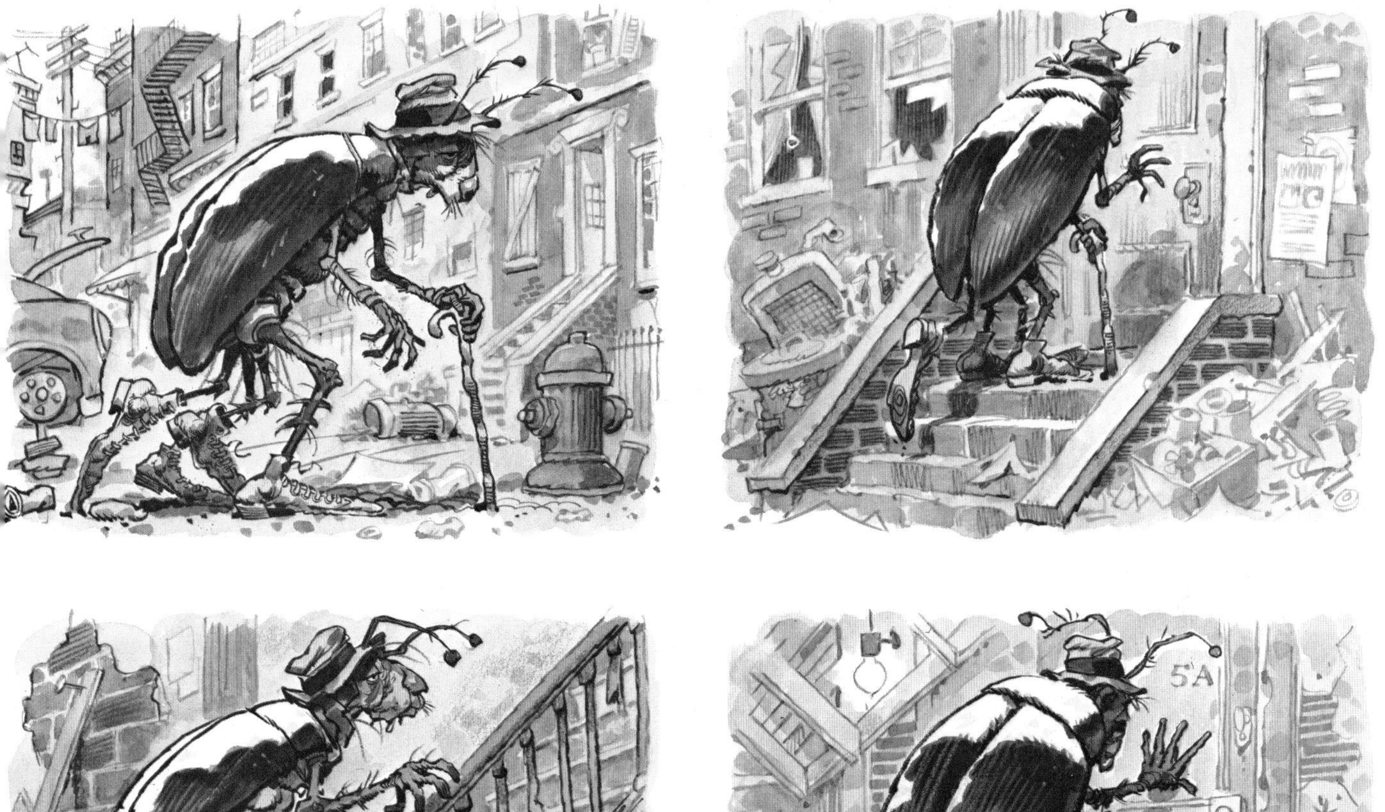
5'A

ARTIST: JACK DAVIS WRITER: AL JAFFEE

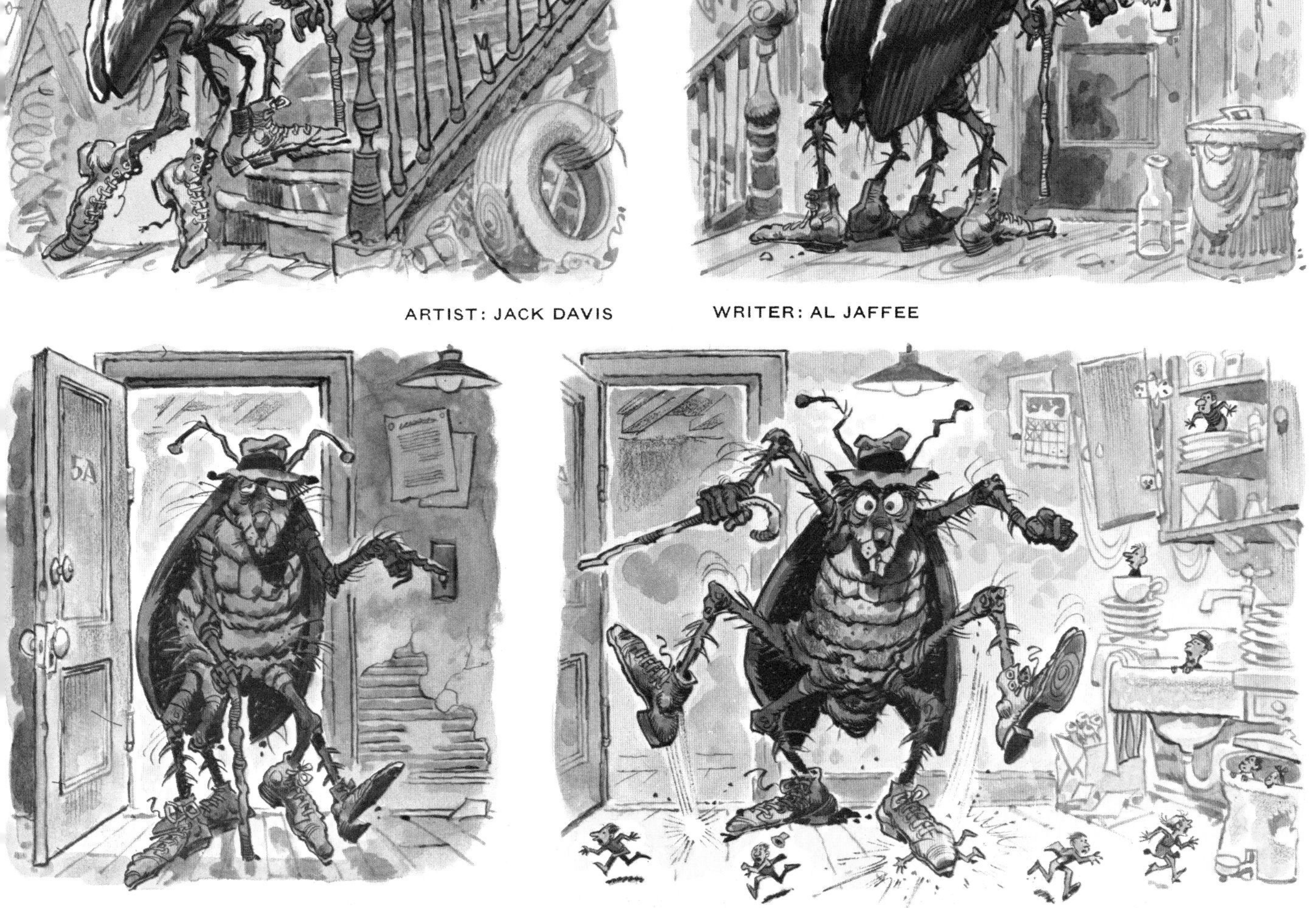
5A

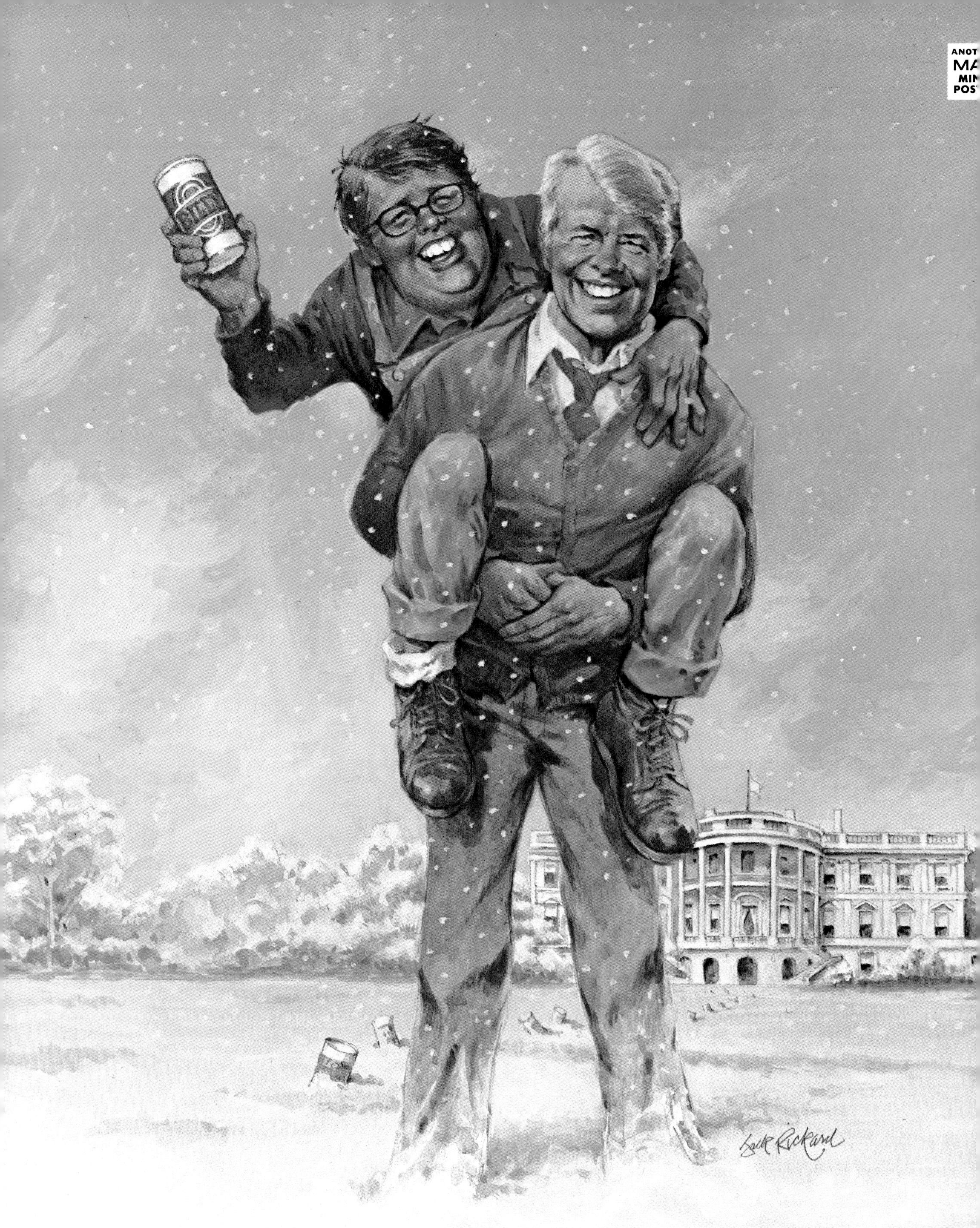
Jack Rickard

"He's sure heavy, Voters...he's m' brother!"

VHAT COLORFUL SPECTACULAR CREATURE IS STILL BEING EXPLOITED . . . EVEN AFTER IT HAS WIGGLED AND DIED?

HERE WE GO WITH ANOTHER RIDICULOUS

MAD FOLD-IN

Fabulously attractive creatures quickly become over-exploited commercially. Leopards, cheetahs, peacocks, parrots, tropical fish and butterflies are good examples. But recently, a new and very special specimen has fallen into this category. To identify this creature, fold in page as shown.

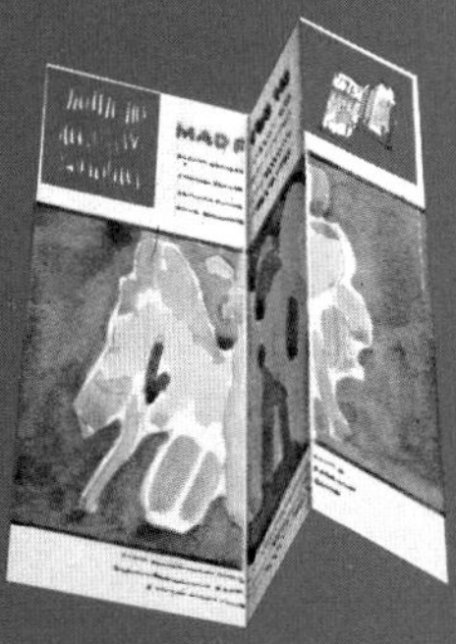

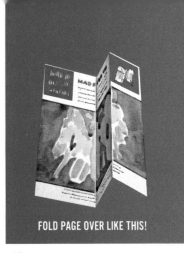

FOLD PAGE OVER LIKE THIS!

A▸ FOLD THIS SECTION OVER LEFT ◂B FOLD BACK SO "A" MEETS "B"

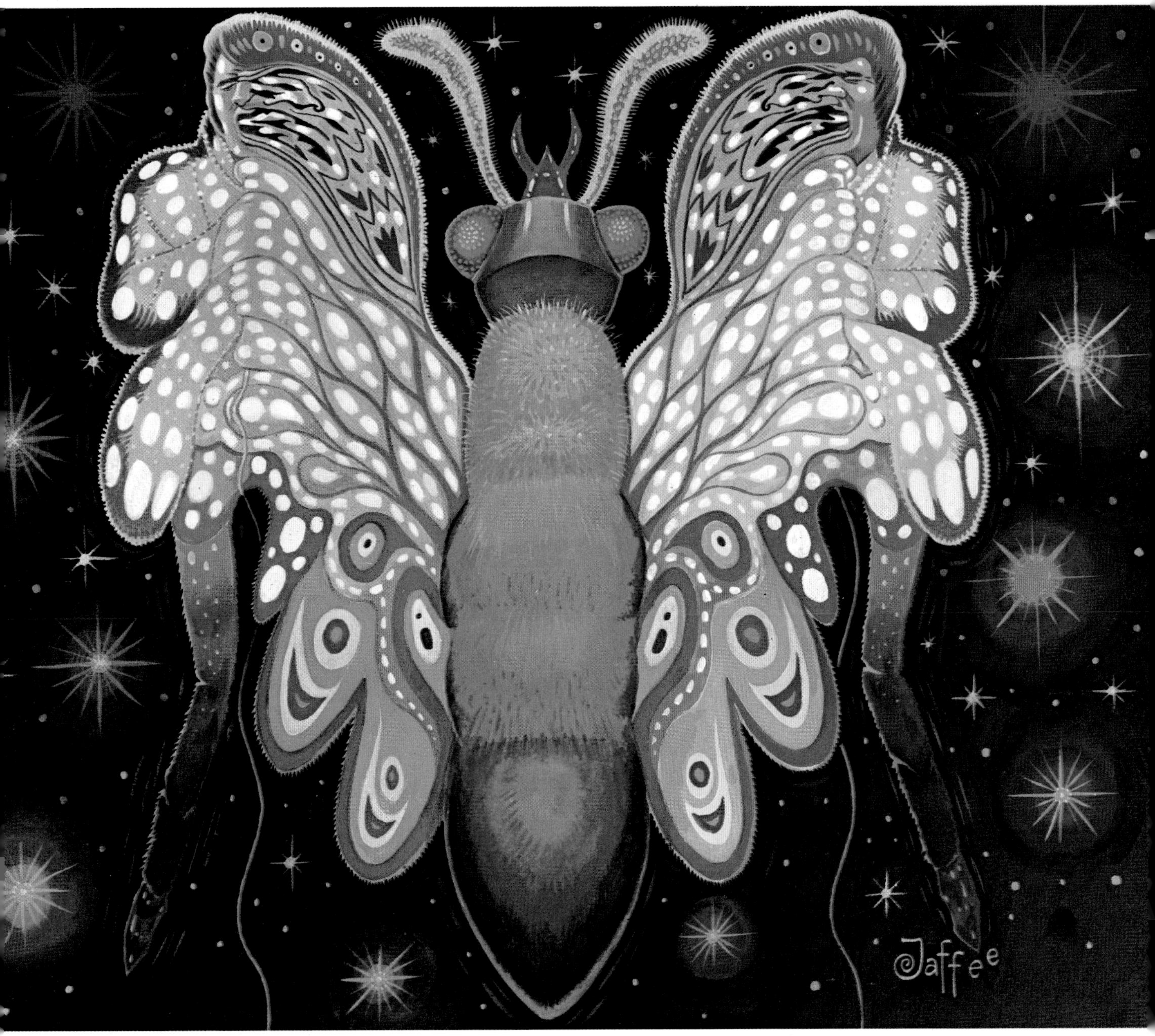
©Jaffee

FABULOUS CREATURES ARE EXPLOITED WHEN ELEMENTS IN OUR SOCIETY, FROM KIDS IN LEVIS TO MATRONS IN MINK, CREATE THE DEMAND

TIST & WRITER:
AL JAFFEE

A▸ ◂B

ONE RAINY AFTERNOON IN THE BLACK FOREST

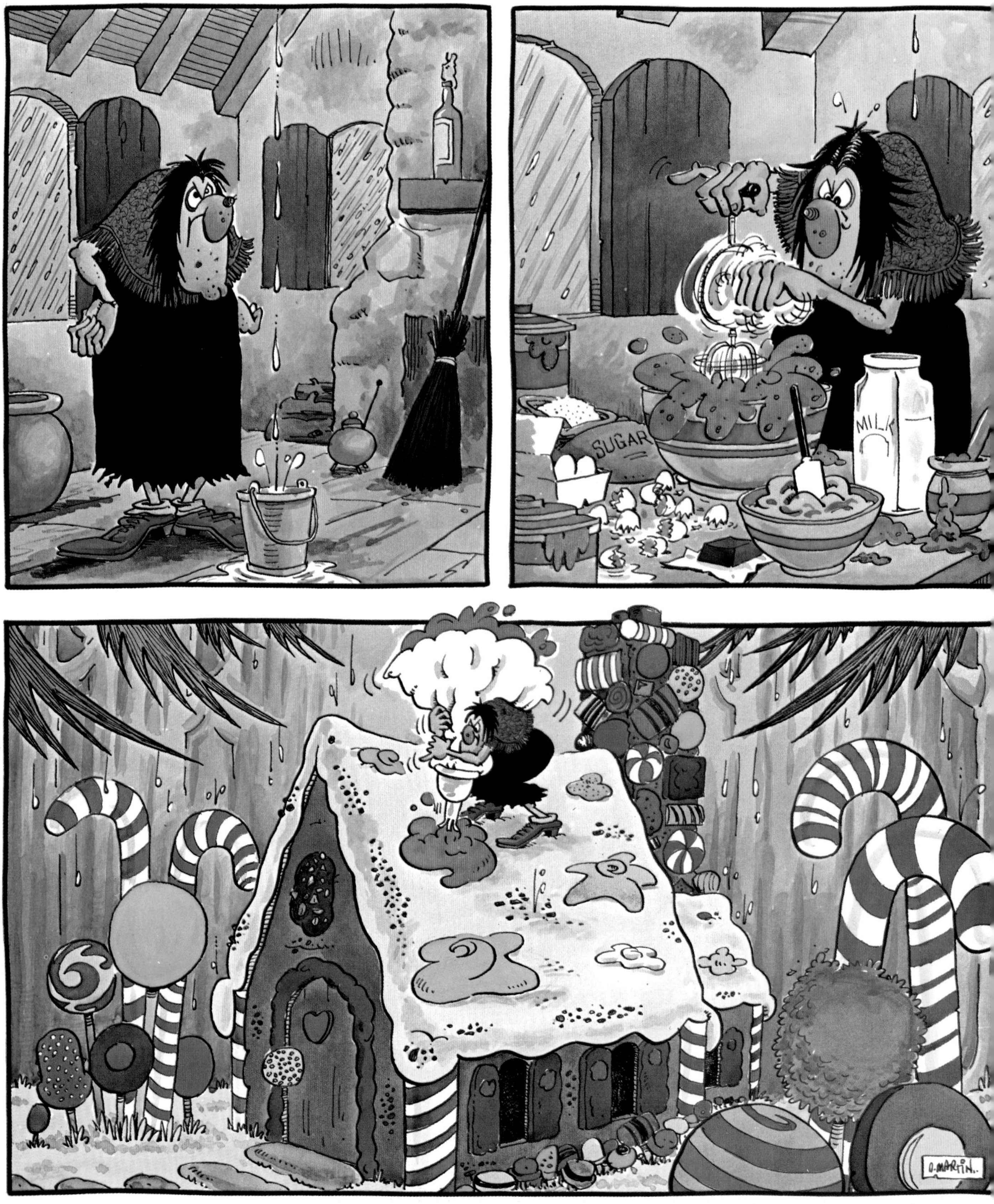
SUGAR
MILK
D. MARTIN

ARTIST: DON MARTIN WRITER: SERGIO ARAGONES

WHAT VOLATILE INGREDIENTS— NOW BEING FORMULATED— ARE SURE TO CAUSE FUTURE CATASTROPHES?

HERE WE GO WITH ANOTHER RIDICULOUS

MAD FOLD-IN

It's always a mystery why human beings are constantly developing new formulas guaranteed to cause future disasters. To find out what one such formula is, fold in the page as shown at the right.

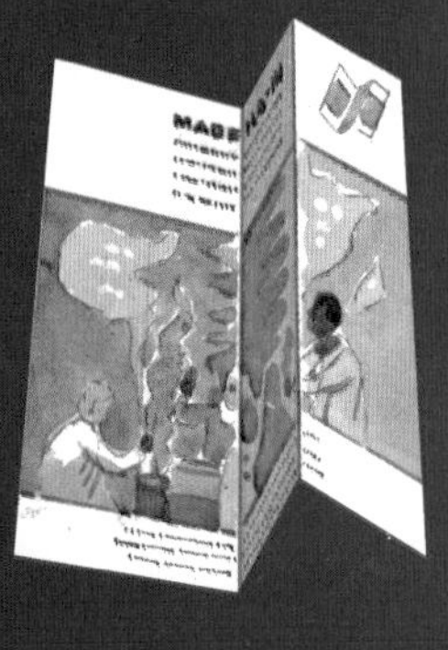

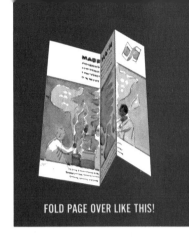

FOLD PAGE OVER LIKE THIS!

A▸ FOLD THIS SECTION OVER LEFT ◂B FOLD BACK SO "A" MEETS "B"

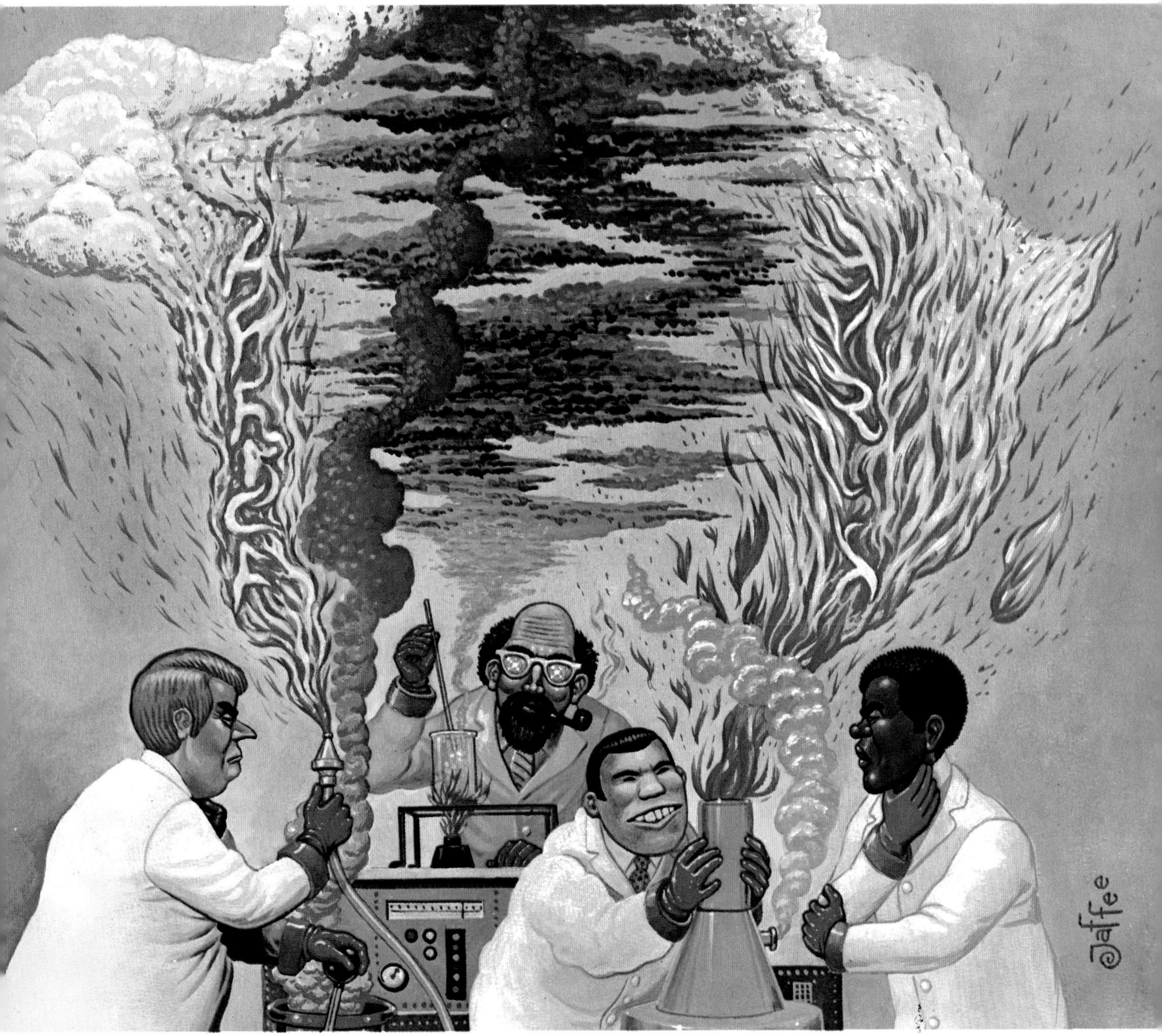
Jaffee

ARTIST & WRITER:
AL JAFFEE

RESPONSIBLE SCIENTISTS EVERYWHERE ARE AFRAID THAT CHINESE, RUSSIAN, ARAB, OR AMERICAN RADICALS WILL ACQUIRE DEADLY WEAPONS. A SPECIAL POLICE FORCE IS NEEDED TO CONTROL THESE ENEMIES

A▸ ◂B

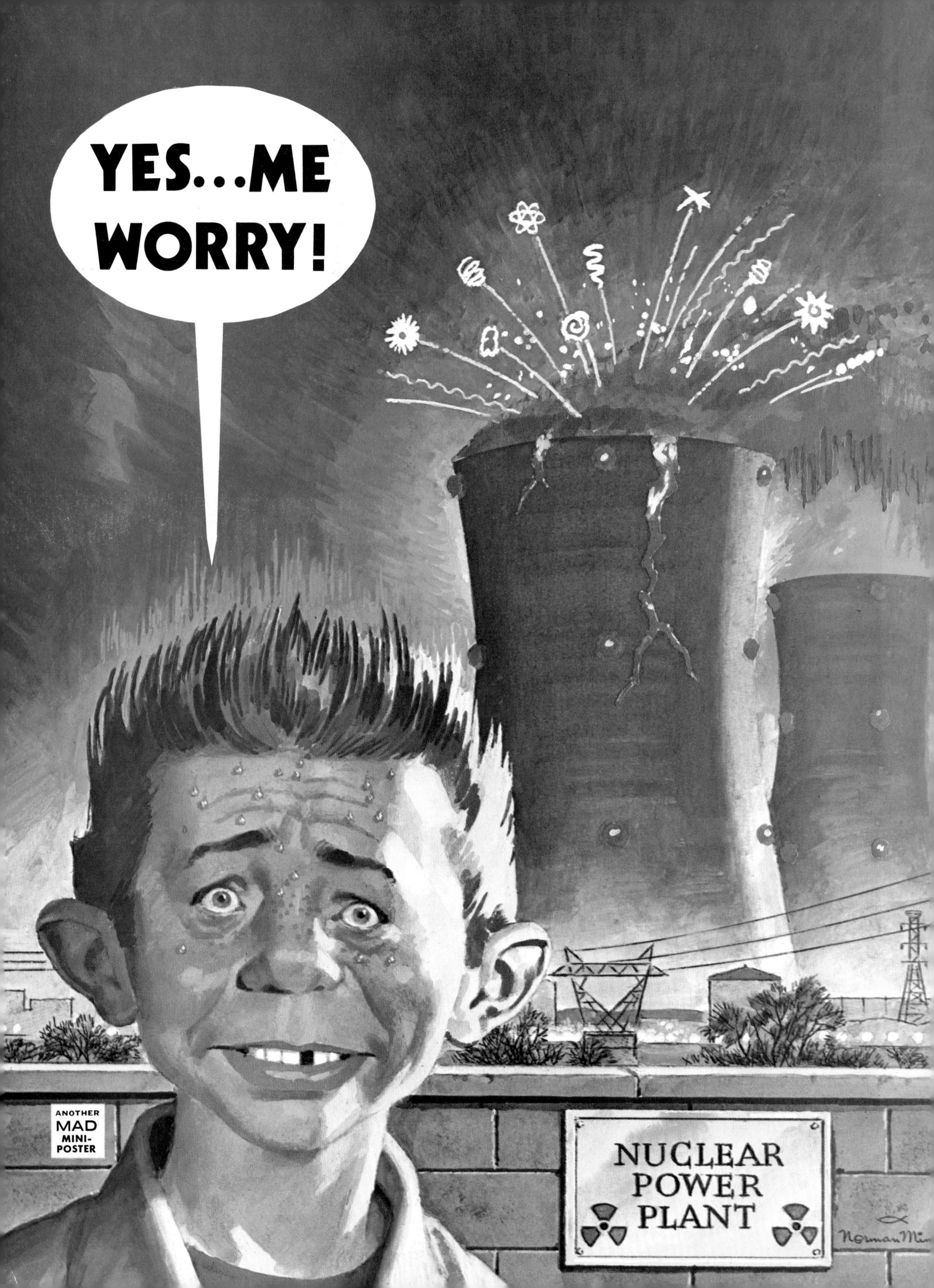
YES...ME WORRY!
ANOTHER MAD MINI-POSTER
NUCLEAR POWER PLANT

A GRAPPLE FOR THE TEACHER DEPT.

There's a new hit show on TV about a teacher and his spaced-out students in a Brooklyn High School. Now, everybody who ever went to school knows that someday, you gotta get out...even if you're spaced out of your gourd. Well, we got to wondering what it will be like when graduation day comes around on...

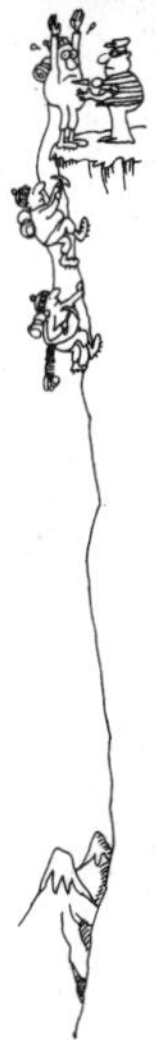

WELCOME BACK, KLODDER

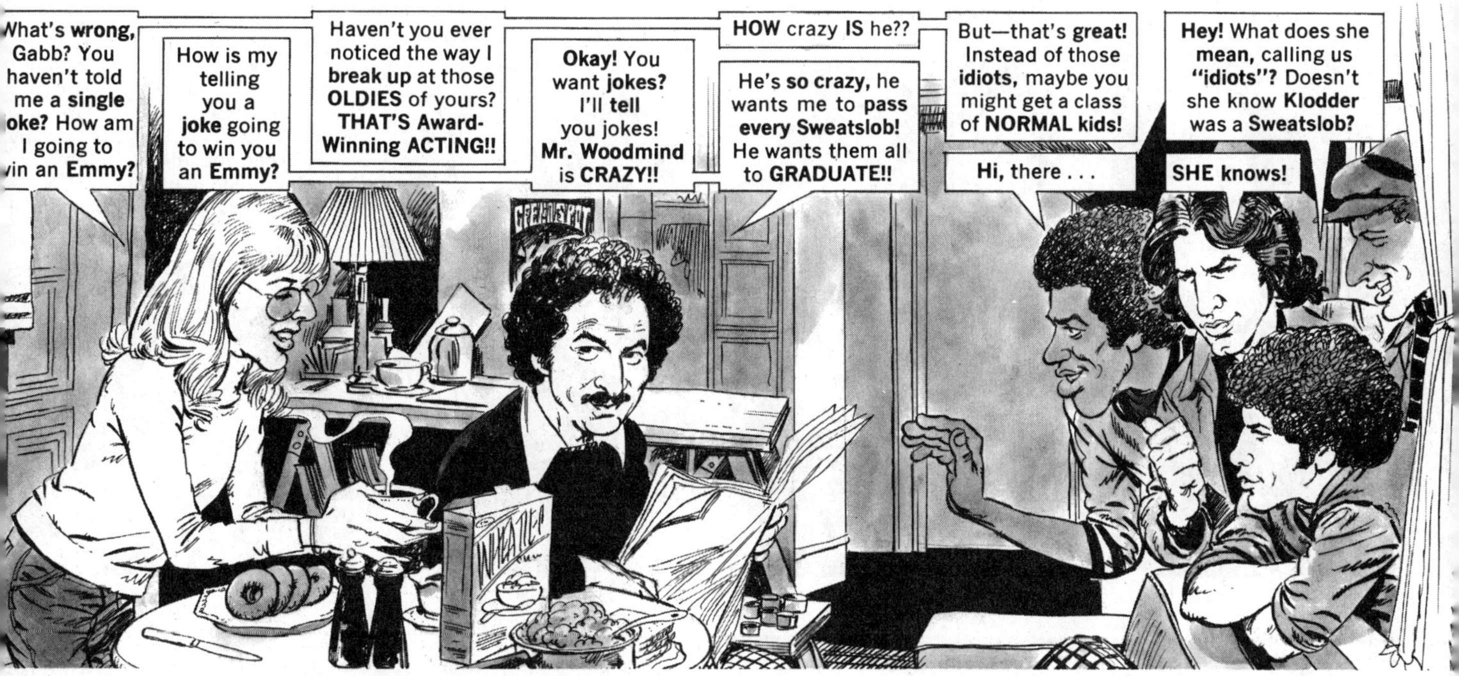

hat's wrong, Gabb? You haven't told me a single oke? How am I going to in an Emmy?
How is my telling you a joke going to win you an Emmy?
Haven't you ever noticed the way I break up at those OLDIES of yours? THAT'S Award-Winning ACTING!!
Okay! You want jokes? I'll tell you jokes! Mr. Woodmind is CRAZY!!
HOW crazy IS he??
He's so crazy, he wants me to pass every Sweatslob! He wants them all to GRADUATE!!
But—that's great! Instead of those idiots, maybe you might get a class of NORMAL kids!
Hi, there . . .
Hey! What does she mean, calling us "idiots"? Doesn't she know Klodder was a Sweatslob?
SHE knows!

ARTIST: ANGELO TORRES WRITER: LOU SILVERSTONE

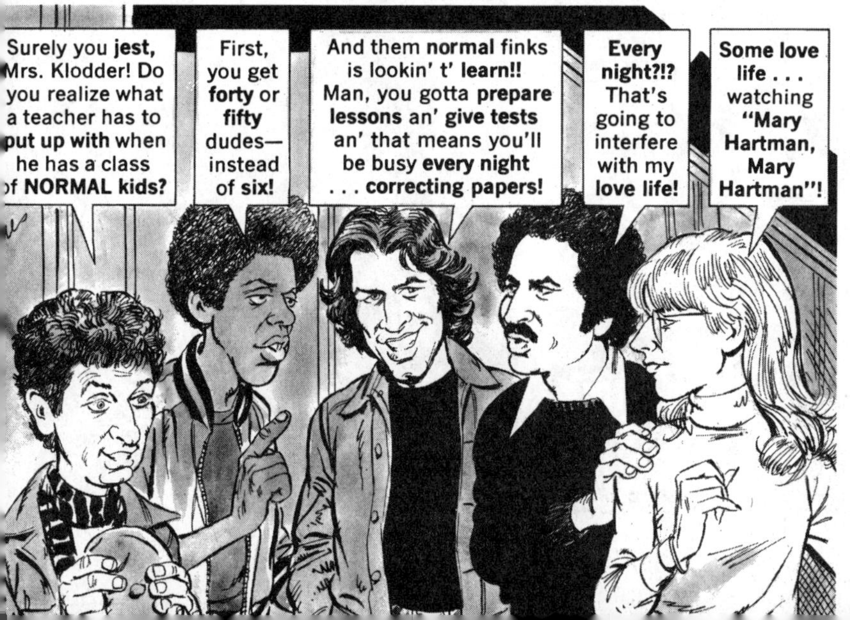

Surely you jest, Mrs. Klodder! Do you realize what a teacher has to put up with when he has a class f NORMAL kids?
First, you get forty or fifty dudes—instead of six!
And them normal finks is lookin' t' learn!! Man, you gotta prepare lessons an' give tests an' that means you'll be busy every night . . . correcting papers!
Every night?!? That's going to interfere with my love life!
Some love life . . . watching "Mary Hartman, Mary Hartman"!

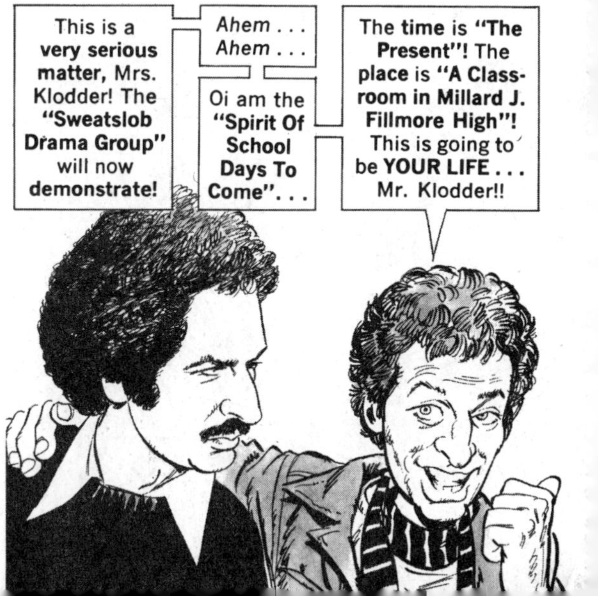

This is a very serious matter, Mrs. Klodder! The "Sweatslob Drama Group" will now demonstrate!
Ahem . . . Ahem . . .
Oi am the "Spirit Of School Days To Come". . .
The time is "The Present"! The place is "A Classroom in Millard J. Fillmore High"! This is going to be YOUR LIFE . . . Mr. Klodder!!

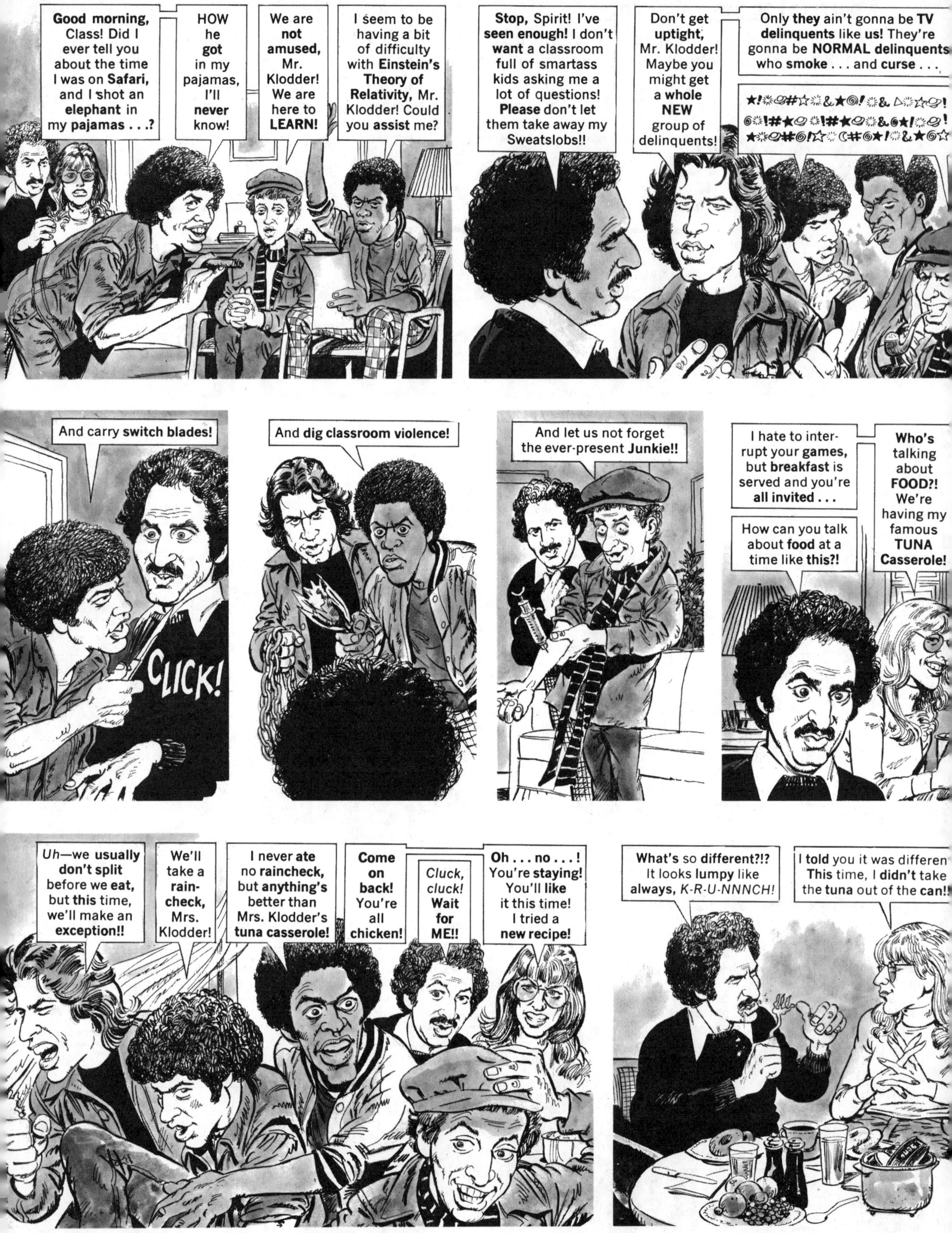
Good morning, Class! Did I ever tell you about the time I was on Safari, and I shot an elephant in my pajamas . . .?
HOW he got in my pajamas, I'll never know!
We are not amused, Mr. Klodder! We are here to LEARN!
I seem to be having a bit of difficulty with Einstein's Theory of Relativity, Mr. Klodder! Could you assist me?
Stop, Spirit! I've seen enough! I don't want a classroom full of smartass kids asking me a lot of questions! Please don't let them take away my Sweatslobs!!
Don't get uptight, Mr. Klodder! Maybe you might get a whole NEW group of delinquents!
Only they ain't gonna be TV delinquents like us! They're gonna be NORMAL delinquents who smoke . . . and curse . . .
And carry switch blades!
CLICK!
And dig classroom violence!
And let us not forget the ever-present Junkie!!
I hate to interrupt your games, but breakfast is served and you're all invited . . .
Who's talking about FOOD?! We're having my famous TUNA Casserole!
How can you talk about food at a time like this?!
Uh—we usually don't split before we eat, but this time, we'll make an exception!!
We'll take a raincheck, Mrs. Klodder!
I never ate no raincheck, but anything's better than Mrs. Klodder's tuna casserole!
Come on back! You're all chicken!
Cluck, cluck! Wait for ME!!
Oh . . . no . . . ! You're staying! You'll like it this time! I tried a new recipe!
What's so different?!? It looks lumpy like always, K-R-U-NNNCH!
I told you it was different! This time, I didn't take the tuna out of the can!!

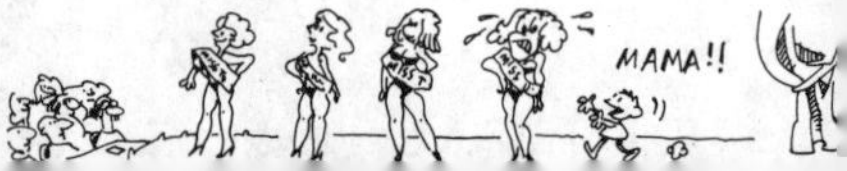
MAMA!!

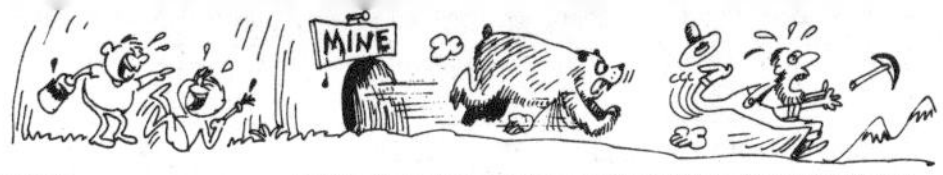
MINE

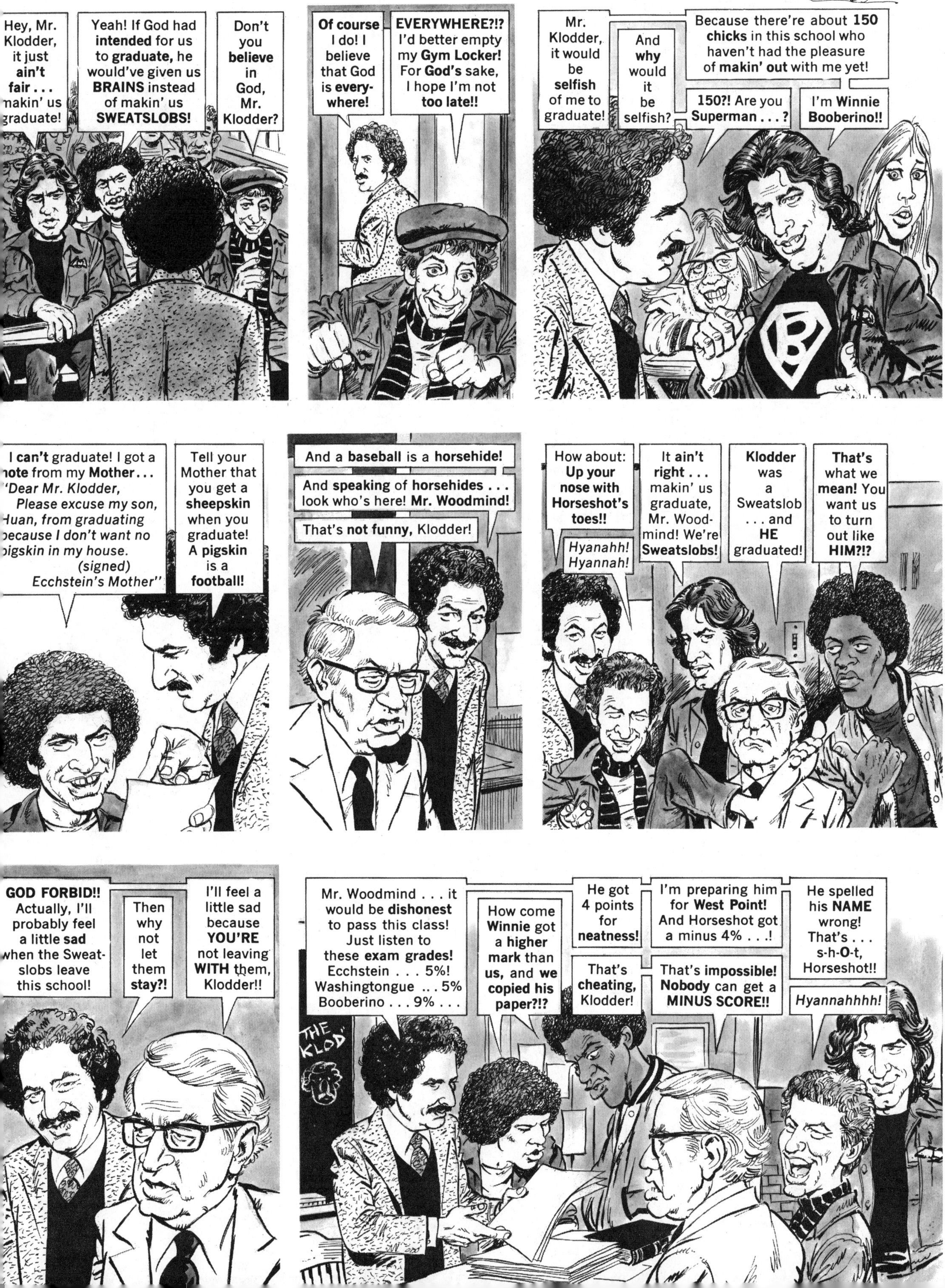
Hey, Mr. Klodder, it just **ain't fair . . .** makin' us graduate!
Yeah! If God had **intended** for us to **graduate,** he would've given us **BRAINS** instead of makin' us **SWEATSLOBS!**
Don't you **believe** in God, Mr. Klodder?
Of course I do! I believe that God is **every-where!**
EVERYWHERE?!? I'd better empty my **Gym Locker!** For **God's** sake, I hope I'm not **too late!!**
Mr. Klodder, it would be **selfish** of me to graduate!
And **why** would it be selfish?
Because there're about **150 chicks** in this school who haven't had the pleasure of **makin' out** with me yet!
150?! Are you **Superman . . .** ?
I'm **Winnie Booberino!!**
I **can't** graduate! I got a note from my **Mother . . .**
"Dear Mr. Klodder, Please excuse my son, Juan, from graduating because I don't want no pigskin in my house. (signed) Ecchstein's Mother"
Tell your Mother that you get a **sheepskin** when you graduate! A **pigskin** is a **football!**
And a **baseball** is a **horsehide!**
And **speaking** of **horsehides . . .** look who's here! **Mr. Woodmind!**
That's **not funny,** Klodder!
How about: **Up your nose with Horseshot's toes!!**
Hyanahh! Hyannah!
It **ain't right . . .** makin' us graduate, Mr. Wood-mind! We're **Sweatslobs!**
Klodder was a Sweatslob . . . and **HE** graduated!
That's what we **mean!** You want us to turn out like **HIM?!?**
GOD FORBID!! Actually, I'll probably feel a little **sad** when the Sweat-slobs leave this school!
Then why not let them **stay?!**
I'll feel a little sad because **YOU'RE** not leaving **WITH** them, Klodder!!
Mr. Woodmind . . . it would be **dishonest** to pass this class! Just listen to these **exam grades!** Ecchstein . . . 5%! Washingtongue . . . 5% Booberino . . . 9% . . .
How come **Winnie** got a **higher mark** than **us,** and **we copied his paper?!?**
He got 4 points for **neatness!**
I'm preparing him for **West Point!** And Horseshot got a minus 4% . . .!
That's **cheating,** Klodder!
That's **impossible!** **Nobody** can get a **MINUS SCORE!!**
He spelled his **NAME** wrong! That's . . . s-h-**O**-t, Horseshot!!
Hyannahhhh!
THE KLOD

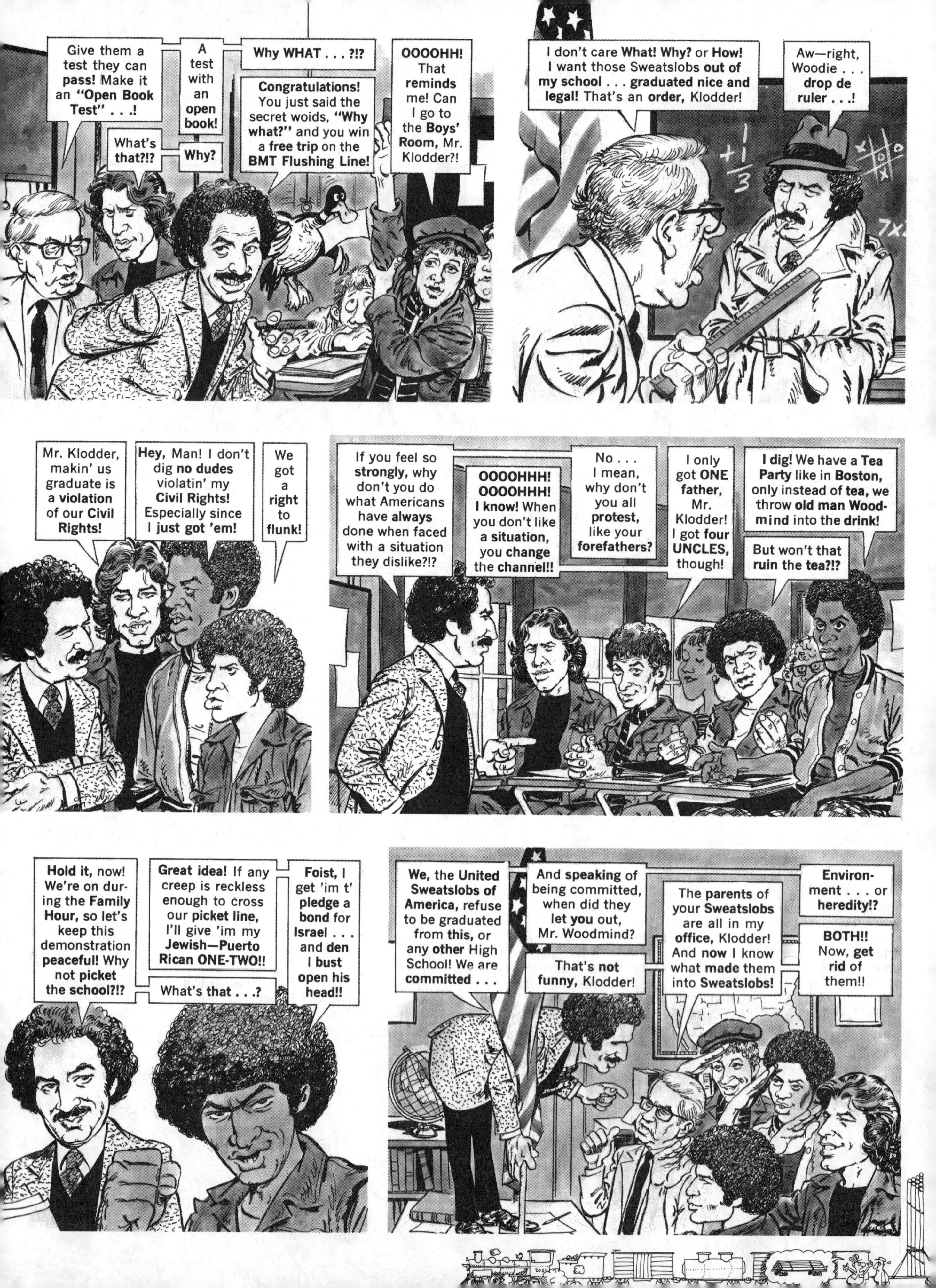

Give them a test they can pass! Make it an "Open Book Test" . . .!
What's that?!?
A test with an open book!
Why?
Why WHAT . . . ?!?
Congratulations! You just said the secret woids, "Why what?" and you win a free trip on the BMT Flushing Line!
OOOOHH! That reminds me! Can I go to the Boys' Room, Mr. Klodder?!
I don't care What! Why? or How! I want those Sweatslobs out of my school . . . graduated nice and legal! That's an order, Klodder!
Aw—right, Woodie . . . drop de ruler . . .!
Mr. Klodder, makin' us graduate is a violation of our Civil Rights!
Hey, Man! I don't dig no dudes violatin' my Civil Rights! Especially since I just got 'em!
We got a right to flunk!
If you feel so strongly, why don't you do what Americans have always done when faced with a situation they dislike?!?
OOOOHHH! OOOOHHH! I know! When you don't like a situation, you change the channel!!
No . . . I mean, why don't you all protest, like your forefathers?
I only got ONE father, Mr. Klodder! I got four UNCLES, though!
I dig! We have a Tea Party like in Boston, only instead of tea, we throw old man Woodmind into the drink!
But won't that ruin the tea?!?
Hold it, now! We're on during the Family Hour, so let's keep this demonstration peaceful! Why not picket the school?!?
Great idea! If any creep is reckless enough to cross our picket line, I'll give 'im my Jewish—Puerto Rican ONE-TWO!!
What's that . . .?
Foist, I get 'im t' pledge a bond for Israel . . . and den I bust open his head!!
We, the United Sweatslobs of America, refuse to be graduated from this, or any other High School! We are committed . . .
And speaking of being committed, when did they let you out, Mr. Woodmind?
That's not funny, Klodder!
The parents of your Sweatslobs are all in my office, Klodder! And now I know what made them into Sweatslobs!
Environment . . . or heredity!?
BOTH!! Now, get rid of them!!

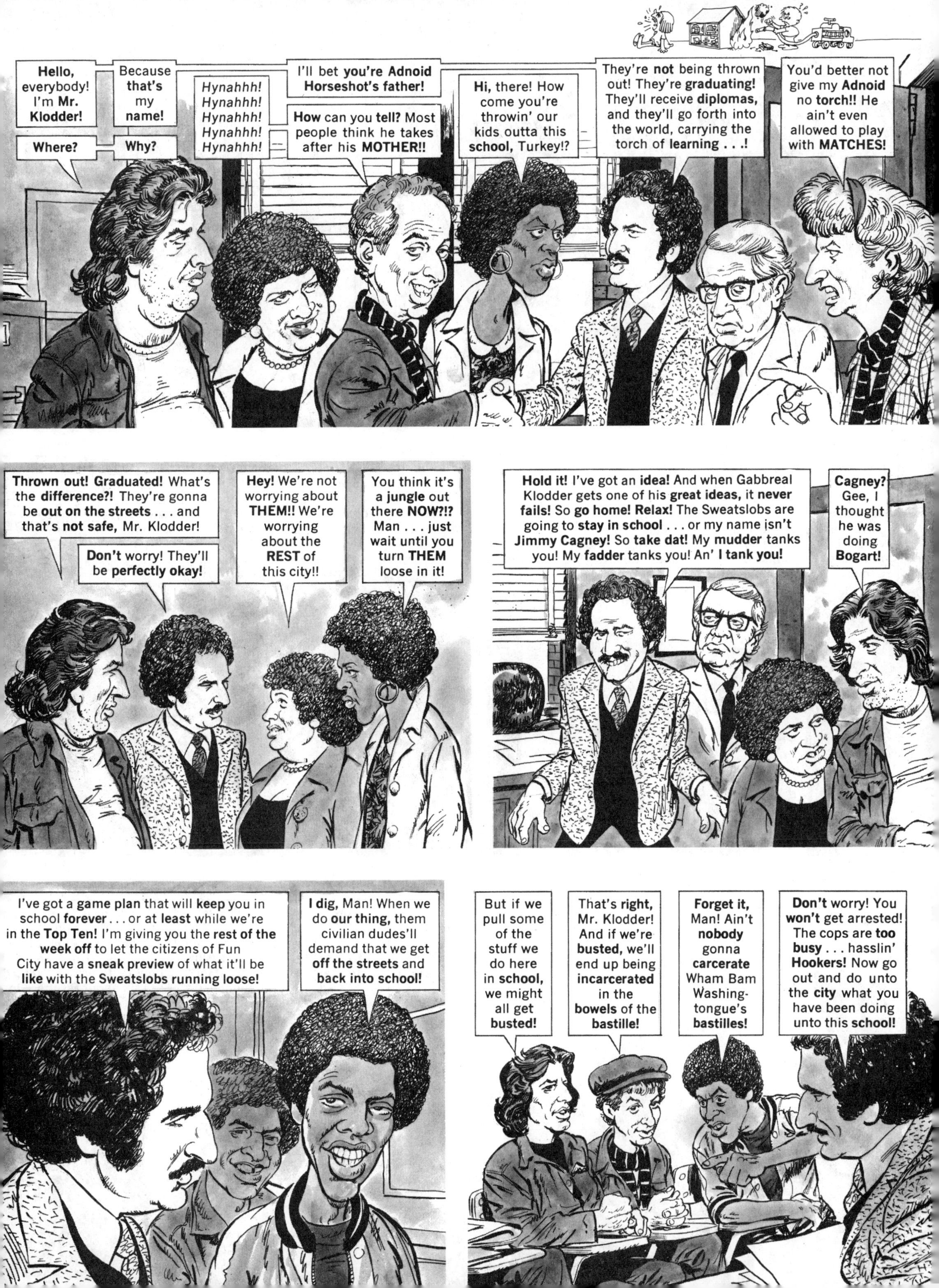
Hello, everybody! I'm Mr. Klodder!
Where?
Because that's my name!
Why?
Hynahhh! Hynahhh! Hynahhh! Hynahhh! Hynahhh!
I'll bet you're Adnoid Horseshot's father!
How can you tell? Most people think he takes after his MOTHER!!
Hi, there! How come you're throwin' our kids outta this school, Turkey!?
They're not being thrown out! They're graduating! They'll receive diplomas, and they'll go forth into the world, carrying the torch of learning . . .!
You'd better not give my Adnoid no torch!! He ain't even allowed to play with MATCHES!
Thrown out! Graduated! What's the difference?! They're gonna be out on the streets . . . and that's not safe, Mr. Klodder!
Don't worry! They'll be perfectly okay!
Hey! We're not worrying about THEM!! We're worrying about the REST of this city!!
You think it's a jungle out there NOW?!? Man . . . just wait until you turn THEM loose in it!
Hold it! I've got an idea! And when Gabbreal Klodder gets one of his great ideas, it never fails! So go home! Relax! The Sweatslobs are going to stay in school . . . or my name isn't Jimmy Cagney! So take dat! My mudder tanks you! My fadder tanks you! An' I tank you!
Cagney? Gee, I thought he was doing Bogart!
I've got a game plan that will keep you in school forever . . . or at least while we're in the Top Ten! I'm giving you the rest of the week off to let the citizens of Fun City have a sneak preview of what it'll be like with the Sweatslobs running loose!
I dig, Man! When we do our thing, them civilian dudes'll demand that we get off the streets and back into school!
But if we pull some of the stuff we do here in school, we might all get busted!
That's right, Mr. Klodder! And if we're busted, we'll end up being incarcerated in the bowels of the bastille!
Forget it, Man! Ain't nobody gonna carcerate Wham Bam Washing-tongue's bastilles!
Don't worry! You won't get arrested! The cops are too busy . . . hasslin' Hookers! Now go out and do unto the city what you have been doing unto this school!

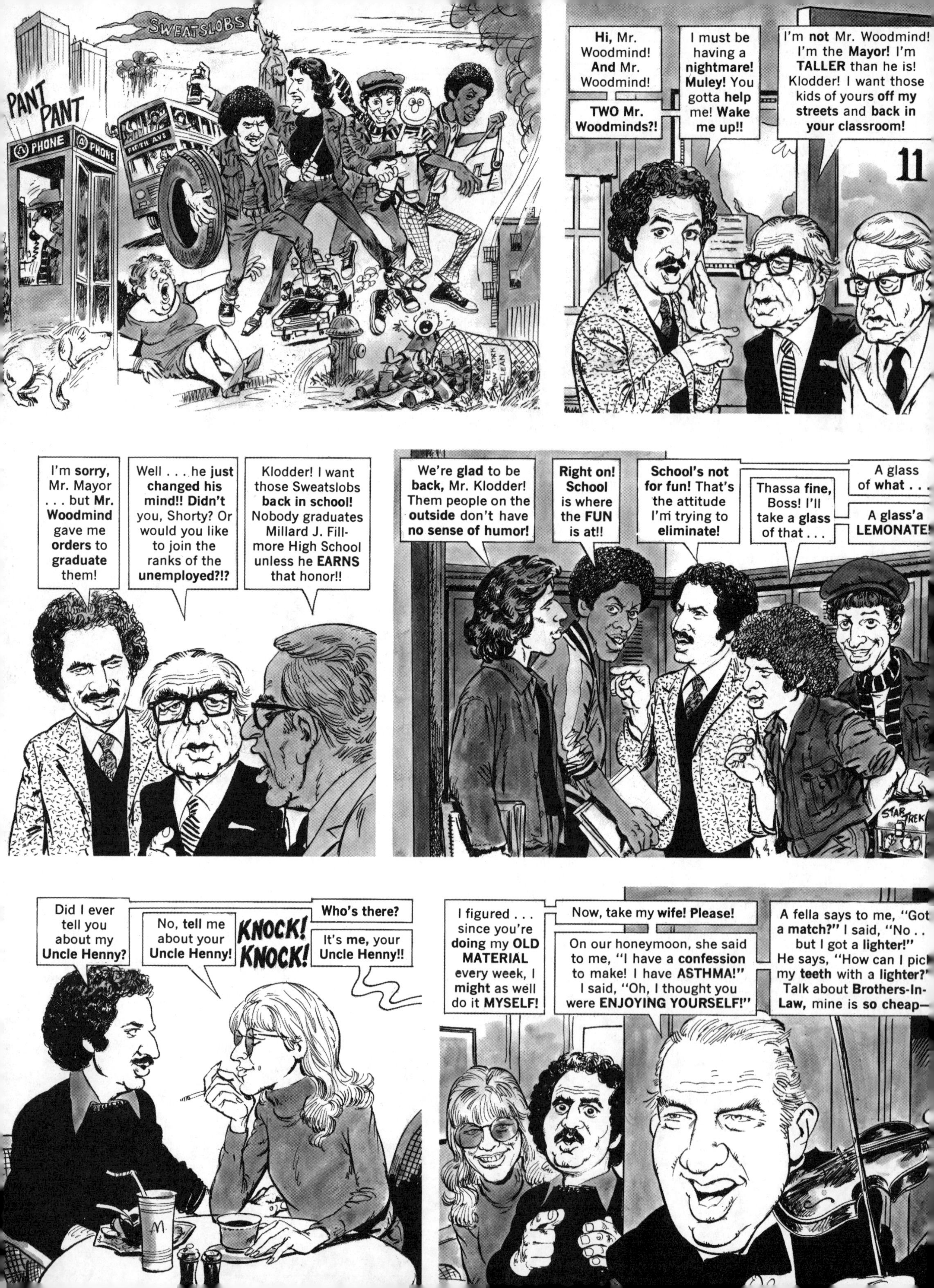
SWEATSLOBS
PANT PANT
PHONE
PHONE
FIFTH AVE
KEEP NEW YORK CLEAN
Hi, Mr. Woodmind! And Mr. Woodmind!
TWO Mr. Woodminds?!
I must be having a nightmare! Muley! You gotta help me! Wake me up!!
I'm not Mr. Woodmind! I'm the Mayor! I'm TALLER than he is! Klodder! I want those kids of yours off my streets and back in your classroom!
11
I'm sorry, Mr. Mayor . . . but Mr. Woodmind gave me orders to graduate them!
Well . . . he just changed his mind!! Didn't you, Shorty? Or would you like to join the ranks of the unemployed?!?
Klodder! I want those Sweatslobs back in school! Nobody graduates Millard J. Fillmore High School unless he EARNS that honor!!
We're glad to be back, Mr. Klodder! Them people on the outside don't have no sense of humor!
Right on! School is where the FUN is at!!
School's not for fun! That's the attitude I'm trying to eliminate!
Thassa fine, Boss! I'll take a glass of that . . .
A glass of what . . .
A glass'a LEMONATE!
STAR TREK
Did I ever tell you about my Uncle Henny?
No, tell me about your Uncle Henny!
KNOCK! KNOCK!
Who's there?
It's me, your Uncle Henny!!
I figured . . . since you're doing my OLD MATERIAL every week, I might as well do it MYSELF!
Now, take my wife! Please!
On our honeymoon, she said to me, "I have a confession to make! I have ASTHMA!" I said, "Oh, I thought you were ENJOYING YOURSELF!"
A fella says to me, "Got a match?" I said, "No . . but I got a lighter!" He says, "How can I pick my teeth with a lighter?" Talk about Brothers-In-Law, mine is so cheap—

Okay, all you clods out there! So you think those "Polish Jokes" that you've been telling are hilarious... and you've been breaking up every time you hear how stupid and imbecilic Poles supposedly are?!? Well, we've got news for you! In Poland, they've got *their* favorite jokes... about *US*! And so, here, direct from the bars and coffee houses of downtown Warsaw, is the latest selection of

AMERICAN JOKES THEY'RE TELLING IN POLAND

ARTIST: PAUL COKER, JR. WRITER: FRANK JACOBS

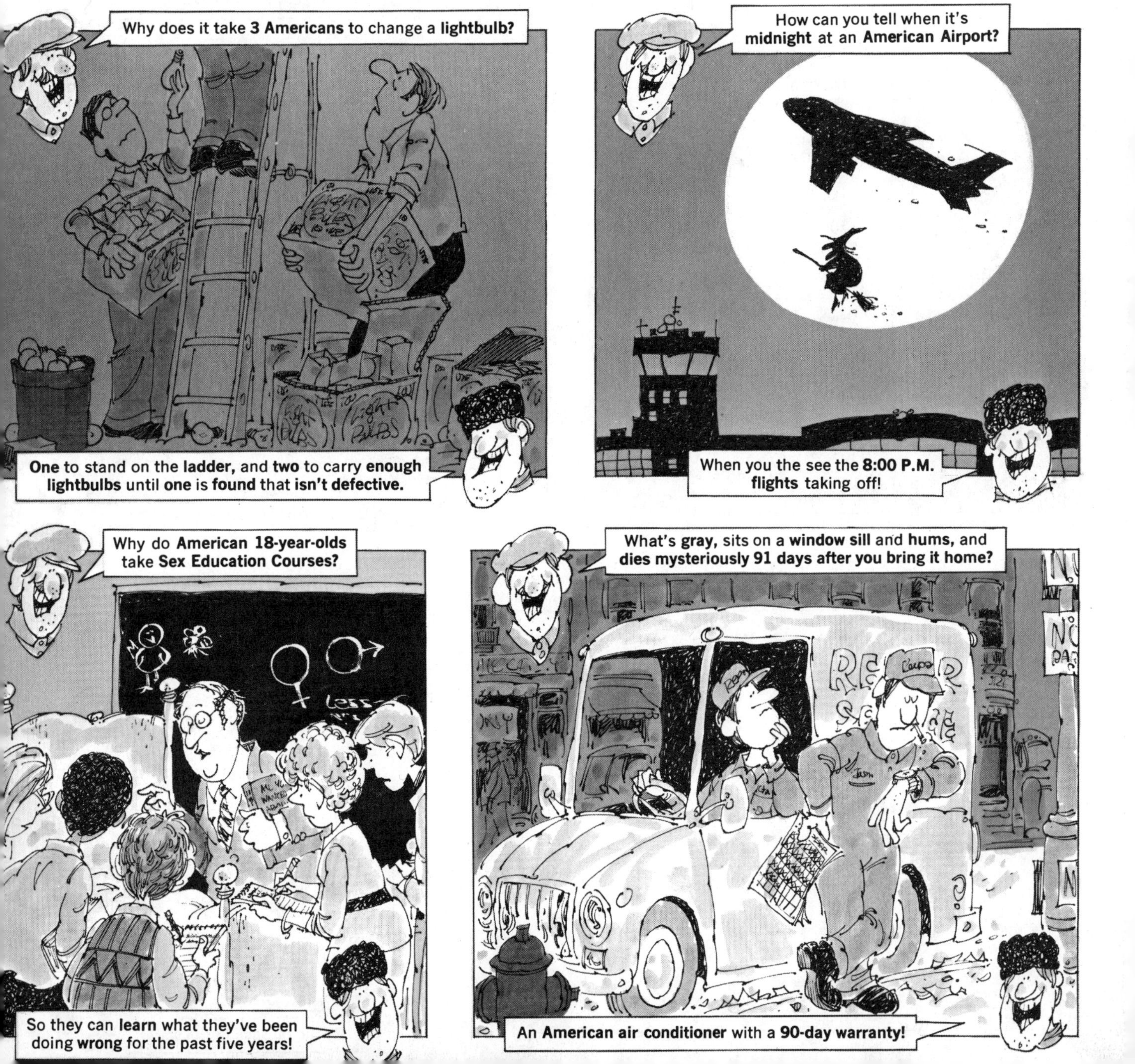
Why does it take **3 Americans** to change a **lightbulb?**
One to stand on the **ladder**, and **two** to carry **enough lightbulbs** until **one** is **found** that **isn't defective.**
How can you tell when it's **midnight** at an **American Airport?**
When you the see the **8:00 P.M. flights** taking off!
Why do **American 18-year-olds** take **Sex Education Courses?**
So they can **learn** what they've been doing **wrong** for the past five years!
What's **gray**, sits on a **window sill** and **hums**, and **dies mysteriously 91 days after you bring it home?**
An **American air conditioner** with a **90-day warranty!**

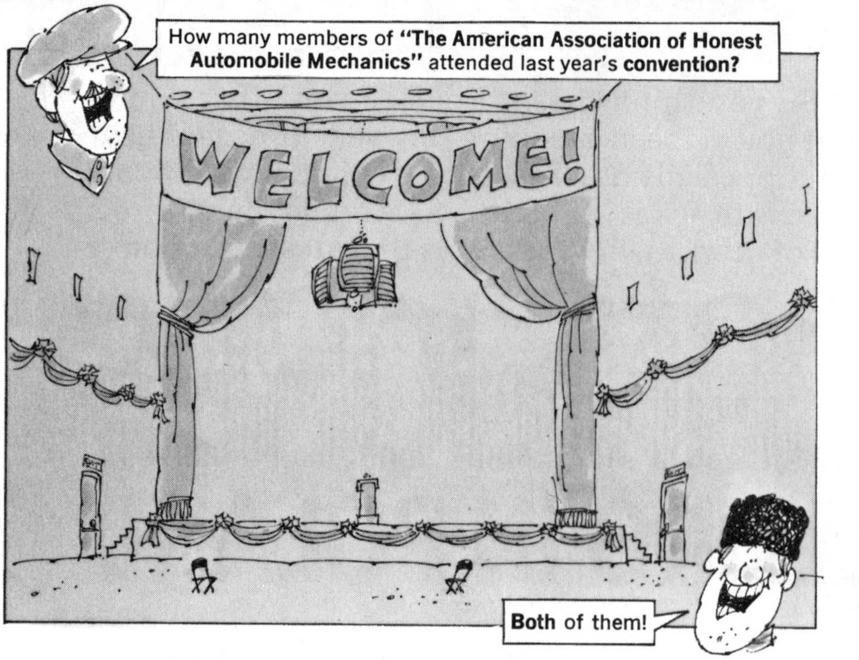
How many members of **"The American Association of Honest Automobile Mechanics"** attended last year's **convention?**
WELCOME!
Both of them!

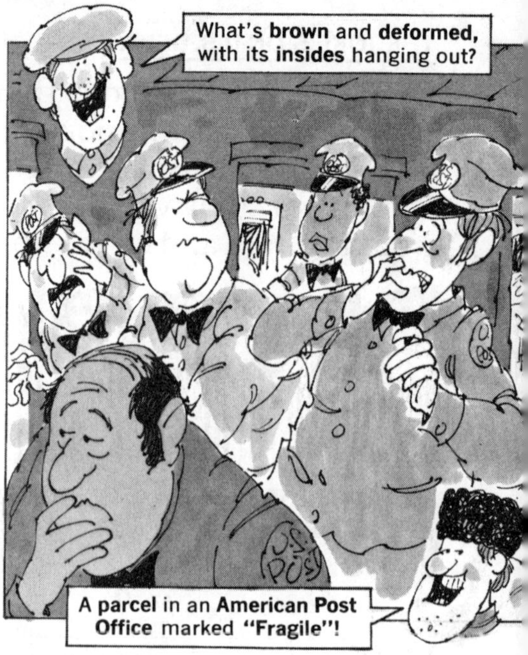
What's **brown** and **deformed,** with its **insides** hanging out?
U.S. POST
A **parcel** in an **American Post Office** marked **"Fragile"**!

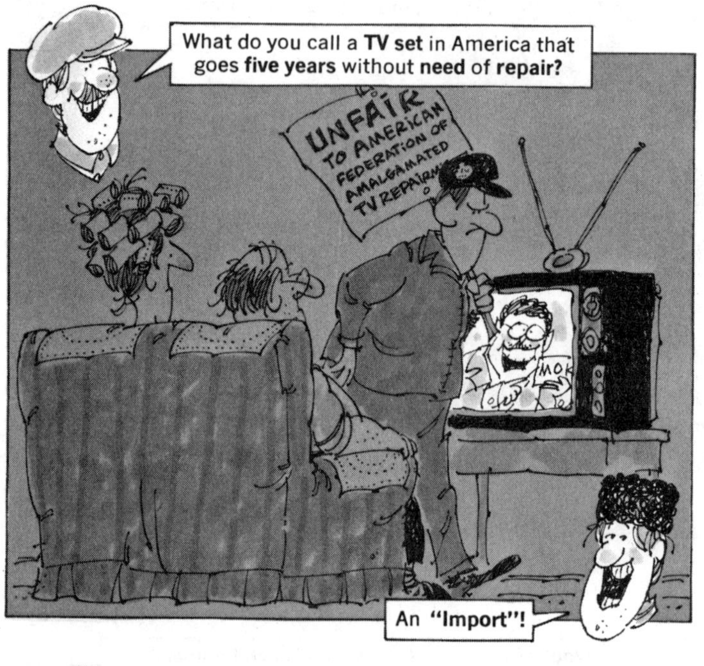
What do you call a **TV set** in America that goes **five years** without **need** of **repair?**
UNFAIR TO AMERICAN FEDERATION OF AMALGAMATED TV REPAIRMEN
An **"Import"**!

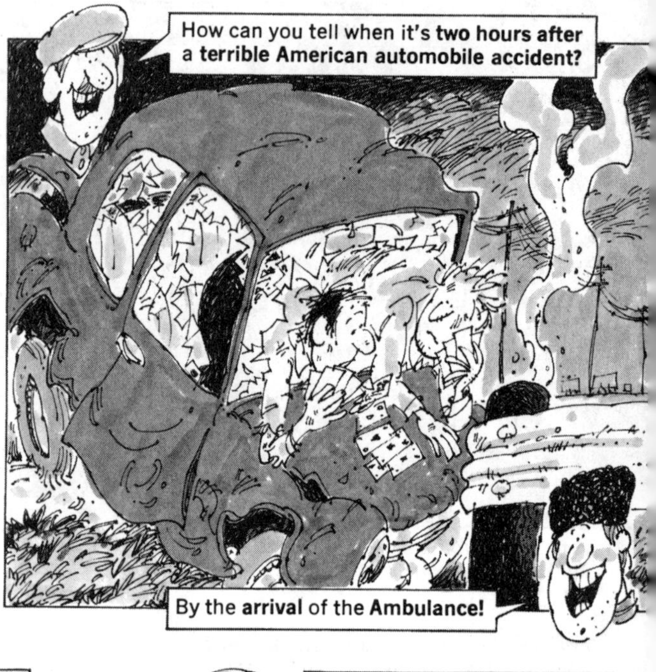
How can you tell when it's **two hours after a terrible American automobile accident?**
By the **arrival** of the **Ambulance!**

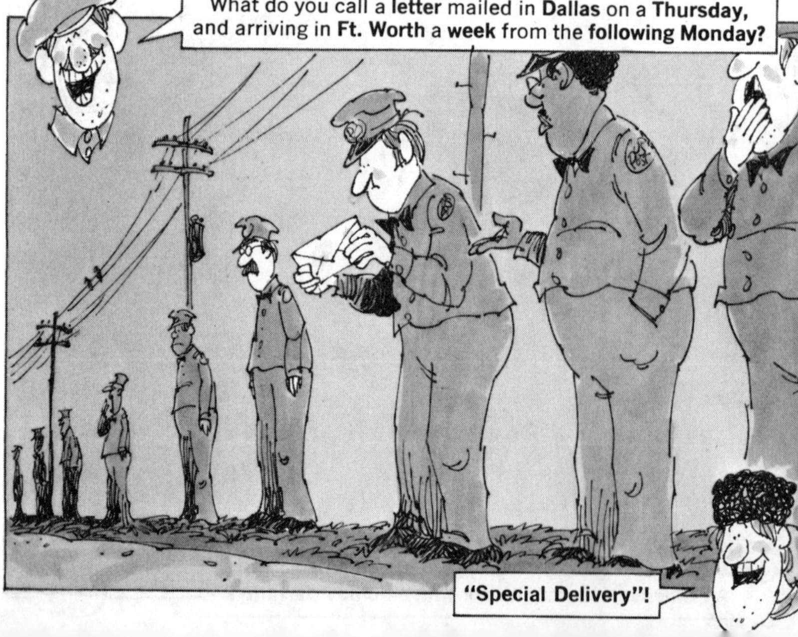
What do you call a **letter** mailed in **Dallas** on a **Thursday,** and arriving in **Ft. Worth** a **week** from the **following Monday?**
"Special Delivery"!

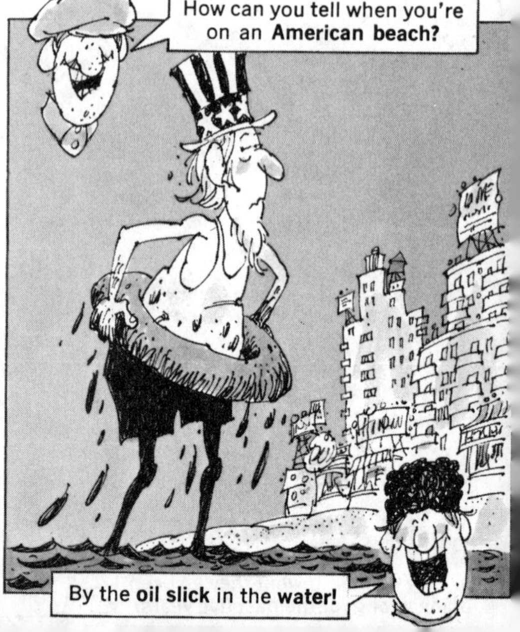
How can you tell when you're on an **American beach?**
By the **oil slick** in the **water!**

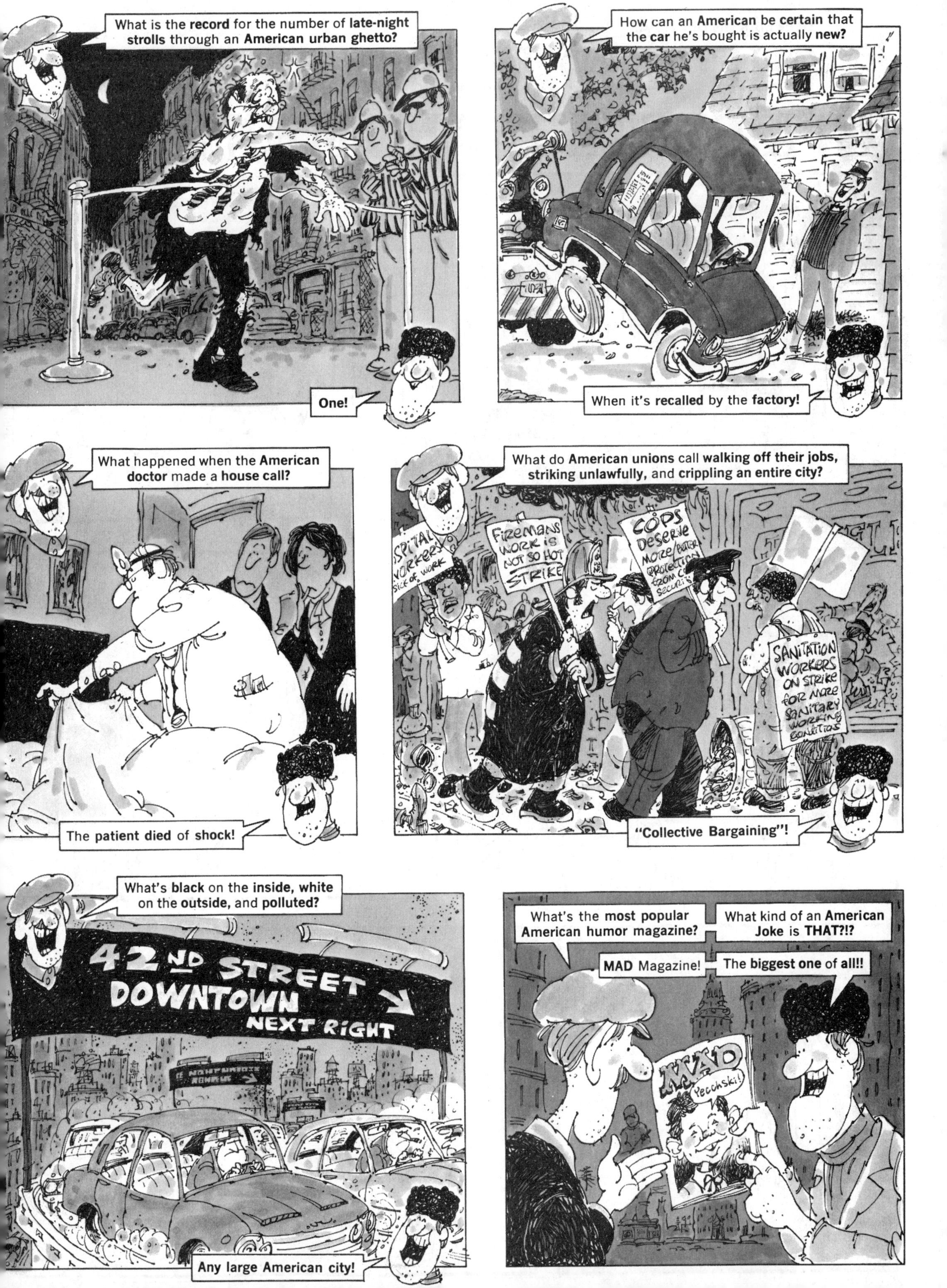
What is the record for the number of late-night strolls through an American urban ghetto?
One!
How can an American be certain that the car he's bought is actually new?
When it's recalled by the factory!
What happened when the American doctor made a house call?
The patient died of shock!
What do American unions call walking off their jobs, striking unlawfully, and crippling an entire city?
SPITAL WORKERS SICK OF WORK
FIREMANS WORK IS NOT SO HOT STRIKE
COPS DESERVE MORE/BETTER PROTECTION
SANITATION WORKERS ON STRIKE FOR MORE SANITARY WORKING CONDITIONS
"Collective Bargaining"!
What's black on the inside, white on the outside, and polluted?
42ND STREET DOWNTOWN NEXT RIGHT
Any large American city!
What's the most popular American humor magazine?
What kind of an American Joke is THAT?!?
MAD Magazine!
The biggest one of all!!
MAD
Yecchski!

DON MARTIN DEPT. PART II

ONE WEDNESDAY EVENING IN A RESTAURANT MEN'S ROOM

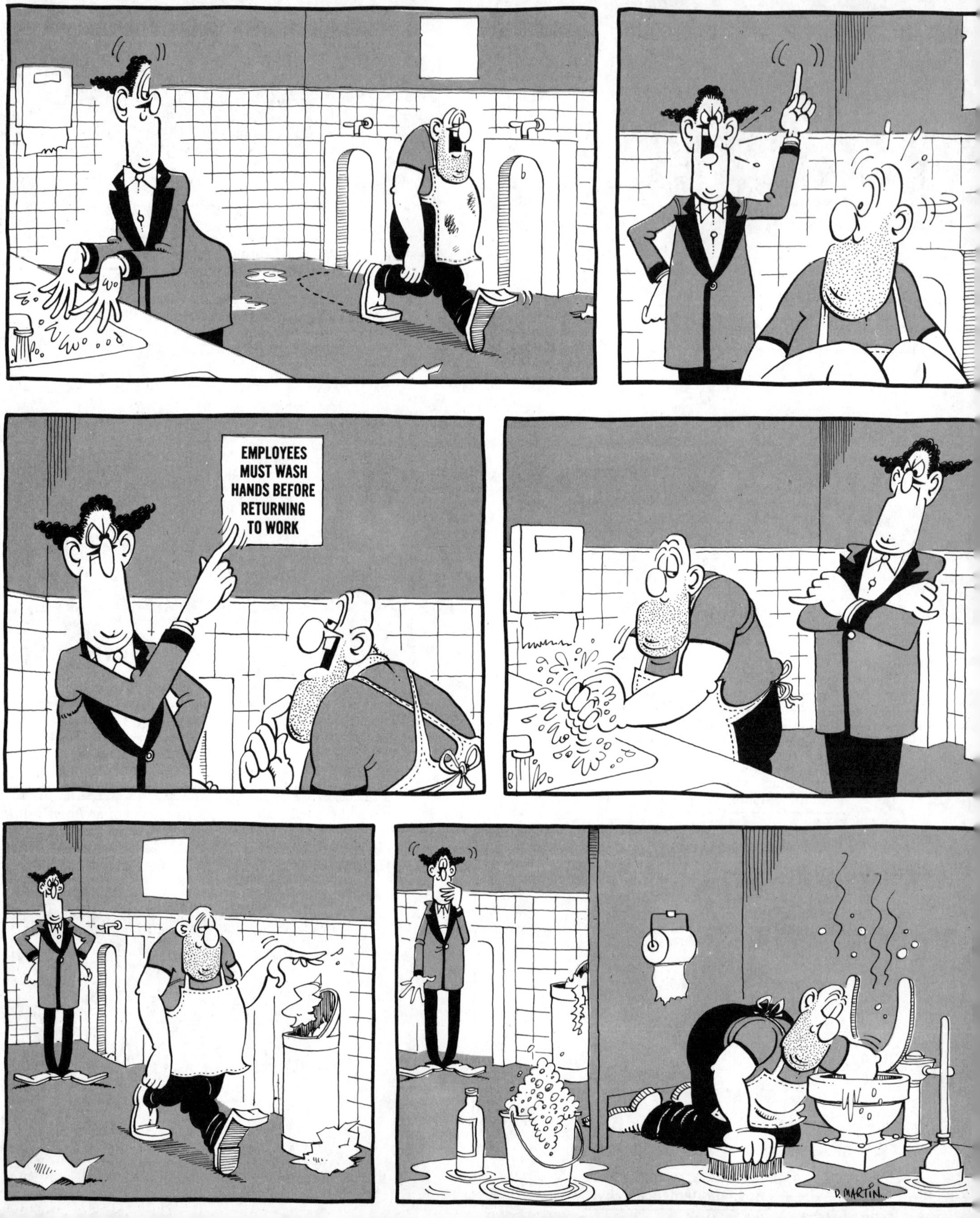
EMPLOYEES MUST WASH HANDS BEFORE RETURNING TO WORK
D. MARTIN

PRIVATE-EYEFULS DEPT.

Once upon a time, there were three little girls who attended the Police Academy . . .

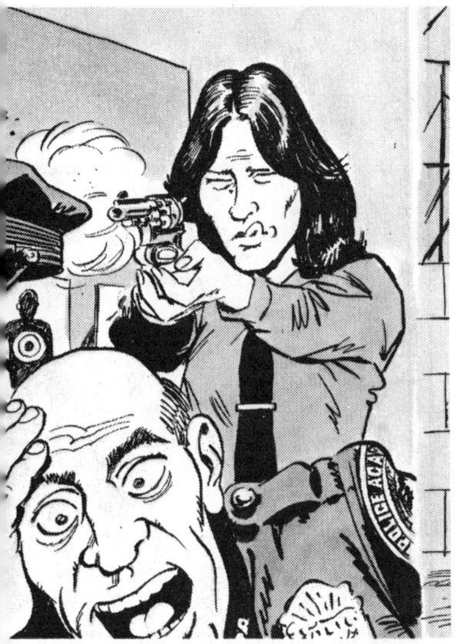

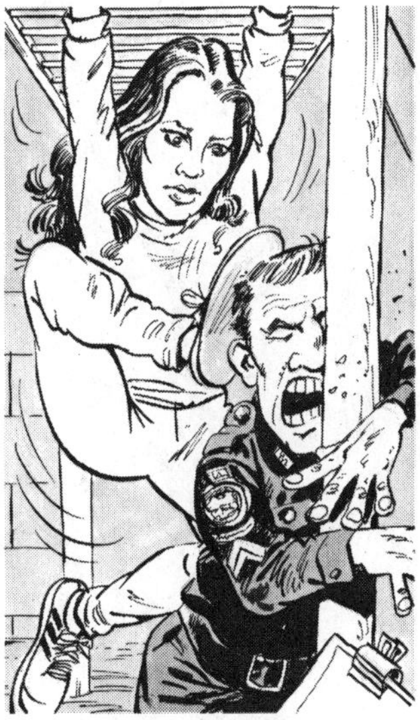

They were graduated and assigned hazardous duties! Hazardous to the rest of the Police Force, that is!

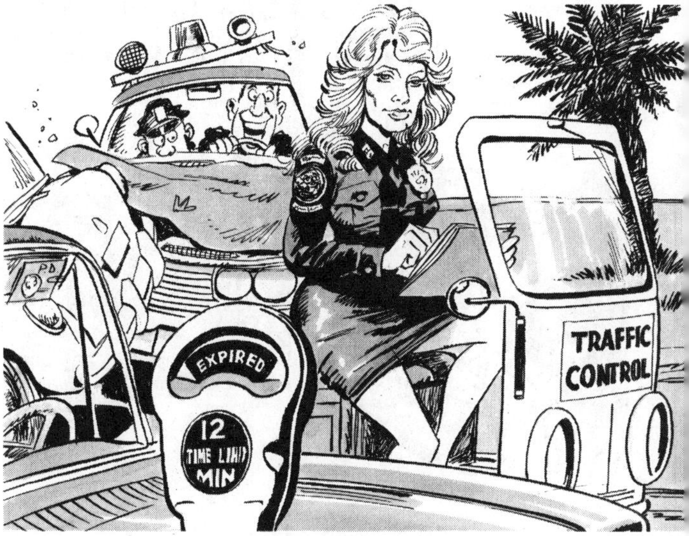
EXPIRED
12
TIME LIMIT
MIN
TRAFFIC
CONTROL

But I took them away from all that, and now they work for me as private detectives. Three glamorous, gorgeous private detectives. How's that for a new angle on fighting crime? My name is Churlie, and I call my girls . . .

CHURLIE'S ANGLES

ARTIST: ANGELO TORRES WRITER: LOU SILVERSTONE

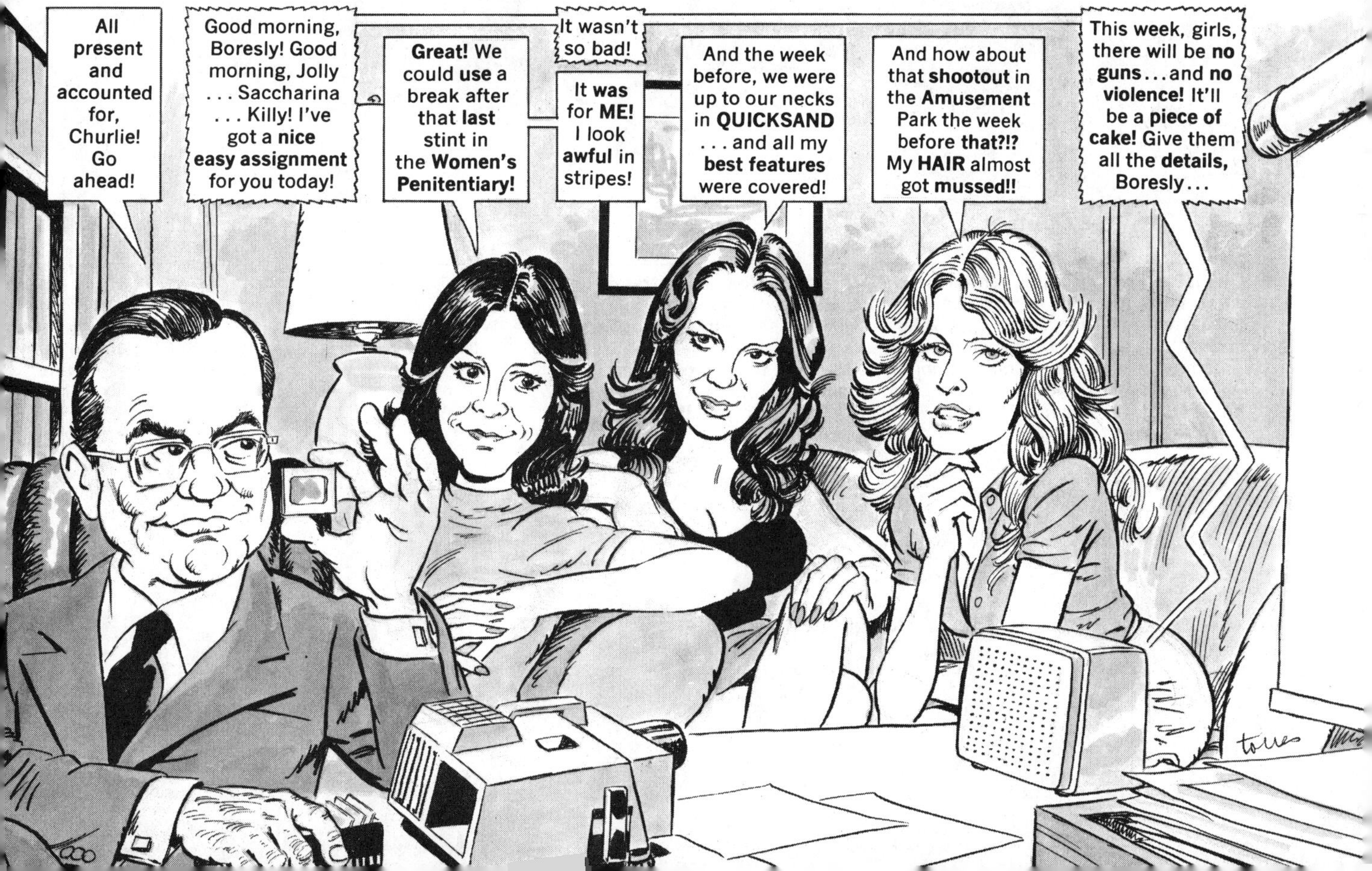
All present and accounted for, Churlie! Go ahead!
Good morning, Boresly! Good morning, Jolly . . . Saccharina . . . Killy! I've got a nice easy assignment for you today!
Great! We could use a break after that last stint in the Women's Penitentiary!
It wasn't so bad!
It was for ME! I look awful in stripes!
And the week before, we were up to our necks in QUICKSAND . . . and all my best features were covered!
And how about that shootout in the Amusement Park the week before that?!? My HAIR almost got mussed!!
This week, girls, there will be no guns . . . and no violence! It'll be a piece of cake! Give them all the details, Boresly . . .

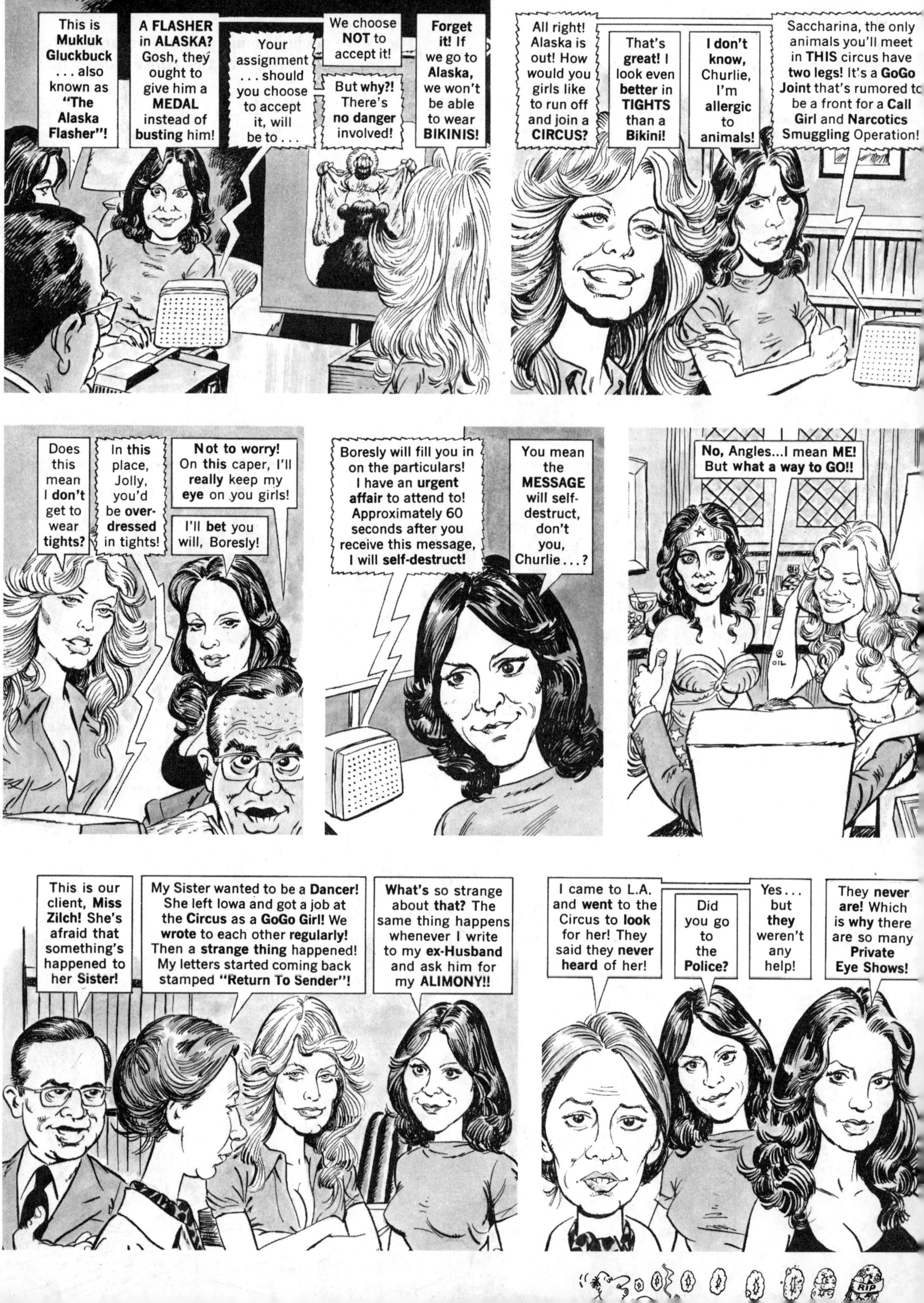

This is Mukluk Gluckbuck . . . also known as "The Alaska Flasher"!
A FLASHER in ALASKA? Gosh, they ought to give him a MEDAL instead of busting him!
Your assignment . . . should you choose to accept it, will be to . . .
We choose NOT to accept it!
But why?! There's no danger involved!
Forget it! If we go to Alaska, we won't be able to wear BIKINIS!
All right! Alaska is out! How would you girls like to run off and join a CIRCUS?
That's great! I look even better in TIGHTS than a Bikini!
I don't know, Churlie, I'm allergic to animals!
Saccharina, the only animals you'll meet in THIS circus have two legs! It's a GoGo Joint that's rumored to be a front for a Call Girl and Narcotics Smuggling Operation!
Does this mean I don't get to wear tights?
In this place, Jolly, you'd be over-dressed in tights!
Not to worry! On this caper, I'll really keep my eye on you girls!
I'll bet you will, Boresly!
Boresly will fill you in on the particulars! I have an urgent affair to attend to! Approximately 60 seconds after you receive this message, I will self-destruct!
You mean the MESSAGE will self-destruct, don't you, Churlie . . .?
No, Angles...I mean ME! But what a way to GO!!
OIL
This is our client, Miss Zilch! She's afraid that something's happened to her Sister!
My Sister wanted to be a Dancer! She left Iowa and got a job at the Circus as a GoGo Girl! We wrote to each other regularly! Then a strange thing happened! My letters started coming back stamped "Return To Sender"!
What's so strange about that? The same thing happens whenever I write to my ex-Husband and ask him for my ALIMONY!!
I came to L.A. and went to the Circus to look for her! They said they never heard of her!
Did you go to the Police?
Yes . . . but they weren't any help!
They never are! Which is why there are so many Private Eye Shows!

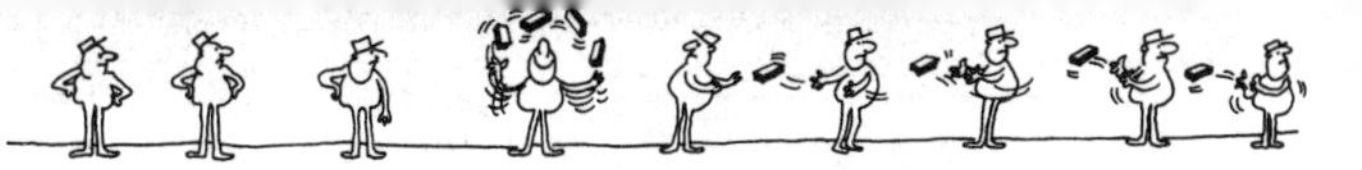

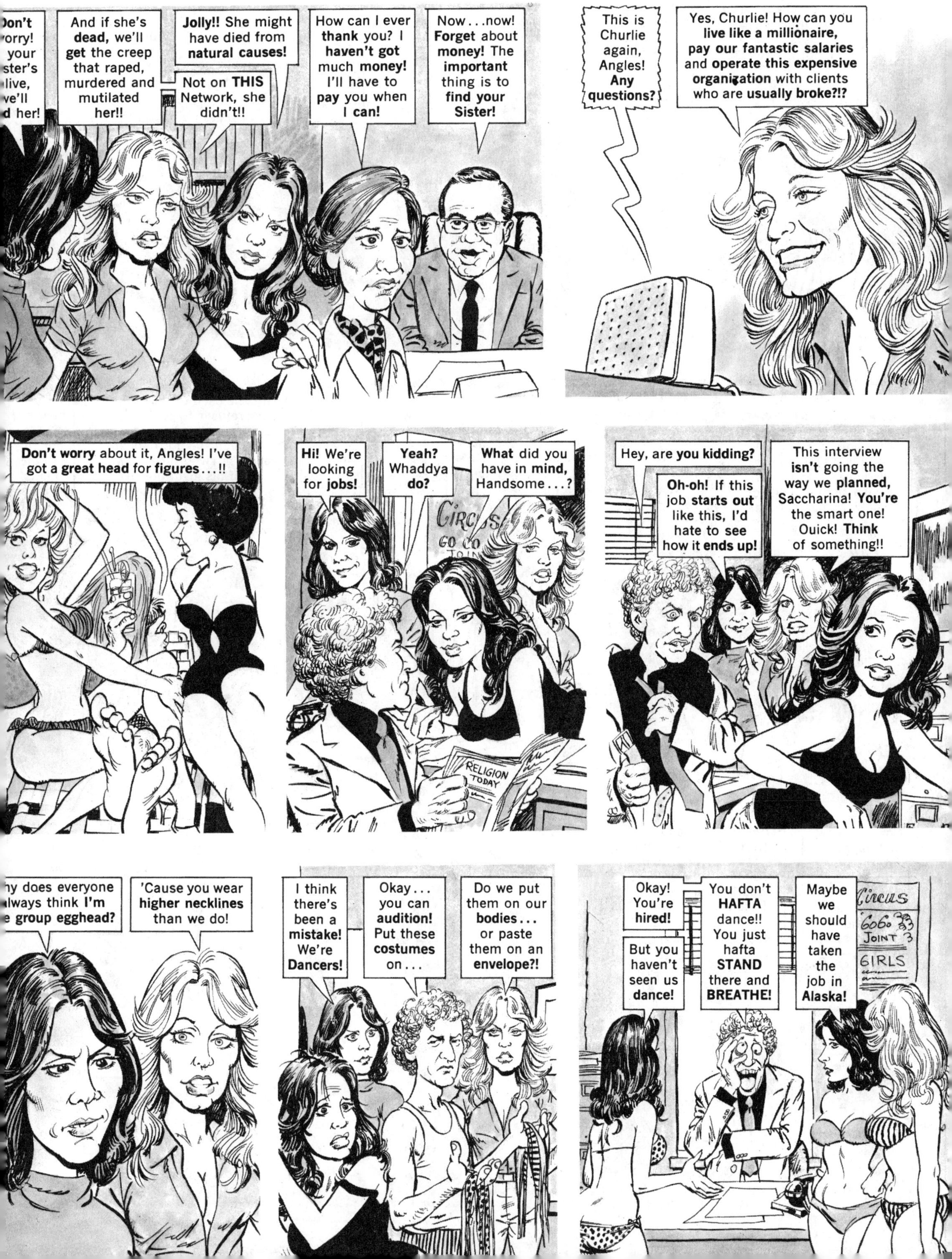

Don't orry! your ster's live, ve'll d her!
And if she's **dead,** we'll **get** the creep that raped, murdered and mutilated her!!
Jolly!! She might have died from **natural causes!**
Not on **THIS** Network, she didn't!!
How can I ever **thank** you? I **haven't got** much **money!** I'll have to **pay** you when **I can!**
Now . . . now! **Forget** about **money!** The **important** thing is to **find your Sister!**
This is Churlie again, Angles! **Any questions?**
Yes, Churlie! How can you **live like a millionaire, pay our fantastic salaries** and **operate this expensive organization** with clients who are **usually broke?!?**
Don't worry about it, Angles! I've got a **great head** for **figures** . . . !!
Hi! We're looking for **jobs!**
Yeah? Whaddya **do?**
What did you have in **mind,** Handsome . . . ?
CIRCUS GO GO
RELIGION TODAY
Hey, are **you kidding?**
Oh-oh! If this job **starts out** like this, I'd hate to see how it **ends up!**
This interview **isn't** going the way we **planned,** Saccharina! **You're** the smart one! Ouick! **Think** of something!!
ny does everyone lways think **I'm** e group egghead?
'Cause you wear **higher necklines** than we do!
I think there's been a **mistake!** We're **Dancers!**
Okay . . . you can **audition!** Put these **costumes** on . . .
Do we put them on our **bodies . . .** or paste them on an **envelope?!**
Okay! You're **hired!**
But you haven't seen us **dance!**
You don't **HAFTA** dance!! You just hafta **STAND** there and **BREATHE!**
Maybe we should have taken the job in **Alaska!**
Circus GoGo JOINT GIRLS

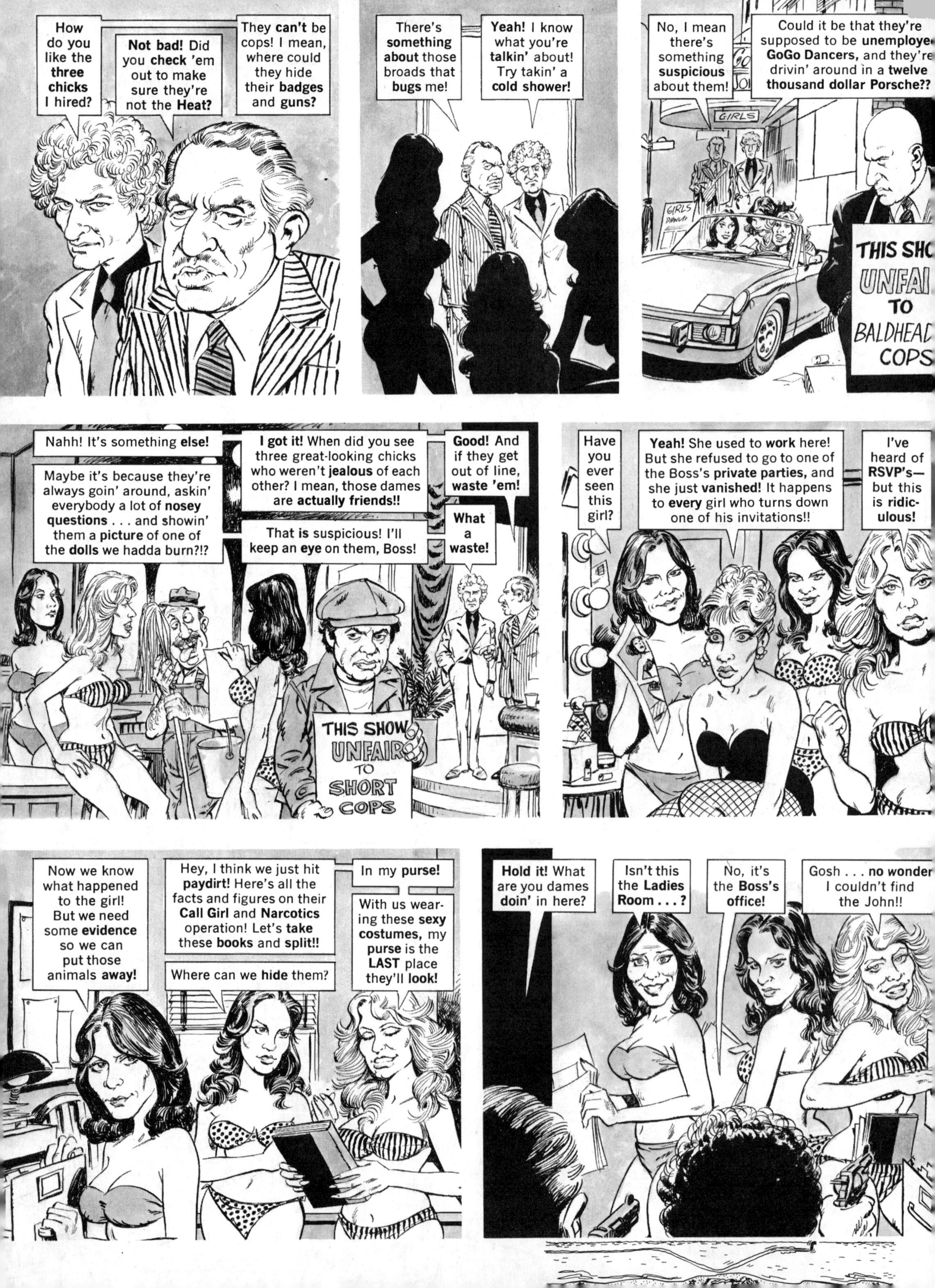
How do you like the three chicks I hired?
Not bad! Did you check 'em out to make sure they're not the Heat?
They can't be cops! I mean, where could they hide their badges and guns?
There's something about those broads that bugs me!
Yeah! I know what you're talkin' about! Try takin' a cold shower!
No, I mean there's something suspicious about them!
Could it be that they're supposed to be unemployed GoGo Dancers, and they're drivin' around in a twelve thousand dollar Porsche??
GIRLS
GIRLS DANCIN
THIS SHO UNFAI TO BALDHEAD COPS
Nahh! It's something else!
Maybe it's because they're always goin' around, askin' everybody a lot of nosey questions . . . and showin' them a picture of one of the dolls we hadda burn?!?
I got it! When did you see three great-looking chicks who weren't jealous of each other? I mean, those dames are actually friends!!
That is suspicious! I'll keep an eye on them, Boss!
Good! And if they get out of line, waste 'em!
What a waste!
THIS SHOW UNFAIR TO SHORT COPS
Have you ever seen this girl?
Yeah! She used to work here! But she refused to go to one of the Boss's private parties, and she just vanished! It happens to every girl who turns down one of his invitations!!
I've heard of RSVP's— but this is ridiculous!
Now we know what happened to the girl! But we need some evidence so we can put those animals away!
Hey, I think we just hit paydirt! Here's all the facts and figures on their Call Girl and Narcotics operation! Let's take these books and split!!
Where can we hide them?
In my purse!
With us wearing these sexy costumes, my purse is the LAST place they'll look!
Hold it! What are you dames doin' in here?
Isn't this the Ladies Room . . . ?
No, it's the Boss's office!
Gosh . . . no wonder I couldn't find the John!!

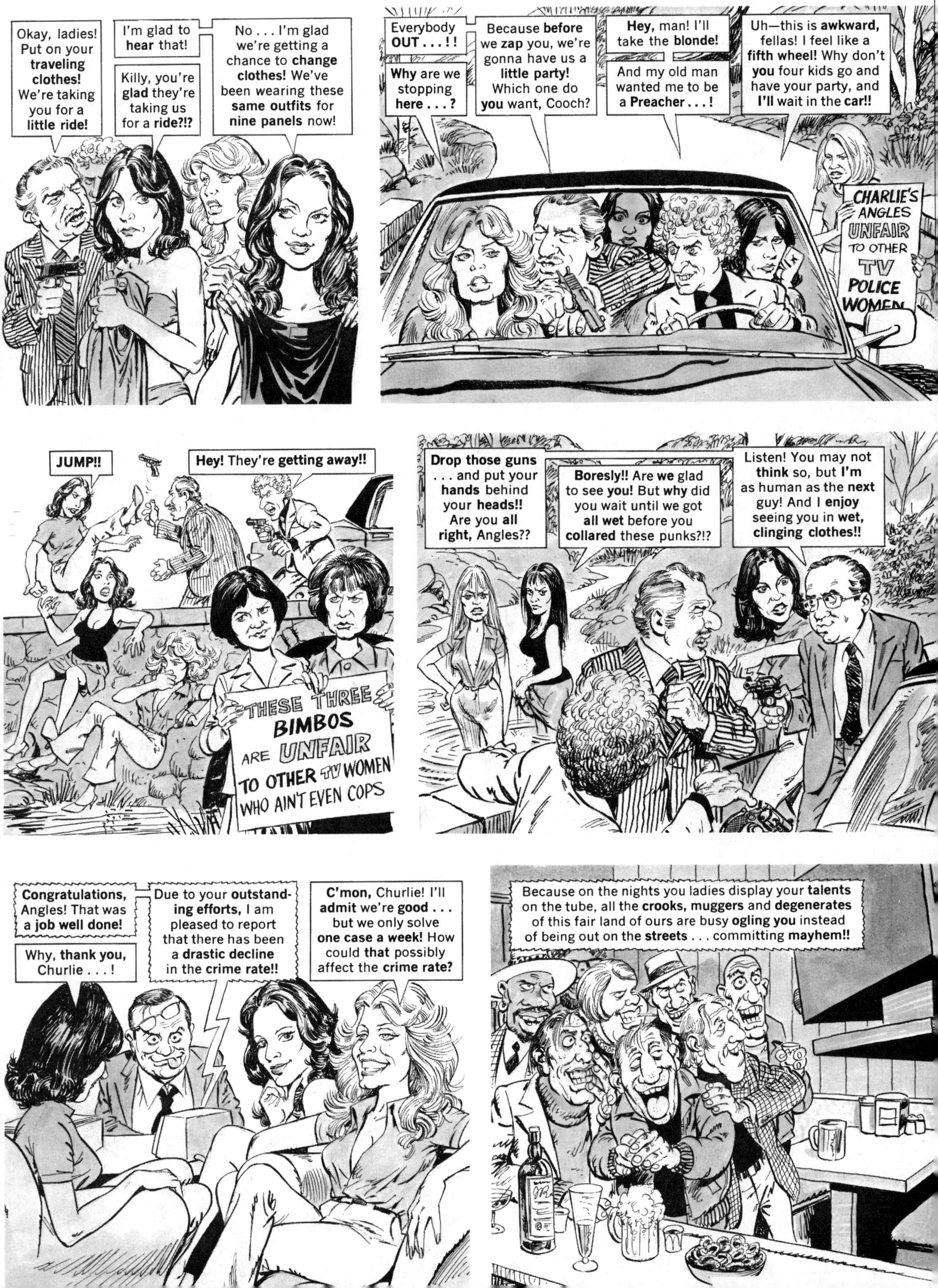
Okay, ladies! Put on your traveling clothes! We're taking you for a little ride!
I'm glad to hear that!
Killy, you're glad they're taking us for a ride?!?
No . . . I'm glad we're getting a chance to change clothes! We've been wearing these same outfits for nine panels now!
Everybody OUT . . . ! !
Why are we stopping here . . . ?
Because before we zap you, we're gonna have us a little party! Which one do you want, Cooch?
Hey, man! I'll take the blonde!
And my old man wanted me to be a Preacher . . . !
Uh—this is awkward, fellas! I feel like a fifth wheel! Why don't you four kids go and have your party, and I'll wait in the car!!
CHARLIE'S ANGLES UNFAIR TO OTHER TV POLICE WOMEN
JUMP!!
Hey! They're getting away!!
THESE THREE BIMBOS ARE UNFAIR TO OTHER TV WOMEN WHO AIN'T EVEN COPS
Drop those guns . . . and put your hands behind your heads!! Are you all right, Angles??
Boresly!! Are we glad to see you! But why did you wait until we got all wet before you collared these punks?!?
Listen! You may not think so, but I'm as human as the next guy! And I enjoy seeing you in wet, clinging clothes!!
Congratulations, Angles! That was a job well done!
Due to your outstanding efforts, I am pleased to report that there has been a drastic decline in the crime rate!!
Why, thank you, Churlie . . . !
C'mon, Churlie! I'll admit we're good . . . but we only solve one case a week! How could that possibly affect the crime rate?
Because on the nights you ladies display your talents on the tube, all the crooks, muggers and degenerates of this fair land of ours are busy ogling you instead of being out on the streets . . . committing mayhem!!

STATUS QUOTES DEPT.

WHEN YOU'RE POOR...

ARTIST: JACK D

WHEN YOU'RE POOR...

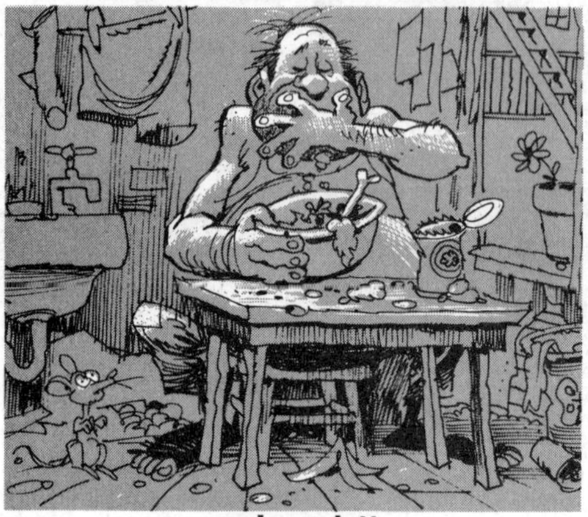

. . . you're a glutton.

WHEN YOU'RE RICH...

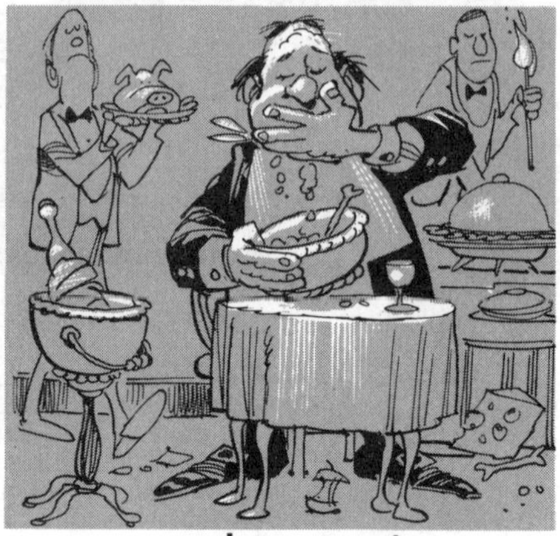

. . . you're a gourmet.

WHEN YOU'RE POOR.

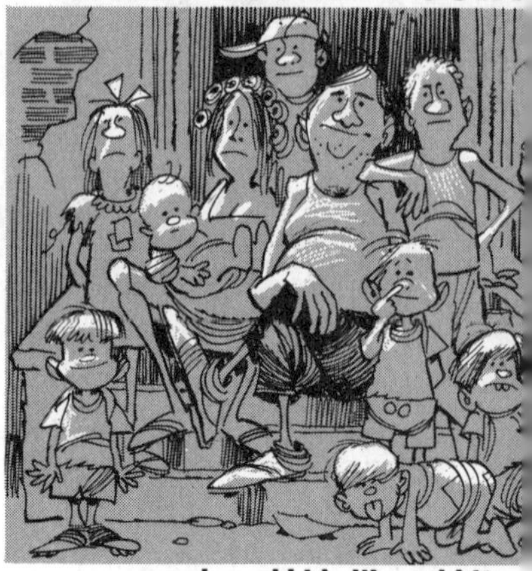

. . . you breed kids like rabbits.

WHEN YOU'RE POOR...

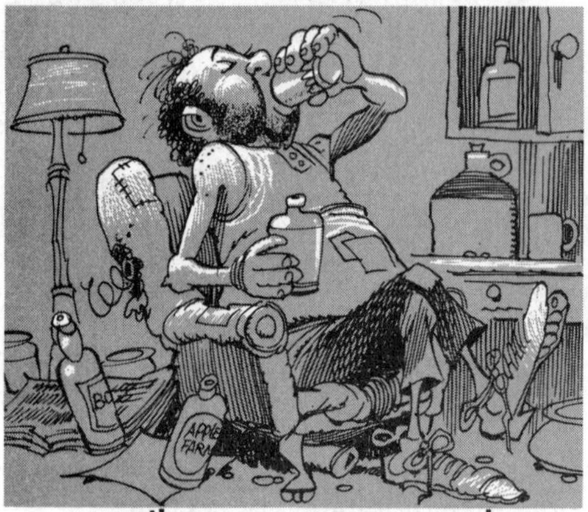

. . . you throw your money away on booze.

WHEN YOU'RE RICH...

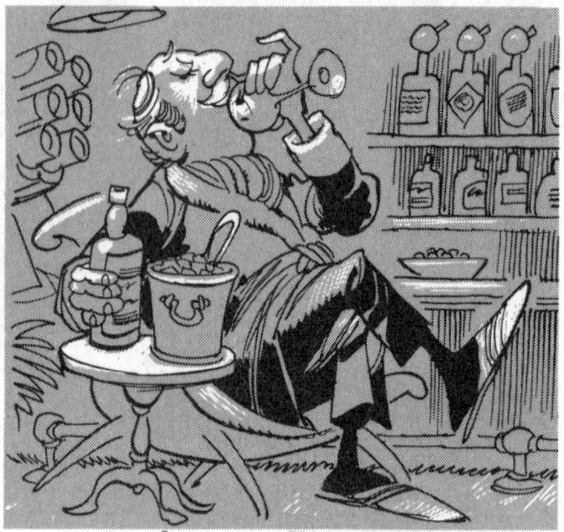

. . . you have a well-stocked bar.

WHEN YOU'RE POOR.

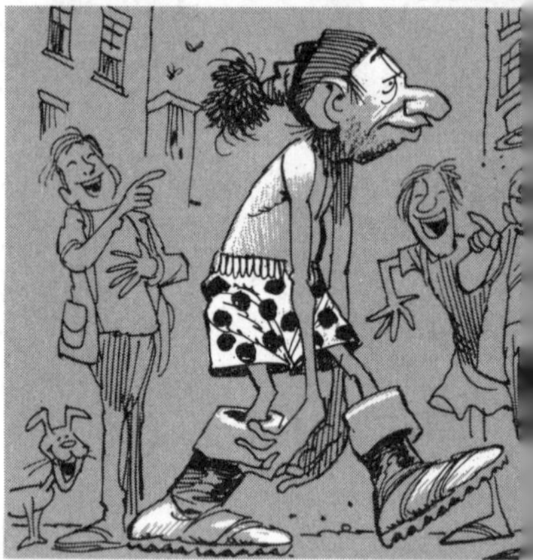

. . . you're the town weirdo.

WHEN YOU'RE POOR...

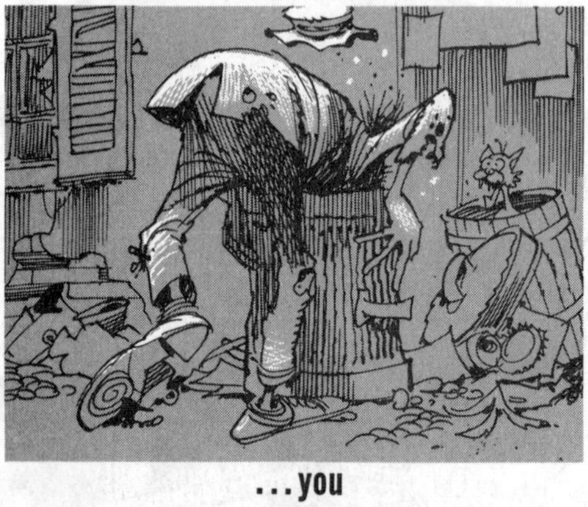

. . . you vomit.

WHEN YOU'RE RICH...

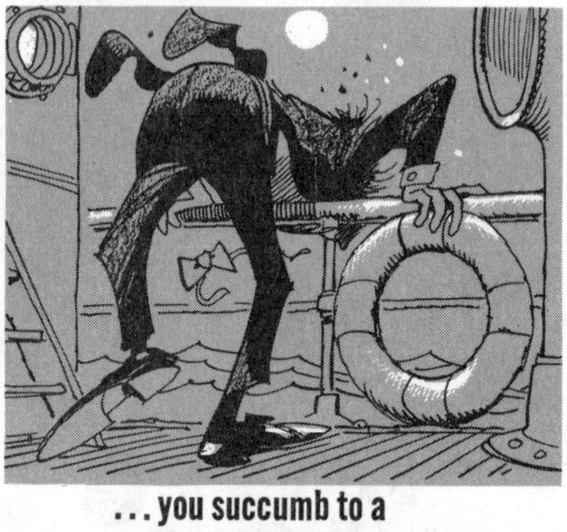

. . . you succumb to a sudden attack of nausea.

WHEN YOU'RE POOR.

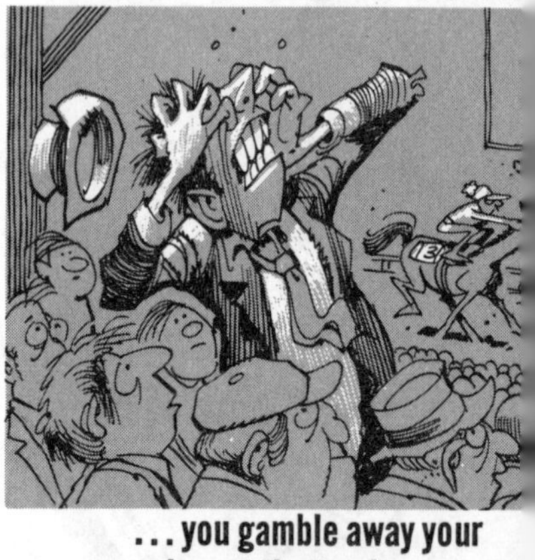

. . . you gamble away your salary at the track.

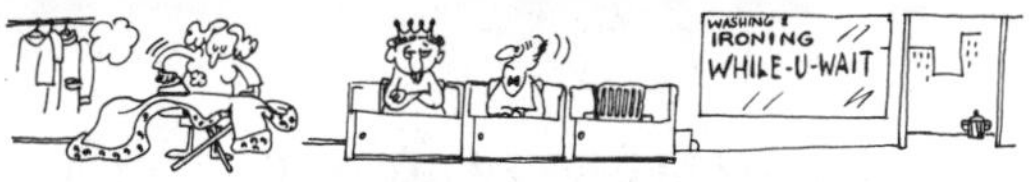
WASHING & IRONING
WHILE-U-WAIT

D...WHEN YOU'RE RICH

'ER: FRANK JACOBS

HEN YOU'RE RICH...

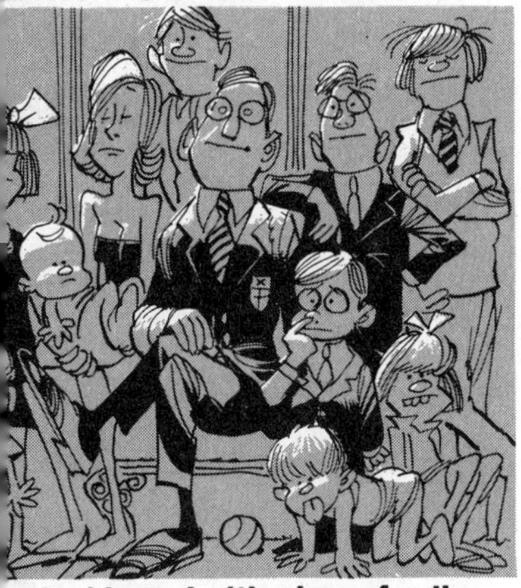

ou're blessed with a large family.

WHEN YOU'RE POOR...

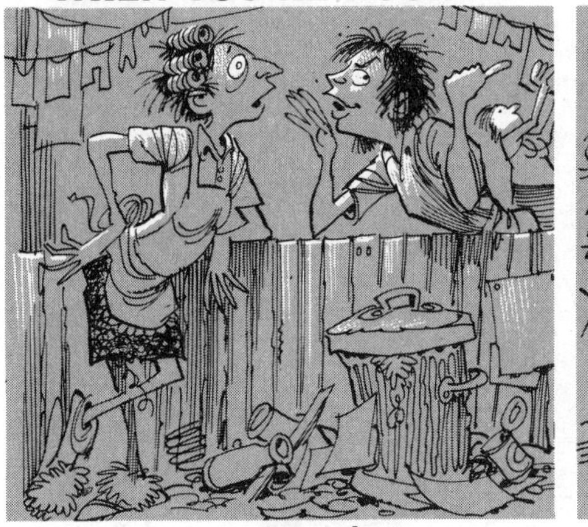

...you gossip.

WHEN YOU'RE RICH...

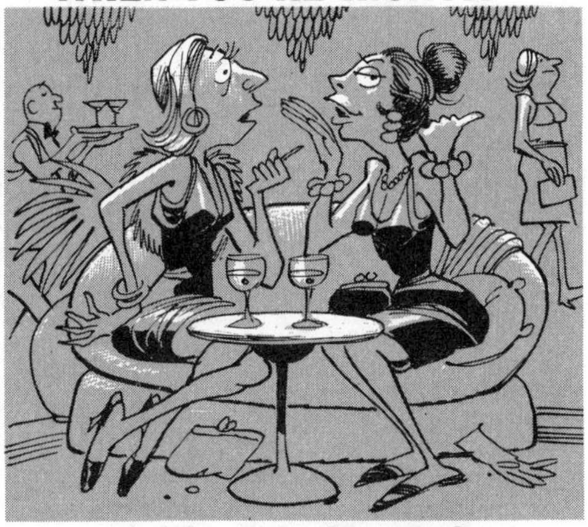

...you bring each other up to date.

HEN YOU'RE RICH...

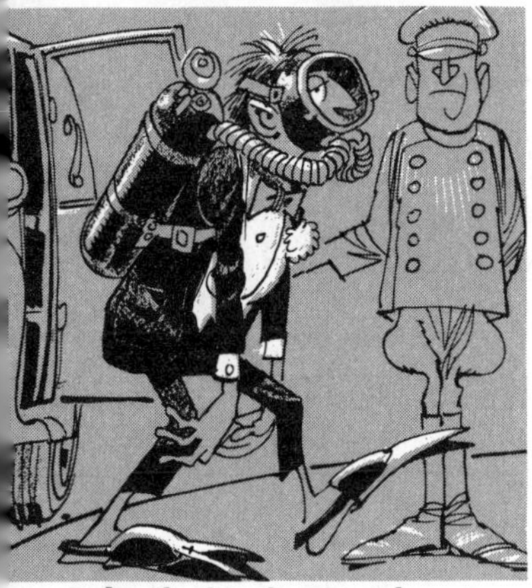

...you're the local eccentric.

WHEN YOU'RE POOR...

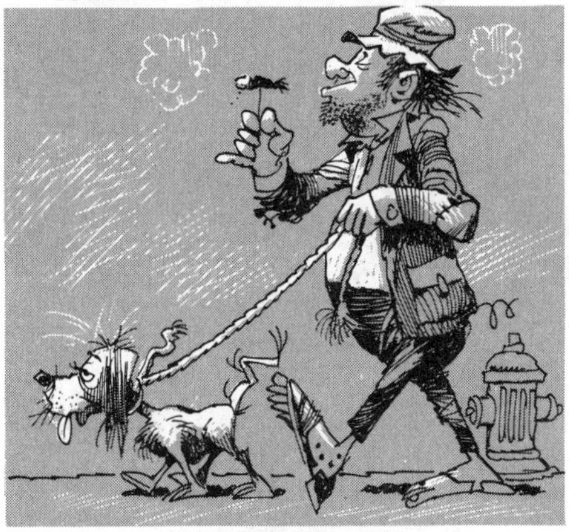

...you own a mutt.

WHEN YOU'RE RICH...

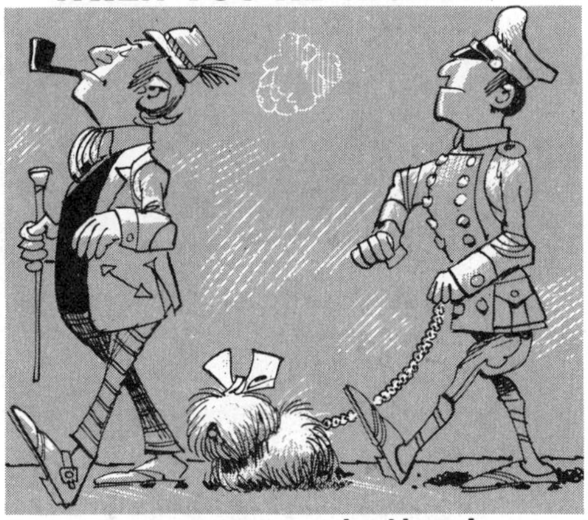

...you possess a mixed breed.

HEN YOU'RE RICH...

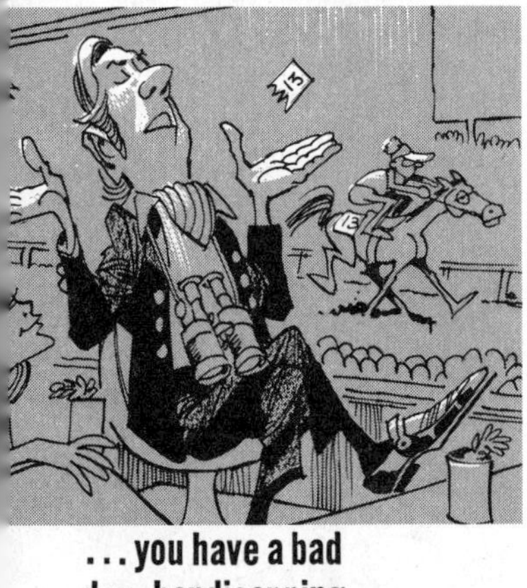

...you have a bad
day, handicapping.

WHEN YOU'RE POOR...

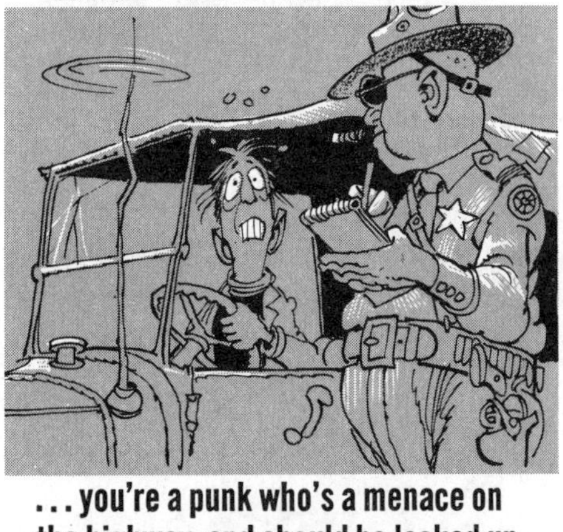

...you're a punk who's a menace on
the highway, and should be locked up.

WHEN YOU'RE RICH...

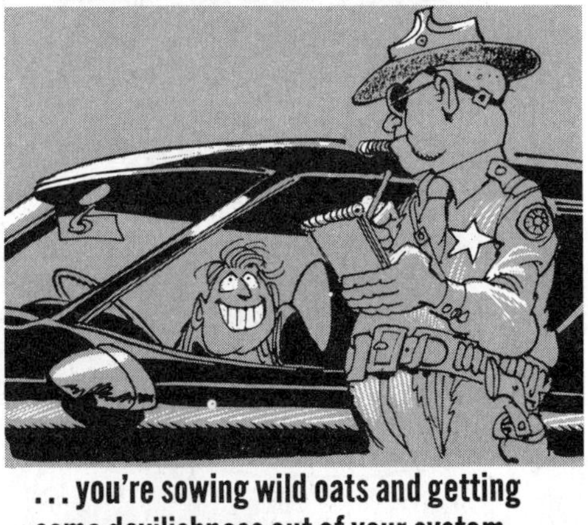

...you're sowing wild oats and getting
some devilishness out of your system.

IT'S STALLONE RANGER! DEPT.

For years, Hollywood made movies about the Fight Game that were loaded with clichés. Recently, however, instead of bringing back another one of those "Joe Palooka" pictures, they made a brand new type movie about the Fight Game . . . loaded with brand new clichés. You'll see what we mean in this version of

ROC

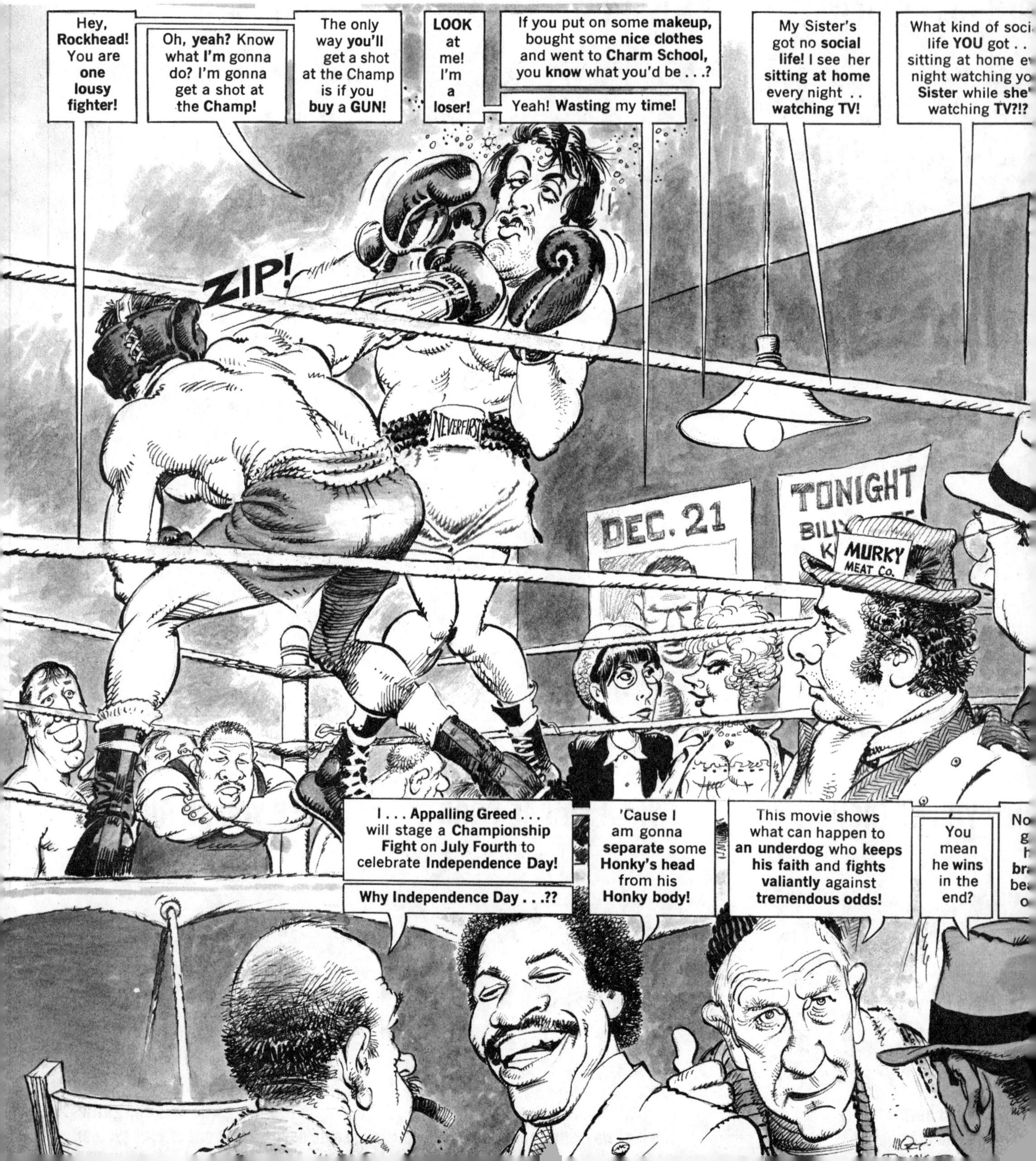

Hey, Rockhead! You are one lousy fighter!
Oh, yeah? Know what I'm gonna do? I'm gonna get a shot at the Champ!
The only way you'll get a shot at the Champ is if you buy a GUN!
LOOK at me! I'm a loser!
If you put on some makeup, bought some nice clothes and went to Charm School, you know what you'd be . . .?
Yeah! Wasting my time!
My Sister's got no social life! I see her sitting at home every night . . watching TV!
What kind of soci life YOU got . . sitting at home e night watching yo Sister while she' watching TV?!?
ZIP!
NEVERFIRST
DEC. 21
TONIGHT
MURKY MEAT Co.
I . . . Appalling Greed . . . will stage a Championship Fight on July Fourth to celebrate Independence Day!
Why Independence Day . . .??
'Cause I am gonna separate some Honky's head from his Honky body!
This movie shows what can happen to an underdog who keeps his faith and fights valiantly against tremendous odds!
You mean he wins in the end?

KHEAD

ARTIST:
MORT DRUCKER

WRITER:
STAN HART

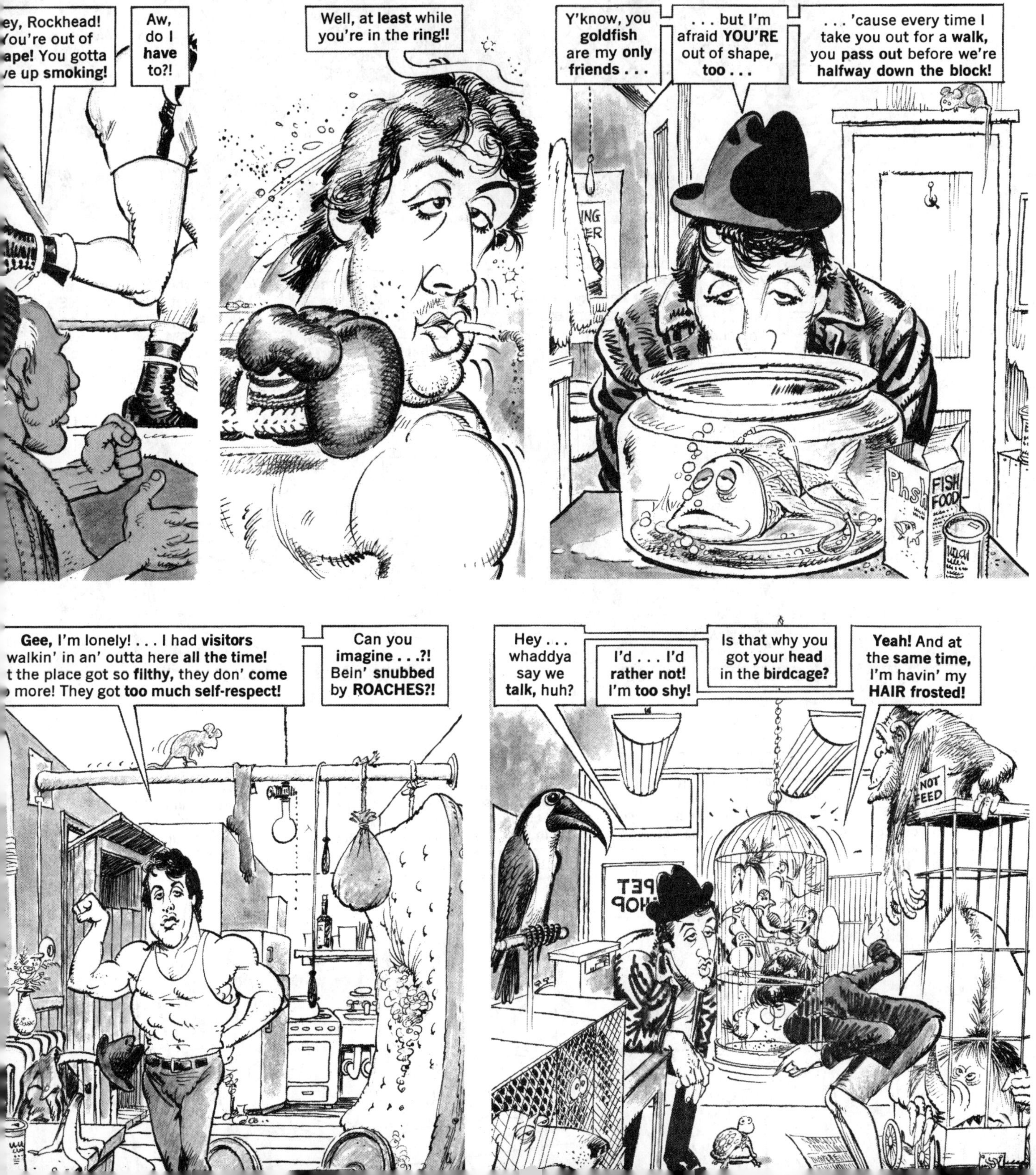

ey, Rockhead! You're out of ape! You gotta ve up smoking!
Aw, do I have to?!
Well, at least while you're in the ring!!
Y'know, you goldfish are my only friends . . .
. . . but I'm afraid YOU'RE out of shape, too . . .
. . . 'cause every time I take you out for a walk, you pass out before we're halfway down the block!
FISH FOOD
Gee, I'm lonely! . . . I had visitors walkin' in an' outta here all the time! t the place got so filthy, they don' come more! They got too much self-respect!
Can you imagine . . .?! Bein' snubbed by ROACHES?!
Hey . . . whaddya say we talk, huh?
I'd . . . I'd rather not! I'm too shy!
Is that why you got your head in the birdcage?
Yeah! And at the same time, I'm havin' my HAIR frosted!
PET SHOP
NOT FEED

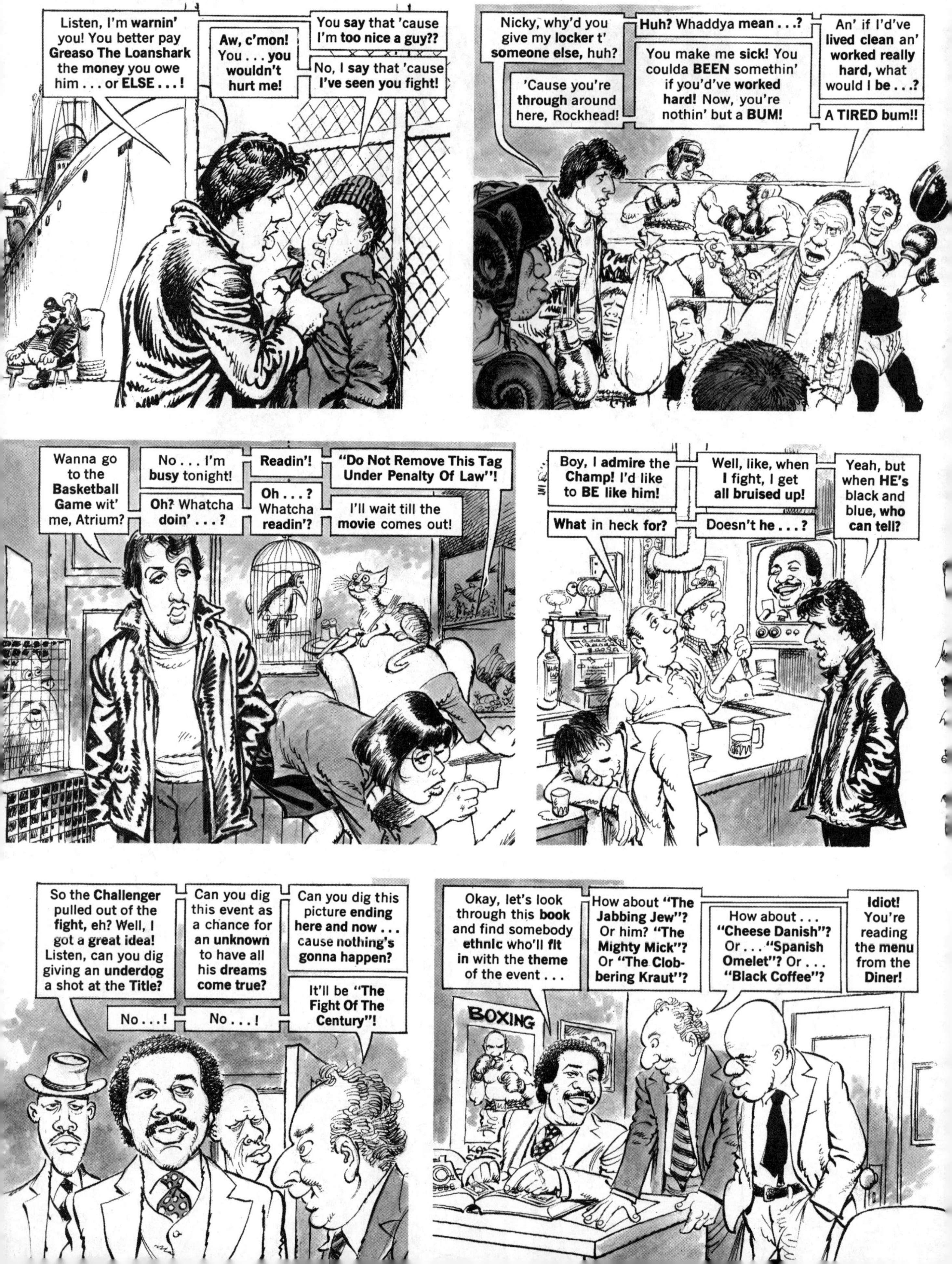
Listen, I'm warnin' you! You better pay Greaso The Loanshark the money you owe him . . . or ELSE . . . !
Aw, c'mon! You . . . you wouldn't hurt me!
You say that 'cause I'm too nice a guy??
No, I say that 'cause I've seen you fight!
Nicky, why'd you give my locker t' someone else, huh?
'Cause you're through around here, Rockhead!
Huh? Whaddya mean . . .?
You make me sick! You coulda BEEN somethin' if you'd've worked hard! Now, you're nothin' but a BUM!
An' if I'd've lived clean an' worked really hard, what would I be . . .?
A TIRED bum!!
Wanna go to the Basketball Game wit' me, Atrium?
No . . . I'm busy tonight!
Oh? Whatcha doin' . . . ?
Readin'!
Oh . . . ? Whatcha readin'?
"Do Not Remove This Tag Under Penalty Of Law"!
I'll wait till the movie comes out!
Boy, I admire the Champ! I'd like to BE like him!
What in heck for?
Well, like, when I fight, I get all bruised up!
Doesn't he . . . ?
Yeah, but when HE's black and blue, who can tell?
So the Challenger pulled out of the fight, eh? Well, I got a great idea! Listen, can you dig giving an underdog a shot at the Title?
No . . . !
Can you dig this event as a chance for an unknown to have all his dreams come true?
No . . . !
Can you dig this picture ending here and now . . . cause nothing's gonna happen?
It'll be "The Fight Of The Century"!
Okay, let's look through this book and find somebody ethnic who'll fit in with the theme of the event . . .
BOXING
How about "The Jabbing Jew"? Or him? "The Mighty Mick"? Or "The Clob-bering Kraut"?
How about . . . "Cheese Danish"? Or . . . "Spanish Omelet"? Or . . . "Black Coffee"?
Idiot! You're reading the menu from the Diner!

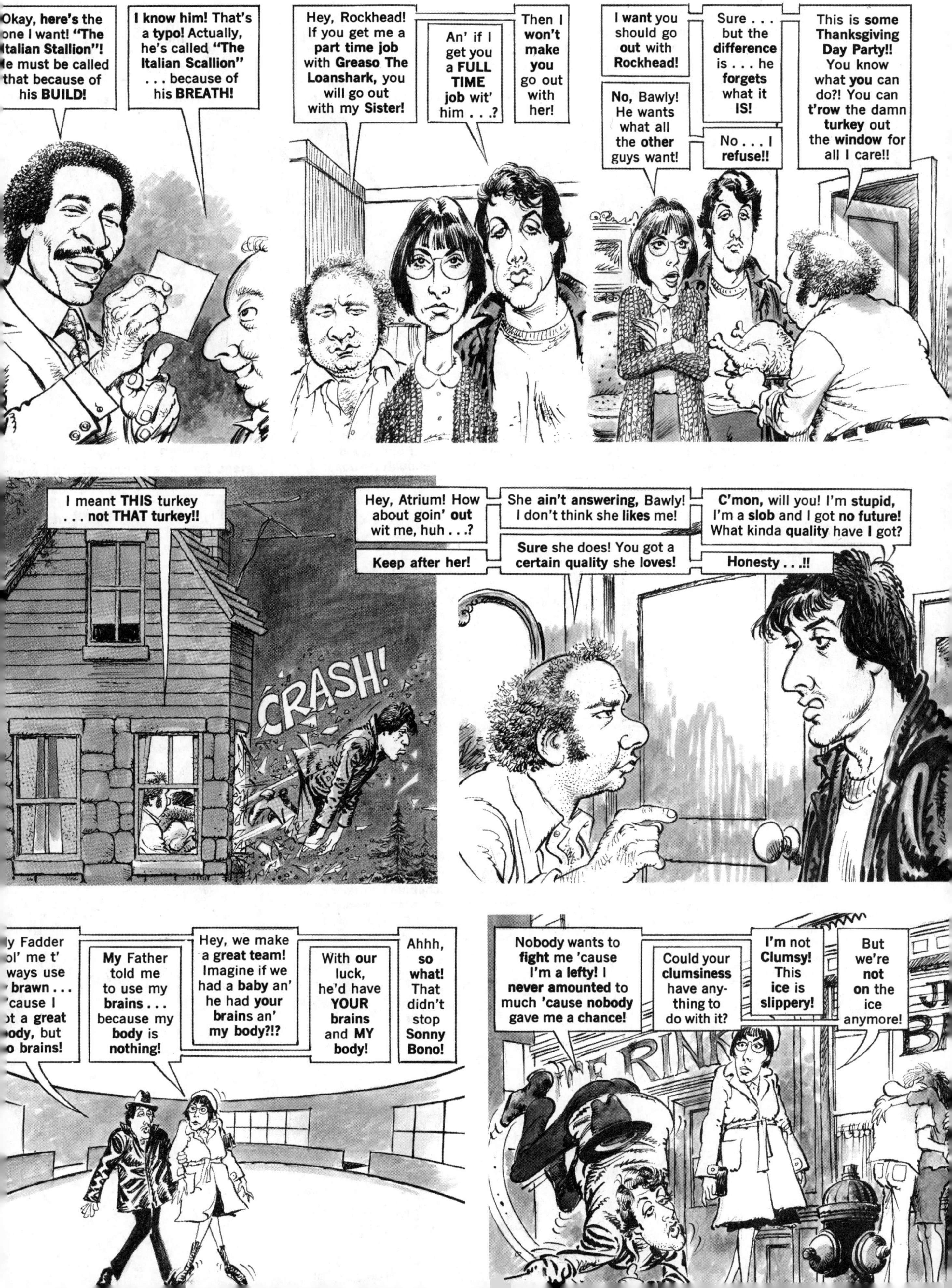
Okay, here's the one I want! "The talian Stallion"! e must be called that because of his BUILD!
I know him! That's a typo! Actually, he's called "The Italian Scallion" . . . because of his BREATH!
Hey, Rockhead! If you get me a part time job with Greaso The Loanshark, you will go out with my Sister!
An' if I get you a FULL TIME job wit' him . . .?
Then I won't make you go out with her!
I want you should go out with Rockhead!
No, Bawly! He wants what all the other guys want!
Sure . . . but the difference is . . . he forgets what it IS!
No . . . I refuse!!
This is some Thanksgiving Day Party!! You know what you can do?! You can t'row the damn turkey out the window for all I care!!
I meant THIS turkey . . . not THAT turkey!!
CRASH!
Hey, Atrium! How about goin' out wit me, huh . . .?
Keep after her!
She ain't answering, Bawly! I don't think she likes me!
Sure she does! You got a certain quality she loves!
C'mon, will you! I'm stupid, I'm a slob and I got no future! What kinda quality have I got?
Honesty . . .!!
y Fadder ol' me t' ways use brawn . . . 'cause I ot a great ody, but o brains!
My Father told me to use my brains . . . because my body is nothing!
Hey, we make a great team! Imagine if we had a baby an' he had your brains an' my body?!?
With our luck, he'd have YOUR brains and MY body!
Ahhh, so what! That didn't stop Sonny Bono!
Nobody wants to fight me 'cause I'm a lefty! I never amounted to much 'cause nobody gave me a chance!
Could your clumsiness have any-thing to do with it?
I'm not Clumsy! This ice is slippery!
But we're not on the ice anymore!

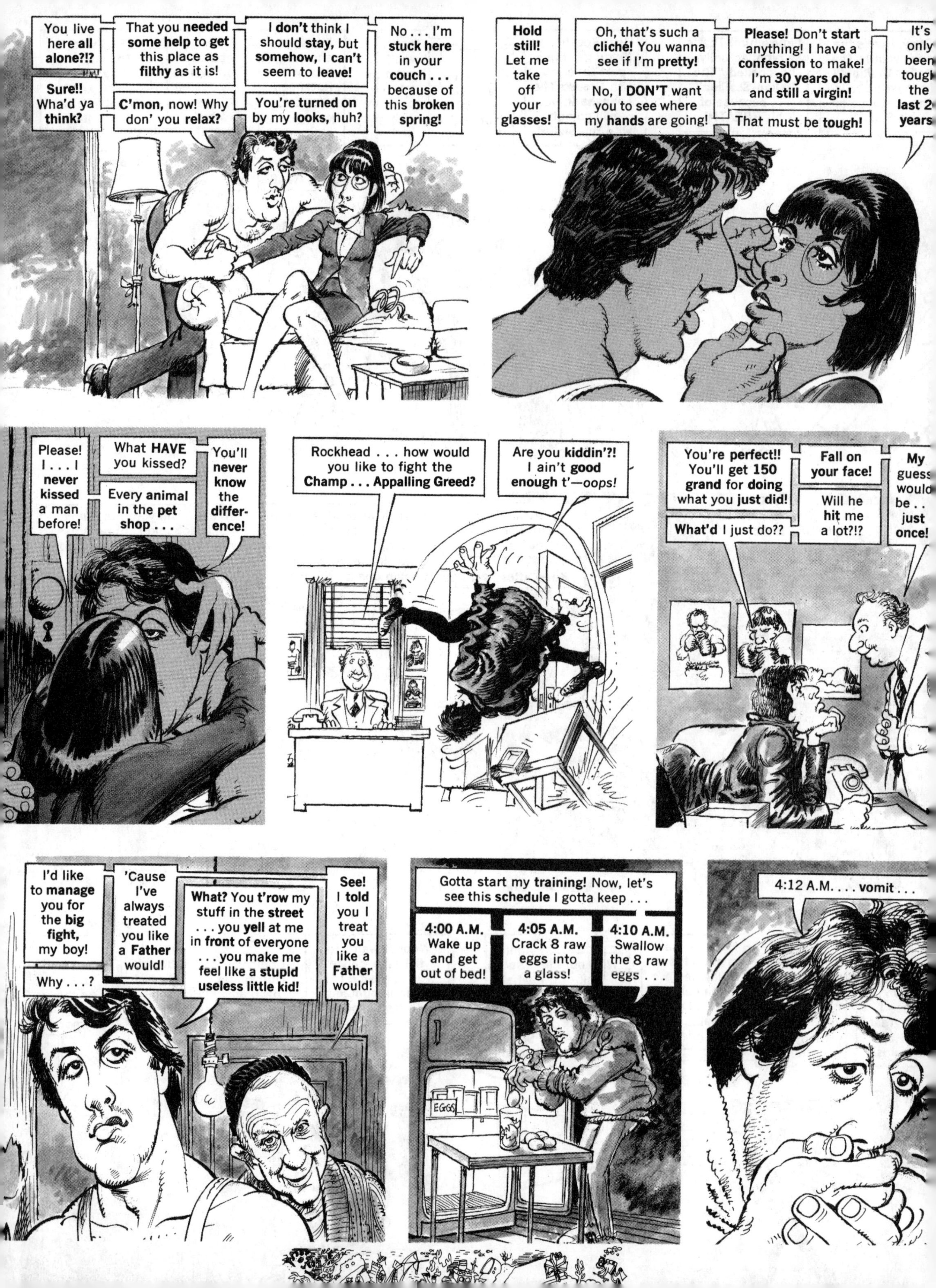

You live here all alone?!?
Sure!! Wha'd ya think?
That you needed some help to get this place as filthy as it is!
C'mon, now! Why don' you relax?
I don't think I should stay, but somehow, I can't seem to leave!
You're turned on by my looks, huh?
No . . . I'm stuck here in your couch . . . because of this broken spring!
Hold still! Let me take off your glasses!
Oh, that's such a cliché! You wanna see if I'm pretty!
No, I DON'T want you to see where my hands are going!
Please! Don't start anything! I have a confession to make! I'm 30 years old and still a virgin!
That must be tough!
It's only been toug the last 2 years
Please! I . . . I never kissed a man before!
What HAVE you kissed?
Every animal in the pet shop . . .
You'll never know the differ-ence!
Rockhead . . . how would you like to fight the Champ . . . Appalling Greed?
Are you kiddin'?! I ain't good enough t'—oops!
You're perfect!! You'll get 150 grand for doing what you just did!
What'd I just do??
Fall on your face!
Will he hit me a lot?!?
My gues woul be . . just once!
I'd like to manage you for the big fight, my boy!
Why . . . ?
'Cause I've always treated you like a Father would!
What? You t'row my stuff in the street . . . you yell at me in front of everyone . . . you make me feel like a stupid useless little kid!
See! I told you I treat you like a Father would!
Gotta start my training! Now, let's see this schedule I gotta keep . . .
4:00 A.M. Wake up and get out of bed!
4:05 A.M. Crack 8 raw eggs into a glass!
4:10 A.M. Swallow the 8 raw eggs . . .
EGGS
4:12 A.M. . . . vomit . . .

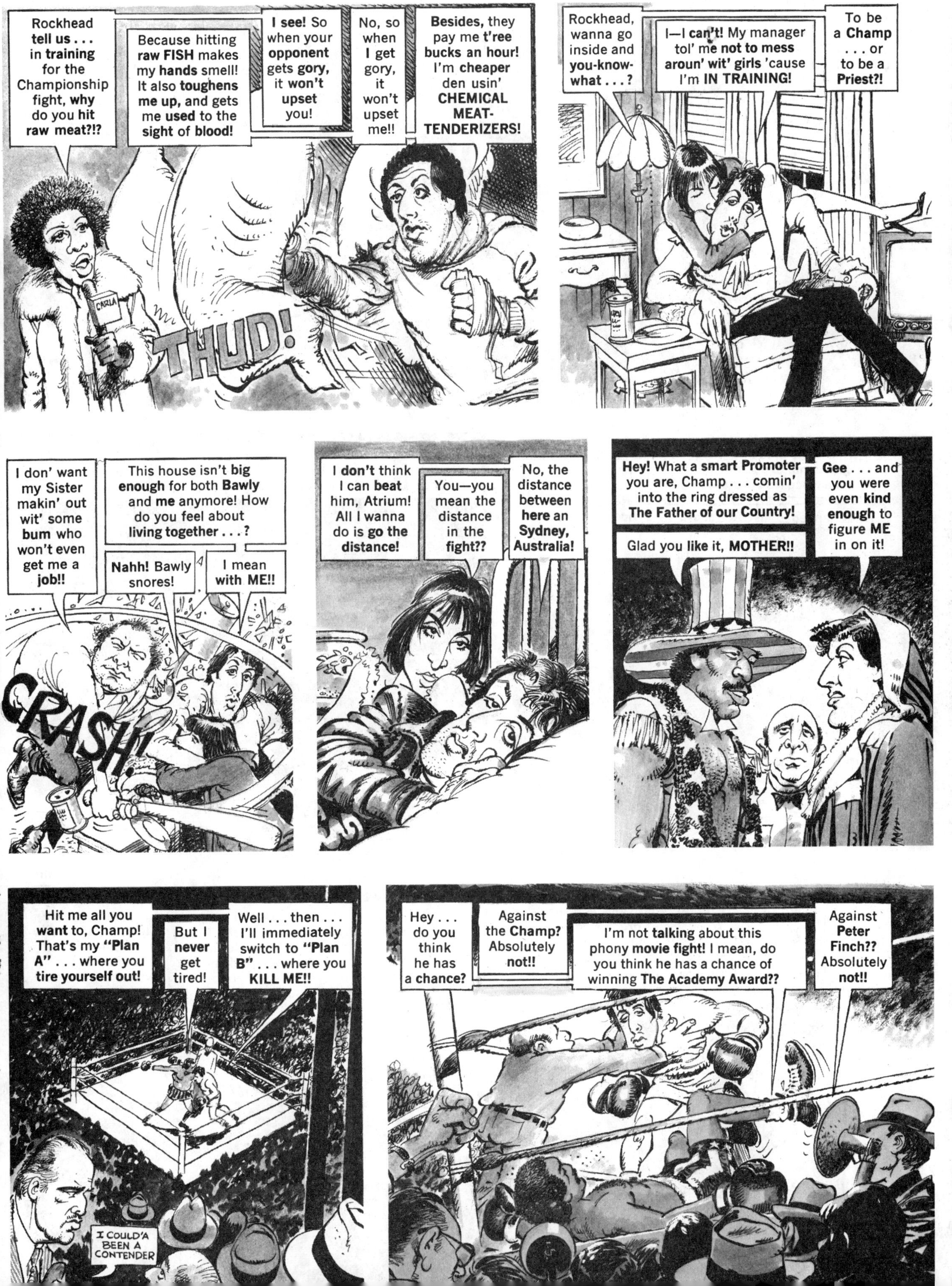

Rockhead tell us . . . in training for the Championship fight, why do you hit raw meat?!?
Because hitting raw FISH makes my hands smell! It also toughens me up, and gets me used to the sight of blood!
I see! So when your opponent gets gory, it won't upset you!
No, so when I get gory, it won't upset me!!
Besides, they pay me t'ree bucks an hour! I'm cheaper den usin' CHEMICAL MEAT-TENDERIZERS!
CARLA
THUD!
Rockhead, wanna go inside and you-know-what . . . ?
I—I can't! My manager tol' me not to mess aroun' wit' girls 'cause I'm IN TRAINING!
To be a Champ . . . or to be a Priest?!
I don' want my Sister makin' out wit' some bum who won't even get me a job!!
This house isn't big enough for both Bawly and me anymore! How do you feel about living together . . . ?
Nahh! Bawly snores!
I mean with ME!!
CRASH!
I don't think I can beat him, Atrium! All I wanna do is go the distance!
You—you mean the distance in the fight??
No, the distance between here an Sydney, Australia!
Hey! What a smart Promoter you are, Champ . . . comin' into the ring dressed as The Father of our Country!
Glad you like it, MOTHER!!
Gee . . . and you were even kind enough to figure ME in on it!
Hit me all you want to, Champ! That's my "Plan A" . . . where you tire yourself out!
But I never get tired!
Well . . . then . . . I'll immediately switch to "Plan B" . . . where you KILL ME!!
I COULD'A BEEN A CONTENDER
Hey . . . do you think he has a chance?
Against the Champ? Absolutely not!!
I'm not talking about this phony movie fight! I mean, do you think he has a chance of winning The Academy Award??
Against Peter Finch?? Absolutely not!!

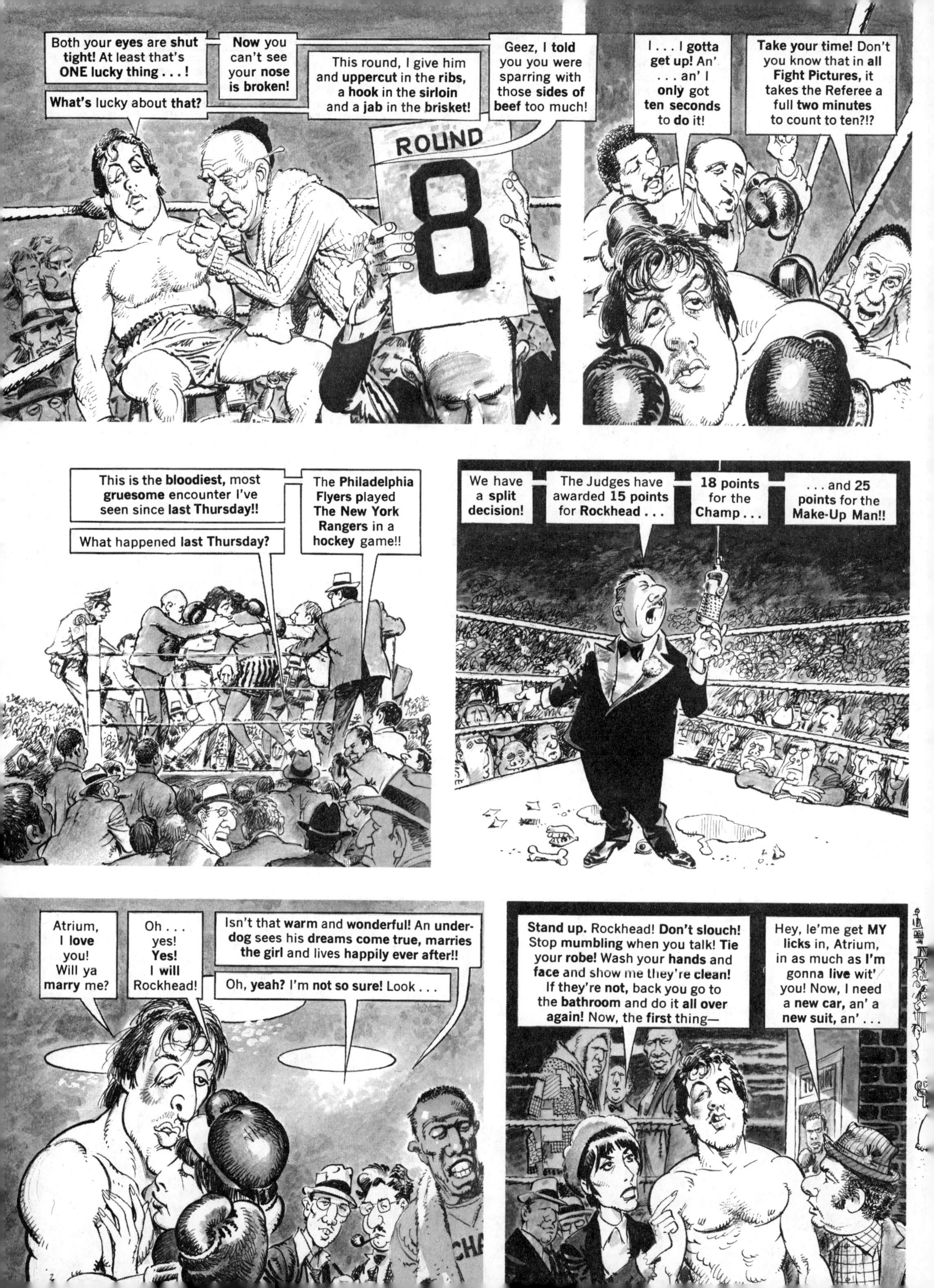
Both your eyes are shut tight! At least that's ONE lucky thing . . . !
What's lucky about that?
Now you can't see your nose is broken!
This round, I give him and uppercut in the ribs, a hook in the sirloin and a jab in the brisket!
Geez, I told you you were sparring with those sides of beef too much!
ROUND
8
I . . . I gotta get up! An' . . . an' I only got ten seconds to do it!
Take your time! Don't you know that in all Fight Pictures, it takes the Referee a full two minutes to count to ten?!?
This is the bloodiest, most gruesome encounter I've seen since last Thursday!!
What happened last Thursday?
The Philadelphia Flyers played The New York Rangers in a hockey game!!
We have a split decision!
The Judges have awarded 15 points for Rockhead . . .
18 points for the Champ . . .
. . . and 25 points for the Make-Up Man!!
Atrium, I love you! Will ya marry me?
Oh . . . yes! Yes! I will Rockhead!
Isn't that warm and wonderful! An underdog sees his dreams come true, marries the girl and lives happily ever after!!
Oh, yeah? I'm not so sure! Look . . .
Stand up. Rockhead! Don't slouch! Stop mumbling when you talk! Tie your robe! Wash your hands and face and show me they're clean! If they're not, back you go to the bathroom and do it all over again! Now, the first thing—
Hey, le'me get MY licks in, Atrium, in as much as I'm gonna live wit' you! Now, I need a new car, an' a new suit, an' . . .

JOKE AND DAGGER DEPT.

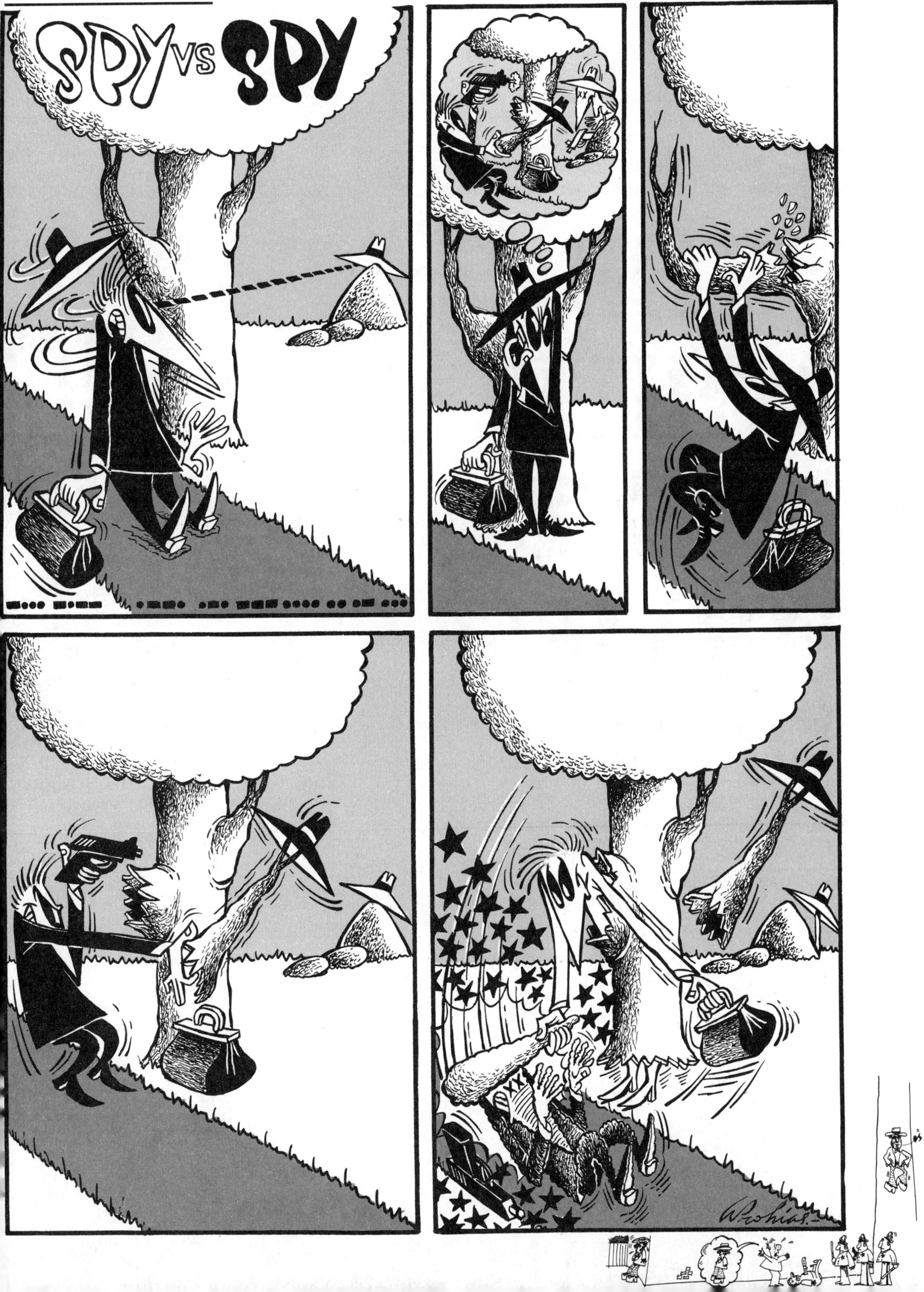
SPY VS SPY
Prohias

BIG TIME OPERETTA DEPT.

A while back, when Richard Nixon was President, we ran a Musical called "The White House Follies of 1972." Shortly thereafter, Spiro Agnew was dumped, 'Watergate' became a household word, and Mr. Nixon resigned. Small wonder that we've been swamped with letters from Washington begging us not to do a Musical about Jimmy Carter. But MAD prides itself on being non-partisan. So here's

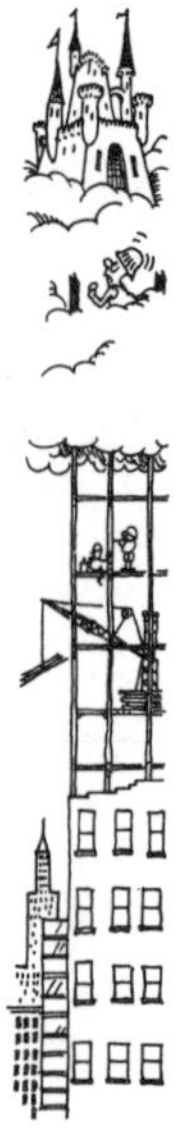

THE WHITE HOUSE FOLLIES OF 1977

ARTIST: MORT DRUCKER WRITER: FRANK JACOBS

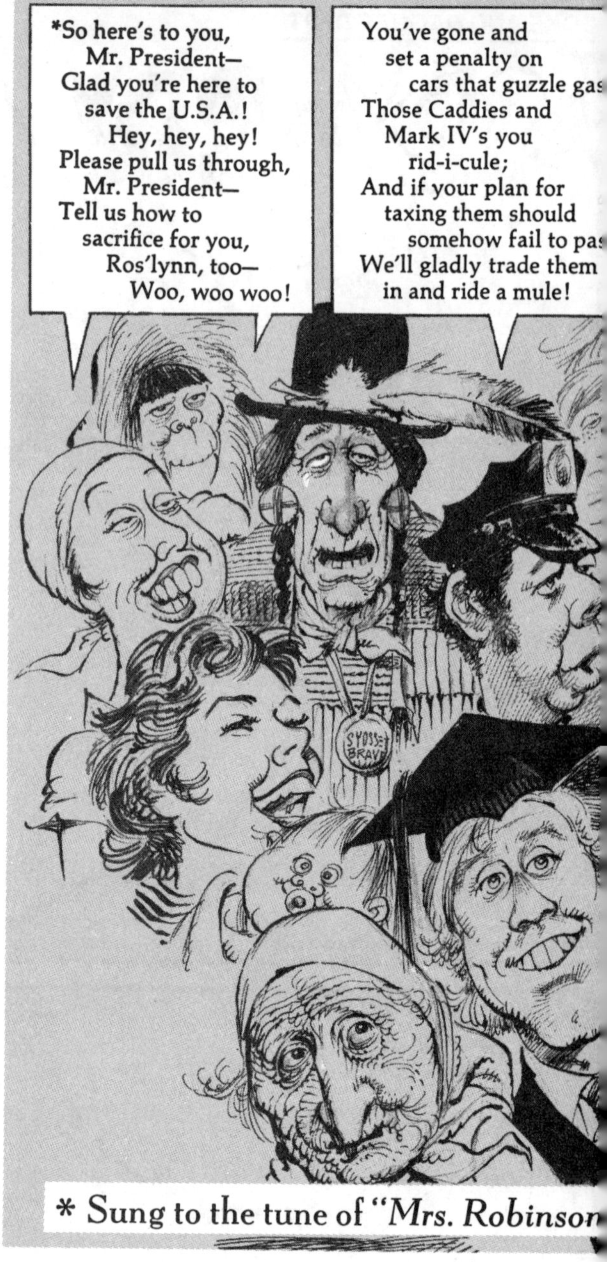
*So here's to you, Mr. President— Glad you're here to save the U.S.A.! Hey, hey, hey! Please pull us through, Mr. President— Tell us how to sacrifice for you, Ros'lynn, too— Woo, woo woo!
You've gone and set a penalty on cars that guzzle gas Those Caddies and Mark IV's you rid-i-cule; And if your plan for taxing them should somehow fail to pas We'll gladly trade them in and ride a mule!
SYOSSET BRAVE
* Sung to the tune of "*Mrs. Robinson*

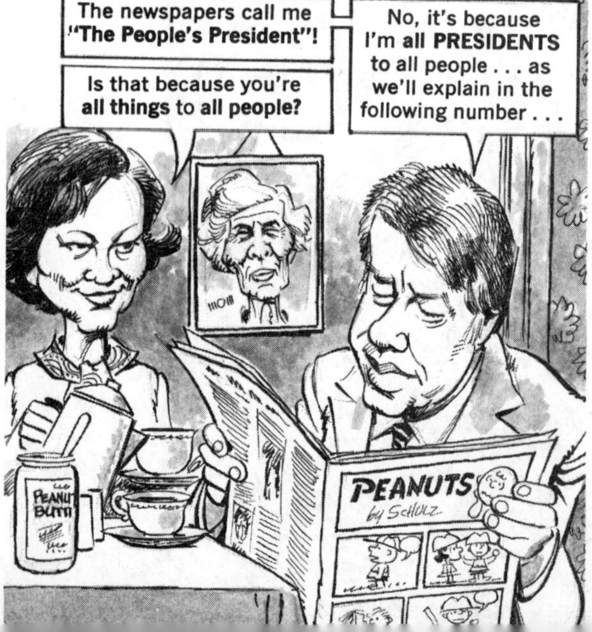
The newspapers call me "**The People's President**"!
Is that because you're **all things** to all people?
No, it's because I'm **all PRESIDENTS** to all people . . . as we'll explain in the following number . . .
PEANUTS by SCHULZ

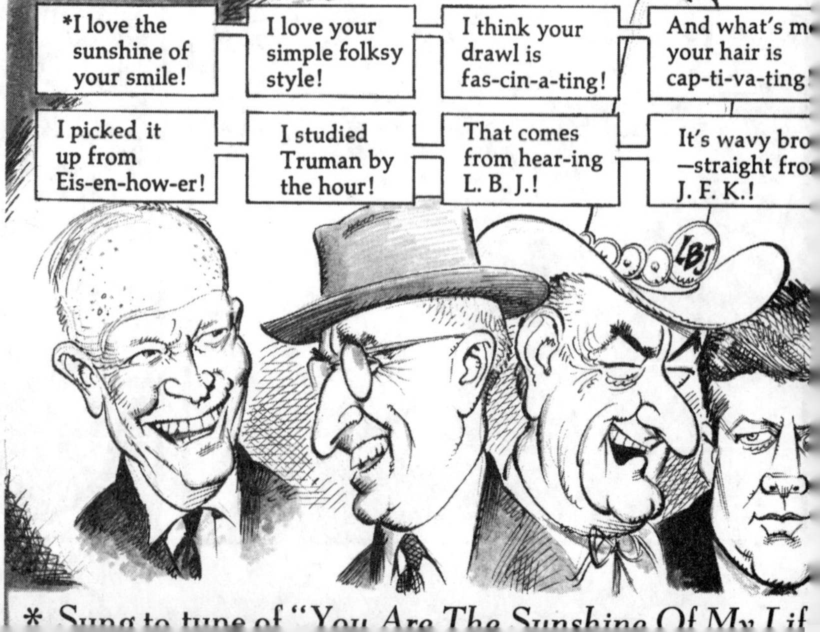
*I love the sunshine of your smile!
I love your simple folksy style!
I think your drawl is fas-cin-a-ting!
And what's m your hair is cap-ti-va-ting
I picked it up from Eis-en-how-er!
I studied Truman by the hour!
That comes from hear-ing L. B. J.!
It's wavy bro —straight fro J. F. K.!
LBJ
* Sung to tune of "You Are The Sunshine Of My Lif

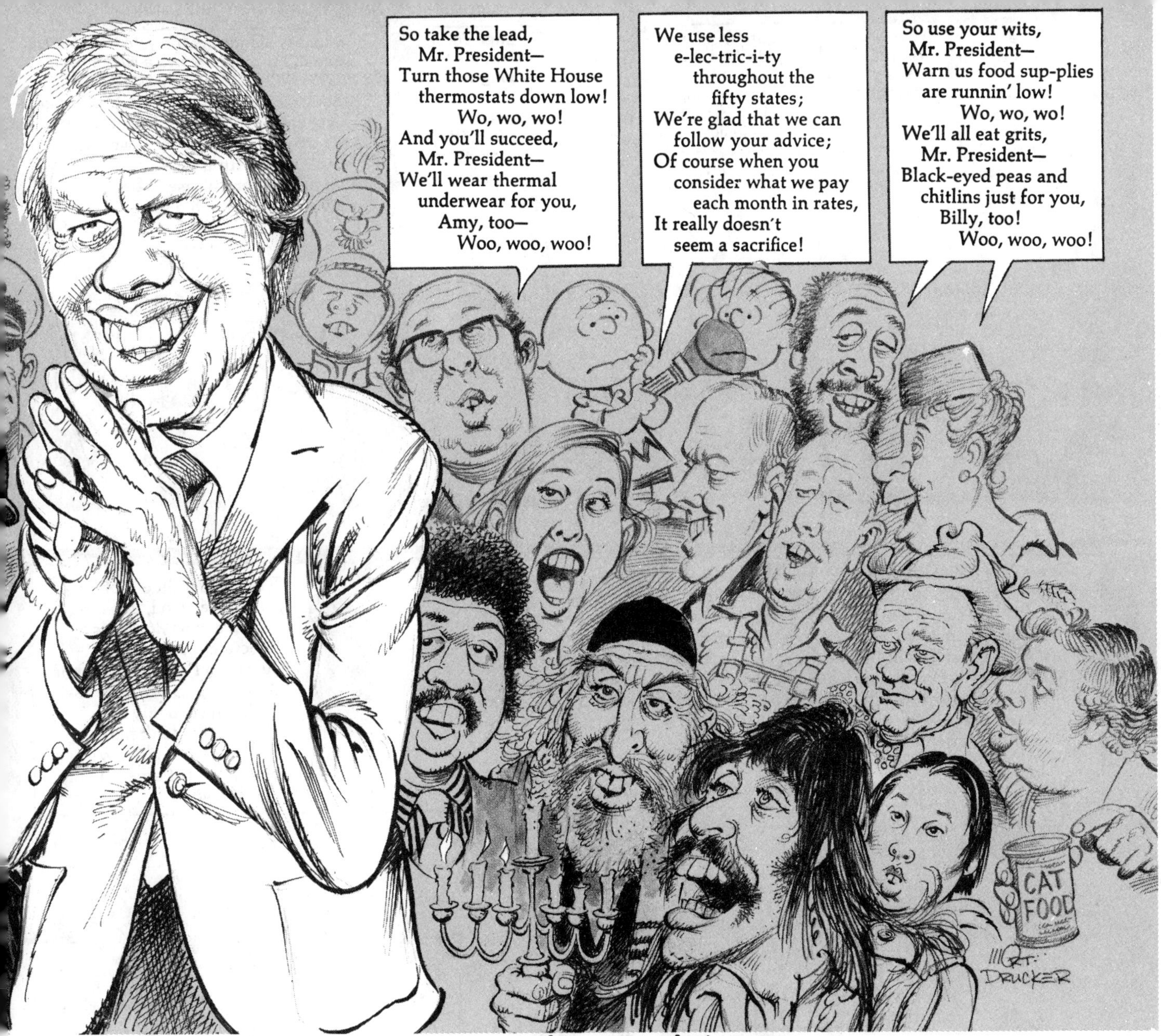

So take the lead, Mr. President— Turn those White House thermostats down low! Wo, wo, wo! And you'll succeed, Mr. President— We'll wear thermal underwear for you, Amy, too— Woo, woo, woo!
We use less e-lec-tric-i-ty throughout the fifty states; We're glad that we can follow your advice; Of course when you consider what we pay each month in rates, It really doesn't seem a sacrifice!
So use your wits, Mr. President— Warn us food sup-plies are runnin' low! Wo, wo, wo! We'll all eat grits, Mr. President— Black-eyed peas and chitlins just for you, Billy, too! Woo, woo, woo!
CAT FOOD
ART DRUCKER

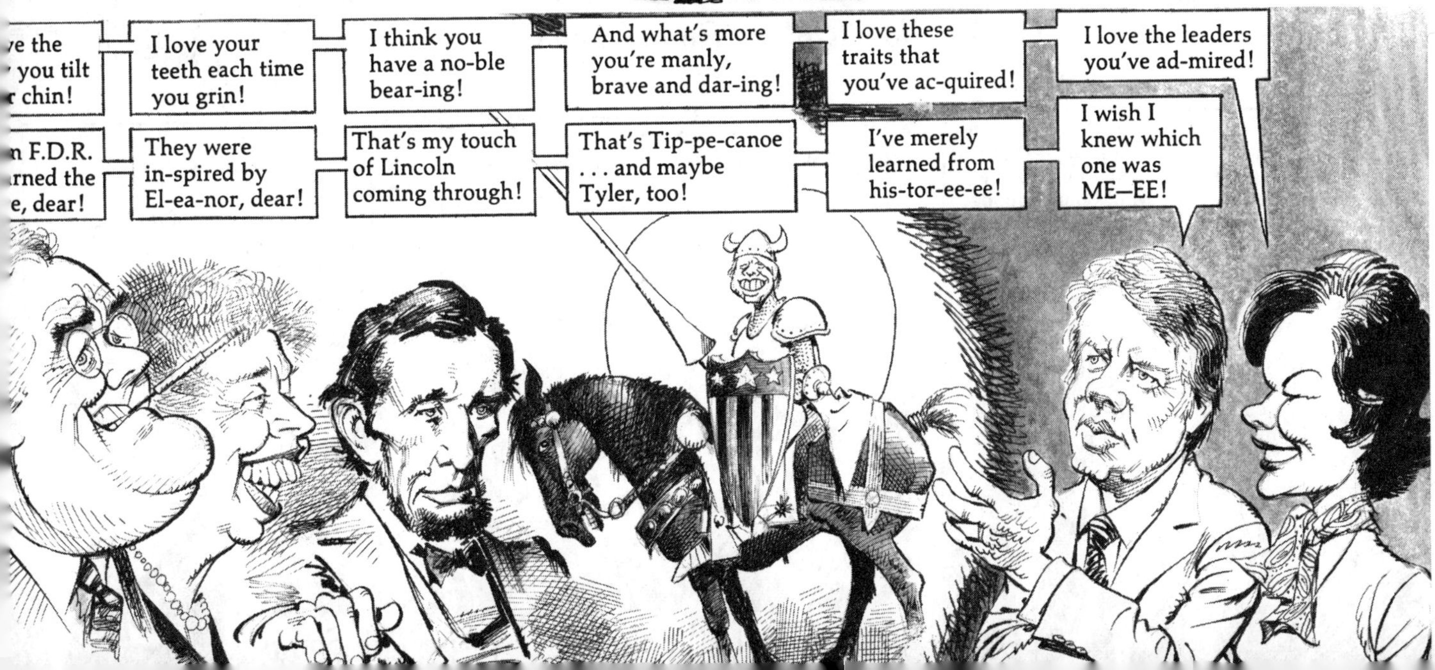

ve the you tilt r chin!
n F.D.R. rned the e, dear!
I love your teeth each time you grin!
They were in-spired by El-ea-nor, dear!
I think you have a no-ble bear-ing!
That's my touch of Lincoln coming through!
And what's more you're manly, brave and dar-ing!
That's Tip-pe-canoe . . . and maybe Tyler, too!
I love these traits that you've ac-quired!
I've merely learned from his-tor-ee-ee!
I love the leaders you've ad-mired!
I wish I knew which one was ME—EE!

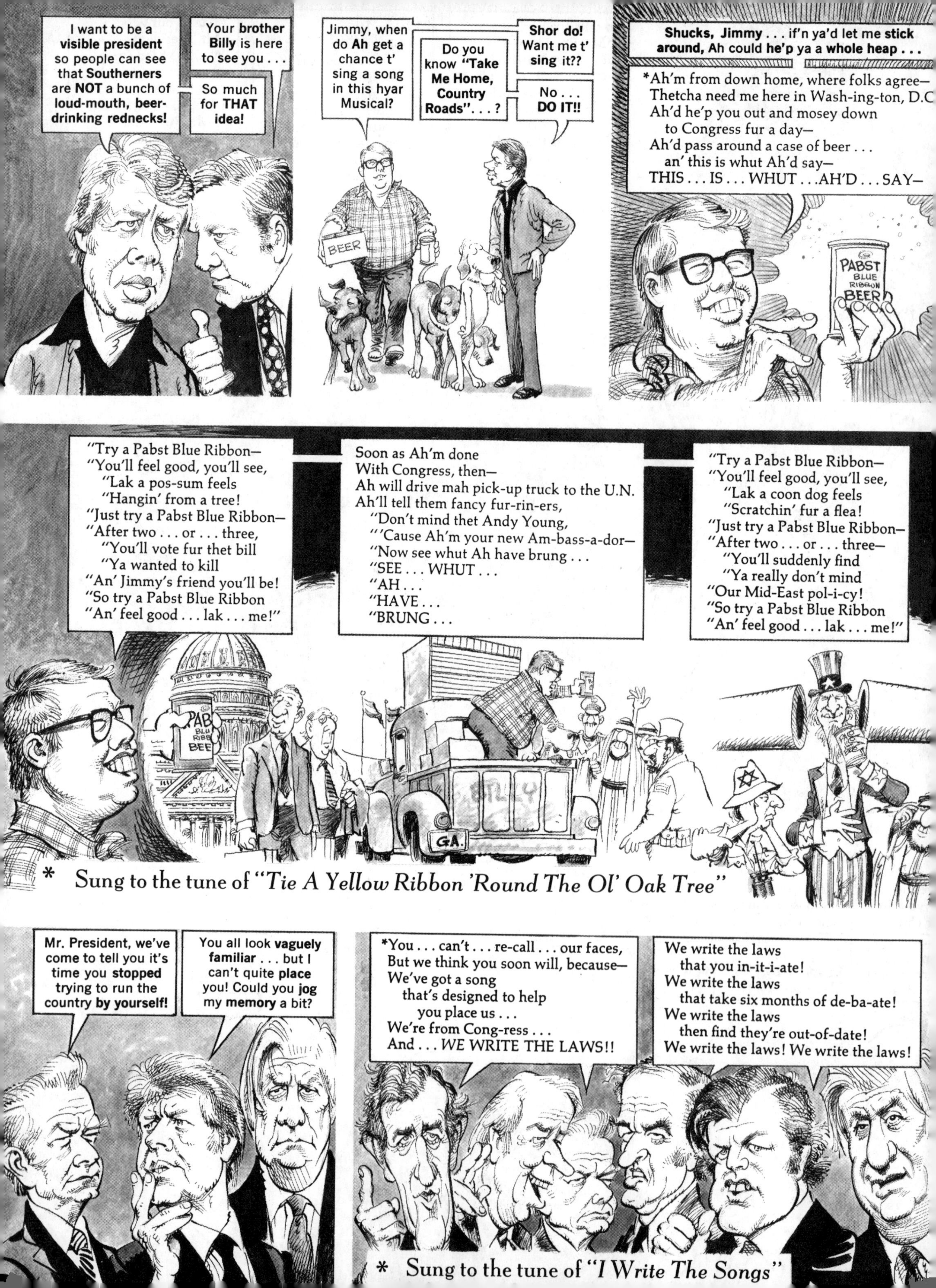

I want to be a visible president so people can see that Southerners are NOT a bunch of loud-mouth, beer-drinking rednecks!
Your brother Billy is here to see you . . .
So much for THAT idea!
Jimmy, when do Ah get a chance t' sing a song in this hyar Musical?
Do you know "Take Me Home, Country Roads" . . . ?
Shor do! Want me t' sing it??
No . . . DO IT!!
BEER
Shucks, Jimmy . . . if'n ya'd let me stick around, Ah could he'p ya a whole heap . . .
*Ah'm from down home, where folks agree—
Thetcha need me here in Wash-ing-ton, D.C.
Ah'd he'p you out and mosey down
to Congress fur a day—
Ah'd pass around a case of beer . . .
an' this is whut Ah'd say—
THIS . . . IS . . . WHUT . . . AH'D . . . SAY—
PABST BLUE RIBBON BEER
"Try a Pabst Blue Ribbon—
"You'll feel good, you'll see,
"Lak a pos-sum feels
"Hangin' from a tree!
"Just try a Pabst Blue Ribbon—
"After two . . . or . . . three,
"You'll vote fur thet bill
"Ya wanted to kill
"An' Jimmy's friend you'll be!
"So try a Pabst Blue Ribbon
"An' feel good . . . lak . . . me!"
Soon as Ah'm done
With Congress, then—
Ah will drive mah pick-up truck to the U.N.
Ah'll tell them fancy fur-rin-ers,
"Don't mind thet Andy Young,
"'Cause Ah'm your new Am-bass-a-dor—
"Now see whut Ah have brung . . .
"SEE . . . WHUT . . .
"AH . . .
"HAVE . . .
"BRUNG . . .
"Try a Pabst Blue Ribbon—
"You'll feel good, you'll see,
"Lak a coon dog feels
"Scratchin' fur a flea!
"Just try a Pabst Blue Ribbon—
"After two . . . or . . . three—
"You'll suddenly find
"Ya really don't mind
"Our Mid-East pol-i-cy!
"So try a Pabst Blue Ribbon
"An' feel good . . . lak . . . me!"
BILLY
GA.
* Sung to the tune of "Tie A Yellow Ribbon 'Round The Ol' Oak Tree"
Mr. President, we've come to tell you it's time you stopped trying to run the country by yourself!
You all look vaguely familiar . . . but I can't quite place you! Could you jog my memory a bit?
*You . . . can't . . . re-call . . . our faces,
But we think you soon will, because—
We've got a song
that's designed to help
you place us . . .
We're from Cong-ress . . .
And . . . WE WRITE THE LAWS!!
We write the laws
that you in-it-i-ate!
We write the laws
that take six months of de-ba-ate!
We write the laws
then find they're out-of-date!
We write the laws! We write the laws!
* Sung to the tune of "I Write The Songs"

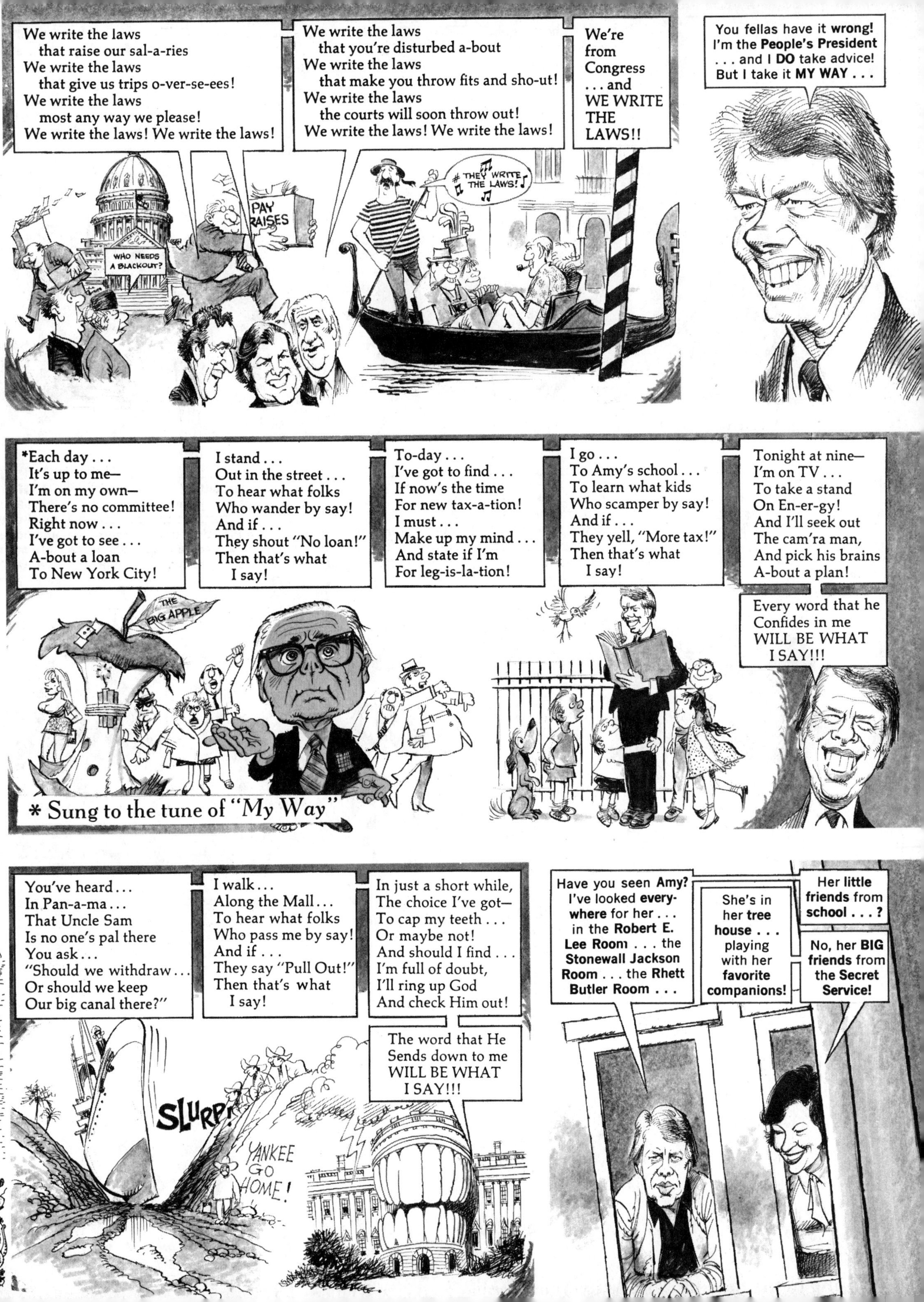
We write the laws that raise our sal-a-ries We write the laws that give us trips o-ver-se-ees! We write the laws most any way we please! We write the laws! We write the laws!
We write the laws that you're disturbed a-bout We write the laws that make you throw fits and sho-ut! We write the laws the courts will soon throw out! We write the laws! We write the laws!
We're from Congress . . . and WE WRITE THE LAWS!!
PAY RAISES
WHO NEEDS A BLACKOUT?
THEY WRITE THE LAWS!
You fellas have it **wrong!** I'm the **People's President** . . . and I **DO** take advice! But I take it **MY WAY** . . .
*Each day . . . It's up to me— I'm on my own— There's no committee! Right now . . . I've got to see . . . A-bout a loan To New York City!
I stand . . . Out in the street . . . To hear what folks Who wander by say! And if . . . They shout "No loan!" Then that's what I say!
To-day . . . I've got to find . . . If now's the time For new tax-a-tion! I must . . . Make up my mind . . . And state if I'm For leg-is-la-tion!
I go . . . To Amy's school . . . To learn what kids Who scamper by say! And if . . . They yell, "More tax!" Then that's what I say!
Tonight at nine— I'm on TV . . . To take a stand On En-er-gy! And I'll seek out The cam'ra man, And pick his brains A-bout a plan!
THE BIG APPLE
* Sung to the tune of "*My Way*"
Every word that he Confides in me WILL BE WHAT I SAY!!!
You've heard . . . In Pan-a-ma . . . That Uncle Sam Is no one's pal there You ask . . . "Should we withdraw . . . Or should we keep Our big canal there?"
I walk . . . Along the Mall . . . To hear what folks Who pass me by say! And if . . . They say "Pull Out!" Then that's what I say!
In just a short while, The choice I've got— To cap my teeth . . . Or maybe not! And should I find . . . I'm full of doubt, I'll ring up God And check Him out!
The word that He Sends down to me WILL BE WHAT I SAY!!!
SLURP!
YANKEE GO HOME!
Have you seen **Amy?** I've looked **every-where** for her . . . in the **Robert E. Lee Room** . . . the **Stonewall Jackson Room** . . . the **Rhett Butler Room** . . .
She's in her **tree house** . . . playing with her **favorite companions!**
Her **little friends** from **school . . . ?**
No, her **BIG friends** from **the Secret Service!**

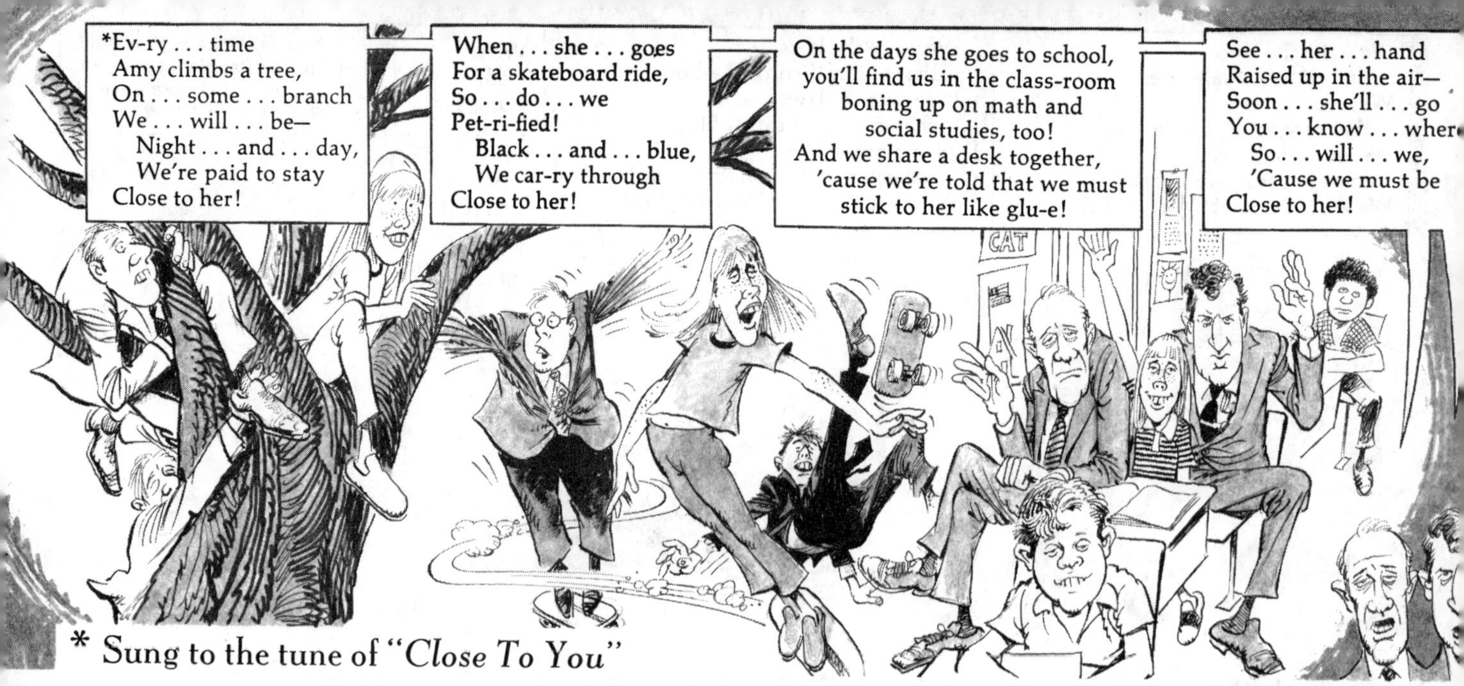
*Ev-ry . . . time
Amy climbs a tree,
On . . . some . . . branch
We . . . will . . . be—
Night . . . and . . . day,
We're paid to stay
Close to her!
When . . . she . . . goes
For a skateboard ride,
So . . . do . . . we
Pet-ri-fied!
Black . . . and . . . blue,
We car-ry through
Close to her!
On the days she goes to school,
you'll find us in the class-room
boning up on math and
social studies, too!
And we share a desk together,
'cause we're told that we must
stick to her like glu-e!
See . . . her . . . hand
Raised up in the air—
Soon . . . she'll . . . go
You . . . know . . . where
So . . . will . . . we,
'Cause we must be
Close to her!
CAT
* Sung to the tune of "*Close To You*"

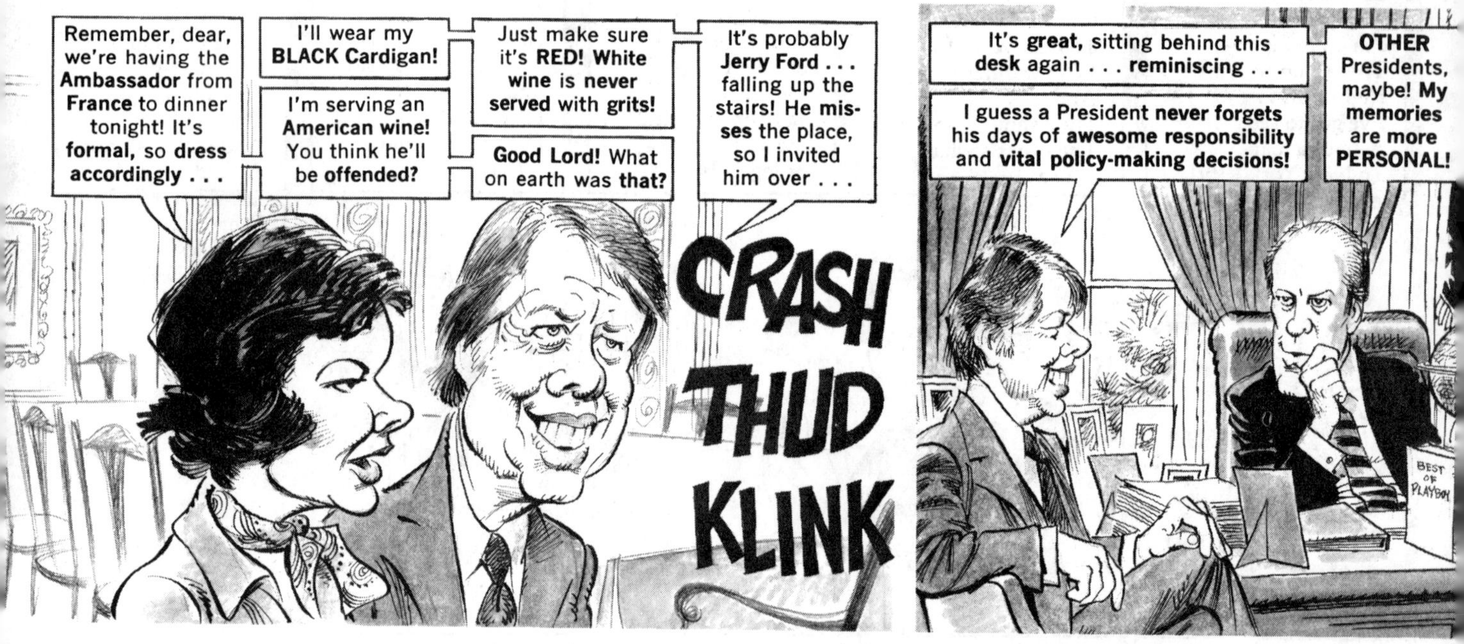
Remember, dear, we're having the **Ambassador** from **France** to dinner tonight! It's **formal,** so **dress accordingly . . .**
I'll wear my **BLACK Cardigan!**
I'm serving an **American wine!** You think he'll be **offended?**
Just make sure it's **RED! White wine is never served with grits!**
CRASH
THUD
KLINK
Good Lord! What on earth was **that?**
It's probably **Jerry Ford . . .** falling up the stairs! He **misses** the place, so I invited him over . . .
It's **great,** sitting behind this **desk** again . . . **reminiscing . . .**
I guess a President **never forgets** his days of **awesome responsibility** and **vital policy-making decisions!**
OTHER Presidents, maybe! **My memories** are more **PERSONAL!**
BEST OF PLAYBOY

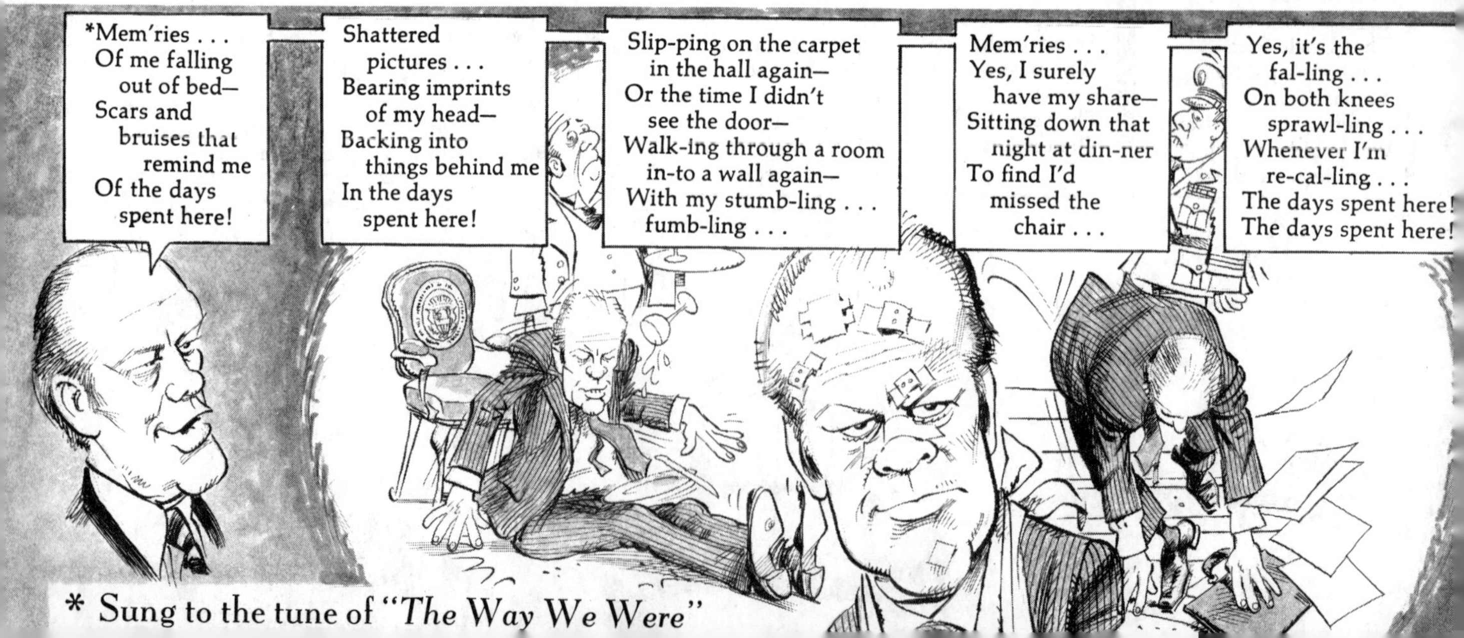
*Mem'ries . . .
Of me falling
out of bed—
Scars and
bruises that
remind me
Of the days
spent here!
Shattered
pictures . . .
Bearing imprints
of my head—
Backing into
things behind me
In the days
spent here!
Slip-ping on the carpet
in the hall again—
Or the time I didn't
see the door—
Walk-ing through a room
in-to a wall again—
With my stumb-ling . . .
fumb-ling . . .
Mem'ries . . .
Yes, I surely
have my share—
Sitting down that
night at din-ner
To find I'd
missed the
chair . . .
Yes, it's the
fal-ling . . .
On both knees
sprawl-ling . . .
Whenever I'm
re-cal-ling . . .
The days spent here!
The days spent here!
* Sung to the tune of "*The Way We Were*"

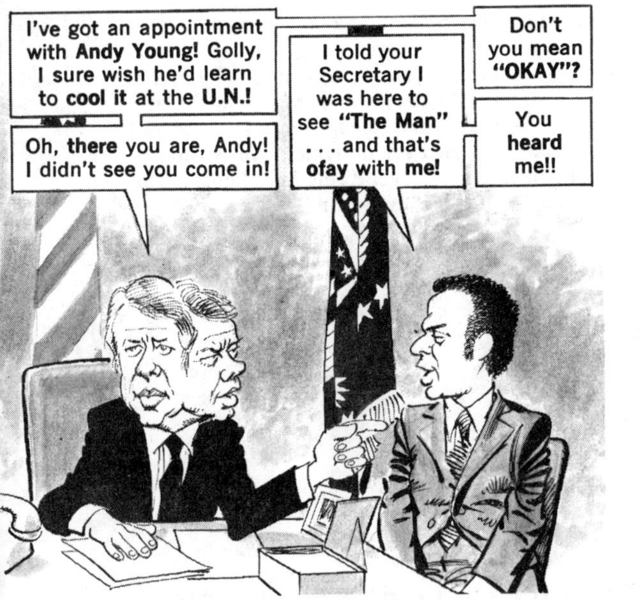
I've got an appointment with Andy Young! Golly, I sure wish he'd learn to cool it at the U.N.!
Oh, there you are, Andy! I didn't see you come in!
I told your Secretary I was here to see "The Man" . . . and that's ofay with me!
Don't you mean "OKAY"?
You heard me!!

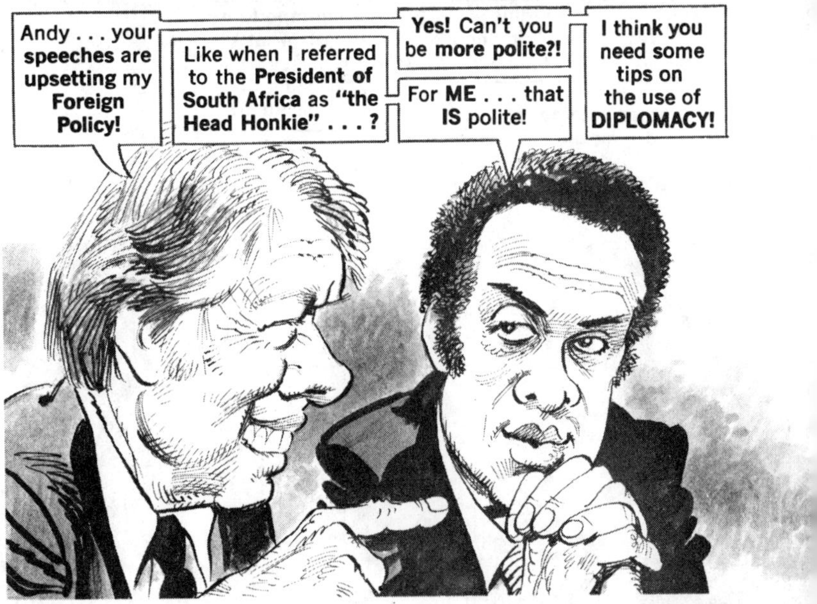
Andy . . . your speeches are upsetting my Foreign Policy!
Like when I referred to the President of South Africa as "the Head Honkie" . . . ?
Yes! Can't you be more polite?!
For ME . . . that IS polite!
I think you need some tips on the use of DIPLOMACY!

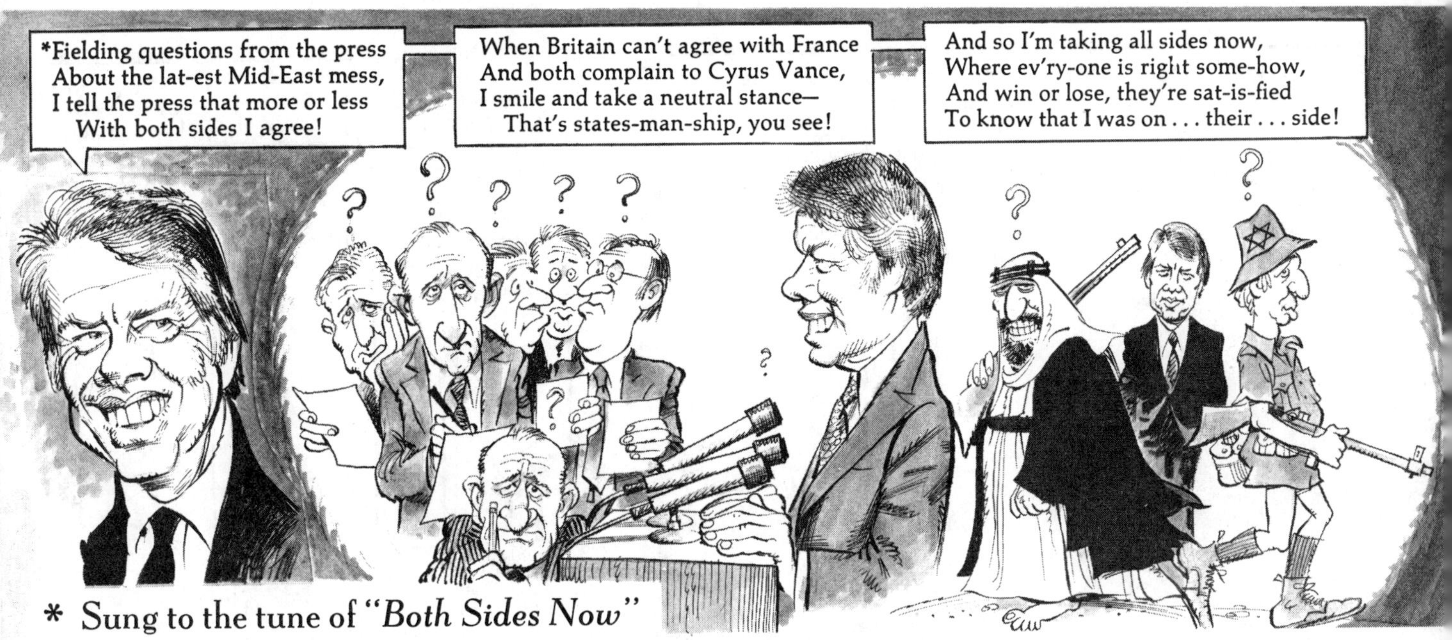
*Fielding questions from the press
About the lat-est Mid-East mess,
I tell the press that more or less
With both sides I agree!
When Britain can't agree with France
And both complain to Cyrus Vance,
I smile and take a neutral stance—
That's states-man-ship, you see!
And so I'm taking all sides now,
Where ev'ry-one is right some-how,
And win or lose, they're sat-is-fied
To know that I was on . . . their . . . side!

* Sung to the tune of "*Both Sides Now*"

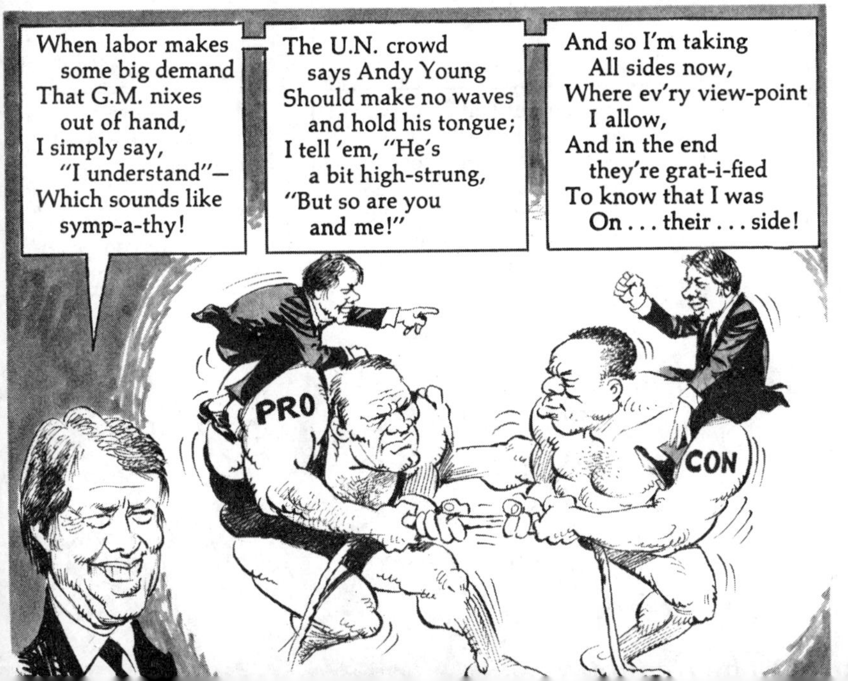
When labor makes
some big demand
That G.M. nixes
out of hand,
I simply say,
"I understand"—
Which sounds like
symp-a-thy!
The U.N. crowd
says Andy Young
Should make no waves
and hold his tongue;
I tell 'em, "He's
a bit high-strung,
"But so are you
and me!"
And so I'm taking
All sides now,
Where ev'ry view-point
I allow,
And in the end
they're grat-i-fied
To know that I was
On . . . their . . . side!
PRO
CON

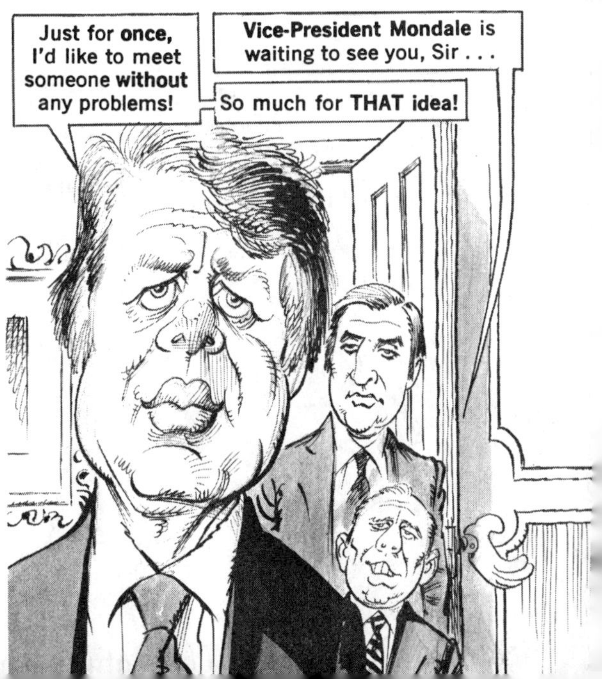
Just for once, I'd like to meet someone without any problems!
Vice-President Mondale is waiting to see you, Sir . . .
So much for THAT idea!

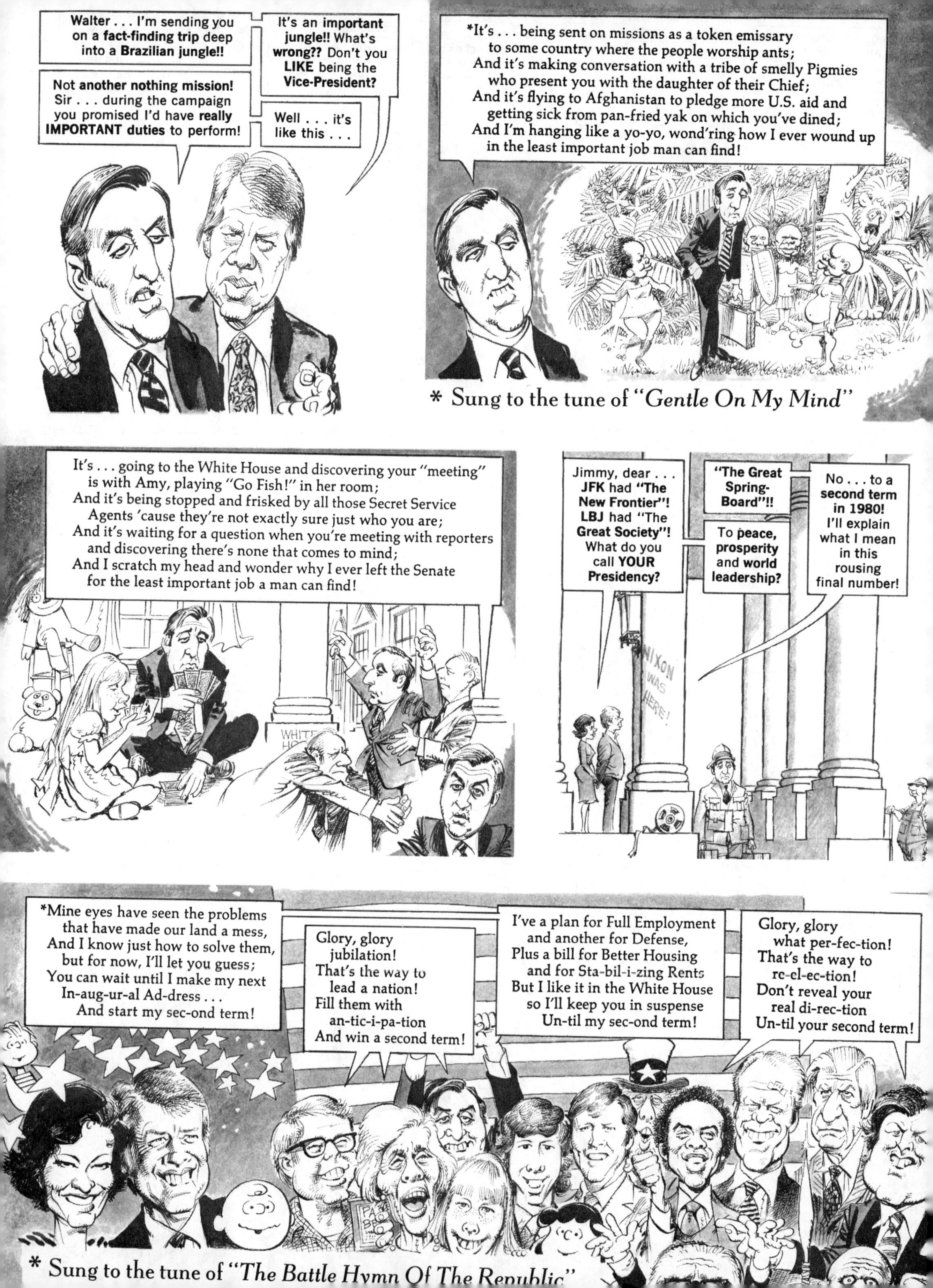
Walter . . . I'm sending you on a **fact-finding trip** deep into a **Brazilian jungle!!**
It's an **important jungle!!** What's **wrong??** Don't you **LIKE** being the **Vice-President?**
Not **another nothing mission!** Sir . . . during the campaign you promised I'd have **really IMPORTANT duties** to perform!
Well . . . it's like this . . .
*It's . . . being sent on missions as a token emissary to some country where the people worship ants;
And it's making conversation with a tribe of smelly Pigmies who present you with the daughter of their Chief;
And it's flying to Afghanistan to pledge more U.S. aid and getting sick from pan-fried yak on which you've dined;
And I'm hanging like a yo-yo, wond'ring how I ever wound up in the least important job man can find!
* Sung to the tune of "*Gentle On My Mind*"
It's . . . going to the White House and discovering your "meeting" is with Amy, playing "Go Fish!" in her room;
And it's being stopped and frisked by all those Secret Service Agents 'cause they're not exactly sure just who you are;
And it's waiting for a question when you're meeting with reporters and discovering there's none that comes to mind;
And I scratch my head and wonder why I ever left the Senate for the least important job a man can find!
WHITE HO
Jimmy, dear . . . **JFK** had **"The New Frontier"!** **LBJ** had "The **Great Society"!** What do you call **YOUR Presidency?**
"The Great Spring-Board"!!
To **peace, prosperity** and **world leadership?**
No . . . to a **second term in 1980!** I'll explain what I mean in this rousing final number!
NIXON WAS HERE!
*Mine eyes have seen the problems that have made our land a mess,
And I know just how to solve them, but for now, I'll let you guess;
You can wait until I make my next In-aug-ur-al Ad-dress . . .
And start my sec-ond term!
Glory, glory jubilation! That's the way to lead a nation! Fill them with an-tic-i-pa-tion And win a second term!
I've a plan for Full Employment and another for Defense,
Plus a bill for Better Housing and for Sta-bil-i-zing Rents
But I like it in the White House so I'll keep you in suspense
Un-til my sec-ond term!
Glory, glory what per-fec-tion! That's the way to re-el-ec-tion! Don't reveal your real di-rec-tion Un-til your second term!
* Sung to the tune of "*The Battle Hymn Of The Republic*"

GOING OVER BARD DEPT.

A MAD TREASURY OF *Shakespeare's Lesser Known Quotations*

ARTIST: HARRY NORTH, ESQ.
WRITER: DENNIS SNEE

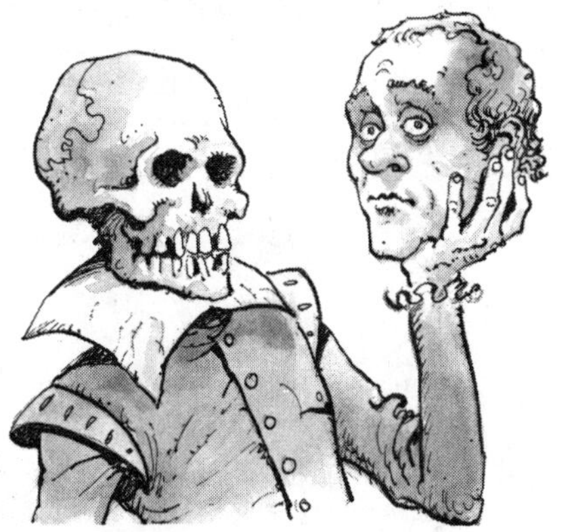

Could Richard stop death? Could Henry? If they were here, you could ask them.

* * *

Of valor, discretion is the better part; of dinner, dessert.

* * *

O! The dawn! Would it only come back in half an hour!

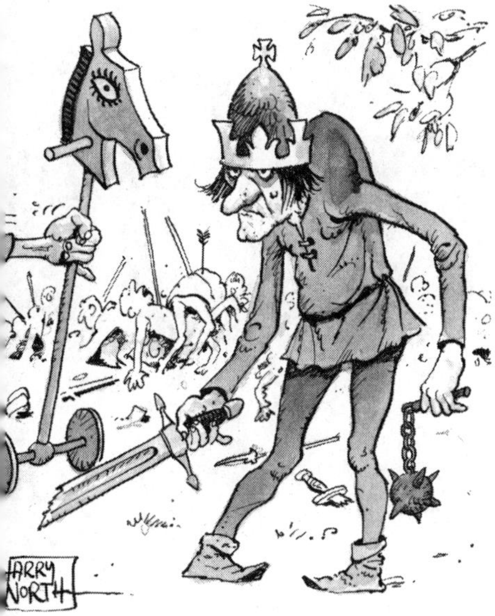
HARRY NORTH

Women, Mercutio, are the itch we gladly scratch.

* * *

In such a night did Orestes take flight, and tripping on a pail, did break his ass.

* * *

Trust not the woman, Horatio, who kisses her husband, then wipes her lips.

* * *

Doth yonder fat man think himself thin? Bring him, then, thy mirror, and none of my mutton.

If your boots are heavy, take them off. But pray, not here.

* * *

You speak of that adultress as if she were a rose, and you but a pound of fertilizer.

* * *

Yea, his evil may live after him, but his best suit he takes to the grave.

* * *

Her tears, Polonius, are as false as thy teeth.

* * *

Youth, in froth and frolic, play. But when age doth come, no elder catches the speedy young tart.

* * *

If something is rotten in Denmark, then haste; get thee to Sweden.

* * *

Talk and talk and talk. Were it not for ears, who would know?

* * *

Judge not Leonard by the length of his beard, nor its color, but by the number of crumbs therein.

* * *

Lo, in Heaven there sits a judge no king can corrupt. Nor will he lend money, save to certain close friends.

* * *

Better a solitary man than relatives in the bathroom.

* * *

A tragic tale is best for winter. In summer, 'tis off to the beach.

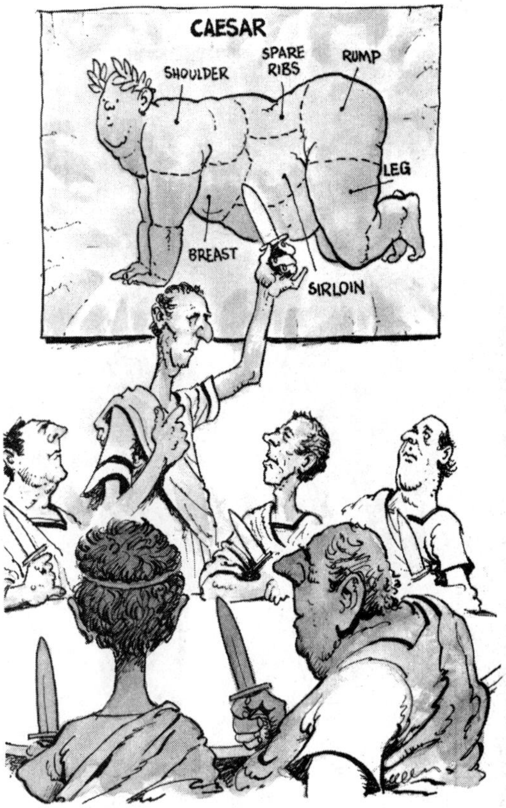
CAESAR
SHOULDER
SPARE RIBS
RUMP
LEG
BREAST
SIRLOIN

Sad, sad, and sad again. His love is gone, but his wife remains.

* * *

In the sight of men, take only your due. But when alone, grabbeth what you can.

* * *

Gladly I would drink the hemlock, my son, but then who would wash the cup? Not you, for sure. The state of thy room announces your talents.

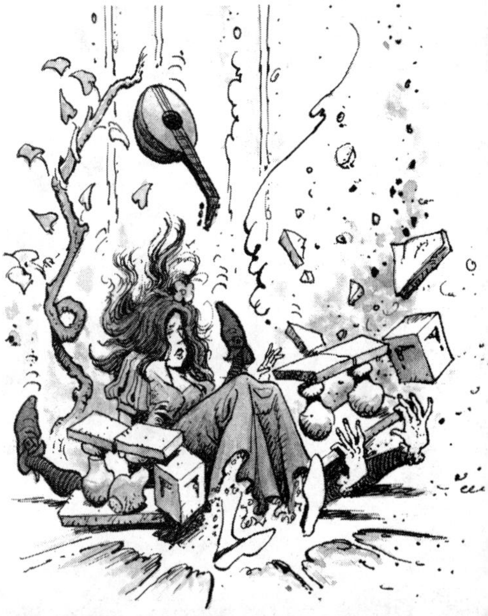

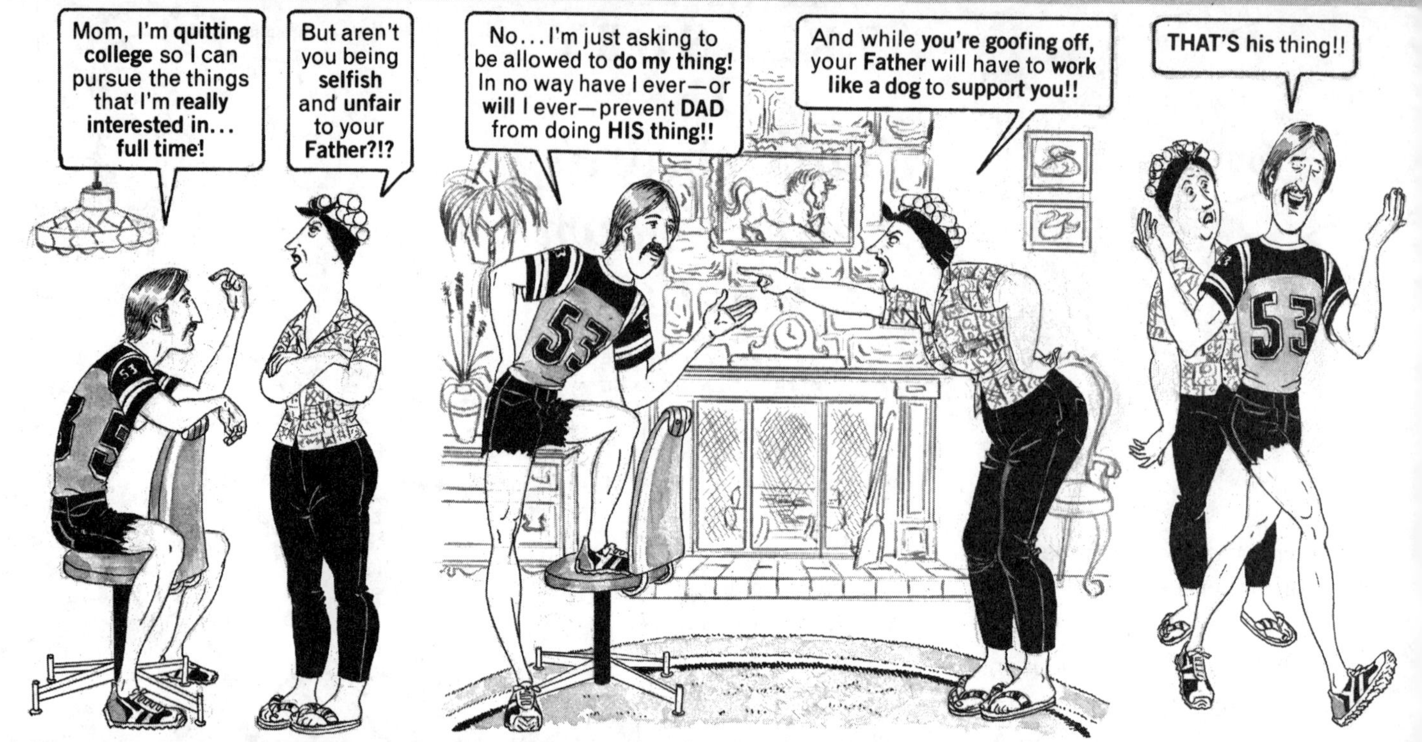

Mom, I'm quitting college so I can pursue the things that I'm really interested in... full time!
But aren't you being selfish and unfair to your Father?!?
No... I'm just asking to be allowed to do my thing! In no way have I ever—or will I ever—prevent DAD from doing HIS thing!!
And while you're goofing off, your Father will have to work like a dog to support you!!
THAT'S his thing!!

BERG'S-EYE VIEW DEPT.

THE LIGHTER SIDE OF... The“

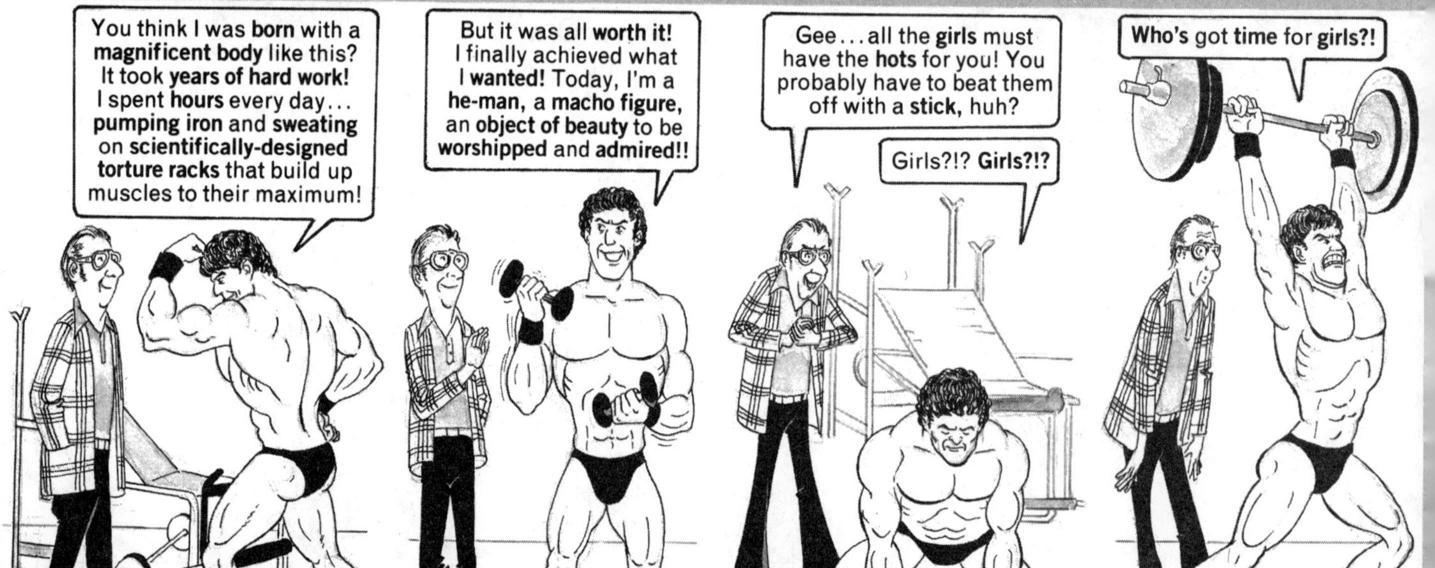

You think I was born with a magnificent body like this? It took years of hard work! I spent hours every day... pumping iron and sweating on scientifically-designed torture racks that build up muscles to their maximum!
But it was all worth it! I finally achieved what I wanted! Today, I'm a he-man, a macho figure, an object of beauty to be worshipped and admired!!
Gee... all the girls must have the hots for you! You probably have to beat them off with a stick, huh?
Girls?!? Girls?!?
Who's got time for girls?!

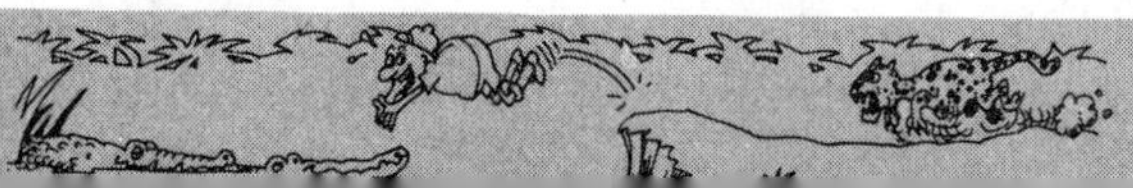

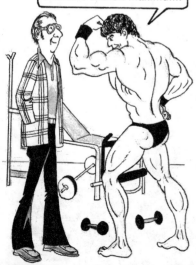

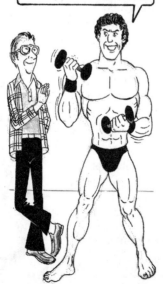

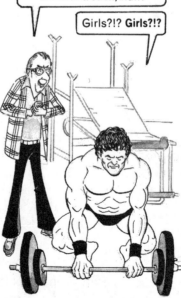

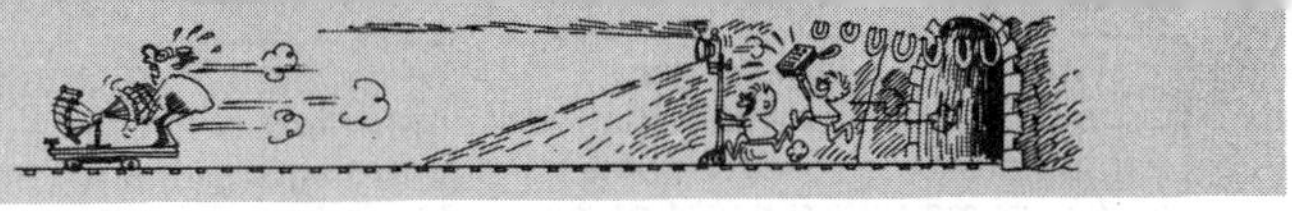

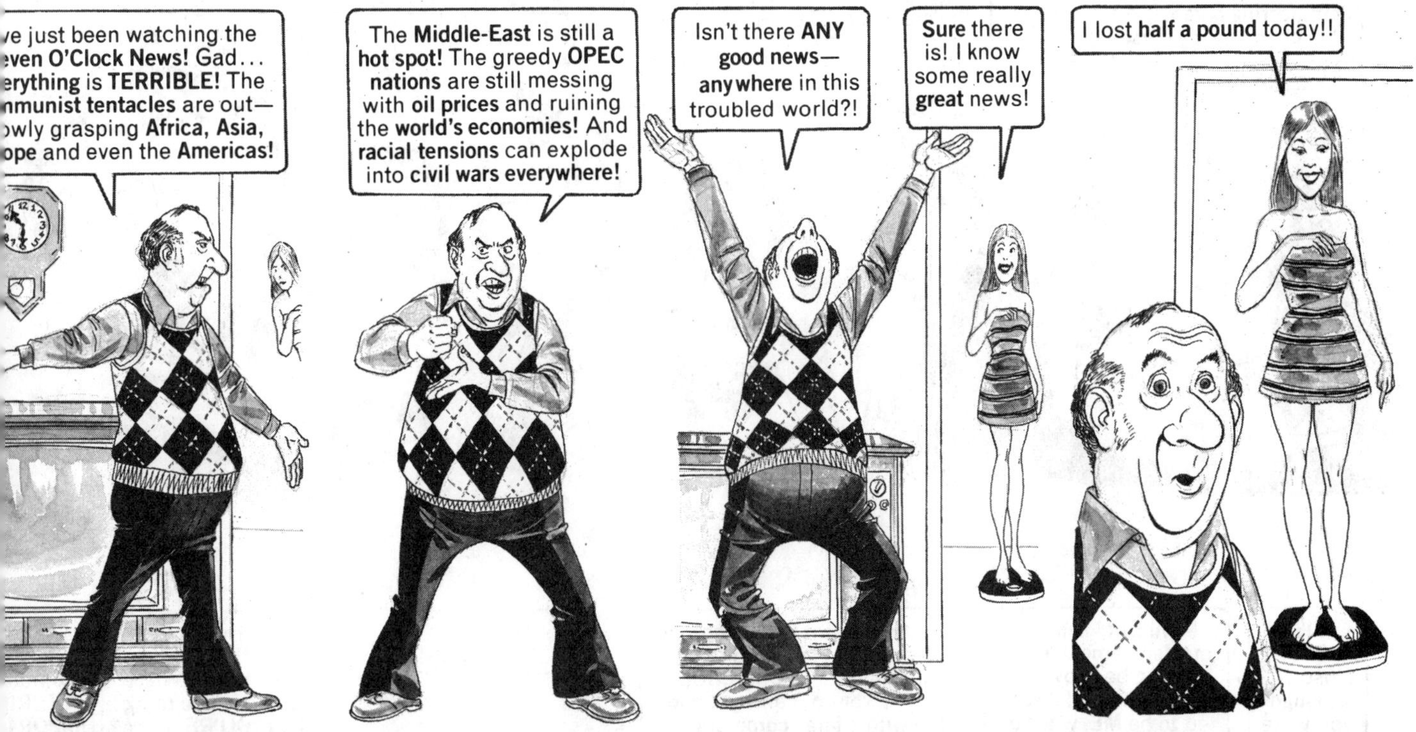

ve just been watching the even O'Clock News! Gad... erything is TERRIBLE! The nmunist tentacles are out— owly grasping Africa, Asia, ope and even the Americas!
The Middle-East is still a hot spot! The greedy OPEC nations are still messing with oil prices and ruining the world's economies! And racial tensions can explode into civil wars everywhere!
Isn't there ANY good news— anywhere in this troubled world?!
Sure there is! I know some really great news!
I lost half a pound today!!

:" Generation

ARTIST & WRITER: DAVE BERG

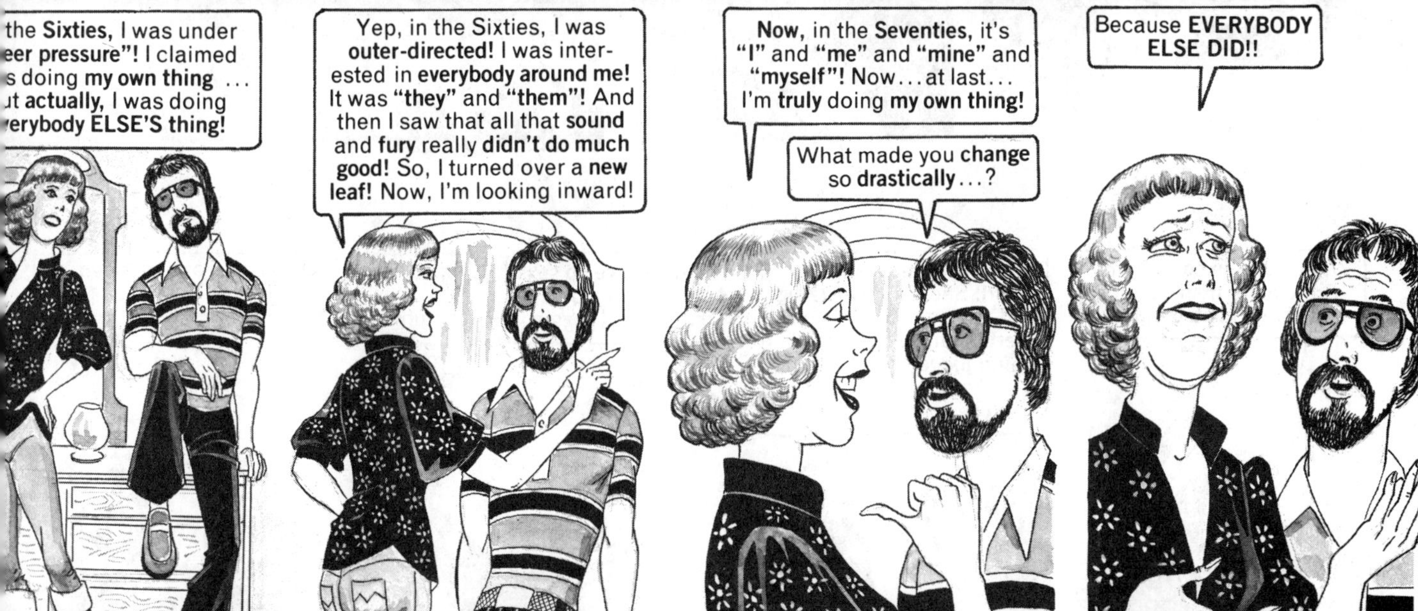

the Sixties, I was under eer pressure"! I claimed s doing my own thing ... ut actually, I was doing verybody ELSE'S thing!
Yep, in the Sixties, I was outer-directed! I was interested in everybody around me! It was "they" and "them"! And then I saw that all that sound and fury really didn't do much good! So, I turned over a new leaf! Now, I'm looking inward!
Now, in the Seventies, it's "I" and "me" and "mine" and "myself"! Now... at last... I'm truly doing my own thing!
What made you change so drastically...?
Because EVERYBODY ELSE DID!!

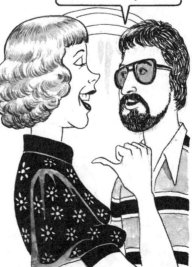

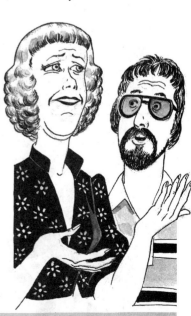

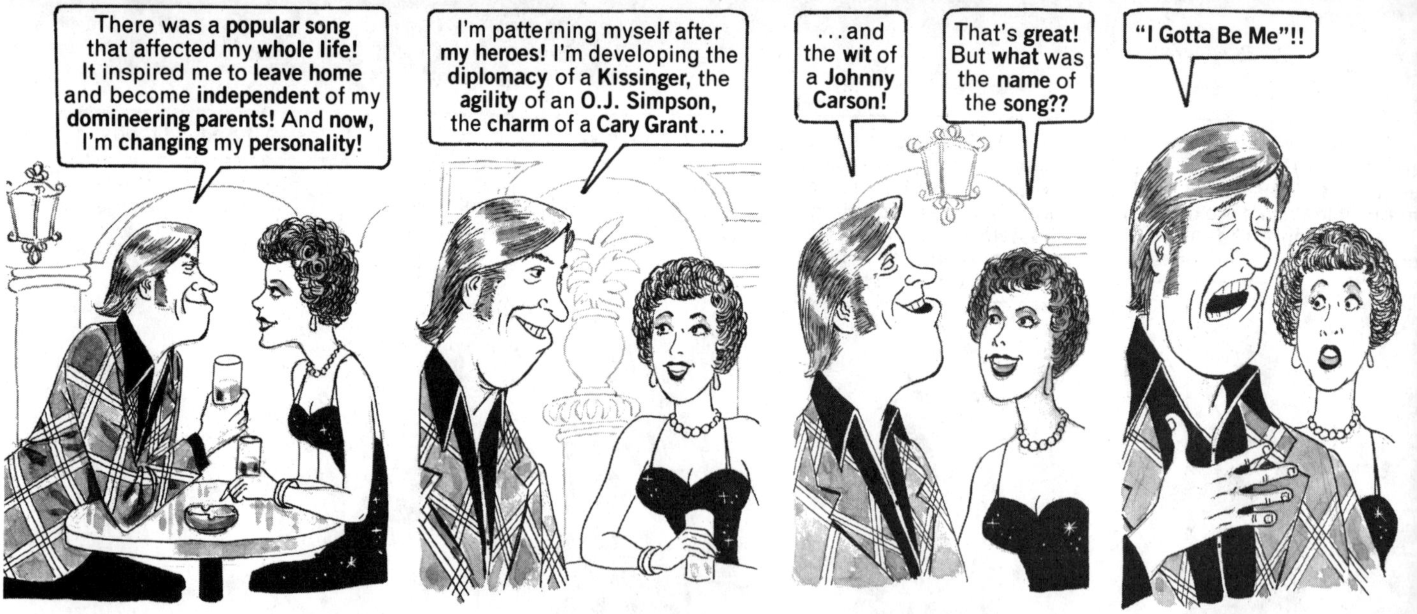
There was a popular song that affected my whole life! It inspired me to leave home and become independent of my domineering parents! And now, I'm changing my personality!
I'm patterning myself after my heroes! I'm developing the diplomacy of a Kissinger, the agility of an O.J. Simpson, the charm of a Cary Grant . . .
. . . and the wit of a Johnny Carson!
That's great! But what was the name of the song??
"I Gotta Be Me"!!

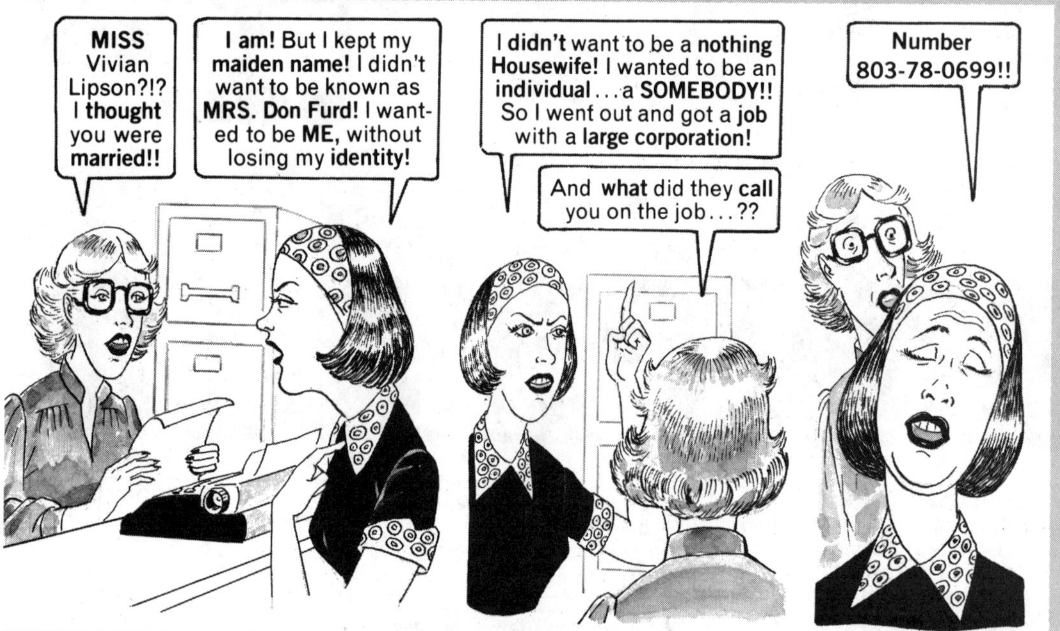
MISS Vivian Lipson?!? I thought you were married!!
I am! But I kept my maiden name! I didn't want to be known as MRS. Don Furd! I wanted to be ME, without losing my identity!
I didn't want to be a nothing Housewife! I wanted to be an individual . . . a SOMEBODY!! So I went out and got a job with a large corporation!
And what did they call you on the job . . . ??
Number 803-78-0699!!

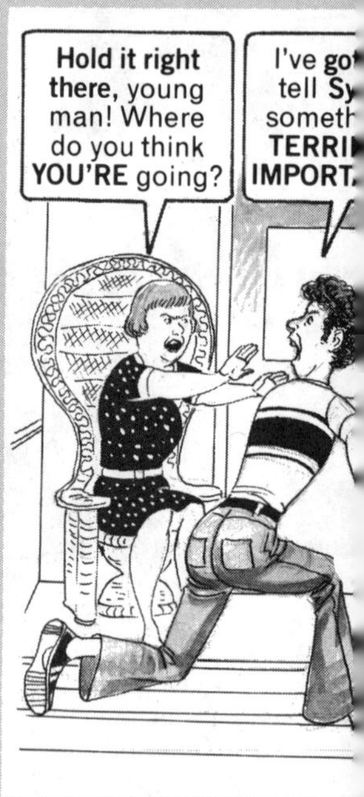
Hold it right there, young man! Where do you think YOU'RE going?

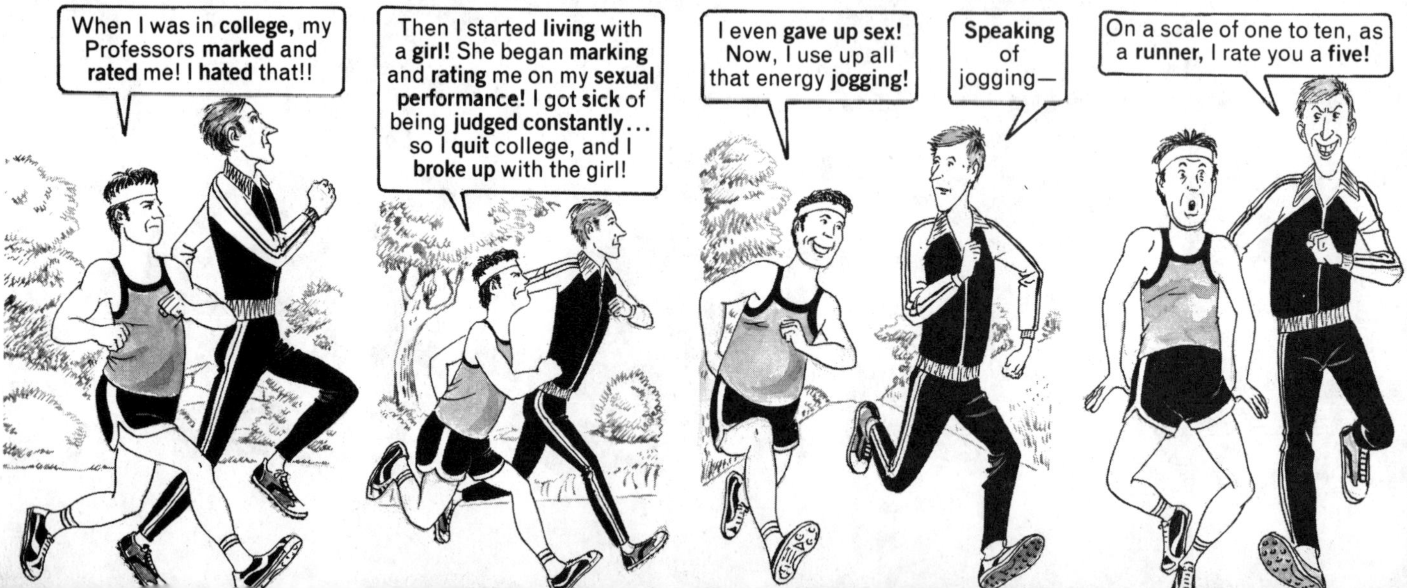
When I was in college, my Professors marked and rated me! I hated that!!
Then I started living with a girl! She began marking and rating me on my sexual performance! I got sick of being judged constantly . . . so I quit college, and I broke up with the girl!
I even gave up sex! Now, I use up all that energy jogging!
Speaking of jogging—
On a scale of one to ten, as a runner, I rate you a five!

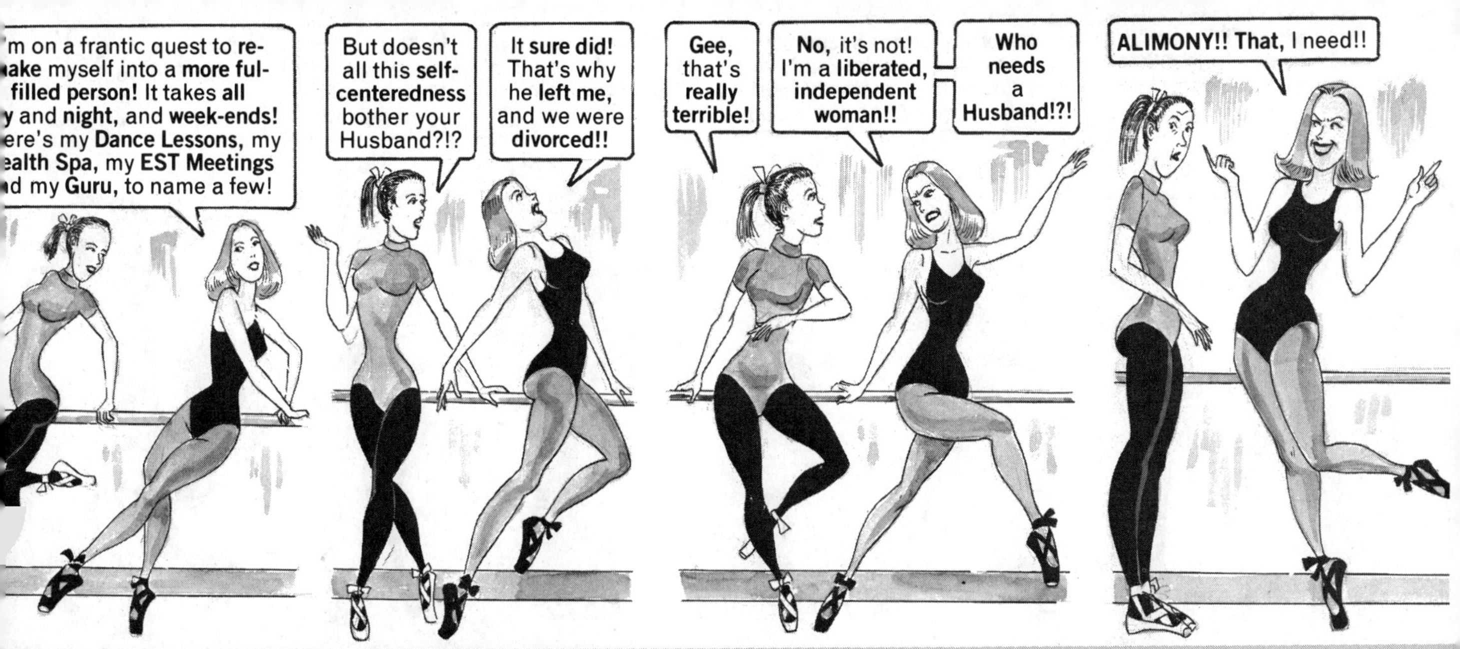
'm on a frantic quest to re-ake myself into a more ful-filled person! It takes all y and night, and week-ends! ere's my Dance Lessons, my ealth Spa, my EST Meetings d my Guru, to name a few!
But doesn't all this self-centeredness bother your Husband?!?
It sure did! That's why he left me, and we were divorced!!
Gee, that's really terrible!
No, it's not! I'm a liberated, independent woman!!
Who needs a Husband!?!
ALIMONY!! That, I need!!

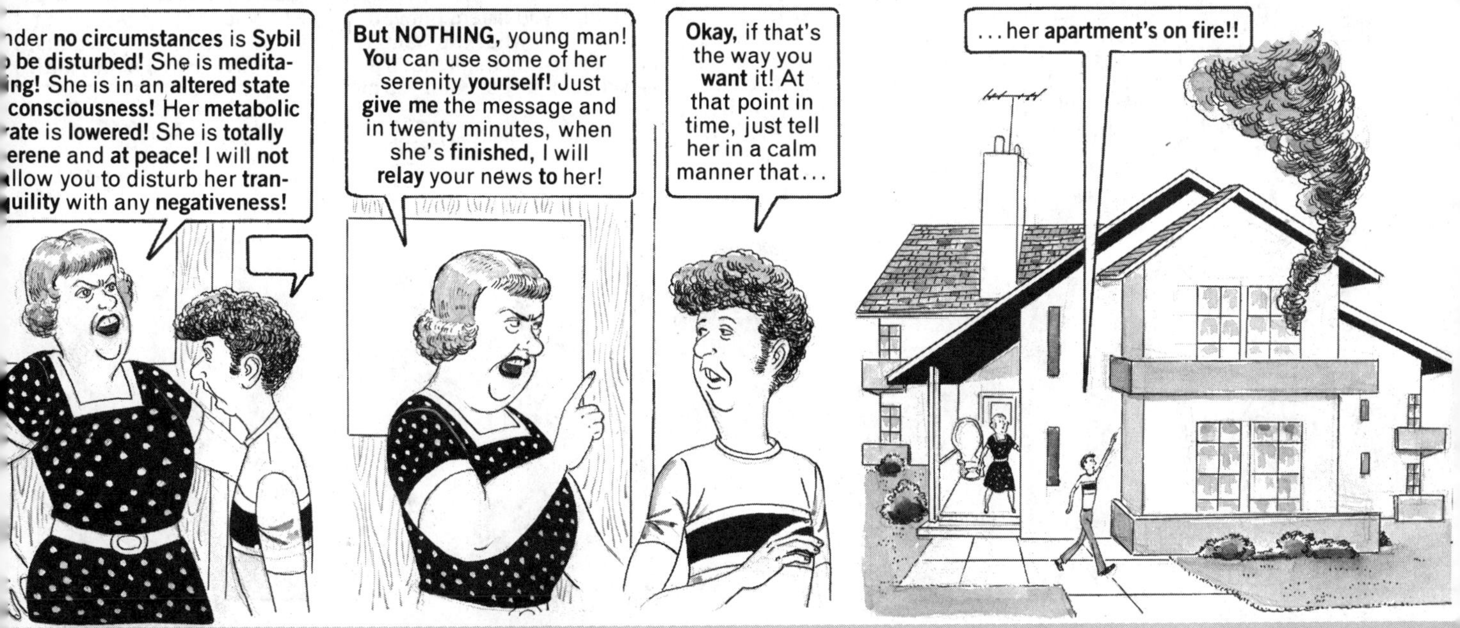
nder no circumstances is Sybil be disturbed! She is medita-ing! She is in an altered state consciousness! Her metabolic ate is lowered! She is totally erene and at peace! I will not llow you to disturb her tran-uility with any negativeness!
But NOTHING, young man! You can use some of her serenity yourself! Just give me the message and in twenty minutes, when she's finished, I will relay your news to her!
Okay, if that's the way you want it! At that point in time, just tell her in a calm manner that...
... her apartment's on fire!!

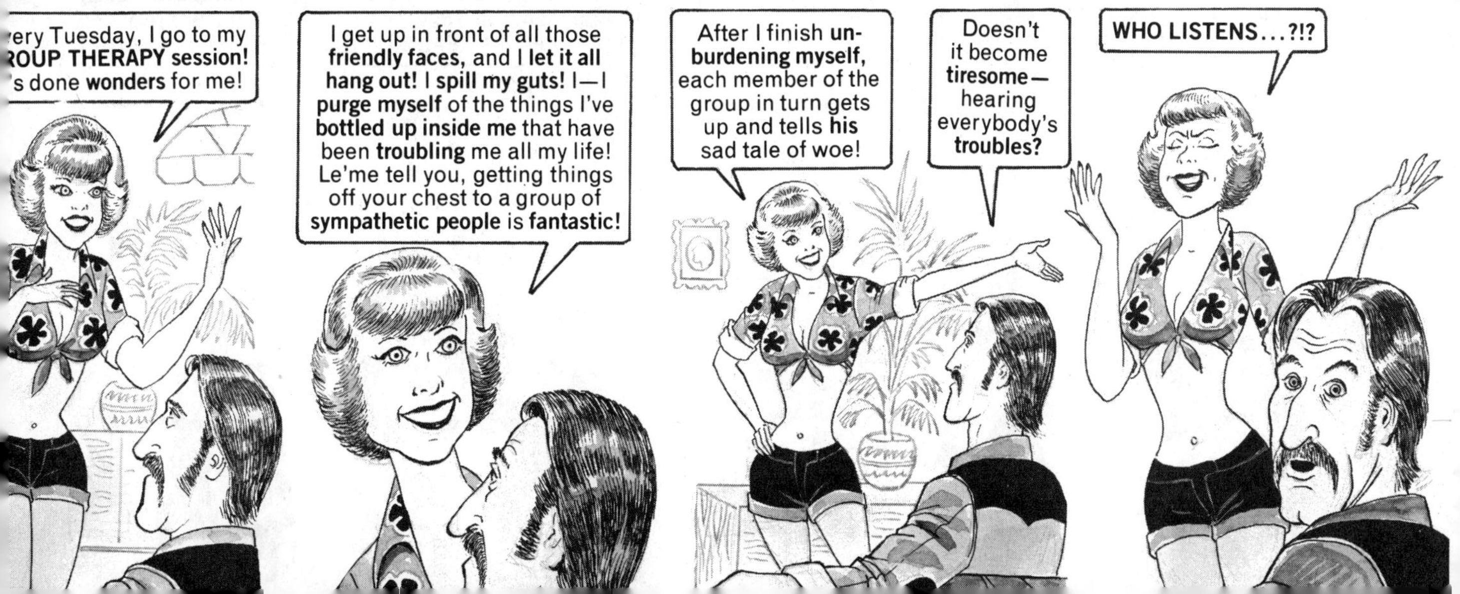
ery Tuesday, I go to my ROUP THERAPY session! 's done wonders for me!
I get up in front of all those friendly faces, and I let it all hang out! I spill my guts! I—I purge myself of the things I've bottled up inside me that have been troubling me all my life! Le'me tell you, getting things off your chest to a group of sympathetic people is fantastic!
After I finish un-burdening myself, each member of the group in turn gets up and tells his sad tale of woe!
Doesn't it become tiresome—hearing everybody's troubles?
WHO LISTENS...?!?

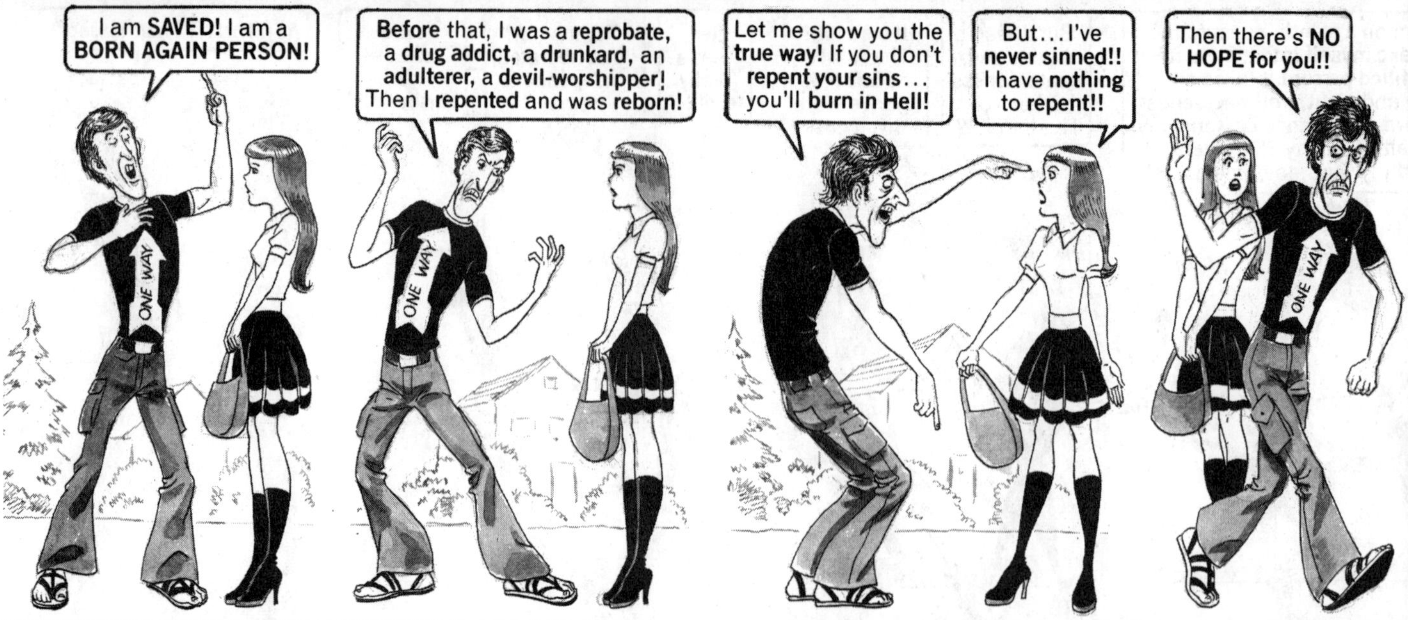
I am **SAVED!** I am a **BORN AGAIN PERSON!**
Before that, I was a **reprobate, a drug addict, a drunkard,** an **adulterer, a devil-worshipper!** Then I **repented** and was **reborn!**
Let me show you the **true way!** If you don't **repent your sins**... you'll **burn in Hell!**
But... I've **never sinned!!** I have **nothing** to **repent!!**
Then there's **NO HOPE** for you!!

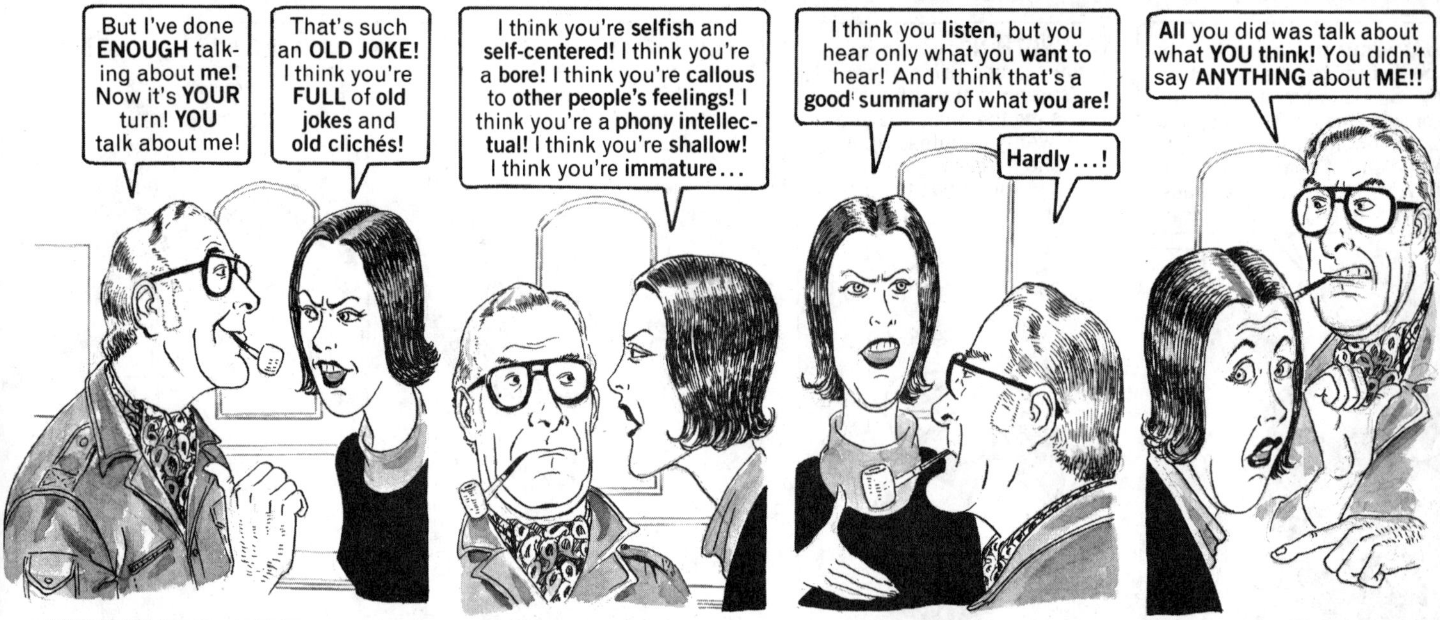
But I've done **ENOUGH** talking about **me!** Now it's **YOUR** turn! **YOU** talk about me!
That's such an **OLD JOKE!** I think you're **FULL** of **old jokes** and **old clichés!**
I think you're **selfish** and **self-centered!** I think you're a **bore!** I think you're **callous** to **other people's feelings!** I think you're a **phony intellectual!** I think you're **shallow!** I think you're **immature**...
I think you **listen,** but you hear only what you **want** to hear! And I think that's a **good summary** of what **you** are!
Hardly...!
All you did was talk about what **YOU think!** You didn't say **ANYTHING** about **ME!!**

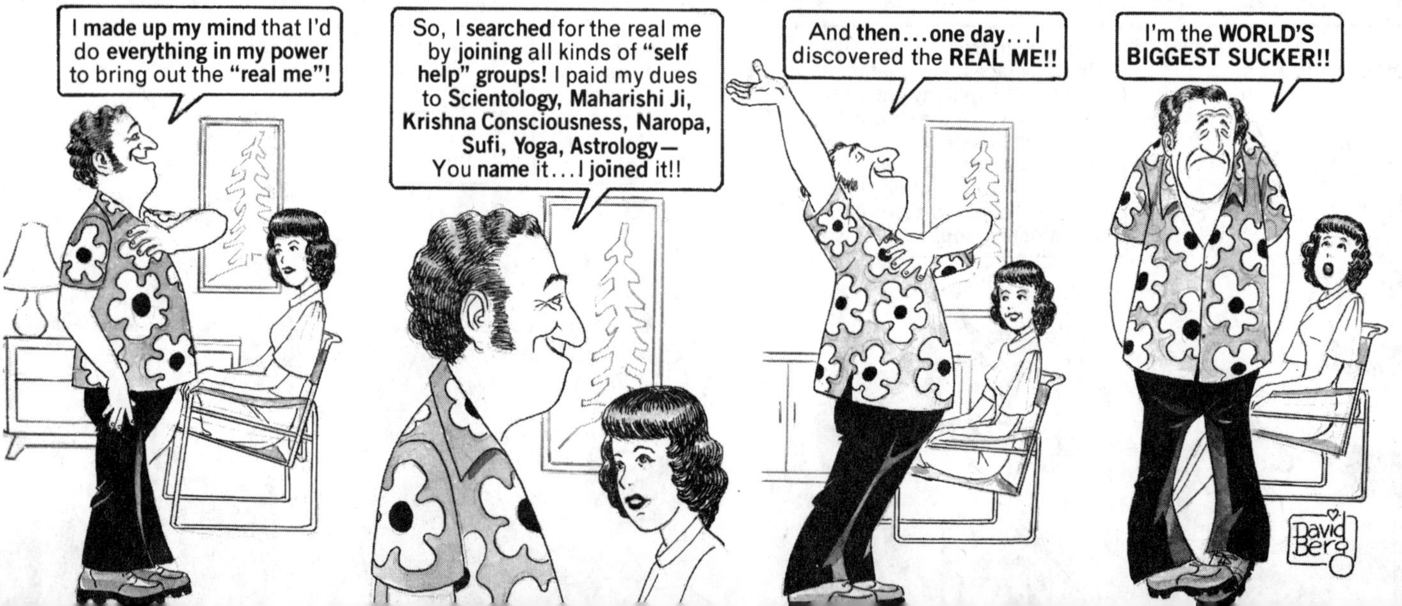
I **made up my mind** that I'd do **everything in my power** to bring out the **"real me"!**
So, I **searched** for the real me by **joining** all kinds of **"self help" groups!** I paid my dues to **Scientology, Maharishi Ji, Krishna Consciousness, Naropa, Sufi, Yoga, Astrology—** You **name** it... I **joined** it!!
And **then... one day...** I discovered the **REAL ME!!**
I'm the **WORLD'S BIGGEST SUCKER!!**
David Berg

SOCKET TO 'EM DEPT.

BEFORE THE ROCK CONCERT

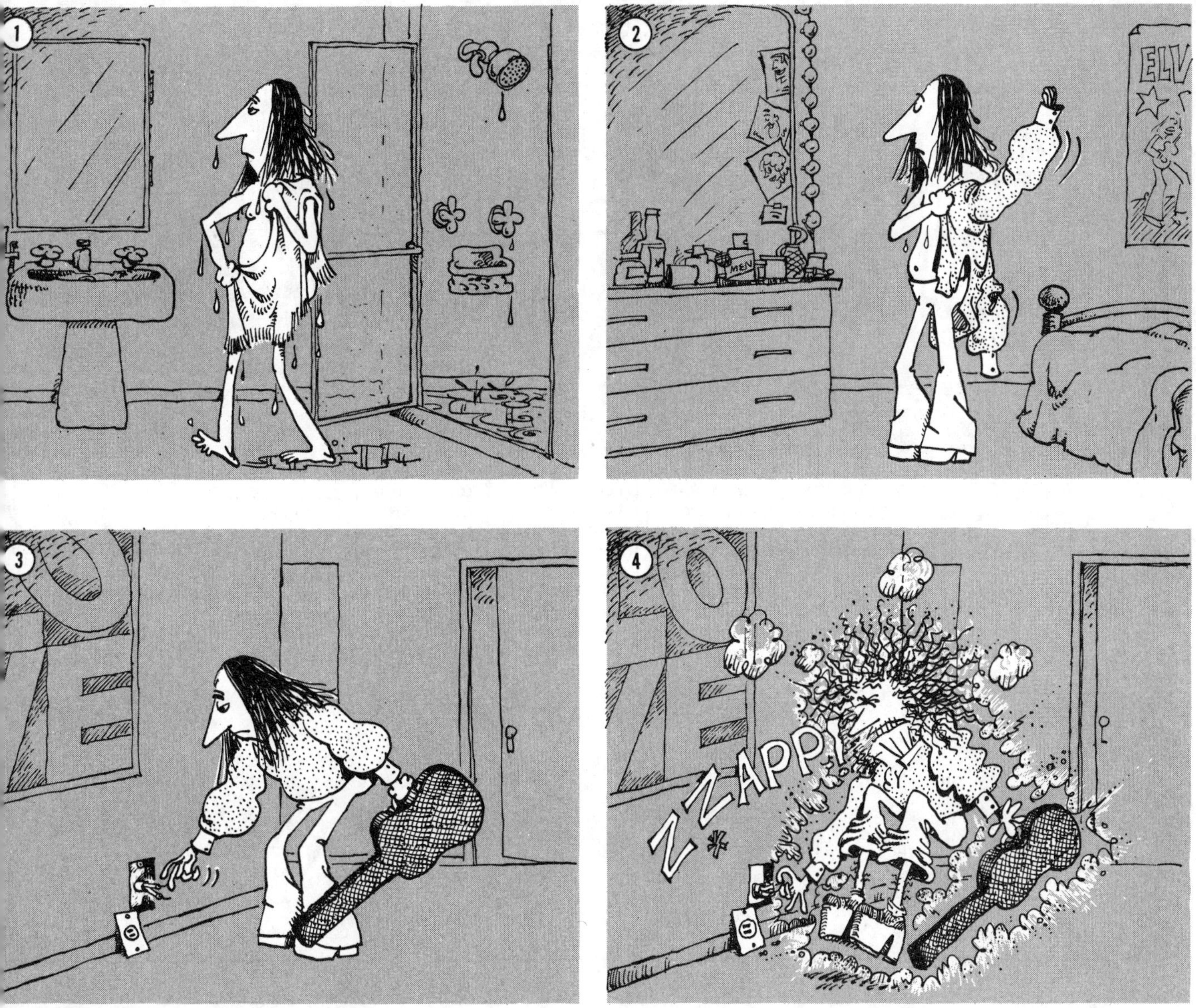
1
2
MEN
ELV
3
4
ZZAPP!

ARTIST & WRITER: SERGIO ARAGONES

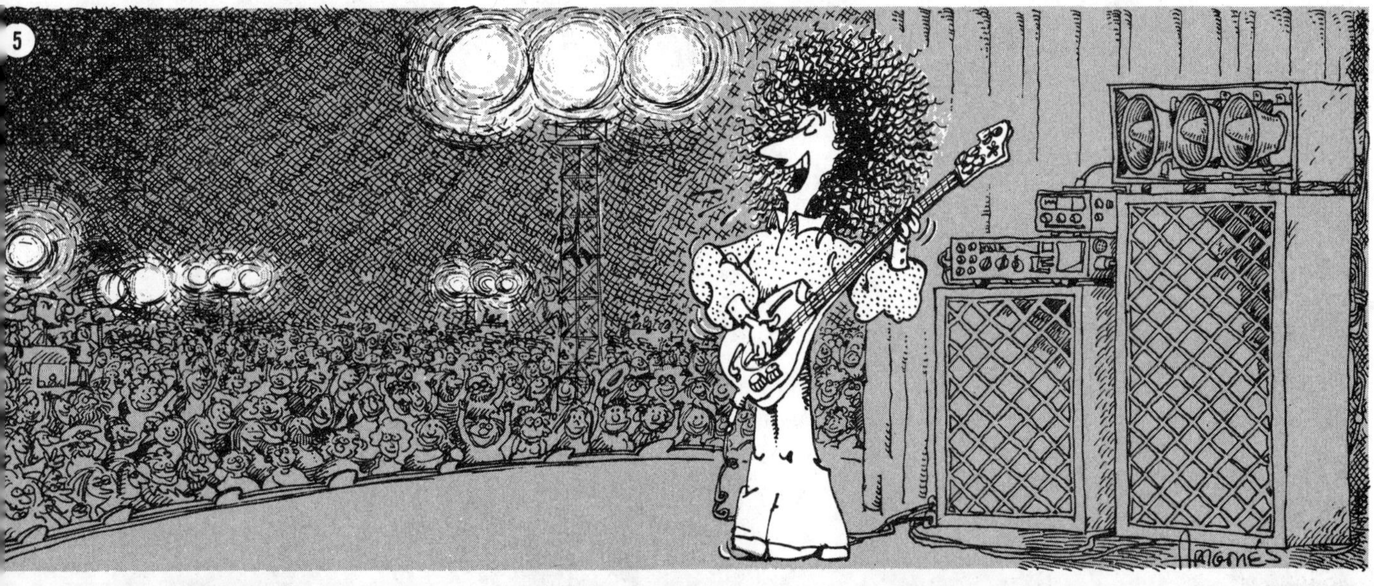
5

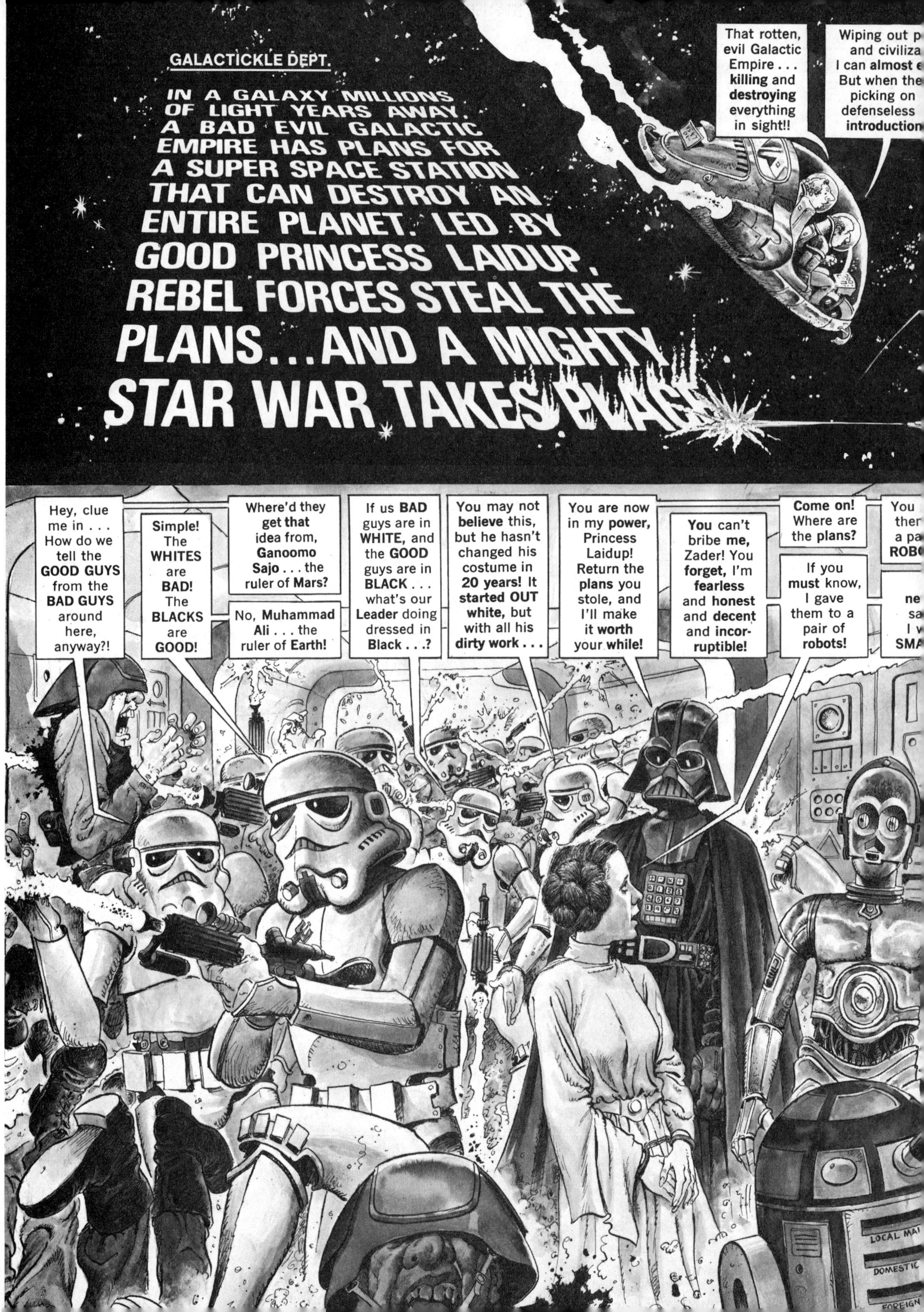
GALACTICKLE DEPT.
IN A GALAXY MILLIONS OF LIGHT YEARS AWAY, A BAD EVIL GALACTIC EMPIRE HAS PLANS FOR A SUPER SPACE STATION THAT CAN DESTROY AN ENTIRE PLANET. LED BY GOOD PRINCESS LAIDUP, REBEL FORCES STEAL THE PLANS...AND A MIGHTY STAR WAR TAKES PLAC
That rotten, evil Galactic Empire . . . killing and destroying everything in sight!!
Wiping out p and civiliza I can almost e But when the picking on defenseless introduction
Hey, clue me in . . . How do we tell the GOOD GUYS from the BAD GUYS around here, anyway?!
Simple! The WHITES are BAD! The BLACKS are GOOD!
Where'd they get that idea from, Ganoomo Sajo . . . the ruler of Mars?
No, Muhammad Ali . . . the ruler of Earth!
If us BAD guys are in WHITE, and the GOOD guys are in BLACK . . . what's our Leader doing dressed in Black . . .?
You may not believe this, but he hasn't changed his costume in 20 years! It started OUT white, but with all his dirty work . . .
You are now in my power, Princess Laidup! Return the plans you stole, and I'll make it worth your while!
You can't bribe me, Zader! You forget, I'm fearless and honest and decent and incorruptible!
Come on! Where are the plans?
If you must know, I gave them to a pair of robots!
You ther a pa ROBO
ne sa I v SMA
LOCAL MAI
DOMESTIC
FOREIGN

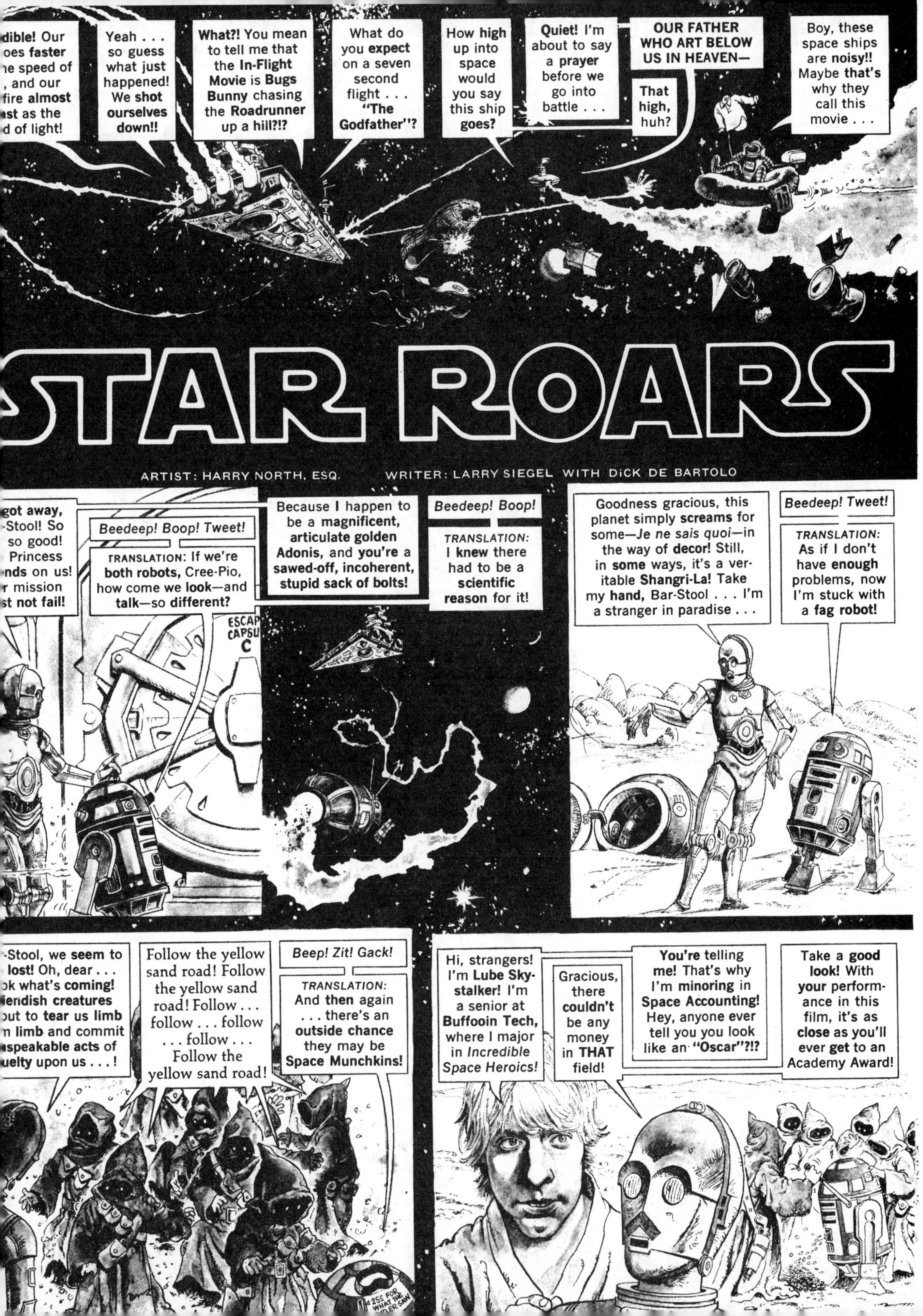
dible! Our oes faster ne speed of , and our fire almost ıst as the d of light!
Yeah . . . so guess what just happened! We shot ourselves down!!
What?! You mean to tell me that the In-Flight Movie is Bugs Bunny chasing the Roadrunner up a hill?!?
What do you expect on a seven second flight . . . "The Godfather"?
How high up into space would you say this ship goes?
Quiet! I'm about to say a prayer before we go into battle . . .
OUR FATHER WHO ART BELOW US IN HEAVEN—
That high, huh?
Boy, these space ships are noisy!! Maybe that's why they call this movie . . .
STAR ROARS
ARTIST: HARRY NORTH, ESQ.
WRITER: LARRY SIEGEL WITH DICK DE BARTOLO
got away, -Stool! So so good! Princess nds on us! r mission st not fail!
Beedeep! Boop! Tweet!
TRANSLATION: If we're both robots, Cree-Pio, how come we look—and talk—so different?
Because I happen to be a magnificent, articulate golden Adonis, and you're a sawed-off, incoherent, stupid sack of bolts!
ESCAP CAPSU C
Beedeep! Boop!
TRANSLATION: I knew there had to be a scientific reason for it!
Goodness gracious, this planet simply screams for some—Je ne sais quoi—in the way of decor! Still, in some ways, it's a veritable Shangri-La! Take my hand, Bar-Stool . . . I'm a stranger in paradise . . .
Beedeep! Tweet!
TRANSLATION: As if I don't have enough problems, now I'm stuck with a fag robot!
-Stool, we seem to lost! Oh, dear . . . ok what's coming! iendish creatures out to tear us limb n limb and commit speakable acts of uelty upon us . . . !
Follow the yellow sand road! Follow the yellow sand road! Follow . . . follow . . . follow . . . follow . . . Follow the yellow sand road!
Beep! Zit! Gack!
TRANSLATION: And then again . . . there's an outside chance they may be Space Munchkins!
Hi, strangers! I'm Lube Skystalker! I'm a senior at Buffoin Tech, where I major in Incredible Space Heroics!
Gracious, there couldn't be any money in THAT field!
You're telling me! That's why I'm minoring in Space Accounting! Hey, anyone ever tell you you look like an "Oscar"?!?
Take a good look! With your performance in this film, it's as close as you'll ever get to an Academy Award!

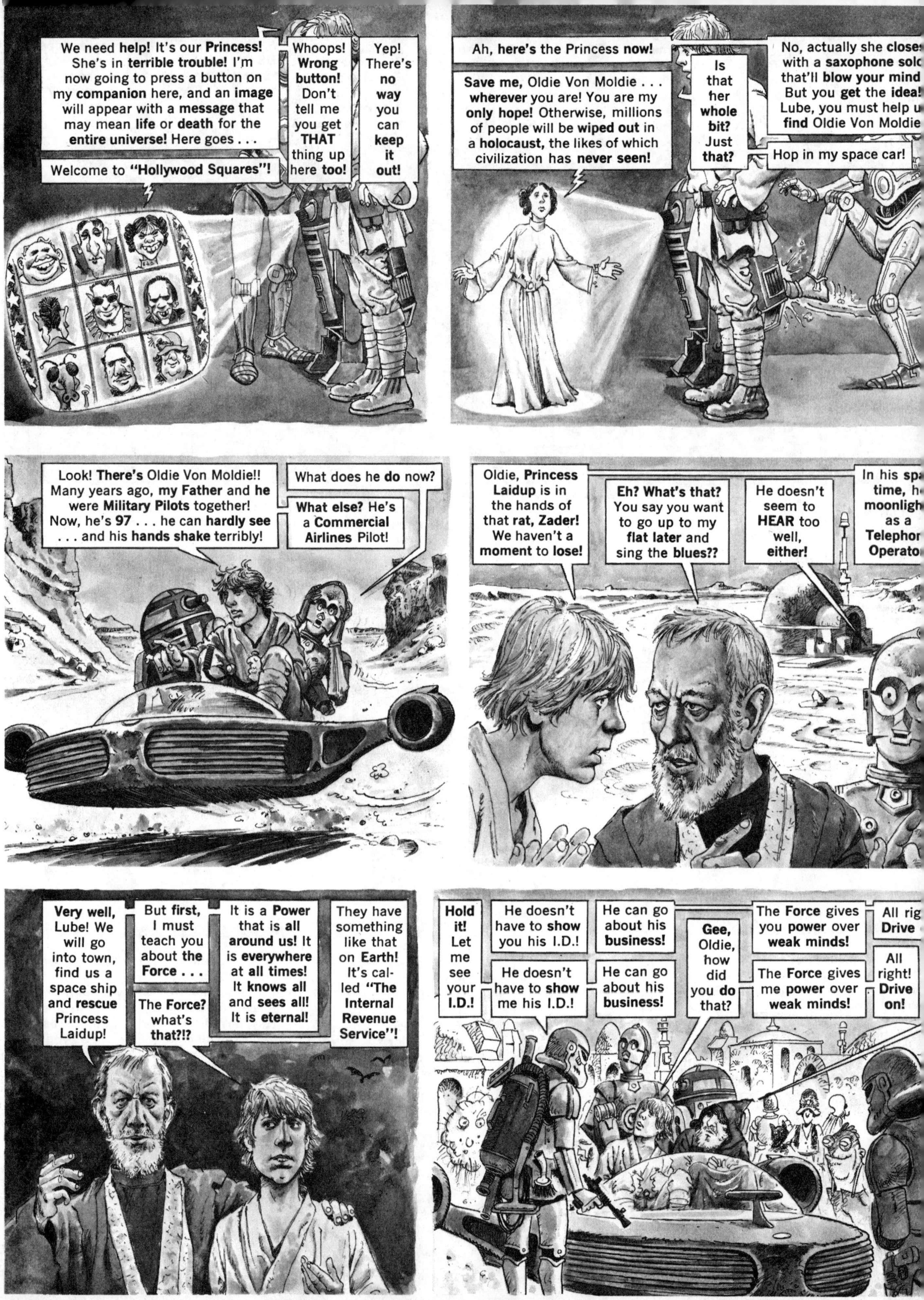
We need help! It's our Princess! She's in terrible trouble! I'm now going to press a button on my companion here, and an image will appear with a message that may mean life or death for the entire universe! Here goes . . .
Whoops! Wrong button! Don't tell me you get THAT thing up here too!
Yep! There's no way you can keep it out!
Welcome to "Hollywood Squares"!
Ah, here's the Princess now!
Save me, Oldie Von Moldie . . . wherever you are! You are my only hope! Otherwise, millions of people will be wiped out in a holocaust, the likes of which civilization has never seen!
Is that her whole bit? Just that?
No, actually she closes with a saxophone sol that'll blow your mind But you get the idea! Lube, you must help u find Oldie Von Moldie
Hop in my space car!
Look! There's Oldie Von Moldie!! Many years ago, my Father and he were Military Pilots together! Now, he's 97 . . . he can hardly see . . . and his hands shake terribly!
What does he do now?
What else? He's a Commercial Airlines Pilot!
Oldie, Princess Laidup is in the hands of that rat, Zader! We haven't a moment to lose!
Eh? What's that? You say you want to go up to my flat later and sing the blues??
He doesn't seem to HEAR too well, either!
In his spa time, h moonligh as a Telephor Operato
Very well, Lube! We will go into town, find us a space ship and rescue Princess Laidup!
But first, I must teach you about the Force . . .
The Force? what's that?!?
It is a Power that is all around us! It is everywhere at all times! It knows all and sees all! It is eternal!
They have something like that on Earth! It's called "The Internal Revenue Service"!
Hold it! Let me see your I.D.!
He doesn't have to show you his I.D.!
He doesn't have to show me his I.D.!
He can go about his business!
He can go about his business!
Gee, Oldie, how did you do that?
The Force gives you power over weak minds!
The Force gives me power over weak minds!
All rig Drive
All right! Drive on!

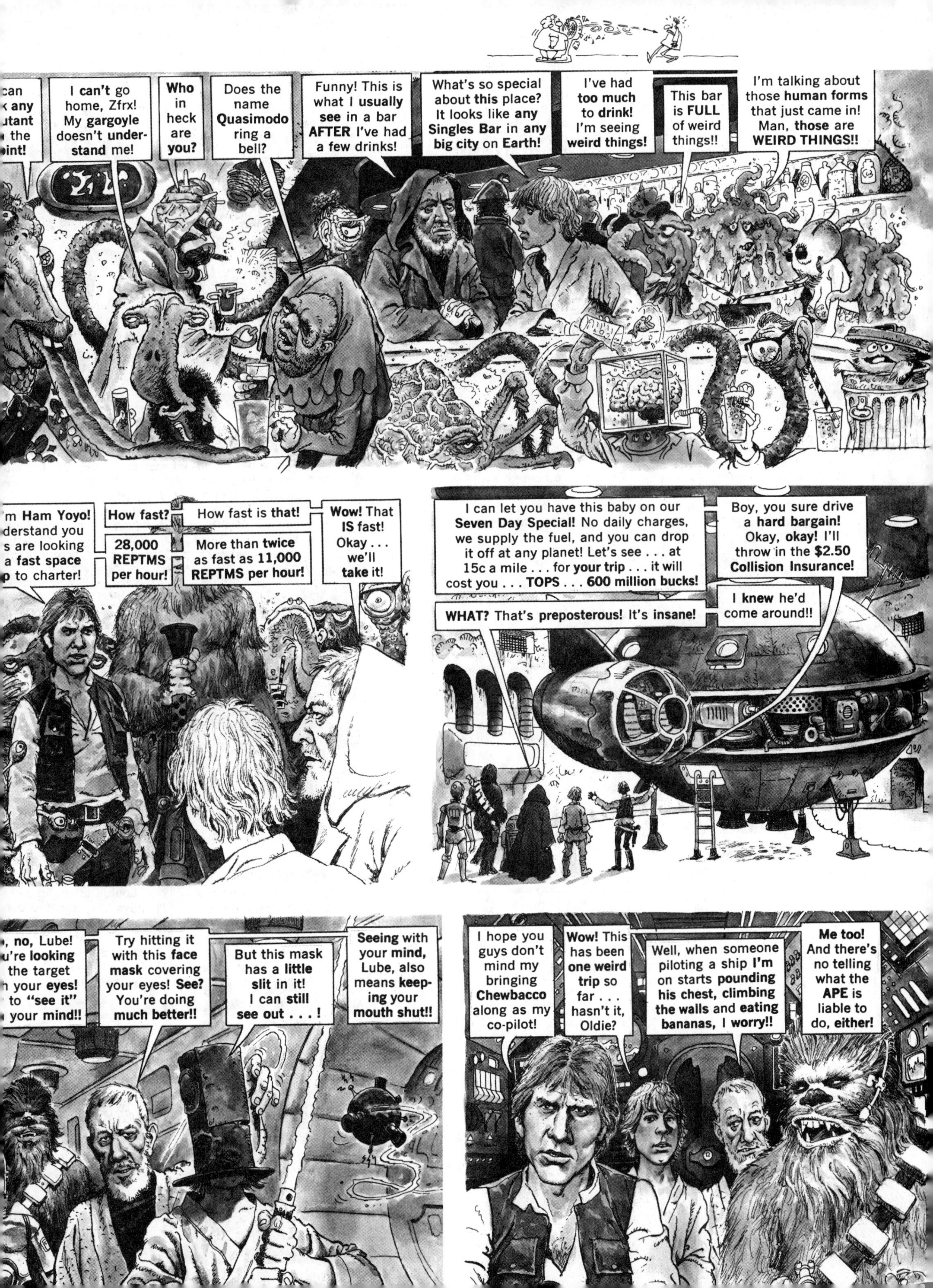
can any utant the int!
I can't go home, Zfrx! My gargoyle doesn't understand me!
Who in heck are you?
Does the name Quasimodo ring a bell?
Funny! This is what I usually see in a bar AFTER I've had a few drinks!
What's so special about this place? It looks like any Singles Bar in any big city on Earth!
I've had too much to drink! I'm seeing weird things!
This bar is FULL of weird things!!
I'm talking about those human forms that just came in! Man, those are WEIRD THINGS!!
m Ham Yoyo! derstand you s are looking a fast space to charter!
How fast?
28,000 REPTMS per hour!
How fast is that!
More than twice as fast as 11,000 REPTMS per hour!
Wow! That IS fast! Okay . . . we'll take it!
I can let you have this baby on our Seven Day Special! No daily charges, we supply the fuel, and you can drop it off at any planet! Let's see . . . at 15c a mile . . . for your trip . . . it will cost you . . . TOPS . . . 600 million bucks!
WHAT? That's preposterous! It's insane!
Boy, you sure drive a hard bargain! Okay, okay! I'll throw in the $2.50 Collision Insurance!
I knew he'd come around!!
no, Lube! u're looking the target your eyes! to "see it" your mind!!
Try hitting it with this face mask covering your eyes! See? You're doing much better!!
But this mask has a little slit in it! I can still see out . . . !
Seeing with your mind, Lube, also means keeping your mouth shut!!
I hope you guys don't mind my bringing Chewbacco along as my co-pilot!
Wow! This has been one weird trip so far . . . hasn't it, Oldie?
Well, when someone piloting a ship I'm on starts pounding his chest, climbing the walls and eating bananas, I worry!!
Me too! And there's no telling what the APE is liable to do, either!

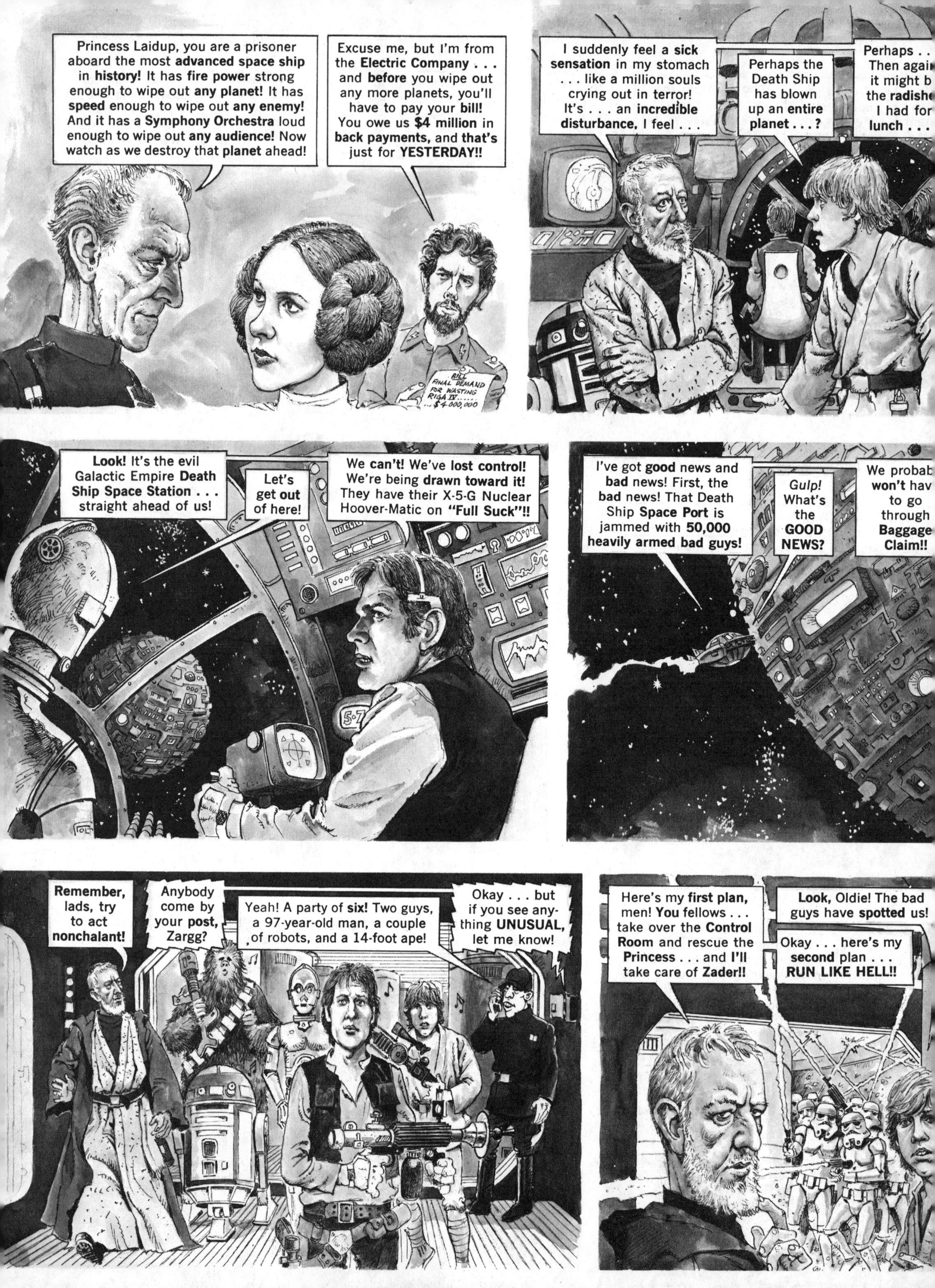

Princess Laidup, you are a prisoner aboard the most **advanced space ship** in **history!** It has **fire power** strong enough to wipe out **any planet!** It has **speed** enough to wipe out **any enemy!** And it has a **Symphony Orchestra** loud enough to wipe out **any audience!** Now watch as we destroy that **planet** ahead!
Excuse me, but I'm from the **Electric Company . . .** and **before** you wipe out any more planets, you'll have to pay your **bill!** You owe us **$4 million** in **back payments,** and **that's** just for **YESTERDAY!!**
BILL FINAL DEMAND FOR WASTING RIGA IV ... $4,000,000
I suddenly feel a **sick sensation** in my stomach . . . like a million souls crying out in terror! It's . . . an **incredible disturbance,** I feel . . .
Perhaps the Death Ship has blown up an **entire planet . . . ?**
Perhaps . . Then agai it might b the **radishe** I had for **lunch . . .**
Look! It's the evil Galactic Empire **Death Ship Space Station . . .** straight ahead of us!
Let's **get out** of here!
We **can't!** We've **lost control!** We're being **drawn toward it!** They have their X-5-G Nuclear Hoover-Matic on **"Full Suck"!!**
I've got **good** news and **bad** news! First, the **bad** news! That Death Ship **Space Port** is jammed with **50,000 heavily armed bad guys!**
Gulp! What's the **GOOD NEWS?**
We probab **won't** hav to go through **Baggage Claim!!**
Remember, lads, try to act **nonchalant!**
Anybody come by your **post,** Zargg?
Yeah! A party of **six!** Two guys, a 97-year-old man, a couple of robots, and a 14-foot ape!
Okay . . . but if you see anything **UNUSUAL,** let me know!
Here's my **first plan,** men! **You** fellows . . . take over the **Control Room** and rescue the **Princess . . .** and **I'll** take care of **Zader!!**
Look, Oldie! The bad guys have **spotted** us!
Okay . . . here's my **second** plan . . . **RUN LIKE HELL!!**

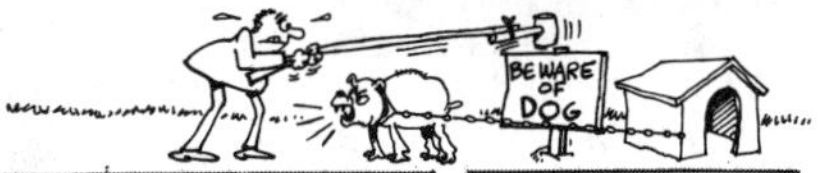
BEWARE OF DOG

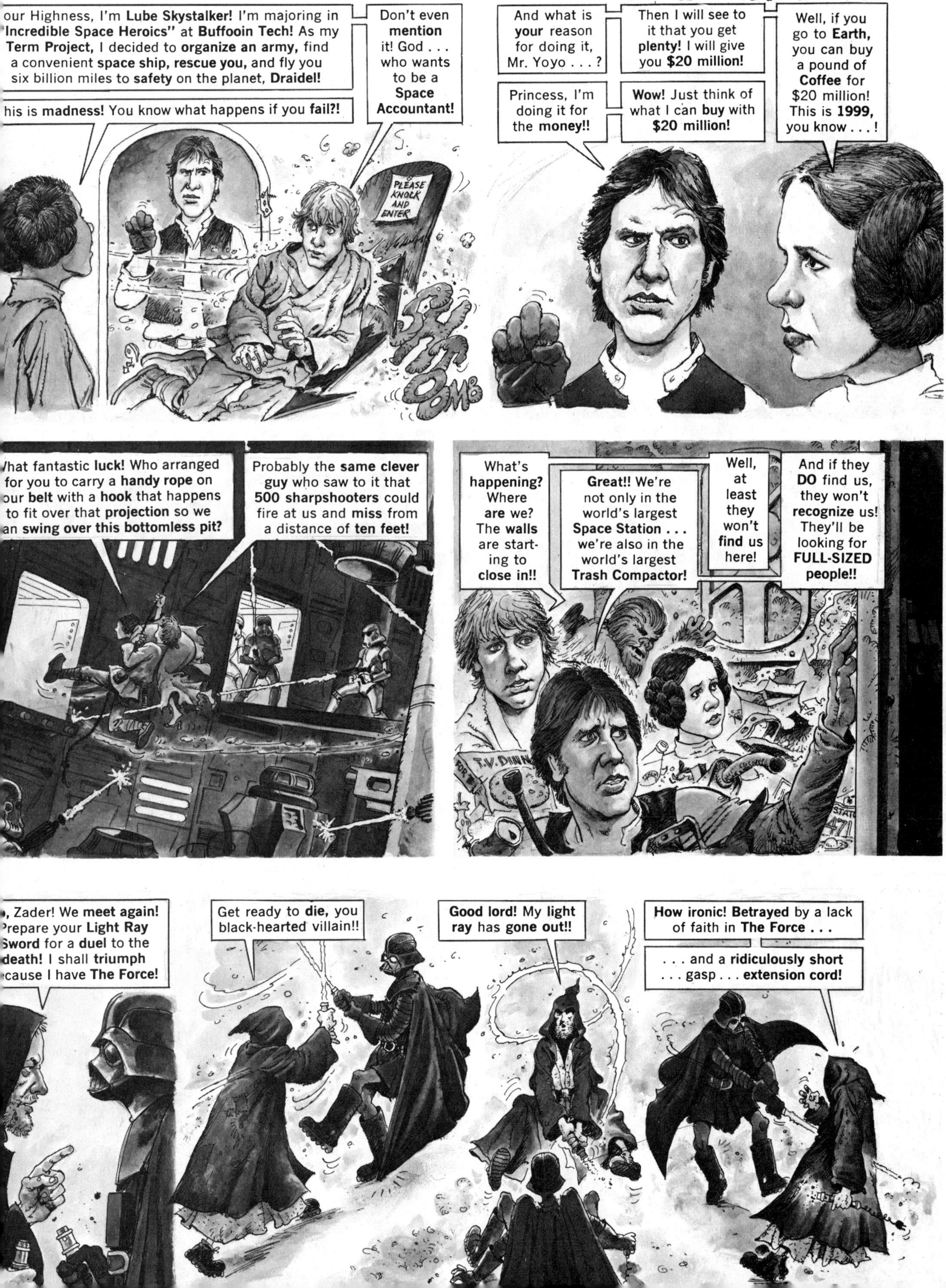
our Highness, I'm Lube Skystalker! I'm majoring in "Incredible Space Heroics" at Buffoin Tech! As my Term Project, I decided to organize an army, find a convenient space ship, rescue you, and fly you six billion miles to safety on the planet, Draidel!
Don't even mention it! God . . . who wants to be a Space Accountant!
his is madness! You know what happens if you fail?!
PLEASE KNOCK AND ENTER
And what is your reason for doing it, Mr. Yoyo . . . ?
Princess, I'm doing it for the money!!
Then I will see to it that you get plenty! I will give you $20 million!
Wow! Just think of what I can buy with $20 million!
Well, if you go to Earth, you can buy a pound of Coffee for $20 million! This is 1999, you know . . . !
/hat fantastic luck! Who arranged for you to carry a handy rope on our belt with a hook that happens to fit over that projection so we an swing over this bottomless pit?
Probably the same clever guy who saw to it that 500 sharpshooters could fire at us and miss from a distance of ten feet!
What's happening? Where are we? The walls are starting to close in!!
Great!! We're not only in the world's largest Space Station . . . we're also in the world's largest Trash Compactor!
Well, at least they won't find us here!
And if they DO find us, they won't recognize us! They'll be looking for FULL-SIZED people!!
, Zader! We meet again! Prepare your Light Ray Sword for a duel to the death! I shall triumph ecause I have The Force!
Get ready to die, you black-hearted villain!!
Good lord! My light ray has gone out!!
How ironic! Betrayed by a lack of faith in The Force . . .
. . . and a ridiculously short . . . gasp . . . extension cord!

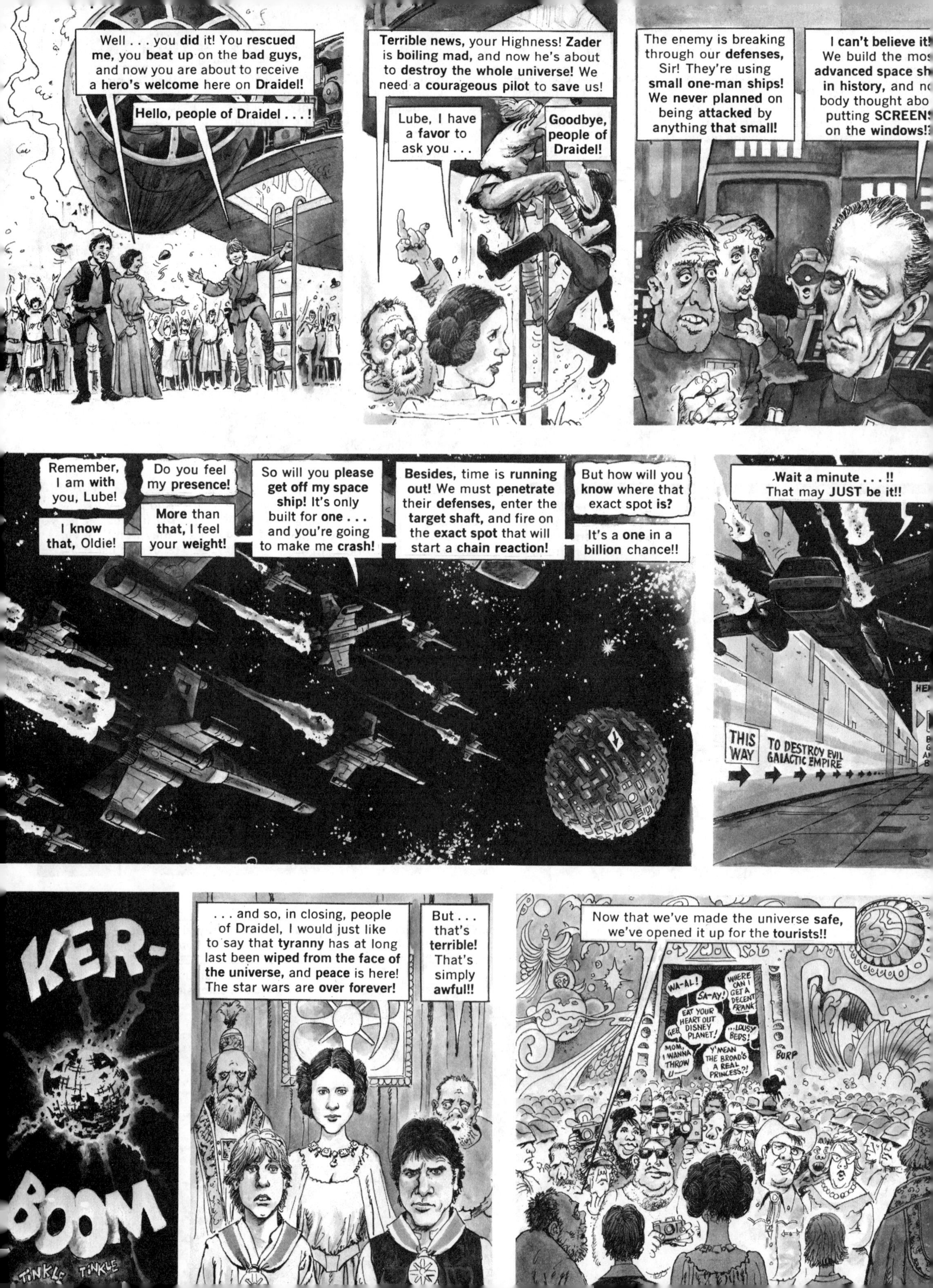
Well . . . you did it! You rescued me, you beat up on the bad guys, and now you are about to receive a hero's welcome here on Draidel!
Hello, people of Draidel . . . !
Terrible news, your Highness! Zader is boiling mad, and now he's about to destroy the whole universe! We need a courageous pilot to save us!
Lube, I have a favor to ask you . . .
Goodbye, people of Draidel!
The enemy is breaking through our defenses, Sir! They're using small one-man ships! We never planned on being attacked by anything that small!
I can't believe it! We build the mos advanced space sh in history, and no body thought abo putting SCREENS on the windows!
Remember, I am with you, Lube!
I know that, Oldie!
Do you feel my presence!
More than that, I feel your weight!
So will you please get off my space ship! It's only built for one . . . and you're going to make me crash!
Besides, time is running out! We must penetrate their defenses, enter the target shaft, and fire on the exact spot that will start a chain reaction!
But how will you know where that exact spot is?
It's a one in a billion chance!!
Wait a minute . . . !! That may JUST be it!!
THIS WAY
TO DESTROY EVIL GALACTIC EMPIRE
KER-
BOOM
TINKLE TINKLE
. . . and so, in closing, people of Draidel, I would just like to say that tyranny has at long last been wiped from the face of the universe, and peace is here! The star wars are over forever!
But . . . that's terrible! That's simply awful!!
Now that we've made the universe safe, we've opened it up for the tourists!!
WA-AL!
SA-AY!
WHERE CAN I GET A DECENT FRANK
EAT YOUR HEART OUT DISNEY PLANET!
GEE
...LOUSY BEDS!
MOM, I WANNA THROW U-
Y'MEAN THE BROAD'S A REAL PRINCESS?!
BURP

DON MARTIN DEPT. PART I

ONE DAY FIVE THOUSAND YEARS AGO

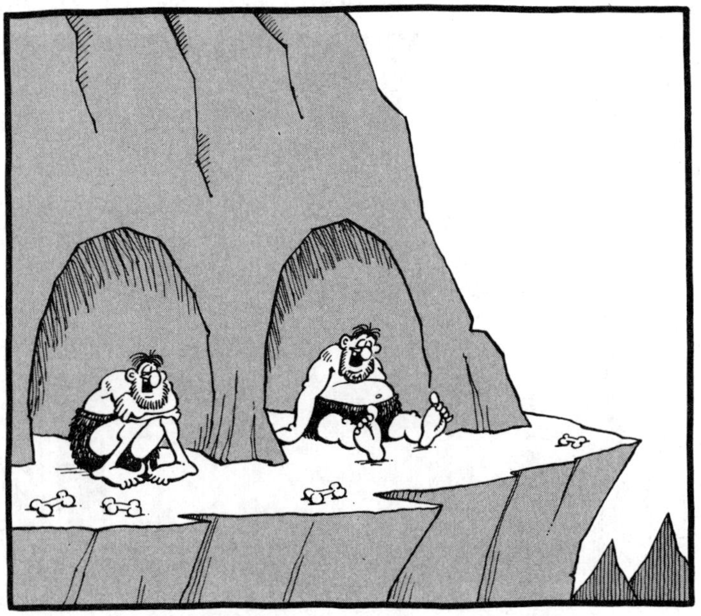

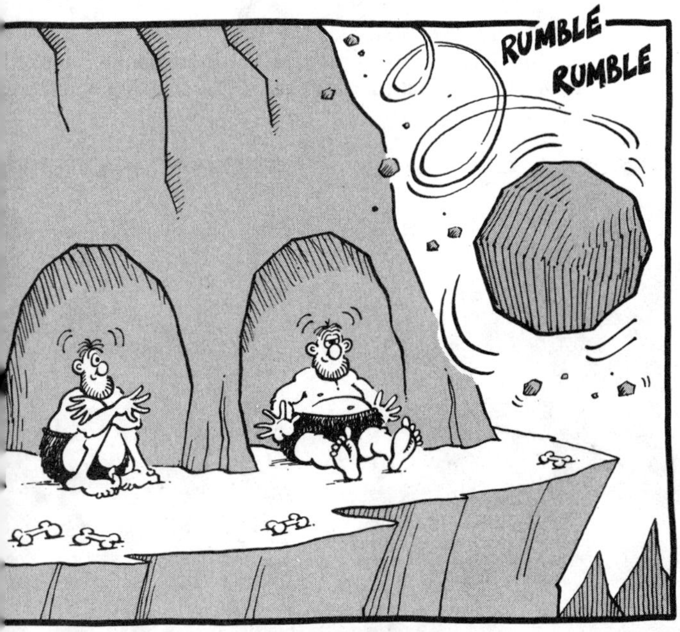
RUMBLE
RUMBLE

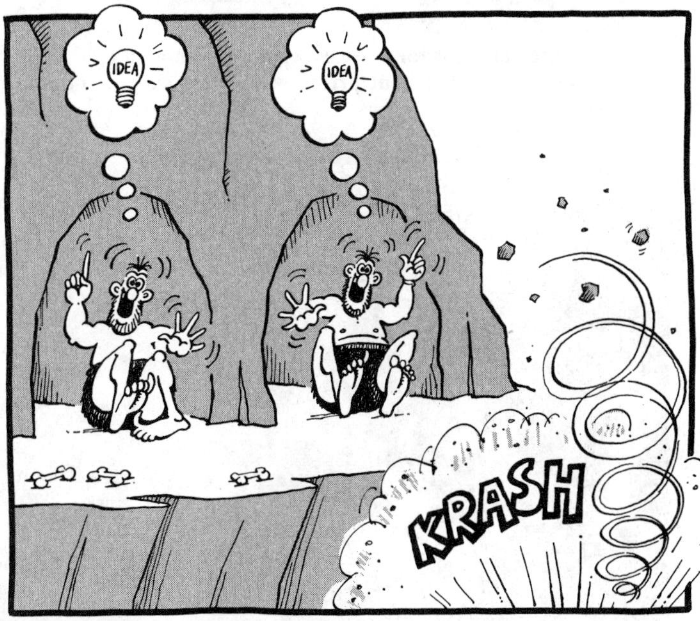
IDEA
IDEA
KRASH

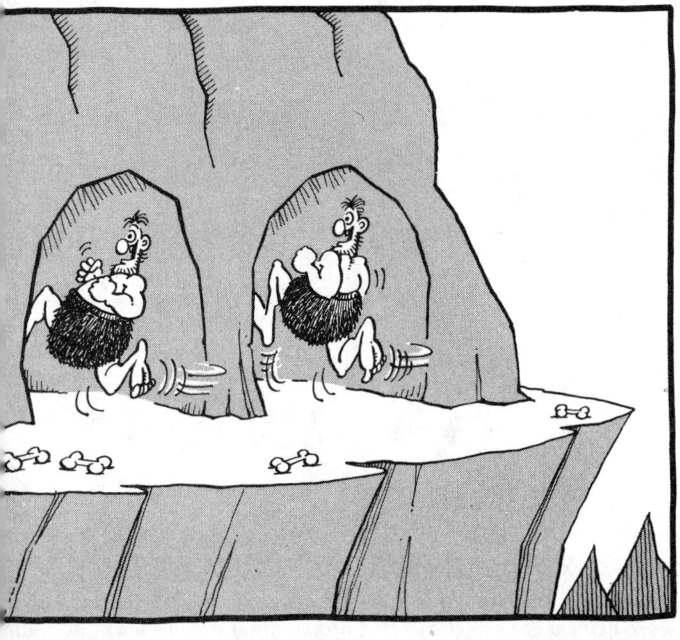

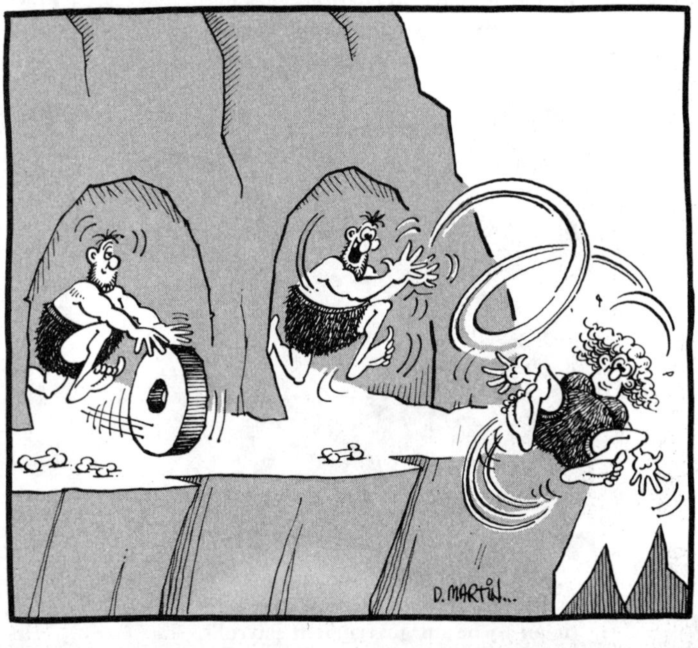
D. MARTIN...

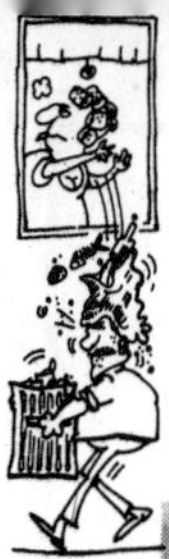

WE SHOULD LIVE SO LONG DEPT.

WE'D LIKE TO SE

ARTIST: JACK

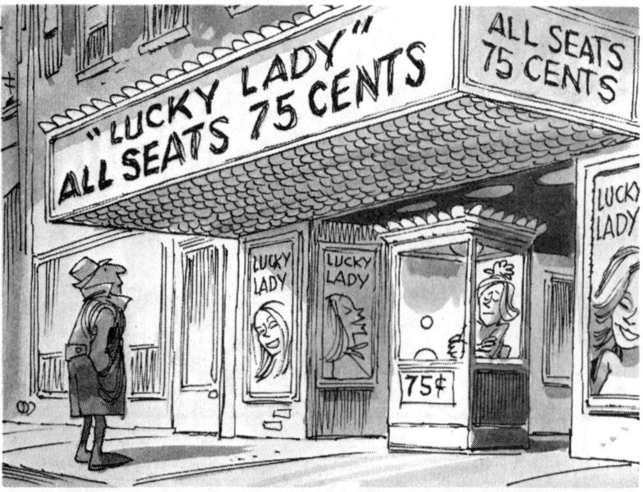
"LUCKY LADY"
ALL SEATS 75 CENTS
ALL SEATS
75 CENTS
LUCKY LADY
LUCKY LADY
LUCKY LADY
75¢

. . . theaters that raise prices when they show biggies like "The Godfather" cut prices when they show a bomb.

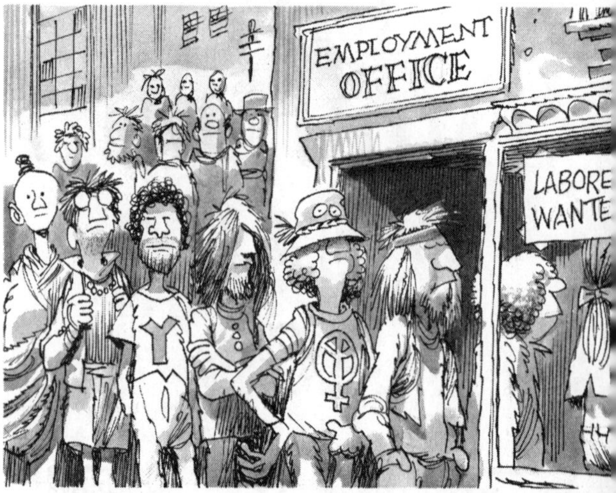
EMPLOYMENT
OFFICE
LABORE
WANTE

. . . those radicals who sneer at the Establishment make i their own without food stamps, welfare or ripping off peo

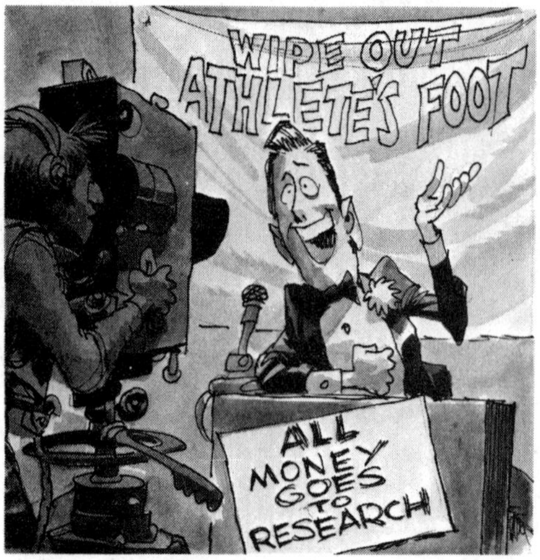
WIPE OUT
ATHLETE'S FOOT
ALL MONEY GOES TO RESEARCH

. . . the money donated to charities goes to the charities instead of the fund-raisers.

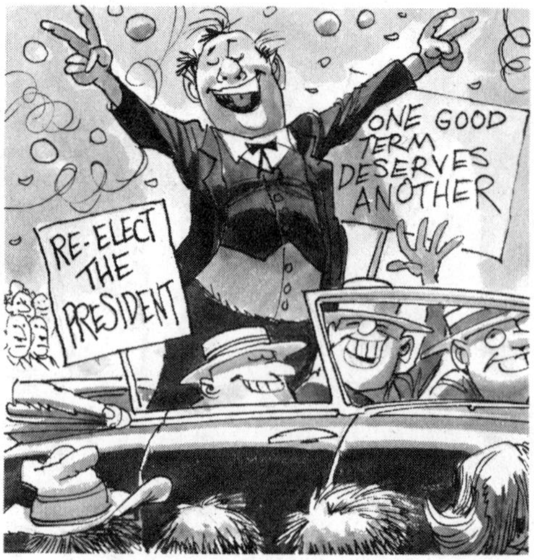
ONE GOOD TERM DESERVES ANOTHER
RE-ELECT THE PRESIDENT

. . . a President doesn't spend the last two years of his term running for re-election.

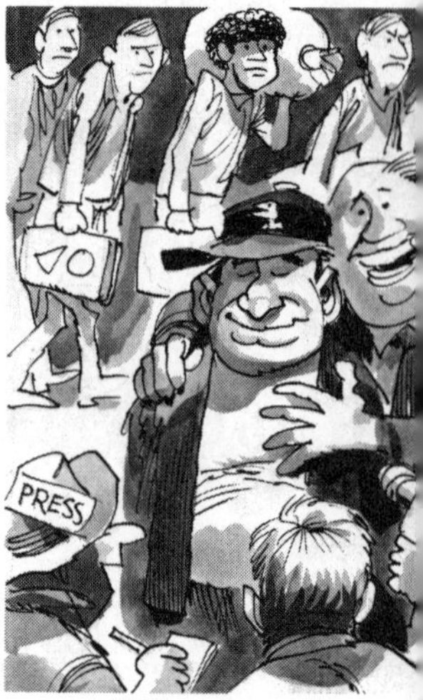
PRESS

. . . a Club Owner fires al players and keeps the Man

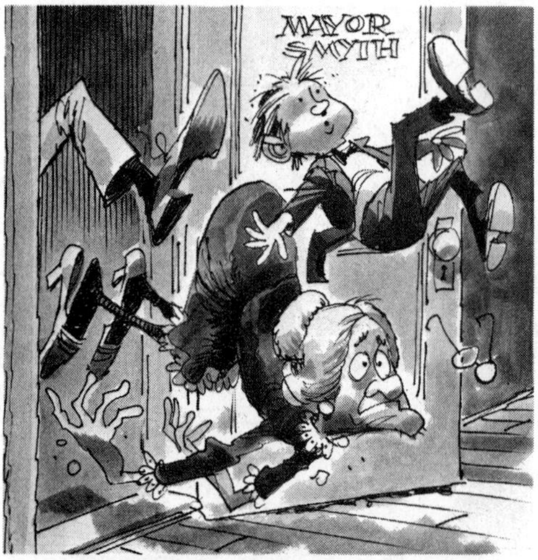
MAYOR
SMYTH

. . . it's illegal for relatives of any politician to be on government payrolls.

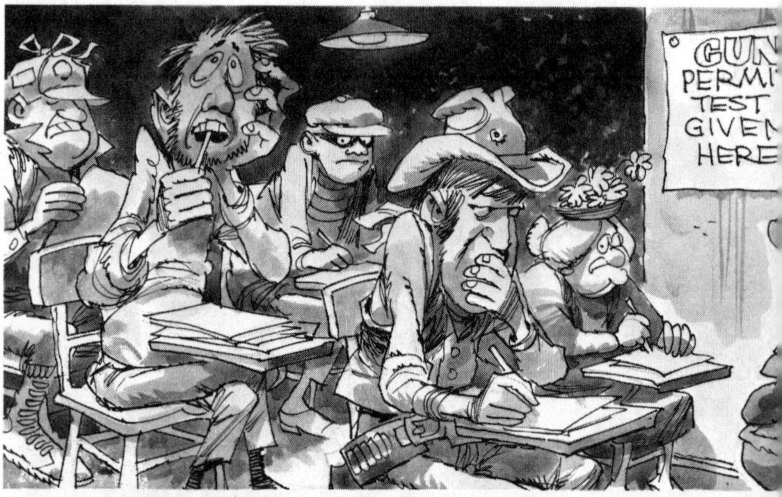
GUN
PERMI
TEST
GIVEN
HERE

. . . a person has to pass a test and get a license to own a gun just li he does to drive a car or get married or any other dangerous undertakin

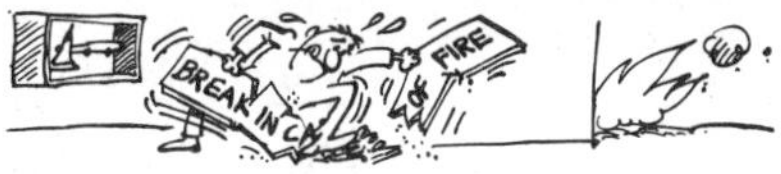
BREAK IN CA
FIRE

'HE DAY WHEN...

E: LOU SILVERSTONE

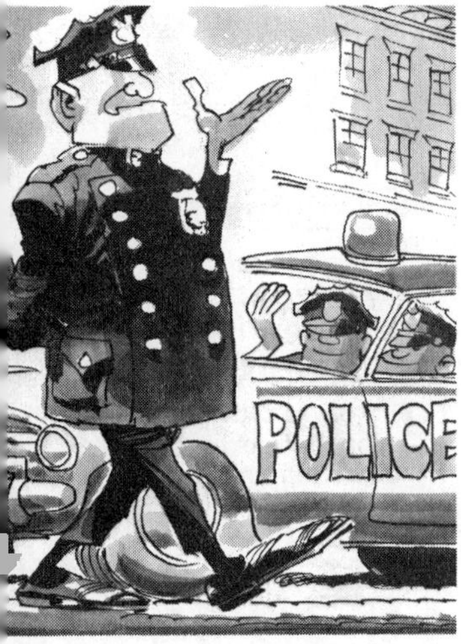
POLICE

there are as many cops on our
eets as there are on our TV's.

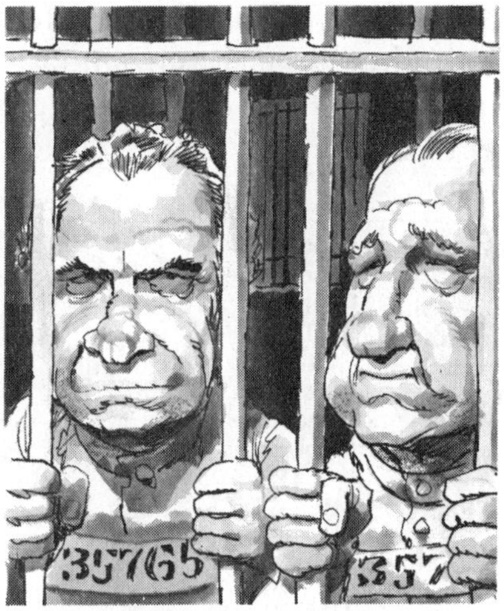
35765
357

...politicians who break the law
are treated like any other crooks.

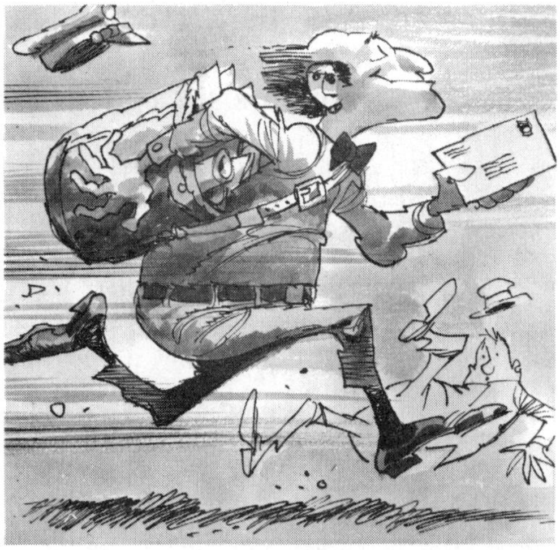

...mail service improves instead of getting
worse every time they raise postage rates.

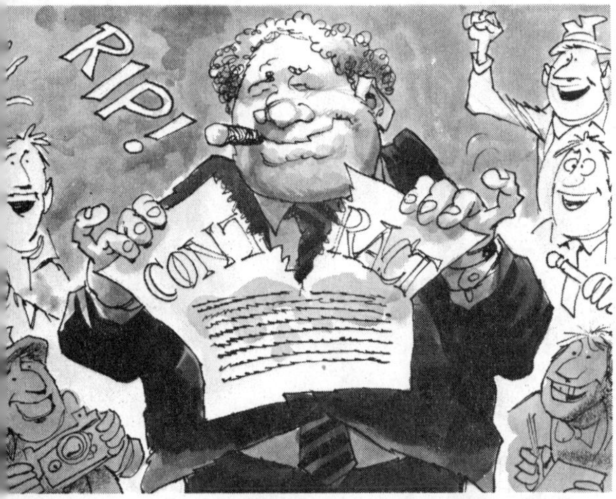
RIP!
CONTRACT

.the head of a municipal union announces that his men
'll take a cut in pay to help a city that's going broke.

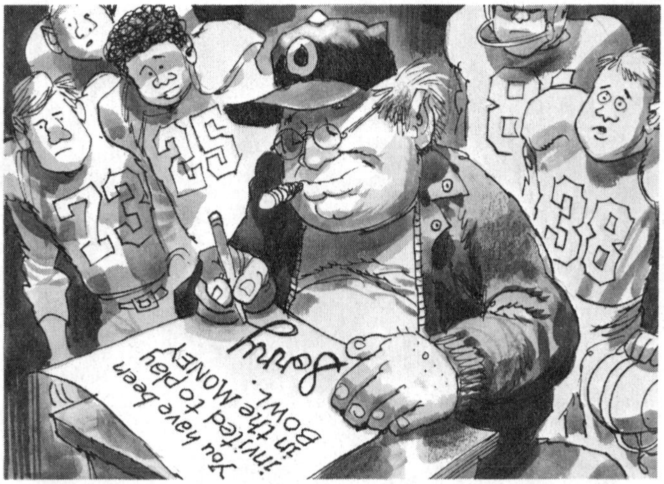
73
25
38
Sorry
You have been
invited to play
in the MONEY
BOWL.

...the coach of a "football factory" turns down a bowl bid
because his players have already missed too many classes.

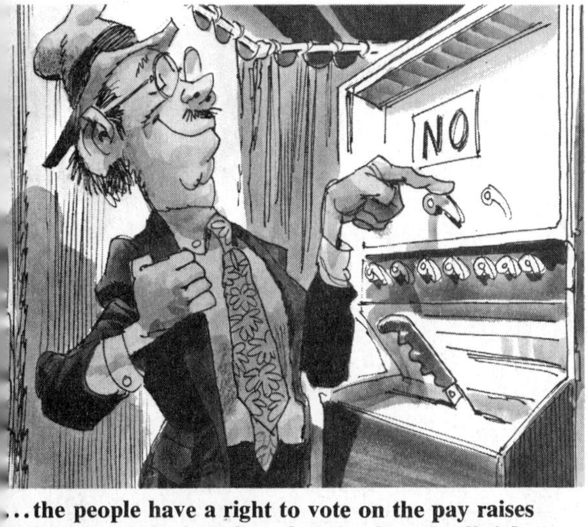
NO

...the people have a right to vote on the pay raises
and gravy train benefits of their elected officials.

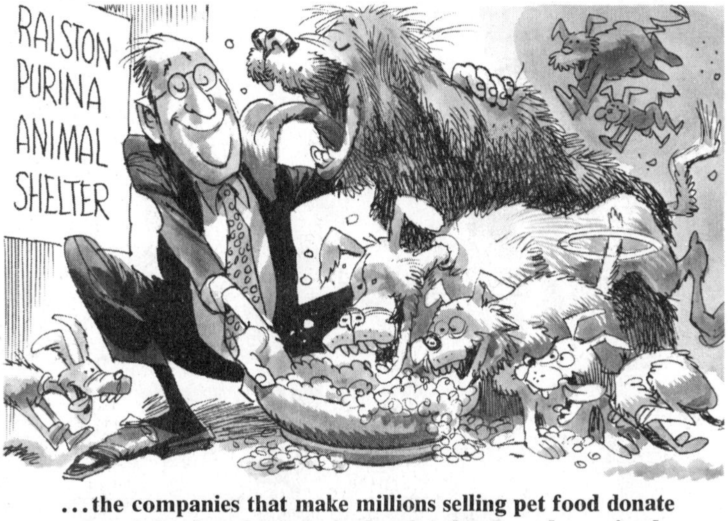
RALSTON
PURINA
ANIMAL
SHELTER

...the companies that make millions selling pet food donate
some of that bread to help feed and shelter homeless animals.

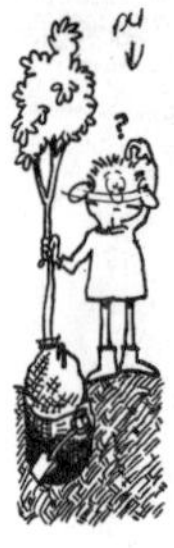

HIGH TRAVOLTAGE DEPT.

Combine a dynamic young TV star with the soundtrack of a hot, exploitable singin group and some "R"-rated dialogue, insure it with some sub-plots from other h films like "Rocky," "American Graffiti," "West Side Story," "Mean Streets," an "Beach Blanket Bingo"... and you've got the formula for one of the biggest block buster movies of the year, right? Wrong! Because the best "hustle" may not be th one they're dancing up on the screen, but the one foisted on us by the producers for making millions on a film that does have spectacular choreography... but no much else! Yep, as far as we at MAD are concerned, you wasted your money on . .

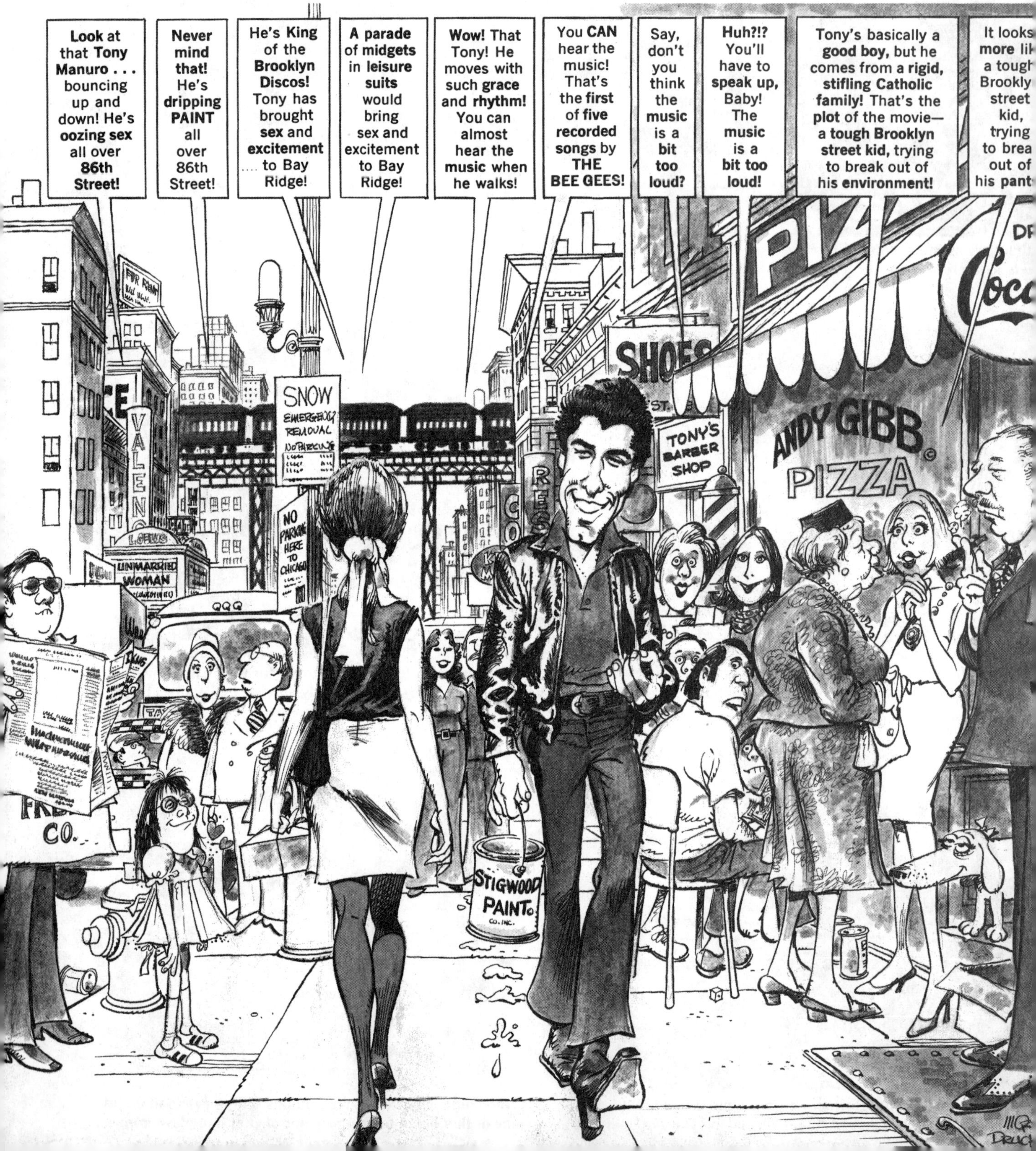
Look at that Tony Manuro . . . bouncing up and down! He's oozing sex all over 86th Street!
Never mind that! He's dripping PAINT all over 86th Street!
He's King of the Brooklyn Discos! Tony has brought sex and excitement .... to Bay Ridge!
A parade of midgets in leisure suits would bring sex and excitement to Bay Ridge!
Wow! That Tony! He moves with such grace and rhythm! You can almost hear the music when he walks!
You CAN hear the music! That's the first of five recorded songs by THE BEE GEES!
Say, don't you think the music is a bit too loud?
Huh?!? You'll have to speak up, Baby! The music is a bit too loud!
Tony's basically a good boy, but he comes from a rigid, stifling Catholic family! That's the plot of the movie— a tough Brooklyn street kid, trying to break out of his environment!
It looks more lik a tough Brookly street kid, trying to brea out of his pant
SNOW
EMERGENCY REMOVAL
NO PARKING
NO PARKING HERE TO CHICAGO
LOEWS
UNMARRIED WOMAN
PIZ
SHOES
TONY'S BARBER SHOP
ANDY GIBB© PIZZA
STIGWOOD PAINT CO. INC.
CO.

SATURDAY NIGHT FEEBLE

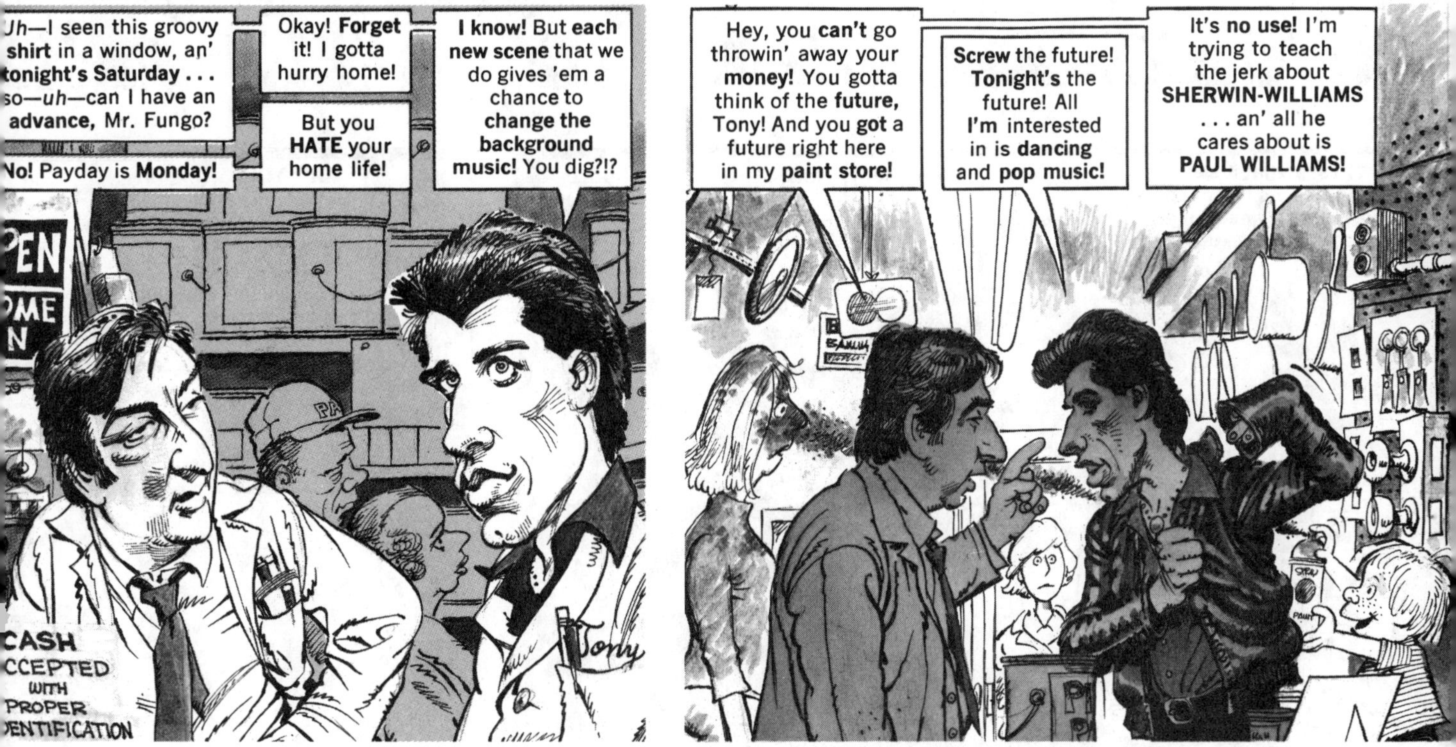

Uh—I seen this groovy shirt in a window, an' tonight's Saturday . . . so—uh—can I have an advance, Mr. Fungo?
No! Payday is Monday!
Okay! Forget it! I gotta hurry home!
But you HATE your home life!
I know! But each new scene that we do gives 'em a chance to change the background music! You dig?!?
CASH
CCEPTED
WITH
PROPER
ENTIFICATION
Tony
Hey, you can't go throwin' away your money! You gotta think of the future, Tony! And you got a future right here in my paint store!
Screw the future! Tonight's the future! All I'm interested in is dancing and pop music!
It's no use! I'm trying to teach the jerk about SHERWIN-WILLIAMS . . . an' all he cares about is PAUL WILLIAMS!

ARTIST: MORT DRUCKER WRITER: ARNIE KOGEN

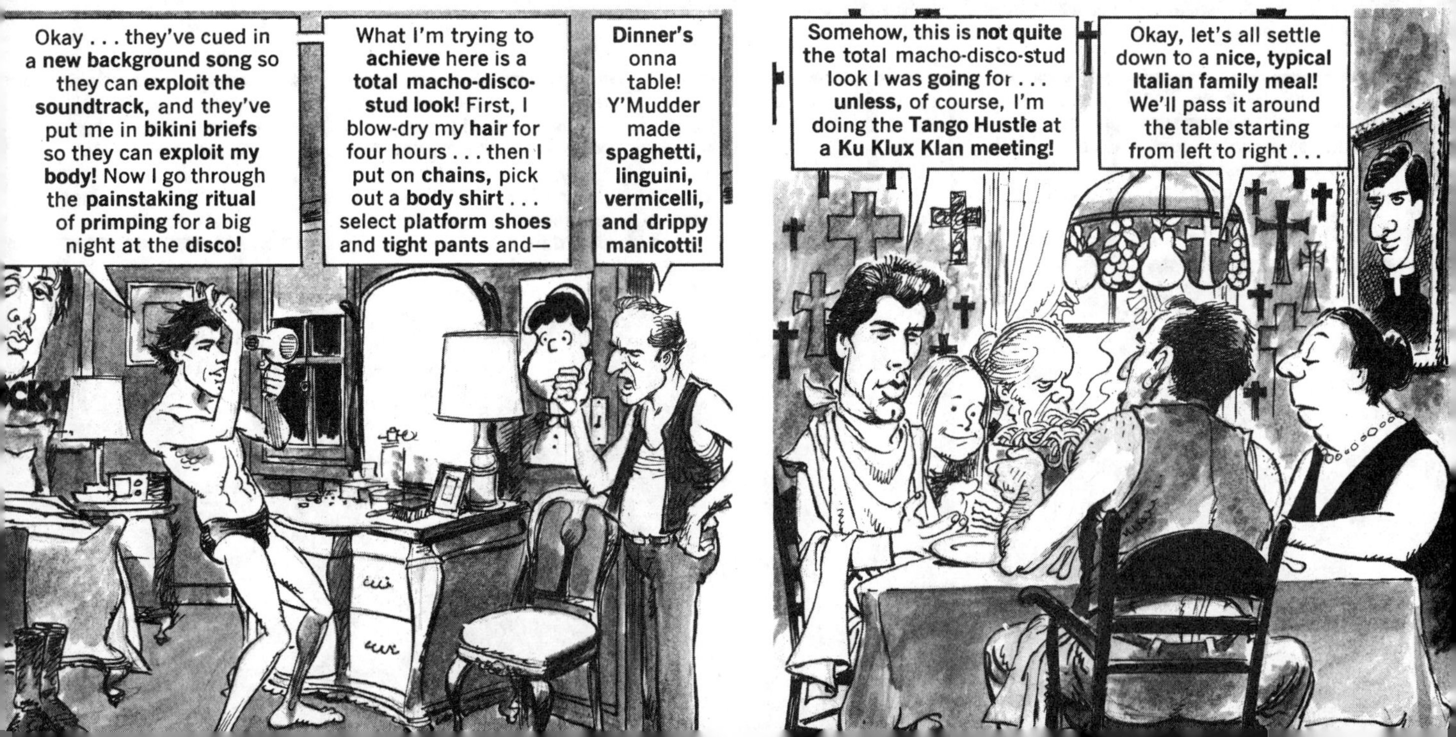

Okay . . . they've cued in a new background song so they can exploit the soundtrack, and they've put me in bikini briefs so they can exploit my body! Now I go through the painstaking ritual of primping for a big night at the disco!
What I'm trying to achieve here is a total macho-disco-stud look! First, I blow-dry my hair for four hours . . . then I put on chains, pick out a body shirt . . . select platform shoes and tight pants and—
Dinner's onna table! Y'Mudder made spaghetti, linguini, vermicelli, and drippy manicotti!
Somehow, this is not quite the total macho-disco-stud look I was going for . . . unless, of course, I'm doing the Tango Hustle at a Ku Klux Klan meeting!
Okay, let's all settle down to a nice, typical Italian family meal! We'll pass it around the table starting from left to right . . .

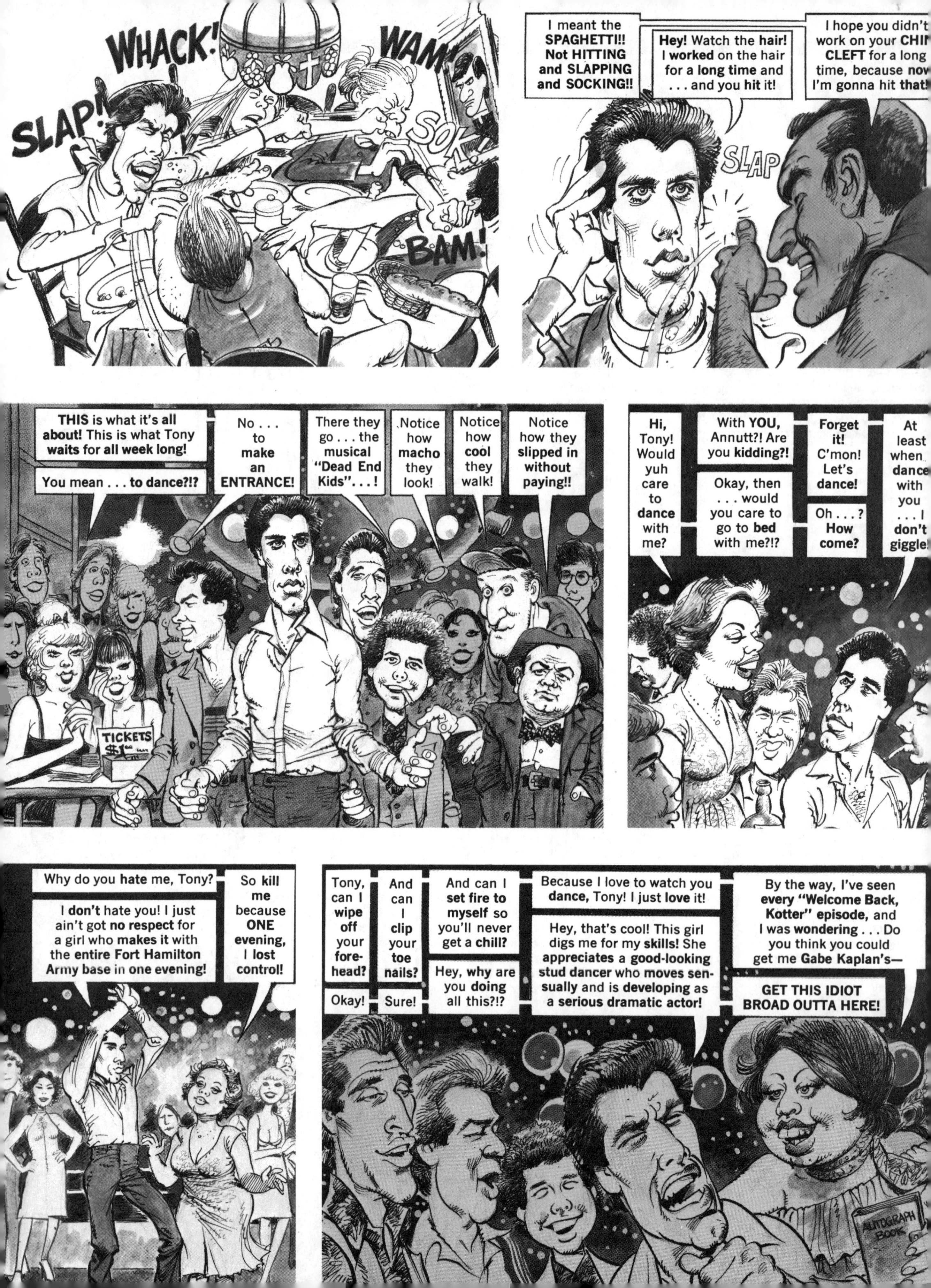
WHACK!
WAM!
SLAP!
SOK!
BAM!
I meant the SPAGHETTI!! Not HITTING and SLAPPING and SOCKING!!
Hey! Watch the hair! I worked on the hair for a long time and . . . and you hit it!
I hope you didn't work on your CHI CLEFT for a long time, because now I'm gonna hit that!
SLAP
THIS is what it's all about! This is what Tony waits for all week long!
You mean . . . to dance?!?
No . . . to make an ENTRANCE!
There they go . . . the musical "Dead End Kids" . . . !
Notice how macho they look!
Notice how cool they walk!
Notice how they slipped in without paying!!
TICKETS $1
Hi, Tony! Would yuh care to dance with me?
With YOU, Annutt?! Are you kidding?!
Okay, then . . . would you care to go to bed with me?!?
Forget it! C'mon! Let's dance!
Oh . . . ? How come?
At least when dance with you . . . I don't giggle!
Why do you hate me, Tony?
I don't hate you! I just ain't got no respect for a girl who makes it with the entire Fort Hamilton Army base in one evening!
So kill me because ONE evening, I lost control!
Tony, can I wipe off your fore-head?
Okay!
And can I clip your toe nails?
Sure!
And can I set fire to myself so you'll never get a chill?
Hey, why are you doing all this?!?
Because I love to watch you dance, Tony! I just love it!
Hey, that's cool! This girl digs me for my skills! She appreciates a good-looking stud dancer who moves sen-sually and is developing as a serious dramatic actor!
By the way, I've seen every "Welcome Back, Kotter" episode, and I was wondering . . . Do you think you could get me Gabe Kaplan's—
GET THIS IDIOT BROAD OUTTA HERE!
AUTOGRAPH BOOK

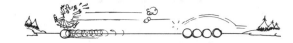

Hey, Double-X! You see that **girl** over here? **That one . . . ?**

Yeah . . . ?

Is she **NEW?**

Nahhh! She looks to be about **twen'y-two** or **twen'y t'ree!**

Don't break my chops, huh? I meant, did you ever see her at the "3001 Spaced Odyssey Disco" **before?!?**

No, Tony, I ain't never did!

Well, **that** chick can **DANCE!!** She don't have the right **PARTNER . . .** but **she can DANCE!!**

You **sure?** The guy looks okay to me!

Forget it! Some dudes are **born to dance!** Others **ain't!**

You gonna ask her to dance, Tony?

Not tonight, Double-X! Right now, we got our **work cut out for us!!**

You mean a **Gang Rumble?**

That's **later!**

You mean a **Gang Bang?!**

That's **later, too . . .**

Tony, what the @#$%¢ are you talking about?!

I'm talking about a **GANG DANCE!!**

Hey, isn't it **amazing** how **200 strangers** in a **Brooklyn Disco** can suddenly **fall in line** and begin doing the most **intricate** and **involved** precision dancing you've ever seen in your life?

It's not so amazing when you realize that **Radio City Music Hall** recently closed, and **half** these dancers are probably **LAID-OFF "ROCKETTES"!**

It's **easy!** Just follow the "dancing footsteps" painted on the floor!

Oh-oh! I think our row is in **deep trouble!**

Why? Is somebody dancing out of step?!?

Even **worse!** Somebody's **DEODORANT** just failed!

Yeah? Whose?

I'm **not sure,** but the term **"Sweathog"** suddenly takes on a great **significance!**

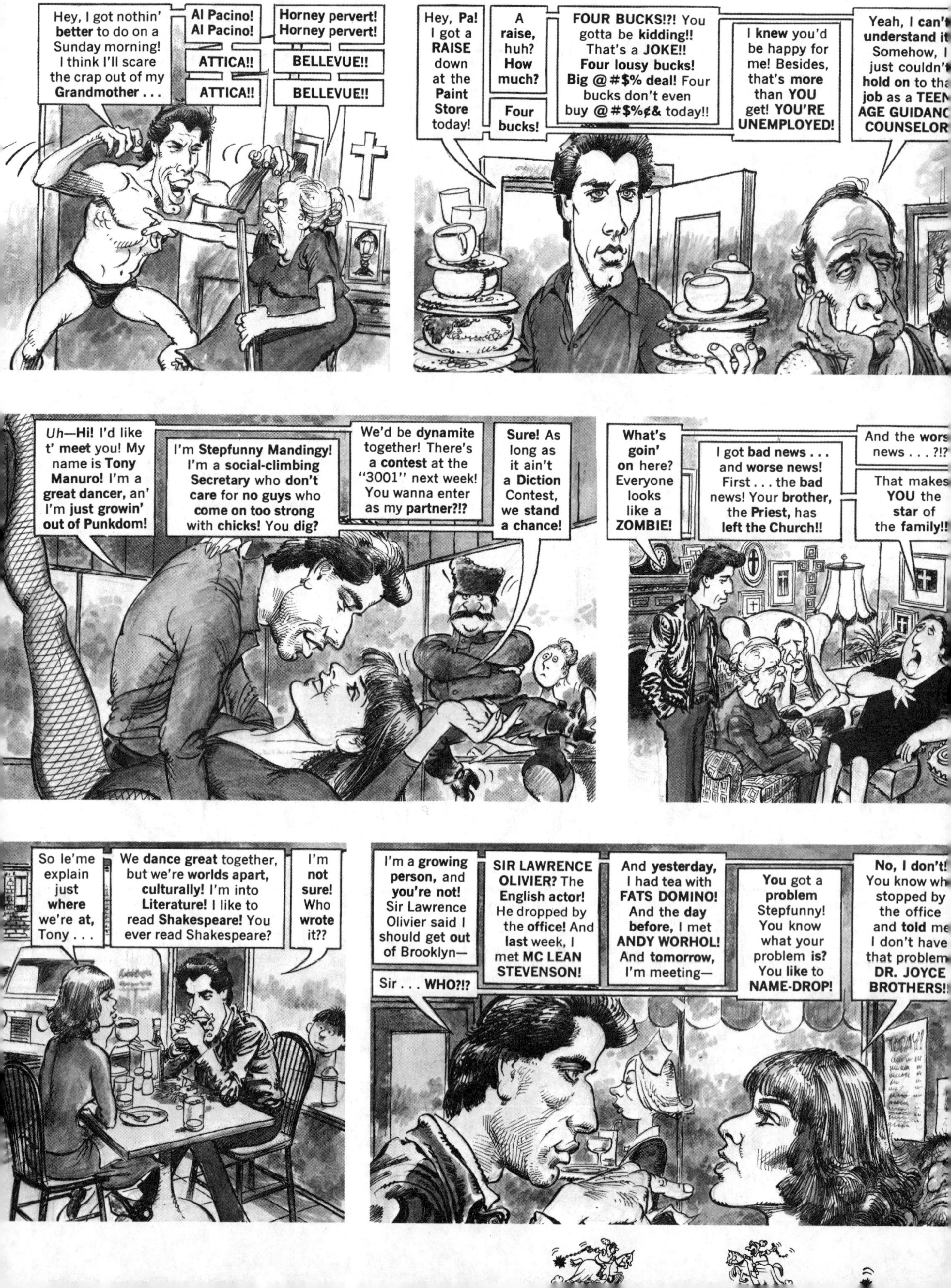

Hey, I got nothin' better to do on a Sunday morning! I think I'll scare the crap out of my Grandmother . . .
Al Pacino! Al Pacino!
ATTICA!!
ATTICA!!
Horney pervert! Horney pervert!
BELLEVUE!!
BELLEVUE!!
Hey, Pa! I got a RAISE down at the Paint Store today!
A raise, huh? How much?
Four bucks!
FOUR BUCKS!?! You gotta be kidding!! That's a JOKE!! Four lousy bucks! Big @#$% deal! Four bucks don't even buy @#$%¢& today!!
I knew you'd be happy for me! Besides, that's more than YOU get! YOU'RE UNEMPLOYED!
Yeah, I can't understand it Somehow, I just couldn' hold on to tha job as a TEEN AGE GUIDANC COUNSELOR
Uh—Hi! I'd like t' meet you! My name is Tony Manuro! I'm a great dancer, an' I'm just growin' out of Punkdom!
I'm Stepfunny Mandingy! I'm a social-climbing Secretary who don't care for no guys who come on too strong with chicks! You dig?
We'd be dynamite together! There's a contest at the "3001" next week! You wanna enter as my partner?!?
Sure! As long as it ain't a Diction Contest, we stand a chance!
What's goin' on here? Everyone looks like a ZOMBIE!
I got bad news . . . and worse news! First . . . the bad news! Your brother, the Priest, has left the Church!!
And the wors news . . . ?!?
That makes YOU the star of the family!!
So le'me explain just where we're at, Tony . . .
We dance great together, but we're worlds apart, culturally! I'm into Literature! I like to read Shakespeare! You ever read Shakespeare?
I'm not sure! Who wrote it??
I'm a growing person, and you're not! Sir Lawrence Olivier said I should get out of Brooklyn—
Sir . . . WHO?!?
SIR LAWRENCE OLIVIER? The English actor! He dropped by the office! And last week, I met MC LEAN STEVENSON!
And yesterday, I had tea with FATS DOMINO! And the day before, I met ANDY WORHOL! And tomorrow, I'm meeting—
You got a problem Stepfunny! You know what your problem is? You like to NAME-DROP!
No, I don't! You know wh stopped by the office and told me I don't have that problem DR. JOYCE BROTHERS!
TODAY!!

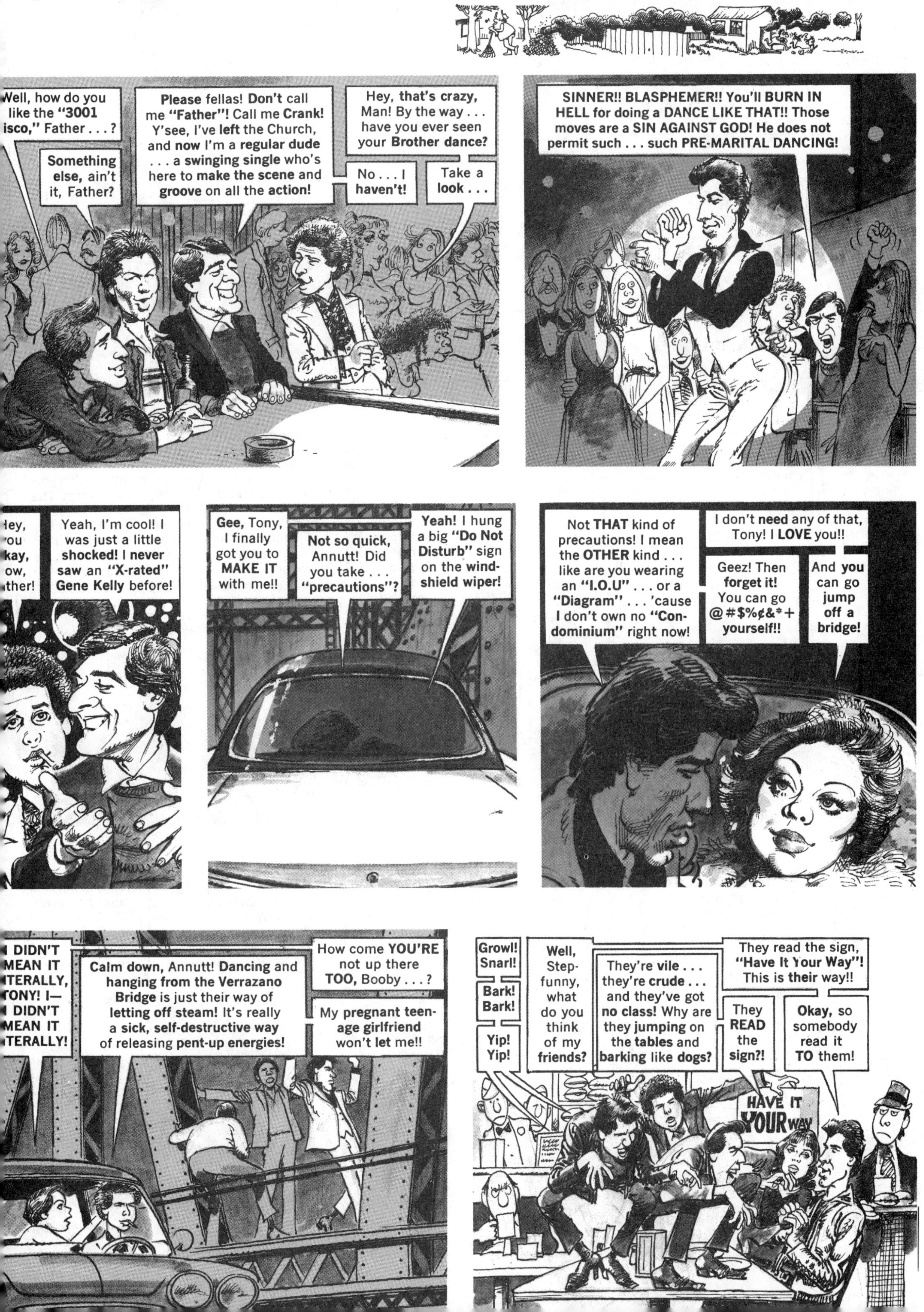
Well, how do you like the "3001 isco," Father . . . ?
Something else, ain't it, Father?
Please fellas! Don't call me "Father"! Call me Crank! Y'see, I've left the Church, and now I'm a regular dude . . . a swinging single who's here to make the scene and groove on all the action!
Hey, that's crazy, Man! By the way . . . have you ever seen your Brother dance?
No . . . I haven't!
Take a look . . .
SINNER!! BLASPHEMER!! You'll BURN IN HELL for doing a DANCE LIKE THAT!! Those moves are a SIN AGAINST GOD! He does not permit such . . . such PRE-MARITAL DANCING!
ley, ou kay, ow, ther!
Yeah, I'm cool! I was just a little shocked! I never saw an "X-rated" Gene Kelly before!
Gee, Tony, I finally got you to MAKE IT with me!!
Not so quick, Annutt! Did you take . . . "precautions"?
Yeah! I hung a big "Do Not Disturb" sign on the wind-shield wiper!
Not THAT kind of precautions! I mean the OTHER kind . . . like are you wearing an "I.O.U" . . . or a "Diagram" . . . 'cause I don't own no "Con-dominium" right now!
I don't need any of that, Tony! I LOVE you!!
Geez! Then forget it! You can go @#$%¢&*+ yourself!!
And you can go jump off a bridge!
I DIDN'T MEAN IT ITERALLY, TONY! I— I DIDN'T MEAN IT ITERALLY!
Calm down, Annutt! Dancing and hanging from the Verrazano Bridge is just their way of letting off steam! It's really a sick, self-destructive way of releasing pent-up energies!
How come YOU'RE not up there TOO, Booby . . . ?
My pregnant teen-age girlfriend won't let me!!
Growl! Snarl!
Bark! Bark!
Yip! Yip!
Well, Step-funny, what do you think of my friends?
They're vile . . . they're crude . . . and they've got no class! Why are they jumping on the tables and barking like dogs?
They read the sign, "Have It Your Way"! This is their way!!
They READ the sign?!
Okay, so somebody read it TO them!
HAVE IT YOUR WAY

Tony, don't you feel limited . . . running around with a bunch of weird, nutsy guys who speak bad English and have bad manners?
Not in a major motion picture! But I don't think I could ever do a TV SERIES with creeps like that!
Taking this day off got me fired, y' know!
I appreciate your helping me move, Tony!
Now that you're moving to your own place in Manhattan, I'll bet you're gonna make it with a lot of ad agency guys and have a lot of sex orgies, huh, Stepfunny?
Wrong!! I'm just gonna continue to become cultured . . . and expand my mind! Why do you think I'm planning to have sex?
Well . . . I don't see no BOOKS strapped on the top of the car!
NEW YORK
Okay—sob—so you found out I've been having sex with ONE GUY! Big deal!!
Listen, Tony, I've had a very emotional day. I'm nervous . . . I'm irritable . . . I'm sick of your jealousy . . . I'm sick of your whining . . . and I'm sick of seeing BRIDGES!!! This is the THIRD BRIDGE SCENE!! Please . . . no more BRIDGES!!
Okay! Okay!! I'm not sore Take it easy! Le'me take you to a spot where you can calm down . . . and relax!!
BROOKLYN
This is it . . .
Thanks, Tony! You sure are sensitive to a woman's needs!!
I like to come here, relax, meditate, and quote statistics that nobody cares about! Like do you know that the bridge towers go up 690 feet! The center span is 4,260 feet long! 49 million cars cross it a year! It's got over six million tons of steel in it! The whole thing was built with a #4 Gilbert Erector Set! And 30 million people have dozed off during this exciting scene . . .
ZZZZZZZZZZZZ!
Make that 30 million and ONE!
Geez . . . these Barracudas are a tough bunch!
Barracudas?!? Aren't these "The Sharks"?
Are you crazy? "The Sharks" is the name of the gang taken directly from "West Side Story"!
So is THIS SCENE!
Hmm! Come to think of it, there ARE similarities! Like a WHITE gang vs. a PUERTO RICAN! And the name of the lead character is "Tony"!
Gee! What else??
I dunno, but I'm getting pummelled! Let's DANCE our way out of here, and figure it out!
Hey . . . where was you?
Yeah, to chicken out of a fight!!
You're not gonna believe this, but I HADDA get out of that scene! I—I had this URGE—
No . . . to stand on some fire escape and sing to Natalie Wood!
BKLY

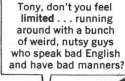

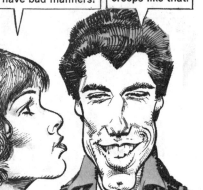

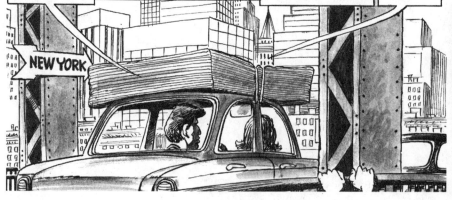

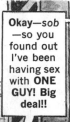

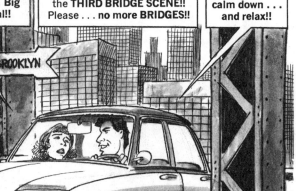

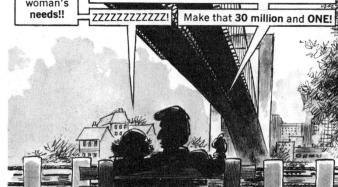

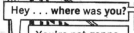

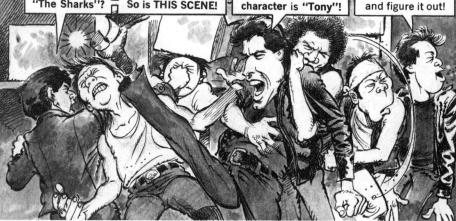

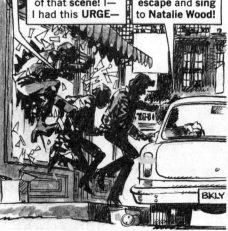

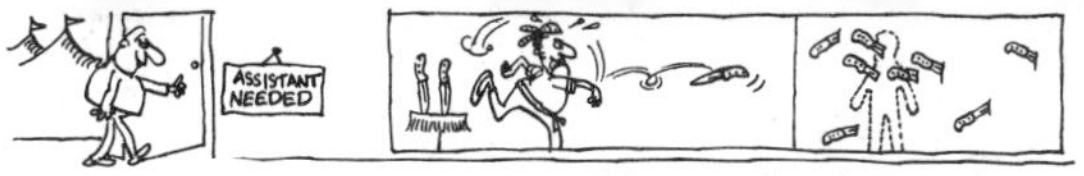

ASSISTANT NEEDED

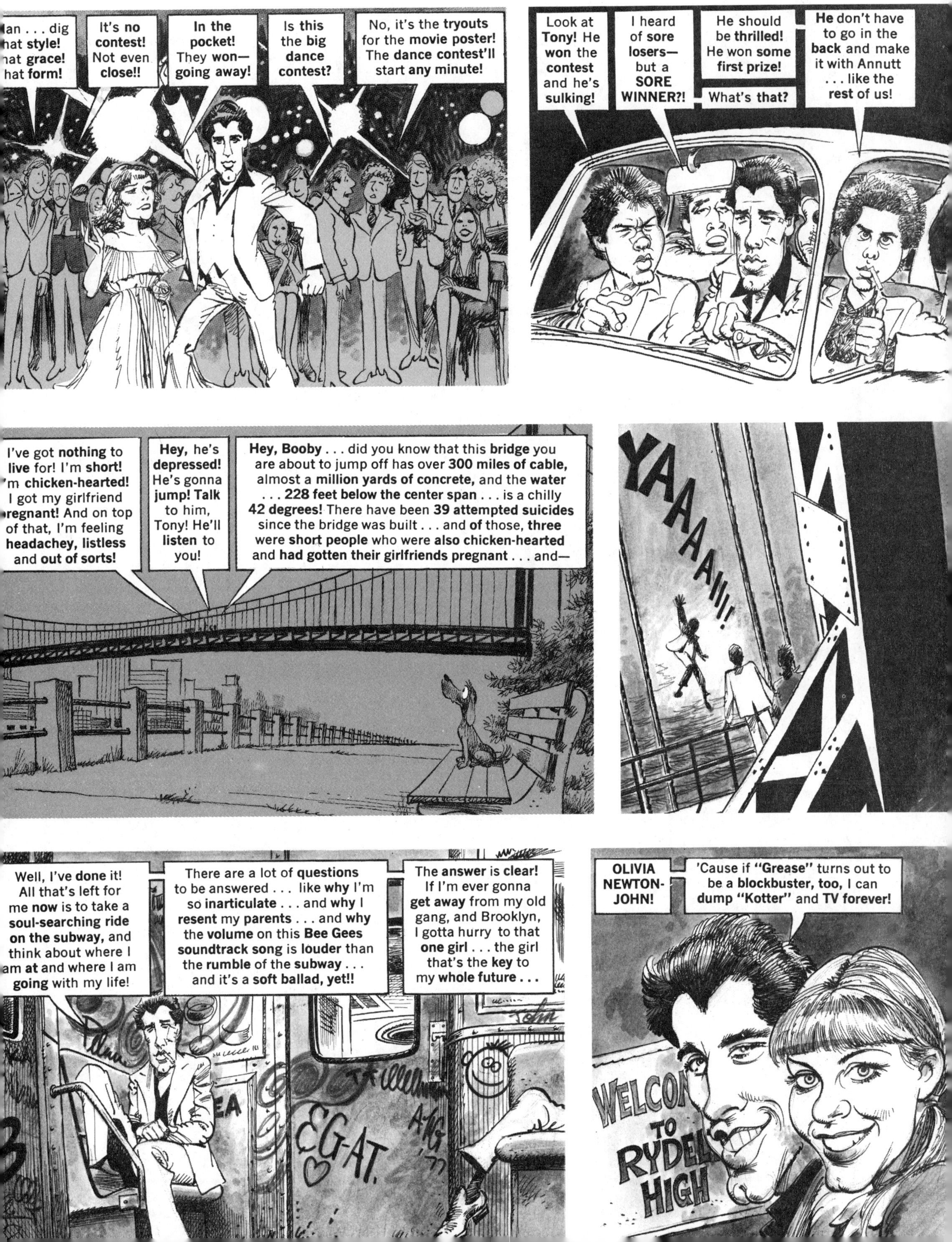

an . . . dig hat style! nat grace! hat form!
It's no contest! Not even close!!
In the pocket! They won—going away!
Is this the big dance contest?
No, it's the tryouts for the movie poster! The dance contest'll start any minute!
Look at Tony! He won the contest and he's sulking!
I heard of sore losers—but a SORE WINNER?!
He should be thrilled! He won some first prize!
What's that?
He don't have to go in the back and make it with Annutt . . . like the rest of us!
I've got nothing to live for! I'm short! 'm chicken-hearted! I got my girlfriend regnant! And on top of that, I'm feeling headachey, listless and out of sorts!
Hey, he's depressed! He's gonna jump! Talk to him, Tony! He'll listen to you!
Hey, Booby . . . did you know that this bridge you are about to jump off has over 300 miles of cable, almost a million yards of concrete, and the water . . . 228 feet below the center span . . . is a chilly 42 degrees! There have been 39 attempted suicides since the bridge was built . . . and of those, three were short people who were also chicken-hearted and had gotten their girlfriends pregnant . . . and—
YAAAAAIII!
Well, I've done it! All that's left for me now is to take a soul-searching ride on the subway, and think about where I am at and where I am going with my life!
There are a lot of questions to be answered . . . like why I'm so inarticulate . . . and why I resent my parents . . . and why the volume on this Bee Gees soundtrack song is louder than the rumble of the subway . . . and it's a soft ballad, yet!!
The answer is clear! If I'm ever gonna get away from my old gang, and Brooklyn, I gotta hurry to that one girl . . . the girl that's the key to my whole future . . .
OLIVIA NEWTON-JOHN!
'Cause if "Grease" turns out to be a blockbuster, too, I can dump "Kotter" and TV forever!
WELCO TO RYDEL HIGH

JOKE-AND-DAGGER DEPT.

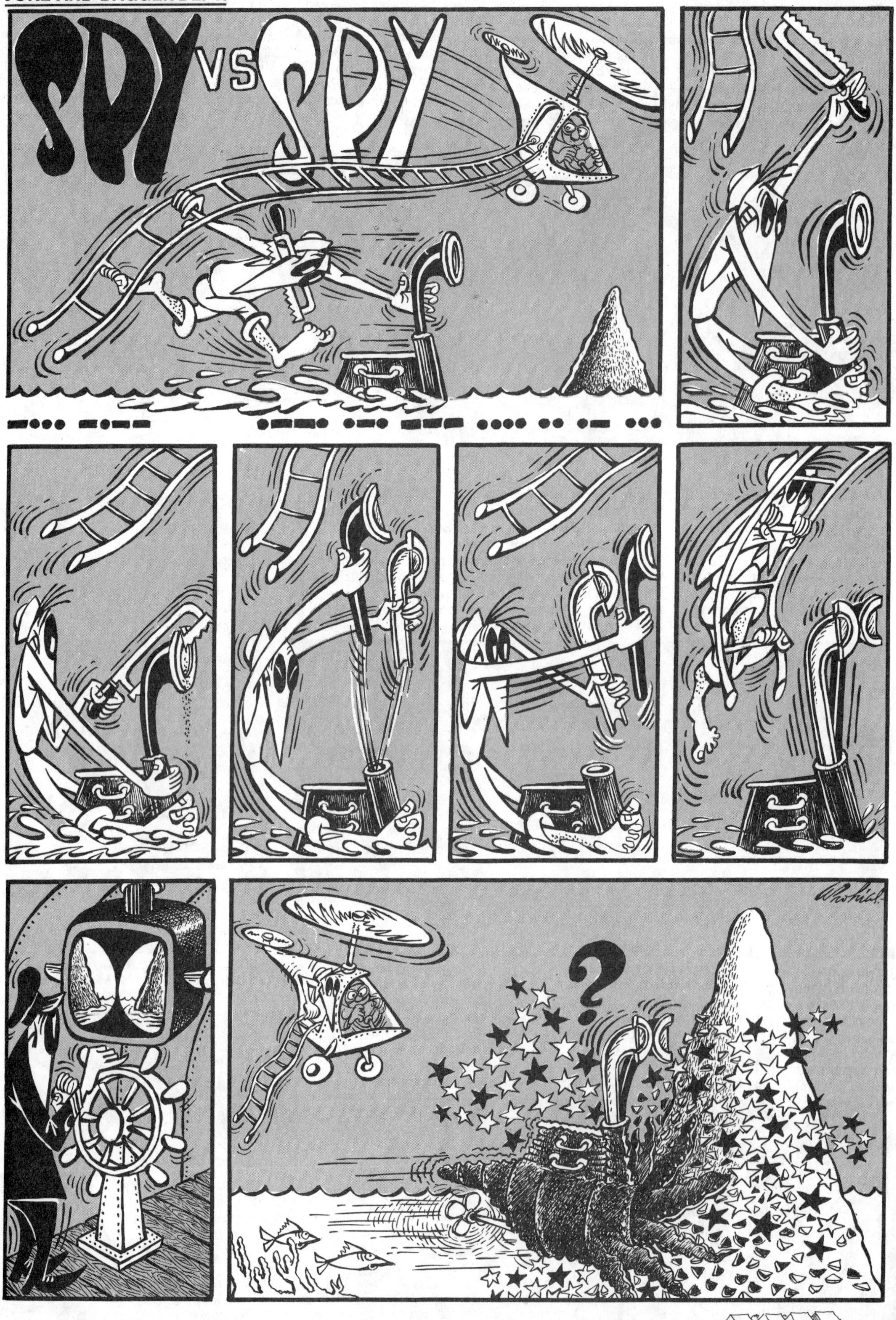
SPY vs SPY
?

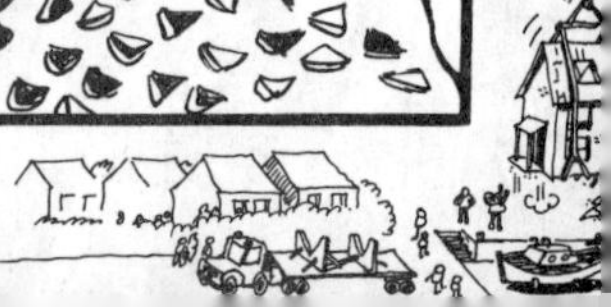

TRIPPING WITH THE LIGHTS IS FANTASTIC DEPT.

A MAD LOOK AT DISCOS

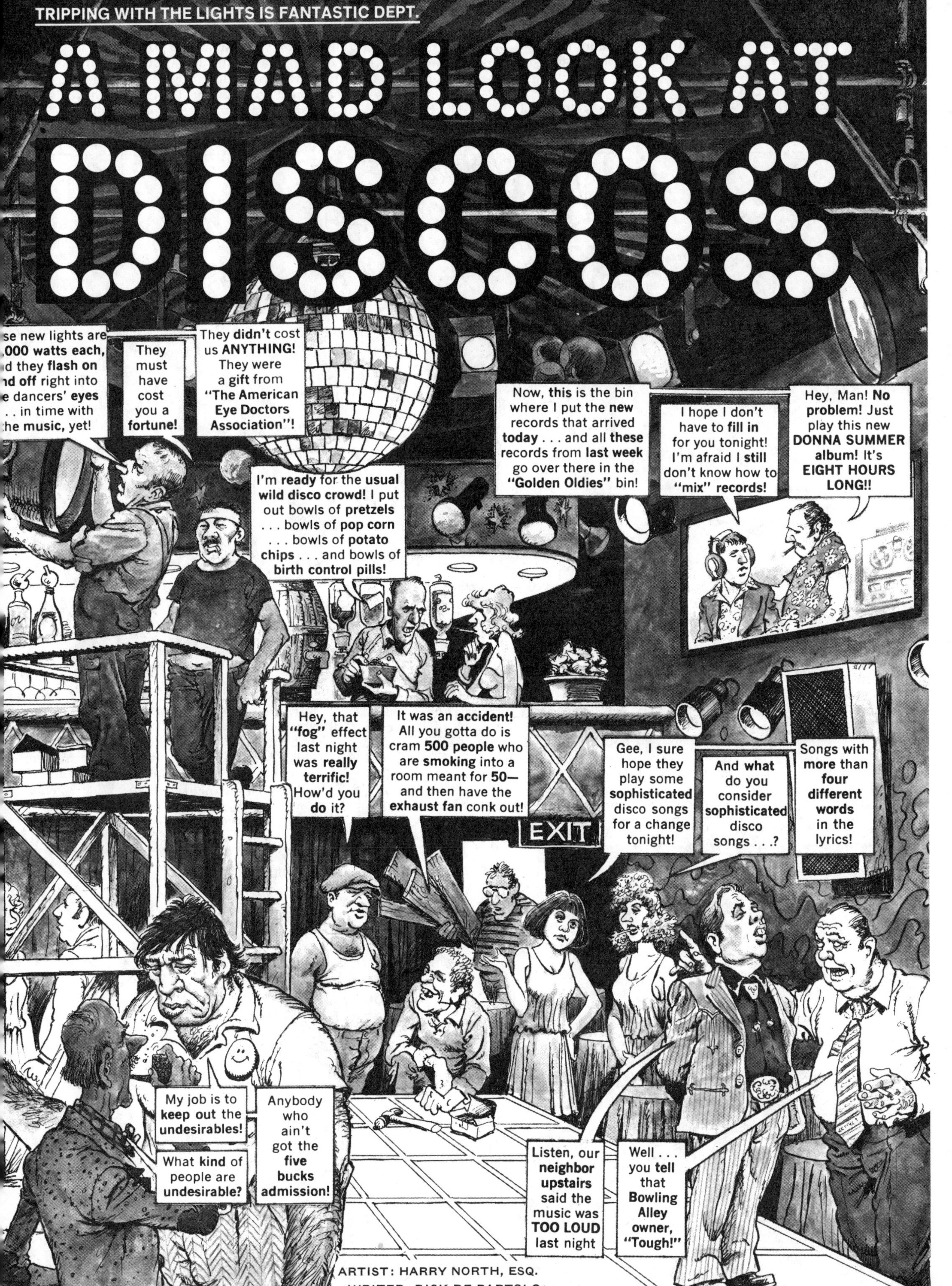
se new lights are
,000 watts each,
d they flash on
nd off right into
e dancers' eyes
. . . in time with
he music, yet!
They must have cost you a fortune!
They didn't cost us ANYTHING! They were a gift from "The American Eye Doctors Association"!
Now, this is the bin where I put the new records that arrived today . . . and all these records from last week go over there in the "Golden Oldies" bin!
I hope I don't have to fill in for you tonight! I'm afraid I still don't know how to "mix" records!
Hey, Man! No problem! Just play this new DONNA SUMMER album! It's EIGHT HOURS LONG!!
I'm ready for the usual wild disco crowd! I put out bowls of pretzels . . . bowls of pop corn . . . bowls of potato chips . . . and bowls of birth control pills!
Hey, that "fog" effect last night was really terrific! How'd you do it?
It was an accident! All you gotta do is cram 500 people who are smoking into a room meant for 50—and then have the exhaust fan conk out!
EXIT
Gee, I sure hope they play some sophisticated disco songs for a change tonight!
And what do you consider sophisticated disco songs . . .?
Songs with more than four different words in the lyrics!
My job is to keep out the undesirables!
What kind of people are undesirable?
Anybody who ain't got the five bucks admission!
Listen, our neighbor upstairs said the music was TOO LOUD last night
Well . . . you tell that Bowling Alley owner, "Tough!"

ARTIST: HARRY NORTH, ESQ.
WRITER: DICK DE BARTOLO

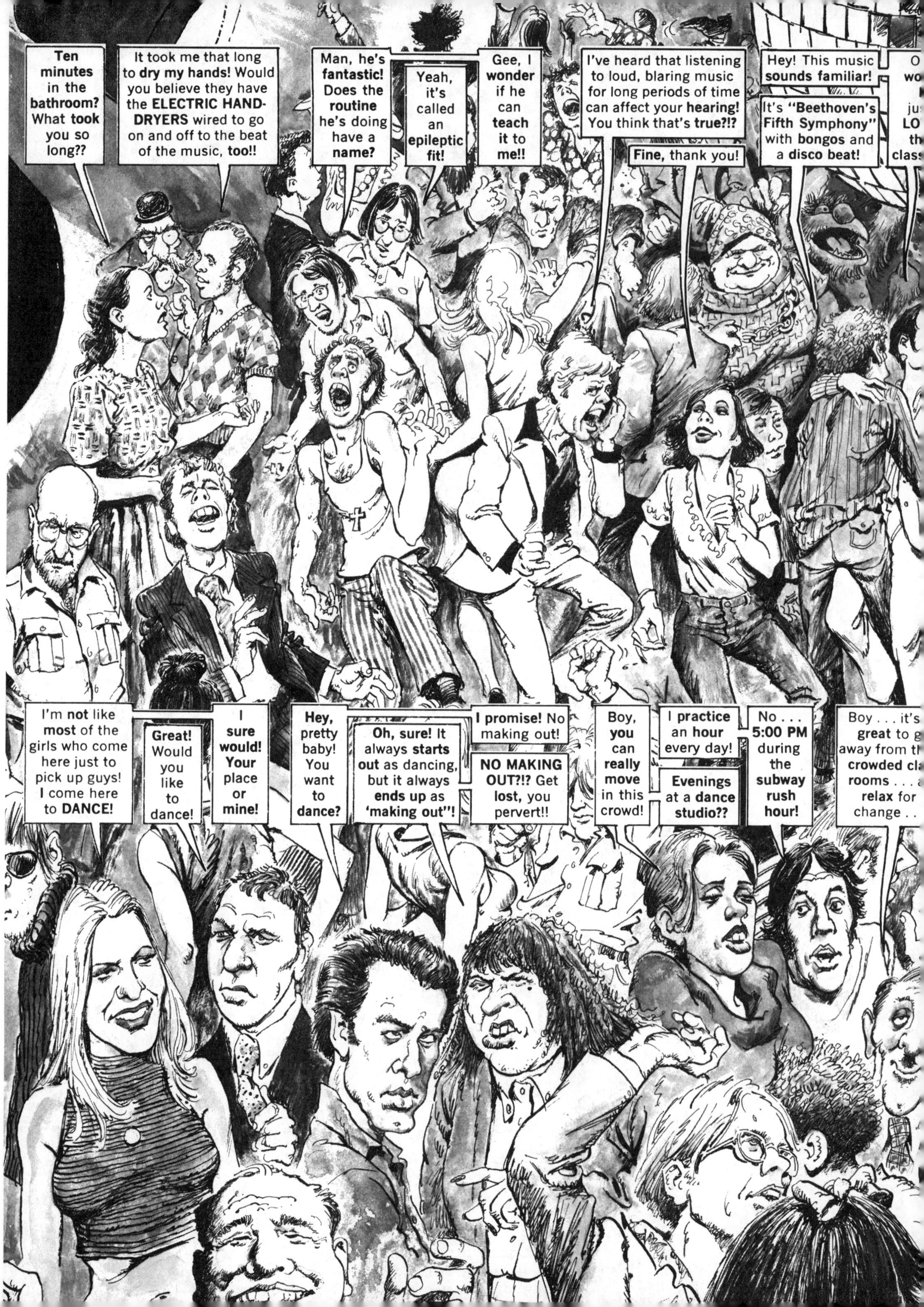

Ten minutes in the bathroom? What took you so long??
It took me that long to dry my hands! Would you believe they have the ELECTRIC HAND-DRYERS wired to go on and off to the beat of the music, too!!
Man, he's fantastic! Does the routine he's doing have a name?
Yeah, it's called an epileptic fit!
Gee, I wonder if he can teach it to me!!
I've heard that listening to loud, blaring music for long periods of time can affect your hearing! You think that's true?!?
Fine, thank you!
Hey! This music sounds familiar!
It's "Beethoven's Fifth Symphony" with bongos and a disco beat!
I'm not like most of the girls who come here just to pick up guys! I come here to DANCE!
Great! Would you like to dance!
I sure would! Your place or mine!
Hey, pretty baby! You want to dance?
Oh, sure! It always starts out as dancing, but it always ends up as 'making out"!
I promise! No making out!
NO MAKING OUT?!? Get lost, you pervert!!
Boy, you can really move in this crowd!
I practice an hour every day!
Evenings at a dance studio??
No . . . 5:00 PM during the subway rush hour!

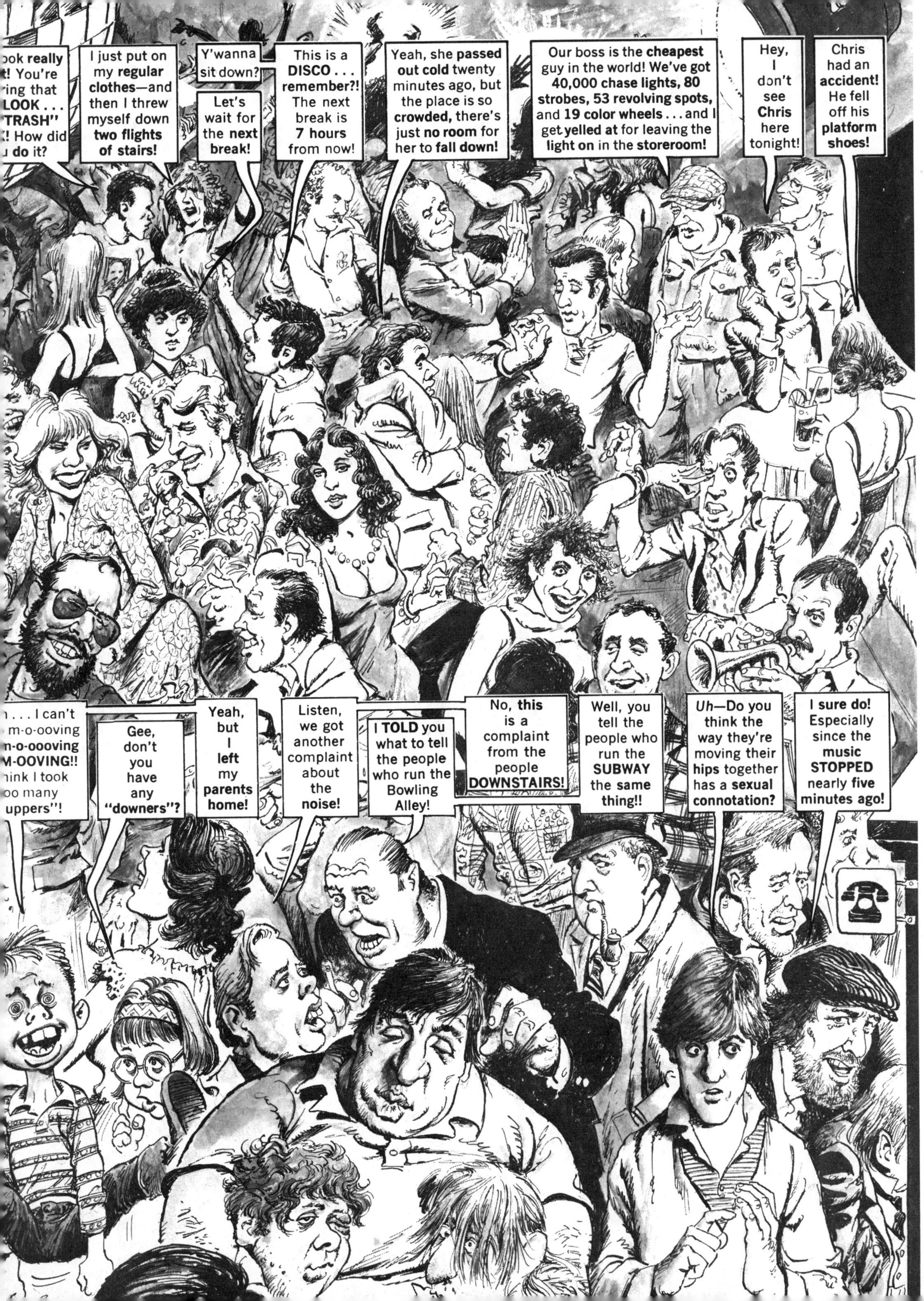
ook really t! You're ring that LOOK . . . TRASH" ! How did do it?
I just put on my regular clothes—and then I threw myself down two flights of stairs!
Y'wanna sit down?
Let's wait for the next break!
This is a DISCO . . . remember?! The next break is 7 hours from now!
Yeah, she passed out cold twenty minutes ago, but the place is so crowded, there's just no room for her to fall down!
Our boss is the cheapest guy in the world! We've got 40,000 chase lights, 80 strobes, 53 revolving spots, and 19 color wheels . . . and I get yelled at for leaving the light on in the storeroom!
Hey, I don't see Chris here tonight!
Chris had an accident! He fell off his platform shoes!
. . . I can't m-o-ooving n-o-oooving M-OOVING!! ink I took oo many uppers"!
Gee, don't you have any "downers"?
Yeah, but I left my parents home!
Listen, we got another complaint about the noise!
I TOLD you what to tell the people who run the Bowling Alley!
No, this is a complaint from the people DOWNSTAIRS!
Well, you tell the people who run the SUBWAY the same thing!!
Uh—Do you think the way they're moving their hips together has a sexual connotation?
I sure do! Especially since the music STOPPED nearly five minutes ago!

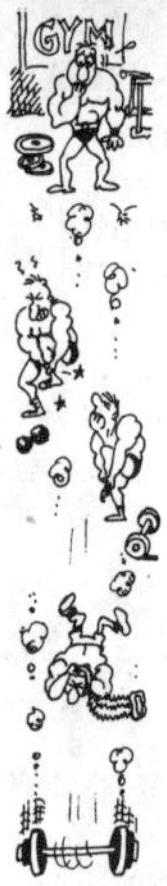
GYM

STATIS-TICKLE DEPT.

MAD'S TABLE OF LITTL USELESS WEIGHT

ARTIST: BOB CLA

198 SQUARE MILES

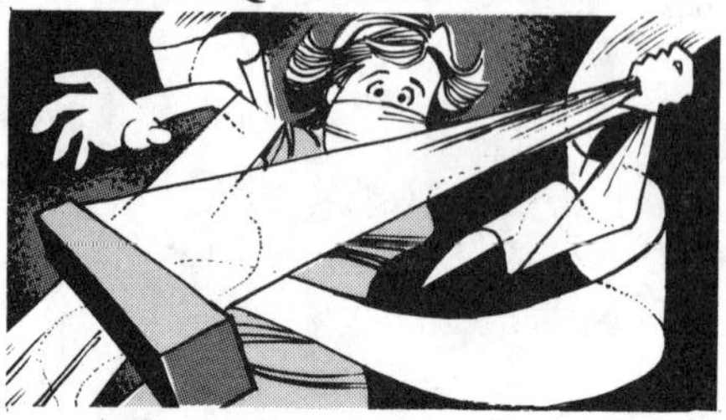

. . . is the amount of "Saran Wrap" the average person overpulls in a lifetime.

2.3 FEET

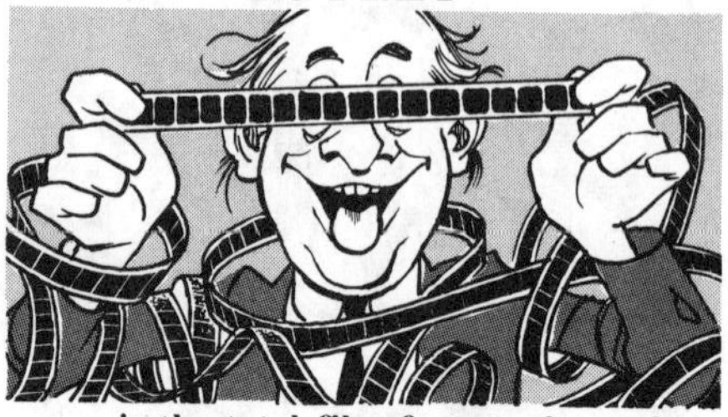

. . . is the total film footage devoted to the plot of an average porno movie.

822 MILLION CUBIC FE

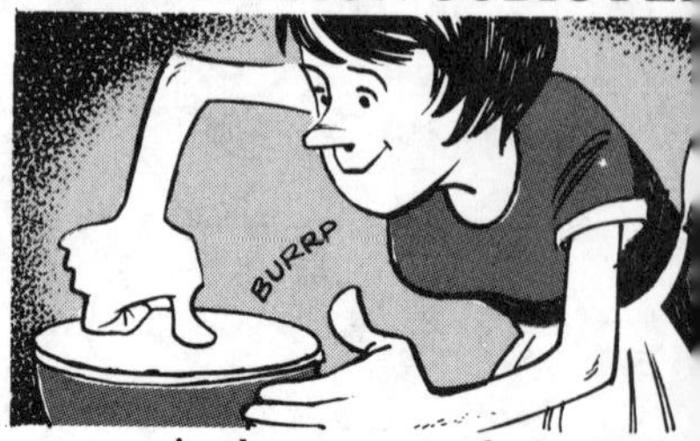
BURRP

. . . is the amount of air displa yearly by the burping of Tupperwa

3.8 MILES

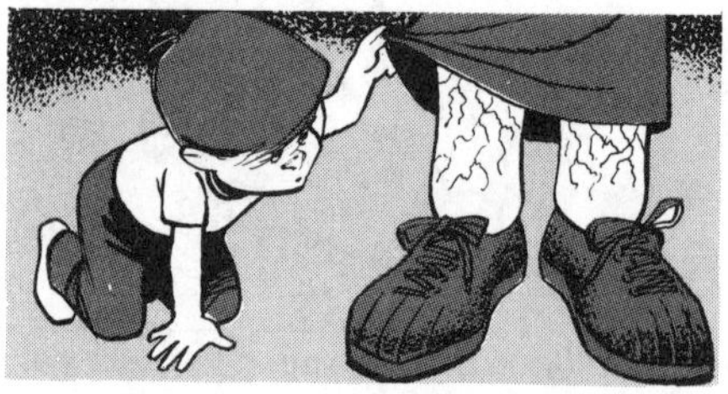

. . . is the average length of all the varicose veins in your Grandmother's legs when they are laid out end to end.

14.2 MILES

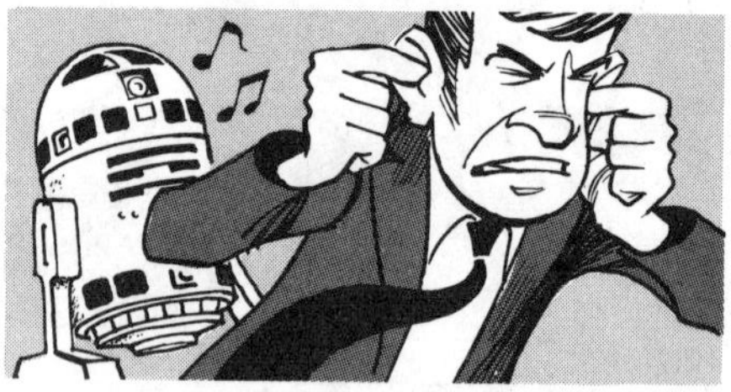

. . . is the average distance traveled by an individual American in 1977 to avoid hearing "The Star Wars" theme.

5.6 OUNCES

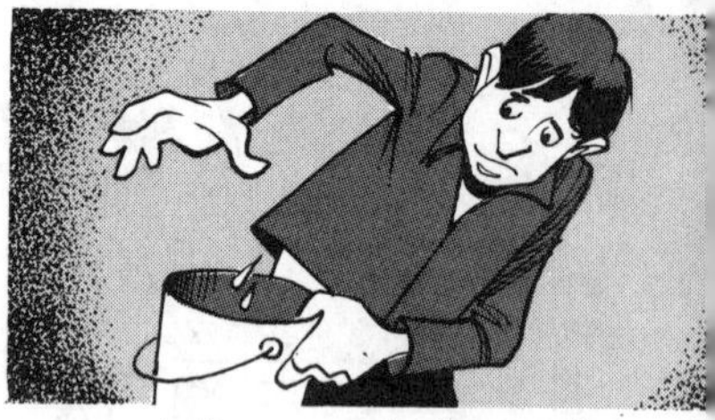

. . . is the amount of sweat from yo armpit that makes it all the way do to your waist over an average ye

3.2 OUNCES

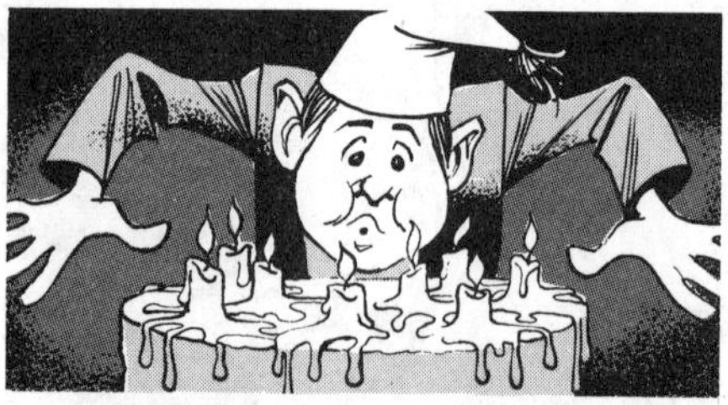

. . . is the average amount of wax that drips all over the icing on a Birthday cake before the candles are blown out.

5.8 CENTIMETERS

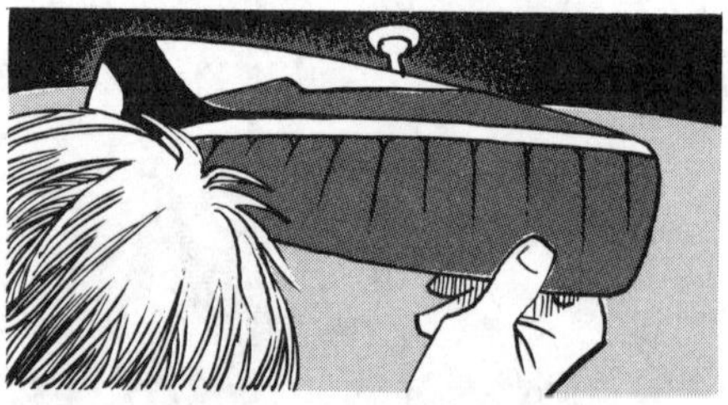

. . . is how far your rear-view mirror always moves from the time you leave your car until you get back into it.

2.3 INCHES

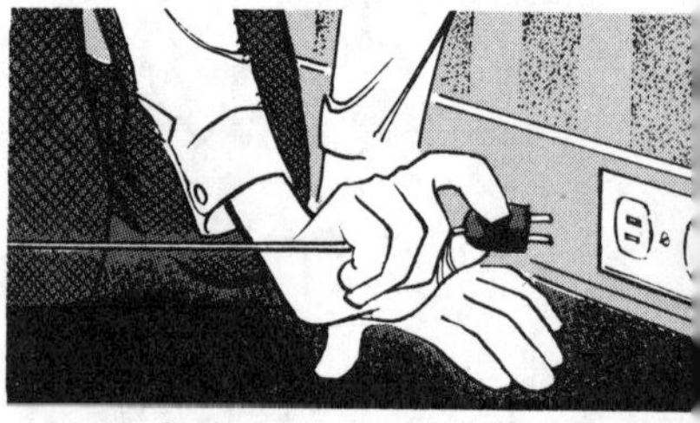

. . . is the average distance between the wall socket and how far the plug of your new appliance cord reaches.

1.1 INCHES

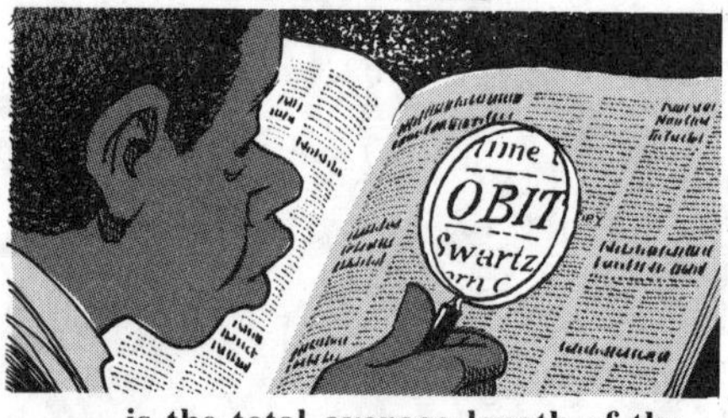
OBIT
Swartz

. . . is the total average length of the "Obituary" of the most famous person you're ever likely to know personally.

3.2 OUNCES

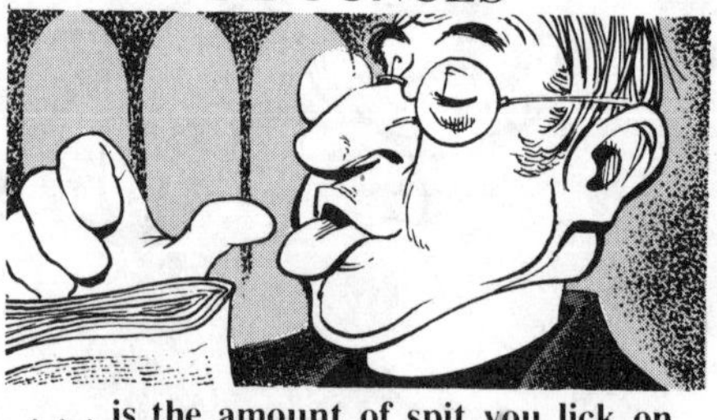

. . . is the amount of spit you lick on your fingers when thumbing through an average copy of the Sunday N.Y. Times.

.571 MILES

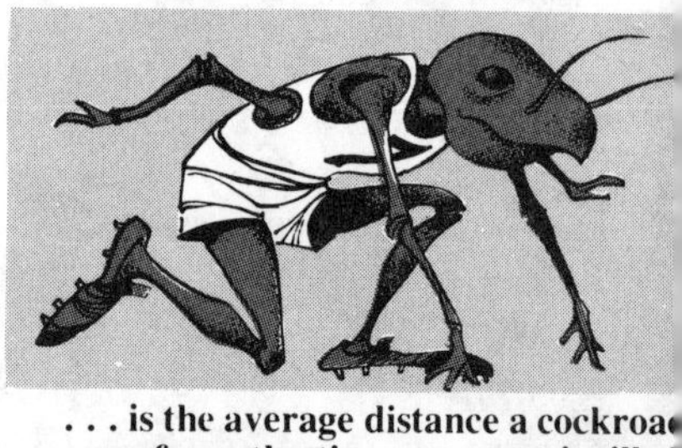

. . . is the average distance a cockroa runs from the time you spot it till t time you finally grab the can of "Raid

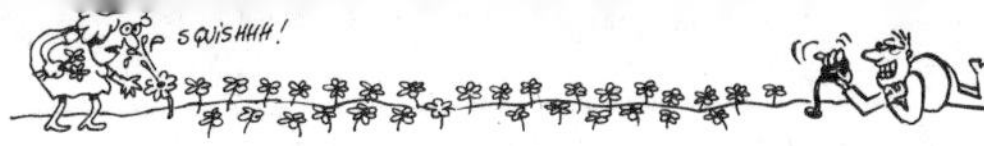
SQUISHHH!

NOWN AND VERY
MEASURES & DISTANCES

ITER: JOHN FICARRA

12.5 GRAMS

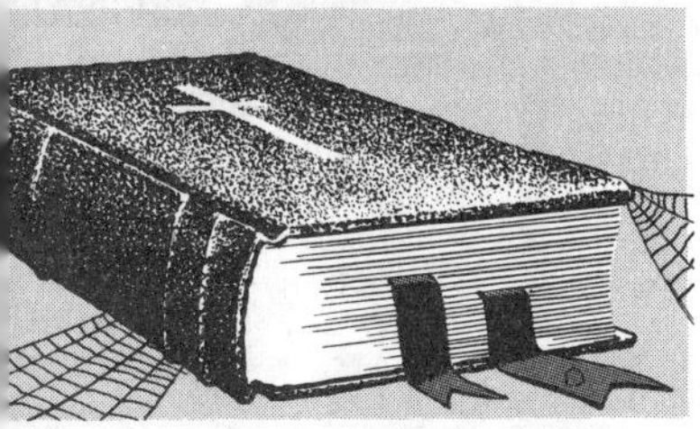

. is the amount of dust that collects
the family Bible between readings.

3.4 INCHES

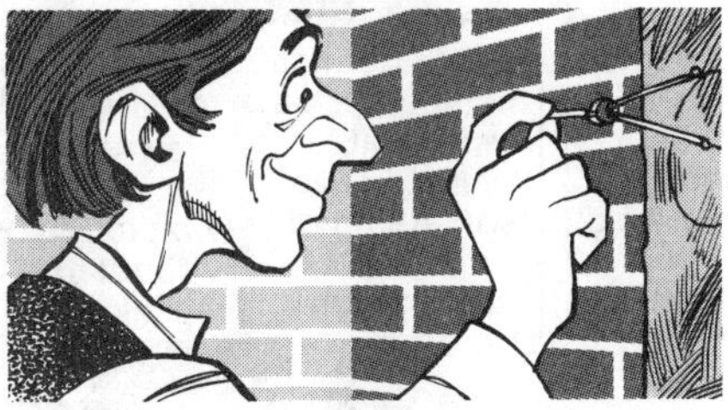

. . . is the diameter of the best part
of the Farrah Fawcett Majors poster.

4.2 GALLONS

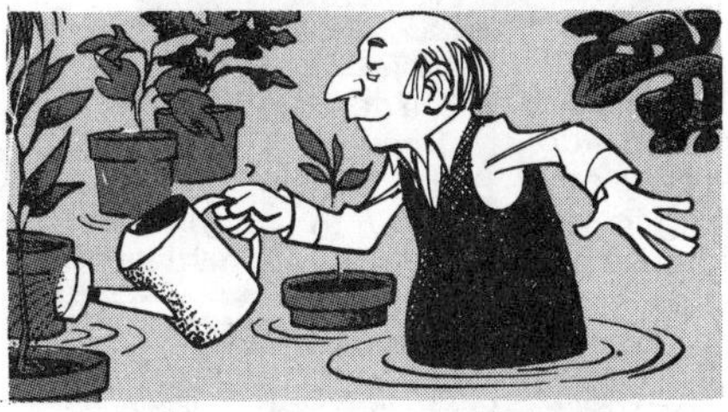

. . . is precisely how much the average
person overwaters his plants each week.

1/2 OUNCE

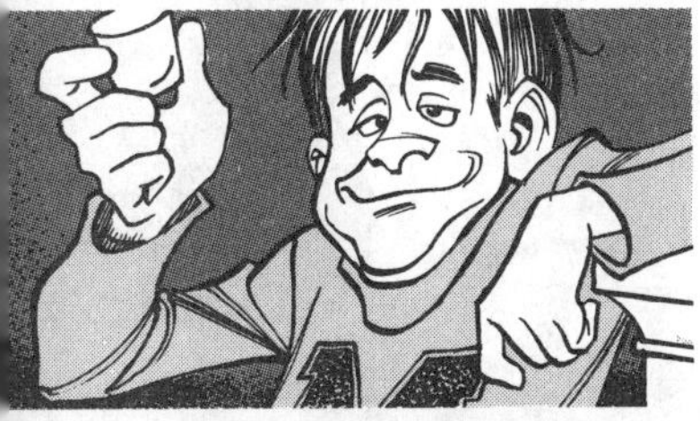

. is the amount of liquor an average
nager drinks before he starts brag-
ng to friends how drunk he really is.

5/8 INCH

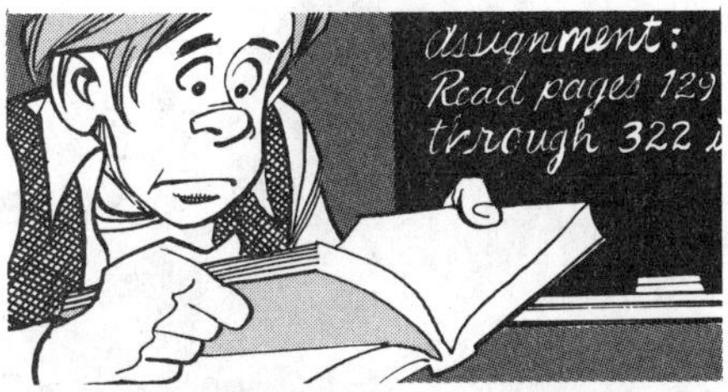
Assignment:
Read pages 129
through 322

. . . is the minimum average thickness of
any book that a Teacher assigns you to
read by the time the class meets again

1/32 OF A POUND

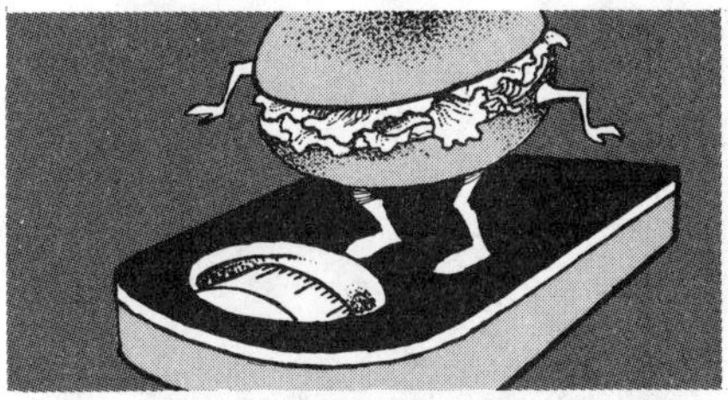

. . . is the average weight of a famous
fast-food chain's "Quarter-Pounder"
hamburger, after it's finished cooking.

127.8 MILES

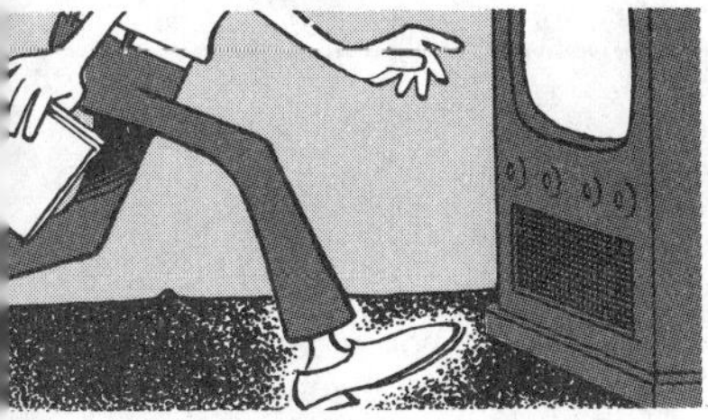

. is the total distance an average
rson walks in his lifetime getting
to change the channel of a TV set.

4.6 BLOCKS

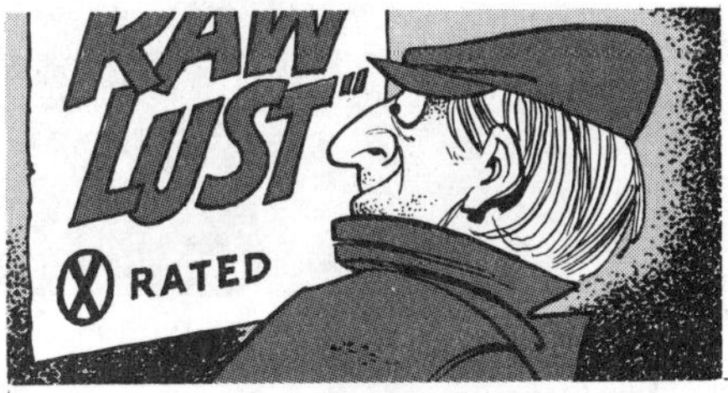
LUST"
X RATED

. . . is how far the average person will
go out of his way just to walk by the
marquee of an X-rated movie theater.

2.1 CENTIMETERS

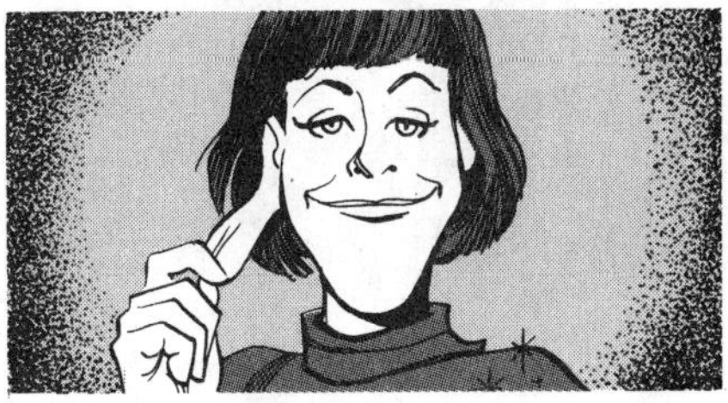

. . . is how much Carol Burnett's right
earlobe is stretched after 11 seasons
of pulling it at the end of each show.

3.7 INCHES

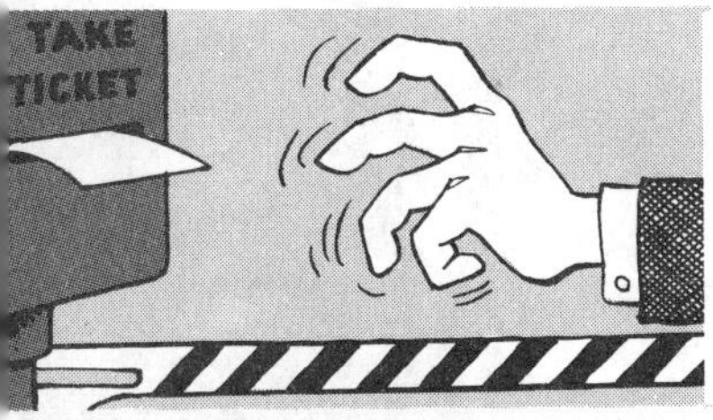
TAKE
TICKET

. is the average distance remaining
tween your hand and the toll booth's
tomatic ticket-dispensing machine.

9.5 GALLONS

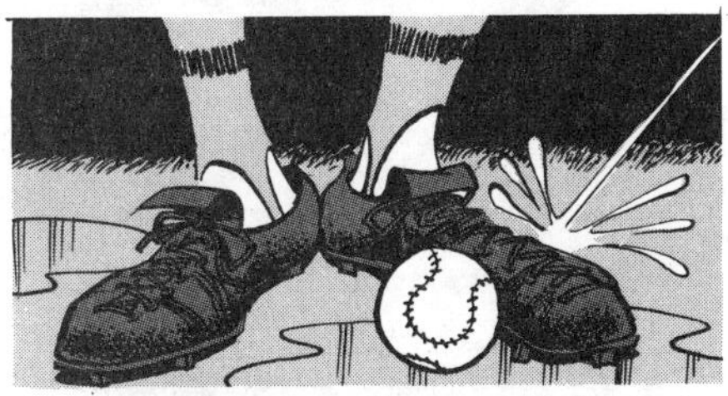

. . . is the amount of tobacco juice and
spit on the floor of a baseball team's
dugout after a Saturday double-header.

12.9 FEET

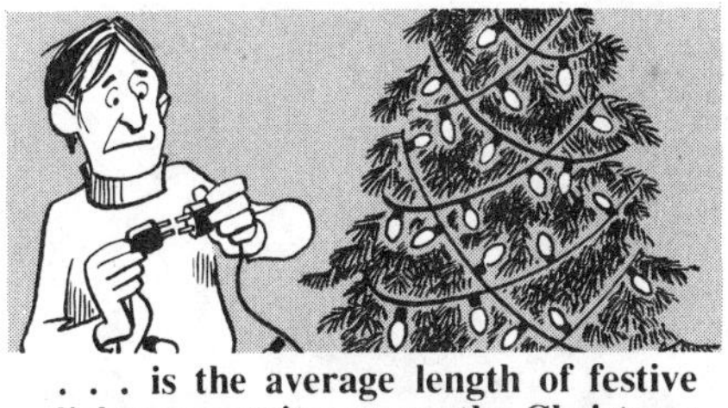

. . . is the average length of festive
lights you string up on the Christmas
tree each year before you realize that
you've started at the wrong end again.

SUPER MARKETING DEPT.

He started out in the Thirties as a comic book hero. Then, he became the star of a movie serial, a radio show, a television series, a Broadway musical, and now...at last...he's the star of a multi-million dollar full-length feature motion picture! Look...up in the sky! It's a gold mine! It's a bonanza! It's

SUPER

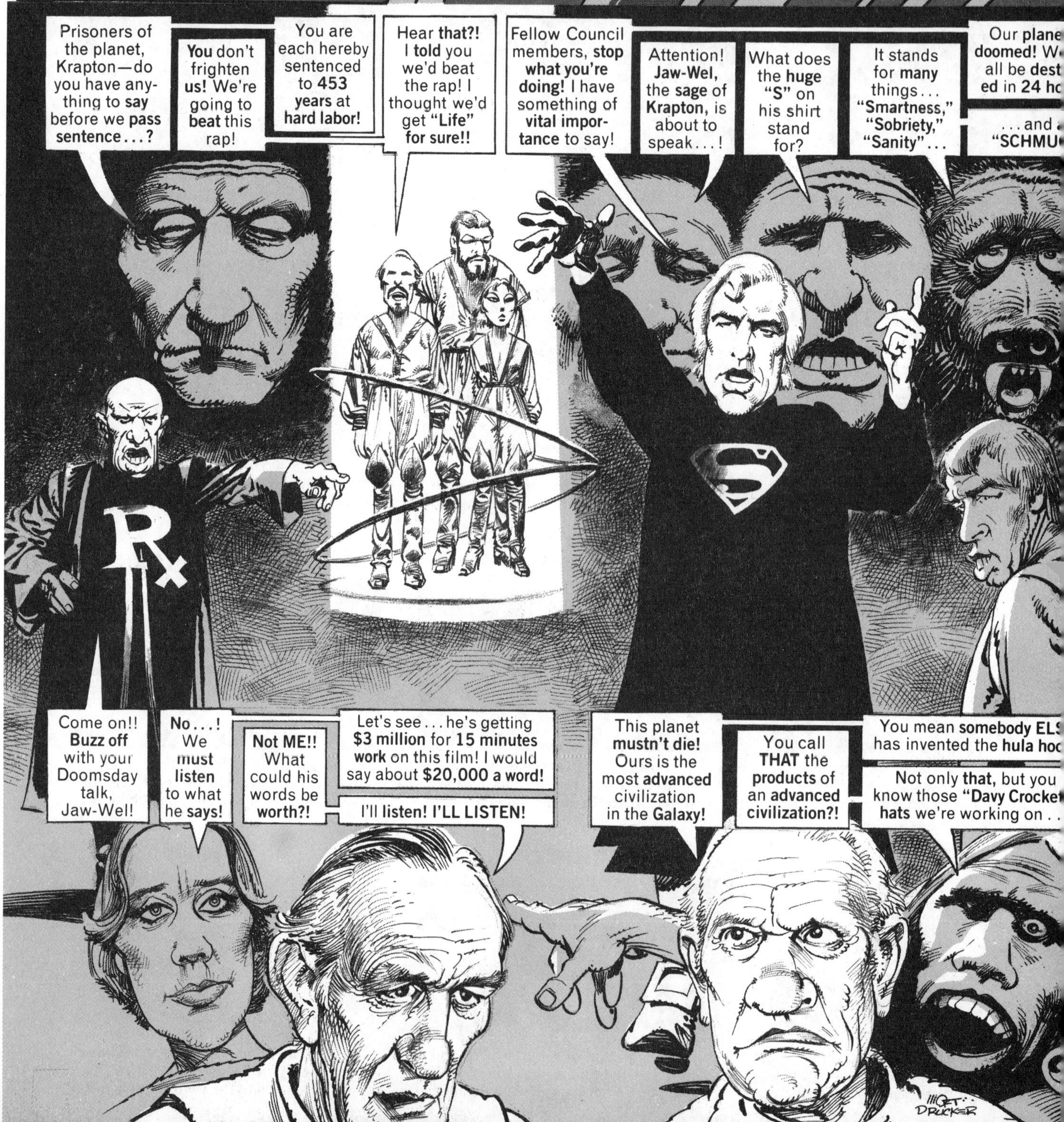

Prisoners of the planet, Krapton—do you have anything to say before we pass sentence...?
You don't frighten us! We're going to beat this rap!
You are each hereby sentenced to 453 years at hard labor!
Hear that?! I told you we'd beat the rap! I thought we'd get "Life" for sure!!
Fellow Council members, stop what you're doing! I have something of vital importance to say!
Attention! Jaw-Wel, the sage of Krapton, is about to speak...!
What does the huge "S" on his shirt stand for?
It stands for many things... "Smartness," "Sobriety," "Sanity"...
Our plane doomed! W all be dest ed in 24 ho
...and "SCHMU
Come on!! Buzz off with your Doomsday talk, Jaw-Wel!
No...! We must listen to what he says!
Not ME!! What could his words be worth?!
Let's see... he's getting $3 million for 15 minutes work on this film! I would say about $20,000 a word!
I'll listen! I'LL LISTEN!
This planet mustn't die! Ours is the most advanced civilization in the Galaxy!
You call THAT the products of an advanced civilization?!
You mean somebody ELS has invented the hula hoo
Not only that, but you know those "Davy Crocke hats we're working on...
MORT DRUCKER

DUPERMAN

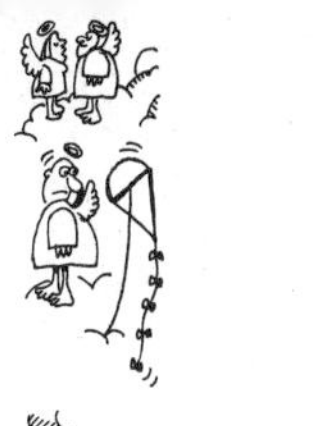

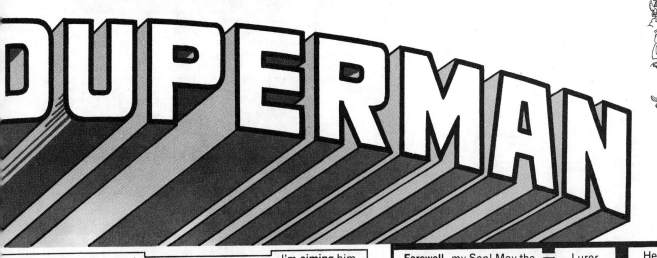

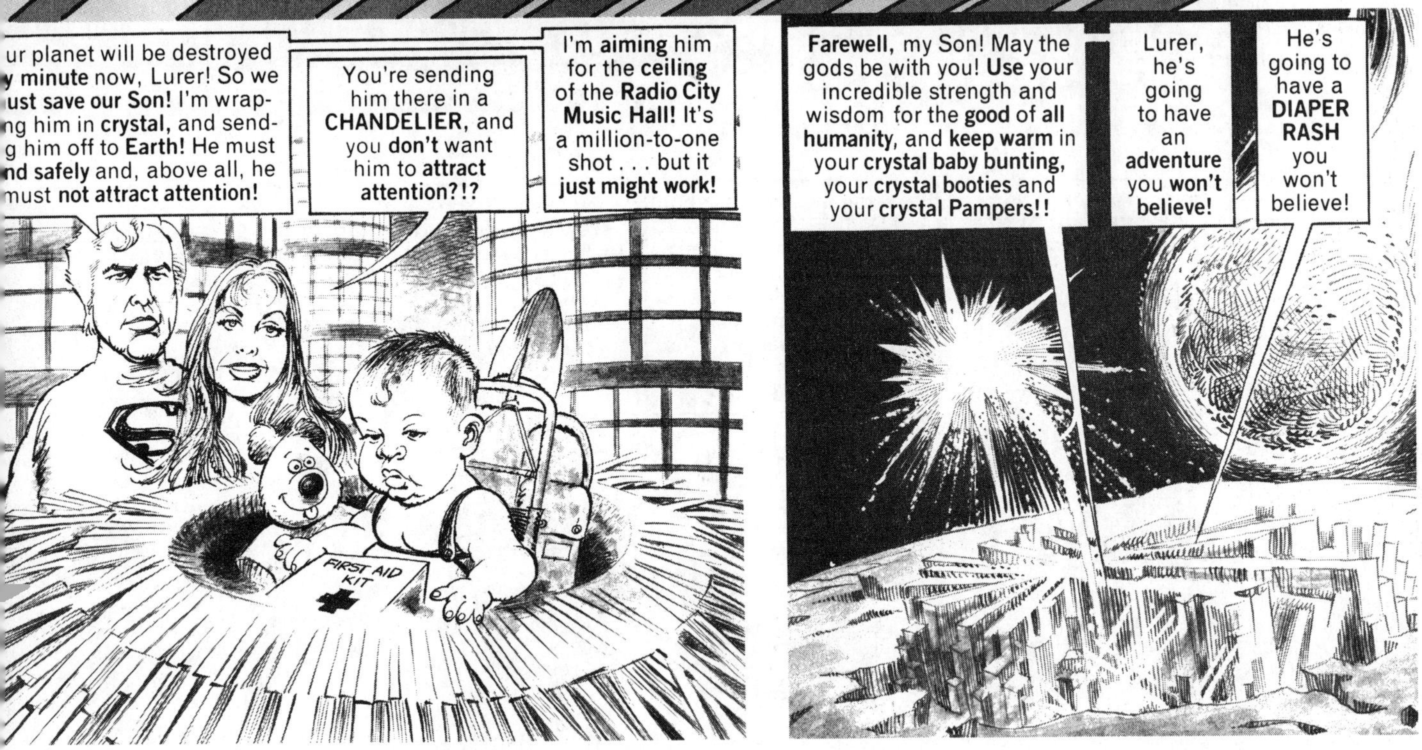
ur planet will be destroyed y minute now, Lurer! So we ust save our Son! I'm wrap-ng him in crystal, and send-g him off to Earth! He must nd safely and, above all, he must not attract attention!
You're sending him there in a CHANDELIER, and you don't want him to attract attention?!?
I'm aiming him for the ceiling of the Radio City Music Hall! It's a million-to-one shot . . . but it just might work!
FIRST AID KIT
Farewell, my Son! May the gods be with you! Use your incredible strength and wisdom for the good of all humanity, and keep warm in your crystal baby bunting, your crystal booties and your crystal Pampers!!
Lurer, he's going to have an adventure you won't believe!
He's going to have a DIAPER RASH you won't believe!

ARTIST: MORT DRUCKER WRITER: LARRY SIEGEL

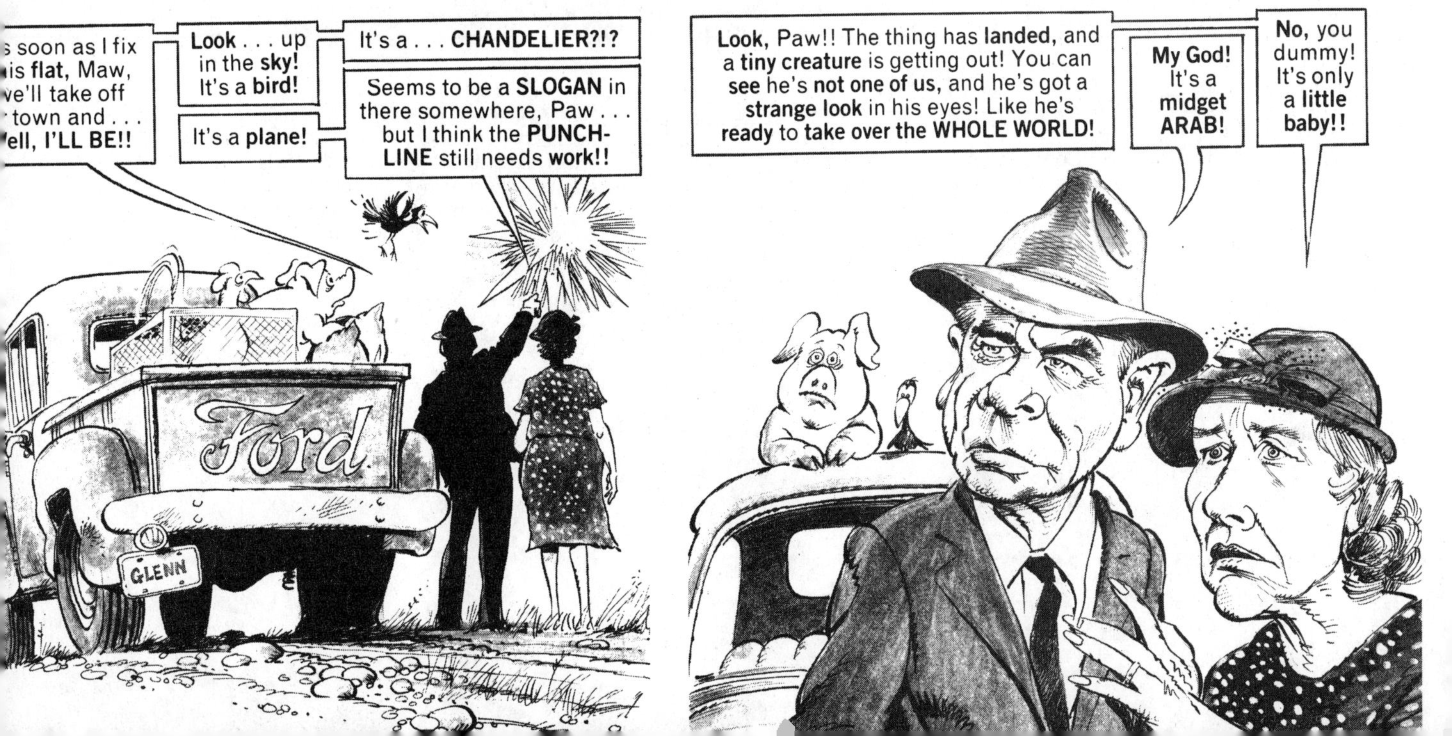
s soon as I fix is flat, Maw, ve'll take off town and . . . ell, I'LL BE!!
Look . . . up in the sky! It's a bird!
It's a plane!
It's a . . . CHANDELIER?!?
Seems to be a SLOGAN in there somewhere, Paw . . . but I think the PUNCH-LINE still needs work!!
Ford
GLENN
Look, Paw!! The thing has landed, and a tiny creature is getting out! You can see he's not one of us, and he's got a strange look in his eyes! Like he's ready to take over the WHOLE WORLD!
My God! It's a midget ARAB!
No, you dummy! It's only a little baby!!

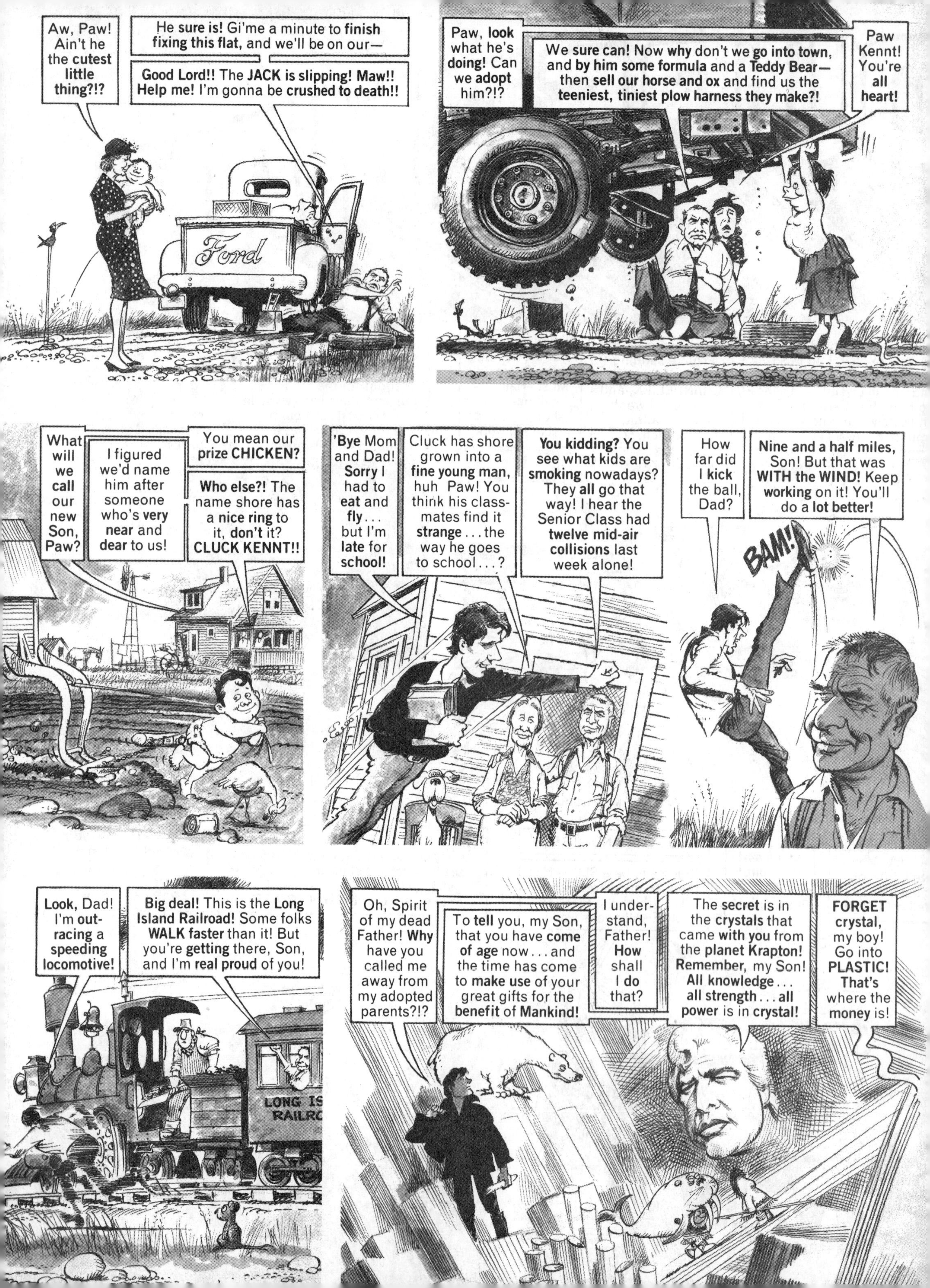
Aw, Paw! Ain't he the cutest little thing?!?
He sure is! Gi'me a minute to finish fixing this flat, and we'll be on our—
Good Lord!! The JACK is slipping! Maw!! Help me! I'm gonna be crushed to death!!
Ford
Paw, look what he's doing! Can we adopt him?!?
We sure can! Now why don't we go into town, and by him some formula and a Teddy Bear—then sell our horse and ox and find us the teeniest, tiniest plow harness they make?!
Paw Kennt! You're all heart!
What will we call our new Son, Paw?
I figured we'd name him after someone who's very near and dear to us!
You mean our prize CHICKEN?
Who else?! The name shore has a nice ring to it, don't it? CLUCK KENNT!!
'Bye Mom and Dad! Sorry I had to eat and fly... but I'm late for school!
Cluck has shore grown into a fine young man, huh Paw! You think his class-mates find it strange... the way he goes to school...?
You kidding? You see what kids are smoking nowadays? They all go that way! I hear the Senior Class had twelve mid-air collisions last week alone!
How far did I kick the ball, Dad?
Nine and a half miles, Son! But that was WITH the WIND! Keep working on it! You'll do a lot better!
BAM!
Look, Dad! I'm out-racing a speeding locomotive!
Big deal! This is the Long Island Railroad! Some folks WALK faster than it! But you're getting there, Son, and I'm real proud of you!
Oh, Spirit of my dead Father! Why have you called me away from my adopted parents?!?
To tell you, my Son, that you have come of age now... and the time has come to make use of your great gifts for the benefit of Mankind!
I under-stand, Father! How shall I do that?
The secret is in the crystals that came with you from the planet Krapton! Remember, my Son! All knowledge... all strength... all power is in crystal!
FORGET crystal, my boy! Go into PLASTIC! That's where the money is!

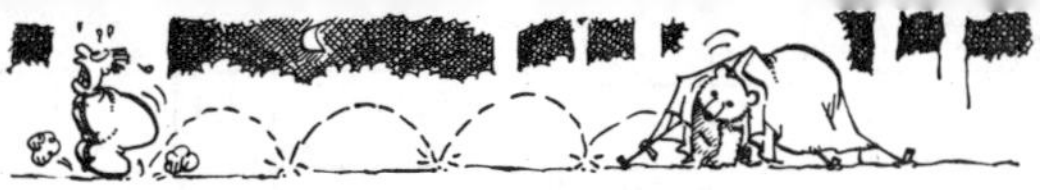

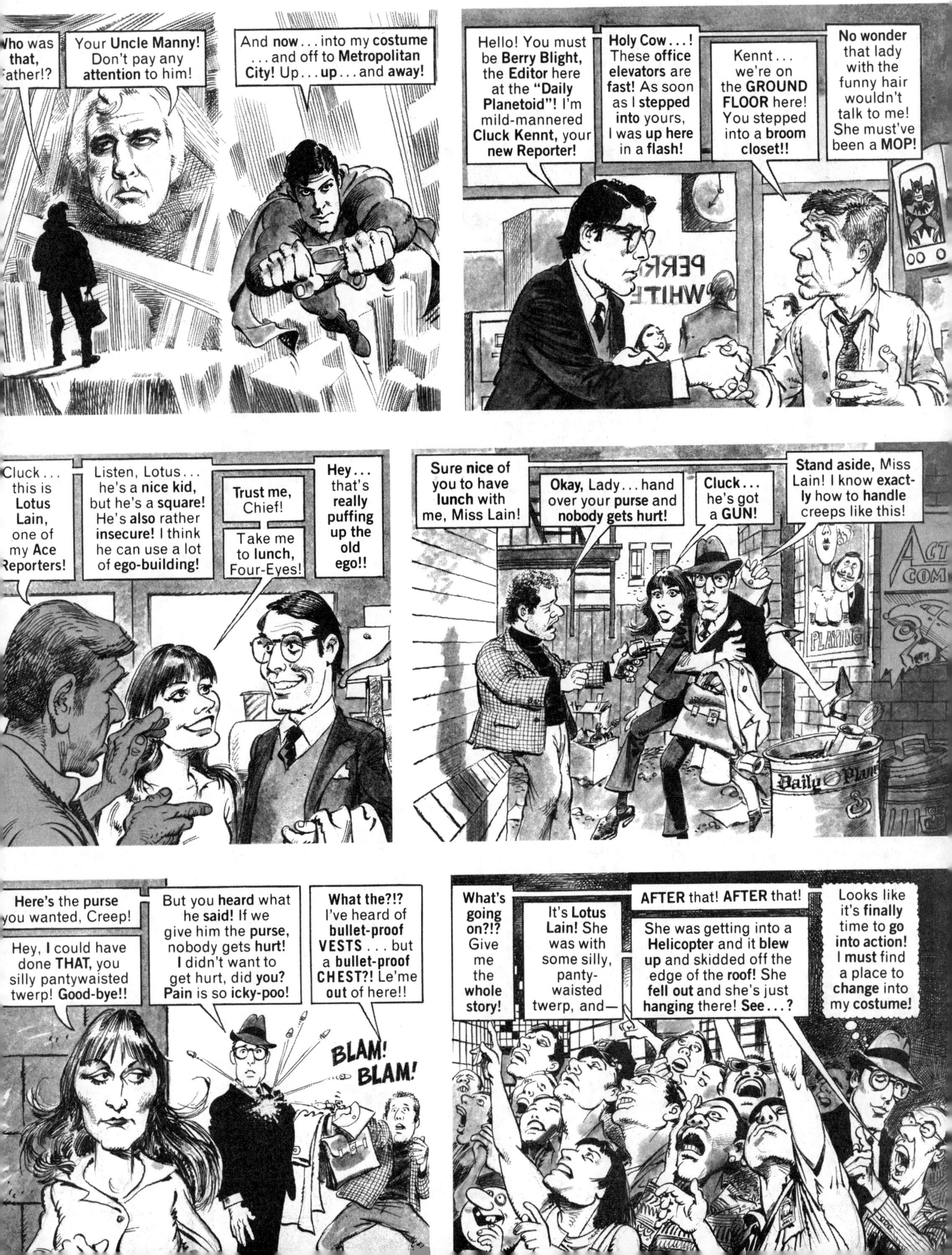

ho was that, ather!?
Your Uncle Manny! Don't pay any attention to him!
And now . . . into my costume . . . and off to Metropolitan City! Up . . . up . . . and away!
Hello! You must be Berry Blight, the Editor here at the "Daily Planetoid"! I'm mild-mannered Cluck Kennt, your new Reporter!
Holy Cow . . . ! These office elevators are fast! As soon as I stepped into yours, I was up here in a flash!
Kennt . . . we're on the GROUND FLOOR here! You stepped into a broom closet!!
No wonder that lady with the funny hair wouldn't talk to me! She must've been a MOP!
PERR WHITE
Cluck . . . this is Lotus Lain, one of my Ace Reporters!
Listen, Lotus . . . he's a nice kid, but he's a square! He's also rather insecure! I think he can use a lot of ego-building!
Trust me, Chief!
Take me to lunch, Four-Eyes!
Hey . . . that's really puffing up the old ego!!
Sure nice of you to have lunch with me, Miss Lain!
Okay, Lady . . . hand over your purse and nobody gets hurt!
Cluck . . . he's got a GUN!
Stand aside, Miss Lain! I know exactly how to handle creeps like this!
PLAYING
Daily Plan
Here's the purse you wanted, Creep!
Hey, I could have done THAT, you silly pantywaisted twerp! Good-bye!!
But you heard what he said! If we give him the purse, nobody gets hurt! I didn't want to get hurt, did you? Pain is so icky-poo!
What the?!? I've heard of bullet-proof VESTS . . . but a bullet-proof CHEST?! Le'me out of here!!
BLAM! BLAM!
What's going on?!? Give me the whole story!
It's Lotus Lain! She was with some silly, panty-waisted twerp, and—
AFTER that! AFTER that!
She was getting into a Helicopter and it blew up and skidded off the edge of the roof! She fell out and she's just hanging there! See . . . ?
Looks like it's finally time to go into action! I must find a place to change into my costume!

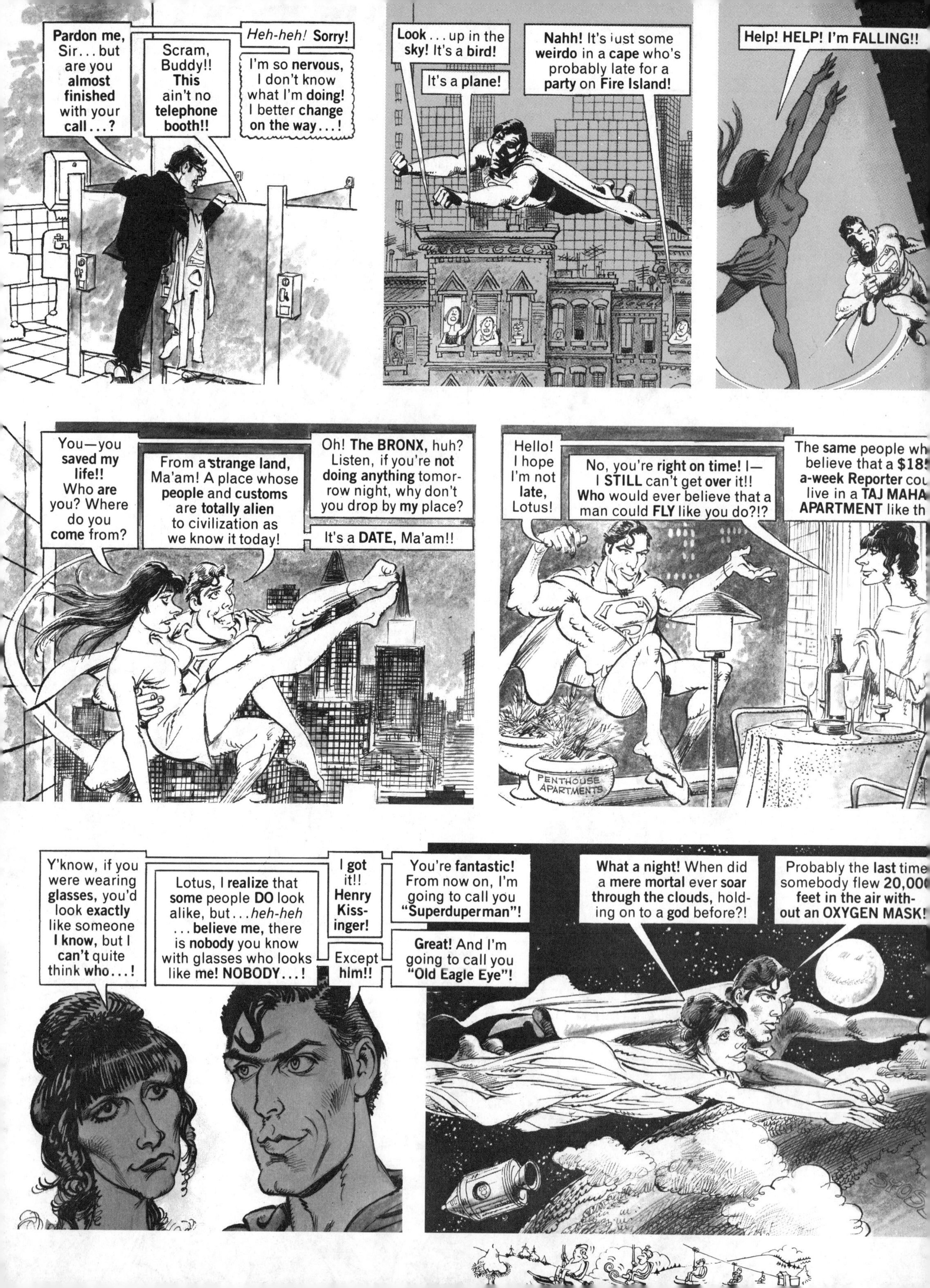
Pardon me, Sir... but are you almost finished with your call...?
Scram, Buddy!! This ain't no telephone booth!!
Heh-heh! Sorry!
I'm so nervous, I don't know what I'm doing! I better change on the way...!
Look... up in the sky! It's a bird!
It's a plane!
Nahh! It's just some weirdo in a cape who's probably late for a party on Fire Island!
Help! HELP! I'm FALLING!!
You—you saved my life!! Who are you? Where do you come from?
From a strange land, Ma'am! A place whose people and customs are totally alien to civilization as we know it today!
Oh! The BRONX, huh? Listen, if you're not doing anything tomorrow night, why don't you drop by my place?
It's a DATE, Ma'am!!
Hello! I hope I'm not late, Lotus!
No, you're right on time! I— I STILL can't get over it!! Who would ever believe that a man could FLY like you do?!?
The same people wh believe that a $18 a-week Reporter cou live in a TAJ MAHA APARTMENT like th
PENTHOUSE APARTMENTS
Y'know, if you were wearing glasses, you'd look exactly like someone I know, but I can't quite think who...!
Lotus, I realize that some people DO look alike, but... heh-heh ... believe me, there is nobody you know with glasses who looks like me! NOBODY...!
I got it!! Henry Kissinger!
Except him!!
You're fantastic! From now on, I'm going to call you "Superduperman"!
Great! And I'm going to call you "Old Eagle Eye"!
What a night! When did a mere mortal ever soar through the clouds, holding on to a god before?!
Probably the last time somebody flew 20,00 feet in the air without an OXYGEN MASK!

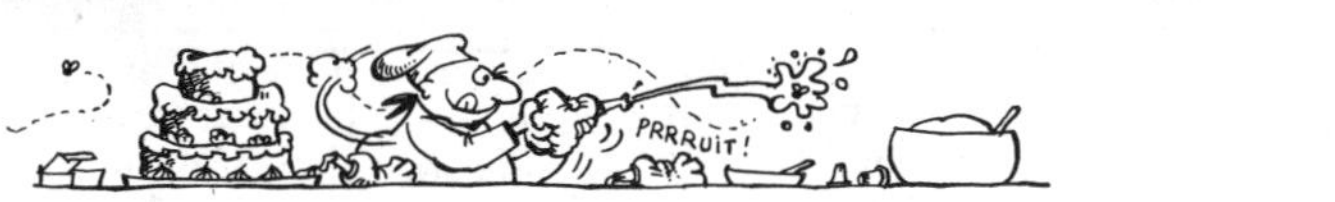
PRRRUIT!

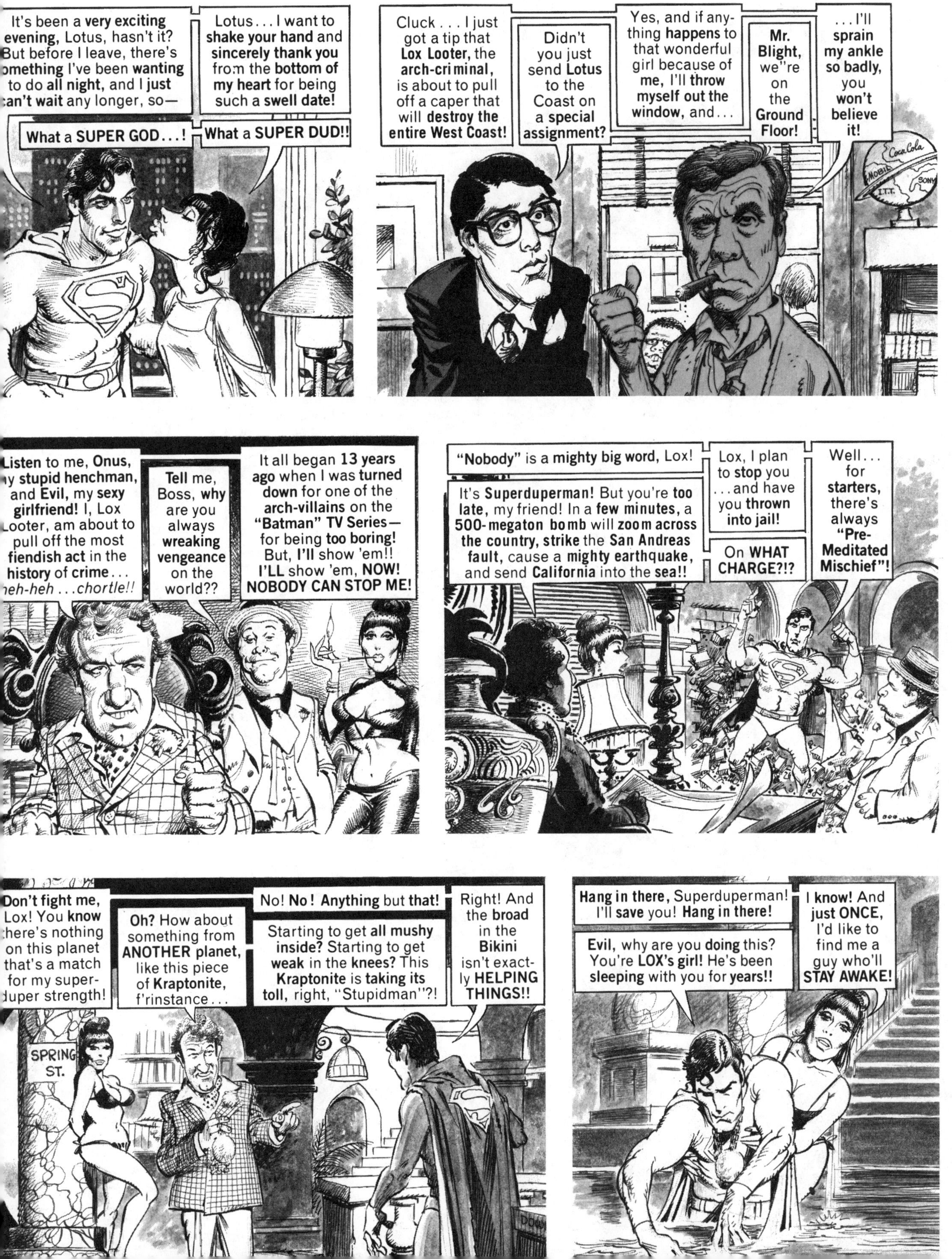
It's been a very exciting evening, Lotus, hasn't it? But before I leave, there's omething I've been wanting to do all night, and I just an't wait any longer, so—
Lotus . . . I want to shake your hand and sincerely thank you from the bottom of my heart for being such a swell date!
What a SUPER GOD . . . !
What a SUPER DUD!!
Cluck . . . I just got a tip that Lox Looter, the arch-criminal, is about to pull off a caper that will destroy the entire West Coast!
Didn't you just send Lotus to the Coast on a special assignment?
Yes, and if anything happens to that wonderful girl because of me, I'll throw myself out the window, and . . .
Mr. Blight, we''re on the Ground Floor!
. . . I'll sprain my ankle so badly, you won't believe it!
Coca Cola
MOBIL
I.T.T.
SONY
Listen to me, Onus, y stupid henchman, and Evil, my sexy girlfriend! I, Lox ooter, am about to pull off the most fiendish act in the history of crime . . . eh-heh . . . chortle!!
Tell me, Boss, why are you always wreaking vengeance on the world??
It all began 13 years ago when I was turned down for one of the arch-villains on the "Batman" TV Series—for being too boring! But, I'll show 'em!! I'LL show 'em, NOW! NOBODY CAN STOP ME!
"Nobody" is a mighty big word, Lox!
It's Superduperman! But you're too late, my friend! In a few minutes, a 500-megaton bomb will zoom across the country, strike the San Andreas fault, cause a mighty earthquake, and send California into the sea!!
Lox, I plan to stop you . . . and have you thrown into jail!
On WHAT CHARGE?!?
Well . . . for starters, there's always "Pre-Meditated Mischief"!
Don't fight me, Lox! You know here's nothing on this planet that's a match for my super-uper strength!
Oh? How about something from ANOTHER planet, like this piece of Kraptonite, f'rinstance . . .
No! No! Anything but that!
Starting to get all mushy inside? Starting to get weak in the knees? This Kraptonite is taking its toll, right, "Stupidman"?!
Right! And the broad in the Bikini isn't exactly HELPING THINGS!!
SPRING ST.
Hang in there, Superduperman! I'll save you! Hang in there!
Evil, why are you doing this? You're LOX's girl! He's been sleeping with you for years!!
I know! And just ONCE, I'd like to find me a guy who'll STAY AWAKE!

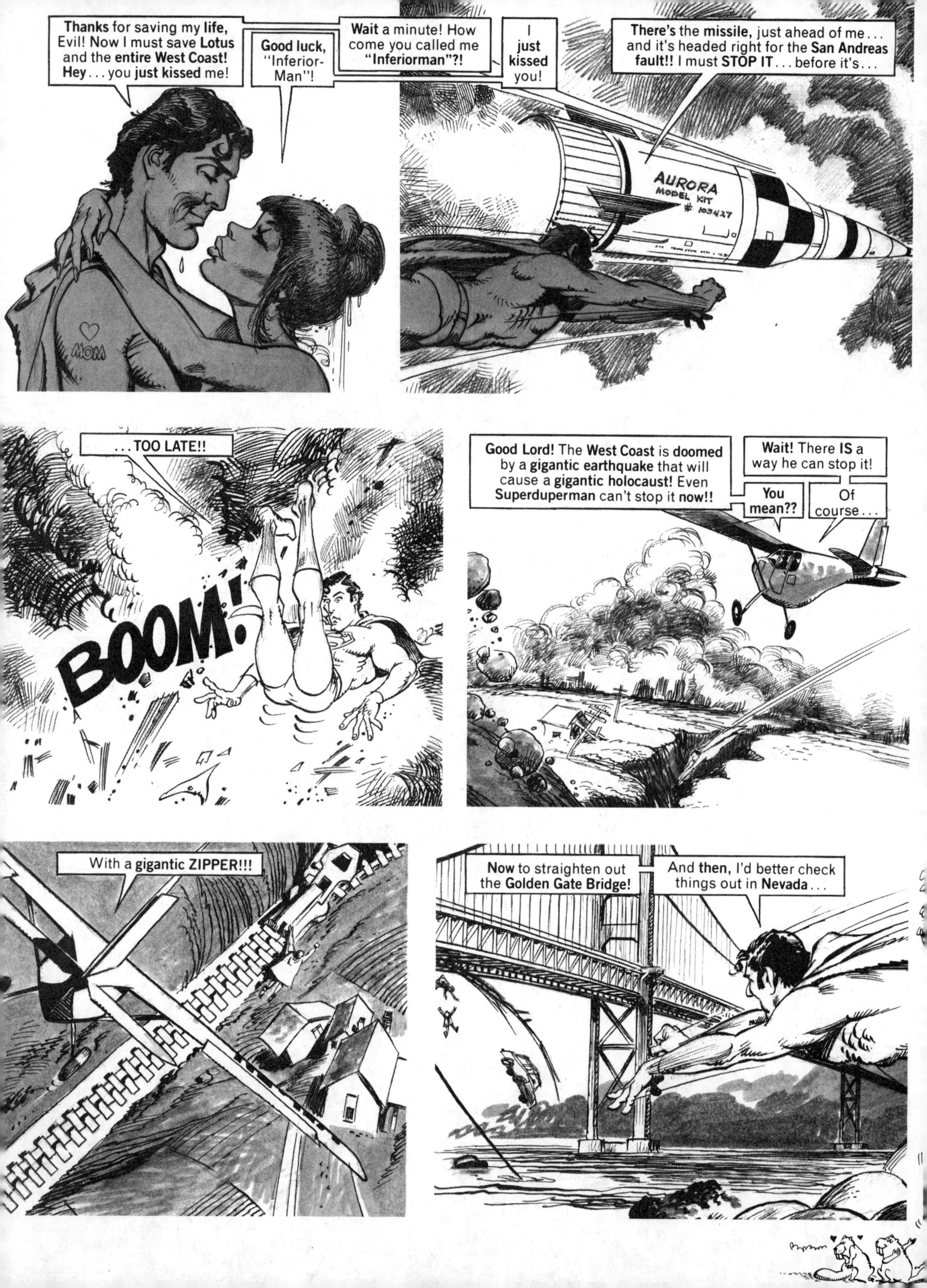

Thanks for saving my life, Evil! Now I must save Lotus and the entire West Coast! Hey . . . you just kissed me!
Good luck, "Inferior-Man"!
Wait a minute! How come you called me "Inferiorman"?!
I just kissed you!
There's the missile, just ahead of me . . . and it's headed right for the San Andreas fault!! I must STOP IT . . . before it's . . .
AURORA
MODEL KIT
103427
. . . TOO LATE!!
BOOM!
Good Lord! The West Coast is doomed by a gigantic earthquake that will cause a gigantic holocaust! Even Superduperman can't stop it now!!
Wait! There IS a way he can stop it!
You mean??
Of course . . .
With a gigantic ZIPPER!!!
Now to straighten out the Golden Gate Bridge!
And then, I'd better check things out in Nevada . . .

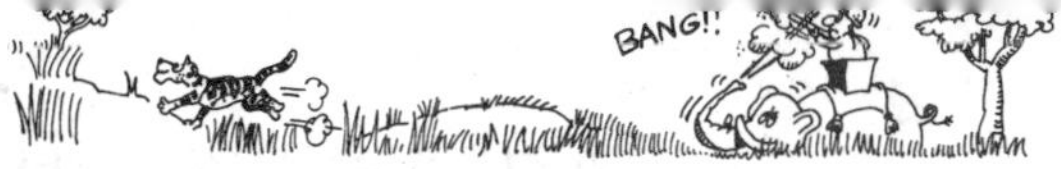
BANG!!

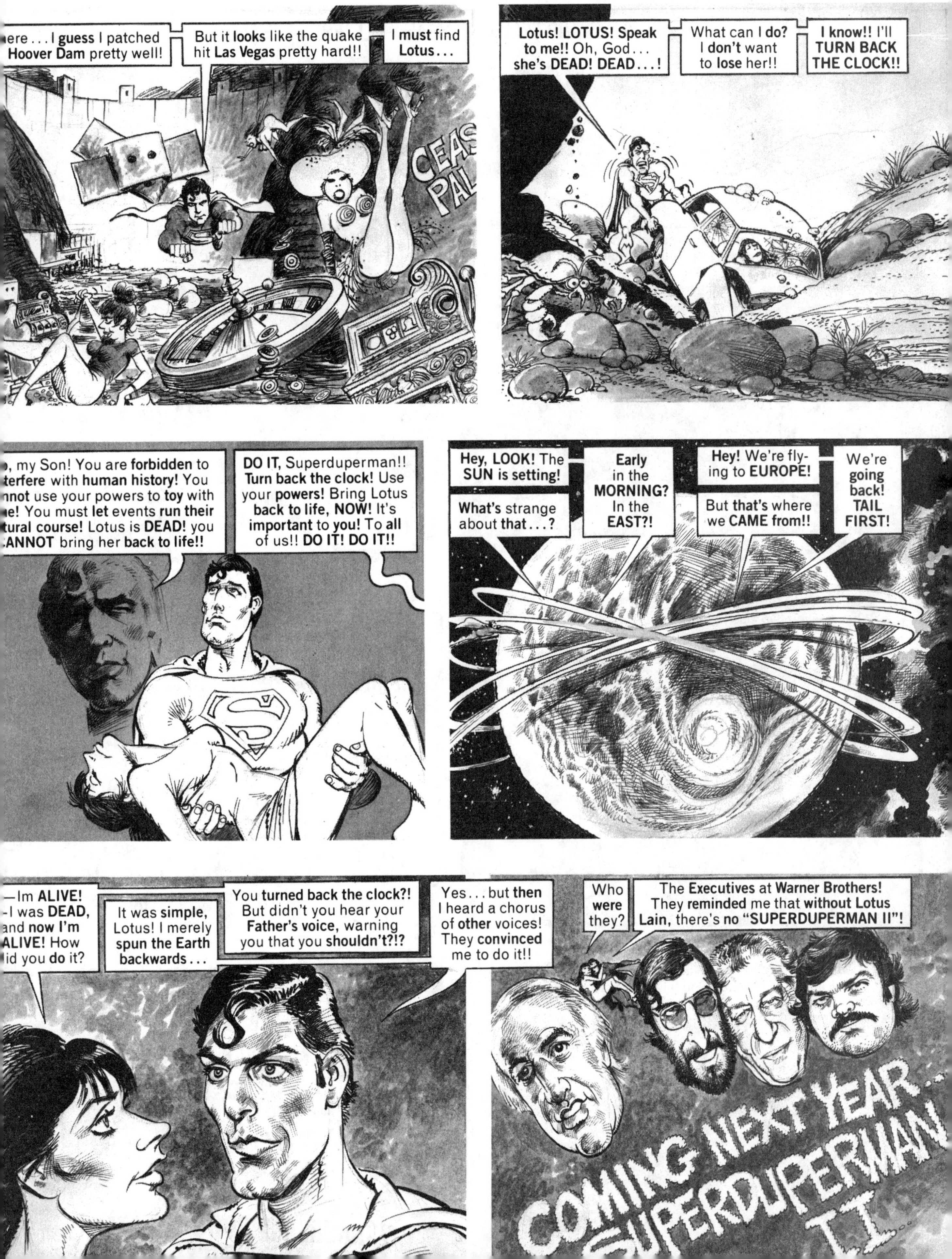
ere . . . I guess I patched
Hoover Dam pretty well!
But it looks like the quake hit Las Vegas pretty hard!!
I must find Lotus . . .
CEAS PAL
Lotus! LOTUS! Speak to me!! Oh, God . . . she's DEAD! DEAD . . . !
What can I do? I don't want to lose her!!
I know!! I'll TURN BACK THE CLOCK!!
, my Son! You are forbidden to
terfere with human history! You
nnot use your powers to toy with
e! You must let events run their
tural course! Lotus is DEAD! you
CANNOT bring her back to life!!
DO IT, Superduperman!! Turn back the clock! Use your powers! Bring Lotus back to life, NOW! It's important to you! To all of us!! DO IT! DO IT!!
Hey, LOOK! The SUN is setting!
What's strange about that . . . ?
Early in the MORNING? In the EAST?!
Hey! We're flying to EUROPE!
But that's where we CAME from!!
We're going back! TAIL FIRST!
—Im ALIVE!
-I was DEAD,
and now I'm
ALIVE! How
id you do it?
It was simple, Lotus! I merely spun the Earth backwards . . .
You turned back the clock?! But didn't you hear your Father's voice, warning you that you shouldn't?!?
Yes . . . but then I heard a chorus of other voices! They convinced me to do it!!
Who were they?
The Executives at Warner Brothers! They reminded me that without Lotus Lain, there's no "SUPERDUPERMAN II"!
COMING NEXT YEAR... SUPERDUPERMAN II

DOUBLE-STANDARD BARERS DEPT.

WE'RE SURE OUR PARENTS AND TEACHERS MEAN WELL WHEN THEY LECTURE US, BUT AFTER LISTI

NO WONDER WE'R

ARTIST: JACK RICK

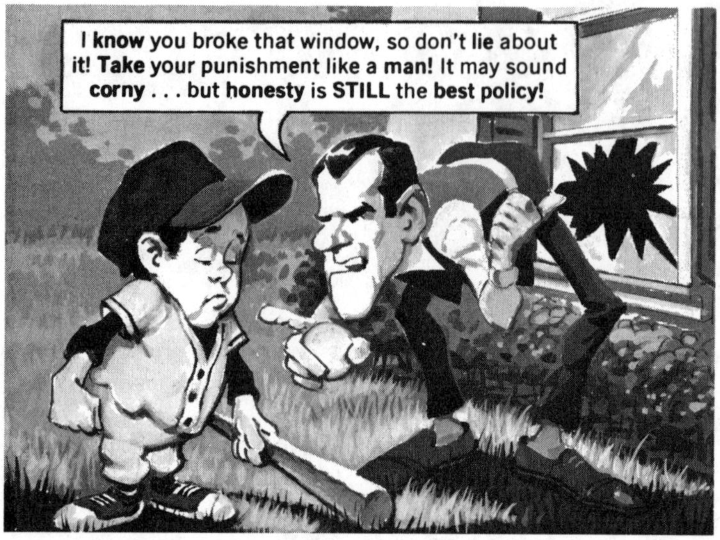

I know you broke that window, so don't lie about it! Take your punishment like a man! It may sound corny . . . but honesty is STILL the best policy!

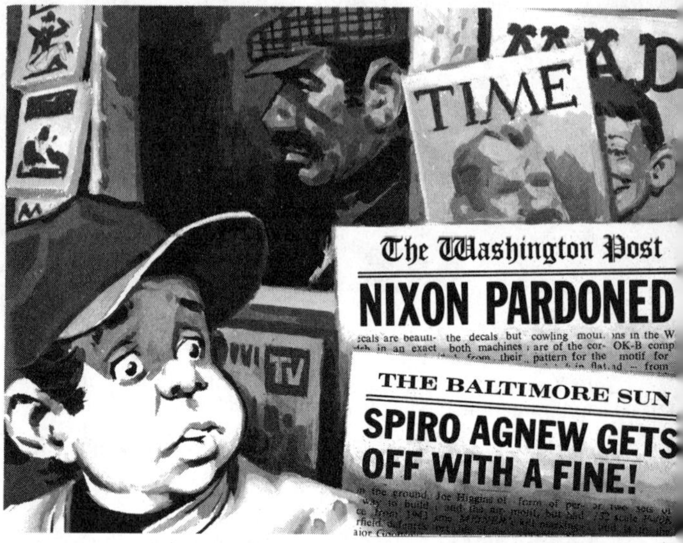

TIME
The Washington Post
NIXON PARDONED
THE BALTIMORE SUN
SPIRO AGNEW GETS OFF WITH A FINE!

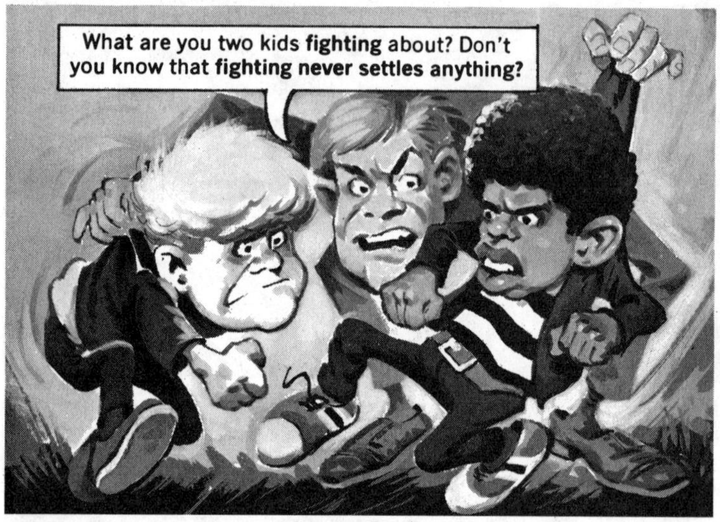

What are you two kids fighting about? Don't you know that fighting never settles anything?

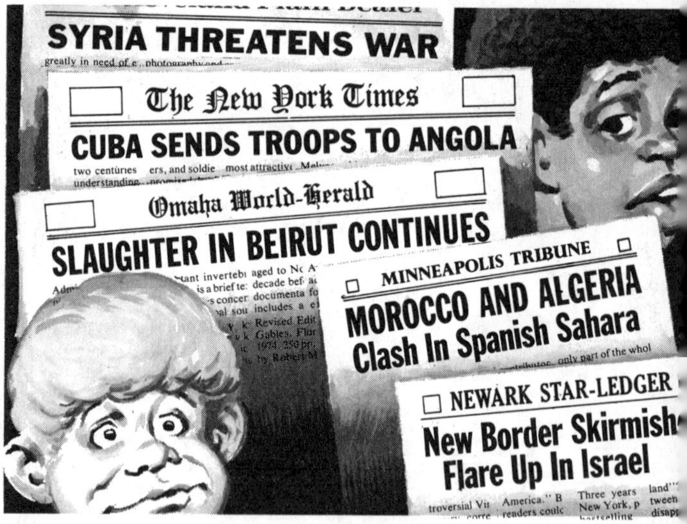

SYRIA THREATENS WAR
The New York Times
CUBA SENDS TROOPS TO ANGOLA
Omaha World-Herald
SLAUGHTER IN BEIRUT CONTINUES
MINNEAPOLIS TRIBUNE
MOROCCO AND ALGERIA Clash In Spanish Sahara
NEWARK STAR-LEDGER
New Border Skirmish Flare Up In Israel

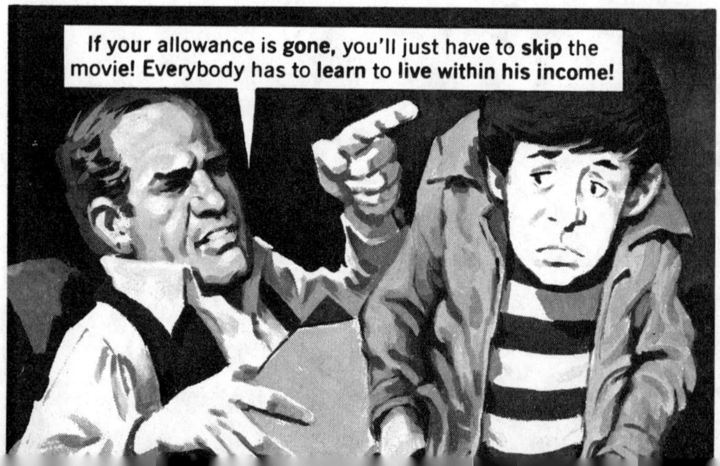

If your allowance is gone, you'll just have to skip the movie! Everybody has to learn to live within his income!

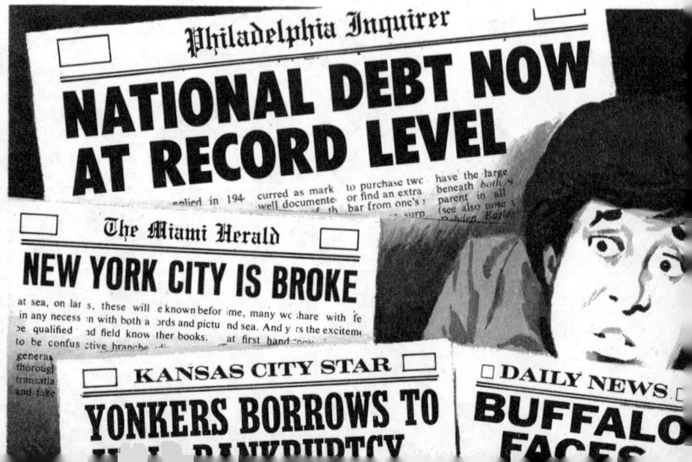

Philadelphia Inquirer
NATIONAL DEBT NOW AT RECORD LEVEL
The Miami Herald
NEW YORK CITY IS BROKE
KANSAS CITY STAR
YONKERS BORROWS TO
DAILY NEWS
BUFFALO

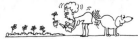

EM AND THEN READING THE WAY IT REALLY IS IN THE NEWSPAPER, ALL WE CAN SAY IS . . .

ALL SCREWED UP!

TER: LOU SILVERSTONE IDEA BY: ALIS ELLIS

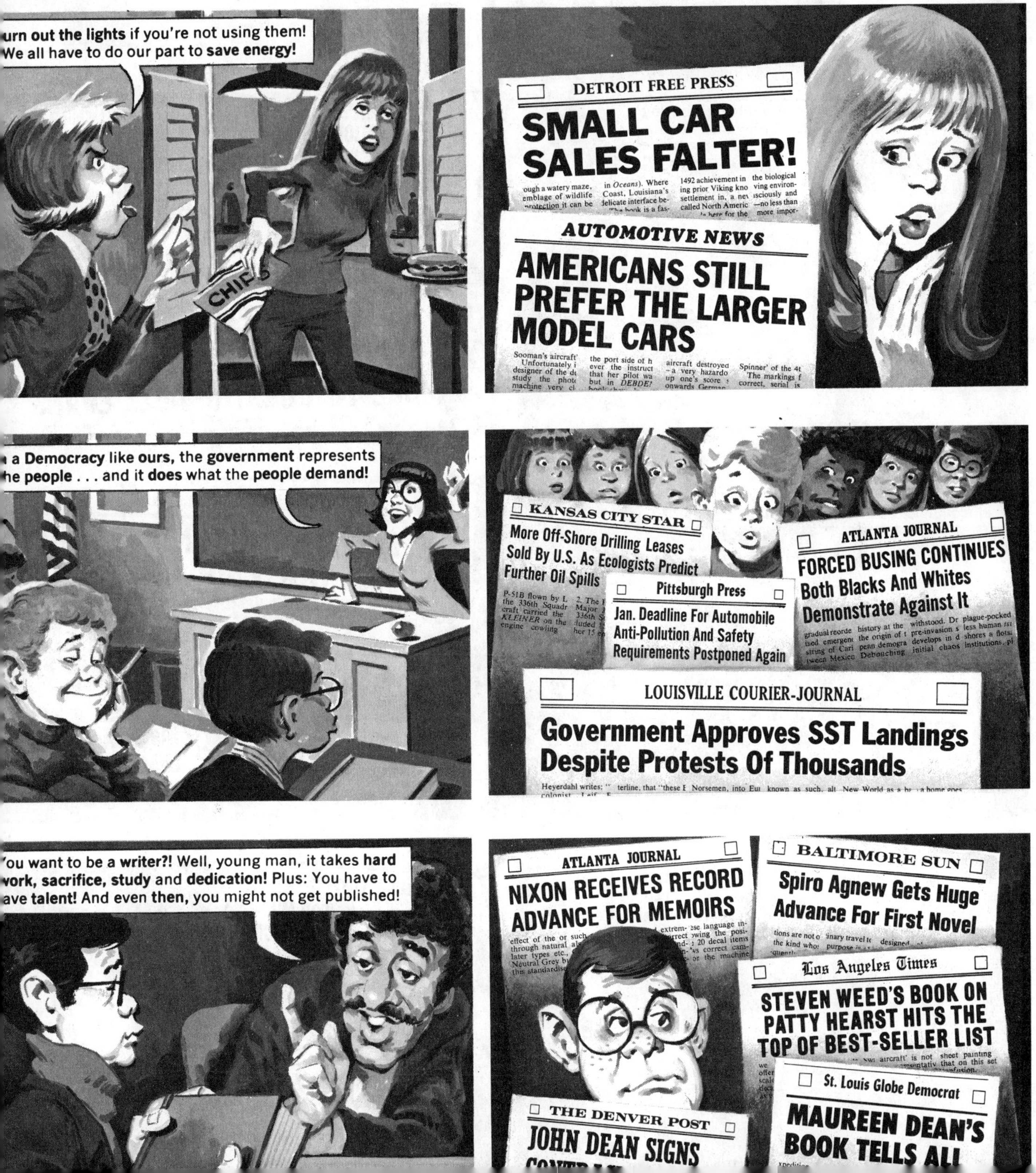

urn out the lights if you're not using them! We all have to do our part to save energy!
CHIPS
DETROIT FREE PRESS
SMALL CAR SALES FALTER!
AUTOMOTIVE NEWS
AMERICANS STILL PREFER THE LARGER MODEL CARS
a Democracy like ours, the government represents he people . . . and it does what the people demand!
KANSAS CITY STAR
More Off-Shore Drilling Leases Sold By U.S. As Ecologists Predict Further Oil Spills
ATLANTA JOURNAL
FORCED BUSING CONTINUES Both Blacks And Whites Demonstrate Against It
Pittsburgh Press
Jan. Deadline For Automobile Anti-Pollution And Safety Requirements Postponed Again
LOUISVILLE COURIER-JOURNAL
Government Approves SST Landings Despite Protests Of Thousands
'ou want to be a writer?! Well, young man, it takes hard vork, sacrifice, study and dedication! Plus: You have to ave talent! And even then, you might not get published!
ATLANTA JOURNAL
NIXON RECEIVES RECORD ADVANCE FOR MEMOIRS
BALTIMORE SUN
Spiro Agnew Gets Huge Advance For First Novel
Los Angeles Times
STEVEN WEED'S BOOK ON PATTY HEARST HITS THE TOP OF BEST-SELLER LIST
THE DENVER POST
JOHN DEAN SIGNS
St. Louis Globe Democrat
MAUREEN DEAN'S BOOK TELLS ALL

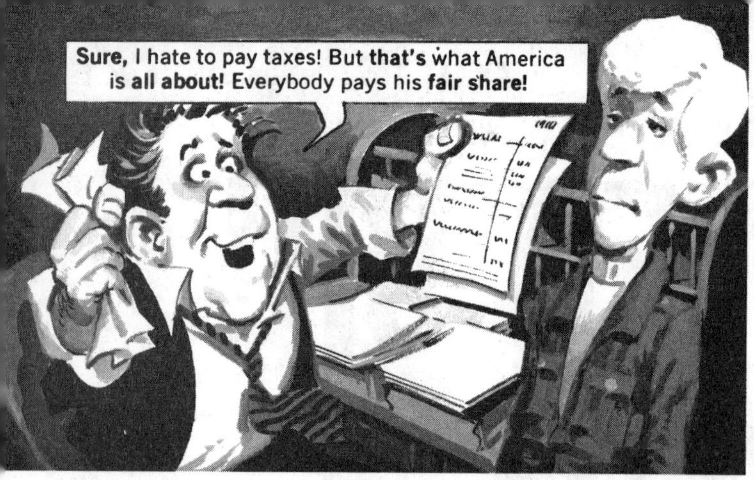
Sure, I hate to pay taxes! But that's what America is all about! Everybody pays his fair share!
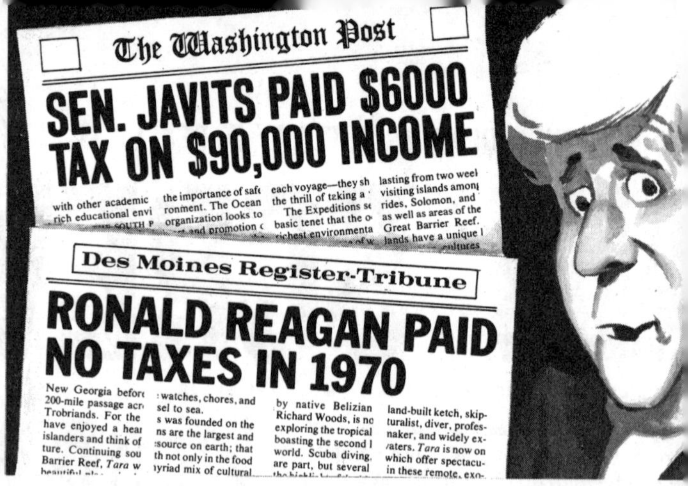
The Washington Post
SEN. JAVITS PAID $6000 TAX ON $90,000 INCOME
Des Moines Register-Tribune
RONALD REAGAN PAID NO TAXES IN 1970
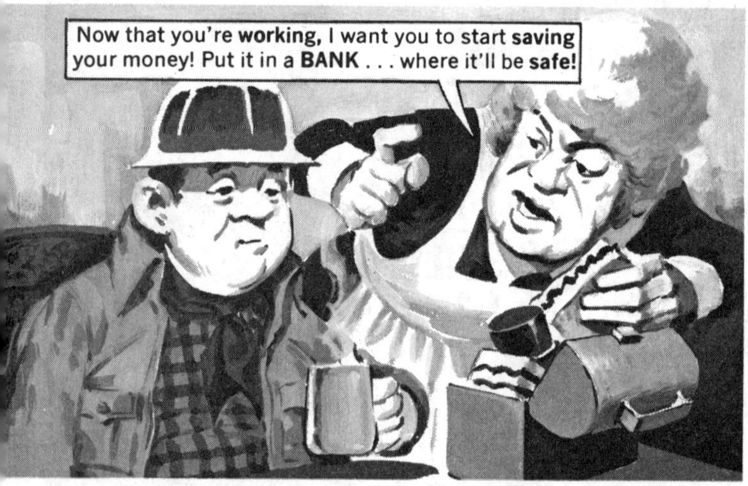
Now that you're working, I want you to start saving your money! Put it in a BANK . . . where it'll be safe!
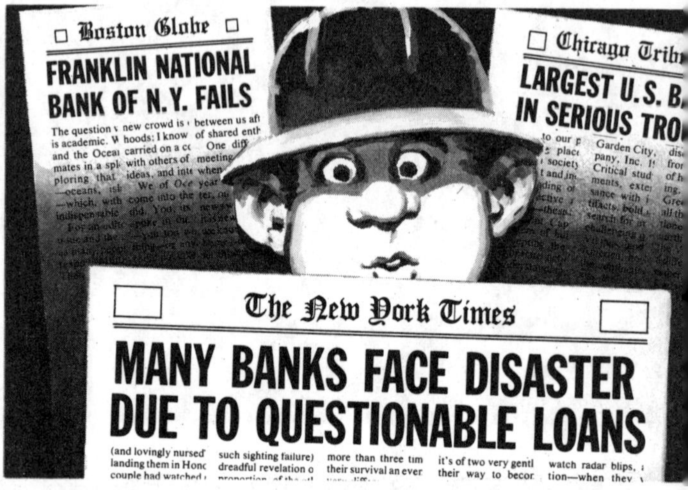
Boston Globe
FRANKLIN NATIONAL BANK OF N.Y. FAILS
The New York Times
MANY BANKS FACE DISASTER DUE TO QUESTIONABLE LOANS
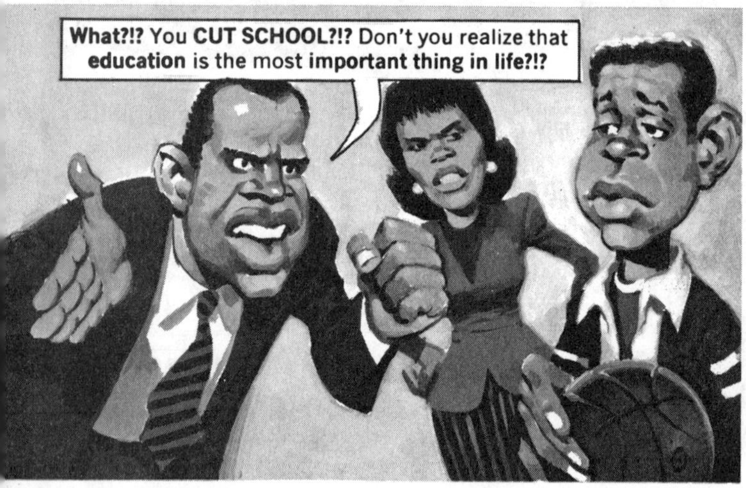
What?!? You CUT SCHOOL?!? Don't you realize that education is the most important thing in life?!?
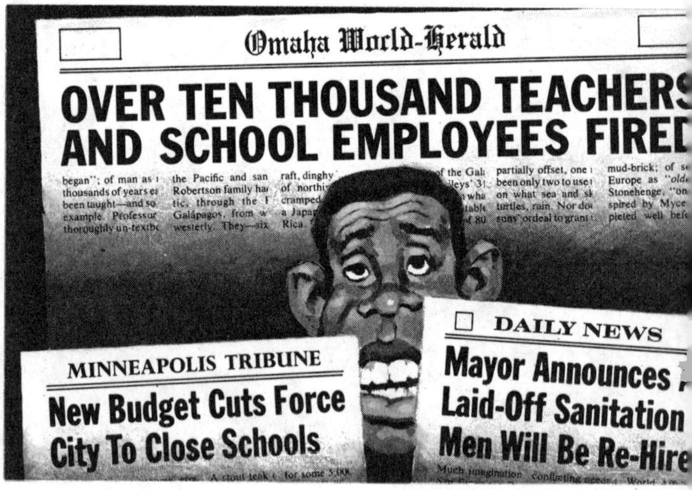
Omaha World-Herald
MINNEAPOLIS TRIBUNE
New Budget Cuts Force City To Close Schools
DAILY NEWS
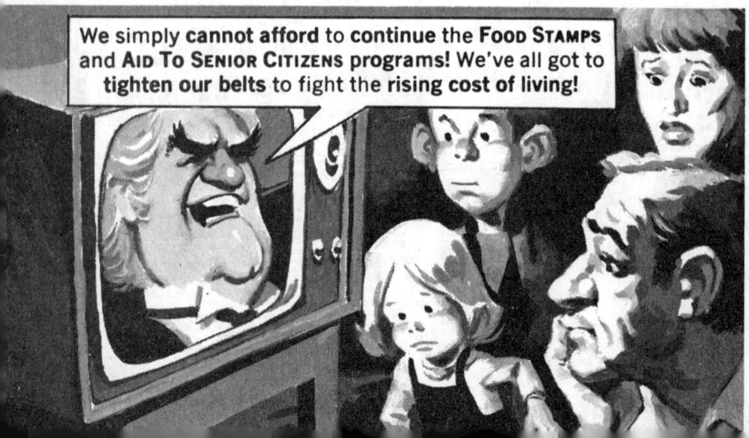
We simply cannot afford to continue the FOOD STAMPS and AID TO SENIOR CITIZENS programs! We've all got to tighten our belts to fight the rising cost of living!
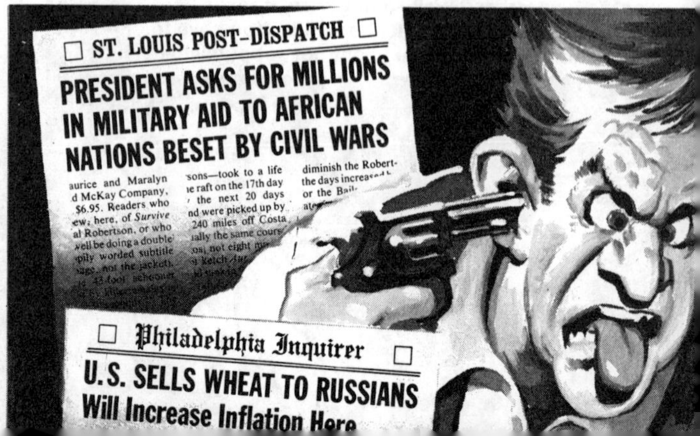
ST. LOUIS POST-DISPATCH
PRESIDENT ASKS FOR MILLIONS IN MILITARY AID TO AFRICAN NATIONS BESET BY CIVIL WARS
Philadelphia Inquirer
U.S. SELLS WHEAT TO RUSSIANS
Will Increase Inflation Here

SIT-COM FROM OUTER SPACE DEPT.

Movies and TV shows about creatures from outer space have always fascinated us Earthlings. They usually feature . . .

. . . a terrifying monster like "The Thing". . .

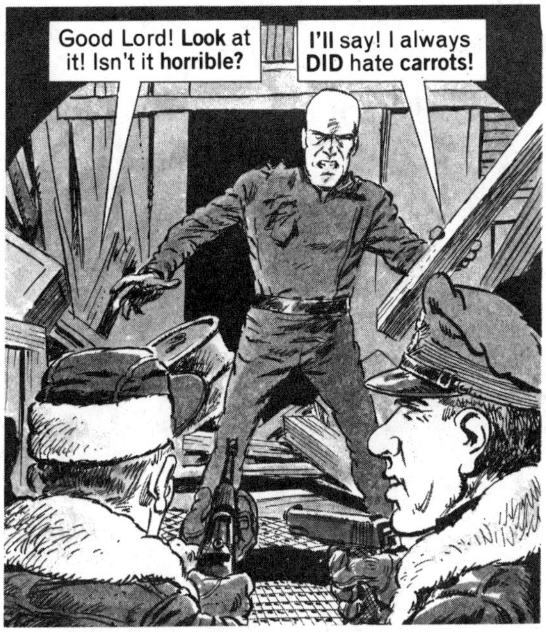

Good Lord! Look at it! Isn't it horrible?
I'll say! I always DID hate carrots!

. . . or frightening aliens like the invaders in "War Of The Worlds"!

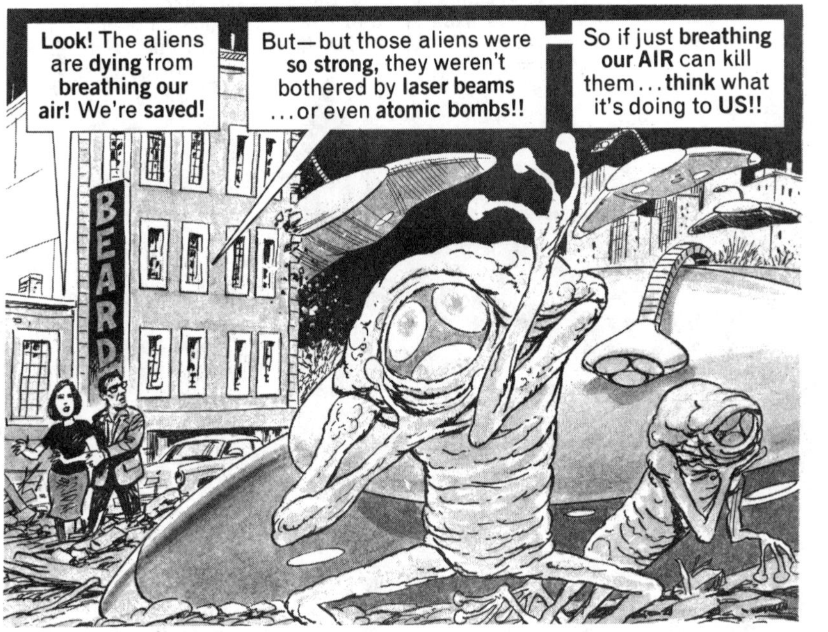

Look! The aliens are dying from breathing our air! We're saved!
But—but those aliens were so strong, they weren't bothered by laser beams . . . or even atomic bombs!!
So if just breathing our AIR can kill them . . . think what it's doing to US!!
BEARD

But those terrifying creatures are a thing of the past. Today, we've got a new breed of outer space monster . . . and the most frightening thing about this new alien is that enough people watch him to make a hit show out of—

SHMORK & WINDY

ARTIST: ANGELO TORRES WRITER: LOU SILVERSTONE

ADDITIONAL DIALOGUE: DICK DE BARTOLO

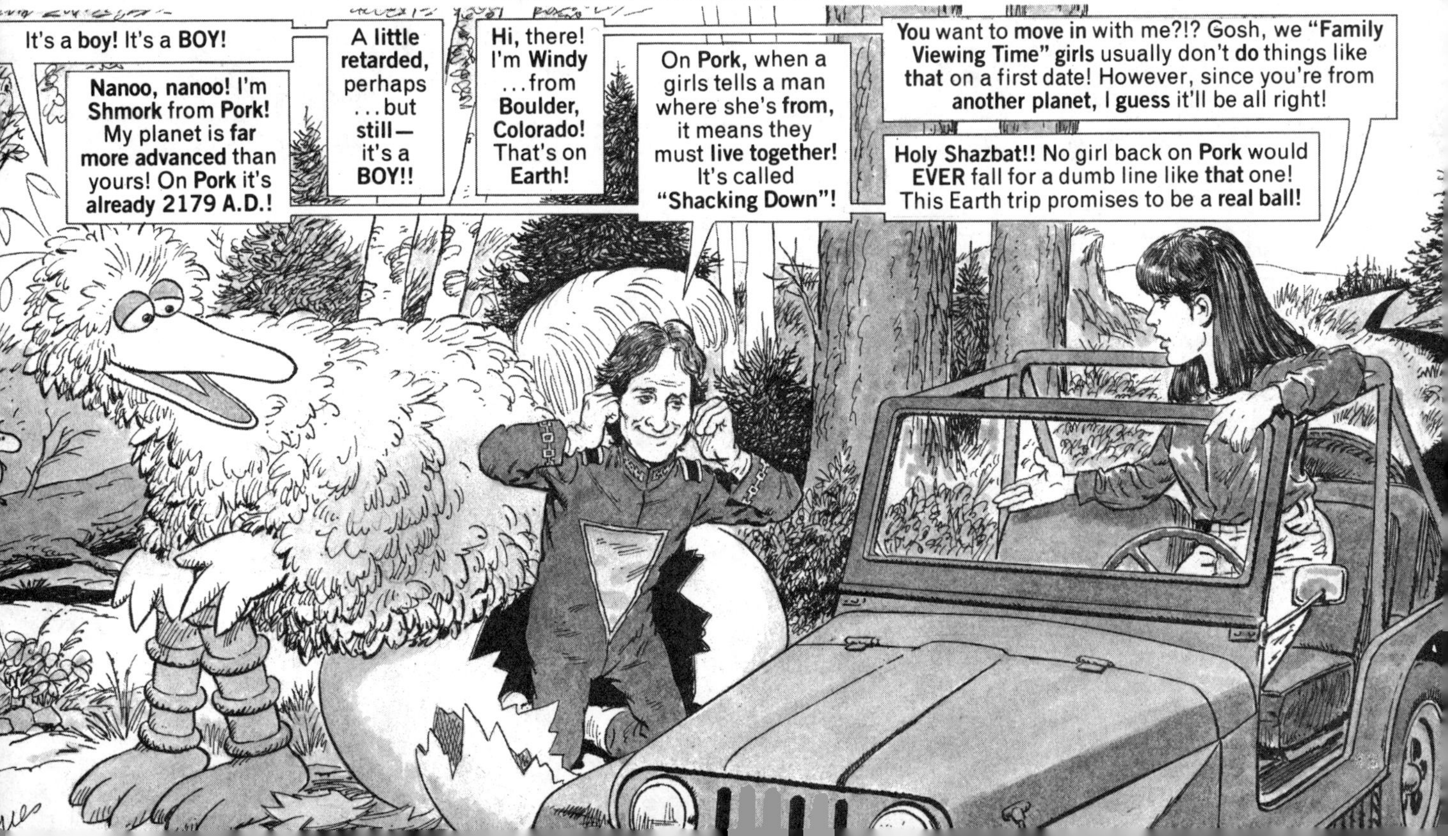

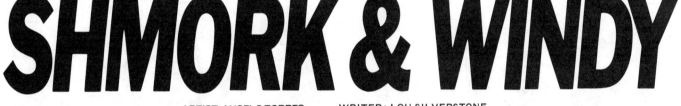

It's a boy! It's a BOY!
Nanoo, nanoo! I'm Shmork from Pork! My planet is far more advanced than yours! On Pork it's already 2179 A.D.!
A little retarded, perhaps . . . but still— it's a BOY!!
Hi, there! I'm Windy . . . from Boulder, Colorado! That's on Earth!
On Pork, when a girls tells a man where she's from, it means they must live together! It's called "Shacking Down"!
You want to move in with me?!? Gosh, we "Family Viewing Time" girls usually don't do things like that on a first date! However, since you're from another planet, I guess it'll be all right!
Holy Shazbat!! No girl back on Pork would EVER fall for a dumb line like that one! This Earth trip promises to be a real ball!

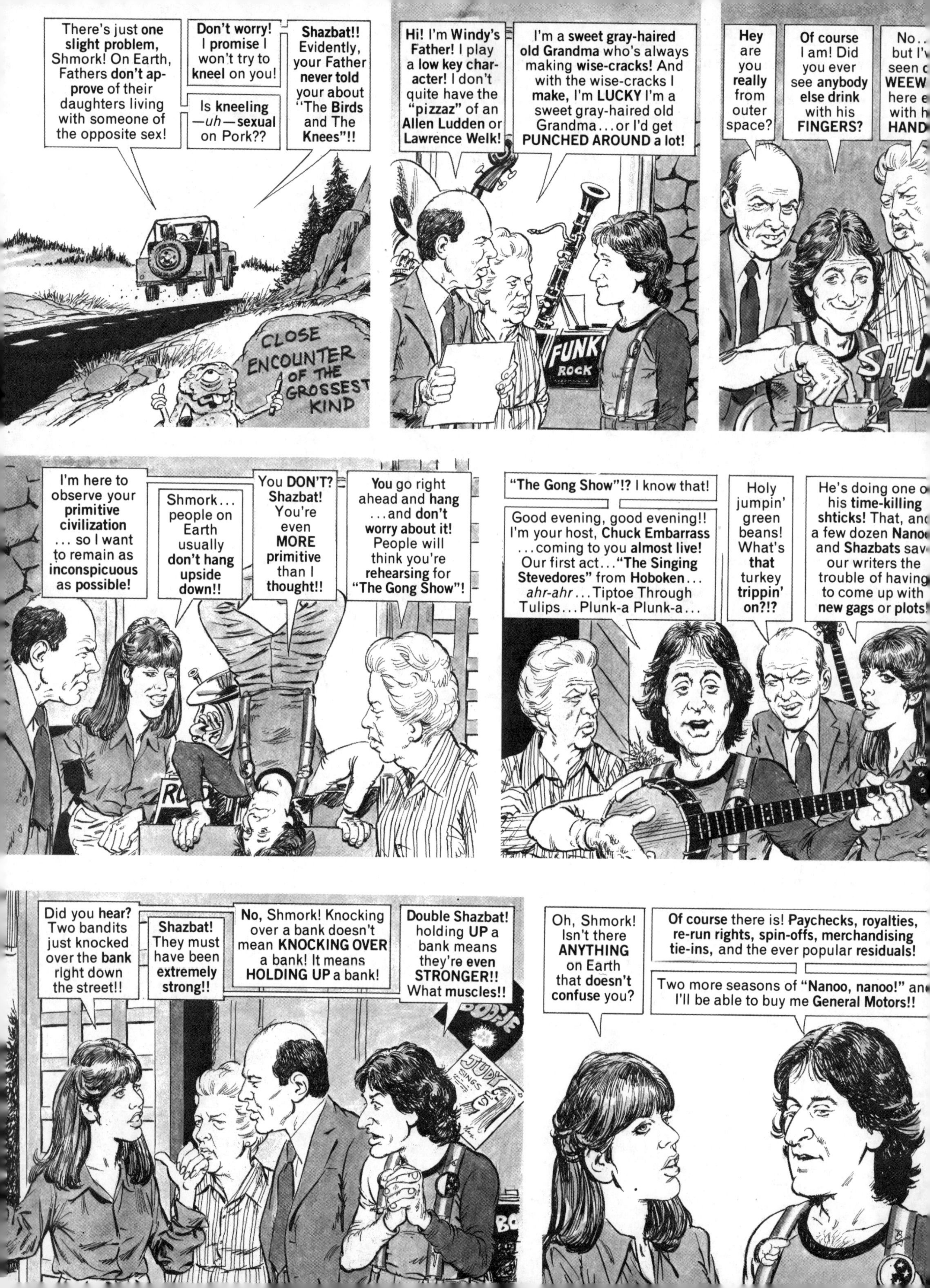

There's just one slight problem, Shmork! On Earth, Fathers don't approve of their daughters living with someone of the opposite sex!
Don't worry! I promise I won't try to kneel on you!
Is kneeling —uh— sexual on Pork??
Shazbat!! Evidently, your Father never told your about "The Birds and The Knees"!!
CLOSE ENCOUNTER OF THE GROSSEST KIND
Hi! I'm Windy's Father! I play a low key character! I don't quite have the "pizzaz" of an Allen Ludden or Lawrence Welk!
I'm a sweet gray-haired old Grandma who's always making wise-cracks! And with the wise-cracks I make, I'm LUCKY I'm a sweet gray-haired old Grandma... or I'd get PUNCHED AROUND a lot!
FUNK ROCK
Hey are you really from outer space?
Of course I am! Did you ever see anybody else drink with his FINGERS?
No... but I'v seen c WEEW here e with h HAND
SHLU
I'm here to observe your primitive civilization ... so I want to remain as inconspicuous as possible!
Shmork... people on Earth usually don't hang upside down!!
You DON'T? Shazbat! You're even MORE primitive than I thought!!
You go right ahead and hang ...and don't worry about it! People will think you're rehearsing for "The Gong Show"!
RO
"The Gong Show"!? I know that!
Good evening, good evening!! I'm your host, Chuck Embarrass ...coming to you almost live! Our first act... "The Singing Stevedores" from Hoboken... ahr-ahr... Tiptoe Through Tulips... Plunk-a Plunk-a...
Holy jumpin' green beans! What's that turkey trippin' on?!?
He's doing one o his time-killing shticks! That, and a few dozen Nanoo and Shazbats save our writers the trouble of having to come up with new gags or plots
Did you hear? Two bandits just knocked over the bank right down the street!!
Shazbat! They must have been extremely strong!!
No, Shmork! Knocking over a bank doesn't mean KNOCKING OVER a bank! It means HOLDING UP a bank!
Double Shazbat! holding UP a bank means they're even STRONGER!! What muscles!!
JUDY SINGS
Oh, Shmork! Isn't there ANYTHING on Earth that doesn't confuse you?
Of course there is! Paychecks, royalties, re-run rights, spin-offs, merchandising tie-ins, and the ever popular residuals!
Two more seasons of "Nanoo, nanoo!" an I'll be able to buy me General Motors!!

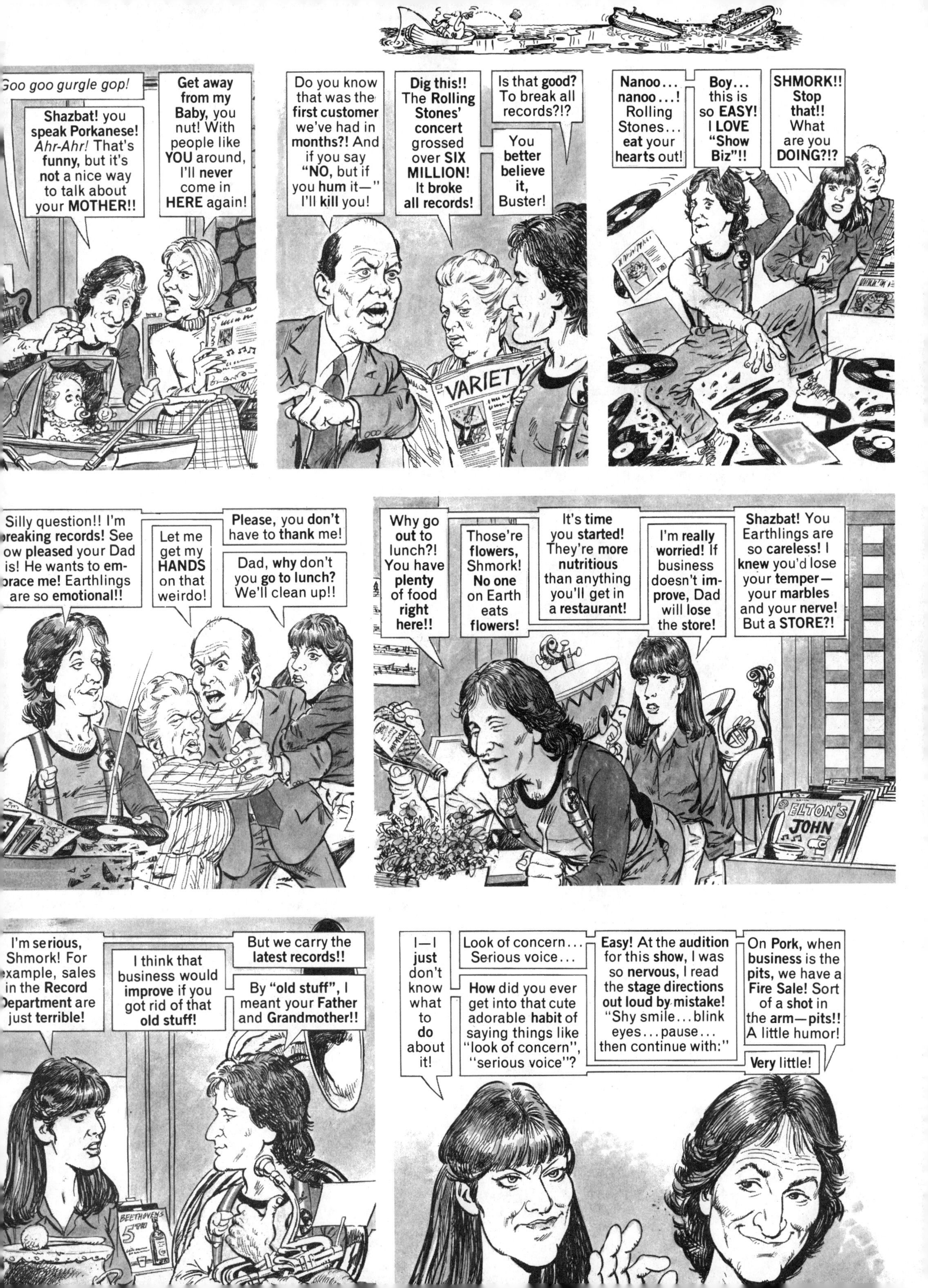

Goo goo gurgle gop!
Shazbat! you speak Porkanese! Ahr-Ahr! That's funny, but it's not a nice way to talk about your MOTHER!!
Get away from my Baby, you nut! With people like YOU around, I'll never come in HERE again!
Do you know that was the first customer we've had in months?! And if you say "NO, but if you hum it—" I'll kill you!
Dig this!! The Rolling Stones' concert grossed over SIX MILLION! It broke all records!
Is that good? To break all records?!?
You better believe it, Buster!
VARIETY
Nanoo... nanoo...! Rolling Stones... eat your hearts out!
Boy... this is so EASY! I LOVE "Show Biz"!!
SHMORK!! Stop that!! What are you DOING?!?
Silly question!! I'm reaking records! See ow pleased your Dad is! He wants to em-race me! Earthlings are so emotional!!
Please, you don't have to thank me!
Let me get my HANDS on that weirdo!
Dad, why don't you go to lunch? We'll clean up!!
Why go out to lunch?! You have plenty of food right here!!
Those're flowers, Shmork! No one on Earth eats flowers!
It's time you started! They're more nutritious than anything you'll get in a restaurant!
I'm really worried! If business doesn't im-prove, Dad will lose the store!
Shazbat! You Earthlings are so careless! I knew you'd lose your temper—your marbles and your nerve! But a STORE?!
ELTON'S JOHN
I'm serious, Shmork! For xample, sales in the Record epartment are just terrible!
I think that business would improve if you got rid of that old stuff!
But we carry the latest records!!
By "old stuff", I meant your Father and Grandmother!!
I—I just don't know what to do about it!
Look of concern... Serious voice...
How did you ever get into that cute adorable habit of saying things like "look of concern", "serious voice"?
Easy! At the audition for this show, I was so nervous, I read the stage directions out loud by mistake! "Shy smile... blink eyes... pause... then continue with:"
On Pork, when business is the pits, we have a Fire Sale! Sort of a shot in the arm—pits!! A little humor!
Very little!

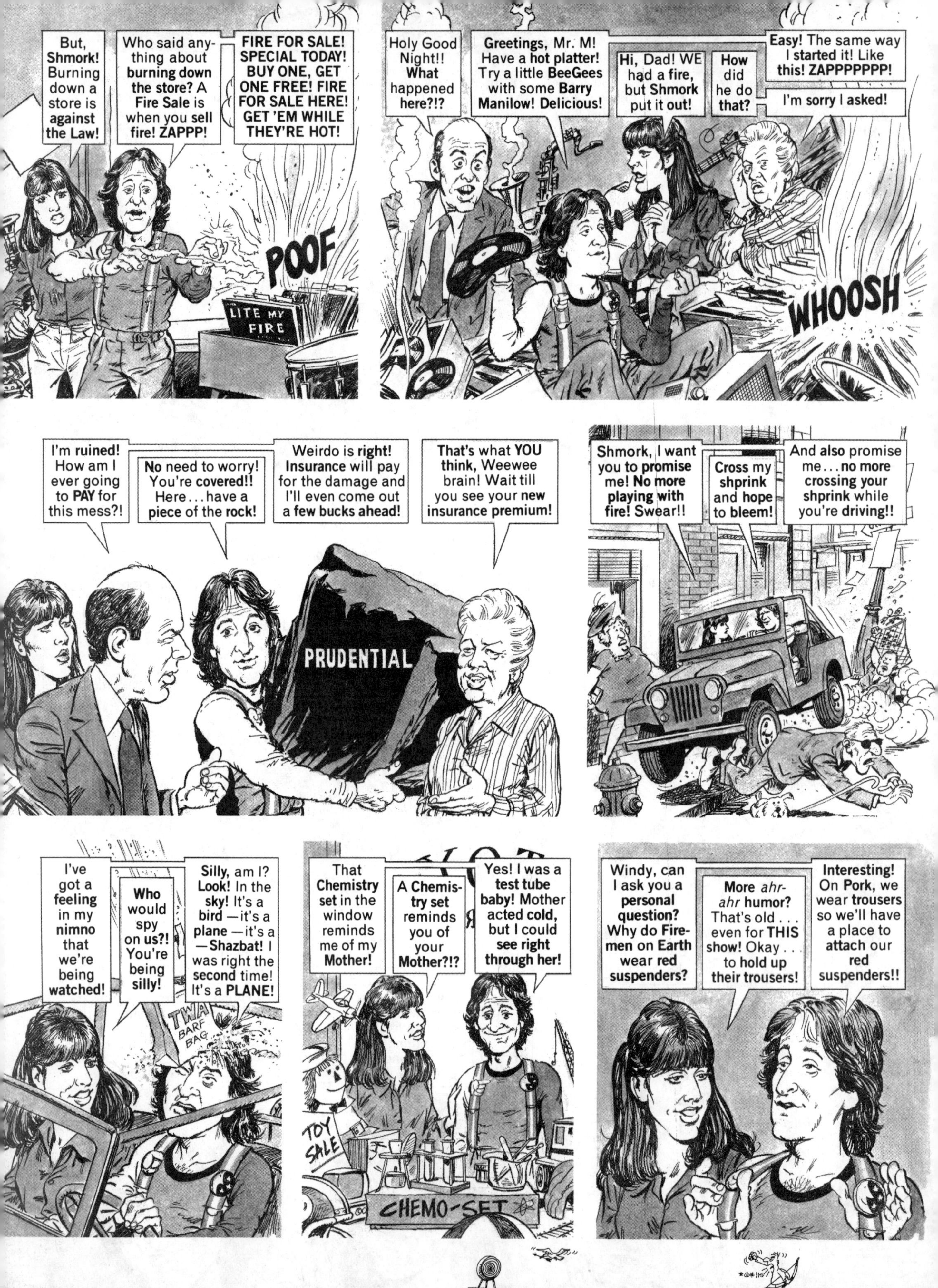
But, Shmork! Burning down a store is against the Law!
Who said anything about burning down the store? A Fire Sale is when you sell fire! ZAPPP!
FIRE FOR SALE! SPECIAL TODAY! BUY ONE, GET ONE FREE! FIRE FOR SALE HERE! GET 'EM WHILE THEY'RE HOT!
POOF
LITE MY FIRE
Holy Good Night!! What happened here?!?
Greetings, Mr. M! Have a hot platter! Try a little BeeGees with some Barry Manilow! Delicious!
Hi, Dad! WE had a fire, but Shmork put it out!
How did he do that?
Easy! The same way I started it! Like this! ZAPPPPPPP!
I'm sorry I asked!
WHOOSH
I'm ruined! How am I ever going to PAY for this mess?!
No need to worry! You're covered!! Here... have a piece of the rock!
Weirdo is right! Insurance will pay for the damage and I'll even come out a few bucks ahead!
That's what YOU think, Weewee brain! Wait till you see your new insurance premium!
PRUDENTIAL
Shmork, I want you to promise me! No more playing with fire! Swear!!
Cross my shprink and hope to bleem!
And also promise me... no more crossing your shprink while you're driving!!
I've got a feeling in my nimno that we're being watched!
Who would spy on us?! You're being silly!
Silly, am I? Look! In the sky! It's a bird — it's a plane — it's a — Shazbat! I was right the second time! It's a PLANE!
TWA BARF BAG
That Chemistry set in the window reminds me of my Mother!
A Chemistry set reminds you of your Mother?!?
Yes! I was a test tube baby! Mother acted cold, but I could see right through her!
TOY SALE
CHEMO-SET
Windy, can I ask you a personal question? Why do Firemen on Earth wear red suspenders?
More ahr-ahr humor? That's old . . . even for THIS show! Okay . . . to hold up their trousers!
Interesting! On Pork, we wear trousers so we'll have a place to attach our red suspenders!!

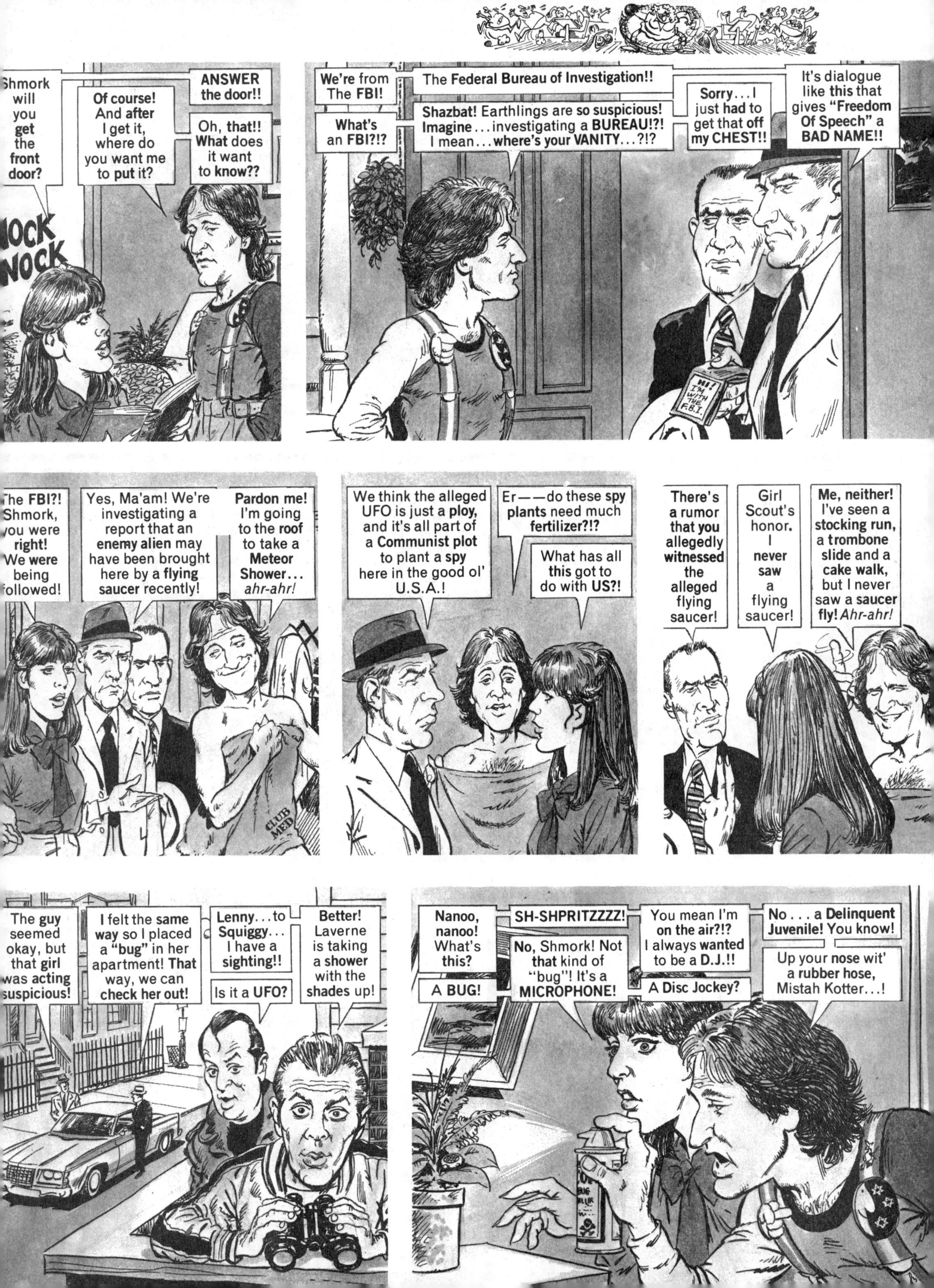
hmork will you get the front door?
ANSWER the door!!
Of course! And after I get it, where do you want me to put it?
Oh, that!! What does it want to know??
OCK
NOCK
We're from The FBI!
The Federal Bureau of Investigation!!
What's an FBI?!?
Shazbat! Earthlings are so suspicious! Imagine... investigating a BUREAU!?! I mean... where's your VANITY...?!?
Sorry... I just had to get that off my CHEST!!
It's dialogue like this that gives "Freedom Of Speech" a BAD NAME!!
HI! I'M WITH THE F.B.I.
he FBI?! Shmork, ou were right! We were being ollowed!
Yes, Ma'am! We're investigating a report that an enemy alien may have been brought here by a flying saucer recently!
Pardon me! I'm going to the roof to take a Meteor Shower... *ahr-ahr!*
CLUB MED
We think the alleged UFO is just a ploy, and it's all part of a Communist plot to plant a spy here in the good ol' U.S.A.!
Er——do these spy plants need much fertilizer?!?
What has all this got to do with US?!
There's a rumor that you allegedly witnessed the alleged flying saucer!
Girl Scout's honor. I never saw a flying saucer!
Me, neither! I've seen a stocking run, a trombone slide and a cake walk, but I never saw a saucer fly! *Ahr-ahr!*
The guy seemed okay, but that girl was acting uspicious!
I felt the same way so I placed a "bug" in her apartment! That way, we can check her out!
Lenny... to Squiggy... I have a sighting!!
Is it a UFO?
Better! Laverne is taking a shower with the shades up!
Nanoo, nanoo! What's this?
SH-SHPRITZZZZ!
A BUG!
No, Shmork! Not that kind of "bug"! It's a MICROPHONE!
You mean I'm on the air?!? I always wanted to be a D.J.!!
A Disc Jockey?
No... a Delinquent Juvenile! You know!
Up your nose wit' a rubber hose, Mistah Kotter...!

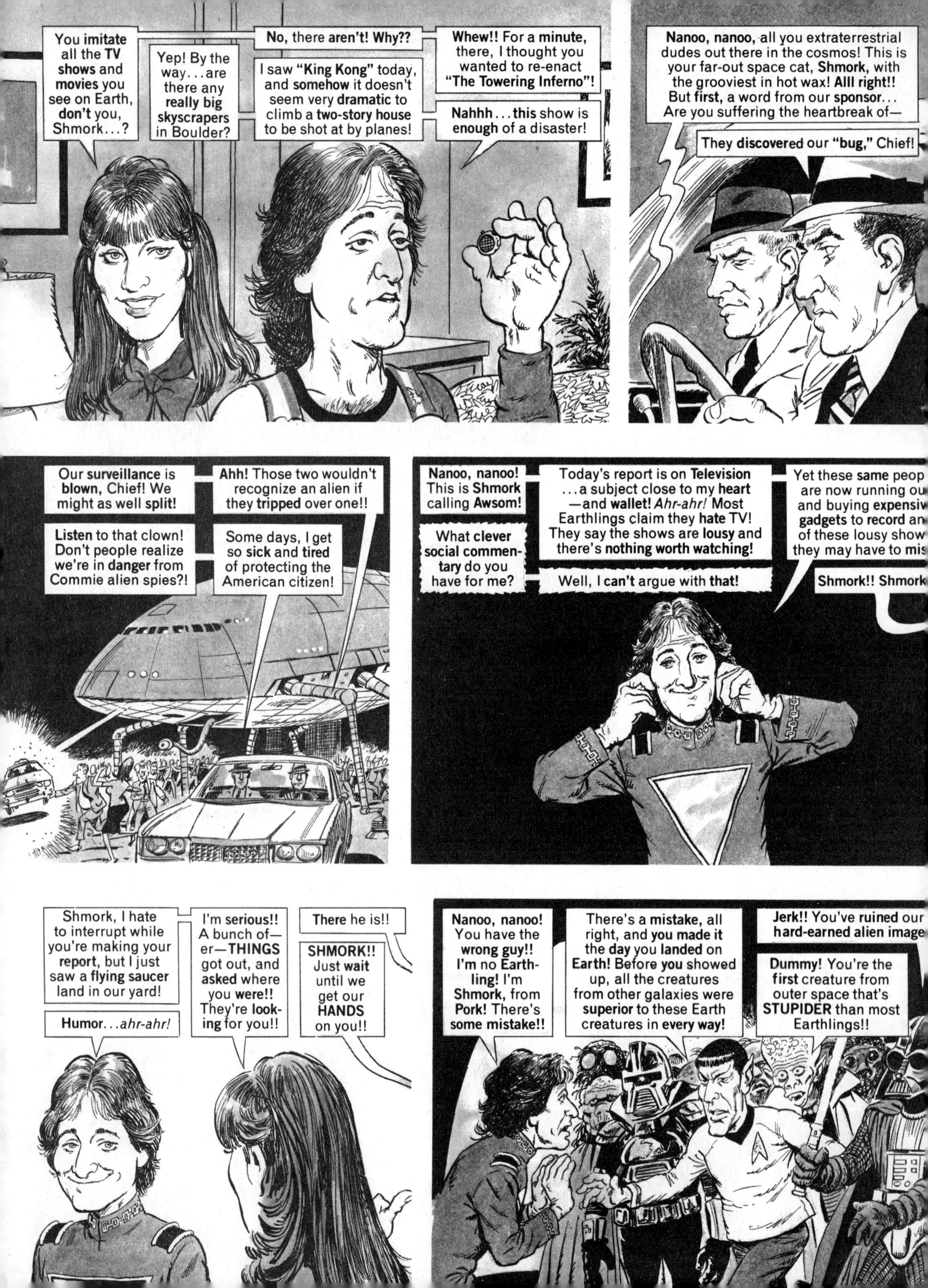
You imitate all the TV shows and movies you see on Earth, don't you, Shmork...?
Yep! By the way...are there any really big skyscrapers in Boulder?
No, there aren't! Why??
I saw "King Kong" today, and somehow it doesn't seem very dramatic to climb a two-story house to be shot at by planes!
Whew!! For a minute, there, I thought you wanted to re-enact "The Towering Inferno"!
Nahhh...this show is enough of a disaster!
Nanoo, nanoo, all you extraterrestrial dudes out there in the cosmos! This is your far-out space cat, Shmork, with the grooviest in hot wax! Alll right!! But first, a word from our sponsor... Are you suffering the heartbreak of—
They discovered our "bug," Chief!
Our surveillance is blown, Chief! We might as well split!
Ahh! Those two wouldn't recognize an alien if they tripped over one!!
Listen to that clown! Don't people realize we're in danger from Commie alien spies?!
Some days, I get so sick and tired of protecting the American citizen!
Nanoo, nanoo! This is Shmork calling Awsom!
Today's report is on Television ...a subject close to my heart —and wallet! Ahr-ahr! Most Earthlings claim they hate TV! They say the shows are lousy and there's nothing worth watching!
What clever social commentary do you have for me?
Well, I can't argue with that!
Yet these same peop are now running ou and buying expensiv gadgets to record an of these lousy show they may have to mis
Shmork!! Shmork
Shmork, I hate to interrupt while you're making your report, but I just saw a flying saucer land in our yard!
Humor...ahr-ahr!
I'm serious!! A bunch of—er—THINGS got out, and asked where you were!! They're looking for you!!
There he is!!
SHMORK!! Just wait until we get our HANDS on you!!
Nanoo, nanoo! You have the wrong guy!! I'm no Earthling! I'm Shmork, from Pork! There's some mistake!!
There's a mistake, all right, and you made it the day you landed on Earth! Before you showed up, all the creatures from other galaxies were superior to these Earth creatures in every way!
Jerk!! You've ruined our hard-earned alien image
Dummy! You're the first creature from outer space that's STUPIDER than most Earthlings!!

HUMOR

$19.95 (Cheap!) FPT
$26.95 in Canada

MAD®

"MAD — a short-lived satirical pulp . . ."
— *Time,* September 24, 1956

"What — Me Worry?" — Alfred E. Neuman, 1996

Alfred E. Neuman does disco? Ecch! In the bestselling tradition of *MAD About the Sixties,* here is a hilarious look back at the "Disco Decade" from America's foremost satire magazine. Illustrated throughout in color and black and white, this MADcap compendium rehashes the best send-ups, takeoffs, and put-ons from the era that gave us Spiro Agnew, smiley faces, and the Bee Gees. You'll be grateful for these dead-on parodies as "The Usual Gang of Idiots" — the artists, writers, and editors of *MAD* Magazine — present classic features from their past. So sit back, grab a Billy Beer, and get down, get funky, and get it on with *MAD About the Seventies.* And may their farce be with you!

DEPARTMENTS

MOVIE TAKEOFFS:
- American Confetti
- The Ecchorcist
- One Cuckoo Flew Over the Rest
- Saturday Night Feeble
- Sleazy Riders
- Superduperman

TV SATIRES:
- Churlie's Angles
- Crappy Days
- M*A*S*H*UGA
- Shmork & Windy
- Welcome Back, Klodder

MAD'S MODERN BELIEVE IT OR NUTS!
SPY vs SPY
SERGIO ARAGONÉS
THE LIGHTER SIDE OF . . .
MAD-ISON AVENUE AD PARODIES
MAD FOLD-INS
DON MARTIN
SCENES WE'D LIKE TO SEE

AND MORE . . .

VITAL FEATURES

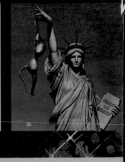

ANOTHER MAD MINI-POSTER

FROM MOM

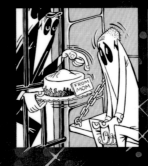

SPY vs SPY

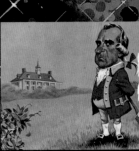

THE NIXON YEARS

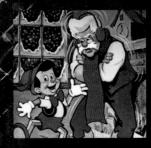

SCENES WE'D LIKE TO SEE

***STAR ROARS:* A MAD MOVIE SATIRE**

SHKLURCH

DON MARTIN

ISBN 0-316-32802-2
90000
EAN
9 780316 328029

Cover design by Steve Snider
Cover art by Jack Rickard

09961945

PRINTED IN THE U.S.A.

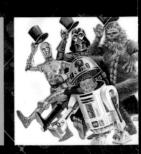

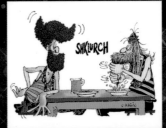